READER'S DIGEST

CONDENSED BOOKS

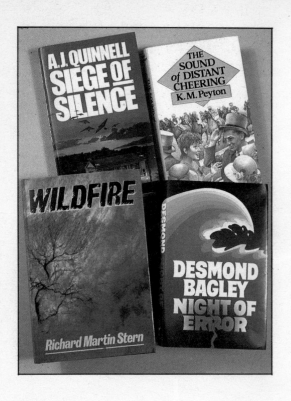

THE READER'S DIGEST ASSOCIATION LIMITED
25 Berkeley Square, London W1X 6AB

THE READER'S DIGEST ASSOCIATION
SOUTH AFRICA (PTY) LTD
Reader's Digest House, 130 Strand Street, Cape Town

Printed by Petty & Sons Ltd, Leeds
Bound by Hazell, Watson & Viney Ltd, Aylesbury

Original cover design by Jeffery Matthews FSIAD

For information as to ownership
of copyright in the material in this book see last page

READER'S DIGEST
CONDENSED BOOKS

WILDFIRE
by Richard Martin Stern

It is summer, and the huge Sanrio National Forest in New Mexico is a cool haven for tourists. But to Ranger J. L. Harmon the forest is a firetrap. No rain has fallen in six weeks. A single spark could set disaster in motion—a disaster that would threaten miles of wilderness, a town full of people, and the one woman who is beginning to mean something special to JL. Suddenly, the flames erupt in the forest—and the stage is set for a terrifying battle between frantic fire fighters and a rampaging inferno.

A powerful story with a factual background from the author of five previous, very popular, Condensed Book selections.

SIEGE OF SILENCE
by A. J. Quinnell

The Central American state of San Carlo is in crisis: within hours of a communist-led coup, the US embassy in the state's capital is under siege, and the ambassador, Jason Peabody, faces cross-examination at the hands of master interrogator Jorge Calderon. Calderon wants names. And he wants them fast. As the hours tick by and the US government tries desperately to devise a rescue plan, the tension in the interrogation room mounts. Gradually Calderon realizes to his dismay that he may have met his match in the cool, resolute American.

Taut psychological drama and superb action are the ingredients of this spellbinding new thriller.

THE SOUND OF DISTANT CHEERING
by K. M. Peyton

This is the story of the changing fortunes of a group of racing people: of Rosy Weeks, a dedicated and hard-working stable girl who dreams of a racehorse all of her own, and who yearns to marry her elusive and self-sufficient boss, Jeremy Cutbush; it's also the story of Jeremy's eccentric and forgetful grandmother, Letitia, who unwittingly plays a major part in altering the course of Rosy's hitherto uneventful life . . .

K. M. Peyton's fine new novel is a gently humorous and touching portrayal of the unpredictable world of racing—a world full of surprises, thrills and heartaches.

NIGHT OF ERROR
by Desmond Bagley

Some lumps of rock from the ocean bed and a notebook filled with cryptic drawings are the only clues Mike Trevelyan has to help him unravel the mystery of his brother's death on a remote Pacific atoll. Determined to know how Mark died, Mike sets out in a 200-ton brigantine to follow his brother's trail across the oceans. A sinister Australian seaman, a singer in a Panama nightclub, and a drunken doctor on a tropical island, all help to lead him to the remarkable truth—and to a scientific discovery of huge potential value.

A gripping tale of skulduggery and suspense on the high seas from this ever-popular storyteller.

Wildfire

A CONDENSATION OF THE BOOK BY

RICHARD MARTIN STERN

ILLUSTRATED BY HODGES SOILEAU

Forest ranger J. L. Harmon is worried. For weeks no rain has fallen, and the vast Sanrio National Forest in New Mexico which he looks after has become a potential firetrap. The towering pines, the aspens, the woodland floor—all are tinder-dry, and it would take only a single spark to ignite them.

Unfortunately, there are people who don't recognize the warning signs. Like Stacy Cummings, who owns a ranch near the forest's edge—too near for JL's comfort. And the Lawry family, camped deep in the forest—deeper than they have a right to be. And Don and Elsie Edwards, a honeymoon couple blissfully unaware of the threat that surrounds them.

Soon they, and others, are to find themselves in the path of a rampaging blaze. To stop its relentless progress, JL has literally to fight fire with fire in a terrifying and unequal battle.

Prologue

The wildland fire that came to be known as Backslope—the name Jay Paul gave it only because every large fire must have a name—began at six twelve pm Mountain Daylight Time on Sunday, June 19, when a single bolt of dry lightning struck a towering ponderosa pinetree deep in New Mexico's Sanrio National Forest.

The electrical charge, following the tree's living inner wood as the most direct path to the ground, easily overcame the tree's resistance, in the process generating unbelievably high temperatures and overheating sap to the point of explosion. The force of this reaction, bursting outwards like a bomb, opened a great, ugly gash through the tree's heavy, platelike bark.

Smouldering pieces of bark were flung from the tree's wound like shrapnel to the forest floor. Some fell harmlessly on bare ground, but some fell on twigs, dry grass or trampled brush. Match-sized flames appeared and, like matches, some flared briefly, consuming what fuel was at hand before dying away.

But one large piece lodged in the snug shelter of a recently fallen and thoroughly dry dead branch, and there, patiently, began to urge its host closer and closer to combustion.

There was no telltale smoke, and no witness to sound the alarm.

Chapter One

Until midafternoon it was a lovely, clear summer Sunday in 1983: a day for swimming in the lakes of the Sanrio National Forest, for fishing the forest streams, for hiking or riding on the mountain trails, for home cookouts in the city of Sanrio, for tennis and leisurely drinks at the country club.

In a shallow, glaciated bowl beneath the summit of Sierra Grande's fourteen-thousand-foot peak, which rises within the forest just north of the city, there was still snow—a reminder of the skiing that had been excellent that season. Elsewhere on the mountain slopes, in isolated meadows above the timberline, tiny blue forget-me-nots and yellow cinquefoil clung to rock and soil, defying wind and temperature extremes to bloom in profusion and welcome hikers staunch enough to reach their elevation.

On the Sanrio side of the mountain there had been no precipitation for weeks, but with heavy run-off from the winter snowpack reservoirs were full, and this year water was no worry, even in this semi-arid land.

Jasper Lightfoot (JL) Harmon saw it differently, but then as fire management officer for the forest, that was his job.

"The brow furrowed with concern," Stacy Cummings said rhetorically, running into him that morning at the Sanrio newsstand. "Problems?" Between them these days there was no longer the kind of wariness that had been present only a few weeks before.

"Lack of rain," JL said briefly. "Six weeks without it."

Stacy studied him. "Now why is that so important?" Her quick smile flashed. "Assume I really want to know."

JL tried not to sound like a textbook. "All the stuff on the floor of the forest—the deadfalls, the fallen needles and twigs—all that, we call fuel. And we classify it ten-hour, hundred-hour, thousand-hour, which means how long it will take to dry out. The light stuff dries first, of course, but after about a thousand hours, everything is ready to burn."

"And six weeks is more than a thousand hours," Stacy said. She nodded thoughtfully. "Luck, Ranger. We'll pray for rain."

JL watched her go, and had an idea that she was aware of it. She wore tight faded jeans, handmade boots and a tooled belt with silver-and-turquoise buckle, along with a light wool shirt.

They had only met how many times—three? but you didn't tend to forget her. Especially not after that first meeting.

That day, eight weeks ago, JL had driven the green Forest Service pickup in from the county road and past the mailbox that read CUMMINGS. The gravel drive, nearly half a mile long, wound in through carefully pruned piñon and juniper. The map JL had seen showed a full section, six hundred and forty acres of Cummings property. Even before he came to the big, sprawling house, with its superb view of Sierra Grande, JL had decided that these Cummings folk had money, pots of it.

Conscious that his Forest Service uniform presented a picture of authority, he told the Spanish maid who answered the door that he wished to speak to the head of the house. The maid hesitated only a moment and then led him inside.

The floor was gleaming terracotta tiles. From the entrance hall he could see into a living room, with heavy, polished furniture and oil paintings on the whitewashed adobe walls, but warm somehow, even intimate. Taste, as well as money, JL thought.

"In here, *señor, por favor,*" the maid said, indicating a small office-library. Then she turned away and walked across the living room towards muffled sounds of talk and laughter. She opened a frosted glass-sliding door.

JL caught a glimpse of water churning in a small tiled pool, of glistening bodies and unrecognizable faces. Suddenly feeling very much out of place, he turned away to wait uncomfortably in the office-library.

After a bit came Stacy Cummings, cool and poised in a white towelling robe, her short dark hair still damp and her brown eyes watching him. He had expected a male head of the house.

"I am Stacy Cummings," she said. "This is my house. What do you want, Ranger?"

Probably no more than in her late twenties, he thought, but with the kind of assurance she hadn't any right to for another ten or fifteen years.

JL gathered himself. "I make it a point to get acquainted with new property owners whose land abuts onto the forest." The words sounded stilted even to his own ears. "But I didn't intend to interrupt."

Stacy's smile was amused, mocking. "Surprised, Ranger? It is called a spa. It is considered therapeutic."

"I know." He allowed annoyance to show. "They're very big in southern California."

"You do get around, don't you?"

"I just wasn't aware," JL said, "that the hot-tub culture had come

11

to Sanrio along with all the beautiful people." He bore down on that last adjective.

Stacy looked at him, the mocking smile no longer showing. "Was that all?"

"Anything else," JL said, "can wait. Have a good spa—or whatever it's called." Exit line, end of their first meeting.

Now, remembering that scene, JL watched Stacy until she turned the corner out of sight. A strange, prickly female, with far more to her than first appeared. Out of curiosity he had asked around and had been astonished to find out that Stacy Cummings was a world champion cowgirl, in addition to having a lot of Texas oil money.

"She's a many-faceted chick," Ken Delacorte, a friend of both, had told him. "Don't sell her short. You don't get to be world champion anything if you've got soft spots."

A little forbidding in a woman, JL thought now, but there it was. He walked out to his pickup and got in, tossing the Sunday paper onto the seat beside him. He thought of going home, but except for the unfinished oil painting on the easel, home had little appeal. Nor had it ever drawn him irresistibly, even when Madge was still there.

"Another woman I could understand," Madge had said. "But how can I compete with mountains and pinetrees? And at your age, still jumping out of aeroplanes!"

"I was a smoke jumper for ten years."

"But you're not a kid any more. Or maybe you are. You don't even want a better job."

"There aren't any."

"Then stay here and grow moss like your trees. I'm leaving."

And so on this Sunday morning, instead of going home, he drove the pickup through the quiet town, into the forest and along deserted roads until he reached the boundary of the wilderness area, a tract in the heart of the forest set aside for special preservation. Here, no cars, structures or roads were permitted. Man was intended to be a transient visitor, one who disturbed nature as little as possible. To reinforce that point, there was a large sign that said NO MOTORIZED VEHICLES ALLOWED.

JL stopped and got out, just to hear the silence. Automatically his thoughts went to the flight he made a while ago, his last real overview of the forest.

With smoke jumper Andy McIlvain as the pilot and JL as copilot, they had taken off in a light plane from the Forest Service airport. JL had sat quietly and let his eyes wander over the terrain below.

Three-million-plus acres of forest lay beneath them, five thousand square miles. An area almost as large as Connecticut and Rhode Island together, with a thousand square miles of wilderness area in its centre—all of it his to care for, to protect.

He knew the forest as he knew the contours of the face he shaved every morning. From the lakes, the creek bottoms and the dry gullies to the pinnacle peak of Sierra Grande itself, he had walked, ridden or flown over every foot of this vast terrain.

The lower elevations of the land were in the piñon-juniper stratum, with isolated cholla cactus here and there. Scrub oak grew on the sharply contoured hillsides. The big trees, the ponderosa pines, came next in the ascending order, and with them, beginning at eight hundred feet, the aspens.

Above the timberline were open talus slopes, slopes formed of rock debris, and bare rock faces—a barren, desolate terrain, hostile, even dangerous, to man. Snow-covered, as they had been that morning, the upper elevations seemed silent and at peace. It was an illusion.

JL glanced at Andy, who was pointing down to their left at a minute clear area beside an open lake. Across the lake a glaciated cliff rose sheer three hundred or four hundred feet. Miraculously, large pinetrees clung to the upper slope, even at the cliff's edge.

"You'll get wind currents off that cliff face," JL said.

"Yep." Andy seemed delighted. "Show you what my new parachute will do. Downwind, crosswind, upwind. Like a modern sailboat. You still want to try it?" he went on. "After all this time, and with all those chair-seat calluses? What'll Madge say?"

Madge had still been with him then. "She won't know until after."

"And Jefferson'll know afterwards too, and he'll be hopping mad." George Jefferson was JL's boss, the supervisor of Sanrio National Forest.

"Could be."

Andy flew for a time in silence. He said at last, "Then why?"

"I want to see for myself how good your new chute is, so I can know what kind of terrain I can send your smoke jumpers into. I don't aim to lose people."

Andy nodded. "OK," he said. "We'll go up in a month or so, and you'll jump. I'll be your jump-mate."

Funny he should think of that now, JL thought, because that morning had been back in the *safe* time, when the snow-covered forest was more or less fireproof. Today it was different. The forest was one large tinderbox.

THE FAMILY'S NAME was Lawry—Les, Cindy Lou and young Tad—and they had driven jolting into the heart of the wilderness area, where no vehicles were allowed, as far as a narrow stretch of the upper Sanrio River, where they had stashed their jeep amid some big rocks, covering it with pine boughs.

"This is how you do it, son," Les told the boy, proud to show off his army knowledge of camouflage. "We always covered our vehicles like this when we bivouacked. You never knew when—there! See?" He pointed suddenly upwards as two low-flying airforce planes roared past, following the course of the river. "They won't catch your old dad as easy as that."

Cindy Lou said, "Old Dad hasn't bothered to tell us yet, hon, why we couldn't have walked in like ordinary folks."

"Because most folks don't come this far into the wilderness," Les said, "so it stands to reason the fishing's better here."

Cindy Lou said, "I didn't even know we had a fishing licence."

"We don't. If anybody comes, we'll say we tried to get one in town but they said they were fresh out."

"Do you always have to behave like a wheeler-dealer?" Cindy Lou said. "What kind of example is that for the kid?"

"He could do a lot worse than copying his old man," Les said. "I haven't done so bad. Now, you two set up the tent and I'll catch us some trout for dinner. Set it under that tree yonder so it won't be seen from the air."

IN ANOTHER PART OF THE WILDERNESS on this Sunday, Elsie Edwards undid the belt of her backpack and gratefully lowered the pack's full weight to the ground. The back of her shortsleeved khaki shirt was wet through with sweat. She stood in silence for a few moments, studying the blue nylon tent pitched beneath the high ponderosa pine. She looked at Don.

"It's not exactly what I had in mind," she said, smiling. "I'm thinking more along the lines of the bridal suite in, say, one of those big hotels in Nice, or perhaps the Dorchester in London."

"We'll get to that kind of thing," Don said. "Maybe for our twenty-fifth anniversary. Or our fiftieth."

Elsie pulled out her shirttails and flapped them vigorously to create a small breeze. "That illustrates one of the differences between us," she said, smiling still. "You're the patient type."

She was a strong young woman in a hurry, this bride of his, Don thought, but he was content. By her very eagerness, she brought a sense of adventure he had lacked. "And for now?" he said.

Elsie stopped flapping the loose shirt, and the quality of her smile changed. "For now," she said, "I suggest you get out of your backpack. I'd say we have all the privacy we need."

THEIR NAMES WERE Frank Orwell and Felipe Vigil. And what they had in common was that both had simply walked away from the minimum security prison at nearby Los Ojos. Then they had stolen a car, walked into a sporting-goods store, subdued the proprietor and walked out again with two hunting knives, a backpack each and $161.11 from the till.

At a self-service store they bought supplies, then drove to the edge of the wilderness, left the car, and headed into the wildland on foot.

"You a real fool man," Felipe said as they walked. "You got one year left, and you walk out. Now you'll get three more. Maybe more than that."

"They got go catch us first. And in the woods there ain't nobody going to catch me. So walk, man, walk."

JL COULD ALMOST HAVE PREDICTED the weather progression that Sunday afternoon. First came a faint thickening of haze behind Sierra Grande's lofty peak. Then a cloud began to form, rising higher and higher, darkening, glowering, gradually emerging as an anvil-shaped thunderhead.

But there was no rain. JL, by now back in his studio at home, brush in hand, swore softly to himself and hoped that all mountain lookouts in this part of the southwest were also watching. Suddenly a jagged lightning streak appeared and seemed to hang quivering, its multiple tendrils reaching down to the forested slopes. Seconds later the thunder reached his ears.

JL waited, and searched the trees, but no telltale smoke appeared. That, he thought, would be too easy. He made himself relax as he turned away from the window to face his easel again.

The scene in the half-finished painting was of the forest, of course: towering ponderosa pines, an aspen touched by autumn gold. Off centre on the canvas was a patch of deep blue sky. No more than a small craggy outcropping of the big mountain was visible, but a sense of its immense presence filled the picture.

JL picked up his palette and then set it down again. The heck with it. With a lightning storm going on right over his forest, it would take a superman to be able to concentrate. He left the studio and headed for the kitchen and a cold beer.

STACY CUMMINGS WATCHED the lightning storm too, and thought of JL Harmon, that oddly complicated ranger. After their first meeting she had asked Ken Delacorte about JL. Ken was a friend from college days who sold real estate in Sanrio now and knew all the gossip. Once, not long ago, he had played football for the Houston Oilers; Stacy felt a kind of athletic kinship with him.

"JL?" Ken said. "He's all right. He's the boss of what they call wildlife suppression in the whole Sanrio forest. Quite a job. And when they get in big trouble other places, he's the head of the team of experts they send out to take over. Quite a guy. Used to jump out of aeroplanes to put out fires."

He still jumps out of aeroplanes, Stacy thought now, remembering.

Some weeks after JL's visit to her house, she had been riding in the heart of the forest on Sam, her big horse, enjoying the coolness, the almost cathedral hush, that surrounded her. As she rode through a clearing in the trees, she came to a stream that emptied into a small glaciated lake beneath a three-hundred-foot cliff. In the lake's placid surface the great mountain was faithfully reflected. A picture postcard, Stacy thought, smiling; and then the smile turned to a frown of annoyance as the growing sound of an aircraft broke the mountain hush.

It came down the valley, well beneath Sierra Grande's peak, a high-wing, high-tail, twin-engine plane that swept over a tiny meadow among the pinetrees on the lake's shore. But her annoyance turned to curiosity as three streamers of weighted yellow-and-orange crepe paper dropped from the open doorway of the aircraft and fluttered towards the centre of the meadow.

The aircraft banked sharply and made a tight circle, and this time, out came one human figure and then a second, and almost instantaneously two multicoloured parachutes blossomed and drifted downwards.

Sam snorted at the sight and pawed the ground. "Easy, boy," Stacy said. "You're no more baffled than I am."

The leading parachute fluttered in the air, seemed to veer off to one side and then dipped, slanting back to its original path. The second chute fluttered and veered in almost exactly the same spot, caught apparently by wind currents coming from the cliff face. It too recovered, but with a jerky movement that left the man swinging like a pendulum.

The first man landed and rolled easily on the ground. The second man hit hard and rose on only one leg, the other held free as he collapsed his parachute. Across the water the two voices came clearly.

"Not bad for an old guy," one of the men said. "You OK?"

"I overcontrolled." It was JL's voice. He lowered the one foot, put a little weight on it and lifted it again. "Clumsy," he said.

"I'll walk out," the other man said, "and send for a chopper."

Stacy touched Sam's flanks with her heels. They trotted round the edge of the lake to the meadow, and she reined Sam in. "We keep running into each other," she said to JL. "You won't need a chopper. Sam can carry two. Come on up."

The other man grinned as he helped JL up behind the saddle.

They rode for a time in silence, Sam holding to his steady, easy walk. At last Stacy said, "Ankle bad?"

"Sprained. Plain clumsiness." JL didn't know what to do with his hands, so he kept them on his thighs.

"You came out to the house that day for a reason," Stacy said unexpectedly, her voice coming to him over her shoulder. "Were you going to explain the facts of life near the forest?"

"Would you have listened?"

"Probably not very well. Anyway, it's my property."

"True."

"I've observed all zoning."

"True again. And you've done a lot of things right. No cedar shingle roof to catch fire from sparks. No undergrowth right up against the buildings."

"I raise horses. I don't want them tangled up in brush."

"But no road out. Only the one-way gravel drive. If there was another car in there, you couldn't move."

"And you want an escape route." JL didn't bother to answer. Stacy wished she could see his face, but she refused to turn in the saddle. "I thought fire people were supposed to put fires out, not run away from them," she said.

With no change of tone JL said, "Is Stacy your real name, like it says on the map?"

"It's my name. It was my daddy's."

"Your daddy's? He named you after himself?"

Caught off balance by the swift change of subject, Stacy chose to smile. "He wanted a boy. But he took what he got. Me."

"I've heard that you're a world champion cowgirl. Barrel racer. Calf roper. Even tried your hand at bronco riding."

Stacy frowned faintly. "What is this? 'This is Your Life'?"

"I try to know my neighbours."

"*Your* neighbours?"

"In a manner of speaking. This is my forest."

"I thought it belonged to the government."

"I care for it."

"And," Stacy said, "on its behalf you resent me, us, with our houses on its fringe. Tell me why." But it was beginning to dawn on her that she already knew the answer. "We're your responsibility, is that it? Fire, flash flood, any kind of trouble, and you bail us out?" She nodded solemnly. "I hadn't thought of it that way before."

Few do, JL thought, but did not say it aloud.

"I think, Ranger," she said, "that I'd like to know more about what you do. And why you do it."

"It's a job."

This time her dark head shook in emphatic denial. "I'm beginning to think it's a great deal more than that." Maybe commitment was the word, she thought, and how many did she know who were really committed to anything?

AS EVENING CAME on that Backslope Sunday, cool dense air began to flow down the flanks of Sierra Grande. Encountering little resistance, it gathered speed, first merely a faint stirring, then a noticeable current, at last becoming a downhill breeze, setting the aspen leaves to whispering as they danced.

Around the base of the lightning-struck ponderosa pine, in response to the moving air, embers again began to glow, some of them rekindling to reach out for more fuel: dry needles, fallen twigs, small branches, a partially rotted log, which, heated, began to smoulder. The large piece of bark beneath the log burst into flame. That was all that was needed to ignite the log.

At first, one man could have stamped out all the flames with ease and, with a single green branch as a broom, swept the smouldering fuel into a harmless pile in a patch of bare earth. Even by full darkness, that same man working quickly could have contained the threat and snuffed it out with shovelfuls of earth.

Chapter Two

Ken Delacorte came to dinner at Stacy's that Sunday evening. "I heard the Brown place next door was for sale," Stacy said. "Next door" was a figure of speech; the properties were contiguous, but the two main houses were more than a mile apart.

"Sold," Ken said. He smiled. "Character who bought it has renamed it El Rancho Costa Mucho, and it did too. The certified cheque he brought to the completion was well up in seven figures. Fellow named Jones, Bartlemy Jones. Goes around in a fancy electric wheelchair." He stopped, watching the sudden change in Stacy's face. "Something I said?"

"The roof just fell in, is all," she said. Her smile was wan. "You couldn't know. An old flame. We parted on something less than a romantic note. Fix yourself another drink."

Ken came back from the bar in a thoughtful mood. He sat down slowly.

"Jones," he said. "You don't like him? Or maybe you don't trust him? Which?"

"Why?"

"Well, aside from buying the Brown place, he's asking too many questions about Bellevue Acres, my development. It's not much, but it's all I could afford to build. It's where I've bet my shirt." He smiled crookedly. "By your standards it's not a very expensive shirt, I'll admit."

"I'll ignore that," Stacy said.

Long after Ken had left that evening, Stacy sat on in the office-library, staring. One wall of the room was floor-to-ceiling bookcases. On the remaining walls were photographs of horses, some with Stacy, some by themselves. She could name each animal and give the place and date of the photo. There were times when it seemed as though her life were there on those walls.

Stacy was then, as JL had guessed closely that first day, twenty-nine, a woman of medium height, smoothly muscled, with boyish hips, slim waist and straight legs. Of her glossy dark hair and brown eyes, her father had often said, "Most likely some Indian in us somewhere, but by golly, not enough to claim a share in any tribe's oil properties, so I've darn well had to find our own."

And he had. He liked to claim that he had tramped and prospected every square foot of Texas, Oklahoma and eastern New Mexico, relying on a God-given gift to know where oil was to be found.

Young Stacy never knew her mother. "I was out in the middle of nowhere . . ." Her father had told her the tale often enough, flagellating himself with the memory. "And that damn well blew at just about the time you began to put in an appearance. I was busier than a bird dog in a stubble field, and your mother said she was all right." He spread his huge hands in helplessness. "You came

through it all right. Your mother didn't. Me, I got another oil well."
The last sentence was said in bitter self-accusation.

It was a strange relationship, father-daughter, no woman in the
house other than hired help. There were women who tried to take
over; the increasing Cummings oil wealth was irresistible. But her
father refused to be trapped.

Stacy did not remember when she had first been on a horse, but
some early incidents remained vivid. There was, for example, the
colt she called Boots, her own, hand-raised from a foal back on the
old home ranch in central Texas. She was not quite fifteen when she
slapped her saddle on him and climbed aboard.

Boots was no longer a foal, and his reactions to the saddle were
anything but friendly. Stacy landed hard on the packed corral dirt.
She got to her feet, dusted herself off and started towards Boots,
who was standing docilely enough, reins hanging.

The ranch foreman walked into the corral. "Better let me take a
little of the edge off him, girl," he said.

Stacy's reaction was immediate. "You," she said in a voice that
shook, "keep your hands off him, you hear? He's my horse, and
nobody but me's going to break him."

There was silence. Then the foreman said slowly, "Now, look
here, young lady. That's no kind of way—"

"You heard her." This was Stacy the father. He climbed the corral
fence and perched comfortably on the top rail. "Well now," he said,
"let the show commence."

It took two more falls, and with each one, young Stacy's chin grew
firmer. She limped back for the fourth try, got stiffly into the saddle
and this time stayed there until Boots, tossing his head occasionally,
walked obediently twice round the corral.

Stacy bent down to pat the sweating neck. "Good boy." Her voice
was gentle.

"Good girl," her father said.

Schooling presented problems resulting in an inevitable clash
of wills.

"Your mother," her father said, "was well educated in the east.
Why she married me, I'm hanged if I know. But she did, and you're
the result, and I'll see that you turn out to be a lady too."

"I'm not interested."

"I didn't ask what you thought. I'm telling you. I'm not going to
see you grow up to be a stable hand."

Not all of what young Stacy considered the unnecessary airs and
graces took, but the product that emerged after three years in Miss

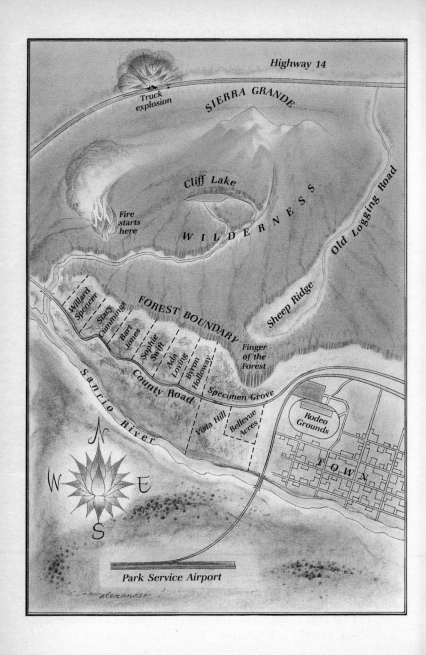

Walker's school in Boston was a different article indeed from the one her father had first put on the plane in Dallas.

"Each time you've come back on vacation," he said, when he met her final homecoming plane, "you've looked a little better. You've turned into a real good-looking filly, and quite a lady. Now, what do you want to do?"

"The university's got a good rodeo team."

"And you're fixing to be a part of it?" Her father nodded. "I guess you've earned it."

At the university there were boys and horses, sometimes in one order, sometimes the other. There were also books, running a poor third except in courses having to do with animal husbandry.

"Some folks," her father said, "like animals better than people. That the way you see it too?"

"People have their uses."

"I don't pretend to understand women," he went on. "But I'm beginning to believe that you're like the man said, a riddle wrapped in a mystery inside an enigma. What do you want, anyway, honey?"

"I'm still looking for it," Stacy said. Simple truth.

She was twenty-two when her father died—as he had lived, violently, his neck broken by a falling length of drill pipe.

Stacy showed no tears in public or in private, but the death left an emptiness she doubted would ever be filled.

To friends there was no noticeable change. "She's a tough one," they would say, in the admiring way that one spoke of an athlete who insisted on playing even when hurt. The result was that no one managed to penetrate the facade.

Bartlemy Jones had assumed a certain importance during this period. He was a big man, as Stacy's father had been big, and solid, but with a strong macho streak that made him as different as different could be from her father.

Stacy Cummings the father had always been willing to go for broke—but only when circumstances demanded it. Bart Jones would take chances merely to be doing what no one else would dare. To Stacy the daughter there was a vast difference.

"You don't have to show off," she once told him. "Not to me, not to anybody."

"You've been alone too much, my girl," he answered. "You get lonely, bitter."

It was a moment of relaxed candour. "Lonely? I've never been lonely in my life. I like some people, but I don't need them."

"Is that supposed to put me in my place?"

"Oh, come off it," Stacy said. "To you, I'm good for a few laughs. Other people don't really matter that much to you."

After what happened on what she still thought of as *that night*, she would have given the world to be able to retract those words. Try as she might, she could never entirely shake the sense of guilt they left her with.

The party that night was like so many others back in Texas: big house, expensive cars in the floodlit parking area. Inside, and out around the pool, white-coated waiters served drink orders, and maids in Mexican skirts silently passed canapés. A Mexican street band played.

Bart Jones was drunk, and there was a dangerous gleam in his eye. They had come to the party together, and now he wanted to leave. The stage was set for trouble and Stacy had known it—that was the part that would not go away.

"Suit yourself, sweetie pie," Bart told her, "but I'm headed back to town and a thick steak."

"I'll go," Stacy said. "If you'll let me drive."

"No dice. You don't always get your way, you know."

"Look," she said, "will you for once in your life be sensible?"

Nothing changed in his face, but a new note came into his voice. "No point in starting now," he said with finality.

She watched him go, smiling and nodding as he made his way through the guests. "Old Bart can really hold his liquor." How often had Stacy heard that? Too often, she thought, and was tempted to go after him for one more try. But she didn't.

AT LEAST IT WAS A ONE-CAR ACCIDENT and nobody else was involved. "He must have tried to take that turn at well over a hundred," one of the state cops said, watching the emergency crew working to cut Bart out of the wreck.

Stacy visited the hospital as soon as she heard the news, but it was days before she was able to see Bart, and her reception then was less than warm.

"Come to say 'I told you so'?" were his first words.

Stacy swallowed hard and managed to hold back what was in her mind. "Anything you need? Books? Magazines?"

"A new spinal cord. Got one?"

It was the first she knew of the seriousness of his injury, and how she managed to hold back the sudden, unexpected tears that stung her eyelids, she would never know.

Texas soured for Stacy after that, with her father gone and now this thing with Bart. Eventually, he was shipped off somewhere for physiotherapy to help him adjust to his new condition. By that time Stacy's college friend Ken Delacorte, having retired from football and finished an unsuccessful ex-athlete assault on Hollywood, was living in Sanrio, selling real estate. And Sanrio, which held no memories, seemed as good a place to settle down as any.

Not, she told herself, that she needed Ken or anyone else, because she was complete within herself, and if, as she knew, that was not wholly true for anybody, it was close enough.

To Sophie Swift, her Sanrio lawyer, she said one day, as she had said to Bart, "I'm never lonely. Not really." And then she had shown the brilliant smile that somehow seemed to mock herself. "I talk to my horses. And they talk back. But don't tell anyone."

"The confidentiality of the lawyer-client relationship," Sophie said, nodding solemnly, and smiled back.

And so here she was, on this quiet Sunday, hundreds of miles distant from Texas and its memories. And there was Bart again, right next door. Too much. Just too much she thought as she stood up and began to turn out lights on her way to bed. One thing was sure: Bart's buying El Rancho Costa Mucho was no accident, no coincidence. That she knew.

BY EARLY MORNING MOONSET, urged on by the night breeze, the growing flames had run downhill and fanned out. Hidden in the deep folds of the foothills and the stands of the forest itself, the fire gathered its strength and force. At last it was large and strong enough to dare the open. Like a monster roaring out of its hiding place, it burst into view. In the darkness it threw its lights and contorting shadows into the sky. Bellowing and roaring defiance, it was suddenly alive, and loose.

AARON SWIFT, ATTORNEY-AT-LAW, and, out of a deep sense of public duty, also federal magistrate, was not sleeping well these nights. At three o'clock on this Monday morning, Debby slept beside him relaxed as a kitten. Indeed, Aaron thought, she resembled a cuddly, purring kitten—wide eyes, softness and all.

Debby was a small-town girl from west Texas who had grown up knowing how to run a house, how to sew a fine seam and how to bake buttermilk biscuits that would almost float off the plate. Debby was, in short, the kind of girl who married dear old dad before women's liberation came along.

Aaron's first wife, Sophie, on the other hand, was strictly one of a kind. Aaron saw her every day in the office they shared, of course, and he had lived with her as her husband for twenty-five years, but he was still not sure that he would understand her. His thoughts kept going back to a night he would just as soon forget.

"Mr. Bumble said that the law is an ass—an idiot," she'd said when he'd told her about Debby. "The law is also a tyrant and a slave master. I have followed its bidding. My fault. That is our problem." As clear and concise as if she were addressing the bench.

"Soph, it isn't—I mean, there isn't any fault. It's one of those things."

"No fault? As in insurance? The dispassionate view? But passion is precisely what we're talking about. You have a passion for young Debby Winslow."

"You make it sound like a—brief."

"That's my failing, Aaron. I don't know how to use the words that demonstrate emotion. They embarrass me. But, believe me, I do have feelings."

"I know."

"Yes. You do. And that is what makes this all the more difficult for both of us. What should I do, try to argue you out of this situation? That would be ridiculous and, even if it succeeded, self-defeating. Our relationship would never be the same again. I can't compete with Debby Winslow. And I know it."

In the end he had left her the ranch and taken an apartment in town. After the divorce they retained their joint practice of law, and through it all Sophie maintained her calm, quiet, decisive presence. It was almost as if she and Aaron had never been more than partners and good friends.

"The quail are back at the ranch," Sophie had told him one recent morning. "And this year they've brought their chicks."

"I'd like to see them."

"You will be welcome any time. Debby too, of course."

And another time, "We have a new foal. Stacy Cummings says he already looks like a quarter horse."

"Stacy knows horses. How's your water this year?"

"Sufficient. But we could use a good, soaking rain."

Now, what kind of conversation was that to be remembering in detail at three o'clock in the morning? Aaron demanded of himself, and heard no answer. Was there some kind of guilt involved, that his mind should keep going over scenes with Sophie?

Beside him, Debby, kittenlike, slept on peacefully.

WILLARD P. SPENCER, also awake early this Backslope Monday morning, felt no sense of guilt, merely annoyance that he should find himself involved in minor financial details. Added to his annoyance was a growing dislike of Sanrio.

The area had been represented to him as an idyllic combination of the grandeur of the Swiss Alps, the charm of Old Mexico and the unhurried restfulness of the Greek islands. An impulsive man, Spencer had taken immediate steps to make a part of this dreamland his own. But the fact of the matter was that Sanrio was merely on the verge of becoming the kind of Palm Springs/Sun Valley locale Spencer had assumed it already was.

At a guess, Sanrio was a town of about twenty-five thousand, with a burgeoning ski industry, a few large and expensive estates like Spencer's, and a long tradition of southwestern informality.

"Backward, ignorant and lazy," would have been Spencer's summing-up. A place where no one gave any thought to breeding or background. Spencer had even been called by his first name on first meeting. Intolerable. Two telephone conversations last Friday had brought it all into focus, and he had brooded unhappily all through the weekend.

The first call was from Aaron Swift. "A couple of things have come up, Willard. Although I'm darned if I know why they were referred to me instead of to you direct."

"Because you are my legal representative here in Sanrio."

"All right." There was resignation in the voice. "Bud Lewis wants to know if you're going to pay the quarterly premium on your homeowner's insurance before the grace period expires."

"Of course I am. The question is ridiculous."

There was a short silence. Then Aaron Swift said, "The second thing is a call from the manager of the bank."

"And what does he want?"

"The last two months' instalments on your personal loan—"

"I am quite aware of that. You may tell him that I intend to see that my loan is renegotiated."

The silence this time was a little longer. Aaron Swift said at last, in a conversational tone, "You know, Willard, when you really put your mind to it, you can be just about as obnoxious as anyone I know." The line went dead.

Spencer placed the second call himself, to John Walters, his estate agent. "What is our situation, Walters?"

"One or two possible leads, Mr. Spencer," he said, "but nothing definite yet. I'm afraid we have to be patient." They were talking about a property with an asking price of a million five, Walters thought: seventy-odd private acres abutting onto the forest, with a four-bedroom main house, an exceptional water supply and stunning views of the mountain range. It was not the sort of property you sold over the telephone.

"Look," said Spencer, "I'm tired of this place, and I want to unload it. It's as simple as that. And you should be thinking of the fat commission you will get, if and when. Keep me posted."

Now, lying fully awake in the early morning, Spencer found that he could recall each of the conversations word for word.

From the other bed, in the dawning light, Angela said, as if they had been talking for some time, "I've been thinking. I've heard both good and not so good about the new Orient-Express, London to Venice. I think we should try it out, Will. Fly over on Concorde, of course. We haven't been to Venice in ages." There was no immediate response, and Angela raised her voice slightly. "Will! Did you hear me, Will?"

"We'll think about it," Spencer said.

JL'S RINGING TELEPHONE brought him instantly awake. "JL here."

"We've got one, JL." It was the dispatcher's voice, professionally calm, speaking from forest headquarters. "It's for real. I sent out two men, and they report it's already out of hand."

"On my way," JL replied. "I'll head for the airport. Have a chopper ready, and a forest map. How close can you get a crew in by vehicle?"

"Within about a mile," the man said. "A crew is on the way."

"Roger," JL answered, satisfied.

In no more than five minutes he was out of the house and starting up the Forest Service pickup. He drove fast, expecting. and encountering no other vehicles. He felt keyed up, eager. With a wildland fire, time was the critical factor. What could be handled immediately by a single crew of twenty men might in only a few minutes require half a dozen crews to dig in, establish a fire line and begin their counter-assault. Wildfire was the enemy, and sensible men treated it with respect.

The chopper was already rolled out and waiting at the Forest Service airport. A single-engine lead plane stood off to one side, near the high-wing Twin Otter from which Andy McIlvain's smoke jumpers operated. In the distance a vintage World War II twin-engine transport stood ready. The illusion, JL thought, was of an airfield in wartime. Well, in a sense it was.

"Ready to roll," the chopper pilot said. "Map and clipboard on your seat."

They swung up over the still sleeping city towards the flanks of Sierra Grande. The big mountain's top was now in morning sunlight, its snowcap a deep pink in the low-slanting rays.

"There she is," the pilot said, and pointed off to their left. The glow among the trees was unmistakable.

The fire area—already about five hundred acres—was midway between the south boundary of the forest, with the large estates adjoining it, and the edge of the wilderness. A breeze coming out of the west-northwest was elongating the burning area eastwards.

"Take her down for a good look," said JL. He folded the map to show the pertinent area and tucked it into the clipboard. He noted date and time, then began to sketch in the fires outlines.

The ride was bumpy. Currents of heated air rose from the ground, tossing the helicopter like a small boat in a choppy sea. JL ignored the jostling and, with frequent ground sightings to make sure of his points of reference, completed his sketching, applying quick shading to spots of heavy flames.

"Take her up now," he told the pilot. "I want an overview to see if anything else is affected."

Nothing else was—at the moment. But that condition, JL thought grimly, was only temporary.

Movement caught his eye, and through the piñon and juniper growth he could see the crew the dispatcher had already sent out: twenty men in yellow shirts and hard hats, walking in single file, far enough apart to avoid accidents from the tools they carried— McLeod hoes, Pulaski axes, chain saws, shovels, brush hooks.

"OK," JL told the pilot. "Let's take her home."

His mind was made up. He knew what was going to be needed.

WHETHER HIS CALL got George Jefferson out of bed or not was a matter of complete indifference to JL when he phoned from the airport. "It's going to be a big one," he told Jefferson, the forest supervisor and JL's immediate superior. "I think we'd better not fool around with a few isolated crews, but put in a full team right away."

This was as far as his recommendation could properly go. A fire team consisted of a complete organization of supervisory personnel and designated specialists, their ranks and responsibilities as specific as those of a military regiment. The overall commander of a fire team was called the fire boss.

There were two levels of fire teams constantly available. The Sanrio team operated only within Sanrio forest. Its designated boss was a man named Jay Paul, newly transferred to the area. The regional, class A, team, which JL commanded, operated on massive fires throughout the country whenever and wherever it was needed. The choice of which team was up to Jefferson.

"How's your ankle?" George Jefferson said. "Still limping?"

"It's fine."

"That was a fool thing, jumping with McIlvain. You know, you're not a kid any more. You're forty-one."

"George," JL said, "this really is going to be big. We need a fire team. Now."

"Aren't you supposed to be going to Idaho?"

JL had totally forgotten. He was signed up for a seminar at the Boise Interagency Fire Centre (BIFC—pronounced biff-see), the nerve centre and information clearinghouse of the nation's fire-suppression efforts. "I was."

"You still are," Jefferson said. "Call the dispatcher. Tell him to get on it. Jay Paul's team can cope."

"Jay Paul's new to the area, George."

"Then he'll have to learn fast."

JL took a deep breath. "George—"

"You want to handle it yourself, is that it?"

"Yes."

"The answer is no. Now call the dispatcher and get the Sanrio team into action." The line went dead.

JL stood for a moment, indecisive, still holding the phone in his hand. Then slowly he hung it up, walked into the radio room and called the dispatcher.

The system worked and worked well—how often had he told himself, and others, that? The lines of authority were established, guidelines in place, all mechanisms ready to go. You took orders from above and saw to it that your own orders were followed on down the line. Period. Into the microphone, to the dispatcher he said, "Call the Sanrio team. I'm bringing a map."

"Ten four, JL."

He put the mike down very gently. It would work, he told himself, because it had to. Jay Paul as fire boss would have immediately available to him a team of specialists and staff, including an air-attack boss, a plans chief, and a fire-behaviour officer to advise on the probable directions the fire would take. There would be a weatherman brought in to forecast climatic conditions, and even a special aircraft carrying equipment for infrared photography. From ten thousand feet, infrared photos could show a spot on the ground one foot square that was smouldering.

At the bottom of it all, the foundation, would be crews of twenty on the ground, the troops who would fight the fire face to face in shifts—an army to be fed, transported, provided with sleeping space and rudimentary sanitary facilities. There would be smoke jumpers and hotshot crews—specially trained teams that followed up the first attack forces.

The dispatcher summoning all this was, properly, the nerve centre of fire-suppression efforts. The Sanrio dispatcher had his office in the forest headquarters, located east of the wilderness and north of the town. He was a carefully screened and trained man, accustomed to what was called the hot seat, coping during extreme burning conditions with as many as two hundred fires a day within the vast area he was responsible for.

But the plain truth, JL told himself, was that he would rather have kept it all in his own hands, which was ridiculous. Or was it? He had seen the fire; others had not.

JL suspected that George Jefferson, who had never in his life jumped out of an aeroplane, still harboured a grudge because of the test jump with Andy McIlvain. In Jefferson's, and Madge's view, it had been merely a dangerous and unnecessary exercise in sheer juvenile romanticism.

Well, maybe it was, but still JL would do it again, because now he knew firsthand just what Andy's new parachute would do. And for that, in JL's opinion, there simply was no substitute.

Suddenly he realized they were going to need Andy and his smoke jumpers on this fire very soon.

On impulse he trotted up the steel stairs to the airport tower for the latest weather readouts. They indicated afternoon thunderstorm activity, but no rain.

"McIlvain's already reported here this morning," the man on duty said. "He's probably called the dispatcher too. He says his guys are tired of sitting on their duffs. You going to use them?"

"Not my decision," JL said, and he went back down the stairs, remembering the keyed-up, eager feelings of his own smoke-jumping days.

The jumpers were an elite group, mostly in their twenties or early thirties, although a few like Andy, who was forty, kept on until they could no longer handle the rigours of the job. They were all

31

experienced wildland fire fighters and all in superb physical condition. Their function was to parachute into terrain too rough for vehicles or helicopter landings; retrieve their "fire boxes" filled with gear they had packed themselves, tools, water when indicated, explosives, radios, food, shelters, in short, everything necessary for isolated wilderness existence and fire fighting (the "fire boxes" were also dropped by parachute after the jumpers were on the ground); stay as long as necessary to subdue whatever fire they had been sent in to attack; and walk out, at least as far as the nearest road reachable by vehicle, carrying their gear which weighed about one hundred and fifteen pounds per man.

During the fire season—in places across the country as early as April or as late as November—teams of smoke jumpers were moved around the country from Alaska to Florida at need, or in anticipation of each area's greatest fire season danger.

That Andy and his crew were already out at the airport, ready to go, was one more indication of the soundness of the planned routine, the *system*, JL reflected as he drove back into town. Still.

He had one more try at George Jefferson, by telephone from his house. "I've seen this fire, George," he said, "and I don't like it. Maybe we don't need the whole regional fire team, but somebody had better be here to look over Jay Paul's shoulder when things start to get rough."

"Namely you," Jefferson said. His voice was heavy with irony and suppressed anger. "Forget it, JL. Now I'm going to tell you just one more time to get on up to Boise, where you're scheduled to be, and stop thinking you're the only one around here who knows anything about fire suppression. Do you understand me?"

JL opened his mouth and closed it again. "I hear you," he said.

"And take your bad ankle with you."

BY MIDMORNING, at the fire command post Jay Paul had chosen— east of the fire's centre and below the wilderness—communications were still being set up, phone lines strung, radio antennae raised into treetops and trucks constantly arriving with supplies. Already the fire lines had been established by crews fanned out in accordance with JL's sketch map.

Out on the line the heat was intense. And the crackling of flames, punctuated by firecracker-like sounds as pine-pitch knots exploded, heightened the illusion of a battle.

Because of the gruelling demands of the job, there are not many women within fire-fighter ranks. But Bessie Wingate, crew chief, big as a big man and as brawny, was a jarring exception. Her crew was one of six ground crews already deployed. Her position was east of the fire's centre, on Sierra Grande's slopes.

"Maybe I ought to take up mud wrestling instead," she was fond of saying, "but, heck, it wouldn't be near as much fun."

On this day she wielded her shovel with grim power and efficiency. The job of the nineteen men under Bessie's command, working with chain saws, axes, brush hooks and shovels, was to maintain a line beyond which their small sector of fire could not pass and, if at all possible, drive the flames back upon themselves; it was hot, dirty, backbreaking and dangerous work.

When the fire began a hundred-and-eighty-degree fishhook turn, Bessie's warning came instantly. "Watch that one! Gus, Joe, get after it! But watch that gully! There's brush in there!"

Feeding on the tangled clutter of brush, and driven by the upslope wind, the fire tore into an area of scrub oak, consuming it with a crackling roar and raced on.

Bessie grabbed the walkie-talkie from her belt. "We've lost our line!" she shouted into it after identifying herself. "That monster is going up the gully, right into the big trees!"

JAY PAUL HAD SPENT FIFTEEN YEARS in fire suppression but was, as JL had said, new to the Sanrio forest. And right from the start he had an uncomfortable feeling about this fire.

"Get some aerial tankers in to douse that gully with slurry," he told his air-attack boss. Slurry is a liquid combination of fire-extinguishing chemicals, far more effective than water, used where ground crews cannot reach. "If we can't cut it off there, we're going to have the whole stand of ponderosas on fire."

Despite himself, some of Bessie's excitement had got to him, and he found it impossible to keep his voice calm. JL now, wouldn't even have batted an eye or raised his voice in the slightest. But, as everybody knew, JL had ice water in his veins.

AT THE BIFC COMPLEX on the outskirts of Boise, JL's first stop was the situation room, where teletyped reports from each area of the United States clacked in constantly. Here was his own Region 3, and the latest situation reports on the fire named Backslope. JL read them quickly. The conflagration seemed to be worse than he had feared: its estimated area was now two thousand acres.

One of the men at the large horseshoe desk recognized him and said, "You've got one going down your way, no?"

JL nodded. "Seems so." His voice was mild, apparently unconcerned. He walked down the hall to the weather room.

Here detailed information from the Weather Service was
received, digested and passed along to regional and forest commands. To one of the meteorologists he knew JL said, "Sanrio.
What's our forecast?"

"Tourist weather." The meteorologist was smiling. "There's a
lovely high sitting right down there, and no nasty storm is going to
move in on that. Dry lightning, but no rain."

JL smiled his thanks and walked out and back to the situation
room. "What's been committed to Backslope?" he asked the man at
the horseshoe desk.

The information was on the wall chart in the form of illuminated
different-coloured pins. "Six crews," the man said, looking over his
shoulder at the chart. "Two helitack crews, two air tankers and a
lead plane."

"Smoke jumpers?"

"No."

Jay was going to need them just for starters, JL thought. Six
crews—a hundred and twenty troops on the line—was not going to
be enough; even from here he could tell them that.

"Are you JL Harmon, from Sanrio?" A girl, in neat Forest Service
uniform.

JL nodded. Recall? George Jefferson wanted him back?

Instead, "They're waiting for you," the girl said. "The seminar is
about to begin."

Chapter Three

Young Tad Lawry was first out of the tent on Monday morning,
leaving his father and mother still in their sleeping bag. Back home
in Texas he was a boy scout and had done considerable hiking and
some camping, but he had never seen big trees like these, nor a
mountain anywhere near the size of Sierra Grande.

And the air tasted strange too, smelling like the trees and the
pitch that had rubbed off on his hand last night while he was helping
his mother put up the tent. And despite what his father had said
about their being all alone in here, there had to be somebody
nearby because he could smell campfire smoke.

His father was a funny guy, and Tad wondered why, after all the
years they had been married, his mother had never seemed to

realize it. "Nobody pushes your old man around," Les Lawry had told the boy once. "And don't let them push you, either."

What that meant was that if you told Pop to do something, he'd turn straight round and do the opposite, simple as that. "Don't drive so fast, Les." And down went the accelerator, almost through the floor. That kind of thing.

Tad studied the nearby stream. It was clear and fast-running. He followed it a few hundred yards, pleased by its gurgling. Round a bend that opened to a view, he stopped. Two deer were drinking, oblivious to his presence. He stood quietly, watching.

A new sound obtruded, the staccato chatter of a helicopter overhead. Both deer raised their heads, then bounded away as if on springs. Tad, remembering his father's caution last night, froze until the sound passed.

ELSIE EDWARDS WAS UP before Don. She peeped out of the blue nylon tent and looked around at the empty forest. She saw only a Canada jay, industriously scratching through the dead campfire. He stopped and cocked his head at her. Pulling on her shirt and shorts, Elsie stepped out into the bright hazy morning. Don followed.

The smell of smoke was faint against the scent of the pines. A campfire? No matter. Elsie breathed deep. "You remember my mentioning the bridal suite in the Dorchester?" she said. "Forget it. This is much better." She smiled. "I think it may be the company."

"I'm flattered."

"You should be." Elsie was silent for a moment, the fond smile still on her lips. "For the record, I don't think I've ever felt so happy in my whole life."

"Wasn't that the idea?"

FRANK ORWELL WAITED impatiently for Felipe Vigil, who had wandered off saying he'd be right back. That was half an hour ago. It was broad daylight now, and high time they got on their way. Orwell was anxious to put as much distance between himself and Los Ojos as he could.

"Hey, man!" Felipe suddenly appeared, breathless, grinning. "You know what I got? A chick, man! A beautiful chick. Wait'll you see her!" He stopped, studying Orwell's expression. "You dig, man? We got a real live woman out here in these woods!"

Orwell stood, indecisive. His mind said to split just as fast as they could. But his loins, after two years of incarceration, refused to listen. He licked his lips. "She alone?"

"There's a guy with her. He doesn't look like much. We can take him easy."

Orwell shook his head. "I don't like it."

"You chicken? Nothing to it. Ten, fifteen minutes, then we on our way. It's been too long, man, too long."

STACY SAW AND SMELLED the smoke when she awakened, and noted that the sun had taken on a strange metallic-orange tinge. The seven am radio news mentioned fire in the Sanrio forest, but reported it was under control. *"No hay problema,"* Stacy told Juanita, her housekeeper, who agreed that those in charge undoubtedly had matters well in hand, and would the señorita be home for lunch?

And that, of course, brought up the subject Stacy had been trying to avoid ever since yesterday—Bart Jones and just what she was going to do about him. In the end, characteristically, she faced the problem head-on and telephoned El Rancho Costa Mucho.

A maid answered, and a few moments later Bart himself was on the line. "I wondered when you'd call." He sounded casual and without guile.

"I didn't know until last night that I had a new neighbour."

"I hoped you'd be surprised. When do I see you? Here, I hope. I don't get around much any more."

"I have work to do this morning," she said.

"Lunch then? I have a good cook."

"Lunch it is. One o'clock?"

Stacy hung up and sat for a little while motionless, staring unseeing across her office. Unreal, she thought; unreal that he's here; unreal that he can still get to me.

AARON SWIFT CAME into the office early as usual that morning. There was already a telephone message from Sophie on his desk, saying that she would be in late, if at all. It was unlike her, and Aaron called the familiar ranch number at once. Her voice sounded all right, and he was conscious of a sharp feeling of relief. "You're OK, then?" he asked.

"I'm fine. It's the fire."

"In the forest? It's way in, deep. Not to worry."

"We're getting ash."

"It's just that the wind is blowing that way."

"Yes. That's what concerns me." Always there was reason, careful logic behind her words.

Aaron said, "You want me to come out, Soph?"

36

"I don't think so. Someone has to mind the store. Besides, what could you do if you came? There isn't anything I can do, either, but I'll feel better just staying here. You can understand that."

Aaron could. More than twenty years of living had gone into that ranch, he thought, both hers and his.

"Will you call me, Soph, if you want me? Promise me that?"

"You didn't have to ask." Her voice was gentle.

The moment Aaron hung up, the switchboard operator buzzed his phone. "Mr. Willard Spencer is on line two."

Aaron sighed and pushed the button. "You are up early, Willard. I was under the impression that you liked to sleep in."

Spencer did not like to be teased. "When there is a fire . . ." he began portentously.

"Oh, come now, it's miles away."

"Nevertheless, I don't like it."

"There's nothing I can do about it, Willard."

"On the contrary, you can find out at once precisely when the grace period of my homeowner's insurance lapses."

Aaron wore his courtroom face. "I have a better suggestion, Willard." He paused, for emphasis. "It is that you write a cheque for your quarterly premium and carry it into Bud Lewis's office. Then there can be no confusion. Now, if you will excuse me—"

He hung up, and instantly the buzzer sounded again.

"Mrs. Swift is on line one."

"Debby, honey . . ." Aaron's voice now held mild protest. The last time he had seen her she had been curled up in a tangle of bedclothes, sound asleep.

"There's a fire, A. I smell the smoke. I'm terrified of fire."

"Tell you what, honey," he said, "you go over to the club for breakfast, and then stay by the pool in the sun. If the fire comes close, you can always dive in."

"I thought maybe you and I could drive somewhere. Maybe up to Santa Fe. We haven't been there for ages."

"Sorry." Aaron's voice was gentle but firm. "I've got work to do. You know Sanrio would grind to a halt without me."

"Oh, you!" There was a smile in Debby's voice. "All right. I'll be at the club."

Being married to Aaron was not exactly what Debby had imagined it might be, even though the sense of financial ease and the status as wife of one of Sanrio's—and the state's—leading citizens was even greater than she had anticipated.

What she sometimes missed was *spontaneity*, the willingness at a moment's notice to drop everything and rush into some innocuous pleasure like a picnic or an unplanned trip. To be honest, she supposed that that kind of freedom could only be a part of irresponsible youth, that the kind of stability Aaron represented came only with the acceptance of duties and obligations. So it all balanced out. Still.

AT THE FIRE COMMAND POST within the forest, plans chief Phil Sommers ran his forefinger along the topographical map. "Getting close to the wilderness," he said, "and unless it's stopped pretty soon, we're going to have quite a mess on our hands. Once it reaches this line, it can fan out."

Jay Paul squinted at the map. In places, he had long thought, this country seemed to stand on edge, and coming as he did from the rolling hills and pinewoods of Georgia, it was a wonder to him that any kind of vegetation, let alone big trees, could gain a foothold in such steep terrain. But there they were, right where Phil's finger was pointing, and they had to be protected.

"No road in?" he said.

"The kind of country it is out there," Sommers said, "McIlvain's smoke jumpers are about the only choice."

Jay shook his head decisively. "It's too rough for them. I've been there, practically on all fours. You can't ask somebody to parachute into that."

Phil Sommers hesitated. "I'm no smoke jumper, but those characters seem to think they can go in just about anywhere."

"No. I won't risk them. I'll see if I can get a slurry drop in there."

Sommers shrugged. "You're the boss. They're predicting wind by noon, by the way."

"I can't help that, either."

Sommers nodded and turned away.

FELIPE VIGIL SAID, whispering, "There they are, see?"

It was impossible not to see, Frank Orwell thought. At that moment in all the world there was only that beautiful girl in his vision—big, but not overweight, with the kind of figure you could drool over in a *Playboy* centrefold.

"What'd I tell you?" Felipe whispered.

"OK," Orwell said. "But we make it fast, you hear me?"

"You got it," Vigil said. He looked round, picked up a large, lethal-looking rock. Then they began their short, savage charge.

38

MRS. TYLER WAYNE came down to her beloved gardens this Monday morning as usual. Manuel and his assistant, Hilario, were already at work, Hilario on hands and knees weeding one of the rosebeds, Manuel with careful skill manicuring the privet hedge that lined the flagstone walk from the big house.

"A lovely morning," Mrs. Wayne said. She was small and slim, with pure white hair beneath the sunshade hat and eyes of intense blue in her still-smooth face. "You do such a lovely trimming job, Manuel. And Hilario doesn't miss a single weed. I am very grateful."

In Manuel's experience, Anglos did not behave in this graceful manner. He and Hilario had discussed it often as they ate their lunches, sitting on the ground in the shade of one of the great Dutch elms the late senator had planted long ago in the sweeping lawns. But then, Mrs. Wayne in many ways was wholly different from any other Anglo either man had ever encountered.

"There is *humo*—smoke—señora," Manuel said. "There is a fire in the forest. It was caused by lightning."

Mrs. Wayne smiled. "That nice Mr. Harmon will attend to it, I'm sure. Now, do you think we might spray the roses, Manuel?"

These days it was more important than ever, Mrs. Wayne felt, that the property be kept in flawless condition, because she was in effect a trustee. Vista Hill, her home for nearly fifty years, and Tyler's for a little more than forty, now technically belonged to the state—Mrs. Wayne's gift in her husband's name, and hers to live in and care for during her lifetime.

"Spraying is good," Manuel said. "With so many beds is maybe a little expensive, señora—"

"That is not important, Manuel. If you think it is good, we will do it. You always know best."

BELLEVUE ACRES, Ken Delacorte was perfectly willing to concede, did not have classy connotations, nor was it intended to. Ken thoroughly approved of the Tyler Wayne estate, as well as Stacy Cummings's pad and all the other homes in that well-heeled category. In fact, after considerable looking around in the southwest, Ken had picked Sanrio as a coming place, a potential Tucson, say, for growth, a place to attract eastern retired wealth. He would have loved to build luxury condominiums, but his finances were simply not up to it—hence Bellevue Acres, a hundred and thirty-six houses, eight to the acre. After all, ordinary folks needed places to live too, as Ken could well remember from his wrong-side-of-town Waco beginnings, before football gave him a hand up.

The houses were not exactly flung together, but they were frame and plywood, with a skin of stucco rather than hand-laid adobe. They were crowded together too, and it was easy to hear your neighbour's TV programme or family arguments. There were lots of kids, and dogs, and bicycles and roller skates.

Ken had no definite idea yet what there was about Bellevue Acres that seemed to be attracting the interest of Bartlemy Jones, who had rolled his fancy wheelchair into the completion when he bought the Brown place, and produced a certified cheque for seven figures as if it were something he did every afternoon.

So he did what many folks in Sanrio did when they were in doubt: on this Monday morning he went to see Aaron Swift.

"This Jones dude," Ken began. "You know him, A?"

"I know him."

"Anything wrong with him?"

"I don't know him well." Then Aaron produced one of his cryptic statements. "He banks at the First."

"So?" Ken puzzled, thought about it. Slowly comprehension dawned, and he began to nod. "They hold our note on the Bellevue Acres property, is that what you're thinking?"

"I haven't said a word, Ken."

Ken thought about it some more. "If they decided to discount it for cash," he said, "to Jones, say . . ."

"Happens that way sometimes. Banks these days do like cash."

There was no need to explain. With interest rates rising, many financial institutions were delighted to sell off older, relatively unprofitable mortgages—even at a discount—for cash, which could then be lent at far higher rates.

"A sharpie in a wheelchair," Ken said. "Is that it?"

"There are slander laws, Ken," Aaron said mildly. He looked out of the window. "Seems the smoke's getting heavier."

Ken stood up. "I hadn't noticed." He nodded. "Thanks, A."

Leaving Aaron's office, Ken went outside into the bright but hazy day. The smoke really was thickening, he decided, but he had other matters to worry about.

In the off-seasons during his professional football years, Ken had put himself through Stanford University's business school, emerging with a degree and a considerable knowledge of business shenanigans. If you had capital, he knew, the possibilities for shady and profitable capers were almost endless.

The bank, the First, where Bart Jones had his no-doubt considerable account, held the underlying note on the Bellevue

Corporation. When Ken had run out of money for the development, the bank had loaned him enough to go on. Because of that, he and the bank were, in effect, partners. And whoever held that note controlled Bellevue's destiny, and that of the mortgaged home-owners living there.

Being a local organization, the bank had established a reputation for fair dealing, if not downright compassion. It tended to view occasional late mortgage payments with understanding, and it had never been known to invoke the due-on-sale clause in each contract, which called for immediate full payment of the outstanding mortgage balance if a house was sold. Rather, it had, as was its privilege, allowed a straight mortgage transfer without renegotia-tion when one of the Bellevue Acres residents sold out; and it had never taken full advantage of fluctuations in the interests standards upon which flexible-rate mortgages are based.

The bank had, in short, consistently behaved like a small-town institution rather than like the big-city giants. In the hands of the First, the underlying note had never represented a threat to the economic wellbeing of Bellevue Acres residents. But in the hands of a stranger, matters might change drastically.

Ken was not by nature a crusader. Blessed with both brains and a splendid physique, he had managed to haul himself up by his bootlaces to a comfortable position in society. But he knew that the world was filled with those who had not been blessed with more than average intelligence, and whose physiques were no bargain, either. The best they could do was struggle through life and consider themselves lucky if they somehow acquired a house of their own in a development like Bellevue Acres. These were natural prey for the sharpies and, despite Ken's basic laissez-faire philoso-phy, letting the cats lose among the caged pigeons did not appeal to him.

He marched into the manager's office at the First and sat down. "A dude named Bart Jones," he said, and studied the man's face. "Making his presence felt in Sanrio, isn't he?"

"You have a point you're working up to, Ken?"

"Our Bellevue Acres note. Are you thinking of selling it? Maybe to Jones?"

The manager considered. "Who told you that?"

"I figured it out for myself."

The manager considered some more. "That's really bank busi-ness, Ken, and we don't—"

"Look." Ken's voice was soft, yet somehow ominous. "I'm asking a simple question and I'd like a simple answer. Are you thinking of selling the note to Jones? Yes, or no?"

The manager swallowed hard. "We're . . . thinking about it." He watched uneasily as Ken got out of the chair and straightened to his full, impressive height. "Was that all you wanted to know?"

"For now," Ken said, and walked out.

Chapter Four

Fighting wildland fires these days is an organized, technical business, with machines and electronic marvels of all kinds. But when you get right down to it, fires are still conquered by the people on the ground, working with hand tools: shovels, axes, brush hooks and chain saws. Fire lines are established by grunting, cursing, aching troops, breathing smoke and hearing the frightful roaring of flames and the crackling of trees and brush as they perish.

They had chosen to make their stand on top of a low ridge. Two crews—one southwest area crew, the other, Bessie Wingate's boys—were spread in a thin line, clearing back everything that would burn, leaving a swathe of bare earth and three-inch stumps as a fire line.

The sun was high and hot, and the fire fighters' yellow Forest Service shirts and hard hats were heavy and uncomfortable. But sparks were flying, and the shirts and hats were protection, so they sweated and they cursed and they chopped, their breath coming in short gasps because they were seven thousand feet up, where oxygen was scarce.

The fire had roared up a narrow break in the rocks to a somewhat level area, spread out, and slowed its headlong progress.

Behind the fire line and above it, a thick grove of big trees, the beginning of the forest's heart, waited helplessly. Birds had long since left, and every other species of forest folk was fleeing now in panic.

One of the southwest crew, Spanish American, swarthy, wiry, with sharp features, waved his McLeod hoe at Bessie. "Hey, *guapa*," he said, and showed intensely white teeth in a broad grin at his joke. The word connotes cuteness, sexiness, and could not have been more inappropriately applied.

"Cut the baloney," Bessie said without rancour.

"OK. How about a beer? Ice cold? How about that?"

"Now," Bessie said, "you're talking." She glanced down the slope at the spreading flames. "But it'll have to wait. That thing's coming straight at us."

"Some like it hot, baby. It comes too close, I got my shelter."

The shelter was simply a sheet of metallic, fire-retardant cloth, with hand and footholds on its underside. In a last-resort emergency, the fire fighter swept a patch of ground bare, lay down and drew the sheet over him, holding the edges of the cloth against the ground and hoping the flames would sweep harmlessly past.

"Me," Bessie said, "I don't aim to get into a fix where I have to use a shelter. And neither will my crew."

Her shovel had not been still a moment. With her strength she uprooted whole plants and even small trees and heaved them back from the area they were clearing. She squinted downhill at the flames. "I don't like it," she said, "not one little bit. Those big trees are too close. I can feel them against my back." She cocked her head towards the fire below them. "Hear that baby roaring at us? It thinks we're meat for the cooking."

ELSIE EDWARDS HAD PULLED ON trousers and a shirt. The need to cover herself was overwhelming, dominating all else.

Don was not dead, as she had feared at first, but he was unconscious. His breathing was steady, and his pulse, as nearly as she could tell by fumbling at his wrist, was regular and strong.

She supposed she ought to be doing something for him, for herself, or about the smoke that was heavier now. But she couldn't seem to get her thoughts in order. She guessed she was in a state of shock, and she was sure she would never lose the sense of shame and degradation that possessed her.

She knelt now beside Don, and her hands made stroking motions on his forehead. Maybe he would die; the blow to his head with the rock had made a dull, ugly thud and he had dropped to the ground without a sound.

Dear Lord, what if he did die? Here in this wilderness?

Don's eyelids fluttered. His eyes opened briefly, unfocused, frightened, and then closed again.

"Don!" Elsie said. "Don, darling. Please!"

His eyes opened again. He stirred. "What's burning?" he said.

"Nothing, darling. It's all right."

It was not all right. That realization was slow in coming, but it burst upon her with impact at last. The smoke was heavy now, too heavy, choking. And as she strained to listen she could hear crackling sounds. She got to her feet and looked around. There—

yes—she could see flames sweeping through the lower branches of a big ponderosa. The sight was terrifying.

"Don! Don!" Her voice was almost out of control.

"Help me up!" His voice was stronger now, and with her aid he struggled to his feet and stood muttering angrily to himself.

Elsie said, "The tent. Shall I take it down?"

"Never mind that." He was standing straight now. "Give me your hand. Let's go."

"But our things!"

His head ached and throbbed. He had neither memory nor knowledge of what had happened, and his vision was still blurred, but his mind was clear enough to realize that there was danger, present and unmistakable. Flight was their only course.

"Never mind our things." He could even smile weakly. "We're what counts."

HALF A MILE AWAY, Felipe Vigil was still babbling happily. "Hey, man, that was some chick, no? She was really built!"

"Drop it, stupid," Frank Orwell said. "Get your mind off that." His voice was harsh. "From here out we're going to need all the thinking both of us can do. Of all the stinking luck!"

"You clicking your teeth, man, but what you saying?"

They had topped a low, almost bare rise. Orwell stopped and looked back. "See that?" He pointed to dark, angry smudges against the hazy sky. "Smoke."

Felipe looked. "So?"

Orwell turned and pointed in the direction they had been walking. "More smoke. See it? What we got is a forest fire, and I've seen a couple and I don't *never* want to see another one up close."

Comprehension came slowly. Felipe looked both ways. "So what we do? You big Anglo hotshot thinker, what we do?"

Orwell waved one hand towards Sierra Grande's lofty peak. "We haul our butts up that mountain just as fast as we can."

MRS. TYLER WAYNE frowned at the whitish flecks that drifted down around her.

"Ash, señora," Manuel said. "From the fire in the forest."

"They should not allow it to come so close," she said. Tyler had known how to deal with such things. He would have spoken to someone in authority. Well, Mrs. Wayne had always found that nice Mr. Harmon to be most agreeable. She thought it would be quite in order if she went to see him about this falling ash.

44

A short time later her chauffeur drove Mrs. Wayne up to the Forest Service headquarters in an ageless shiny black limousine. Mrs. Wayne, in hat, white gloves and a summer frock, went inside to call upon JL and ended up in George Jefferson's office. Jefferson got up promptly to greet her.

"My gardener," Mrs. Wayne said, "tells me that there is a fire in the forest."

"Yes, ma'am."

"The young lady down the hall tells me that Mr. Harmon is in Idaho."

"Yes, ma'am."

"Mr. Harmon's card, which he was good enough to give me, says that he is fire management officer for the forest."

"Yes, ma'am."

"Then," Mrs. Wayne said, "I fail to understand why he is not here, managing this fire. Ash is falling in my garden."

WILLARD SPENCER'S FIRST INCLINATION was to ignore Aaron Swift's suggestion about paying his insurance. He was not accustomed to running errands such as carrying cheques to someone's office.

A second look outside, however, at the strange copperish tinge of the sky had convinced him to set his pride aside for this occasion only. Accordingly, cheque in pocket, he presented himself at the Lewis Insurance Agency and demanded attention.

Bud Lewis himself appeared. "Here," Spencer said, and held out the cheque.

Lewis made no move to take it. "The due date on your invoice was May eighteenth, Mr. Spencer. The grace period ended Friday, June seventeenth. Today is June twentieth. Your homeowner's policy has lapsed."

"You joke, of course," Spencer said.

Nothing changed in Bud Lewis's face.

With determined calm Spencer said, "Very well," and held out the cheque again. "Reinstate the policy."

Still nothing changed in Lewis's face. "There is a fire in the forest, Mr. Spencer. This is hardly the time to issue, or reinstate, a homeowner's policy."

There was silence.

Spencer said, "Do you realize what you are doing? You are leaving my property unprotected."

"I am saving my underwriters a possible considerable loss," Lewis said. "That is my prime consideration."

LES LAWRY SAID, "It's a rotten nuisance. We go to all the trouble to come into this wilderness, and now they let a fire get started. We'd better pack up and drive back out."

Cindy Lou said, "A fire means a lot of people. Suppose they see us driving out? That sign said no motor vehicles allowed."

"Doesn't mean a thing. Anybody asks, we say we didn't see it."

Tad said, "Pop, if there really is a fire, a big one, I mean . . . well, here's this stream. If the fire gets bad, we could all get in the water. I've read about that."

"You just stick with your old man," Les said. "We'll be fine. It's just a nuisance. If the rangers had been on their toes, it wouldn't have happened. We pay our taxes, and this is what we get. Now, let's start packing the jeep."

BART HAD MELLOWED, not much, but some: that was Stacy's early reaction when she arrived at his house for lunch. Maybe adversity had given him a touch of humility, although the word seemed a strange one to use in connection with Bart Jones.

The lines of his face had somehow softened and lost a bit of their harsh arrogance, but his eyes had retained what she had always thought of as the kind of cold fierceness one found in the eyes of a bird of prey. What did I ever see in him? she asked herself.

"I must say," Bart exclaimed as he showed her into the broad living room, handling his electric wheelchair with skilful ease, "that you chose nice country for your retreat."

"No retreat," Stacy said.

"New life, then?"

"Something like that."

"Breeding horses? That's too tame for you, Stacy. A little wine?"

She accepted the glass. Then, as usual, her impulse was to come straight to the point. "Why are you here?"

She had almost forgotten his lopsided grin, the expression of a boy caught with his hand in the cookie jar. "You," he said.

"Come off it, Bart. Nobody ever meant that much to you."

"You underestimate yourself."

She had forgotten too how infuriating he could be sometimes. "All right," she said, "let's talk about something else."

"Like what?"

Remembering Ken Delacorte's visit the night before, she said, "Bellevue Acres, for starters."

"Real estate's a little out of your line, isn't it?"

"Ken Delacorte's an old friend."

Bart sipped his martini. "Good football player."

"But no businessman, is that what you're saying?"

"Bellevue Acres is a nickel-and-dime operation."

"And you're used to big deals, is that it?"

"There aren't too many things I can still do, and I need some fun out of life. You'll grant me that?"

"I don't know if I'll grant you much of anything," Stacy said.

IN HER LOGICAL, ANALYTICAL WAY, Sophie Swift on this Backslope Monday occupied herself as if she were organizing a law case about to go to trial. One prepared for the worst, she had always believed, and then one could allow oneself to hope for the best. Sitting in the June sunlight on the patio, a legal pad on her lap, she listed steps to take if the fire threatened her home.

First and foremost, the horses. The mare, Impatient, and her foal would go together in the horse trailer. The other two horses could be tethered behind the trailer and led slowly to safety. Her favourite paintings would go in the rear of the station wagon. The silverware she would put into pillowcases and carefully lower to the deepest part of the swimming pool. Certain file drawers containing her own and Aaron's records over the years also should be loaded into the station wagon.

Surveying the list, she smiled ruefully when she discovered that she had made no provision for clothing. No doubt Debby, if she had thought to make any list of priorities, would have included clothing first. Sophie decided there was a message for her in that realization.

The wind had shifted, Sophie noticed, and ash was no longer falling around her on the patio. She studied the big mountain and noted the usual summer afternoon clouds beginning to take shape.

Sophie and Aaron had met at Stanford law school and had carried on a courtship that by most standards, Sophie conceded, would have been unexciting in the extreme. They married the evening they graduated and spent their honeymoon studying for bar examinations.

Their marriage, she supposed, had been more intellectual than romantic, and in her unworldliness Sophie had assumed that was sufficient. Obviously it was not, and she had had no idea that the pain of that discovery would be so intense.

With a final appraising look at Sierra Grande, she got up and carried her list inside. A cup of tea while she waited for further developments, she thought, would help to pass the time.

She was leaning against the kitchen sink, sipping her tea, when

Aaron walked in, wearing a strained, sheepish grin. "Just thought I'd check to see that everything was OK," he said.

Sophie turned so that her back was to him and put her teacup carefully in the sink. She wanted suddenly to laugh aloud, to squeal, to sing, to do all manner of girlish things she had seen female television contestants do when a winner was announced. Instead, turning again and smiling faintly, she said, "That was good of you, Aaron. But I think everything is under control. Would you like a cup of tea?"

THERE ARE FEW SIGHTS ON EARTH as terrifying as a wildfire on the loose when faced close up from ground level, which is the view fire fighters customarily have. Jay Paul, at his command post within the forest, was far removed from the fire perimeter, and guiltily happy to be where he was.

On the other hand, as fire boss there was no avoiding the responsibilities that came with the job, and by noon of this first day he was close to despair. It seemed to him that everything that could go wrong, had.

North of the fire's centre, wind-driven flames had attacked Sierra Grande's west flank. They had overpowered the crews there, and were now racing towards the east-west line of Highway 14, which had once seemed too distant to worry about.

To the south, towards the estates adjoining the forest, the flames coming downslope were advancing slowly but with apparent steadiness. And to the east of the spot where the fire had started, the monster was well into the wilderness. A good share of the problem, of course, was the presence of that great mountain Sierra Grande.

Around its mass, winds twisted and swirled in no immediately discernible pattern. At ground level, miniature whirlwinds picked up burning brush and fallen debris, flinging them across open ground to ignite the lower branches of big trees. Dry pine needles flared like tiny torches, creating their own updraughts of hot air, which spread the fire.

Another worry: the pilot of the chopper that had taken in one of the crews reported catching glimpses of maybe half a dozen people in the wilderness. If the report was accurate, it was up to Jay Paul to see that they were found and rescued.

And now came word that a new area, over near a small lake that lay within the wilderness, had somehow ignited and was burning furiously.

"Andy McIlvain's still waiting," Phil Sommers told Jay Paul. "You want him to go in with a few of his people?"

"I'm saving the smoke jumpers. All of them."

For what? Phil Sommers thought. Christmas?

ON THE PHONE FROM SANTA FE, the regional supervisor, George Jefferson's boss, said, "Looks like you've got a bad one, George."

"This time of year, no rain. You know how it goes."

"I see you've got your Sanrio team on it. What about JL's regional team? Think you'll need him?"

"Could. The weather's against us. And I'm beginning to get civilian complaints."

"So am I. Some expensive real estate is threatened, George. Expensive people own it. Fellow named Spencer, Willard P. Know him?"

"As much as I want to." In a reassuring voice Jefferson added, "We'll get it whipped."

"I'm sure you will."

For that last comment, Jefferson thought as he hung up, read, "You'd better!" He called to his secretary in the outer office. "Get off a message to BIFC. We want JL back here."

IN PLACES, THE FIRE ADVANCED SLOWLY; in other places, wind-driven, it rushed forward in quantum leaps from a piñon here to a juniper there, to a scrub oak further upslope already brought to the point of combustion by the rising currents of heated air.

Bessie Wingate, still working in tandem with the southwest crew, swore at the flames and at her men. With her, fighting a fire was a personal vendetta, no quarter asked or given. "Had me a house once," she had been heard to say one night at a bar called The Antlers. "Wasn't much, but I'd built it, me and Ted, and it was mine." She never explained who Ted was, and no one had the temerity to ask.

"A fire come busting over the ridge. There went the house. And Ted. The darn fool let himself get burned to death. What the heck, long time ago. Let's have another beer."

Now, moving into a new area of the fire line, Bessie was all business. "Gus, you and Pete take that chain saw over yonder and take down that stand of piñon. The rest of you fan out and get hacking and scraping. I want this ground slicker than a baby's behind; nothing left for that beast down there to feed on."

To a neighbouring crewman, the wiry Hispanic from the south-

49

west crew, Bessie said, "You're doing a good job with that McLeod." The tool was a modified, highly efficient hoe. "What's your name?"

"Eloy Jaramillo."

"Tell you what, Eloy. After this is all over, I'll buy you a beer at The Antlers. You know where that is?" Bessie's shovel continued to move as she spoke. "In fact, you keep on working like that, maybe two beers. How about that?"

"Muchas gracias."

"That's OK," Bessie said. "A job like this separates out the men from the boys."

THE TEAM THAT LATER sifted carefully through the situation reports and listened to direct testimony decided that at this point, late afternoon of that first day, Backslope, estimated at something over ten thousand acres, could have been contained by quick, decisive action.

Jay Paul had his troops deployed, his communications in place and his air attack organized and operating. But Andy McIlvain's smoke jumpers remained on the ground; two hotshot crews were in the wrong places, doing routine line work; and although ground tankers were available within striking distance, none had been summoned because of Jay Paul's exaggerated respect for the rugged terrain.

As dusk gathered, the air tanker slurry drops slowed and then stopped altogether, and the wind and temperature conditions that had nurtured the fire's beginnings the night before resumed their encouraging effects.

Chapter Five

The moon that Monday night was almost full and hung low over the eastern plains. To Frank Orwell, leading the way up Sierra Grande's flank, it resembled a gigantic eye, fixed on them, spotlighting their progress. Here, above the timberline, there was no place to hide from its scrutiny, and he felt naked, exposed.

Felipe Vigil, panting along behind in the thin, cooling air, said, *"Basta!* Enough! What we trying to do, set some kind of record?"

They stopped. Orwell was breathing deeply. "With that fire," he said, "this mountain's going to be crawling with people. You got that?"

"So what are we? *Brujos?* Spirits?"

"We," Orwell said with heavy scorn, "are escaped convicts."

"And we wear signs that say so? Or these men here to fire-fight, they carry pictures of us? You crazy, man! All they care about is fire. They not interested in us."

Orwell thought about it. The guy had a point, he told himself in surprise, and almost said so. But instead of speaking, he merely nodded agreement.

"So what we do now?" Felipe said.

"We'll work around the mountain, spend the night up here and then early in the morning go down and see how things look on that side of the forest."

"Going to be cold."

"Yeah." Orwell wondered if there would be resistance.

Instead, "OK," Felipe said. "I just keep thinking about that chick. She here, she'd make me warm."

DON AND ELSIE too had stopped climbing and running, Don at the limit of his endurance. His headache remained, throbbing unbelievably with each heartbeat, blurring his vision.

"I think we're above it now," he said, panting, sitting exhausted on the ground.

The snapping of flames and the crashing of falling branches reached them clearly from down the slope. The rising smoke was heavy, choking.

"Are we safe here?" Elsie said. She was two selves, she thought, and felt hysteria was near. One of her recognized the danger and worried about Don's condition. The other still could neither believe nor comprehend what had happened to her.

"I don't know what happened," Don said, his voice weak. "I can't remember anything except your saying that you'd never been happier." He looked at Elsie then.

Suddenly she was crying, without a sound—no sobs, no gasps of breath, merely her face screwed up and tears running down the sides of her nose from eyes that were wide open.

"Elsie!" Don said. "Baby!" He reached for her weakly.

"I'm all right," Elsie said. "All right. Honest."

Don closed his eyes, took a deep breath, then willed himself to focus on the girl's face. "What happened?"

Elsie shook her head. She fought back tears and wiped her cheeks with the backs of her hands. She shook her head again in stubborn silence.

51

"Baby," Don said, his voice patient now, "you have to tell me. We promised to share, remember? Whatever happened to you happened to me too, but I can't remember. . . . Something, somebody . . ." He shook his head in exasperation. "It won't come to me."

"You were hit on the head," Elsie said. "Two men . . ." She too closed her eyes, and opened them. It was somehow easier now. "Yes"—the words came slowly—"you have a right to know what happened." She told him.

IF MOM HADN'T TOLD POP to slow down, Tad thought, Pop wouldn't have done just the opposite and, as always, driven faster, and they wouldn't now be stuck.

"Of all the luck," Les Lawry said, and swung his legs out to stand up and have a look.

Cindy Lou got out and stood unmoving, almost rigid. "I'm scared, Les. The smoke is heavier. There's fire, and it's close. I can almost feel it! We never should have come here!"

"Oh, shut up! Tad, come here. Let's see what we can do."

With one wheel off the ground and the jeep's frame resting solidly on a big, half-buried rock, there wasn't anything they could do, Tad decided, but he did not say so aloud—that would only make it worse.

"Maybe we can lift it off," Les said.

It took two futile tries, and it was Les who called a halt. "No dice," he said. He was red in the face and puffing. "These old jeeps are heavy. That's why they stand up. In the army—"

"Les!" Cindy Lou's voice was rising. "Over there! Look! I can see the fire!"

So could they all. In the gathering dusk, first the brightening glow, and then the flames themselves were suddenly visible through the trees, angry orange-red in colour, the fire's voice a crackling roar.

"Oh, Lord!" Les said. "Let's get out of here!"

Cindy Lou said, "Our things!"

"Forget the things, Cindy Lou. Just get out of that jeep and come on! Tad, you lead!"

"Which direction?"

"How do I know? Just away!"

JL CAUGHT A COMMERCIAL FLIGHT out of Boise, and landed in Albuquerque, where a Forest Service aircraft waited to take him to Sanrio. Along the way he ordered the pilot to fly low over the fire.

52

At first glimpse, it was just a red glow in the distance, as harmless-seeming as the comfortable glow in a fireplace on a winter evening. But as they flew closer, JL could almost hear the roaring sounds of conflagration—the crackling of huge trees, the rushing of winds. On the ground, he knew, strange, threatening shadows would be leaping and cavorting against shifting curtains of thick smoke. Around the flaming area, men and machines would be fighting to create a perimeter of containment, a firebreak across which the fire could not travel.

"Offhand," the pilot said, "I'd say you had your work cut out for you."

JL's eyes remained on the fire. "We'll whip it," he said. Because we have to, he thought. There is no other way.

Late as it was, George Jefferson was waiting in his office at headquarters when JL arrived.

"How's your ankle?" Jefferson said.

"It's fine, George," JL said. "Just fine. When I'm sitting on my butt, it doesn't bother me a bit."

"Did you make smart remarks like that at BIFC?"

"I just sat and listened."

Jefferson closed his eyes for a few moments. When he opened them again, he said, "OK, it's been a long day. Albuquerque called, regional office; and Mrs. Tyler Wayne came in." He looked curiously at JL. "She a friend of yours?"

"I like her. When she has questions, I answer them. She's out of touch, but—"

"If she wanted to pick up the phone and complain to three, four people, old senatorial cronies of Tyler's, the Secretary of Agriculture would be down on us inside the hour. That's how out of touch she is. Ashes were falling on her roses, and that is definitely not allowed."

JL nodded as patiently as he could. "I'll bear it in mind."

"You do that. Now, how does it look out there?"

"Bad. And it's going to get worse."

Jefferson leaned back in his chair and gestured towards the map of the forest on the wall. "Show me."

At last. JL walked over to the map. With his forefinger he traced an irregular elliptical outline, its major axis running east-west, with a horn-shaped projection in the northwest, where the flames had worked their way around Sierra Grande's flank and were headed for the highway. "This is roughly the area of the open fire—"

"How many acres? At a guess?"

JL shrugged. "Must be close to fifteen thousand. I haven't seen the infrared photos, but I'd guess that here and here—between the south boundary of the wilderness and the line of large estates— there are probably other areas already smouldering and ready to combust."

He moved his finger to the big mountain's eastern flank. "When the morning sun begins to heat up the ground and starts to create air currents, the upslope wind will enlarge this area. Lots of timber up there."

"Can you stop it?"

"We'll try." He moved his finger again, to the south. "But here's the big problem. Too close to houses, that development—"

"Bellevue Acres?"

"Right." JL paused. "All those houses, all those kids. And then, if we aren't careful, the town itself."

Jefferson nodded. "And the Wayne place—Vista Hill," he said, "and all those other big estates abutting the forest?"

"They'll get the de luxe treatment." They wouldn't really, and both men knew it. The fire-suppression effort JL would direct would try to protect all property; whatever favouritism might be shown would be based on general, not specific, good.

"All right," Jefferson said, "it's all yours. Have the dispatcher call in what you need."

As JL walked outside to his pickup he felt unshackled, finally turned loose on the job he knew and liked best. He glanced up into the sky to see the reflected glow of the fire—his enemy. Preliminaries over, he thought: now to the main event.

JAY PAUL WAS SITTING at a folding table staring glumly at a map. Electric lights had been strung from the portable generator here at the command post in the forest. Radio antennae had been mounted high in nearby trees. From a catering truck not far away, cooking smells blended with the smell of smoke. In the deep shadows men were lying on the ground, blanket-wrapped against the chill of this high-country June night.

Jay Paul looked up, saw JL, automatically began to smile in relief, and then, as full realization came, suddenly looked less than happy. "They called you back . . . you're taking over."

JL pulled up a chair and sat. This was the hard part. "Look," he said, "for near twenty-four hours you've been working your tail off—"

"And getting nowhere."

"Well, maybe we can change that. Let's see your last situation reports. Then you go off and have yourself a cup of coffee. You might have somebody bring me one too."

Taking over like this was never easy, either for those doing the taking or for those being superseded, and sometimes it could be downright destructive to general morale. But there was no help for it.

JL began reading Jay Paul's latest reports, which showed clearly a deteriorating situation. As he read and considered his options he glanced from time to time at his watch. On major fires, briefings for supervisory personnel were held on a strict schedule: twice daily, at 0430 and at 1630. The predawn briefing time was approaching fast.

Once, young in the fire-suppression business, he had found it incongruous that a fire boss should sit quietly, apparently doing nothing, while the world was going up in flames and troops on the lines were breaking their necks to hold what territory they had. But he had long since learned that the fire boss, like the commanding general of an army, performed best when he had the time to study and think.

It was close to briefing time when Jay Paul reappeared. His face was set and sullen. "Orders, boss?"

JL deliberately gathered together the papers he had been reading and got out of the chair before he answered. "Yes," he said. "The first one is to get that chip off your shoulder. You're not going to do me any good in that frame of mind." He waited a moment and watched a subtle change in Jay's face. "Now," JL said, "let's go find out where we stand."

To JL, the twice-daily briefings were valuable in ensuring that all supervisory personnel knew what was going on throughout the entire effort. In this instance, he was particularly interested in the people themselves and their attitudes.

First came the roll call. JL, with Jay Paul slightly behind him, sat off to one side, watching as each hand was raised, identifying the face that went with it. Next, from Phil Sommers, plans chief, came a background brief of fire-suppression progress to date.

Somewhere behind JL a low-pitched voice said, "Pitiful little, with good movement backwards."

JL recognized the voice as Andy McIlvain's. Stifling the temptation to look round, JL faced resolutely forward. At his shoulder Jay Paul muttered to himself.

The fire behaviour officer came next, followed by the meteorologist. The line boss, second in tactical command, followed, and JL attended to him carefully. A bright boy, in JL's opinion, marked to go far.

His name was Ben Hastings, college educated, a forestry major specializing in plant biology. Trim, neat, he handed out assignments that were as neat as himself.

Again Andy's voice behind JL. "And what about us? We lepers?" This time the voice was not low-pitched.

JL, without turning his head, said, "I'll talk with you later, Andy. Simmer down." Then he rose.

He spoke to them all, deliberately keeping his voice calm.

"You've held the lines for twenty-four hours," he said. Not true: they had lost their lines in a dozen places, but his voice held no hint of criticism. "Now we've seen how it's developing, we'll see what we can do to make sure that it doesn't get out of hand."

His voice altered subtly.

"They brought me back from Boise because I wasn't learning anything. It wasn't that I knew it all, I just wasn't listening. I was back here instead of there, so they said, 'Might as well send him home, he's no good to us here.'"

There were smiles, and a general sense of relaxation. JL's voice changed again, to a brisker tone.

"All right, let's get at it." He pointed at Andy McIlvain, Jay Paul, Phil Sommers and Ben Hastings. "I want you four, Andy first. Alone."

JL could have written Andy McIlvain's résumé from memory: a degree from Cal Tech in aeronautical engineering; forty years old; unmarried; winter-season ski instructor; thirteen years as a smoke jumper, the last eight as crew foreman; department commendation for a new parachute design; impatient.

"What's your beef?" JL said.

"You've got a fire. I've got a crew of smoke jumpers, good ones—"

"The best." JL nodded.

"And we've been sitting on our behinds, pitching cards into a helmet. I told Phil Sommers we could go into that terrain! Duck soup! With the new chute, even you could make it!"

"Thanks."

"But Jay Paul says he won't risk us. You've lost a whole square-mile section because he wouldn't let us go in at the start."

"All right," JL said. "You've made your point. Now I'm here, and we'll use you. That's a promise. You're loaded up?"

"Gear lashed down, men ready to suit up."

"Back to the airport," JL said. "I'll call you."

Chapter Six

In full daylight on Tuesday, this second day, the scene was wholly different from what it had been twenty-four hours earlier. Sierra Grande's towering peak was still plain against the limitless sky as winds above the ten-thousand-foot level swept it clean, but lower, the pall of smoke hung like smog, ugly and threatening.

From the town no flames were visible, and even from the big houses abutting the forest, like Vista Hill and Willard P. Spencer's now uninsured estate, stands of ponderosa pines screened the actual conflagration from view. But fire was there, and it made its presence felt in the smoke it generated, thick, in places choking, seeping through closed windows and doors, leaving its distinctive smudgy prints on whitewashed walls and garden trellises.

Overhead in the forest there was an almost constant din as air tankers swept past at near treetop height to discharge their loads of slurry in ragged clouds. On the forest's fringe, where terrain permitted, bulldozers carved firebreaks and ground tankers pumped water by the ton. But in rougher, steeper country sweating, cursing line crews dug and chopped and scraped the ground clean by hand, hoping their lines would hold and that no errant wind gust would catch a burning branch and carry it across the cleared area into a fresh stand of trees.

Andy McIlvain was in the spotter's seat of the Twin Otter this Tuesday morning, abaft the open fuselage door. Headset and mike in place, and his head well out of the open window, he scanned the forest below. On the wooden bench that lined the starboard side of the bare cabin, eleven smoke jumpers sat, suited up and wearing their two parachutes each. One thing, Andy was thinking. When old JL got into the act, things began to happen.

"We can handle these two quadrants," JL had said on the phone. Both men, though miles apart, were studying copies of a reference map as they talked. "But up in that northwest corner, I can't get trucks or choppers in."

"We can go in," Andy said.

"Yes, I think you can." JL did not hesitate. "I just want that line held so it can't fishhook and cause us trouble. Got it?"

"Duck soup."

"OK. Get on it. But save part of your crew in case we need you somewhere else as well."

"Charge!" Andy said, and hung up.

AGAIN AARON SWIFT had not slept well, and vague guilt feelings continued to run through his mind. The previous afternoon at the ranch, after finishing the tea Sophie had made for him and listening to her plans and preparations, all logical and sensible, Aaron had gone back to his office. There was a call from Debby at the club, and as he went about returning it he could picture her, young and shapely in one of her scanty bikinis, stretched out beside the pool.

"A," Debby's breathless voice had said on the phone, "would you feel like having dinner here tonight? Everyone says the new piano player is super."

"Why not?" Aaron said. "I'll bring along my fiddle and we can watch Rome burn from there."

"You say the funniest things sometimes," Debby said. "I never know when you're teasing."

That night, lying awake in the predawn blackness, Aaron was not at all sure that he knew, either.

At this office that second day of Backslope, he heard, as usual, pretty much all that was going on in Sanrio.

JL was back in town and in charge of the fire, which was all to the good. But it seemed to Aaron that during the night the fire had spread, and that was all to the bad.

Around midmorning the film star Ada Loving, Sanrio's resident celebrity, arrived at Aaron's office unannounced. Reports of her impressive figure, Aaron decided, had not been exaggerated.

Ada Loving had purchased a home in Sanrio—or it had been purchased for her: details were unclear. In an interview with the local newspapers she had said she was enchanted by the climate and the scenery and the friendliness of the folks who lived in Sanrio. The area would burgeon and prosper mightily as soon as its charms became more widely known—something she was going to help happen.

"My business manager," she told Aaron, "advised me that in any kind of emergency you were the person to depend on."

There was shrewdness behind this careful facade, Aaron decided. Ada Loving was obviously of the opinion that sexy actresses were not supposed to be intelligent, and behaved accordingly, but glimpses of her real self showed through. "Flattering of him," Aaron said. "Do you have an emergency?"

"I don't know. Does this fire count? In Malibu it would."

"Happily," Aaron said, "this is not Malibu yet. And so far, the fire is merely a fire, no threat to life or property."

"But it could be?"

"With bad luck, very bad luck, it could be."

"You kid me not. Thank you for that." The celebrated blue eyes were steady. "Who is in charge? And how do I meet him?"

"To make sure a little extra care is taken of your property?" Nothing changed in Ada Loving's friendly smile. "Why not?"

"Matter of viewpoint." Aaron wore his courtroom manner. "The forest supervisor is named George Jefferson. He's the top of the local totem pole."

As Ada Loving left his office, Aaron decided that the view from the rear precisely balanced the view from the front, a miracle of anatomical engineering.

JL GLANCED AT THE NOTE Jay Paul handed him. "A burned-out jeep? In the wilderness?"

Jay Paul nodded. "One of the smoke jumpers found it."

"No people?"

Jay Paul shook his head.

"Get a chopper in. See if it can spot them." JL's voice was doubtful. "If they know they're not supposed to have driven in, they may not want to be seen. If they have a choice, that is. One thing about a fire: it smokes out a lot of things, including people."

ELSIE EDWARDS CAME CAUTIOUSLY back into the uppermost fringe of the big trees, where Don sat on the ground, resting, eyes closed, against one of the massive trunks. There was a purple bruise behind his right ear, where he had been struck, but the continuing throbbing ache included his entire head. The fact that he was conscious indicated that it was probably no more than a mild concussion. But, oh, how his head ached!

He opened his eyes as Elsie approached, and what he saw in her face took his attention away from his own condition.

"What is it? You look as if you'd seen—"

"I have. I—did!" Elsie was holding herself as tightly in control as she could. "They're above us! They're still on the mountain!"

"The same two men?"

Elsie caught her lower lip in her teeth and nodded.

"Did they see you?"

Her head moved sideways, a jerky, mechanical motion.

"Then we're all right here," Don said, "unless the fire comes up the slope."

"It—does, doesn't it? Move upwards, I mean?"

"Sometimes. Maybe. We'll just have to wait and see."

REPORTS AND PHOTOGRAPHS were all very well, but in JL's opinion there was no substitute for looking at the situation yourself. Sitting now in the Forest Service helicopter, he studied the fiery battlefield below with an appraising eye. The situation, he decided, was less than good.

By giant leaps, in terrain too steep for bulldozers, one front of the fire was advancing up Sierra Grande's slopes, in its savagery obliterating all low growth and leaving the big pines as naked and blackened skeletons. Further on, in an area of dense underbrush, ominous smoke tendrils were rising, testimony to the hidden build-up of temperatures that, unopposed, could rise steadily until the entire area suddenly took flame.

Even ground crews were useless here because of the impenetrability of the tangled growth. In a situation like this, you gambled on what appeared to be the lesser of two bad choices.

The aircraft's radio crackled and Andy's voice came through. "Northwest corner here. Eleven men with gear on the ground, taking positions. They'll be in touch. I'm heading home."

JL plucked the hand microphone from the control panel bracket. "Roger," he said. "Stand by."

Still holding the microphone, he glanced out of the window at the smoking undergrowth, then called Ben Hastings, the line boss. He read off a set of coordinates from the map he kept in a clipboard on his lap. "That area we wanted to clean out with controlled, prescribed burning," he said, "got it?"

"Got it."

"It's smoking now. Before it reaches flash point, I want it opened up so ground crews can get at it."

"Roger," Ben Hastings said. "Spaced explosives—will do. I'll take care of it."

JL was pleased by Ben's immediate understanding of the problem and the solution. "Any word from the people with that jeep?"

"Negative," said Ben. "The chopper is still sweeping the area. My guess is they're keeping under cover."

"Then they're making the wrong choice. Over and out."

He signalled to the pilot, who nodded and took the helicopter off in a new direction. Soon they came over the tiny opening in the trees where Andy's smoke jumpers had gone in. The pilot stared at it in awe. "You mean they went in there? By parachute?"

"Good men," JL said. He pointed. "There they are."

The jumpers were spread out in a thin, spaced line, with saws and hand tools, cutting a wide, clean firebreak. One of the men on the ground looked up and waved, thumb and forefinger held in a circle. JL waved the clipboard in reply.

They flew further north, and JL, pointing down, said mildly, "Our one real bright spot—that highway. Natural firebreak."

The highway was two full lanes wide, with a mown verge supporting only low grass and cactus insufficient to feed fire.

"We won't have to worry about containing the fire there," JL said. Be thankful for small blessings, he told himself, and resumed study of the map he had been marking as they flew.

Containment, that was the key: surround the monster; force it to exhaust its fuel and burn itself out. It sounded simple enough, but JL had often thought that the process of containment, particularly in mountainous terrain and with swirling wind currents, was a great deal like trying to pin down a blob of mercury on a flat surface. You applied pressure, and immediately what you were trying to contain separated into parts that skittered off in new directions. Here, in country too steep for machines, you fought the beast hand to hand, constantly aware that it might at any time outflank you, or leapfrog your position.

The pilot said suddenly, "You ever feel you've got a fire you can't whip?"

"No," JL said, and mentally crossed his fingers at the lie. "You whip them all eventually."

"Tonight," the pilot said, "I'm going to pray for rain."

JL nodded. "We'll take whatever help we can get."

RIGHT AFTER BREAKFAST Stacy went out to the corrals surrounding her big barn. Pancho, her stable hand, immediately appeared, to follow on her rounds. Pancho was fifteen, small and wiry, with strong, horse-sensitive hands. He wanted to be a jockey, and his postage-stamp racing saddle, a present from Stacy, rested proudly on its own rack in the tackroom, bright and polished.

"The smoke's not bad yet," she said to him, "and if it doesn't get any worse, we'll be OK. But I want you to stay out here, Pancho, and if the horses start getting spooked, let me know immediately." She studied the boy. "Big responsibility. Can you handle it?"

"*Sí, señorita, con gusto*—with pleasure."

Stacy smiled, and reached through the corral fence to snap her fingers in summons to Sam, who walked over and presented a velvety nose to be stroked.

"You help keep track of things too, Sam," Stacy said. "If there's any problem, we'll get you all out in plenty of time."

As she walked back towards the big house she reflected that they were all treating what was happening in the forest as something distant, remote, as if it were not real. She wondered if civilian populations looked on war in the same way—until it actually descended upon them and shattered their lives.

She realized that she had been aware for some time of the staccato sounds of a helicopter, and she looked up now as the sounds suddenly increased in volume and the craft swept overhead. Automatically she waved, and saw an answering wave, and a face looking down. Looked like JL, she thought. Funny, but since she'd heard he had come back to take charge, she could feel a definite strengthening of her sense of security.

Soon afterwards she heard the explosions, muffled, deep sounds, as of large doors being shut on distant, empty cupboards. She looked towards the forest, saw the columns of smoke rising and felt her first real intimations of unease.

AS JL AND BEN HASTINGS had anticipated, the spaced explosives, lowered by helicopter and detonated by remote control, had blown a rough but open path through the tangle of brush and ground clutter. They had also spread tendrils of fire and smouldering fuel in all directions. The two hotshot crews that attacked the area, one from either side, had their hands full.

Gordy Walker, chief of the closest hotshot crew, inevitably approached a new assignment with extreme caution, thereby causing suppressed snickers among his men, who knew that within minutes old Gordy would be furiously charging their objective. It was suggested that Gordy's mother had been frightened by a burning bush, and that she had passed along to her child a hatred of anything that caught fire.

Now, muttering to himself between commands, he spread his crew around in pairs, to douse whatever was already on fire and to widen and clean out the pathway break the explosives had left. "Slow and easy," he told them. "There's still smoke coming out of some of that brush." To an experienced crew like his, totally unnecessary advice.

Terry Young, the crew's free spirit, said, "Yes, *sir!* Will do, sir!"

"Same to you, mister," Gordy said without rancour.

BEN HASTINGS TOOK a deep breath and approached the table that was serving as JL's desk. "Yes, Ben?" JL said.

"We've lost our north fire line."

JL leaned back in his chair. He forced his face to remain calm. The one sector he had considered secure, he thought, was now just one more danger point, with no further barriers like the highway to contain the monster. "The fire jumped the road?"

Ben shook his head. "Not exactly. A trucker apparently panicked, had an accident and spread a tanker loaded with gasoline across the highway. It blew up, of course."

JL blinked, but that was all. A freak accident, happens one time in a million, maybe. No matter. It was done. "And the trucker?"

"They may find pieces of him, and they may not."

Still JL showed no emotion. Slowly he nodded. "All right, Ben. Get dug in on a new line as best you can." Dismissal.

Ben opened his mouth and then closed it again. In silence he turned away. The man was not human, he thought, totally without feelings. Unbelievable.

JL picked up the latest situation report in front of him, and found that he could not concentrate. How many more dead would there be? he wondered, and then he told himself, We're at war, and in a war there are casualties. It was scant comfort.

There was a new sense of urgency at the 1630 briefing. Phil Sommers, plans chief, spoke sombrely of the fire's progress during the previous twelve hours, and neither the meteorologist nor the fire behaviour officer could add any word of cheer.

"And it's not going to get any easier," JL said, addressing the group. "No rain in the forecasts, probable wind, the usual afternoon thunderstorms with dry lightning." His manner, he knew, appeared almost unconcerned. But would it have helped to present a face of gloom? "All right, let's get on with it." As he turned away he beckoned Ben Hastings and Jay Paul.

The two men followed him in silence back to his desk. "Ben and I are going for a little jeep ride," JL told Jay. "You take over here. We'll be in touch on the radio."

Ben drove; JL, map and clipboard on his lap, hung on with his free hand. "More than twenty thousand acres so far," JL said. Despite himself, a little of his worry sounded in his tone. "If we get strong winds out of the east . . ." He shook his head.

"There's a lot of forest west of here," Ben said, nodding. "It could burn all the way across Arizona if it really got out of hand. Do we want more line troops?"

"Think it would help?" JL, the teacher, was making the pupil think for himself.

Ben's answer came slowly. "Not really. Not now."

"Neither do I." There was approbation in JL's voice. "Turn here. Uphill. Let's have a good look at this sector."

They were approaching the lower slopes of Sierra Grande now. Bessie Wingate, leading her crew down the trail, stopped at JL's signal and walked over to the jeep.

"How's it look?" JL said.

Bessie was dirty and tired and unwilling to make small talk. "Stinks," she said. "That thing has pushed us halfway up the mountain, whipping us every foot of the way. I told Jim McColl— his crew relieved us—that as far as I can see, we've lost this whole sector and we might as well admit it and cut our losses." Beneath her yellow hard hat the belligerence on her face was plain. "And just what do you think of that?"

JL listened, his face expressionless. He knew such anger would be gnawing at the innards of every man in the crew; fire becomes a personal enemy, capable of arousing sheer hatred.

"Another two hundred yards, maybe," Bessie went on, "and it'll run out of fuel anyway. Timberline. We're wasting manpower fighting for that last little bit."

JL agreed. "Send one of your men back up to tell McColl to let that sector go and pull his crew over to protect against the fire fishhooking into fresh timber when the downslope breeze begins near sundown."

"I," Bessie said, "will be thoroughly skinned. Whoever heard of anybody listening to the poor slobs on the fire line?"

"And you," JL said, "catch some food and some rest."

"Aw . . ." Bessie said. "We could go on all night, if we had to."

JL smiled. "We'll need you tomorrow. Let's head down, Ben."

Ben drove in silence for a time, his face thoughtful. "Sacrificing a little timber for morale, is that it?"

"A good trade-off," JL said. "And her idea does have merit." He pointed in the direction of the estates. "Let's see what the situation is over by Vista Hill. I want to reassure Mrs. Wayne."

A short time later they were out of the forest, driving along the county road. As they pulled into the Wayne estate they saw two gardeners hard at work. They watched the jeep curiously, saw JL and waved. JL waved back.

"Right up to the big house," he said.

As he drove Ben thought, On the lines are hundreds of men—and a few women—in a battle against the destroyer, fire. And here are JL and I, the top command in this war, driving up to a big house to speak with an old lady. Unreal.

"It's her forest too," JL said, as if he had been reading Ben's thoughts.

Mrs. Wayne came to greet them as they got out of the jeep. "How thoughtful of you to stop by, Mr. Harmon," she said, "just to reassure me, I know. Tea? Sherry?"

"Thank you, no, ma'am, I'm afraid we're a little pressed for time," JL said, as he and Ben sat down in the chairs offered.

"I quite understand. And I do want to say how much safer I feel now that you are back from—was it Idaho?" Her manner was thoughtful. "Tell me, Mr. Harmon, is this fire the result of what I believe you call prescribed burning? I recall my husband once had occasion to take that up with the Secretary of Agriculture."

"No, ma'am," JL said. "Prescribed burning had nothing to do with this fire." He was his usual calm, pleasant self, and yet Ben could sense now a new feeling of urgency. "As a matter of fact, ma'am," JL said, "if we had been allowed prescribed burning, this fire might well not have become what it has."

Mrs. Wayne thought about it. "I'm afraid I don't understand."

JL explained about the fuel that accumulated on the ground in the forest, and about the uncontrolled second growth they had had to open with explosives, all of it contributing to the threat of a large conflagration if and when, as had happened, dry lightning struck or someone was careless with a campfire. With prescribed burning, that dangerous ground clutter would have been taken out long before any threat of fire was imminent. But the Forest Service had repeatedly been forbidden to conduct prescribed burning in the Sanrio forest. Too many citizens like Senator Tyler Wayne were frightened by it.

Mrs. Wayne remained thoughtful, and when JL was done she said, "I see. I was not aware of all the ramifications, Mr. Harmon, and I thank you for informing me."

JL stood up. Ben rose with him. "We just wanted to make sure that everything was all right here, ma'am," JL said guilelessly.

"And I do appreciate it," Mrs. Wayne said.

Back in the jeep, going down the long drive, Ben said, "You were making a pitch. Will it do any good?"

"If George Jefferson's right," JL said, "she can pick up the phone and call a couple or three senators, and they'll listen."

"And maybe, just maybe," Ben said, "we'll be allowed to care for this forest the way it ought to be cared for."

"Worth a try," JL said. Then he added, "Who's this?"

A large station wagon was pulling alongside them on the county road, the driver obviously wanting to talk. "Humour him," JL said.

Ben pulled over and stopped, and they waited while the driver climbed importantly from the station wagon and approached them.

"I am Willard P. Spencer," the man said. "You are approaching my property."

JL smiled noncommittally.

"I wish to have a crew of your men," Spencer said, "patrolling the perimeter of my land to see to it that this inexcusable fire does not damage my property. I have been in touch with your regional office in Albuquerque, and they assure me that everything possible will be done to protect my holdings."

"It most certainly will, Mr. Spencer," JL said.

Ben sat quiet, expressionless.

"And now if you will excuse us," JL added, "we'll get on with seeing that it's done." He waved as they drove away.

They rode for a little time in silence. "Good Lord," Ben said. "Is he real?"

"Not only real," JL said, "but there are lots more like him."

As they rounded a bend JL pointed ahead. "Stop here," he said, and wondered at the sense of urgency he felt.

Stacy, in her customary jeans and boots, was standing beside the Cummings mailbox, a bundle of mail in her hands. "I heard you were back," she said, and added without embarrassment, "I felt better knowing that you were in charge."

JL tried and failed to think of a reply. He was conscious that Ben was watching him closely.

Stacy glanced towards the forest. "Am I shying at shadows, or is it worse?"

"I'm afraid it's worse. But still not to worry."

"My horses?"

"I've thought of that."

"We'll cope." She studied his face with a strange intensity, and it was as if Ben were not even there. "And after it's all done," she said, "you can come over one night and tell me about it."

"I'd like that."

Stacy said then, as if suddenly embarrassed, "Clouds over there." She pointed her finger. "Rain?"

JL shook his head. "Unhappily, no."

"So," she said, "all you can do is hope."

JL's faint smile appeared. "That's about the size of it. We have a lot of practice at hoping. Ben, let's get back to work."

"Luck," Stacy said, and watched them drive off.

In the jeep the radio came alive with Jay Paul's voice from the command post, saying, "Come in, JL. Come in." There were undertones of hysteria behind the words.

JL picked up the microphone and spoke his name. "Over."

"We've got a new breakout," Jay Paul said. "Beyond Highway 14. Isolated. It's either spontaneous or incendiary. And Los Ojos prison reports two convicts missing." The words were coming faster and faster. "Maybe they're responsible. Maybe they—"

"Slow down," JL said, breaking in. "You're racing your motor. Have the convicts been spotted? Over."

"Negative."

"Then they could be anywhere. Have you sent an attack crew into the new area?"

"Not yet. I wanted to—"

"Then send one in. Now. And forget the convicts under the bed. Over and out." JL hung the mike on its dashboard hook and leaned back in his seat. "You heard," he said to Ben. "Do you think we have an arsonist at work?"

"Not likely. I don't have too much faith in statistics, but very few fires in the west are incendiary." JL knew the facts as well as he did, Ben was thinking, but JL didn't ask questions without reasons. Suddenly Ben's voice altered. "Oh," he said, "I see what you mean. Jay comes from the southern pinewoods, and there they have up to fifty-five-per-cent incendiary fires."

"And habit dies hard," JL said. A bright boy, Ben, he thought.

The other man shook his head slowly. The sky was darkened by smoke, the taste of conflagration was in the air, and JL could go from detail to detail and yet still keep the big picture in mind. "You don't miss much, do you?" Ben said. There was admiration behind his words. After a moment he added, "Why don't I drop you off at your house? Jay and I can take the night shift and you can catch some sleep. Anything urgent comes up, we'll phone."

JL thought about it. "How do you and Jay get along?"

"Well enough."

"Who's your relief man?"

"Jerry Weinstock."

JL knew him. He was reliable. "Turn your line boss duties over to him," JL said, "and you hold Jay's hand. I don't want to replace him unless I have to." It was a ticklish situation he was creating, he knew, because Jay was technically Ben's superior. On the other hand, in merely this one day, JL had learned who was the better man. He glanced at Ben. "Any argument between you and Jay on something you think can't wait," JL said, "I want you to call me pronto."

"Will do."

But sleep did not come easily for JL that night, which was unusual, because he had trained himself to sleep just about anywhere, any time. He could not shake the memory of Stacy Cummings saying that she felt better because he was in charge, nor the warmth in her voice when she said that after it was all over they would talk. He tried not to read meaning into her words, and instead found all manner of ridiculous possibilities running around in his mind.

He also tried not to think that if George Jefferson had allowed him to handle the fire from the start, the crews on the line would now be simply cold-trailing—patrolling the perimeter to make sure that nothing started up again out of the near-dead ashes—instead of still fighting step by step in the sharp, acrid, choking smoke, facing terrifying nighttime flames.

ON THE MOUNTAIN, near the timberline, the evening breeze coming off the snow probed the trees and set aspen leaves to whispering. It was cold.

"So now we stuck up here on this mountain," Felipe Vigil said. "How long we stay here?"

Frank Orwell resented the implication that it was all his fault. "You saw the fuzz when we tried to go down. State fuzz too. Not just local yokels."

"So now they know we here."

"Not necessarily. If we stay out of sight, they may think we got off the mountain ahead of them and are halfway to Arizona."

"Yeah, and we freeze tonight for sure. How about a fire?"

"No way. Those fire-fighting crews maybe couldn't care less whether or not we're up here, but they spot a fire and they'll be up here fast to put it out. Then what do we do?"

"You big-shot Anglo brain, you tell me."

"Walk, and try to stay warm. Think about the Anglo chick." Orwell smiled. "Matter of fact, I could do some of that myself."

LES LAWRY WAS MORE exasperated than usual. He and his family had been tramping through the forest for hours, darting for cover each time they heard the whine of the searching helicopters. No one was going to put Les Lawry in the slammer if he could help it.

"Come on, Cindy Lou," he said. "Why can't you watch where

you're going? I look round and there you are, either on your face—"

"Mom's hurt her ankle, Pop," Tad said. He dropped the branch he was using as a walking stick and knelt beside his mother in the moonlight, trying to remember his first aid.

"Damn it!" Les said. "Can you walk, Cindy Lou? Tell me that. Can you walk?"

"I think we're going to need help, Pop," Tad said. "I don't think she'd better even try to walk."

"Well, she can't just sit here!"

"I'm sorry, Les," Cindy Lou said. "I didn't mean to twist it."

"OK, OK. Let me think." Les looked at the boy. "You're the boy scout. You got any ideas?"

Tad had been thinking about their situation for a long time. He said now in a hesitant voice, "I think we're safe enough here."

"What makes you think that? Speak up, boy. How come out here in the middle of a forest fire we're all of a sudden safe?"

Tad looked round at the blackened desolation. "It's all burned over. There's nothing left to catch fire."

"He's right, Les," Cindy Lou said.

Les too looked round. "OK, maybe we're better off here than I thought." Grudging admission. "What now?"

"Maybe we'd better just stay here," Tad said, "until it gets light."

"Then what?"

"We can lay out a signal for a helicopter to see."

"Oh, Les!" Cindy Lou said. "Then they can help us."

"Yeah." Les thought about it. "But they'll want to know about the jeep." His face brightened suddenly. "Got it! We'll say we were trying to get away from the fire, and that's why we drove in here. To save our necks. How about that? True, isn't it?"

Tad looked at his mother. Cindy Lou looked at the ground. Neither spoke.

"OK," Les said, in command once more. "Now Tad, you see about getting a nice level place and sweep it clean of ashes. Use a branch. A tidy camp, that's what we want. And we'll just stay here until morning. That's the way I see it."

I'M NOT BEING LOGICAL," Elsie Edwards said. "I know that. And I'm not being brave, either. I'm being just what I've always hated—stupidly, helplessly female."

"You're doing fine," Don said. "Just fine." Words were so painfully inadequate, he thought. He tried to smile.

"How's your poor head?" Elsie asked. Her voice was calmer now.

"Better. Really. I can focus now." Almost true. The terrible throbbing had subsided to a constant, lesser ache, and his mind felt clearer. He tried to sound calm, competently objective. "We're very close to the timberline," he said. "Above it, we're safe from fire, but not from those—rapists." It was difficult to say the word aloud.

Elsie sat silent, for the moment unable to speak.

"The problem is," Don continued, "the only place we can be completely safe is below the fire. And"—he attempted a lighter touch, accompanied by a wry smile—"the trouble is that I don't see quite how we're going to get there from here."

Elsie took a deep breath. Her eyes searched Don's face. "We can't go up or down. That's what you're saying, isn't it?"

Don said slowly, "Pretty much."

"We can't go up," Elsie said, "because you're thinking of me. So am I. But I'm thinking of you too. They'll do again what they did to me. But they'll kill you. They're that kind of animal. One of them almost used his knife on you before. This time they'd do it."

Don closed his eyes briefly. "The evening breeze blows downhill," he said. "That's how it happens in these mountains. It may hold the fire, at least temporarily. And there's a moon. We can move further on round the mountain, just below the timberline, as we are here."

"But how far? There's that lake you've told me about. And the cliff above it. We'll have to go up when we reach that."

Don nodded in silence.

Elsie tilted her head towards the fringe of trees and the open mountainside above them. "What will *they* be doing?"

"Probably the same thing."

"So we'll meet?"

"We'll try not to." Don shook his head angrily. "That's the best I can give you at the moment, baby."

AARON SWIFT WAS HAVING ANOTHER bad night, lying awake in the darkness.

At last Debby turned to him and said, "You're worried, A. I've been watching. Is it the fire?"

"Imagination," Aaron said. "Yours."

"No." Debby's voice was definite. "Yesterday you said that funny thing about bringing your fiddle and watching Rome burn. You were talking about that emperor with the funny name, weren't you? The Roman one?"

Aaron was silent, vaguely shamed. He had no business teasing

71

her with references she would only partly comprehend. She deserved better than that.

"And you haven't been sleeping," Debby said. "I've been listening, and I know. I can always tell."

Aaron said gently, "That means you've been awake too. Why?"

"I don't like the smoke. And I'm worried about you."

Aaron thought of the absurdity of himself, a middle-aged man, trying to cope with a young woman's unease and having not the faintest idea how to go about it. He said, "At least you have reasons. I don't."

"Honest? There isn't anything bothering you? Anything I've done? Or maybe haven't done?"

"Nothing. I'm just being difficult, honey. Forgive me."

"It's all right, A. Honest. You know I love you. And I depend on you too. That sounds funny, doesn't it, but it's so."

There was a new note in Debby's voice now, an urgency arising from Aaron knew not what source. And the words she spoke were strange and puzzling too.

"You've been . . . funny lately. Not, you know, funny ha-ha, but funny different."

"How? In what way?"

"I don't know. I'm not a big brain, A. You know that already. But I . . . feel things even when I don't understand them."

True enough; her almost extrasensory perception was sometimes startling. "I know," he said. Smiling in the darkness, he added, "In other times, you might have been burned as a witch."

Debby giggled. "You say the funniest things. I don't always understand them, A, but I can tell when you're laughing at me. Like now." She snuggled warmly against him. "Thank you for talking to me."

"I didn't say anything."

"Yes, you did. You said a lot. Goodnight, A."

In no time at all she was asleep, curled as always in her kitten position, her breathing deep, untroubled. It was almost dawn before Aaron himself found sleep.

Chapter Seven

Backslope made the local TV7 news early that Wednesday morning, with spectacular air shots taken from the TV chopper, and caustic commentary from the station's ace newsman, Carter Norris. "TV

Seven has attempted to contact JL Harmon, Forest Service fire management officer," Norris's solemn voice said, "but all efforts have failed. And the fire is no closer to being controlled now than it was at this time yesterday. Sanrio residents are beginning to wonder if the town itself is in danger."

By this time, JL was back at the command post. Within minutes of the telecast George Jefferson was on the phone.

"Is it?" Jefferson asked.

JL, with the reports from the 0430 briefing in the forefront of his mind, said, "Is it what?"

"TV Seven is beginning to wonder if the town is in danger."

"Carter Norris reporting?"

"He has a big following, JL. Folks believe him."

"They believed Chicken Little too. The town is not in danger unless . . ." He left it hanging.

"Unless." Jefferson said the word musingly, fully understanding its implications. He said, "Unexpected, violent wind shift?"

"That could make things difficult."

"What's your weather forecast?"

"More of the same. No precipitation in sight."

"Injuries?"

"It's all in the status reports, George."

"I've read them. Between the lines, too. Do you want to replace Jay Paul? If you do, go ahead. I made a mistake. I admit it."

"I'm keeping him on a tether. He may be all right yet."

There was a silence. Jefferson said at last, "I'm getting pressure, JL. All the way from the governor in Santa Fe."

"Do you want to replace *me*, George? Ben Hastings is a good man."

"I won't even answer that. How's your ankle?"

"And I won't answer that, George. That all?"

JL hung up and leaned back in his chair to look up at Andy McIlvain, the smoke jumper foreman. "You got a beef?"

"I've got thirteen men, counting myself, unassigned for today."

"I need you on standby."

"Come on. You know what it's like sitting around. Maybe we could—"

"I don't know where I'll need you," JL said, "or what I'll want you to do. But I want you in reserve, available. So go on back to the field and toss more cards into a helmet. But be ready to suit up in a hurry."

Andy let his breath out in a sigh. "George Jefferson would pass

73

out if he knew how you run a fire, part by the book, part by the seat of your pants." He shook his head in slow wonderment.

As Andy left in his jeep, daylight scarcely begun, Stacy Cummings came up, riding her big gelding as if she and the horse were one. She stepped down from the saddle, leaving the reins dangling, and came over to the table where JL sat. She was unsmiling. "Don't get up. I'll sit for a moment." She pulled up a camp chair and sank into it, obviously ill at ease.

"I'm sorry to bother you." She hesitated. "But some things . . ."

"I'm glad you came."

There was silence between them. Stacy broke it. "I heard that pompous fool on TV," she said. "I wouldn't talk to him."

"But you, like everyone else, want to know how it's going." JL nodded. "I don't blame you. Well, here's the picture: we've taken a licking so far. It was bad yesterday, and we lost more ground during the night."

"And you don't like to lose," Stacy said. "Neither do I." She paused again. "Any help from the weather?"

"None. If anything . . ."

"Wind change?" Stacy caught the look of surprise that crossed his face. "I've been thinking too," Stacy said. "Best case, worst case. You know."

JL regarded her seriously. "You do look at things, don't you? Yes, we may have a sudden, strong wind change."

"How bad is that?"

"Depends what we can do between now and then. If the fire crowns—that is, if it rises into the tops of the big trees and begins spreading from treetop to treetop, above the reach of fire fighters on the ground, we'll be totally at the mercy of the wind."

"You're thinking about my side, aren't you?" Stacy said. "Mine and Bart Jones's, Willard Spencer's, Sophie Swift's, Bellevue Acres, Vista Hill—and the town beyond?"

"I'm afraid I am."

"You're moving some men into that side," Stacy said. "I rode through and saw." She stood up. "Thank you. I admire honesty."

"I'll see that you have warning," JL said. "If it's necessary."

"Thank you for that too."

She got up, walked to her horse and swung lightly into the saddle. She faced JL again. "That date we have"—she smiled briefly—"to talk things over when all this is done." She hesitated. "As far as I'm concerned, it's still on."

"I'm looking forward to it," JL said, and he smiled openly.

MRS. TYLER WAYNE left Hilario and Manuel working carefully in what she thought of as her English garden—primroses, foxgloves, Canterbury bells—and went back up to the house to rest.

Even .without air-conditioning, which Mrs. Wayne disliked, it was cool inside. The broad porch overhang shielded the house from the high sun in summer, and the thick whitewashed adobe walls kept the inside temperature at a pleasant level day or night. In addition, Vista Hill enjoyed a cooling breeze even on days when the air down in town was still.

A maid brought Mrs. Wayne a glass of iced tea, which she sat sipping quietly. Sierra Grande, its remaining snow patch coming into view and then disappearing as smoke clouds swirled, dominated the middle foreground. Mrs. Wayne had always thought of the great mountain as guardian of the valley, and as such it held both her attention and her respect. Once, in her younger days, she and Tyler had climbed the mountain and eaten a picnic lunch just beneath its peak, while they gazed in awe at the broad land laid out before them, the horizons impossibly distant.

In the near foreground now she could clearly see Bellevue Acres with its bustle and its clutter. She had considered attending the city council meeting at which the licence to allow a higher density of houses on the estate had been discussed, and had decided against it.

Tyler, she had thought many times since, would have gone, argued forcibly against change, and probably carried the evening. Perhaps she had let him down by not following suit. No matter; it was done now, and if she found the view distasteful, she could always look in another direction.

She glanced up as the maid approached carrying a telephone extension. As she handed the phone to Mrs. Wayne she said, "A Senator Bronson calling from Washington."

Mrs. Wayne was smiling as she raised the phone. "Hello, Will."

"Myra. How good to hear your voice. It's been a long time."

"I'm not one of your constituents, Will." The smile was in her voice now. "You don't need to butter me up, even though I love it. You have something in mind?"

There was hesitation. "You have a fire in the Sanrio forest," the senator said.

"We do indeed."

"Is it being properly handled? I have had reports, complaints."

"I believe so, Will. I know the young man in charge, and I consider him eminently qualified."

"Bureaucrats become entrenched, Myra. You know that as well as anyone. They become careless, set in their ways . . ."

"Like politicians, Will. Only some politicians, of course."

The senator's tone changed. "Are you all right, Myra? I'm worried about you. The reports I have of this fire—"

"No doubt exaggerated, Will."

"Nevertheless," Bronson said, "I am going to call the secretary and ask for a report, on your behalf."

Mrs. Wayne was thinking of JL and what he had told her. "You might also tell him, Will, that if it were not for his ban on what I believe is called prescribed burning, I understand that this fire might not have reached its present proportions."

Was there hesitation? "I will mention that," the senator said.

You do that, Mrs. Wayne thought as she hung up. Looking out at the smoke, she felt a little better.

BESSIE WINGATE SAID to no one in particular, "If you ask me, this thing is determined to burn the mountain clean, right up to the timberline. You, Pete, and Stinky, haul yourselves over yonder with that saw and take down that lone pine. It could be a stepping-stone if the wind carried a burning branch to it."

Bessie and her crew were back on the fire line on the upper slopes of Sierra Grande, after a fitful night camped out at forest headquarters.

Through the trees above which they were cutting their firebreak, a perpetual glow marked the approaching flames, with an occasional bright burst as a pitch-filled piñon went up like a torch. The sounds of the fire were constant, a roaring, crackling furnace sound, punctuated now and then by the crash of a huge tree collapsing.

The heat reached them too, carrying with it the smoke fumes that could be, as Bessie knew, all too lethal; carbon monoxide concentration in wildland fires could rise to more than eight hundred parts per million, more than enough to cause death. Taking a brief glance downhill towards the fire front, Bessie saw two figures dodging among the trees on a course parallel to, rather than away from, the flames. Her first thought was that some fire fighters had lost their marbles and, in panic, their sense of direction as well. She raised her voice in a great shout.

"Come out of there, you fools! You're too close to the front! Head uphill! Uphill!"

The running figures disappeared, and Bessie, leaning briefly on her shovel to wipe the sweat from her forehead with one dirty shirt sleeve, said, "Well, I'll be . . . now who in tarnation would be wandering around down there with a fire front coming uphill at them like a mad bull in a field?"

ELSIE AND DON EDWARDS never heard the sound of Bessie's voice; it was drowned out by the roar of the fire, and so they ran on, as close to the approaching fire line as they dared.

At this elevation, somewhere around nine thousand feet, the air seemed to contain less oxygen than smoke, and their breath came in great gasps. To Don, whose head had become again one huge aching throb, running at all was sheer torture.

For Elsie, the feeling was that of being on a treadmill in a nightmare. I'm going mad, she thought. One moment they were alone in their own tiny place in the forest. The next, the world was turned upside down.

She was aware that Don was stumbling now, close to the limit of his endurance. She was suddenly aware too that the faintly cooling breeze on her cheeks had shifted direciton and was coming now from above them on the mountain, and that the flames below them were further away than they had been.

Elsie caught Don's arm and slowed him down to a walk. "I think," she said through gasping breath, "that we're—safe. For now. Sit down. Rest." And when he had sunk to the ground like a doll unhinged, she knelt beside him and touched his cheek with great gentleness. "Poor baby," she said. "Rest. I'll—have a look."

Don sat where he was, his arms on his bent knees and his head bowed over them. He no longer had any idea where they were, or any clear picture of what had happened during the past few hours. He seemed to remember that at one point Elsie had whispered urgently. "There they are again! They're still here!" But his head throbbed so violently now that he could not be sure what was real and what mere fantasy.

Sitting unmoving, eyes closed, he tried to remember at least the contours of the mountain he had studied so carefully on the topographical map. The way they must have come, with the body of the fire on their left and below them, they were travelling clockwise round the mountain's mass. So far, so good.

They had not yet come to the cliff he remembered from the map. It had appeared to hang over a mountain lake, the edge of the cliff not far below the timberline. It was possible, he thought, that the fire might have been thwarted by that cliff area, and that beyond it he and Elsie might be able to descend to safety.

Elsie was suddenly back. She was breathless again, but her expression had lost some of its tenseness. "Nothing," she said, and in the single word there was triumph. "When you're ready, we can go on." She dropped to her knees beside him. "Oh, darling, I think—"

"Well, well, well," said Frank Orwell's voice, "will you look who we've got here?"

He and Felipe Vigil stepped out of the shadows. Each man held a knife. Orwell gestured menacingly with his. "If you're thinking of getting up," he said to Elsie, "just do it slow and easy. And you, buster, just stay right where you are."

Elsie put her hand on Don's shoulder. "Don't," she said. "Whatever you're thinking, don't. You . . . can't."

"You think good," Felipe said. "Real good."

Elsie took a deep breath. "What do you want?"

"Why, honey, we liked the sample." This was Orwell. "We been talking about it. You'd be real pleased if you knew."

Elsie was silent, motionless, still kneeling beside Don. She looked from man to man, studying the faces. There was, she thought, no pity, none. Her mind felt strangely analytical.

"Stand up," Orwell said.

Don said, "No. No, damn it! What kind of animals are you?"

"Hush," Elsie said. "Please hush, darling." She rose from her knees and straightened herself.

"Now move away," Orwell said, and watched Elsie obey.

"Run!" Don said.

"Better not." Orwell again. He had moved quickly and now dropped to one knee, pressing the point of his knife against the side of Don's neck. "Unless you want to see his throat cut."

Elsie closed her eyes briefly. She opened them again. "Please, darling. Don't do anything. No matter what. He'll do it."

"She catches on good," Orwell said. He made a small gesture with his free hand. "OK," he said to Felipe, "she's all yours."

Felipe held his knife with practised ease. He gestured with its glittering blade. "You hear the man, chick? Is good. The shirt—take her off."

Don said, "Don't—" He stopped as Orwell's knife point broke the skin and a thin trickle of blood rolled down his neck.

"Please, darling! Please!" Elsie's voice came out almost in a scream as she started to pull the shirt from her trousers.

To the two men she said, "Just leave him alone. Please. I'll do what you say."

"You bet your sweet life you will," Orwell said. "Now, get those clothes off or—"

The sound was a blend of roar and scream, highpitched, hoarse, filled with fury and entirely terrifying. Bessie Wingate, enormous and overpoweringly visible in yellow hard hat and grimy yellow shirt, her shovel clutched in one hand, burst out of the forest shadows on a dead run. "You bastards!" Her voice echoed through the trees. She headed towards Felipe.

Felipe was agile. He sprang back from Elsie, and the knife in his hand seemed alive as it flashed in the air. "*Qué vaya*, fat one! Beat it before I cut your gizzard out!"

Bessie did not hesitate. She swung her shovel with the full strength of both brawny arms in a broad arc, edge forward. It nearly severed the arm Felipe flung up to protect himself, and—continuing almost unchecked—slammed into his side.

The knife fell unnoticed to the ground as Felipe staggered no more than two paces backwards and collapsed.

Bessie faced Orwell, who had risen to his feet. "Now you, you little—" She advanced, shovel held at the ready.

Orwell turned and ran.

Chapter Eight

By early afternoon, the party around Ada Loving's swimming pool was in full swing. Ada herself, tanned to smooth flawlessness, wore a stunning white bikini. Of the twenty guests at the party, all but one had been imported from Hollywood. The lone exception was a man named Leon Sturgis, who wore carefully faded jeans, ostrich-skin cowboy boots and a shortsleeved Sulka shirt.

"Tax shelter with cash flow is the name of the game," he told a group round the portable bar, "and if you can have it, and enjoy yourself in a place like Sanrio, why, that's a licence to steal."

"Smog for smoke," one of the imports said. "I'm not sure you gain much. They both make you sneeze."

"Smoke's temporary," Sturgis said. "There's the difference."

Ada, despite her costume, was not insensitive to the anomaly of her poolside party-as-usual while the countryside burned. On the other hand, the charter flight and rented limousines to carry guests from the airport had been all arranged, and last-minute cancellations were bad public relations, so the decision had been made to carry on as planned. Profits from the sale of $250,000-and-up

apartment blocks yet to be constructed were not to be taken lightly.

Ada had often wondered who really controlled the purse strings and made the decisions; not that it mattered as long as she was paid as agreed, and on time.

Sturgis, drink in hand, wandered over from the bar. "They've sent us a pretty dead group," he told Ada in a quiet voice. "What can we do to stir them up? A drive through the forest?"

"You've heard that there is a fire going on?" Ada's voice too was quiet, and her smile did not fade.

"Sure. We'll show it to them firsthand."

"Include me out," Ada said. "Folks here are taking it seriously. So am I."

Then Ken Delacorte arrived, looking round curiously at the strangers, nodding to Ada and giving Sturgis a cold stare.

Ken had met Ada a few times during his short stint in Hollywood, and since her move to Sanrio he had squired her around on occasion, often enough to suspect that beneath the gorgeous exterior was someone worth knowing. He had never met Sturgis, but he had encountered dozens like him, always on the fringes and on the make: human jackals, in his opinion.

Sturgis made his position clear at once. "You're in real estate too," he said, then indicated with a nod of his head the people round the pool. "But these are our pigeons."

"Pluck them clean for all I care," Ken said. "But I think you"—he spoke now directly to Ada—"would do well to think about where you might go if things get completely out of hand."

"Paul Revere," Sturgis said. "Warning us that the British are coming?"

"Are things going to get out of hand?" Ada said.

"They could. We all hope they won't, but that's a big fire."

"The Forest Service clowns screwing up, as usual?" Sturgis said.

"You know," Ken said, "some day somebody is going to pick you up, Sturgis, and set you down so hard you'll find your teeth on the ground. I might even do it myself. Now go play with your Hollywood pigeons."

Ada watched Sturgis walk off, still wearing his easy smile. She said, "You're not usually that belligerent, Ken."

"I don't usually talk to toads like him."

Ada was silent for a few moments. Slowly she turned on the famous Loving smile and gestured towards the bar. "Would you like a drink? It is, after all, my house. On paper, anyway."

Ken looked across the pool area to Sturgis and the other guests. He looked again at Ada and shook his head. "Just don't let too much of them rub off on you," he said. "Wave the body around all you want. That isn't you—just something you happen to have been born with. But hang on to the real part. Keep it the way you'd like it. Do I sound like a preacher man?"

"Strangely enough," Ada said, "you don't. I'll bear it in mind."

JL WAS LEANING FORWARD IN HIS chair, staring glumly at the latest infrared photos with Ben Hastings. "Here, here and here"—JL's pencil moved quickly—"we have open flames, these black areas. We're moving in men to block their spread where we can."

"Slurry drops?" Ben said.

"Slurry drops are fine, but you can't hold a long fire front with them alone."

"That means backfire?"

JL nodded. "I think that's the answer. I've called in a chopper fitted with helitorch equipment capable of setting one along a prescribed line." He reached out and pulled over a map. "A limited backfire right here." He drew a line running southwest to northeast above the area called Sheep Ridge, a long, low-rise strategically located just to the north of the town and the line of estates bordering the forest. "I want you behind the helitorch in another chopper, calling the shots. And we'll need a hotshot crew on the scene to keep it contained."

Ben studied the markings on the map and brought to mind the terrain, which was hilly, with thick brush and scattered piñons.

The logic of a backfire here was irrefutable, he thought; by preemptive burning, scorching to the ground the area JL had marked before the actual danger arrived, they could deny the fire further fuel if it burst at last from the deep forest, and perhaps, in that sector at least, stop it in its tracks.

On the other hand, there were always dangers. "If the wind shifts—" Ben began.

"The longer we wait, the more likely a wind shift becomes," JL said. "So get onto it. I've got some thinking to do."

He sat quietly at the improvised desk long after Ben had gone. It grieved him that the forest hush was now constantly disturbed by the clamour of men and equipment—jeeps, trucks, ground tankers, bulldozers, and the sudden painful sounds as living trees came crashing to the forest floor.

In each major fire too, situations arose that could not have been foreseen, leaving a residue of what JL could only look upon as personal failure. Early this morning, for example, one of the chopper pilots had seen ground signals in the wilderness—rocks set out in a geometric pattern—and when he hovered to investigate, he saw a man, a woman and a boy waving frantically and motioning for him to land nearby. As machinery is forbidden in the wilderness, the pilot simply radioed a report, and eventually a rescue party was sent in on foot. JL was not told until it was too late to interfere, and the incident left a bad taste. It would, no doubt, be retold as an example of Forest Service insensitivity.

Thoughts of the situation involving Bessie Wingate, the honeymoon couple and the two escaped convicts continued to bother him too, although by no conceivable standards could he or any of his people be considered even vaguely culpable.

"Clear case of self-defence," the state police lieutenant had reported, after talking to all the witnesses. He shook his head slowly. "What kind of a woman is this, anyway? A runaway truck couldn't have done more damage to that guy Felipe."

"She's been on the fire line almost four days now," JL had explained, "and when you've been at it that long, you work up a pretty fair head of steam. You don't fool around any more."

Felipe was now in intensive care in the hospital. The other convict was still on the loose and was bound to turn up again with his knife; he had to be considered dangerous.

JL shrugged and sat up straight to study the map again. The

backfire he had sent Ben to set up was a gamble. That could not be denied. Wind change was coming: the high-pressure ridge that had sat over them these last few days was stirring itself and beginning to move east. But *if* the wind direction held steady for only a little time, the odds in favour of the gamble were high.

It was how these things were done, he thought—little by little and bit by bit, precariously establishing a bastion beyond which the flames could not spread, holding that area securely and at the same time throwing men and equipment into a new sector, there to fight for fresh ground from which to launch new attacks. On a minor fire simultaneous assaults on all fronts were possible. But piecemeal attack was the only way to fight Backslope.

He remembered trying once to explain that to Madge. It had been a waste of time. And here came thoughts of Stacy again, because she would have understood. Suddenly he realized that his image of Madge was fading. The picture of her in his mind, like a dream upon awakening, had lost much of its form and colour. She belonged in another world.

So be it.

STACY STRIPPED, BUNDLED UP HER clothes and tossed them into the hamper. Much as she loved horses, she detested people who always smelled as if they had just come from the stables. She remembered that it had not always been so.

"We have a house," her father had told her one evening long ago, "and we have a horse barn. They aren't the same. When you come to the dinner table, by golly, I won't have you stinking of horse sweat!"

Sometimes, she thought as she headed for the shower, the sound of his voice came back to her so vividly it hurt. And once the memories began, they were difficult to shut off.

She remembered another evening now, much later but also dinnertime. The two of them were sitting alone at the big polished table with lighted candles and silver candlesticks. "Why haven't you ever married again?" Stacy had asked.

"I'm too cantankerous," her father had said, and showed his fond, crooked smile.

"I'm serious."

Her father studied her across the table. "Trying to find a clue to something in yourself, honey?"

"Maybe. I don't know."

"I'm luckier than most," her father said then. "I found one

84

woman, the right one. Darn few do. Darn few like me, that is. I'm a loner, I suppose. I like folks, but I want a little distance between us. There's something of that in you too."

Stacy smiled sheepishly. "I know."

Her father took his time before going on. "Horses aren't a substitute for people, honey," he said gently, "and winning prize saddles isn't the be-all and end-all. Maybe you're beginning to find that out too."

Of course, Stacy thought now, there was usually a connection between remembered conversations and the present. In this instance, the connection was her lawyer and neighbour, Sophie Swift.

On the telephone earlier, Sophie had said, "I wonder if it would be convenient for you to meet me this afternoon, Stacy? Say five thirty? I realize that with this fire—your worry about your horses, I mean—I am troubling you, and I'm sorry. I don't usually impose."

Stacy had never heard Sophie this close to incoherence. "Of course I'll meet you. Where?"

"I thought maybe the lounge of the inn. It's quiet there."

"Fine," Stacy said. "We can talk."

SOPHIE WAS WAITING at a table for two in one corner of the lounge, sitting very straight in the upholstered wing chair. She could not remember when she had felt like this—so helpless and indecisive. Nor until now had she realized how alone she was in this wide world. Her invitation to Stacy was a cry for help.

Looking up, making herself smile, she said, "Thank you for coming," as Stacy approached.

"It's good to see you. Even as neighbours we don't—"

"And thank you for not asking if anything is wrong. Of course it is. You already understand that."

The waiter arrived. Stacy ordered a glass of white wine. The interruption was welcome. "You and Aaron?" she asked.

"Of course."

"I'm not very good at these things, Soph, not very good at all."

The other woman sighed. "I'm supposed to be good at it," she said. "Lawyers are very good at telling clients what to do, how to run their lives. Now it's case of *Physician, heal thyself*. And I don't know how to cope."

Through the large windows across the lounge the mountain rose grandly, shrouded in smoke. Stacy stared at it. "When things get out of hand," she said, "they seem to do it all at once, don't they?" She looked again at Sophie. "I wish I had wise advice, Soph, I really do. But I don't."

"I like Debby," Sophie said. "She's good for Aaron."

"You are generous."

A faint smile appeared and was quickly gone. "The fact is that I hate her too. Isn't that an ignoble confession?"

"I didn't even hear it," Stacy said.

It was as if she had not spoken. Sophie's thoughts ran their course unhindered, as if words too long forcibly contained had finally burst free.

"You take for granted what you have," she said, "until one day you lose it. That is trite, but true. I have seen it with clients to whom the prospect of losing liberty exists merely as an abstraction until the verdict is handed down and they are led away. Then, all at once, realization takes place, and it is shattering."

It was embarrassing to listen to, Stacy thought, and yet in a strange way she was glad that it was she whom Sophie had chosen for her confidences. Her reactions astonished her too. Instead of detachment or even slight amusement, what she felt was pure compassion for another human being in pain. It was a feeling she had previously reserved almost entirely for horses.

"I think another glass of wine, Soph," Stacy said when at last the spate of words slowed. "And then why don't we have dinner here? I've heard that the food is good."

DROPPING FIRE FROM THE SKY is always a risky business, Ben Hastings thought, as he surveyed the forest below from his seat in the helicopter. Too many variables. A hundred and fifty yards ahead flew the helicopter-helitorch that would drop flaming gelled gasoline on Sheep Ridge, the scene of the backfire that JL had planned. Ben wore a headset and mike attachment, leaving both hands free.

He spoke into the mike now. "You're right on course," he said to the leading helicopter. "Start your fire on the far side of that next low ridge, and hold it steady as you go. Do you read me? Over."

"Roger. Over."

"The backfire line we want is a little more than a quarter of a mile long," Ben added, "terminating well before the heavy tree growth begins. I'll give you ample warning."

"Roger. Piece of cake. Over."

I hope so, Ben thought.

When they were able to look over the low ridge ahead, Ben saw the hotshot crew standing on the ground ready as ordered—spaced along the line of fire and well below it for safety's sake. Gordy Walker was in charge of the crew, which was something of a comfort, because if anything were to go wrong, Gordy would see that his men bust a gut to cope.

And then the first stream of flame dropped from the flexible hose that trailed beneath the helitorch, and Ben watched the hanging fire reach the ground. Instantly a clump of brush was ablaze. As the line of flaming gelled gasoline moved on, the men on the ground moved closer to the fire line to attack scattered flames that had been started downslope.

So far, so good, Ben thought, and resisted the impulse to cross his fingers.

Into the mike he said, "You're bang on target."

JL's chosen front for the backfire was strategic: far enough downslope from the heavy stands of big trees that windblown sparks would not easily reach them, yet far enough above the large private holdings that they too would be well protected.

As the helitorch approached the end of the backfire line, Ben spoke again into his mike. "On the rise of that next ridge," he said, "cut off your fire. We want to give the ground troops plenty of room to get round the end and keep it from spreading into those big trees."

"The rise of the next ridge—will do."

Ben let out his breath in a long sigh. He had not realized how tense he had been. Watching the helitorch approach the rise, he whispered to himself, "OK, cut it off, and we can go home."

But the string of fire continued, and through Ben's headset the pilot's voice came clearly, "Shut off, damn you. Shut off!"

"You're too far!" Ben said into the mike in sudden alarm.

"I know it! The valve's stuck! It should—"

"Then turn back! Stay away from those big trees!"

The helicopter was now right on the edge of the big trees, at an elevation of perhaps forty feet, and trying to turn back, but it was losing altitude at an alarming rate.

"Pick up!" This was the helitorch pilot's voice coming loud and clear in Ben's headset. "Up, up, up, damn—" The words were his last. Suddenly, where the helitorch had been there was only a ball of fire, rising incredibly.

The blast of rushing air rocked Ben's own chopper. Three of the big trees instantly burst into flame. Several more followed. On the ground, Gordy Walker led his hotshot crew at a dead run towards the inferno.

Ben's pilot took their chopper up and, banking, headed away from the scene. "We can't do anything here," he said.

Speechless, Ben nodded in agreement and closed his eyes.

IT WAS STILL LIGHT, and the sun low in the western sky had turned a copper colour by the time Stacy drove home from the inn. Along the way she paused on the county road to stare at what seemed to be a new area of fire—in the base of the stand of big trees that extended down towards the town and the large property holdings.

It was while she sat there studying the heavy smoke that the green Forest Service pickup came slowly by. She waved, and the truck stopped. JL was behind the wheel. "Yes, it's a new outbreak," he said. "Something we could have done without."

He was bone tired; that was Stacy's first judgment. There were deep lines round his eyes, and his shoulders did not seem quite as erect as usual. "Are you off duty?" she asked.

"For a while. I was having a look round here on my way home."

"Come with me," Stacy said, "and I'll give you a drink."

They sat in Stacy's living room at opposite ends of the big leather sofa. JL sipped his drink gratefully. "What happened?" she said, and listened quietly to the tale of the abortive backfire.

"The pilot's shutoff valve stuck, he fussed with it and flew too close to a stand of big trees," he said, summing up. "We swung and we missed, and killed a man in the process."

"And you blame yourself?"

JL shook his head. "Blame," he said, "is for hearings and investigations. What I have is the responsibility. I'm the fire boss, and it happened on my fire."

"Do you resent that?" Stacy asked curiously.

JL thought about it. "Not exactly resent. I'd rather just answer for my own performance. But somebody has to run the show"—a small, self-deprecating smile appeared—"and I seem to be out there leading the parade and making the decisions."

"But you'd really rather be alone?"

"Yes," he answerd truthfully.

The beeper on JL's belt gave out its sudden shrill signal. He silenced it as he stood up. "I'll use your phone, if I may?"

Stacy waved him towards the office-library. Another loner, she thought, watching him go. Like her father, like herself.

"There's more to JL," Ken Delacorte had once told her, "than you may think on first meeting."

"You know him well?" Stacy had asked.

"I don't think anybody does. I've hunted and fished with him, played poker with him—I've even seen his paintings, but I don't know him well."

It was the first Stacy had heard of JL's painting, and she asked Ken more about it. "Watercolours? That kind of thing?"

"Not on your life. Oils. Big canvases. I'm no connoisseur, but I've wandered through a gallery or two and I've seen a heck of a lot of forest scenes hanging in them that didn't give me half the jolt in the belly that one or two of his do."

"Does he exhibit?"

"Nope. Fighting fires is his thing. Madge—that was his wife—didn't like his painting *or* his fire fighting. So she left."

It was the first Stacy had heard of Madge.

JL came back from the office-library. "I'm afraid I have to get back. We've been expecting a front and it's moving in."

"Fronts," Stacy said, "sometimes bring rain."

"This one won't. It's warm, dry air, wrung out by passing over the Arizona high country. No moisture left. Just wind and pressure change." He finished his drink. "I am grateful for the little time of relaxation. And the drink."

"*De nada.*"

JL shook his head in slow wonder. "Funny," he said. "We used to strike sparks, you and I. We don't seem to any more."

"I've noticed that too."

"I wonder why."

"Maybe it's just that the fire's more important."

The slow smile appeared. "Maybe that's it."

IN THE TOWER of the Forest Service airport, Andy McIlvain had just listened to the latest weather forecast. He pondered it as he went back down the stairs to the main hangar.

The men he had parachuted in over thirty hours ago were back now, having held their sector until danger of fire had swept past. Then, gathering their gear and hoisting it to their shoulders, they had hiked out. They were now repacking their chutes and reloading fire boxes against the certainty of another drop.

Unable to sit still any longer, Andy called to one of his crewmen. "The front's coming," he said. "I've seen the infrared photos, so I have an idea what it'll mean, but I want to see the actual scene. I'll be gone maybe thirty, forty minutes."

He walked out to the field, where his own single-engine aircraft was parked. Once airborne, he felt free and loose and easy, sharing with the ravens and eagles the ability to look down on the world and see its true dimensions.

Dominating the earthbound scene, of course, was the big mountain, still proudly thrusting its rocky peak above the smoke. In one section below the timberline, even as he watched, the flames spread inexorably upwards, and no fire-fighting crews attempted to stop, or even slow, their progress. JL had obviously written off that fringe of trees as not worth the effort.

Andy flew over the cliff in front of which he and JL had jumped, and noted, as he had expected, that the vegetation-free rocky face had been a natural barrier beyond which the fire could not pass.

He took the aircraft up in a wide, swinging turn until his view was from a position above the mountain's peak, and the full extent of the fire called Backslope was spread beneath him.

The total fire area was roughly elliptical in shape, its major axis extending east-west, its minor axis running almost due north-south. Airborne estimates were mere guesses, but it looked to him as if the fire had grown to cover an area about fifteen miles long and perhaps ten miles deep: a hundred and fifty square miles, or—he did quick calculations—in the neighbourhood of ninety-six thousand acres!

North of Highway 14, where the gasoline tanker had exploded, the fire had established a bulge, against which Andy could see ground crews fighting a desperate holding action. At the moment, the wind was against the crews, driving the open flames further north.

The southern line of the fire was almost straight, except for an expanding area of flames at the base of a finger of the forest that pointed towards the Bellevue Acres development and the town beyond. Along that southern line, the wind aided the efforts at suppression, although, as Andy could clearly see from his eagle-eye view, the crash of that helitorch had been a near thing indeed, and only immediate action by the hotshot crew on the spot had kept the fire from spreading out of control among the big trees. So far, then, the eastern flank of Sierra Grande was secure; the fire's penetration from its starting point had not proceeded east or northeast beyond the Sheep Ridge area.

But as he began a second, larger circle, one more item caught Andy's attention, and at this he stared long and unhappily.

To the northwest there was no smoke, which was momentarily puzzling, since the fire beyond Highway 14 was being pushed by a southerly wind. A trail of smoke from that fire should by now have stretched north and northwest.

There was, of course, only one explanation: the anticipated wind shift had arrived, and the smoke arising from the bulge beyond Highway 14 was being blown back upon itself; so everything was about to be reversed, and what had been secure to the south would soon be in jeopardy. Andy reached for the mike and called the tower at the airfield. "Can you patch me through to JL?"

The tower could. JL's voice came through loud and clear.

"I'm up here at fifteen thousand," Andy said, "and if you want to chew me out for leaving the field, at least wait till I report. There is no smoke, repeat, no smoke beyond the fire line in the northwest quadrant. Got it?"

JL's weary voice conveyed instant comprehension. "I think I can work it out. A major wind shift." He added, almost to himself, "Just what we don't need."

FRANK ORWELL, up on the mountain, was not lost; on the contrary, he knew all too well where he was—between a rock and a hard place. Below him, and coming closer, were flames. Above him he could hear the voices of a fire-fighting crew cutting a break, grunting with their efforts. And from time to time, almost as if calculated to torment him, the voice of that wild woman with the shovel sounded off, echoing through the trees and drowning out even the crackling sounds of the approaching flames.

The heat and the smoke were both increasing, and try as he might, Orwell could stifle neither the urge to cough nor the growing terror that was gnawing at his guts. Again and again he thought about Vigil. Incredible! That woman had swung the shovel right from her heels, and if Orwell lived to be a hundred he would never forget the sound when the shovel blade made contact.

And so, hating himself for refusing to dare the open, he crouched like a rabbit and took one cautious step backwards after another in the growing darkness, while the flames came closer and the heat and the smoke became almost unbearable. Sooner or later, he told himself, he would reach the point of daring to stop, of advancing and showing himself. But not yet.

He wiped the sweat from his eyes with the back of his wrist. Just a little further, and then he would make his stand.

He took one more step backwards. It was his last.

Rock crumbled beneath his weight. He tried to throw himself forward, but he felt himself falling, where and into what he had no idea. And then he was in free-fall, cartwheeling into space over the cliff above the small lake. The scream he heard was his own.

THEY FOUND THE BODY within the hour. One of the southwest area crewmen, a Chiricahua Apache, spotted it lying on the rocks at the edge of the small lake. The crew chief radioed in the information, and two men—one of them a state policeman—worked their way with a packhorse through burned-over forest to the site.

The policeman squatted on his heels for a closer look. "At a guess," he said, "I'd say we've got the second one who walked away from Los Ojos. Fellow named Orwell." He stood up and squinted at the cliff wall. "Long fall," he said.

The other man said, "Did he fall, or was he pushed?"

"You know," the policeman said, "as far as I'm concerned he fell, and that's where I'm leaving it. Couldn't have happened to a nicer guy. Let's get him on the horse."

"THE WIND CHANGE will work to our advantage here and here," JL said to Ben Hastings. Bent over the table, JL indicated on the map the north and northwest sectors of the fire. "It will push the flames right back to burned-over territory, where they'll die for lack of fuel. We can pull crews out of there and bring them down here, where the new danger will be." His finger indicated the southern fire boundary, near Sheep Ridge. "We've asked Albuquerque to send in another helitorch, just in case."

Ben closed his eyes. He could still see that sudden fireball as the helitorch-chopper slammed into the ground and exploded. He could still hear the pilot's voice, cut off in midsentence. He said, "Another backfire?"

"If we have to." JL studied Ben carefully. "You'd rather someone else flew in the following chopper and called the shots?"

Ben shook his head. "I'll do it." He took a deep breath. "And I'll get some trucks to start moving crews down that old logging road through the wilderness area."

JL permitted himself the faintest hint of an approving smile. He nodded. "Get to it, then. And keep me informed."

Jay Paul came up as Ben left. Jay said, "I'm pretty much extra baggage round here. If you—"

"We don't keep extra baggage around," JL said. "So you're going to work. Have a look at this sector." He tapped the map and waited until Jay bent over it reluctantly. "Sudden wind shift. Northwest," he said. "What will that do down here?"

Jay straightened. "Push the fire down towards those big houses. But you've already figured on that." His voice was resentful, that of a small boy being asked the obvious.

"And over here to the east?" JL asked.

Jay Paul glanced at the map. JL's finger pointed to wooded terrain on the big mountain's flank. "I don't know," Jay said.

"And neither do I for sure. But suppose the wind bringing sparks around starts the fire moving east to south? What about the crews working that southern quadrant?"

Jay Paul looked again at the map, with careful interest now. He said, "They'd be caught. They wouldn't stand a chance."

"So," JL said, "we want to see that that doesn't happen. You go out to the airfield. Show Andy McIlvain what we've got, and let him pick a spot where he can put in a crew to guard against that kind of encirclement. I want you to fly along with them, and once they're on the ground, give them instructions for placement. From the air you'll have the whole picture, and they'll be down among the trees and rocks, working almost blind."

JL sat quietly for a little time after Jay Paul, still doubtful but now determined to try, had headed for the airfield. Jay was a good man, JL told himself, or he wouldn't be here. How good a man, they would find out.

BESSIE WINGATE HERDED HER CREW into the back of the first truck, giving the last man a helping shove on the rump that almost carried him the length of the truck floor. Then Bessie heaved herself mightily over the tailgate and took a quick look round.

"We got room for one more!" she bawled. She spotted a familiar face. "Come on, Eloy!"

Eloy Jaramillo, the little fire fighter from the southwest crew, had become separated from his team and was standing nearby. Bessie caught his arm and hoisted him up bodily, as by a crane. Then she hammered with her fist on the cab's top. "Let's go! We got a full load!" The truck lurched off.

One of Bessie's crew said, "Sure beats walking. But where we going?"

"Wind change, jughead," Bessie explained, "so we go down to see that those rich dudes sitting around their swimming pools don't get singed."

Bessie settled herself comfortably in the truck. "Funny stuff, wind," she said meditatively. "You can't see it, but you can sure as heck see what it does. I've watched it grab up a burning branch, carry it halfway to hell and gone and drop it in the middle of some area you thought was secure, and—bang! You've got a new fire front, just like that."

Bessie was warming to her subject now. "I seen wind come out of nowhere too," she went on, "just when the fire you're fighting is whipping you good, and all of a sudden it's like somebody dropped an asbestos curtain, and the fire stops, tries to go back but can't and then dies down for lack of fuel.

"There's just no figuring it. But one thing that's for sure: whenever you get wind and a fire together, you'd better watch your step every minute."

THE FRONT-RUNNING GUSTS that heralded the wind change were welcome to the crews still manning the fire line in the north, beyond Highway 14. The flames they faced now wavered and lessened in force; here and there they even withdrew over areas already burned and faded for want of fresh fuel.

In the sky to the northwest, high, thin cirrus clouds, like the banners of an approaching army, announced the main front. The wind picked up; gusts became stronger. Down on the southern front, JL knew, those gusts would be carrying sparks and burning fuel into fresh, untouched areas. And down there it was not only trees but houses as well that would be threatened.

Chapter Nine

Early Thursday morning, Jay Paul climbed up behind Andy McIlvain into the Twin Otter. In the almost-bare fuselage, now crowded with the jumping crew, there was only a single wooden bench and the spotter's place for seating. They put Jay on the floor next to the open doorway and, using a cargo sling, attached him to one of the fuselage stringers. He tried not to be obvious about grabbing another stringer for support. By the time they were airborne, Jay's hand holding the stringer was numb from the pressure of his grip.

He watched Jake, Andy's number two man, in the spotter's seat, and Andy McIlvain in the open doorway, as they searched the ground for a drop site. Craning his neck, Jay looked down too and saw only treetops and rocks, and was sure that a drop was not possible.

But Andy, pointing, said, "Over there! We can circle and come upwind to it! Duck soup!"

Jake nodded and spoke into his mike, directing the pilot.

Jay Paul swallowed hard as Andy, paired with another jumper, took his place at the open doorway. Almost casually the spotter tapped Andy's shoulder, and Andy launched himself from the aircraft. Moments later his partner followed. Jay closed his eyes in relief when the two chutes deployed and the men began their guided descent to the chosen spot.

When, two by two, all the jumpers were gone, Jake left his spotter's seat to begin wrestling boxes towards the fuselage door. As the aircraft repeated its careful circling, he pushed them out two at a time. With difficulty, Jay unsnapped his cargo sling from the stringer and began giving Jake a hand. And when all the boxes were gone, Jay took another cautious look out from the doorway. It was then that the two airforce fighters appeared out of nowhere and swept past beneath them.

"WE WERE AT TWELVE HUNDRED FEET," Jake reported later to JL, "and none of us saw a thing when those two came under us. I thought we'd hit something. Their turbulence bounced us like a cork in a heavy sea. I saw Jay Paul make a grab for a stringer, miss, start to slide towards the doorway, make another grab and this time catch hold and hang on so tight his hand was all bloody when he finally hauled himself back. He was scared witless and so was I. Just fun and games for the fighter boys."

JL permitted himself the briefest of smiles. Then he turned to Ben Hastings, who was standing nearby, listening.

"All right, tell me about Sheep Ridge," JL said. "Did you get your crews in place?" He sat back in his chair to wait.

Ben told him. The trucks, using an old, abandoned logging road through the wilderness, had reached the Sheep Ridge area, discharged their human loads and made a fast run back to pick up more.

"We spread the men thin at first," Ben told JL, "but as more and more came down, we thickened up the line, and began to make a solid stand. By then, the wind had swung completely round and the fire was coming right down the ridge at us." He watched JL nod with understanding, and knew that he was remembering fires when he had been the one to watch the flames coming at them.

"You know what it's like. The fire's got the wind behind it. But we've got plenty of troops to man the line," Ben said. "Right now, it's a standoff." He extended both hands, fingers crossed. "I almost hate to say it, but I think we can bring it under control."

JL nodded. He hoped Ben was right. But until they were cold-trailing the embers, he'd reserve judgment.

"Well, you'd better get back there," he said. "And keep the pressure on the crew chiefs. Keep me posted." He watched Ben turn away, and stopped him. "One more thing," JL said.

Ben stood quiet, waiting.

"It's a standoff now," JL said finally, "but you could lose that line."

"Yes, sir. Depends on the wind."

"I think," JL said slowly, "that you'd better start thinking about evacuating Bellevue Acres, just in case. All those kids, pets . . ." He shook his head. "With the big places, you tell them to get in their cars and drive off. With that development, you'll have a roundup problem on your hands. Got it?"

"Got it," Ben said.

JL nodded once again. "Good man," he said, and immediately seemed embarrassed that he had uttered such praise.

AARON SWIFT, IN HIS ROLE as federal magistrate, considered the case in his office. Les Lawry was standing before him, with a uniformed man from the county sheriff's office waiting nearby.

"The jeep in the wilderness is yours?" Aaron said.

"Well," Les said, "I guess you could say that. I mean, it was." He tried to smile. "What's the big deal?"

"We'll talk about that in a moment," Aaron said. "Right now I'd like to know what you were doing in the wilderness?"

"Well," Les began, "there was this fire. It was really burning up a storm, and I thought, Les, you'd better get the family the heck out of this. So we hightailed it away from those flames just as fast as we could. Why, there wasn't time to think about it at all, you see what I mean?"

"Not quite," Aaron said quietly. "As I understand it, there was the entire night to think about it. The first night, when you camped well inside the wilderness. What about that?"

"You mean," Les said slowly, "we were where we shouldn't of been? I mean, we didn't see—"

"The tracks of your jeep, Mr. Lawry, lead immediately past a very legible sign forbidding any kind of machinery within the wilderness area. As a matter of fact, you had to take down part of a fence in order to drive through."

"Why, that couldn't of been me, Judge. It had to be somebody else. As a matter of fact, we saw—"

"I am not really amused, Mr. Lawry," Aaron said. "Blatant lies tend to have quite an opposite effect on me."

"Why," Les said, "you can ask Cindy Lou and Tad—"

"Would you ask them to perjure themselves too?" Aaron leaned back in his chair while the question hung unanswered in the air. "You see," he went on, "I can refer this case to a US district court. That could turn out to be a great deal more than you may have bargained for. Perjury, for example, is a criminal offence. Or, I can deal with the matter myself. Do you have a preference?"

Les hesitated. "Well now," he said at last, "I don't see why we can't work this out right here, Judge. The jeep's a write-off, no good to anybody. So why don't we just leave it at that, and forget the whole thing? Now wouldn't that be the sensible thing to do?"

Aaron's voice took on an edge. "No, Mr. Lawry, it would not. Write-off or not, your jeep is a piece of machinery. It is within the wilderness, and you caused it to enter quite unlawfully. You will now remove the jeep, all of it."

"But Judge, that would mean having a truck go in, and that would break the rules again, wouldn't it?" Les, having scored a debating point, was smiling now. "So why don't we—"

"No one but you mentioned a truck, Mr. Lawry."

Les was frowning now. "But you want the jeep out of your woods, don't you?"

"That is correct. You will remove it. At your expense."

"What am I supposed to do, carry it on my back?"

"Precisely how you do it, Mr. Lawry, is a matter of complete indifference to me—as long as it does not involve taking more machinery into the wilderness area. The last transgressors had their jeep hauled out by mule team."

Les said, "Hire a wagon and a mule team and enough men to pick a jeep up and haul it out? Do you realize what that would cost?"

"You might have thought of that beforehand. You may go now, Mr. Lawry. The sheriff will accompany you."

ADA LOVING DROVE a leased sky-blue Mercedes 380 SL, top down. In sandals, skintight slacks and a crisp white shortsleeved blouse, she parked behind Ken Delacorte's aged Ford and went into the real estate office.

Ken was at his desk, staring at a map. He stood up to acknowledge her presence, and then sat down again as Ada sank gracefully into a visitor's chair. She was unsmiling.

"I'm scared, Ken," Ada said, the words coming out too fast. "The fire's gotten too big and too close. And everybody else seems to be pretending it doesn't mean a thing. That's the scary part."

Ken smiled. They had not seen each other since the brief time at Ada's pool.

"Did you come to have your hand held?" he asked.

"It would be a welcome relief from the hands I usually have to contend with." Again the words came too fast, tumbling over themselves. "Are we safe, Ken? Can they control that—monster?"

Monster was the right word, Ken thought, then said, "You do have it bad, don't you, baby?"

Ada said in a slower, calmer voice that nonetheless seemed to emphasize her fright, "I was in a fire once. I was five. The fire department didn't arrive until it was too late, and I can still close my eyes and remember standing with my mother, watching the whole house go up—with my crippled aunt inside screaming. I've been terrified of fire ever since."

Ken was silent.

"I'm afraid to be alone," Ada said. "I want a man on the scene."

"What about Sturgis?"

"Be serious, Ken. He isn't a man. He's a piece of typecasting."

"And the Hollywood pigeons?"

"They decided to cut their losses. They sent them back in the chartered plane this afternoon."

"They?"

"Whoever backs the show. I'm hired help, not part of the management."

Ken said slowly, "There's a dude in town name of Bart Jones, goes around in an electric wheelchair. This sounds like his kind of operation."

"I've met him," Ada said. "But whether it's his bankroll or not, I don't know. I'm paid in cash for showing up, and that's an end to it." The famous eyes watched Ken steadily. "And if you think it's a pretty sleazy way of making a buck, why, I agree."

Ken took his time. "What do you want me to do, tell you everything is going to be OK?"

Ada said, "Coming from you, it would help. You're real. You're not make-believe, like the ones I spend my time with. . . . Can I stay here?" She gestured round the small office. "I don't know how to type. I don't know how to file things, either, but I do know the alphabet and maybe I could figure it out."

Ken studied her carefully. "You're serious," he said.

"I told you, I'm scared to death. I'd run, but I wouldn't know where, and besides, then I'd be alone again. Please, Ken. Let me stay. That's all I ask."

BART JONES'S VOICE on the phone, Stacy thought, was hardly subdued, but there was a quality of restraint in it she had not heard before.

"It's short notice, I know," Bart said, "but it was just sprung on me too. Duane Semple—name mean anything?"

"It rings a very faint bell. Why?"

"Oil," Bart said. "Gypsum. Uranium, back when it was worth something, and a couple of up-and-coming high-tech industries."

"What about him?"

"I'm invited for dinner," Bart said, "and I'd take it kindly if you'd keep me company."

Stacy paused. This was unexpected. "Why me?" she said. "Don't you know anybody else?"

Nothing changed in Bart's voice. "For one thing, Duane knew your daddy, and liked him. So being with you puts me in good company."

"I'm flattered."

"For another, I thought you might want to get in a word for Ken Delacorte's nickel-and-dime housing operation before Duane takes it over. Or I do."

Stacy was silent, thoughtful. "When is this dinner?"

"Tonight. Black tie. It's a thirty-minute drive to Semple's spread. I'll pick you up a little before seven. Of course, if you'd like to give me a drink first . . ." He left the sentence hanging.

"Oh, all right," Stacy said.

"That's my gracious girl."

JL STUDIED THE LATEST infrared photographs while Ben Hastings sat close by, watching. The 1630 briefing was well behind them, but JL had given no sign that he was planning to rest.

"You had maybe two hours' sleep last night," Ben said. "Are you thinking of knocking off some time tonight? You look beat."

"I don't like it," JL said, ignoring the question, "and that's the truth." The photos were setting off alarm bells in his mind. Things seemed to be improving to the north, but in the south the situation was still in doubt. And the most recent weather report wasn't helping JL's peace of mind.

"There's a storm in the Gulf of Mexico now. They're calling it Charley," he said, "and it's beginning to flex its muscles. They say we're probably in for another wind shift. And stronger winds." He tapped the topographical map also spread on the table. "If that happens I think we'd better buy some insurance."

99

Ben looked where JL's finger rested on the map. "Sheep Ridge?" He was frowning.

"Below. Between the ridge and these houses."

"Are you still thinking of another backfire?"

"If we get a wind shift away from town. Not otherwise."

Ben was silent, thoughtful. He said at last, "You don't trust our Sheep Ridge fire line?"

"I don't trust anything in this whole fire." JL looked again at the infrared photos. "These pictures can tell us where some small spot is smouldering on the ground. Fine. I'm glad to know it. But they can't tell us if it's going to become open flame, because that depends on what the air on the ground is doing, on the humidity, on the kind of fuel that's being heated, on a dozen other factors." He paused. "What it boils down to is my judgment that Sheep Ridge is too tricky in these conditions to take chances with—any chances. This"—he drew his finger across the infrared photograph between Sheep Ridge and the houses to the south of it—"is our best defensive line. It's also almost our last before we get into the housing development, and then the town. I want that line held, and a well-placed backfire will give us the chance to take out that insurance I mentioned." He looked up at Ben. "Unless you have a better idea."

Ben spread his hands helplessly. "I don't, but—" He stopped.

"Go on," JL said. "But what?"

"You're playing a hunch, aren't you? That something more will go wrong and we won't be able to hold the line we already have?"

"I am. I admit it. So I want to hedge my bet with another hundred acres deliberately sacrificed. It's not the kind of thing that's in the book, but this is my best judgment."

Ben nodded, suddenly easier than he had been for some time. "I'll go along with that," he said. "But I've got a suggestion. Let me call in Jerry Weinstock, my night man, to back me up here while you go home and get some rest. We'll shout if we need you." He watched JL's hesitation, and then his slow nod of assent. "We won't let you down," Ben said.

ON THE PHONE from the Sanrio Volunteer Fire Department a voice said to the Forest Service dispatcher, "We've got a roof afire at grid number A8-B6. Our pumper's on the way."

"A8-B6. Roger." A very brief pause. "Byron Holloway? Off the county road?"

"That's it. He just called it in."

"Damn!" the dispatcher said. The Holloway place, one of the large houses adjoining the southern boundary of the forest, was the closest to the Sheep Ridge fire line. "That means the fire's jumped our line. Much obliged, Sanrio. Your people will have company."

BEN HASTINGS TOOK THE NEWS over the phone while he was sitting in for JL. "OK. We'll get onto it," he said, after listening quietly. As he replaced the receiver two thoughts crossed his mind. The first was that JL had to be psychic, and the second was that with the fire in this position, the proposed backfire was now out of the question.

He was just about to phone JL when a second call came through from the Sanrio dispatcher. Ben listened with growing incredulity. "You're sure you have the coordinates right?"

The dispatcher's voice was calm and unhurried. "Commercial aircraft usually know where they are. This one spotted flames and took bearings to check himself."

"Roger! Thanks." Ben hung up and instantly dialled JL, who came out of a deep sleep to answer the telephone. But he seemed to take in what Ben repeated about the two new outbreaks.

"Send a car for me," he said. "I'm too groggy to drive."

"It's on its way."

Ben hung up. He sat back in his chair to stare at the area map and ponder. The wind had shifted again, as predicted. From almost dead out of the northwest, it had swung to the northeast, with occasional gusts from the east. The new fire reported by the commercial aircraft was east by northeast of Andy McIlvain's position. And headed in his direction. It just didn't seem possible that sparks from the fire line they were already holding could have blown so far to start fresh trouble. But there it was.

Ben had the uneasy feeling that even though he didn't know the answers, he ought to be taking action anyway. It occurred to him to wonder if this was the kind of dilemma the man in ultimate command was constantly facing—to move or not to move and, if so, in which direction? He felt a guilty sense of relief when the car he had sent for JL arrived, and JL himself came to pull out a chair at the table and sit down, wearily.

"You were right," Ben said. "About Sheep Ridge, I mean. Somehow it did get past us to the Holloway house. We're trying to hold it there."

"It can happen, sometimes in funny ways. How about the other houses?"

Ben moved the map closer, so they both could see. "So far we're

OK. But Andy's sector could cause trouble." His pencil indicated the area reported on fire by the commercial aircraft. "The other outbreak is clear over here."

JL shook his head. "Could be anything. A lit cigarette tossed away, a campfire not completely dead." He spread his hands. "Get on the radio to Andy and warn him. If this new fire isn't too big, he can handle it. But tell him to be careful. He could get caught in it." JL looked again at the map. "What exactly is his position? Your last fix?" He watched Ben's pencil touch the contour lines on the map that encircled heavily wooded terrain above Sheep Ridge. "And the nearest ground crew?" The pencil touched paper again.

JL made a rough measurement between the two marks. "Well over a mile," he said, "a darned rough mile." He paused reflectively. "Whose is the nearest crew?"

"Gordy Walker."

JL nodded approval. "Throw your next best crew in with them. Who would that be?"

"Big Bertha. We brought her down from the north yesterday."

"Bessie Wingate?" JL smiled. "Move her in. We want to get to Andy if we can."

ADA LOVING'S MERCEDES followed Ken's Ford into the drive of his house. Ada got out and walked with him in silence to the front door. As she watched him put his key in the lock she said, "Think of me as a stray cat that followed you home because it had no place else to go."

"It's OK," Ken answered. "I can smell the smoke too."

Ada, searching refrigerator and cupboards, found eggs and bacon, a can of chopped chillies, some onions and tomatoes. The full, dazzling smile appeared.

"A feast," Ada said. "Stand back. *Huevos rancheros*, or a reasonable facsimile, coming up."

Her hands were deft and sure, and there was no hesitation in her manner.

"You know your way around a kitchen," Ken said.

"Where I grew up," Ada said, "there weren't any restaurants, or supermarkets with frozen food. Mom worked all day. So did Pop. So I did the cooking. The glamour bit came later."

Over their meal, Ada told him more about herself. "I taught myself to dance," she said, "by sitting through Ginger Rogers movies three or four times then practising like mad. I stole a baton from the local high school. I gave it back eventually, but by then I

102

was good enough to win a couple of competitions and a college scholarship. Lucky for me, baton twirling was real big then." She smiled suddenly. "I didn't have it so tough. Not really."

"Tough enough," Ken said.

"You got your brains beat out playing football so you could make it to college, and then business school."

"I got paid for it."

"Let's say we're about even. I'll clean up these things."

"We'll both do it."

"No," Ada said. "Every night after dinner, Pop would offer to help and Mom would say, 'No thanks.' That's the way I like it."

She stacked the dishes neatly and carried them to the kitchen. Ken was pushing his chair back from the table when he heard the crash. He reacted instantly, crossing the room in two long strides. In the kitchen doorway he stopped.

Ada was standing quite still, the wreckage of the dishes on the floor around her. Her eyes were wide and seemingly unfocused. "I'm—sorry," she said in a distant, automatic voice.

"What scared you?" Ken said.

Her eyes closed, and slowly opened again, back in focus now. "Look out of the window."

Ken walked over to where she stood. Outside, against the black of the sky, not too distant flames were plain, flaring.

Ken stared at them for a few silent moments, then turned back to Ada. "A shame. But it has nothing to do with us. They'll get it under control."

Ada gathered herself with visible effort. "I'm all right. Honest. Where's the broom?"

When she'd cleaned up the mess, she came into the living room and sank gracefully down on the sofa. "Silly," she said. "Some people are afraid of cats. Did you know that? Ailurophobes, they're called. I guess I'm a pyrophobe. I'm sorry."

"Nothing to be sorry for. And talk about it as much as you need to. I can stand it."

"Yes," Ada said, "you can stand a lot. That's obvious. I plant myself on your doorstep like a kitten nobody wants, and you take me in as if it happens all the time. You're a nice, sweet guy."

"The world is full of guys who would give their right arm to have Ada Loving knock on the door."

"But you don't make passes, either."

"Magnificent self-control, not lack of interest."

"If you'll let me," Ada said, "I'm going to stay here tonight.

Maybe even—who knows?—a number of nights." Her eyes watched him steadily.

"You're welcome to stay as long as you like."

BESSIE WINGATE HERDED HER MEN into position alongside Gordy Walker's crew. "All right," she told them, "this is where we start earning our C rations! Let's get the lead out!" To Gordy she said quietly, "What gives? We were told to get up here on the double."

Bessie was half again as large as Gordy, and a woman besides, but between them there was a strict sense of equality. Gordy explained about the new fire that had broken out near Andy McIlvain's position. When he was done, Bessie was already at work with her shovel, grunting as she dug and heaved. "That Andy's a heck of a good man. They're all good men."

Gordy too was hard at work. "You can say that again."

"So all we got to do is move this old mountain," Bessie said, "or at least this hunk of it, cut down a few trees, clear out some low growth and put out a few fires on the way, right?"

"You've got it," Gordy said. Bessie loved to exaggerate, but the funny thing was, she tended to come up with performances to match. In Gordy's book, Bessie was the genuine article.

"Eloy," Bessie shouted to the fire fighter from the southwest crew, who was standing nearby. "We still don't know where the rest of your guys are, so you just stick with us."

Eloy grinned and nodded, conserving his breath for his labour.

"Real good little man," Bessie confided to Gordy. "Kind of a mascot I guess I sort of adopted!" She raised her voice again. "All right, you lazy jugheads, let's see some action! We got folks waiting for us!"

STACY RODE HOME from dinner at Duane Semple's house in the big chauffeur-driven car Bart Jones kept for such occasions. She was in a thoughtful mood that—for a wonder, she thought—Bart acknowledged by keeping silent until she chose to speak.

"I don't like him," Stacy said at last, and turned in her seat to study as best she could Bart's face in the late evening light. "But you expected that, didn't you?"

"The dinner wasn't intended to be a lovefest."

"Semple wants to see Ken about Bellevue Acres. Why? And why try to use me as an intermediary?"

"Because Ken believes you. He might not believe me, and he doesn't know Duane."

104

It had the ring of truth. After a pause Stacy said, "Why does he want to see him? What shenanigans does he have in mind?"

"Don't make it too complicated," Bart answered. "Duane just wants to size him up. It helps to know the man you're going to tangle with."

"So he wants Ken to come to him."

"Because he doesn't get around even as well as I do."

True enough. Stacy had been shocked to find that Duane Semple was an obviously sick man, moving from room to room in the huge house only with enormous effort. He made her think of a great, bloated spider, waiting for its prey.

"Your daddy and Duane went around and around a couple of times," Bart said, as if reading her mind. "It pretty much was a standoff. I think that's why Duane liked him. He never met many he had to deal with on even terms." His voice changed. "How about it? You'll deliver Ken?"

"I'll leave it up to him."

Later she sat alone, still in her long dress, at the desk in her office-library, strangely hesitant to pick up the telephone and call Ken with this odd invitation.

She told herself that she disliked the feeling of being manoeuvred into the position of—face it—Judas goat, in a sense leading Ken to the slaughter. It was, of course, a ridiculous concept, because Ken was a grown man, well able to fend for himself. She picked up the telephone and placed the call.

Ken was a long time answering, and when he did his voice was a trifle breathless.

"I've interrupted something?" Stacy asked, then quickly added, "Forget that. None of my business. Look, Ken, do you know a man named Duane Semple?"

There was a short silence. "I know *of* him," Ken said. "I've never met him. He plays in the big leagues."

"He wants to meet you."

There was another silence.

"Bart Jones took me to Semple's for dinner," Stacy explained. "They want me as go-between. What they're after is . . ."

"Bellevue Acres," Ken said. "It figures. Milk it dry, raise the mortgage rates until the people are driven out, then tear the houses down to build their fancy condominiums." His voice was quiet, with anger in its depths.

"That doesn't make much sense," Stacy said.

"It does, because that land already has a zoning licence, and they

106

won't face any hassle with the city council about whether and what they can build. That's worth quite a bit to them."

Stacy was thoughtful. She said at last, "What will it do to you?"

"Personally? Nothing I can logically object to. It will put money in my pocket when they buy me out, as they'll have to. Or cut me into their project."

"And never mind the folks with all the kids and the dogs being pushed out?"

"That's about it. When does Semple want to see me?"

"Tomorrow night. Dinner. He dresses. Will you go?"

"I'll be there."

AT THE COMMAND POST early on Friday morning, JL studied the latest radar-enhanced satellite photographs handed him by the weather service meteorologist assigned to Backslope. It was evident that the tropical storm named Charley had gone past the simple muscle-flexing stage and now, packing winds close to a hundred miles an hour, was a full-blown hurricane. The problem was to figure out in which direction the storm was going to go.

Charley could decide to stay offshore well out in the Gulf, in a sense just spinning his wheels but causing winds far inland to back and veer insanely. Or he could come romping ashore and break up into smaller wind systems. He might even be obliging enough to bring some moisture with him. Meantime, we'll simply have to try to cope, JL thought. His telephone rang, and he reached for it. It was Ben Hastings, who was patrolling the fire line. "We've had a bad accident," Ben said. "A southwest crewman, name of Eloy Jaramillo. Been working with Bessie Wingate's crew since the truck lift down from the north line—" His voice stopped.

JL said, "And?"

Ben said slowly, "He thought he'd better get back, find his own people. He got—cut off. Used his portable shelter and the fire went over him, but he's burned. Bad."

JL closed his eyes briefly. He nodded. "OK," he said, carefully keeping all pain from his voice. "I want to be kept informed."

"Right." Ben's voice changed. "Gordy Walker and Bessie—they're tearing that mountain apart. That's the good news."

JL said, "There's more bad?"

"Andy McIlvain and his people. They're fighting a rearguard action uphill towards the timberline—"

"If there's any doubt at all, I want them to cut and run. Tell Andy I said so."

Chapter Ten

It was the last ironic twist Sophie Swift would have imagined, and confronting it taxed her self-control to its limits. The situation was compounded by the fact that, as she had told Stacy, she liked young Debby, Aaron's wife, who appeared unannounced at her door.

"A doesn't know I'm here," Debby said, "but I had to talk to someone, and you're the wisest person I know. May I come in?" Young and vulnerable and obviously in over her head.

They sat in the study, where Sophie and Aaron had sat so many evenings, reading, talking or just listening to music.

"I had no idea where he was," Debby said, "until he walked up to me at the club and said 'Hi'. Can you imagine my shock?"

Sophie said in a kindly tone, "I'm not sure I understand. Whom are you talking about?"

"Johnny Joe Ames. We went to high school together. He was my date for our senior dance. He gave me a corsage."

The girl's mind, perhaps under strain, Sophie thought, jumped about aimlessly. Sophie kept her face as expressionless as she could. "And after that?"

"He went off to college and then joined the navy. Men do." As if that explained it all.

"And now he's here in Sanrio?"

"Well, not exactly. He just came to see me. That isn't wrong, is it? I mean, it isn't as if I was seeing him on the sly. It was right there at the club, with lots of folks around me."

"It sounds quite innocent to me."

"I wouldn't want A to think I was going behind his back. I *like* A. I really do. He's awful good to me."

Sophie knew that Debby had probably married Aaron for the things she had never had: financial security and comfort, the wisdom and easy decisiveness of an older man willing to relieve her of all responsibilities.

But the youthful fire had been missing, and until Johnny Joe suddenly reappeared, she had not realized how much she had missed it. It was as simple as that.

As if to underline Sophie's thoughts, Debby said, "Johnny Joe is . . . well, Johnny Joe, if you see what I mean."

Sophie said slowly, wanting no misunderstanding, "Perhaps you'd better tell me."

Debby took a deep breath. "I'm not very good with words, but, well, you see a person you haven't seen in a long time, and all of a sudden you start remembering things you thought you'd forgotten." Her eyes clung to Sophie's face, pleading for sympathy.

"Like the senior dance and the corsage?"

"You do understand, don't you? I was sure you would."

Sophie kept her face carefully composed. She said, "Sometimes things or events from long ago seem more important at first remembrance than they actually are, Debby."

"I know. And I've thought about it a lot. That's why I came to you." Debby's smile was hesitant. "I mean, you're a lawyer."

"True."

"You represent people, and, well, I've thought about it a lot. If Johnny Joe asks me to go with him . . ."

"Where, Debby?"

"I don't care. Anywhere. I'll go." There was finality in the words and the tone.

Sophie blinked. It was the only expression of emotion she allowed herself. "And what is it you want me to do?"

"Explain to A for me. I'm not good with words like he is. I feel things, but I don't know how to talk about them."

There was silence. Out in the front hall the grandfather clock that had belonged to Sophie's grandparents chimed the hour. Sophie listened until the last echoes had died, then she said, "Has Johnny Joe asked you to go with him, Debby?"

"No, but he will. I know it." Her smile this time was confident, brilliant. "You can tell."

"I would rather you asked someone else to speak for you."

"No. Please. I know you. And you know A. And I wouldn't know who else to go to."

"I could suggest someone."

"Please," Debby said. "Don't do it for me. Do it for A. I wouldn't want to . . . hurt him."

BESSIE GOT WORD of Eloy's burns by walkie-talkie, as did Gordy Walker. "Poor little stinker," was Bessie's immediate comment. "I didn't even know he'd gone!" Gordy, telling about it later, swore that the stout handle of Bessie's shovel bent like a toothpick beneath the sudden force of her emotion. "Blast it, Gordy," Bessie said, "I told him to stay with us!"

"He's in the hospital," Gordy said. "You want to go see him, I'll cover for you."

"You talk like a man with a paper head," Bessie said, almost savagely. "We got folks waiting for us over yonder. Let's stop clicking our teeth and get to them." She worked in furious silence for a time before she spoke again. "This damn fire," she said.

AT SIXTEEN THOUSAND FEET, well above Sierra Grande's rocky peak, the reconnaissance plane bucked and jumped in heat-produced updraughts. "That," the pilot said, looking down, "is quite a little bonfire. Can you take it all in with your wide-angle lens?"

"Just about," the photographer said. "JL won't get the detail we usually give him—"

"Detail is the last thing JL's worried about now. He's thinking in miles, not acres. Look yonder. Another house . . ."

In point of fact, it was not a house that had suddenly erupted in flames, but the cabana at the end of Ada Loving's swimming pool.

"Look at that baby go," the pilot said, "and I'll bet that won't be the last of them. In the meantime, we've got ringside seats."

KEN DELACORTE GOT THE WORD by phone from one of the local volunteer firemen. "Thanks," he said, and turned to Ada. "Sorry, baby," he said, "your cabana—"

"I don't care. Feed the whole house to the monster. Maybe it will keep some other house from going up."

"I'll go over—"

"No. *Things* aren't important. Only people matter."

Ken said gently, "It's OK. You're—"

"I'm not being hysterical, Ken. I mean it. I've been broke. Stony. It's uncomfortable, but it doesn't really matter. But when you lose somebody who counts—a friend, maybe a part of the family—then you see what really is important. That's why I don't want you going near the place. It's . . . unlucky. It's nothing but a joint to attract suckers for their money." She smiled suddenly, the full, brilliant smile. "Think I could go back to baton twirling?"

"I think," Ken said slowly, "that you could do anything you put your mind to, baby, and do it superlatively well."

STACY WALKED PAST THE SPA on the way to her bedroom to dress for the second dinner at Duane Semple's place. She had not been in the spa for a long time now, and it passed through her mind that the day JL had come to talk to her and interrupted the party was indeed a while ago, and much had changed, of which the fire and, to a lesser extent, the spa had become only symbols.

Showered, powdered and perfumed, Stacy padded to her

110

cupboard to decide which evening dress to wear for this occasion. How long had it been since she had dressed two nights in a row for dinner? That too was somehow a symbol of change, and she could imagine how her father would have teased her.

"When you put your mind to it, honey," he would have said, "you really can turn into an eastern dude. I'm proud of you."

And if she had explained the situation to him, he would have told her to follow her instincts. Well, she had a pretty fair idea that this evening Ken was going to put his concern for the folks who lived in Bellevue Acres ahead of his own best interest and, in effect, spit in Duane Semple's and Bart Jones's collective eye, by his own admission stepping into competition he couldn't really hope to match. So that left her own choice pretty plain, didn't it?

She could stay strictly on the sidelines. It was, after all, none of her concern; she bred and trained horses, nothing more.

Or she could declare herself into the game by offering Ken the financial backing he needed. She'd probably lose a bundle, but the more she thought about what Bart and Semple were trying to do, the more she got her dander up.

By the time Bart's car and driver arrived, and Bart himself wheeled up the walk to her front door, Stacy was keyed up, as she always was before competition, and smiling as if she hadn't a care in the world. "We've time for a drink, I think," she said, and stood aside for the wheelchair.

Glass of wine in hand, and the smile still holding steady, Stacy said, "I heard on the radio that the fire got Ada Loving's place."

"So I understand. Pity." Bart's eyes watched her warily.

"Your house, wasn't it?" A guess, pure and simple, but, Stacy thought, on the basis of what she knew from Ken, a good guess.

"Why do you say that?" Bart's face showed nothing.

"Part of the long-range operation, wasn't it? Famous movie star picks Sanrio for her hideaway. And, of course, acts as a magnet to draw in potential investors? Bellevue Acres with zoning licence already approved, the ideal site for new, fancy condos? You aren't going to tell me it's coincidental. Daddy taught me to look at a horse's teeth before I accepted the age as represented."

Bart's eyes did not leave her face. He lowered his glass slowly. "Your daddy had a lot of pep. He had a lot of business sense too. You inherited the first. Did you get the second as well?"

"I've never had to find out. Things have always been pretty easy."

Bart smiled at that. "A few busted ribs, dislocated shoulder, a broken wrist—"

"They don't count. It's the big things that have always been easy. For most folks they never are. They're always trying to get out from under and never can."

"Look, lady, don't quote Thoreau at me, about 'lives of quiet desperation'. He never knew what desperation was."

"Have you?" Instantly she wished she could recall the question.

Bart now wore his crooked smile. "I've had my moments," he said, "of wishing. And hating."

He finished his drink. "We should go, if you're ready."

KEN DELACORTE TIED HIS BLACK TIE and turned to find Ada holding out his dinner jacket. Smiling, he shook his head slowly. "How many men would believe this scene?"

"I not only believe it, I like it. I just don't like your going."

"You know where I'll be. And you know it's important."

Ada helped him into the jacket and smoothed the shoulders fondly. "I believe what you say." She waited until he had turned again to face her. Idly she brushed a nonexistent speck from his lapel. "You don't even know this Semple character, do you?"

"Only by reputation."

"I've heard of him too. Big bucks."

Ken said, "You're making a point?"

Ada nodded slowly. "In a funny way," she said, "I'm talking about you and me. I don't mean any ties or commitments. It's just that you and I are one kind of people, and well, the Semples are another. I'm probably talking out of turn. I learned a long time ago that men don't like to be told what they aren't, so I'll shut up if you want."

"No. That's the last thing I want."

The blue eyes searched his face. "OK," Ada said then, and took a deep breath. "You're a decent person, and there aren't very many of those. You're not out to cheat anybody, because you wouldn't want to be cheated yourself. Isn't that what the Golden Rule says? Do unto others . . ."

"I guess that's one way to put it." Ken was smiling.

"But the Semples of this world don't work that way. They figure everybody's out to get them, so they just do it first, and hardest. That's why I say we're one kind of people and they're another. We can't compete with them, because the only way would be by behaving as they do. And I've stopped trying, because even if I made it, I wouldn't like it. That's all."

There was a short, understanding silence between them.

"I'll remember it, baby," Ken said. "And . . . thanks."

IT WAS A SINGLE TALL LODGEPOLE pinetree clinging precariously to one of Sierra Grande's steep upper slopes that did it. Higher on the mountain a rock slipped beneath the boot of one of Andy McIlvain's smoke jumpers.

The rock rolled, starting a minor slide, loosened the pine's already frail grip on the mountainside, and slowly, almost majestically, its topmost needles already blazing from contact with a flying burning branch, the tree began its fall.

By the time it crashed to the rocky ground, breaking apart as it hit, its lower branches too were ablaze, and what had been an open if hazardous escape route for Andy and his people was now closed. Instantly the entire area was ablaze.

"Make like mountain goats!" Andy shouted. "Head for the timberline! Move it!" Already scrambling up the slope himself, he poured information into his walkie-talkie. "Tell JL we're high-tailing it out of here. You'll find us up top with the goats. I hope. Over and out."

GORDY WALKER HELD HIS WALKIE-TALKIE at an angle so Bessie too could hear Ben Hastings's report.

"That area's cut off," Ben's voice said. "Chopper observation reports Andy and his people above the fire area and for the present safe. Break off your operation as it goes now, and start establishing a north-south line to seal off where the jumpers were working. We'll let it burn itself out to the timberline. Over."

Gordy looked up at Bessie's sweat and smoke-stained face. "Blast it," Bessie said, and shrugged in resignation.

Gordy suppressed a smile. "Roger," he said into the walkie-talkie. "North-south it is. Let her burn. Over and out." He looked at Bessie again. "Now do you want to knock off the go see Eloy?"

Bessie shook her head. "I'll wait till change of shift. Way I probably look now, I'd scare him into a coma. Let's turn these raggedy troops round and get them going."

FROM THE BROAD TERRACE OF Vista Hill, Mrs. Tyler Wayne looked out at the great mountain across her favourite grove of specimen trees, so modestly begun so long ago. A black walnut had been the first planting, she remembered, a gift from a now-forgotten visitor from Nebraska. It had arrived by truck, neatly balled, and Mrs. Wayne and Tyler had discussed at length where to have it put, never guessing that it would be the beginning of what became almost a private forest of carefully tended exotic plantings. Eucalypti from California, rhododendrons from Scotland, locusts, ashes, ginkgoes and others that had delighted visitors for years.

It was a pity the development had been built so close to the grove. Tyler would no doubt have seen to it that such a thing would not occur, but there it was. On the other side the finger of the forest offered protection against any encroachment. When they made their first plantings, Mrs. Wayne often thought, there had been only open land where Bellevue Acres now was, and who could have dreamed that such change might take place?

But it was Sierra Grande that held her attention now. As she saw the forest destroyed before her, she wished there were something she could do about those facing devastation if the fire spread further. All theose people in Bellevue Acres, all those children— what would happen to them if the fire came all the way down?

She closed her eyes in sudden pain, and opened them again only with reluctance. For a long time she stood quite still, staring at reality, knowing that it would not go away. At last, slowly, she turned and walked back into the big house. There she seated herself at a table in the library and picked up the telephone.

"This is Mrs. Tyler Wayne," she said in a steady voice to the young woman at Forest Service headquarters. "I wish to speak with Mr. J. L. Harmon, if you please."

JL's voice on the line was polite, but there was obvious fatigue and faint impatience in its depths. "Yes, Mrs. Wayne?"

"I have been watching the progress of the fire down what I believe is referred to as the finger of the forest. Can you stop that fire, Mr. Harmon? I should like an honest answer."

"We're doing all we can, Mrs. Wayne. But these winds . . ."

"The answer then is no? I was afraid it would be."

"Mrs. Wayne—"

"Please. I did not call with a plea but rather with a suggestion. If that finger of the forest is lost, then the grove of specimen tree plantings you have been kind enough to admire in the past will also be destroyed. It is inevitable."

"I'm sorry—"

"Please, Mr. Harmon, I am not finished. That grove, as you know, abuts the development. If the grove is destroyed because the finger of the forest is lost, the development is certain to go as well. No doubt you have already considered this?"

"I'm afraid we have."

There was a picture of Tyler Wayne in a silver frame on the table. Mrs. Wayne looked at it now, expressionless. She said, "If you were

114

to burn my grove now, Mr. Harmon, before it is in immediate danger, could you control the blaze and keep it from reaching those houses?"

JL sat unmoving. He said slowly, in a gentle voice, "The answer, Mrs. Wayne, is probably yes. But I can't promise."

Mrs. Wayne's eyes had not left the picture. "Then burn the grove, Mr. Harmon. You have my permission." She hung up. "I'm sorry, Tyler." It was no more than a whisper.

BEN HASTINGS, SUMMONED, said, "Good Lord! You mean it? When I was a kid, we used to make field trips to that grove. There're two trees from the Himalayas, and a specimen from way up the Amazon."

"There's no other way," JL said. "Just make it a good, clean burn, as successful as possible. That's the least we can do."

He sat for long moments after Ben drove off. Fires, JL thought, brought out the best and the worst in people. Correction: in some people. Right now for example, although nothing would show on the surface, Mrs. Tyler Wayne was crying inside. And when the blaze actually began, which would be at any moment, she would be standing at a window watching, compelled by the same motive that would make her hold an old, loved pet dog's paw while he was put to sleep—so he would not die alone.

And then there were the Willard Spencers and the Les Lawrys, very different types indeed.

JL looked at his watch: evening was coming on fast, and there was still too much unfinished business.

"I ASKED YOU TO COME OUT HERE, Aaron," Sophie said, "because the office is something less than . . . neutral ground. Also, I knew that we would want privacy."

"Mysteriouser and mysteriouser," Aaron said. He glanced at his watch. "It is after hours. Is a drink in order?"

"Please," Sophie said, "I'd prefer that you waited."

Aaron settled back in his chair and sat quiet but alert.

"I have a client, Aaron," Sophie said. "This client is not of my choosing. You must believe that. I tried to avoid the engagement and in conscience was unable to. Have you guessed already that my client is Debby?"

"I was beginning to see the light, Counsellor." It was his dry courtroom voice, agreeing to a stipulation in order that matters might proceed.

115

"There is a young man," Sophie said, "who has turned up unexpectedly. His name is Johnny Joe Ames."

"Someone out of the past, no doubt."

"They were high school sweethearts."

"How romantic."

Sophie's lips tightened, and there was a sudden colour in her cheeks, but her voice remained calm. She said, "They are romantic, and young, as once upon a time we were. We have, I suppose the phrase is, grown up, become mature. I don't believe they have. Debby still retains—"

"If you're saying that in many ways Debby is immature," Aaron said, "I shall so stipulate. And the swain?"

"I haven't met him, but . . ." Sophie spread her hands.

Aaron forced himself to relax a trifle. He shook his head. "I think we can read between the lines. Go on."

"Debby is not carrying on an affair, Aaron. She tells me that she has behaved . . . honourably, and I believe her. But if Johnny Joe asks her to go away with him, as she is certain that he will, she will go."

Aaron was silent and still. He said at last, "She wants out?"

"Just that. Nothing more."

There was a longer silence. In the hallway the grandfather clock ticked loudly. "You may tell your client, Counsellor," Aaron said at last, "that she is welcome to an uncontested divorce. Is that satisfactory?"

Sophie closed her eyes. She opened them again and nodded. "Thank you, Aaron." She drew a deep breath. "Now would you like that drink?"

It was as if the question had not been heard. "Oh, Soph!" Aaron said suddenly. "Why did it have to be you?"

BESSIE WINGATE, silent and ponderously graceful, came into the hospital room almost on tiptoe, and stood quietly looking down at Eloy, motionless beneath his bandages.

Eloy had been caught virtually in the middle of a raging inferno, Bessie had been told. He had tried to use his fire shelter, but it had split as he tugged it over himself, or he hadn't stretched it taut. or maybe some other blasted thing. Anyway, what difference did it make now? This was all that was important.

Eloy's eyes opened and came slowly into focus. What showed of his mouth began to spread in a weak smile. "Hi, big mama." It occurred to him in a dreamlike way that this was the first time he

116

had called Bessie to her face by the name he had carried in his mind for days, but it didn't matter now. "I screwed up, didn't I?"

"You want argument?" Bessie said, and shook her head. "I'm real sorry, Eloy." She reached into one of her jacket pockets. "I didn't think you'd go for flowers or anything like that, so I brought you a beer." She took out a can of cold beer and set it on the table beside the bed.

The weak smile reappeared. "When I get out," Eloy said, "and we go to The Antlers, I'm going to do the buying. OK?"

"You got a deal."

"You get to them smoke jumpers?"

Bessie shook her head. "But they're OK," she said, hoping that it was true. "They hauled it for the timberline when things got too hot."

Eloy's eyes closed. He opened them with an effort. "They shoot me full of, you know, all kind of stuff." He waggled his head gently towards the intravenous tube. "You know?" he said.

"Sure. Makes you sleepy. That's good. You sleep, Eloy." Bessie's big hand touched his arm gently. "Hang in there."

His eyes were already closed as she let herself out of the room and walked down the hallway to the nurse's station. There she stopped and stood, large and motionless. "How about it?" she said looking down at the seated nurse.

"Patient Jaramillo?" the nurse said. "He's doing quite well."

"Cut the bull." The words hung in the air like a growl.

The nurse took a deep, uneasy breath. It was as if suddenly she faced a mother bear, a grizzly maybe, asking about one of her cubs and wanting a straight answer. *Now.*

"I'm not the doctor," the nurse began. She stopped. Wrong approach. "I don't know. He may make it," she said. "He may not."

Slowly Bessie seemed to relax in acceptance. "OK," she said. "If that's the way it is." She turned away, then immediately turned back. "Thanks," she said, and turned away again to walk massively and expressionlessly down the corridor.

IN BELLEVUE ACRES a small crowd gathered to stare at the fire in Mrs. Wayne's grove of specimen plantings. "Lord," one man said. "They might have warned us if it's that close."

Ben Hastings drove up, braked to a stop and did not even get out of his jeep. Immediately he was the centre of the small crowd's attention. "I just wanted to tell you that we've set that fire. For your protection. It's a firebreak, to try to make you safe."

The man who had spoken up said, "To *try* to make us safe! That sure is poor reassurance."

"We're doing our best for all of you, but just in case—"

"Here it comes," the man said. "Can't you people do anything right?"

"Just in case," Ben repeated flatly, "you might start thinking about what you'll want to take *if* we have to evacuate you. I don't think we will." Mentally he crossed his fingers. "But we can't control the winds."

A pregnant woman said, "Oh, no! You can't mean it! Everything we have is right here! We—"

"I wish," Ben said, "that I could tell you different."

Chapter Eleven

Duane Semple's property was enclosed by a well maintained four-strand barbed-wire fence. A high masonry wall surrounded the house itself. "If he has a coat of arms," Stacy told Bart, "it ought to show paranoia rampant, don't you think?"

"You've got your spurs with the big rowels on tonight, haven't you?" Bart said.

Stacy patted herself. "No gun," she said. "No knife. Just me."

The car drew smoothly to a stop at the entrance to the big house. Behind them Ken's car swung into a parking place, and Ken got out. "OK," Stacy said, "let the festivities commence."

Semple was not a big man, and he was obviously in frail health, but there was no mistaking his air of authority. His greetings were easy and gracious.

"Delighted to see you again, Miss Cummings." He smiled at Ken Delacorte. "I spent a large part of one afternoon in Texas Stadium, Mr. Delacorte, admiring your abilities on the football field. My pleasure was dampened, though, by the fact that I was sitting in the owner's box, and the Dallas Cowboys do not enjoy losing."

"I didn't think anybody did," Ken said. "I know I don't."

Semple's nod was almost imperceptible. He waved a hand towards the butler. "What will you drink, Miss Cummings?"

Her father, Stacy thought, would probably have understood the ground rules of this meeting, as Ken and Bart seemed to, and she did not. Men were supposed to be direct and to-the-point. Somebody had turned conventional wisdom inside out.

Before dinner there was talk of the Sanrio fire, the current

118

baseball standings, and New Orleans restaurants. Bellevue Acres was not mentioned. Over soup the talk turned to a new television series, the national budget deficits and the Sante Fe opera.

"Anyone interested in what we came here for?" Stacy asked as the main course—beef Wellington—was served.

"Her daddy didn't have much patience, either," Bart said.

"Humour me, please, Miss Cummings," Semple said. "My digestion is somewhat delicate, and I try to avoid controversial subjects at mealtimes."

Stacy was aware that Ken was watching her, expressionless, and that Bart Jones wore an amused smile, which annoyed her. She took a sip of wine and tried to think of something bright to say. "Good beef," she came up with finally. "Well hung and from first-rate stock. Hard to come by these days."

Without looking directly, she saw that Bart's amused smile had faded and that Ken wore an expression of approval. "Cross-breeding experiments," she went on, "genetic engineering . . ." She shook her head. "Hard to keep up with."

Semple said, "You are against interference with nature, Miss Cummings?"

"I breed horses," Stacy said. "I go after the results I want, so the answer is no, I am not against changing things. As long as the change benefits instead of hurting people." She smiled suddenly. "You see, I'm really a very simple person."

"I am beginning to doubt it very much," Semple said. "A touch more wine, perhaps?"

In the large living room after dinner there were coffee, cognac and, for Duane Semple, a cigar as well.

"Now to business," Semple said. "Undoubtedly you have a price in mind, Mr. Delacorte?"

Stacy noted Ken's alert expression. The contest had begun.

"A price for exactly what?" Ken said.

"For your interest in Bellevue Acres, of course," Semple said.

"The property," Ken said, "the houses, the people, including the kids and the dogs? The home-built barbecues that smoke and that funny-looking badminton court? My share of all of it?"

"Oh, come on," Bart said from his wheelchair, "let's not be mawkish. This is a business proposition."

"For you, yes," Ken said. "I see it differently."

Semple said, "I think that is understandable. The project was your idea in the first place, and you worked to bring it to fruition, which involved surmounting a number of obstacles, I am sure."

"Such as getting a zoning licence," Ken said. "That's really what you're interested in, isn't it?"

"Having the zoning licence in place is helpful," Semple said. "There is no question about that."

"Getting the people out," Ken said, "won't present much of a problem, will it? Jack up the interest rates as high as you can, which means increasing the mortgage payments. Make a few extra bucks in the process, and all of a sudden the peasants have gone and you have nice empty land where you can put up your fancy condominiums. Then the real profits begin."

Semple, wholly unperturbed, admired the long, even ash on the end of his cigar. "Your business school studies were not in vain, Mr. Delacorte," he said at last. "I return to my original question. Undoubtedly you have a price in mind?"

"My interest in Bellevue Acres," Ken said, "is not for sale."

"Indeed?" Semple's tone contained no indication of surprise. "You are already skating on rather thin financial ice, Mr. Delacorte," he said. "We took the trouble to ascertain that. A few obstacles placed in your way, perhaps litigation of some sort or the sudden discovery that certain building codes had not been properly adhered to—expenses arising from matters such as these might cause that thin financial ice to collapse."

"I don't think so," Stacy said.

Ken said sharply, "Stay out of this."

"I think freshman year was the last time you tried to tell me what to do," Stacy said. "It didn't work then, and it's not going to work now." Her glance included them all. "Daddy used to say that it was pretty hard to sit by and watch a bully, in this case apparently two bullies, picking on folks who couldn't fight back. I feel the same way. So—"

The butler, a cordless telephone in hand, coughed politely and said, "Excuse me, sir, but there is a call for Mr. Delacorte."

Semple said, "If you would rather take the call in my library, Mr. Delacorte, please feel free."

Ken merely shook his head and reached for the telephone.

It was Ada. Her voice, under tight control, came clearly. "The fire's broken loose," she said. "I'm not being hysterical. It's on the radio. It's blowing like mad and—"

"On my way." Ken handed the phone back to the butler. "Sorry," he said to Semple, and looked at Stacy as he stood up.

"Right with you." Stacy was already on her feet. Her eyes swept over Semple and Bart Jones. "You get the message," she said.

120

BILLY BOB BARKER, the mayor of Sanrio, was neither a bold nor a profane man. He was a pharmacist by trade, and a peaceable soul by nature. But he felt that crises demanded extraordinary emphasis. "Damn it, George," he told the forest supervisor on the telephone, "I knew this was going to happen. JL is a nice fellow and all that, but apparently he's over the hill, and now we've got a real mess on our hands. Pete Trujillo's market is about to go, they tell me, and if it does, you know what's next?"

George Jefferson's mind was on a number of other matters. "You tell me, Billy Bob."

"The Sanrio Propane Company, that's what. What we'd have left of downtown would be nothing but a big hole in the ground."

The second light on George Jefferson's phone was blinking. "I've got another call now, Billy Bob. I hope it's JL. I'll get back to you as soon as I can."

It was JL. "We've got a mess down here, George. No question about that. Our airport tower is measuring heavy wind gusts shifting through an arc that takes in a good share of the town. Willard Spencer's house is going. We can't save it. The Cummings place is probably next—"

Jefferson said, "What about that propane storage tank?"

"The city's going to have to take care of that. We're throwing everything we have in a curved line from Sheep Ridge and the Vista Hill grove round to the estates."

"All right," Jefferson said. "Keep at it and keep me posted. Anything you need . . ."

"I'll shout." There was a short pause. "And, George, if you're thinking of replacing me . . ."

"You keep at it. It's still your baby."

Jefferson broke off the connection, then dialled Billy Bob's number.

"It was JL," Jefferson said, "and things are not good."

"You replacing him, George?"

"I am not. He's the best we have. Now, here's what you do."

Billy Bob listened. He said at last, "That propane tank—"

"It's a nasty situation," Jefferson said. "No argument. But we have our hands full. Your people can do the job as well as we can."

"And if the fire jumps your line?"

"Then you'd better give thought to dynamiting some houses near the city limits to protect the rest of Sanrio."

"George!"

"I know," Jefferson said. "That's where my house is too."

WILLARD P. SPENCER was close to apoplexy. "The governor will hear of this outrage," he told Ben Hastings. "Washington will hear of it! I demand that my house and property be protected!"

"Fine," Ben said. He beckoned one of the crew chiefs. "Get that hose hooked up to the swimming pool, and see that the well pump keeps running until it sucks air."

"That well," Spencer said, "cost fifteen dollars a foot to drill. And if you burn out the pump—"

"Move it, *amigo*," the crew chief said. "We got work to do and you're in the way." He squinted through sooty eyes at Spencer's immaculate polo shirt, blazer and flannels. "Was I you, I'd be hauling out the family silver and heading for far places."

Angela Spencer took her husband's arm and urged him to one side. "They won't listen to you, Will," she said. "I believe we'd do well to take some things and move to the inn temporarily."

"You don't understand, Angy."

"Quite possibly not. But I can't see that you are accomplishing anything by staying here. The house is obviously threatened, and we may lose it, insurance or not, so—"

"What do you know about insurance?"

"We have none. Isn't that correct?" There was no answer. Angela had expected none. "So," she said, "I think we might well go to the inn. We'll need night things, at least, and you'll want your toilet kit and shaver. We'd best get them while we can."

SOPHIE SWIFT HAD THE STATION WAGON packed in accordance with the list she had made. With some difficulty she had hooked the horse trailer to the station wagon and urged the mare inside. The foal had followed. The other two horses were tethered behind the trailer, already restive in the gathering smoke.

Sophie did not consider herself an emotional female, and perhaps this was merely one more flaw in her make-up; but now, faced with the logical necessity of abandoning the house she and Aaron had built together and filled with memories, she found herself very close to tears. It was beginning to seem that the life she had once considered so organized and well balanced, so securely built, was now crumbling.

Inside the horse trailer the mare whinnied and stamped a nervous hoof. The two tethered geldings stirred anxiously.

"Easy, boys," Sophie said, but she too was conscious that time was running out and that the sensible thing to do was get into the station wagon and drive away. Still she hesitated.

122

Through the trees at the forest's edge she could see flames and hear their crackling menace. The mare in the trailer whinnied again and stamped angrily. The tethered geldings tugged at their ropes.

"All right," Sophie said at last. "You're right. Time to go."

AARON SWIFT WALKED OUT OF the home he and Debby had shared into the eerie near-darkness, flickeringly lit by the flames of Backslope. It occurred to him to hope that since things had been bad for so long, the chances were that any change would almost have to be for the better.

And things had been bad. First there had been and still was the fire. Raised in this country, Aaron knew what an agonizingly long time it would take for the forest to replenish itself.

Then of course there was Debby, who had already packed, wept sincerely over their farewells and gone off with her Johnny Joe. Aaron had long approved of the ease with which the laws of New Mexico allowed a husband and wife to decide jointly that they had made a mistake, and almost without further ado to go their separate ways. But now that it had happened to him, and not as a result of his own decision, he saw matters a little differently.

Foremost, of course, Debby's leaving was a blow to his ego. He was honest enough to admit this, and to admit as well that he had done precisely the same thing to Sophie, which left him ruefully contemplating Aaron Swift as a man who deserved sympathy from no one, including himself.

And now, as the final blow, there was the news on the radio that Backslope was out of control here, on its southern end, had just destroyed Willard Spencer's property and was probably fast closing in on the ranch he and Sophie had built together.

Sophie was still at the ranch. Aaron was sure. She would be ready to leave, but she would not do so unless the danger had become too imminent, and Aaron did not think it had quite yet.

And here he was, nursing his wounded pride and pretending to mourn the departure of a young wife whom he had teased for her shortcomings. "You," he told himself aloud, "had better put your priorities in order, Counsellor." And with that he walked quickly to his car, got in and set out for Sophie's.

SITTING AT THE COMMAND POST TABLE was no longer possible. JL pushed back his chair and stood up. To Ben he said, "You stay here. I've got to get out there and see for myself." He started for the jeep. "I'll keep in touch."

"Take somebody with you," Ben said. But JL was already gone.

As he drove JL studied the map in his mind, setting against it the reports that had continued to flow in. Sheep Ridge first, he decided. He'd give a lot to be able to put Ben in charge of that sector, but Ben was needed right where he was. Then who?

He took the microphone from its bracket on the dashboard. "Find Jay Paul. Tell him to get over to Sheep Ridge. I want him there. Over."

Ben's voice was comfortably calm. "Roger."

"And get your relief man, Weinstock, and give him the sector to the west, where the estates are."

Again the comforting, "Roger."

"Over and out for now." JL hung up the mike and concentrated on driving.

KEN AND STACY were speeding along the county road near the Holloway place. By the furious glare of the fire they could make out what was left of the house: two standing walls pierced by a gaping doorway and a large hole where a window had been.

Stacy said unexpectedly, "Serves us right. All of us. Building that close to the wildland."

"JL's tub-thumping has got to you, has it?"

"Now hold on," Stacy began automatically, and stopped. "OK," she said in a different tone. "The answer is yes."

There was a long silence, unbroken until they rounded the last bend in the road and approached Stacy's drive. Then, "Ken, look!"

It was the Spencer house, still in flames. And in a scene from hell, the moving figures of fire fighters threw enormous shadows against the curtain of smoke rising from the forest trees.

"Ada was right," Ken said. "The wind—look there, that shower of sparks and burning branches!"

"Let me out at the end of my drive," Stacy said, remembering JL's dislike of the long, curving one-way entrance. "I don't want you stuck up by the house not able to turn round."

"OK." Ken looked at her gravely. "I'm not going to try to tell you what to do," he said, "but if it comes to a choice between you and your horses . . ."

"I'll take care of it."

"I know you will, but what I'm trying to tell you is to take care of yourself as well, you hear?"

"I hear." Stacy's voice was unexpectedly soft. She put her hand on his arm. "Stop worrying."

124

"Fat chance. You're—" He stood on the brakes as a car burst out of the entrance to Stacy's drive and almost rammed them. Ken could see that a woman was driving. "Juanita!" Stacy was already out of the car, racing to the other. When she reached it she bent to the window.

"The fire!" Juanita's words almost ran together. "And Pancho. That *chico!* He thinks of nothing but the horses. He is letting them out of their stalls. . . ."

Stacy half turned to wave at Ken. "Beat it! You too, Juanita!"

She turned then and began to run up the curving drive, uncertain on the high-heeled sandals, holding the long skirt above her knees. At last she burst into the parking area and found the house still intact. She swerved and ran towards the horse barns.

She saw Pancho. He was bareback on a big grey gelding, clinging like a burr, controlling the animal with a hackamore rope instead of a bridle. He saw Stacy, and his face split wide in a white-toothed grin. "*Vámonos, señorita!* Let's go! There is a hackamore on Sam! And the horses are loose!" He gestured to them milling in the shadows.

Good boy, Stacy thought, and ran towards Sam, who stood patiently, the rope hanging to the ground. The smell of smoke was thick now, choking. The milling horses whinnied in panic.

Stacy seized the hackamore rope, and then looked down in disgust at the long, impossible dress she wore. "Hold it, Sam," she said, and dropped the rope. With both hands she tore the dress up to the waist, and let the bottom half drop to the ground.

She seized the rope again, and a handful of Sam's mane. "Move it, boy! Let's go!" And as the big horse took his first jump forward Stacy vaulted onto his back. "Get them moving, Pancho!" She pursed her lips, whistled shrilly and waved her free arm. "*Yeeeeay!*" And another whistle.

"Not the drive!" she shouted to Pancho. "Down the hill, away from the road!" There would be cars, maybe fire trucks, too much chance of collision. "Take them past Mr. Jones's house, towards the Swift property!"

SOPHIE SWIFT OPENED THE DOOR of the station wagon and started to get in. In the trailer the mare whinnied and stamped loudly again. "Easy!" Sophie said automatically, but hesitating there in the darkness, she too was conscious of something she could not comprehend. She searched the trees for the cause.

It was a sound, but it was also a feeling, as if the earth itself were shaking beneath her feet. And suddenly, amid the shadows, there was a running horse, and another, and then a bunched mass and a thunder of hoofs. A shrill whistle cut through the sounds without warning, and a voice raised above the din shouted, "You go on, Pancho! Take them towards Vista Hill!"

Sophie, only partially comprehending, could see then a big grey gelding, and on his back, hunched forward like a jockey, a small human shape that shouted, "*Aaaiiie! Arriba! Vámonos!*" A thin brown arm waved a coiled rope as the grey leaned obediently into his turn, forcing the mass of horses to the new direction. They galloped off into the darkness.

And here, on Sam, came Stacy, to rein the big horse to a skittering stop as she surveyed the situation: Sophie beside the station wagon, with the horse trailer behind and the two geldings in tow.

"Turn the geldings loose," Stacy ordered. "I'll take care of them. You have the mare and the foal in the trailer? Good. Get going. Luck." She half turned on Sam's back to stare at headlights coming up the drive. "Who's this?"

Sophie too was staring at the headlights, as if mesmerized. She could make out the shape of the vehicle behind the lights only dimly, but somehow she *knew*—

"Turn the geldings loose!" Stacy commanded sharply, and Sophie stumbled to the rear of the horse trailer to obey.

She heard Stacy say then, "Oh, it's you! Good. About time. Get that wagon and trailer out of here! Pronto!" And again the shrill whistle sounded as the two geldings moved free and Stacy disappeared into the darkness.

Sophie hurried back to the station wagon. Inside the trailer the mare was whinnying in terror. "We're going!" Sophie almost screamed, and towards the now stopped headlights she called, "Is it you? Is it?"

"You lead," Aaron's calm voice said. "I'll follow. It's going to be all right, Soph."

"Oh, thank God!" As she scrambled into the car seat and switched on the engine, Sophie had no idea whether she had said the words aloud, or only in her mind.

FROM HIS VANTAGE POINT well above the timberline on the great mountain, Andy McIlvain could look down almost as if from the cabin of his plane, with a broad view of Backslope's vast area. He could watch the surging flames as wind gusts buffeted them, and

126

although the distance was too great to hear any sounds, he could imagine the tumult on the fire lines.

It seemed the war was being won; that much was clear. In the northwest the first wind shift had driven flames back across Highway 14 into territory already burned. There the flames were expiring from lack of fuel. In the northeast and east, Gordy's and Bessie's crews had cut a fire line that was holding. By now, Gordy and Bessie and their people had probably been brought down to the one remaining area of great danger—Sheep Ridge and the finger of the forest—where fire threatened the big estates, the housing development and the town itself.

It was the way these things worked, Andy thought; gradually you got one part of the area under control, then another, and yet a third; and as these conquered territories became joined, the fire shrank until at last, as now, you were in a position to throw everything you had into the last breach in your line.

His eyes still on the scene before him, he lifted his radio and called the dispatcher. "Patch me through to JL," he said. When the familiar voice acknowledged, Andy said, "Call me your eye in the sky. I've got a clear view of the entire battlefield."

JL, driving with one hand and manipulating the jeep's mike with the other, felt an immediate surge of hope. Andy with a view of the whole area—nothing could be better. Were they beginning to get the breaks at last? "I'm in a jeep," he said, "trying to cover the entire line. Mrs. Wayne's grove that we backfired—is it holding as a break?"

"As of now. Bellevue Acres is still intact."

"And down the finger area?"

"Troops fighting a rearguard action. And I suggest that if you're thinking of another backfire to protect the town, you'd better get to it quick. There's that empty parking lot by the rodeo grandstand, and if you set your backfire with that lot behind you . . ."

"Got it. And Andy . . . stay right where you are."

"Aye, aye, sir."

ADA WAS WAITING in front of the house when Ken drove up. She greeted him with an unsteady, welcoming smile. "I'm sorry," she said, taking his arm. "I—"

"You did just right. It's bad."

"What do we do now?"

"I get out of this soup and fish and into jeans and go over to Bellevue Acres."

"To do what? And why? That's so close to the fire line!"

"Slow down, baby. Those are my houses. In a sense, they're my people too, and—"

"But what can you do?"

Ken had taken off his dinner jacket and was undoing his tie. He stopped and looked at Ada. "Not a thing—except be there."

Ada shook her head, as if to drive a bad dream away. "OK," she said then. "But I go too."

"Now look—"

"You look," Ada said, and her voice was firm. "I know the place. It's full of kids. Kids worry. I'm good with kids." She smiled. "I used to be one. Maybe I still am. Where you go, buster, I'm tagging right along."

COMING BACK from Duane Semple's house, alone in the rear seat of the big car, Bart Jones switched on the radio, tuned to the local station and immediately wished he hadn't.

"And while it is not yet known how many thousands of acres the fire has consumed," an announcer's voice said, "it is now apparent that Sanrio itself is threatened, and desperate measures are being taken in the town's defence."

Desperate measures unspecified, Bart thought, and switched off the sound. He doubted if he would get a more coherent account, and in any event he was about to see for himself just how serious the problem had become.

In the front seat the driver reacted as if the thoughts had been spoken aloud. Without turning his head, he said, "Do you think it's safe, sir? To drive to the house, I mean?" It was a mistake.

"We'll find out, won't we?" Bart said. Always he reacted instantly at the first hint of a challenge. "Just keep driving. I'll tell you when or if we're going to stop."

JL BRAKED THE JEEP to a sliding stop on a dirt road that overlooked the town. The air was filled with flying sparks and ash and acrid smoke. He surveyed the area swiftly but carefully, wanting no oversight to turn into a mistake.

There was the parking area, acres in extent, that Andy had mentioned, bare dirt and patches of grass, which would amount to nothing as supporting fuel. Next to the parking area was the ancient wooden rodeo grandstand.

Beyond the rodeo grounds the town itself began, only scattered houses at first, but further on more houses crowded together, divided by narrow streets as old as Sanrio itself. Once flames reached those houses, there would be no stopping the conflagration. On the other hand, JL thought, if they could hold it here, it just might spell the beginning of the end for his voracious enemy.

He plucked the microphone from its bracket, identified himself and his position, sent out another call for Jay Paul, ordering him from Sheep Ridge "on the double", and hung up.

While he waited he reviewed the situation in his mind. He had no panacea, he thought; indeed, with the winds what they were, he could be sure of absolutely nothing.

A short time later Jay Paul drove up and got out of his own jeep. Immediately JL pointed to the finger of the forest. "We're fighting a losing battle there. All we're doing is slowing the fire's progress. But we *are* doing that, and that gives us a little time."

Jay Paul listened in silence. Since flying with the jumpers, JL thought, Jay had seemed to mature. It was strange how quickly it could happen. No matter. JL pointed again, in the direction of the town this time. "Those two parallel roads," he said, "thick piñon and juniper growth between." Jay Paul nodded.

"Below the lower road," JL went on, "there's that parking area and the grandstand. Then the town begins." He paused. "And it's all downwind." He waited.

"So we burn out the piñon and juniper between the roads," Jay said. "If we do it fast enough, it will give us a firebreak as wide as the space between the roads, *plus* the parking area to protect the town." He paused. "And the grandstand?"

"Explosives," JL said. "Take it right down flat. Lumber lying on the ground we can handle if it starts to burn. Flying sparks from a standing grandstand can go right over our heads and start setting roofs afire in town."

Jay Paul thought about it briefly before he nodded. JL liked that moment of contemplation instead of blind obedience.

"You're in charge," JL said. "I want to see the rest of the line firsthand. You can reach me on the radio."

KEN WAS SURROUNDED as soon as he got to Bellevue Acres. Head and shoulders above the group, he was easy, friendly, in the face of what looked like incipient hysteria. "How's it going? OK?"

The man who had complained previously to Ben Hastings said now, "No, it's not OK! Look at all those burning branches flying around! You call that OK?"

Behind him two or three men had their garden hoses out and

were spraying the roofs of their houses. "I think," Ken said in a voice that had altered subtly, "that you'd better get off your duff, mister, and hitch up your hose and fall to with the rest of them. Let the women pack up, just in case."

"And just how will we know when to run? Tell me that!"

"The Forest Service people will get word to you."

"I wouldn't trust those clowns to do anything. That's—"

"Mister," Ken said, his voice very quiet now, "I'm trying to be friendly, but you're making it hard. If you keep stirring these people up, you're going to have real trouble on your hands, starting with me." He paused. "Is that clear?"

The man hesitated. Slowly he nodded. "OK." He turned away and said to the woman behind him, "Where's our hose?"

Ken looked around at the group. "Any more questions?"

Ada, standing a small distance away, took a deep breath. To a nine-year-old boy she said, "Hi. What's your name? Jimmy? OK, Jimmy, how's about you get a bucket. Fill it with water. Then get a couple of tin cans, and you and I will set up an auxiliary fire brigade."

"You nuts or something? What can we do?"

"What we can do," Ada said, "is keep our eyes open for burning twigs, like that one over there. And when we see one, we dip up water in our tin can and douse the twig. OK?"

"Where'll you be?"

Ada tried to keep her eyes from the flames in the finger of the forest beyond Mrs. Wayne's blackened grove. "I'll be right here, Jimmy." She took another deep breath. "Promise."

ON THE MAP IN HIS MIND JL visualized the fire line as beginning somewhere in the forest above Stacy's section of land and stretching east-southeast through a part of the Swifts' property and Ada Loving's, dipping down to include the Holloways' and Mrs. Wayne's specimen grove, then rising northeast across the finger area and above the county road.

"Give or take a half mile," he said aloud to himself, and called for Andy McIlvain.

From the timberline Andy's voice came in loud and clear.

"Your end position is near that El Rancho Costa Mucho place— and then, you're right, it runs pretty much the way you thought, staying above the county road. On the western side, by the big houses, they've got a job on their hands, but it looks as if they may contain it."

"I'll have a look-see," JL said. "Over and out."

The shortcut he took was no more than a deer path, but in low gear and with four-wheel drive the jeep bounced and hammered its way through the low brush.

Suddenly, there was the end of the fire line, ground crews at work with hand tools, and two bulldozers pushing loose debris out of the fire's way.

JL stopped and got out. As far as he could see in the smoky murk and dust, men were working almost shoulder to shoulder, cutting their firebreak. JL caught sight of Jerry Weinstock, whom he had told Ben to put in charge of this sector, and made his way towards him.

Jerry was tall, cadaverous, all whipcord and sprung steel, now filthy, smoke grimed and obviously near exhaustion. But he waited quietly in his reserved way, his eyes steady on JL's face.

"Can you hold the line?" JL said.

"We'll hold it." No hesitation, no doubt.

JL nodded, then turned away, and with no further words made his way back to his jeep. The radio was crackling as he got in.

"Jay Paul here." There was anger in the voice. "The mayor objects to the backfire. And to blowing the grandstand."

A new voice came on the radio.

"Look here, JL. If they blow up that grandstand, how do we stage a rodeo this year? Answer me that. All that tourist trade and traffic—"

JL pressed his microphone switch, shutting off reception. "Jay?"

"Jay here." JL could picture the mike suddenly plucked from the mayor's hand.

"Carry on with that backfire," JL said. "I'm on my way." He started up the jeep's engine with a roar. Pushing the vehicle as fast as it would go through the brush, he thought of all kinds of things he might say to His Honour the Mayor.

And then all at once in his headlights, in the dimness of the forest growth, he saw what he could not for an instant really believe— Stacy, in the shreds of an evening dress, bent low on Sam's withers, herding two other horses ahead of her and running straight towards what JL knew was an area aflame.

He blew the jeep's horn and shouted, but the apparition was already gone into the gathering gloom.

JL, reacting automatically, spun the wheel, bore down hard on the throttle and set off in pursuit. The mayor, the backfire—both would have to wait.

THE HORSES SENSED THE FLAMES ahead before Stacy saw them, and without warning one of the Swift geldings screamed, turned suddenly and ran headlong through a solid mass of piñon and juniper branches without slowing. The other gelding followed.

Sam at full gallop spun as only a cutting horse can, and tore off in a new direction, heading instinctively for the county road. Stacy had no saddle horn to grab, so she settled for a firm handful of Sam's mane, which she almost pulled out by its roots as she struggled to retain her balance. "Sam! Ho, boy!" Wasted breath. With no bit in Sam's mouth to control his flight Stacy was helpless, clinging as best she could as they crashed through low branches and across the bottom of a dry gully.

Up the far side without slowing the mad pace, and there in the darkness a low, solid pine branch scraped Stacy from Sam's back as cleanly as one scrapes snow from a boot sole.

She hit the ground and, rolling limply, fetched up against a dumped pile of debris by the side of the road. She lay motionless as Sam thundered off into the night.

A STATE POLICEMAN flagged down Bart's car. "Sorry," he said, leaning in at the lowered rear window. "It isn't safe to go on."

"I live in there."

"Maybe you did," the cop said, "but it's a fair bet there isn't anything left to live in now."

"That I'll see for myself. And I'll take full responsibility."

"Look, mister, my orders are to—"

The radio in the police car across the road came alive with a hollow sound, and a voice spoke in police radio jargon. The cop turned away and walked quickly to the vehicle.

"Let's go!" Bart said, and when the driver hesitated, "You heard me!"

The big car rolled down the county road.

It was a scene of desolation, and even Bart, not customarily sensitive to his surroundings, was shocked by the smoking destruction of what had been a green, living forest.

"*Madre de Díos*," the driver implored. "*Señor—*"

"Just keep going," Bart said.

They rounded a broad curve and, astonishingly, came upon a stand of tall, still living trees, flames now attacking their helpless perimeter. Wind gusts rocked the treetops, and a burning branch flew across the road and narrowly missed the car.

"*Señor—*" the driver said again.

"Shut up!" Automatic response. And then in a louder, far more urgent tone, "Stop! Stop the car, hear?"

The body by the side of the road showed clearly in the headlights, naked legs white in the glare.

"Good Lord!" Bart said. And then, "Don't just sit there, damn it! Get out and fetch her here! Jump!"

The driver set the brake and opened the door. Reluctantly he stepped out. The woman looked dead, he told himself; and he had no desire to touch her. Around him the wind wailed and shrieked with the sound of souls in torment.

From the car Bart's voice bellowed, "Get going!"

One careful step, and then another, trying to look in all directions at once; and so it was that the driver saw and avoided the large burning branch that flew towards him and crashed into the car, starring the windscreen as if from a hammerblow. Suddenly the car was engulfed in flames.

Without even looking back, the driver turned and fled.

IN ROUGH WOODED COUNTRY a jeep was no match for a western-bred horse. JL, having lost the trail, was pursuing Stacy merely by guesswork now. He plunged on, ignoring the brush and the small branches that snapped against the windscreen.

There was fire to the right of him and fire ahead, so close he could feel its heat. He came to the dry gully Stacy had crossed, took its steep bank at an angle that almost overturned the jeep and, all four wheels churning, scrambled up the far side. Brush ahead suddenly burst into flame, and he floored the accelerator.

For a moment the heat of the flames seemed to sear his flesh, but the moment passed, and he was through and clear, bouncing out onto the county road, where Bart's automobile stood burning. He stopped then, jumped out and ran as close as he could.

Bart had managed to get the rear door open. Now, dragging himself by his hands, his clothing afire, he was making his tortured way towards the verge of the road. He saw JL, and instantly his expression of grim determination changed to triumph.

"Get her!" His words came out as a croaking scream as he lifted one hand to point. "Get her out of here! Never mind me!"

JL glanced towards the side of the road where Stacy's body lay motionless, seemingly lifeless. Stunned, he moved towards the body, slowly at first, and then broke into a trot. He scooped her up, finding her limp in his arms as he ran back to the jeep and set her gently in the front bucket seat. Then he turned back to Bart.

134

Bart's head was down, but it came up again, still wearing that expression of triumph. "Now get out of here!" Bart said, gesturing at the trees. "Look!"

Near the edge of the stand a stately pine, aflame from trunk to top, was beginning a slow, inexorable death fall towards the road.

"Go!" Bart croaked. His head collapsed on the dirt.

JL ran to the jeep and jumped in. A few yards to a safer spot, he told himself, and then he could go back. He was starting away when a crackling, tearing sound announced that the last of the big tree's restraining roots had torn loose. In the jeep's mirror JL could see the tree itself, gathering speed as it fell.

He floored the accelerator, and even at that surging speed felt the heat of the burning branches as they crashed across the road behind him. He looked in the mirror again and saw no Bart, no car, only the rising flames of a funeral pyre filling the road.

He drove on, his mind numb.

BESSIE WINGATE, summoned to the jeep by JL's waving arm, her shovel still in her hand, stared at the limp body in the front seat. She took in JL's stricken expression and nodded decisively.

"I'll take care of her. You tend to your backfire." She tossed the shovel into the rear seat as she squeezed herself beneath the jeep's steering wheel. She added angrily, "Will this slaughter ever stop?" and thought of Eloy Jaramillo, poor little guy.

The jeep roared off into the night.

Chapter Twelve

JL moved like a man in a dream towards the spot where his boss, George Jefferson, Mayor Billy Bob Barker and Jay Paul stood waiting. On his way he noticed automatically that the backfire had been set between the two parallel roads, burning upwind from the parking area and the grandstand, and that the towering fire in the finger of the forest had progressed.

"We're wiring charges under the grandstand," Jay Paul said.

"Good." JL spoke in a normal, calm tone, as if they were merely discussing the baseball pennant races.

"You OK?" Jefferson said. "You look skinned up."

JL shrugged, indicating that what had gone before was unimportant. "Jerry Weinstock has his end anchored, secure. This is what we have to worry about." His broad gesture included the finger area, the burning backfire, the town. He looked at Jay Paul. "Who's setting the charges?"

"I called down Gordy Walker and one of his crew, Terry Young."

Jefferson watched a burning branch flying through the air in the direction of the grandstand. "Better get them out of there."

JL held out his hand for Jay's walkie-talkie. He pressed the mike button. "JL here. Come in, Gordy. Over."

It was Terry who answered. "Hi, boss."

"How much longer?" JL said.

In the background Gordy's voice said, "Tell the man ten minutes. Maybe a little more."

"You're catching sparks," JL said.

Again Gordy's voice. "Ten minutes. We want a complete job."

JL closed his eyes and nodded. "You got it." He handed the walkie-talkie back to Jay Paul. "Ten men," he said, "with pack pumps. Douse whatever lands on or near the structure." He turned to Billy Bob. "Get your city fire engine at the far edge of the parking area. When she blows, there'll be sparks flying."

"I'm against this," the mayor said. "I want to go on record—"

"Noted," JL said. "So now get your pumper in place."

FROM HIS MOUNTAIN PERCH Andy McIlvain studied the situation with experienced eyes. At last he raised his walkie-talkie.

"It's blowing merry hell up here," Andy reported to JL. "And I imagine it is down there too. Your west flank is holding. Whoever's in charge there—"

"Jerry Weinstock," JL said.

"He looks in fair shape. Bellevue Acres looks reasonably safe too. The backfire by the parking area—"

"That's where I am."

"Figured." Andy's voice took on a new, warning note. "There's more wind coming at you, pappy. I can see the smoke north of you lying out flat. You'd better blow that grandstand quick."

"Got it," JL said. "Over and out." He handed Jay Paul the radio and looked at Jefferson. "You heard? OK." He jerked his head sideways at Billy Bob Barker but spoke still to Jefferson. "Kick his backside if you have to, but get that town fire engine in position. Those homes are going to need all the protection they can get."

Then JL turned away and was gone, headed at a brisk trot for the grandstand. Bending low, he ran in under it.

Beneath the grandstand JL switched on his helmet light and made his way as quickly as he could towards the lights further in that marked Gordy and Terry Young's location. Reaching them, he found Terry wiring a charge to one of the uprights.

Gordy said, "We'll bring her down, not blow her up. Take out these supports and she'll collapse like a house of cards."

One of Gordy's crewmen scrambled in towards them. "You're still clear overhead. The structure hasn't caught yet. But pack pumps won't hold what's flying around. That wind is *blowing!*"

Gordy moved quickly to the next upright to wire his charge.

JL followed him. "You've got a reel of wire? Good. You, Terry, take it on out and hook it up. We'll hook onto it here when we've got the charges set. Now beat it."

And then JL and Gordy were alone, working with careful haste. Gordy said, "Old guy I knew once drove a nitroglycerine truck in the oil fields back in the '30s. Got a dollar a mile, big wages then. Got paid every night. Spent it every night too. Man has to be crazy to take a job like that, no?" He threw a quick glance at JL, and in the light of his helmet lamp his face showed a faint smile.

JEFFERSON SAID TO BILLY BOB, "I'm not going to tell you again. Get that pumper in place!" He watched a burning juniper branch fly through the air and land almost lazily among the darkened grandstand seats. He waited, but no flames appeared.

Billy Bob said, "We can post more men in the grandstand, can't we? I mean, to put out any fires that could start?"

"We could not!" Jefferson's voice was sharp now. "If that firetrap ever begins to go—" He stopped, his eyes still fixed on the spot where the juniper branch had disappeared. "Oh, Lord!" he said softly. "There she goes!"

One moment there was a small column of smoke; then, incredibly, the smoke turned into flame that ran along a wooden seat and jumped to the next row. Within moments an entire section of seats was ablaze.

Jefferson turned, grabbed a walkie-talkie from a man in a yellow hard hat and pressed the microphone button.

"Jefferson here," he said. "The stands are on fire. Get out. Repeat, get out!"

Terry, outside on his knees attaching the detonator to the wire he had carried with him, said, "They're coming as fast as they can."

"Damn it—" Jefferson began.

And here came Gordy on a dead run, to slide to a stop in the gravel and hunker down to inspect Terry's connections. "OK." He nodded judiciously. "That ought to do her."

"Look at JL," Terry said. "For an old man, he motors pretty good."

JL was running towards them awkwardly, holding one arm with the other hand. His voice was raised in a shout that reached them clearly. "All set! Blow it!"

Terry pressed the detonator handle. There was a dull harrumphing sound. For a moment nothing happened, and then the whole flaming grandstand structure seemed to shudder, and with slow dignity collapsed inwards upon itself in a fiery mass. All that remained when it had settled was a low-lying pile of shattered lumber, burning as a fire burns in a grate.

Out of breath, JL ran up to Jefferson, whose eyes were on the burning debris. "Town pumper on the way," Jefferson said. "It can handle that." He looked at JL. "What happened to your arm?"

JL made a sharp gesture, dismissing the question, and turned to survey the scene. The burned-over area between the two roads was still glowing, still throwing wind-driven sparks and burning branches into the air, but with the grandstand no longer there the threat was gone. Beyond the upper road, in the finger of the forest, the force and fury of the fire were slowly diminishing for want of fresh fuel. The town fire engine arrived, clanging noisily, and firemen set about subduing what was left of the burning grandstand.

Jefferson watched JL. He was still holding his arm. Jefferson turned to Gordy Walker. "What's wrong with him?"

"A timber burned loose and fell on his shoulders as we were wrapping up."

Jefferson blinked. "It was that close?"

Gordy's face and voice were expressionless. "Let's say we didn't have a lot of leeway."

Reaching into the jeep with his good hand, JL switched on the radio and took up the mike. "Patch me through to Jerry Weinstock." And when the connection was made, "Still holding?"

No hesitation. "We'll hold it," Weinstock said.

"Good man." JL's voice held its customary calm. He switched back to the dispatcher and said, "Now get me Andy McIlvain up on the mountain."

It was not over yet, he thought, not quite, but despite everything they had the upper hand now, and unless Andy had bad news the outcome was no longer in doubt.

Andy's voice said, "That was quite a cliffhanger, but never mind. You pulled it off. The town looks good from here."

"And the rest of the way round?"

"You're under control. Little flare-ups here and there, but what the heck, you'll have those to contend with for days."

True enough. But it was still good news. "Over and out," JL said, and called the dispatcher again. "Now Ben Hastings." And when Ben's voice came on, "How are we at the development?"

"So far, OK. They're packed up, ready to get out if they have to." Ben hesitated. "Your friend Delacorte wants somebody official there, but . . ."

"Yes," JL said in sudden understanding. In the end, he thought, it all came down to people, individuals—not forests or trees or paintings on canvas—individual persons. Like Stacy. "Tell Ken I'm on the way," he said. "You can reach me there."

AS JL PULLED UP IN THE JEEP, Ken Delacorte was easily visible, towering above the householders, directing hoses here and there, smiling, encouraging, praising. Nearby, Ada Loving was totally occupied with the kids, who scurried to and fro at her direction.

"Breaking her in to harness?" JL asked when Ken joined him.

"That'll be the day." Ken's smile disappeared. His eyes studied JL's face intently. "What's the word?"

JL could savour the moment. Once again they had fought the beast and won. They had lost a great deal, but they had learned some things too, and in the process had prepared some good young people, like Ben Hastings and Jay Paul, to take over. So it was no standoff; it was victory, and he could say it with pride. "You're safe. We've got it whipped. You can tell them that."

BESSIE WINGATE, now cramped into store clothes and scrubbed until she shone, was coming out of a room at the hospital as JL, his arm in a sling, walked down the corridor. Bessie stopped. "What happened to you?" She shook her head. "Never mind. You look like you'll live."

JL was smiling faintly. "I expect to."

"Somebody," Bessie said, "said they heard you were quitting. I said, 'That's a lot of baloney.' You get a taste for smoke, and like a drunk, you can't give it up." She flipped one large hand in a parting gesture. "See you at the next one," she said, and rolled off down the corridor.

JL watched her go. Bessie was about as subtle as a fist in the mouth, and nothing was going to change her, ever.

He glanced up at the number of the room Bessie had been visiting, knocked on the partially open door and went in.

Stacy was propped up in bed, her left arm in a cast, but her face reflected no pain and her eyes watched him steadily.

JL looked round the room at the vases of flowers. "I guess I ought to have brought something."

"You know better. You're the reason I'm still here at all."

"Your friend is. Was. Jones."

Stacy shook her head gently, as if to drive that thought away.

"I just wanted to see how you were," JL said.

Stacy was smiling faintly, almost certainly reading his thoughts. "You whipped it," she said. "I knew you would."

"We were lucky."

"Yes." The faint smile was gone, but amusement remained in her eyes, and something else. "The harder you fight," she said, "the luckier you get. I've noticed that too. Shall we add that to the list of things we have to talk about?"

"That list," JL said, "is getting pretty long." He took a deep breath. "What I mean is—"

"That it's going to keep on growing," Stacy said. "Yes. I've been thinking too. It's going to take a very long time to talk our way through it."

From sparks that had flown between them, JL thought suddenly, to—this. Hard to believe. But also more pleasant to think about than he would have thought possible. He said slowly, "Maybe we won't reach the end of it."

Stacy's smile had returned, but its amusement was replaced by pure warmth. "We'll have fun finding out," she said. "Together."

RICHARD MARTIN STERN

Firsthand experience is a trademark of Richard Martin Stern's intensely realistic fiction. *Wildfire*, his sixth novel to appear in Condensed Books, is a case in point, for Stern himself battled against forest fires when he was a teenager in California. "My family had a place near the Angeles National Forest," he explains, "and whenever there was a fire, the ranger would come and ask for volunteers. Once you've seen a forest fire close up," he adds, "you don't forget it!"

A stickler for authenticity, Stern thoroughly familiarized himself with the latest fire-fighting methods before he wrote *Wildfire*. He also took the trouble to make a special flight over New Mexico's vast Gila National Forest in the company of a team of smoke-jumpers, the trained men who, in the United States, provide a crucial service by parachuting in to fight fires in areas inaccessible to motor vehicles. He says of the flight: "It was quite an experience. I was sitting on the floor right next to the open doorway—there is no door—and watched the first two men go out, and my stomach went with them! They were jumping from twelve hundred feet into a place that looked no bigger than my hand. And they did it!"

The starkly beautiful countryside of New Mexico is something else the author knows intimately. For twenty years he and his wife Dorothy have lived in the hills of Santa Fe in a house they designed themselves, "with lots of glass and a view of three mountain ranges." Though both Sterns are native Californians, they are clearly devoted to their adopted home in the southwest. "There's a sense of space out here which we love," he explains. "Some days you can sit on the portico and feel as if you're looking for ever."

In their spare time he and his wife, who have been married for nearly fifty years, enjoy walking and travelling. Over the years Mrs. Stern has learned to keep a detailed journal of their trips, which her husband refers to when he needs facts and figures on faraway places for his books. However, when Dick Stern went up with the smoke-jumpers, Dorothy kept her feet firmly on the ground!

SIEGE of SILENCE

A CONDENSATION OF THE BOOK BY

A.J. QUINNELL

ILLUSTRATED BY BRIAN SANDERS

Jason Peabody has his faults. He's cold, unemotional, some would say forbidding. But he's also a man of exceptional qualities, and it is these that are to be tested as never before when he faces the greatest crisis of his life in his new post as US ambassador to San Carlo, Central America.

In the chaotic aftermath of an overnight communist coup, Peabody finds himself facing crack Cuban interrogator Jorge Calderon, who is hell-bent on extracting from him the names of collaborators in a plot against Castro.

The Cuban is confident, for he holds a trump card. He knows of the one weakness that Peabody has kept hidden from the world; the one painful memory that could bring him to his knees and make him talk. . . . Can the ambassador hold out until rescue forces arrive?

The tense psychological battle between captive and captor is traced with chilling accuracy in Quinnell's thought-provoking new novel.

PROLOGUE

Jason Peabody. *San Carlo City, San Carlo.*

As I enter the room in the Venezuelan ambassador's residence, the hostility is tangible. It radiates, and my skin prickles with the sensation. I find it agreeable.

The room, lit by two oversized chandeliers, is full of people, uniforms and medals, long dresses and diamonds, sober suits and polished shoes. All the hallmarks of a diplomatic reception.

The Venezuelan ambassador approaches, his plump body cut diagonally by a red sash, his hand outstretched, a smile stuck on his face like peeling tape.

"Excellency, so good of you to come—an honour."

His handshake is damp. I utter the ritual words. "Thank you, Excellency. Congratulations on this auspicious day. My apologies for being late; work you understand."

"No matter."

A waiter approaches with glasses on a silver tray. I take one.

"We waited," the ambassador adds ingratiatingly. "Would you mind?"

"Of course."

I step forward and silence works its way through the room. I am the focal point of resentful looks. Some are curious. If they expect a speech they're wrong. I raise my glass and glance at the ambassador. "Your Excellency." I nod towards a cadaverous figure in the corner. "Mr. Foreign Minister; ladies and gentlemen. On this the occasion of the National Day of Venezuela, San Carlo's respected neighbour, I would like to offer a toast to President Lusinchi." I raise the glass high, murmur, "President Lusinchi," and take a sip amid the chorus of response. God, I hate champagne. My task completed, I quickly move away towards the French windows.

Out on the broad portico the air is sweet with the aroma of jasmine and bougainvillaea. Flagstone paths weave through beds of plants and flowers and tall palms. A shadow materializes into the form of a guard sauntering along a path, submachine gun slung over one shoulder. It typifies the situation in San Carlo—violence in paradise.

Behind me I hear the murmur of conversation, the clinking of glasses and the braying laugh of the British ambassador.

Then a voice, close by, interrupts my thoughts. "I'm told you prefer Scotch, Excellency."

I turn to find the Venezuelan ambassador behind me. He holds out a glass and I exchange it for the champagne.

"Do I disturb you?"

"No, I stepped out to escape the hubbub."

He smiles conspiratorially and gives a theatrical sigh. "Ah, these receptions.... But then we have both been diplomats long enough to bear them ... to close our ears and merely nod at regular intervals, and smile when required."

He waits for an answer, but I'm in no mood for small talk. I shrug, hoping he will go away. I'm disappointed.

"I wanted a word with you in private, Excellency. I heard a disturbing rumour this evening."

"Oh?"

"Yes. Apparently you are considering sending home all dependents and non-essential personnel."

Irritation washes over me. Damn! A confidential chancery meeting in mid-afternoon and by early evening the word is out to every embassy in the city and doubtless right through the government. It's the blabbering wives, of course.

I speak to him coldly and formally. "Understand, Excellency, I have been US ambassador here for just one week. Naturally I have had meetings with my senior officials, including those from Military Aid and Security. I have to examine all aspects of the situation and at this time I have taken no firm decision as to repatriation. It is, therefore, as you say ... merely a rumour."

"I understand. May I speak to you not as a diplomat ... that is to say in a straightforward way?"

"Sure."

There is more braying laughter from the room behind. He takes my arm. "Shall we walk in the garden?" He gently propels me down the steps onto a path. I hate people touching me, and extricate my arm.

"You are very experienced and knowledgeable, Señor Peabody. Even your Spanish is of fine quality. Permit me to say, that is rare for an American."

"I thought you were not going to talk as a diplomat."

He is unruffled. In the semi-darkness his teeth show in a smile. "The compliment was sincere. However, now to the matter. In spite of your experience and length of service, I believe I'm right in saying that this is your first posting as chief of mission."

"Correct."

"I, on the other hand, have been an ambassador for over twenty years, although I now find myself in a backwater like San Carlo." He glances at me, perhaps looking for sympathy. Not finding any he continues. "As the doyen of the diplomatic corps here, I feel I have the unwritten privilege to offer advice to new ambassadors ... especially in matters concerning the diplomatic community."

I insert a warning into my voice. "And you're going to offer me unsolicited advice?"

"Not really, Señor Peabody. I'm just going to point out to you certain consequences that may arise if you do issue a repatriation order."

Curtly I say, "I told you it's only under consideration."

"Exactly, and what I have to say may have a bearing. Such an order can have three possible consequences: first, to start a snowball effect among other embassies, particularly as it is your government which is propping up the regime here in San Carlo with its aid. The second effect would be to weaken morale among local people ... the government and the civil guard ... the business community. And thirdly, such an announcement could only give encouragement to the Chamarrista rebels and their friends in Cuba."

We turn a corner on the path and are confronted by a patrolling guard; spectral in a paramilitary uniform. He stands to one side at semi-attention as we pass.

"The point is," the Venezuelan continues, "none of the other chiefs of mission have seriously considered such a move. They feel that President Vargas has things under control here in San Carlo."

I gesture over my shoulder with a thumb. "Armed guards, day and night. It's hardly a normal situation. Besides, you forget that it's we

Americans who are the prime targets. I'm aware of the consequences if I decide on repatriation."

. The path turns again towards the lights of the residence and the faint sound of music.

"Of course, Señor, and naturally with the great American aid and large covert presence here you must have more and deeper information than the rest of us."

There is condescension in his voice. The man really is a fool. I've had enough.

"That's exactly right, Mr. Ambassador. I'll make my decision based on that information, and at that time I'll inform you prior to the others—as a common courtesy."

We are facing each other on the path. I am about a head taller. Having lost the point, his face carries a sullen look. He opens his mouth to argue but I cut him off. "My thanks for a pleasant evening. Goodnight."

I walk up the path leaving him mute behind me. I feel good.

LATER THE SAME EVENING, I'm back in my quarters at the US embassy. It's luxurious, but it's a prison. From my study window I look across the roof of the staff apartments to a high wall. Floodlights illuminate the wires running across its top and the television cameras at each corner. Yes, it's a prison. We are forty-two souls locked into our compound. Even the glass in front of me is bulletproof. This is what I am now: the most important man in the country apart from the president; and I'm a prisoner. The position makes me a target of any crazed commie—or any other crazy.

If the Chamarristas do attack, I'll do the job fast. With our new aid package and the new military trainees from Fort Bragg, the rebels will be swept away. Then to his surprise San Carlo's President Vargas will have to face elections and, with enough money and influence, a decent government—or a decent general—will run the country on decent lines.

Through the thick glass window I hear the faint, single chime of the cathedral clock. It reminds me of my fatigue, and I walk through to the bedroom. At last the maid has remembered to put the flask of chilled mineral water on the bedside table, together with a glass. Ten days I've been here and wasted a vast amount of time teaching the residence staff the fundamentals of hygiene and comfort. My predecessor must have lived like a pig. But it's to be expected. He was very lax in his policies, in his personal and general discipline and in his reports.

148

The maid has also remembered to turn down the bed and lay out clean pyjamas. She was astonished when I told her, "Clean pyjamas every night—and clean sheets." God knows how Calder used to live. The whole residence stank of cigar smoke until I had all the air-conditioning filters changed and banned smoking.

Suddenly I notice the glass is not clean. I go back into the bathroom, rinse it, pour water and take two pills. Then I brush my teeth. It's a pleasurable duty. I use a "water pik" and enjoy the tingling sensation of the tiny spray against my gums. Churchill used one. I read it in his memoirs.

In bed I pick up a tract of the Sandinist revolution. I have trained myself, no matter how tired, to read for half an hour before sleep. In that time I can read twenty pages. In rough terms it means thirty books a year. Just from that half hour!

When the half hour has passed I switch off the light and rearrange the pillows. I rarely have difficulty sleeping and I am sinking into unconsciousness when the bedside telephone rings. It is Gage, chief of station. His voice is nervous. He's had to take a difficult decision in ringing me at this hour. He mumbles apologetically that the CIA deputy chief of station has an unsubstantiated report that a large column of Chamarristas has passed through the village of Paras, twenty miles northeast of San Carlo City. Gage is sorry to wake me but to his knowledge Bermudez, the rebel leader, has never brought his men this close to the capital before.

I ask the obvious question. "Have you discussed this with our chief of security?"

A painful pause, then, "No, sir. Mr. Fleming went to a party at the Brazilian embassy. I rang there but he left an hour ago—they don't know where he's gone."

Again I feel resentment towards my predecessor. His laxity has rubbed off on all the staff. There should be strict procedures: a 1:00 am curfew and hourly whereabout reports between sunset and that time.

Gage's tentative voice again. "I checked with the national guard headquarters, sir. They dismissed the report as nonsense. They have a garrison in that village ... but I thought I'd better call you, sir ... your standing instructions ..."

"Gage, you did right. Stay in touch with the CIA and the national guard. Call me if anything develops, and meanwhile let Fleming know that he's to report to my office at 8:00 am ... sharp!"

I replace the receiver and just as I do so, I remember something. I immediately call Gage back and instruct him to go and wake Colonel

Sumner, the military attaché, and get him to meet me in fifteen minutes. "Tell him to come to the tank," I say. "This has got to be confidential."

SUMNER MAKES IT to the tank in twelve minutes. He looks sleepy but I note with approval that he's dressed in a well pressed suit and tie.

I'm standing at the large wall map. I've stuck a red pin on the dot of Paras.

"Sorry to get you up, Colonel. I've ordered coffee." I tap my finger on the map. "There's an unconfirmed report that Chamarristas have passed through this village heading for the city."

With the heels of his hands he rubs his eyes and nods. "Gage told me. Also that the national guard discount the rumour. That village is well garrisoned and it lies at the foot of a steep valley. There's no way a large column of rebels could move through there undetected."

"Unless the garrison was from General Lacay's brigade."

There is a tap on the door and it opens to reveal a young Mestizo with a tray on which there are two steaming mugs of coffee. He puts it on the table and withdraws. I gesture towards it. Sumner drinks gratefully, then says, "You're suggesting that the garrison may have collaborated with the Chamarristas?"

"It's a possibility. This morning at your briefing you talked about Generals Cruz and Lacay. You were saying that just recently Cruz has been in more favour with President Vargas than Lacay. You also said that Lacay is still bitter over Vargas's decision to post all the new military trainees to Cruz's brigade."

Sumner is looking very sceptical. He drinks more coffee and says, "Mr. Ambassador, let's slow down a bit. You're talking collaboration by the national guard. That's way out. Those guys know that if the Chamarristas ever take power, they've had it. It's like hitching a ride across a river on an alligator's back. Halfway over you get eaten."

"OK. Let's wake somebody else." I point to the telephone. "Get Tessler over here and find out exactly where that report came from."

IT TAKES TESSLER twenty minutes to appear. He is rumpled and in a foul mood. I don't care. He might be the chief of station, but I'm the ambassador. I don't bother ordering coffee for him; merely instruct him to check out the report.

He is on the telephone for a surly ten minutes. Then he hangs up, sighs dramatically and says, "We have informers in most villages. They're very low grade stuff. They get a little monthly stipend and a small bonus when they come up with something. This guy in Paras

150

hasn't had a bonus for over a year so I guess he's trying it on. Anyway consider his report worthless. If the Chamarristas are trying to move close to the city, they sure as hell wouldn't use that route."

He's young and cocksure and barely makes the effort to be respectful. I glance at Sumner. He is gazing at the wall map. I can read both their minds: I've been here ten days and I'm panicking.

Casually Tessler takes out a packet of cigarettes and lights one. He knows the new regulations and he watches me enjoying his insolence. I am about to coldly tell them both to go to bed when the telephone rings. Sumner picks it up, listens for a minute, then says, "Call immediately if anything else happens."

He hangs up, turns and says, "Two bridges on the Tekax River and one on the Chetumal have been blown up."

Offhandedly Tessler mutters, "It happens all the time."

We are all studying the map. Very thoughtfully, Sumner turns back to the table, picks up the telephone and while he dials he explains to me, "That call came from Major Anderson who heads up our military advisers. I must check something."

I'm irritated that he reminds me who Anderson is. I take it out on Tessler. "Kindly put that butt out."

He grinds it into an ashtray. Tomorrow I'll give orders to clear the whole damn building of ashtrays.

Sumner speaks urgently into the mouthpiece. "Paul, what's Vargas doing?" He swings to look at the map. "Hell! I could've guessed. Listen—can you talk him out of it...? Because it could be a set-up.... No, I'm not. Look at the map. Let's take the worst case scenario. Suppose the Chamarristas have deliberately drawn General Cruz towards the mountains. Then they blow the bridges so that Cruz and his brigade are effectively cut off from the capital. If President Vargas now orders General Lacay to retake the bridge-heads, it'll give Lacay the chance he's been waiting for. He'll send half his force, far too many for the job. Yes, persuade Vargas to pull those units back. Let Cruz look after himself.... It could be coincidence rather than a set-up, but for the moment, just tell Vargas it's bad tactics. Get back to me."

He hangs up and Tessler says incredulously, "Hey, you think General Lacay has collaborated with the rebels?"

Sumner sighs. "Well ... maybe ... just maybe, if Bermudez got to him."

Tessler laughs in derision. I cut him off by asking Sumner, "Colonel, following your worst case scenario, what would be the next step?"

He points at the map. "Lacay has already thinned out the city's defences by sending an over-large force to retake the bridgeheads. He would have sent those units and commanders who have the least loyalty to him. So now he sends loyal units to the airport and other strategic sites. He puts his best—and most loyal—officers and units into position to engage the presidential guard when the Chamarristas attack the city."

Tessler is shaking his head in disbelief. To me the next step is obvious. We must monitor all troop movements in and around the city. I am about to state that when the telephone rings. Sumner picks it up.

"Paul, yeah..." He listens for a minute during which his body hunches lower in the seat. Then, "Hang on, he's here."

He cups a hand over the telephone, runs his tongue over his upper lip and says nervously, "Mr. Ambassador, we have a crisis situation. Units of General Lacay's brigade are moving towards the airport, the presidential palace, the radio station and the police barracks." At this moment I can only think of the rank, detestable incompetence of those around me. Nausea almost overwhelms me. Then, into the petrified silence drops the distant rumbling of gunfire. Suddenly I am calm.

I HAVE NEVER BEEN in such a situation before. Since Teheran and Beirut some of our best minds and a lot of money have been devoted to embassy security, but now I discover how plans, honed to perfection over years, can go abruptly wrong.

It starts with the discovery that the chief security officer, the economic counsellor, their wives and several other middle rank staffers are all out of the compound, at a big party at an industrialist's beach house ten miles up the coast. This, in total contravention of standing instructions.

Well, it's happened. Now the palliative of action. Within minutes procedures are being followed. The crisis team is assembled. In the absence of Fleming, Gage and Marine Gunnery Sergeant Cowder take charge of the compound security. I draft the first cable to Washington. There is satisfaction in knowing that it will get a lot of people there out of warm beds, and that very shortly a similar crisis meeting will be taking place in the situation room at the White House.

There are now eight of us in the tank and information is flowing in. Chamarrista units have already linked up with elements of Lacay's brigade and are assaulting the presidential palace and the police barracks. They already have the radio station, and taped messages by Bermudez are going out over the air proclaiming the revolution and urging an end of all resistance. Apparently there are roadblocks in most streets and anything moving is shot at. My concern now is embassy security. Thank God I made that my first priority on arrival and reviewed all procedures.

We have a squad of fifteen marines commanded by Cowder the "gunny". We have sandbagged machinegun emplacements on the roofs of the chancery, a staff apartment block and the residence. They cover the three wide abutting streets. The compound walls are three feet thick and reinforced with steel. They are topped with wire which is now electrified. In addition to the marines we have a team of twelve bodyguards and security guards.

The main gate to the compound is solid steel and there is a machinegun emplacement built into the top of the wall at its left. There is a guardhouse inside the gate manned by our marines, and another outside manned by a platoon of San Carlo national guards. I am informed that the latter are still in place.

Inside the compound we number forty-two of whom twenty-seven are Americans, including seven women. Momentarily I wish that I had given the repatriation order yesterday. I am worried about the women. Apart from the crisis team the rest of the embassy staff and dependents are gathered in the cafeteria. I order mattresses and blankets to be sent there.

Are we in immediate danger? I think not. Although the telephone system has now broken down we are getting continuous reports by radio. The British embassy which is close to the police barracks reports that resistance there is dwindling. Major Anderson radios that fighting around the presidential palace is fierce, with many casualties, and that the Chamarristas appear to have the upper hand. He doubts whether Vargas and his crowd will survive the night. He expects the siege to be over by dawn, and other pockets of resistance in the city to die out a few hours later.

I review the possibilities. General Cruz and his brigade can't play any part in the fighting for several days. By that time the city will be in the hands of the combined forces of Lacay's brigade and the Chamarristas, and he will have no chance against them unless he has the active support of American troops. So now I have two paramount problems: what advice to give Washington as to active American involvement, and what to do in the event of violence against the embassy compound.

The second problem is more immediate. I discuss it with Sumner, Gage and "Gunny" Cowder. We agree that it is unlikely any coordinated attack will be made on the compound. The Chamarristas are the most extreme of all Central and South American terrorists but once they see the prospect of power they will not wish to totally alienate the gringos. They will go through the motions of seeking détente. The only danger is posed by undisciplined units who, in the heat of the moment, may act stupidly.

Both Gage and Cowder see no difficulty in holding off such units, particularly as they will only have light weapons. Sumner considers any threat to the embassy as unlikely. Bermudez, the Chamarristas' leader, will be wary of direct American intervention and will risk nothing to precipitate it.

Anyway, I decide to check our defences and, with Gage and Cowder, I make the rounds. I am comforted. I then look in on the cafeteria and am reminded of pictures of the wartime blitz in London. Mattresses and blankets are laid out at one end of the room. Wives and secretaries are checking through the food supplies. I gather them around and say a few words.

"You know that the city has been overrun by terrorists with the collaboration of certain units of the national guard. I perceive no immediate danger. Our lives will be disrupted for a time until the situation clarifies. Meanwhile I want you to remain calm and do all you can to help."

There are murmurs of assent and I continue, "I'd be glad if someone would take charge here." The political counsellor's wife, a small, birdlike woman, nods her head vigorously.

Satisfied, I leave and walk across the compound to the residence. Out of the air-conditioning it's moist and hot. There's only the occasional sound of gunfire. I am sweating slightly and resolve to take a quick shower and change my shirt. There is a faint paling of the eastern sky. It will be dawn over Cuba. Bitterly, I visualize the celebrations over there.

Half an hour later, back in the tank, we all listen to the radio. Bermudez, on the air live now, proclaims the revolution victorious. He has a highpitched educated voice. I have seen photographs of him. Small and thin with a black moustache and thick-lensed glasses. Only twenty-eight years old, but looking older. He announces the death of the dictator Vargas and the arrest of dozens of henchmen. They are to be tried by people's courts. He orders the immediate surrender of all other Vargas functionaries. He praises General Lacay and all "loyal" elements of the national guard who forthwith are joined as brothers with the Chamarristas in an "Army of National Liberation" which will crush all reactionary elements!

I've heard all this before. He's just dusted off Castro's old manuals.

He praises and thanks the Cubans for their aid. Curiously he makes no mention of the United States. No message of hate. Maybe he will be conciliatory.

A long telexed message comes in from Washington, obviously drafted by an idiot. There are scores of questions demanding immediate answers. Most of them are inane such as: "Give Sit. Rep. morale and sentiments local population." What am I supposed to do? Take a clipboard and wander around the city asking everybody how they're feeling?

I do the rounds again. There is a strange gaiety in the compound. Early fears have been transformed into the excitement of anticipation. But the mood changes abruptly when lookouts report the approach of a convoy of five trucks, heading towards the compound down Avenida Santanda.

From the tank we can watch on television monitors as they pull up at the main gate. The trucks are full of national guardsmen. A colonel climbs down from the cab of the front truck. Sumner recognizes him as an aide to General Lacay. He approaches the gate and speaks into the intercom requesting to be allowed into the compound. Sumner looks at me for an order. I nod and he instructs the marine guard to open the small door let into the gate. Together with Gage, Sumner and I walk out to meet him.

It is barely dawn, but the colonel wears very dark sunglasses. He greets Sumner, then turns to me and says, "Excellency, I am sent by the revolutionary council to assure you of the safety of the American presence in San Carlo."

Stiffly I reply, "Inform General Lacay that I hold him personally responsible for this outrage."

The colonel nods vigorously. "Of course, Excellency. That is why I am here—sent personally by General Lacay. The situation at the moment is ... well, fluid. There is some indiscipline among the Chamarristas. They are vengeful. General Lacay needs time to impose order. Meanwhile all Americans—including some of your own staff who were at a party up the coast—are being collected by our own units and guarded by a large contingent of disciplined national guards."

"Why were they not brought here?"

He is carrying an ebony swagger stick which he taps against the top of his polished boot.

"The route was dangerous ... and General Lacay is worried about security here."

Sumner interjects. "Why? We are well defended. And Chamarristas only have light weapons."

The colonel taps his boot in agitation.

"No. They took the presidential guard armoury. They have mortars, field guns and anti-tank rockets."

Sumner's face turns sombre. He is about to say something when I cut in. I don't like being a bystander to this conversation. "Can't Lacay disarm them?"

"Not yet, Excellency. There must be much discussion first with Bermudez and the other Chamarrista leaders. Meanwhile there is danger to all Americans. You are, not unnaturally, hated by the Chamarristas. They blame you for the Vargas dynasty. General Lacay is concerned. He has sent me with a hundred of our guard to protect the embassy—until arrangements can be made for repatriation."

"Very kind," I comment sarcastically. "You can deploy them around the outside of the walls."

He shakes his head. "Excuse me, Excellency. They must be inside the compound. Only then can we be sure the Chamarristas will not molest you."

Sumner's reply is emphatic. "No way, Colonel. They stay outside."

At that moment there is a distant thump. Sumner's head jerks in its direction, then he looks up at the gunny on the roof of the guardhouse who has binoculars to his eyes.

Sumner is about to call when there is the crump of a loud explosion. I feel a slight pressure in my ears.

"Mortar!" the gunny shouts down. " 'Bout three hundred yards away over Santanda. Came from somewhere near the stadium."

I say quietly to Gage, "Get moving, fast. Tell them to start burning documents immediately—and all the women are to go into the vault."

He runs off towards the chancery.

The colonel is very agitated. "Excellency! We must enter the compound. I urge you to lower your flag. It incenses them. We must replace it with ours."

The idea is repugnant and I dismiss it with an angry wave of my arm. There is another distant thump and we all turn. A few seconds later another explosion, louder and closer.

Laconically the gunny calls down, "Hundred yards. They're ranging in. You guys better take cover."

We move quickly into the guardhouse. The colonel has a grip on my arm now. I smell garlic as he says urgently, "Think of the others.

156

The women. Those fanatics have over a dozen mortars ... and rockets that will blow through your gates. Señor, if we run up our flag they will stop firing ... and Señor, if I order my men to defend the compound from outside I doubt they will do it. Sorry, Señor. I think they will not sacrifice their lives for Americans."

There's another explosion from the opposite direction. Grimly Sumner states, "We're bracketed. They have the range and can lob them right in."

I try to keep my face calm. Furious at myself for having to do it, I decide to compromise. Sumner is watching me urgently. The colonel is tapping his boot again with the stick. I wish I could penetrate those glasses and see into his eyes.

Formally I say, "Very well, Colonel. Your men may enter the compound. I will lower the American flag, as you request, but will permit no other flag to be raised in its place. I suggest you send an officer to tell those imbeciles out there to stop firing, or face the consequences from my government. ... Sumner, go and see to the disposition of his men!"

Sumner and the colonel file quickly out of the guardhouse. I remain, wanting to be alone for a moment, probing my decision. I hear the rumble of the huge gates and the revving of engines. I walk to the door and watch as the trucks move into the compound. Two of our security guards start pulling the gates shut behind the vehicles. The colonel is talking to Sumner and the gunny. They look surprised as he turns and walks briskly out through the narrowing gap between the gates. Puzzled I watch the guardsmen pour out of the trucks. They are all armed with submachine guns. There have been no more explosions.

Suddenly, like the end of a losing chess game, the moves click in my head. The guardsmen are scattering in disciplined groups. They're carrying Russian submachine guns. San Carlo's national guards are supplied with US M3s.

There were only three mortar rounds. The colonel had known there would be no more. They were a mere persuasion to his argument. The gunny and Sumner are looking around them in bewilderment.

I have been tricked. I feel neither panic nor anger, but deep humiliation. I watch the act played out.

Sumner and the gunny already face a circle of guns. Sumner is watching me in consternation. I look up and see the colonel's guardsmen already on the roofs of the residence and chancery covering our machinegun emplacements.

157

Suddenly there is a noise at the gates. Half a dozen of our security guards are frantically pushing them open. An order is shouted in Spanish, bullets clang off steel, and our guards are tossed about screaming.

Sumner and the gunny have thrown themselves to the ground. They are still circled by guns. There is silence. I look back at the gates. Six bodies: corpses twisted on the concrete.

In all my long life I have never seen a corpse. Someone is shouting, and I wrench my gaze away. It's the gunny lying on his side, one hand on the butt of his holster pistol, his face a mixture of fear and something else ... yes, determination. He is looking at me.

"Sir! Do we fight?"

In an instant I scream back. *"No!"*

I have not even thought. No considerations, no process of logic enters my head. The chess game is lost—why smash up the pieces?

A man approaches the guardhouse. On his shoulders are the bars of a lieutenant. He is very tall and wide with a boxer's face. His black hair is crew cut—very rare for a Central American. He loosely carries a submachine gun in his left hand. He is grinning widely.

"Excellency." He taints the title with insolence. "Tell your marines and any others to lay down their weapons or they will die."

My frustration is gone. I only feel icy rage.

"Are you in charge of these killers?"

He nods equably.

"Then I protest in the name of my government and all humanity and..."

"Shut your mouth, pig!" His grin is gone. He raises the gun and points it at me. As I look at the tiny black hole he says, "Give the order, or I fire. How I would love to shoot you, honourable Excellency!"

He will not shoot. I know it. I think I know it. Alive, I am a hostage. Dead, I am retribution for this scum and all the rest. But he will shoot others. I look at Sumner. He is sitting on the concrete, his arms around his knees watching me forlornly. I nod at him. "Colonel, go with the gunny and tell them to lay down their weapons."

He and the gunny scramble to their feet and, still surrounded, move off towards the chancery. I am praying that the incinerators have done the job. That all the documents are ashes. I have to keep the imbecile in front of me talking.

"Who are you?"

He grins again, and bows elaborately. "Carlos Fombona."

I recognize the name. During the past week and in pre-arrival briefings I have seen it often in reports. He is a lieutenant to Bermudez. Known for cruelty.

His smile widens as he lowers his gun to the ground. Still grinning he unzips his combat blouse and shrugs it off. Underneath he wears a white T-shirt emblazoned across the front, like a student's, with a red, jagged bolt of lightning. Underneath is a portrait of Lenin. He unzips his camouflage trousers and steps out of them, revealing a pair of faded student's jeans. He shouts an order and I look around as other guardsmen in the compound discard their uniforms. They all wear T-shirts covered with Marxist slogans.

Fombona picks up his gun and walks forward. There is pleasure in his eyes as he says, "I have nothing to do with Bermudez or any of them. Me and my friends here are acting alone. We are..." a dramatic pause "...militant students!"

He leans forward, his face inches away. "Militant students of the revolution."

I laugh derisively. "Sure. Forget the charade. Within hours you and your crowd will be thrown out. You think my government will stand by after this outrage? You think we've learned nothing?"

He shrugs. "We also have learned."

He turns and shouts an order and some of the "students" jump into a truck. They reappear carrying several packages. One of them comes over to us and gives Fombona what resembles a heavy canvas flak jacket. A thin black wire trails from it to a small plastic box. Fombona hefts it with satisfaction. "Put this on."

I shake my head.

"Put it on, pig, or I'll call some of my men to force you."

There is no doubt he will, so I turn and he slips it onto my arms and up over my shoulders. It is heavy and smells musty.

There are several canvas straps hanging on each side of the front. Carefully he ties them, pulling the jacket tight around me.

"Don't worry, Excellency, soon you will get used to it. You will be wearing it night and day."

He moves back trailing the black cord and hands the small box to the student. The wire is about five yards long. Fombona points at the jacket and says, "That garment is packed with three kilos of plastic explosive. The wire is connected to a detonator. You will wear it all the time. Awake, asleep—every American pig in this compound will be wearing one." He points at the student. "Pedro will always be by your side. At the first sign of a rescue attempt Pedro will turn that button."

The man is crazy! We are twenty-seven. If they blow us up,

159

twenty-seven students go with them. Acidly and with pleasure I point this out. His face is very serious. He nods solemnly.

"Pedro is prepared to die for the revolution. So are the twenty-six others. They volunteered. Hundreds volunteered. What is twenty-seven when thousands have died already?"

I look at Pedro. Young, thin ... almost emaciated. He holds the little box in his hand as though it is sacred. I believe it. He will die. The jacket feels like lead. I can imagine watching him as he turns the button. Imagine the flash of extinction.

Fombona is studying my face. He reads the belief in it and nods in satisfaction.

"And now, Excellency, we have to make sure that the chief pig in his White House pigsty understands that too. The photographers will be here tomorrow. Soon you will be famous. Your photograph and your lovely new jacket and your faithful attendant will be in all the newspapers. You will be the most famous pig in the world."

DAY ONE

JASON PEABODY. *San Carlo.*

The photographers have come and gone. Now Fombona has brought me to the guardhouse. I'm standing in the doorway of the main office, and for a moment I hesitate.

There's a hippy in the room. I look around. No one else. He slouches in a chair behind the desk, one leg up on an arm rest, swinging. He is wearing frayed jeans and a black T-shirt. His hair, reddish blond and curling slightly, falls almost to his shoulders. There is a newspaper on the desk in front of him and a stack of files with black covers. The clod Fombona pushes me from behind and I stumble into the room. I feel a jerk on the wire and then the little suicide guard is beside me.

The hippy studies me, then says to Fombona in Spanish, "Take that jacket off him and get rid of the kid."

Fombona moves past me with his submachine gun. I have never seen him without it. He is shaking his head. "No. He wears it every second."

The hippy sighs, swings his leg to the floor, stands up and stretches languorously; then he moves around the desk towards me. He's wearing cowboy boots! I'm tired. I hardly slept at all last night. Is all this a fantasy?

160

He starts to untie the thongs holding on my jacket. I glance at Fombona. He is watching in astonishment.

He snarls, "Leave him alone. You can talk to him. Nothing else!"

Oblivious to Fombona the hippy continues unlacing the thongs. Fombona's face tightens in rage. I watch him as he raises the submachine gun and with great deliberation aims it straight at the hippy's back.

The hippy smiles and then astonishes me. In perfect, British accented English he says conversationally, "Spare the rod and spoil the child. The trouble with all students, militant or otherwise, is an occupational lack of discipline."

It must be a fantasy! The hippy reaches forward with both hands. I feel the weight of the jacket being lifted from my shoulders. I put my arms back and it slides down. The hippy hands it to the kid, pats him on the shoulder, and pushes him gently out of the door. Then without even glancing at Fombona, he walks briskly back to the desk, his boots clomping on the concrete floor.

Fombona is quivering with rage. He swings the muzzle of his gun to cover the hippy and moves forward two paces. The hippy appears to be reading the newspaper. When he looks up it is directly at me. He points a finger at the chair opposite.

"Excellency, kindly sit down. We have much to discuss and our time may be limited."

There is a silence. At any second Fombona will fire. I am certain. I look into the hippy's eyes, trying to detect any sign of fear. There is absolutely none. Abruptly I know that this man's life is in my hands. I walk forward slowly but positively, past the gun barrel. I have the sensation of moving over ice. I sit down. The chair squeaks—shrieks in my ears. The hippy smiles and says over my shoulder to Fombona, "Comrade, on that uncomfortable journey in your sealed supply truck I noticed some bags of your wonderful San Carlo coffee. Please arrange to have two mugs sent over here ... very strong. And again in an hour."

He has gone too far. Yesterday I watched Fombona beat one of his own men half to death because of a minor infraction. Now I can imagine his finger tightening on the trigger. I have an ache in my back. I wish to move even slightly but I stay rigid. There is total silence.

Seconds pass. My nerves jangle at the scrape of a boot. There are rapid footsteps and a door slams. I will not show my relief. I cross my right leg over my left and adjust the crease of my trousers.

The hippy notes the action, smiles and says, "I have learned never

161

to argue with such people. Debate gives them a false sense of importance."

I am pleased. I have managed to control my trembling. Casually I say, "Had I not moved when I did he would have shot you."

"That's very probable."

I don't know how to answer that. He was close to death and knows it. I believe he may even be savouring it. The whole emotion is alien to me.

The silence grows while we study each other and then he says, "My name is Jorge Calderon." He says it as though I must know it. And with a terrible mental explosion I realize that I do know it. Has my face registered the shock? I pray not. I simply look at him. Then he shrugs, leans forward and says, "I'm from the—"

I cut him off. "—the Cuban Directorate of Intelligence. Jorge Calderon, rising star . . . one of Castro's whiz kids."

I've won a tiny victory. He smiles and leans back. As an expert on pre and post Castro Cuba I am very familiar with the top echelon of their government. Jorge Calderon, under thirty—he looks much older—one of the new generation of leaders brought in by Castro to regenerate his damned revolution. The man in front of me is both brilliant and dangerous. An intellectual revolutionary; the worst kind. His father was Spanish, a wealthy painter. His mother a Scotswoman. The father left Cuba shortly after the revolution. Mother and child stayed on. Calderon trained as a lawyer and went straight into intelligence, becoming a brilliant analyst and interrogator. . . . He sure as hell doesn't look it. He might have shambled off the campus at UCLA. What is he doing here?

He pushes the newspaper across. It's the *Herald Tribune* dated the previous day. I look down at my own face. I quickly read through the article. The militant students have set our ransom at two and a half billion dollars.

I look up. "They're crazy!"

"I agree." Calderon's face is serious.

"Does your presence here in San Carlo mean that your ever-meddling Cuban government is behind this demand?"

"No. My presence here has nothing to do with the Chamarrista revolution, nor with your embassy."

"What, then?"

He waves a hand dismissively. "We'll get to that." He points at the newspaper. "Two and a half billion dollars is not in fact unreasonable. Morally your government owes them money."

"That's ridiculous."

He prods at the article. "Over the past fifty years three US corporations, with the active aid of successive US governments have raped this country. Just as they have raped others in the region. If Universal Foods had paid a fair price for their half million acres of prime land, and if Andana and General Metals had paid normal royalties for their ores, then at least three billion dollars would have accrued to the State of San Carlo. Bermudez is being generous ... he's offering half a billion discount."

"I don't need a lesson in the history of Central America. Anyway Bermudez won't get a cent from my government."

"He doesn't expect to. At least, not directly."

"What do you mean?"

He grins. "Bermudez is a realist—and a Marxist. Even if he holds onto the country he's facing a disaster. It's bankrupt. It's over-populated, with one of the lowest per capita incomes in the world. Where will he get money? The World Bank? It's controlled by your government. So are most of the other international aid agencies. He has the example of Cuba and Nicaragua in front of him. Because of their ideologies they get nothing."

He's supposed to be brilliant but he talks rubbish. I'm unable to keep the derision from my voice. "Where *will* he get funds from then—Russia? He's crazy. So are you."

"I'm not. He might be. But he has a plan. Of course the militant students are a charade. Bermudez knows that their demand will never be paid. Meanwhile stalemate. The students have demonstrated what will happen to you and the other Americans in the compound if any rescue is attempted. By the way, one of your aircraft carriers, the *Nimitz*, is already sitting on the horizon. But it's a question of firepower being impotent."

He gives me comfort with this news. I say, "Maybe my president doesn't see it that way."

He runs a hand through his hair. "I hope for your sake he does. Anyway assume a stalemate. After a while Bermudez, through third parties, will offer a solution. He'll let it be known that the students will release the hostages if an international aid package of one billion dollars is put together, say over five years. Oh, the suggestion could come from anywhere, even the Red Cross. Obviously due to pride and politics the USA cannot be seen to contribute even a single cent; but these things can be arranged. It will contribute all or most of it."

Again he is waiting for me to comment. I am tempted but determined not to give one clue as to what I think. Instead, I say, "So what's all the talk about? I thought you had nothing to do with it."

"I don't. I'm just indulging myself in curiosity. I wish Bermudez well. And even if he made a mistake taking you people hostages, the mistake benefits Cuba."

He pushes the newspaper away and as he puts a black file in front of him, there is a knock at the door. He shouts, "Enter!" and as the door opens I smell the rich aroma of coffee. I recognize the young man who carries the tray. He is a Mestizo employed in the kitchen on menial tasks. He is nervous and avoids looking at me. After he leaves, Calderon pours the coffee. Without asking me he puts three lumps of sugar in my mug and a little milk.

"That's how you like it, I understand."

"How do you know?"

He sips at his coffee. "I've been finding out a lot about your personal habits."

"Why?"

"Because I'm going to be spending a lot of time with you."

"Why?"

He taps the file and smiles very pleasantly. "Excellency, you're going to tell me about Operation Cobra."

JORGE CALDERON. *San Carlo.*

It's going to take time. I hate this elegant, foppish man; sucking the blood of whole nations and peoples in the false name of democracy. I loathe him with his crisp suit, perfectly knotted tie and groomed hair. He'd been attached to the kid for three days but he looks as though he's just walked out of a barber's shop. It's hot in there and he sits without a glimmer of sweat. He was probably terrified during the business with Fombona but he concealed it. Now when I mention Operation Cobra he merely looks politely puzzled. He's very good. I have to be careful and very cautious; interrogation is seduction, and like seduction is an art form. The subject must be prepared with great patience. I recall the Russian instructor Kubalov. All that rubbish with drugs. The subject gets turned into a babbling monkey and all you get is monkey chatter. It's an insult to the art. Interrogation is a long fencing match. Probing for an opening, and recognizing it when it comes. Above all, you must *know* the subject, his mental strengths and weaknesses, his fears and desires and conceits. You must know him better than your mother or child or lover. Your knowledge becomes his weakness, and you must be the strength he is drawn to. When the subject finally talks he should weep with relief.

From our intelligence sources we know that the Americans have launched an operation against Castro, codenamed "Cobra". After so many operations and codenames, they begin to lose imagination. Fidel knows that two of our top people have collaborated with the CIA. He has ordered me to find out who the traitors are.

From this Peabody I need only one name. In a conspiracy one name leads to the others. He knows the names because he advised on the operation before he was posted to San Carlo, but he will be difficult. In the file in front of me is a single positive weapon. It is the weapon to break him but it must be used at precisely the right moment. Too early and the wound will not be severe enough. Too late and it could be fatal.

I watch his face. Like his clothes it is all in order. Smooth cheeks, neat eyebrows, brown eyes with identical crease lines at each outer corner. A perfectly straight long nose that certainly has never been broken. Thin lips, parted now, showing very white, even teeth. A wide, cleft jaw. His dark hair is short, flecked with grey and carefully combed straight back. He is sixty-three but looks ten years younger. He would be attractive to women. He has the arrogance of intellect and the dignity of the position it has given him in life. If I undermine the dignity, the arrogance will collapse.

But with this man it would be fatal to rush. I give myself twenty days. I would like more and maybe I will get it. Maybe I will get less but I will pace myself, and Peabody, for twenty days.

I open the file in front of me and say, "We are both intelligent men. I know a lot about you and assume you know about me. I have an advantage. I've been studying your file for many days now."

Peabody shrugs, reaches for his cup, and takes a delicate sip. I harden my voice. "Operation Cobra is yet another attempt by your government to de-stabilize mine. Operations mounted against us by the CIA now number in the twenties. They have all failed and so will this." I tap the file emphatically. "You were the top expert on Cuba. You were certainly consulted about this operation."

In a bored voice he says, "I'm a foreign service officer. I have nothing to do with the CIA."

I turn two pages of the file. "In the past three months you attended at least a dozen meetings at Langley. Peabody, you people underestimate us. I don't mind telling you that eighty per cent of our budget is devoted to our USA department. In addition the KGB give us a vast amount of information that relates to Cuba. I know exactly what your role has been over the past months and your connection with the CIA and Operation Cobra. There is no point denying it!"

165

Good. I've made him angry. He stands and leans over the desk, thin lips compressed. He points a finger at my face.

"Deny? Why should I deny or confirm anything to you? By international law this compound is sovereign territory of the United States of America. You are guilty of an invasion of US territory. If you have the impertinence to try to interrogate me, Calderon, you will get nowhere. The only thing I have to say to you, as a Cuban official, is to protest at your presence here."

He sits down and looks past me at a spot on the wall above my head. His mouth is set in a straight line. Good. The interrogation has started well. He is addressing me by name. He has taken the first rung up the ladder. He thinks he will go no further. Now is the time to start him up the next few rungs.

There's an inner room within the main office and I stand up and walk over to it. I open the door. There are two high windows with bars on them, and four bunks. It was obviously built to act as a detention room if necessary. I turn; he is watching me intently.

I say, "You will not have to wear that explosive jacket again. You will be separated from the others and will live in here." I indicate the empty room. Did I see a flash of relief in his eyes? If so, it was not about the jacket. The other hostages are being held in two big rooms in the chancery; men in one, women in the other. Peabody is a private man. The thought of being alone pleases him. He will shortly be less pleased.

"Peabody, I'm going to come back in a couple of days. In the meantime I'm going to give orders to Fombona. The bunks will be cleared out of the room and a straw palliasse put on the floor. A bucket will be provided. There will be another bucket with water to drink from and for washing . . . but no soap. You will get one meal a day—thin soup, rice, beans, plantain, cabbage and so on. Occasionally some stewed meat or fish."

His face is no longer impassive. "You expect me to live like that?"

"Yes, Peabody. Thanks to people like you who put people like Vargas into power and keep them there, millions of campesinos in this country and in Latin America live exactly like that. They sleep on dirt floors, defecate in buckets, drink only water and eat the sort of food you'll be eating." I continue. "You are to take off your clothes and leave them on the desk. You may keep your underpants on. I suggest you do that as soon as I leave. Fombona will have orders to forcibly take them off if you are still wearing them when he arrives. That would be undignified. He would enjoy it."

I cross the room to the outer door, open it, turn back and say,

"When I come back we'll talk about Operation Cobra and the traitors in my country. You will tell me about them. Be sure of it. One way or another."

He takes a step back, coming up against the desk. "You would torture me . . . ?"

I shake my head. "No, Peabody. I never use torture. It's usually counterproductive. Also no drugs. Drink your water and eat your food without fear."

He thrusts an arm towards the inner room. "Forcing a man to live like that is a form of torture!"

I laugh. "Peabody, even being in love is torture . . . you should know that."

DAY THREE

Jason Peabody. *San Carlo.*

My rage has subsided. It has taken a full day and night. During that time the rage has been refined into hatred. Rage is meaningless. Hatred is wonderfully logical.

I read him easily. I am not a half-educated reactionary, or a dimwitted agent. I can control my mind and he will not tamper with it. He expects to take away my dignity. He is a devil in his perception, for it is my solitary weakness. It's why the rage consumed me. Not discomfort, but the loss of dignity. Standing in my shorts, thin and almost naked, while that animal Fombona sneered and laughed. I have always been conscious—over-conscious—of my thin legs. Ever since childhood.

It's true I have not made friends easily. Scarcely at all. I don't know why. It was always so. Solitary people often take solace in style and order. He has seen that already. So he tries to pry me away from my dignity. But he miscalculated. A man will endure much if sustained by hatred.

He does not know, cannot know, how intensely I hate him and the man and the system that sent him. He will not find me pleading for comfort. I pray this will end; but he will never know it.

I have eaten what they call food. Logic forced me to eat it and I did so. I need physical strength, and the hatred helped me force it down and keep it there. Later I felt a twisting in my bowels, then more indignity at the bucket. He has thought about all of this.

What did he mean, "Being in love is torture . . . you know that . . . ?"

167

Is it in that file...? All those years ago? I doubt it. I have never spoken about it. Even now it is painful to remember.

I am sitting on the straw palliasse with my legs drawn up under my chin. I think about Operation Cobra. Of course I know all about it. I virtually planned the whole thing. Calderon is right. It's the most significant move against the Castro regime since the Bay of Pigs. In October Castro will go to Moscow for the big anniversary celebration, and then the bastard will find out what it's like to be on the wrong end of a coup d'état. The thought gives me immense pleasure.

I'll be able to return to Cuba again. I can never think of that island without a picture of her coming to my mind. Strangely, in recent years the picture has changed in subtle ways, some of her features becoming more distinct. Sometimes in dreams all I can see are her lips and eyes, as though all her other features have been burned away by a bright light. I wonder at the significance. It was the eyes that watched me, always strangely mournful; and the lips that used to touch me, always soft, even in passion. My memory moves back across two decades. The pain, never diminishing, spreads through me yet again. For me the gift of memory is nothing but a curse.

JORGE CALDERON. *San Carlo.*

Inez stands naked by the window and I change my mind again. It was not a mistake to bring her with me. We have made love. Is it that which draws me to her? Only the physical? I partly wish it were, for then I would be able to control my feelings, and her. But part of me, the darker part, knows that it is my lack of control over this woman that attracts and fascinates and draws me to the edge.

She turns and walks to the bathroom. Her walk is a strut, almost boyish, but the body is outrageously female; its curves a miasma distorting the eye. I told her that once and she asked me what the word meant and laughed when I told her. "A vapour rising from a marsh, corrupting the air of the mind." Set on a long neck her face appears innocent in its dark beauty. She always holds her head proudly high.

I met her three months ago during an interrogation. Her husband of two years was a subversive. We had turned him and a month afterwards he was found hanging by his neck from electric cord from his kitchen ceiling. I suspected foul play and Inez was the first I interrogated. My first question was whether she knew of any reason why he might have killed himself? Her answer was direct and devastating.

"Certainly. I left him for his friend. He couldn't exist without me. He was boring."

His friend turned out to be also boring but he did not kill himself when she moved in with me a few weeks later.

After a minute she comes out of the bathroom carrying a mirror. She stretches out on her back at the foot of the bed, across my legs. I get a vivid impression of our situation. She is a dangerous animal in a circus cage ... a tiger. I am the trainer, the showman who dares to enter the cage without even a whip or a chair. He controls the beast with only his personality. That control is balanced on the edge of the sharpest mental blade. One sign of weakness and the balance is tilted.

The bedside telephone rings. It is one of Bermudez's aides. Excitedly he tells me that the Americans have just announced a total sea and air blockade against San Carlo, to come into force at dawn. Any ship crossing a three-mile coastal limit will be sunk; any aircraft approaching to within ten miles of San Carlo airspace will be shot down by fighters from the aircraft carrier *Nimitz*. There is a plane leaving for Cuba in an hour. Do I want seats? I decline and hang up. As I expected, the Americans have reacted swiftly. They will not allow a military buildup in San Carlo. I look at my watch: 7:30 pm. The supply truck which takes me into the compound leaves in half an hour. I had meant to leave Peabody languishing for another day, but now I may have less time than I expected to extract those names from him. I pull my feet out from under Inez, scramble out of bed, and start dressing.

Petulantly she asks, "Where are you going?"

"The compound. I'll have to stay there till morning."

"What about me?"

I gesture at the television. "There'll be some video films on. Order a meal from room service."

She is sitting up on the bed looking hostile. "Maybe I'll go out somewhere to eat."

"No. The streets are still dangerous. Eat in the hotel ... or go to the airport. There's a plane to Managua in an hour. If you want I'll fix you a seat on it. There won't be any more for some time."

She is silent, considering it. Do I want her to go?

I finish dressing and pick up the canvas bag holding my files. At the door I turn to look at her. She is kneeling now, looking at her face in the mirror.

I open the door and she says, "Leave me some money."

"Why? You can sign for anything."

She looks up at me. We are in the cage. Very quietly she says, "I may decide to pay the waiter in kind."

She is probing for a weakness. Casually I reply, "Money is short."

I close the door behind me. Five paces down the corridor I hear a splintering crash as something hits the door; presumably the mirror. The animal is still in the cage.

COLONEL SLOCUM. *Washington, USA.*

I, Silas Slocum, have been in the US army for twenty-eight years and nothing like this ever happened to me. I'm at Anacosta, and there's a limousine waiting at the foot of the helicopter steps with a smart airforce captain standing alongside. As I reach the bottom he salutes crisply and opens a rear door. I'm puzzled as all hell, but I duck into the limo, the door clunks shut and we glide away. There's a guy in a dark suit sitting next to me.

He holds out a hand. "Good to see you again, Colonel."

I get clobbered by yet another shock. I'm looking at Mike Komlosy, national security counsellor to the president. But what's he talking about? He's never seen my face before.

"Mr. Komlosy, I know who you are. I've seen you on TV and in the papers. But I never met you."

"Sure you did. April 25th, 1980. A bar in Raleigh, North Carolina, the night after the hostage rescue failure in Iran. You were drunk. You talked a lot."

I remember hazily. I'd got drunk out of frustration. There was this bearded guy sitting at the bar next to me, and I'd sounded off. "You had a beard?"

"Yes. I was in Raleigh doing advance work for the election. You'd come out of Fort Bragg military academy and you talked for about two hours. Colonel, a lot of it made sense to me. It stuck in my mind. So did your name. For a career army officer you kinda speak your mind.... Anyway, I soon forgot all about you ... until around midnight last night."

"How so?"

"San Carlo."

Ding dong! The bells ring. For six days now I've followed the news about San Carlo and just before I left Bragg I heard the news of the blockade. It was a good move. "You're gonna get the embassy people out?" I ask.

Komlosy sighs. "It's a major option. But there are problems."

He reaches into his pocket for a packet of cigarettes and offers me

170

one. I shake my head. He lights up and blows smoke against the glass partition at the back of the driver's head.

"Colonel, last night the chairman of the joint chiefs of staff briefed the president and the National Security Council on a possible plan to rescue the hostages. As I listened I kept thinking about your words, your ideas, all those years ago. Now, I'm a lawyer by training, and not really competent to comment on the plan, but it seemed to me that, like the Iranian operation, it was ingenious but over-complicated."

I can't help it. I laugh. "I'll bet. If the Joint Special Operations Agency planned it, then the Normandy landings were a beach party in comparison. But what am I here for?"

He blows more smoke, then impatiently mashes the cigarette out. "After the briefing the president asked his military aides what they thought. They were all enthusiastic."

"Sure they were! They're not about to criticize the chairman of the joint chiefs."

"Exactly. Well, I persuaded the president that we should have another opinion ... a maverick opinion."

"Aha ... so *that's* what I'm here for."

"Exactly."

The idea warms me. "Do I get to meet the president?"

"I doubt it. The briefing was taped and recorded. You'll watch it, think about it and then make your comments to me."

I'm disappointed. "Then I go back to Fort Bragg?"

"We'll see."

We are turning into the White House.

The gate is heavily guarded. One of the men peers through the window at Komlosy, nods respectfully, and waves the driver on. We move slowly to an entrance that's covered by a canopy like a door to a fancy restaurant. Inside there's another secret service guy sitting at a desk. He throws a semi-military salute.

Komlosy nods vaguely and walks on. I follow, surprised by the lack of formality. He stops at a door with a cipher-lock on it, and twists the dial. There's a click, and he pushes the door open. I follow him into an office. Secretaries at typewriters, a guy talking on a telephone. We pass through it into another office, this one equipped with word processors and a girl working a Xerox machine.

Komlosy says to her, "Hi, Gail. Ask Rogers to come into the sit. room, will you?"

Then we go through another door and we're inside. This small, cramped room is the nerve centre of the White House; of the whole damned country! There's a polished wooden table with a dozen chairs around it. One wall is covered by large television screens. There are several telephone consoles and there's a large map of the world on the other side of the room.

I hear a knock on the door and a small man comes in. He wears thick frameless glasses and a rumpled suit. Komlosy introduces him. "Ken Rogers. One of my staffers. He'll work the equipment. Ken, this is Colonel Slocum."

We shake hands. Komlosy looks at his watch. "The briefing lasts about forty minutes, after that I'll see you in my office."

He goes out. Rogers indicates a chair at the head of the table. There's a pad of lined yellow paper and some ballpoints in a silver mug. Also a flask of water and a glass. I sit down as he walks to the television console, pushes a button, then leaves.

The figure of a uniformed general appears on the screen. Behind him, to the left, is a diagram headed "Embassy Compound". To his right a large scale map of San Carlo. He is one handsome guy. Square face; greying, tailored hair; thrusting jaw, his voice a blend of honey and cut glass. For ten minutes I'm mesmerized by it. Then, as the individual words penetrate, my toes begin to curl. After thirty minutes I have a pain in my guts. After forty minutes I've a pain in the brain.

The briefing ends and I gaze down at the yellow pad. I haven't taken a single note. I look up at the blank screens and imagine the president and his advisers sitting at this table listening to what I've just heard. I stand up and start to pace. I try to wipe my brain clean. I glance at the map on the wall. San Carlo is so small they had to print the name out into the Caribbean.

An idea comes to me. Not in a logical way. It just appears in my head and washes away the last of the confusion. But who's going to buy it? The president will listen only to his generals ... unless ...

Rogers opens the door and silently taps his watch. I follow him through into Komlosy's office. He is slouched back in his chair, behind a vast desk, a telephone in one hand and a cigarette in the other. He waves at a chair, replaces the receiver and grinds his cigarette out into a stub-filled ashtray.

"What do you think?"

"It won't work."

He runs a hand through his hair. He looks close to exhaustion. "Why not?"

"That plan has less than a thirty-per-cent chance of success. I can give you a dozen detailed reasons why."

"And in the few minutes since you watched that briefing you've formed a totally different plan?"

"You got it."

"Don't be flippant, Colonel."

I stand up. "Mr. Komlosy, sir. You may as well have it straight. You watched that briefing last night with the president and all the brass. On the surface it's damned impressive—to a civilian. But the bottom line is really whether you want to get those hostages out alive or in body bags."

He lights another cigarette, staring at me.

I stare back. "If you care ... get me in to see the president."

I expect scorn. I get a contemplative look. "And then?"

"And then I can persuade him that if he follows the plan his generals have drawn up, there's a seventy-per-cent chance those hostages are going to die. You personally can't tell him that. Admit it!"

I am angry and I guess it shows. Komlosy is looking up at me, tapping his nails on the polished desk. He asks, "And *you* can tell him?"

"Damn right. I'm a soldier. He's my commander in chief. It's my duty to tell him. You brought me here—so let me talk to my president!"

He's looking past me now. He's really considering it. Slowly, so as not to interrupt his thoughts, I sit down again. In spite of his exhaustion this man gives off all the vibes of power. I guess there's only a one in ten chance, but it was worth a shot.

He asks, "Colonel, that plan is wrong for all the reasons you talked about in Raleigh?"

"And more."

He sighs. "OK, Colonel, I'll give it a try." He stands up. "Wait here. Don't get your hopes up."

He goes out. I get up and start to prowl around. It's a plush office; real leather chairs and the picture on the walls are so awful they must be expensive.

The door opens and a young woman comes in carrying a tray. She gives me one of those smiles they paint on Barbie dolls. She puts the tray on the table and I walk over and sit down. She leans over, picks up the jug and pours. The jug bears the presidential seal.

"Cream? Sugar?"

"No thanks, just as black as my face, lady."

She laughs nervously and backs off towards the door. "Call me if there's anything else."

"Sure thing."

The coffee's good. I drain the cup and pour another, then put my mind to work. If the chance comes I must be ready.

Twenty minutes later Rogers is at the door crooking a finger. The chance has come.

He walks with an important spring-heeled step, up some stairs and along a couple of corridors. We come to a large wooden door. There's a secret service type outside. He opens it. Rogers murmurs "Good luck," and turns away. I go in to find Komlosy standing alone in a small room. His voice sounds loud in the hushed atmosphere.

"Colonel, we're going in to see the president now. Tonight is a rare chance for him to have dinner alone with the first lady, so try to keep it brief."

I nod and he turns to a door and opens it. We go through. It's true. It is oval. Large, but kind of intimate.

My attention is immediately riveted on the man sitting at a desk in front of a tall window. There's a dark blue flag behind his shoulder. Komlosy coughs. "Colonel Slocum, Mr. President."

I snap out a crisp salute and see the brief impact of shock on the president's face. I realize that he has not been told that I'm black. Was it an oversight on Komlosy's part, or deliberate?

The president recovers quickly, rises, and comes round the desk. His smile is genuine as he holds out his hand. His grip is firm. He puts his other hand on my shoulder and urges me towards a group of low chairs. We sit down. Komlosy has pulled a chair up and is sitting off to my left. I'm excited but not nervous. The president is looking at the slab of medals on my chest.

He says, "Colonel Slocum, your many decorations tell me that you have long been a courageous defender of our country. Now, Mike here tells me that you're worried about some aspects of the San Carlo rescue plan. Tell me about that."

I decided that I may as well start as I mean to go on. I look the president in the eye. "Sir, Mr. Komlosy asked me to keep this brief because you're shortly going to have dinner. Sir, either dinner gets cold or you only get to hear part of what I need to say."

I slid a glance at Komlosy. He's looking unhappy. The president glances at his watch, purses his lips and gives me a long, level stare. Finally he says, "Colonel Slocum, if I believe that what you're telling me is important, then my dinner can wait."

First hurdle over. I take a deep breath.

"Sir, I have been a soldier for twenty-eight years. The American soldier, airman and sailor is as fine as any in the world and better

174

than most. And yet, in the past thirty-five years our country has had far too many military failures. Take Grenada for example. Grenada was a mess."

"What was wrong with Grenada?" The president is watching me intently now.

"Well, sir, we used a steamroller to crush a walnut. And in the process the roller got knocked about a bit."

"How so?"

"We took unnecessary casualties. For one thing, all the services wanted in on the act. We should have done it with a thousand paratroopers. We had so many men running around they were in danger of colliding with each other. Ostensibly we went in to protect the lives of our medical students. It took us forty-eight hours to secure them. It should have taken two. The only smart idea the generals had was to keep the media out. They saved themselves a scandal."

The president smiles slightly, reaches for the phone, and punches a button on the console.

"Julie, would you please tell my wife I'm going to be held up? No, I can't say for how long."

Then he gets up. He walks to a cabinet and opens it. Inside are glasses and bottles. Over his shoulder he says, "Colonel, I generally mix myself a martini at this time of the evening. Mike enjoys one. How about you?"

"Yes, sir. Thank you."

He mixes the drinks carefully. Komlosy walks over and collects his. The president hands me a glass and perches on the edge of his desk.

I take a sip. It's dry enough to numb my tongue. "Great martini, sir."

He smiles. "Now, Colonel, I'm going to hear you out. Don't think I agree with everything you say, but tell me, briefly, why that so-called mess happened."

I martial my thoughts. "Sir, in one word . . . technology."

He is looking reflectively into his glass. I go on. "We rely too much on it, sir. Our top command neglect the simplest and most fundamental rule of war: battles are won by soldiers on the ground. We were beaten in Vietnam by an enemy comprised solely of infantry because we were blinded by computers, sensors, avionics, electronics and all the other tricks in the bag. The first and last rule for a commander is to get his men into contact with the enemy in the most efficient way. But our generals are trying to fight without contact. That can't be done unless you go nuclear."

He nods. "OK. Following that line, what do you think is wrong with the rescue plan?"

I drain my glass. "Well, sir, to be frank, it stinks...."

JASON PEABODY. *San Carlo.*

I hear a slight clatter and open my eyes. The cell is lit by a single unshaded bulb hanging from the centre of the ceiling. There are no shadows. No movement. But I heard a noise. I hold my breath and listen. There's a slight sniffling. Something catches my eye, hanging over the rim of the food bucket by the door. It twitches. The food bucket topples slowly onto its side and something slides out. I press myself back against the wall. It's a rat—black—about ten inches long. It moves, disappearing behind the bucket. I can feel pain and realize I'm clenching my fists so tight my nails are digging into my palms.

Keeping my eyes fixed on the bucket, I shout, "Guard!"

It comes out barely louder than a squeak. The bucket moves again and I push myself away into a corner. "Guard!" This time it's a scream. *"Guard!"*

I hear the sound of the outer door, then footsteps. It's an eternity, then the lock turns and the door opens. The guard is young; a round-faced teenager. He holds his submachine gun ready. He sees me crunched into the corner. I point at the bucket. The muzzle of his gun swings towards it.

The rat moves. It's hurtling across the floor towards me. I throw myself to one side, and through my fingers see the rat concertina itself into a tiny hole in the corner where I was standing.

The guard is laughing uproariously. My hands are wet from the sweat on my face. Horror is replaced by rage. I scream at him, "Shut your mouth!"

He looks at my face and whatever he sees there stills his laughter. He covers me with the gun and moves back a step. Then with a sneer says, "Frightened by a little rat? Don't worry, Excellency, you are too skinny. You won't make him a good dinner."

I'm still thinking of a retort as he goes out chuckling and the key scrapes in the lock.

I feel crushingly alone. His footsteps recede and the outer door closes. I look quickly at the hole in the corner. Is there a snout there? No. I check the rest of the room. There are two other holes, a bit smaller but I have to block them. With what?

A brief inventory. Apart from my shorts there is nothing, and they

176

won't block all three holes. Besides, they are the last of my dignity. I look down at the palliasse. Straw and sackcloth. It's all I have. I squat down and start tearing the palliasse apart. I don't think about my future sleep; with those holes unblocked there will be no sleep. I tear three strips of sackcloth and roll them tightly round bundles of straw. I unpick the crude stitching and bind the bundles tight. It takes me half an hour to get the sizes right and the holes firmly plugged. As I force the last one in I am pervaded by a sense of relief. I loathe rats.

I kick the remains of the palliasse back against a wall and sit down. I wonder how long it will take a rat to chew through a plug of straw and sackcloth. A week? A day? An hour?

When will Calderon come?

DAY FOUR

Jorge Calderon. *San Carlo.*

I climb out of the back of the supply truck. Fombona saunters up with a young guard. They tell me about Peabody and the rat. Fombona says, "He's terrified. Turn out that light and put a dozen rats in with him—he'll babble in minutes."

This is an interesting development and it could be crucial to the next stage. I give Fombona his orders. For a moment he's dumbfounded, then he spits on the ground in disgust.

"You're wasting your time. Give me a few hours with him and he'll be singing."

"Do what you're told. You know your orders."

There is a hesitation. This one is another beast in a cage. I look steadily into his eyes, and after a minute he drops his gaze and turns away with a curse.

I glance around the compound. Already the militant students are losing their attentiveness, groups of them playing cards as they smoke long cigars. Fombona is getting overconfident. I'll inform Bermudez.

I walk slowly towards the guardhouse. A group of prisoners is being led out from the chancery. Six women all attached to their suicide guards—girls who look to be in their late teens. Would they really blow themselves up? They look cheerful, talking loudly to each other as they walk. Their prisoners are morose and silent, looking at me with contempt.

Once in the guardhouse I don't immediately unlock the cell door. I put my files in a desk drawer and sit down, analysing my strategy. After five minutes three guards arrive. They are carrying buckets and brooms and a shovel. They are grumbling good naturedly. I unlock the cell door and open it. Peabody is standing in front of me, almost naked, a look of hatred on his face.

"I'm told there's a problem with rats here." I gesture at the guards. "They'll put rat poison in the holes, then plaster them up." I point at the bottom edge of the door. "There's a gap there. They'll put a board and make it flush with the ground. They'll disinfect the whole room and spray it with insecticide. Your food bucket will be disinfected." I notice the torn up palliasse. "They'll bring you a new palliasse and whitewash the walls."

His expression hasn't changed. "Am I supposed to be grateful?" he sneers at me. "I'm not some common criminal. You forget who I am."

I turn, and give the guards their orders. They lead Peabody out and sit him in front of the desk in the outer office. His face is impassive, and he watches silently as I close the door, go behind the desk, and take out my files from the drawer. I put them on the desk.

I look up. He has a small superior smile on his face. Airily he waves a hand at the cell door. "Calderon, I know what you're trying to do."

"What?"

"The carrot and the stick. It won't work. You think you're so smart but I can read you. First you come on hard to soften me up. Then you're pleasant. It's standard technique by people like you to confuse and disorientate. You don't give a damn if there's rats in there and I get bitten to death."

"You're wrong. I don't use that technique."

"So what technique do you use?"

"There's no real technique. I try to persuade, to enlighten even."

He snorts cynically. "And you're going to enlighten me?"

I open a file and select a page and start reading: "I spent thirty-three years in active service as a member of the Marine Corps.... During that period I spent most of my time being a high class muscleman for big business, for Wall Street and for the bankers. I helped make Mexico and especially Tampico safe for American oil interests in 1914. I helped make Haiti and Cuba decent places for the National City Bank to collect revenues in.... I helped purify Nicaragua for the international banking house of Brown Brothers in 1909 to 1912. In short I was a racketeer for capitalism..."

I look up at him. "Do you know who wrote those words?"

"Certainly. General Smedley D. Butler."

"And?"

"And what?"

"Don't you have a comment? Don't you find it a damning indictment?"

Peabody gives a bored shrug. "So there was capitalist exploitation.... We're a capitalist country and it's been government policy to support our businessmen internationally. Sometimes in the past there have been excesses. That's part of history. Over the decades capitalism has become more enlightened." He leans forward. "During those same decades communism has degenerated into mental oppression."

I leaf through the file and start to answer but he cuts me off.

"Listen. You want to judge a country by its historical crimes? Who decides how far you go back? Fifty years? A hundred? A thousand? You're going to blame a Spaniard today for the Conquistadores? You're going to blame me for the slave trade?" He points a finger. "Or you? What were your ancestors doing?"

I find my anger rising. "Communism is the antithesis of slavery."

"Oh yes? Preach that in the Gulags."

I'm going down the wrong road. This man is impervious to logic. He's sixty-three years old and I'm not going to argue him out of something he's never been argued into. He's too clever. I have to go back and open him up from the beginning. He's talking again, confirming my thoughts.

"Calderon, you're crazy. You think you're going to sit there and convince me? Convert me to communism so I'll spout a couple of names that I don't know anyway? You're not crazy . . . you're stupid."

With a sigh I replace one file with another. It's far too early to use my weapon but I must prepare him for it. I open the file and read out a woman's name: "Amparo Flores."

I look up and see the shaft strike into his eyes. I've scored. He struggles to react normally. "What?"

"Amparo Flores. The reason you hate communism and particularly Cuban communism."

Now there is silence. I wait for him to break it. He doesn't. He sits mute. With a single name we are no longer strangers. There is a haggardness in his face. He has five days' growth of speckled grey beard, and his hair is unkempt. For an irrational moment I feel sorry for him. It passes and I look down at the file again.

I intone, "Between May 1958 and March 1959, subject had a sexual liaison with Amparo, daughter of Juan and Nani Flores. They became betrothed during the first week of March. Amparo Flores arrested March 28th '59 for anti-revolutionary activities. Subject recalled to Washington May 4th '59. Amparo Flores died of cerebral thrombosis May 11th '59."

"That's a lie!"

The words are a scream. He's on his feet, hands on the desk, leaning over it, and the tirade goes on for several minutes; a litany of hatred and pain. Until it finishes with a finger stabbing at me and the words, "You murdered her! Cuban filth! You, you, *you!*" He swings away and, trembling, walks to a small window across the room and stands with his back to me.

I expected a reaction but the intensity surprises me. Softly I remark, "I was just an infant at the time."

His shoulders are still moving from the passionate outburst. I hear his tight voice.

"You... them. No difference. They breed scum like you to replace scum like them."

Is it the time now? No, too early. He is not broken, not yet reliant. I affect a conciliatory tone.

"It was a time of much passion ... and vengeance ... and excess. She was denounced as a spy."

Peabody turns, walks slowly back and sits down. His voice is normal again. "They killed her because she was close to me. She was nineteen years old."

I must draw closer now. "From the way you reacted to her name you must have loved her deeply." I want a reaction but his face is set. "I'm told she was a great beauty...."

Still no reaction. Time to move on.

"Peabody, Batista had an extensive secret police network. We inherited most of their files. Some of them are fascinating. I'll indulge you and quote from yours."

I turn some pages in the file and begin to read: "November 10th 1958. Subject: Jason R. Peabody. Political counsellor, US embassy. Further reports have come from informants that Peabody continues to make favourable comments during his social life on the Castro bandits. It is also known from other sources that he gives negative advice to Ambassador Smith who, however, takes little notice of this advice."

I close the file and look up.

Peabody says, "Batista was a fool and obviously so were his intelligence people."

I shake my head. "No, Peabody. Some of them were good. It's

interesting psychologically. You arrive in Cuba in '56 a young, idealistic foreign service officer already speaking fluent Spanish. You fall in love with a local girl and plan to marry. Then comes the revolution. Your fiancée is arrested. At that time your government is trying to reach a working agreement with Castro—trying to keep Cuba within its sphere of influence. Outraged at the arrest, you lose all objectivity and become a nuisance to your embassy. You are recalled. I guess at that time your career was just about over. Then comes the tragedy of your fiancée, the deterioration in US-Cuban relations, and Fidel's historic embrace of Marxism. Your career picks up again, but now with a difference. Your whole existence is directed against Cuba, Castro, and above all, communism. Whatever idealism was in you had imploded to nothing."

He is not looking bored, but neither is he totally fascinated. I decide to lighten the atmosphere. "Let's have some coffee."

His upper lip curls. "More carrots."

I smile and shout the order to the guard.

DAY FIVE

JASON PEABODY. *San Carlo.*

I'm raising the mug. The rich, deep smell of the coffee drifts into my nostrils. My mouth salivates. And I understand in one startling moment: this is the sensation of an addict at the end of deprivation. Five days only, and my fingers shake and the mug rattles against my teeth.

He is watching. With those sleepy eyes that see everything. I carefully take two sips and lower the mug. The guards have finished cleaning the cell and gone. He inspected it as though it were a queen's boudoir. I stayed sitting at the desk. I make another protest at my detention, at the appalling conditions. He listens attentively and then informs me airily that all the other hostages are in good health and not being mistreated. I ask him what's happening outside. He spreads his hands.

"Nothing. Stalemate. Your government is issuing threatening statements and its puppets are dancing up and down on strings parroting protests."

He's lying, of course. There must have been developments. Several times today I've heard jets fly overhead. They can only come from the *Nimitz*. But he will tell me nothing, a deliberate strategy to keep me off balance, and it's working. I *am* off balance. Yet there have been times in my life when all I wanted was solitude. Now I understand that, when enforced, it changes its character. I'm getting a glimmer of the horrors of incarceration. And Amparo. *Amparo.* It was hearing that name emerge from his lips.

This man in front of me, this boy, is more than cunning. He has in him a strange power. A few hours ago, had anyone told me that this boy could extract information from me, I would have thought them insane. Now, thank God, I understand the danger. I must be always on my guard.

He says, musingly, "You devote your whole career, your whole life, to an anti-communist crusade, with great emphasis on Latin America and Cuba in particular. You become almost a recluse. You have no friends. You write anti-communist books which are widely acclaimed by your capitalist intelligentsia. Tell me, Peabody, when did you last make love?"

I'd been lulled by the cynical but accurate biography. I grasp for a retort. I ask, "Why do you tint your hair?"

He grins amiably. "I don't tint it, Peabody. I squeeze lemon juice on which streaks it as it dries in the sun."

"Why?"

"It suits me."

"You look damned ridiculous."

He shrugs, still smiling. "You don't find me attractive?"

God, is *that* what he thinks? The fool!

"I find you repulsive in every way. Now it's getting late. I'm going to sleep."

He looks at his watch and nods in surprise.

"OK. But one more question. For the last three or four years, whenever you've been in Washington you've made frequent trips to Dulles airport without flying out. On average about once a week. You get there about seven in the evening and leave an hour later. You've never been observed talking to anyone. Generally you just sit in the arrivals hall. Sometimes you have coffee or a drink. Then straight home. It puzzled our analysts. Why, Peabody?"

That's going to be the last shock today. I feel unsteady as I stand up. I walk towards the cell and manage to say, "Your questions are boring. I prefer my own company."

Trying not to rush, I go into the cell and close the door. The tart smell of whitewash is in my nostrils. Has he guessed? Even he could not guess. Can he look into my head? I hear the scrape of his chair. I pray he won't come in.

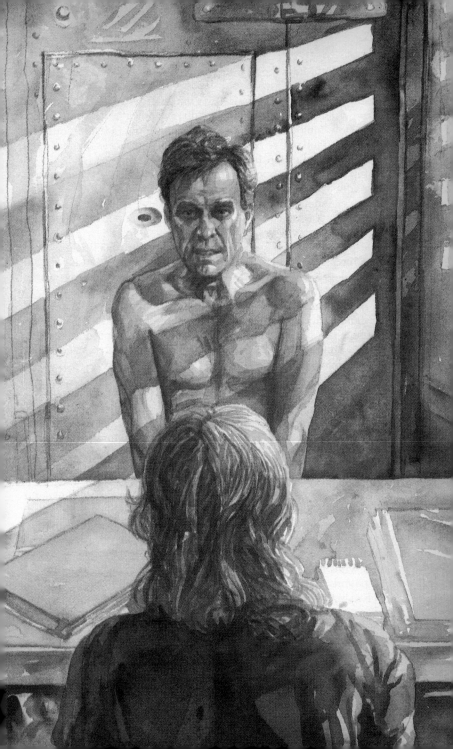

With relief I hear the key turn in the lock, then his voice. "See you in a day, or two, or three."

I sink down onto the palliasse. My limbs are weak. How much does he know? How can he know? I feel dirty. I look at my thin legs. I am dirty. How long can this hell last? Eating muck, washing out of a bucket. And today I've been through emotional shocks that have left me drained and exhausted....

Amparo is sitting opposite me. She lifts her head and I'm looking at the golden olive of her face, framed in jet black silkiness. The picture has never faded. What would Calderon know or understand? I've never made love since I left Cuba. Why should I need anything after her but a memory?

Despite the heat I shiver as I remember the shock I felt when Calderon asked his question about Dulles airport. I feel shame that anyone, let alone he, could ever crawl so close to my mind as even to ask that question.

Five days in this cell. The word "cell" startles me. It sounds like it feels and it rhymes with hell. Five solitary days and the loneliness sharpens my senses. I look at my feet. Dirt growing between the toes.... How well Calderon knows me. Each day the grime grows and humiliates me. Five days gone. How many more?

COLONEL SLOCUM. *Washington, USA.*

I savour the memory. There's not much else to do. My room is on the tenth floor but the view is confined to a heavy rainstorm. In two days I've seen enough TV re-runs and soap operas to want to go out and strangle every producer in the land.

The memory eases the boredom. It's of the president's face. I'd finished telling him what was wrong with the rescue plan. I'd kept it brief. I'd explained the over-complications. The plan, as it stood, involved five simultaneous operations: a ground assault, an airstrike to take out the city's electricity generator, another air attack on the main army barracks, a helicopter-borne assault into the compound itself, while helicopter gunships were "sanitizing" the area round the compound to discourage reinforcements.

I had highlighted the one word: "simultaneous". It's much loved in military jargon. What would happen, I asked, if because of miscalculation, or bad luck, just one of those operations failed to be simultaneous?

Then came the moment. The president said, "The joint chiefs have emphasized that this is to be a major military operation."

I took a breath. "Sir, with respect, World War Two was a major military operation. This is an itsy bitsy little one."

The memory is of his expression when I said that. I quickly went on. "It's an operation to secure a small compound right by the sea and only twelve miles from a major base of operations—the *Nimitz*. To release twenty-seven people from the clutches of a semi-trained bunch of youths and chopper them back to base."

"You make it sound easy."

"It is."

He said sceptically, "What about the explosives strapped to our people?"

I answered firmly. "There aren't any, sir, that's just a bluff."

"How can you know?"

"I'm ninety-nine per cent sure. South Americans aren't all religious fanatics who believe eternal paradise follows suicide. You might find one or two nuts in ten thousand who'd blow themselves up—but not twenty-seven. Besides, those guys are not stupid. With twenty-seven people wired up the chances of an accidental explosion are enormous. Why risk it? Those jackets just contain padding."

"You can't be positive."

"No, sir. But anyway, your generals' plan gives them around sixty seconds to make up their minds, so even if there are no explosives they could still shoot our people. The way I'd do it they would only have ten seconds or less. It would be late at night and most of them would be asleep. There would be a few seconds of noise and confusion then we'd have our people and the compound secured."

Komlosy decided it was time to assert himself. He asked, "How would you get in, Colonel?"

Without taking my eyes off the president I replied, "Silently. By ultralights."

The president was puzzled. "Ultralights?"

"Yes, sir. Motorized hang gliders. We take off from the *Nimitz* and climb to around eight thousand feet approaching the coast, cut the engines and glide right in."

The president was still puzzled. "But those things are made of cloth and metal tubes. I've seen them on TV. They're just bicycles with wings and sewing machine engines!"

"Yes, sir." I knew I'd got to be persuasive. "But you could say that parachutes are only made of cloth. I've been experimenting with ultralights for months. They're simple and effective."

He nodded thoughtfully. "How many men would you take?"

"Twenty, at most."

"But they have over a hundred in the compound."

"Sir, each of my guys is worth ten of theirs. In that sense we'd outnumber them two to one."

A long silence, then the president mused, "It all sounds so very simple ... twenty men." He glanced at his watch and said to Komlosy, "Mike, I'm going to sleep on this. We'll discuss it tomorrow. Keep Colonel Slocum on hand ... and incognito."

So I got sent up to this hotel room and now I've kicked my heels for two whole days. Komlosy's phoned once on each day. I guess to check I'm still here. To my questions he just answered, "Wait." That's one habit I never really mastered.

I pick up the *Washington Post* and read the news for the third time. It's all front page stuff. UN resolutions; messages of solidarity; silence from Moscow. I drop the paper. I'm trying to decide whether to ring down for a hamburger and fries when there's a sharp tap on the door. I open it to find Komlosy holding a brown paper bag.

"Hi."

He brushes past, casts a look round the room and then goes into the bathroom. He comes out with two glasses, puts them on the bedside table, sits on the bed, points a finger at the sole chair and, from the bag, produces a bottle of Johnnie Walker Black Label.

I sit down and watch as he pours two healthy slugs. He passes me a glass and raises his own.

"Cheers, Colonel. Here's to us."

"Cheers."

I drink and, trying to casual, ask, "We got it?"

He grimaces at the neat Scotch. "Not exactly. Not yet. The two plans are to go forward side by side. At a later stage the president will take a decision on which to use."

"Uh huh. What now?"

"You go back to Fort Bragg tonight. Assemble your team and start training. You're to report to General Simmons. He'll provide back up engineering to build a mock-up of the compound. You got your basic plan ready?"

"Sure, sir."

I walk across the room, lift a corner of the mattress, pull out a sheet of cardboard and lay it on the bed. It shows a plan of the compound marked with several crosses and arrows. He studies it.

"That's it?"

"That's it. What do you want? A computer printout? That's it, unless of course the intelligence situation changes. What's happening on that?"

He drains his glass. "We could have got lucky, Colonel. We'll know in a day or two, but we might have an agent on site."

"In the compound?"

He nods. "But we're not sure yet. I'll be coming to Fort Bragg in a few days. I'll tell you more then. How soon can you be ready?"

I've been waiting for the question. "I'd like three weeks."

"OK. That's good. The other plan calls for five to six weeks minimum."

He looks at his watch. "I've got to get back to the White House. A car will pick you up at six and take you to the airport. You'll be flown back to Fort Bragg." He hands me an embossed card. "Simmons has been given special authority, but if there are any problems he can't handle, ring that number. I'll see you in a few days."

"OK, sir. There's just one more thing." I show him a report in the paper which tells how the *Nimitz* is sitting on the horizon. "Mr. Komlosy, that's acting as a reminder to those student guards to keep on their toes. Plus all the over-flights, it's counter-productive. They should be kept to a minimum."

He thinks for a moment. Then, "I agree. I'll try to make the president see that."

I show him to the door and watch him stride down the corridor. Back in the room I check my watch. An hour to kill before the car picks me up. I start going through names in my head. I'll need four squad leaders. The names pop up quickly. I'll talk to them before I select the rest of the team. I try to picture the situation in the compound. It's been a week now, and the guards will be getting a little bit sloppy. Within three weeks they'll be bored out of their skulls.

I try to imagine the feelings of the hostages right now. Twenty men, seven women. I sure hope I'm right about those explosive jackets being nothing but dummies.

DAY SIX

JORGE CALDERON. *San Carlo.*

Inez is still sleeping. She is lying with her head cradled on one arm. When she's asleep her face looks even more angelic than when she's awake. I brush the hair away from her forehead and feel tenderness—or is it love?

She stirs and opens one eye.

"Inez, I'm leaving soon for the compound."

"When will you be back?"

"Tonight."

The eye closes. I bend down and kiss it. She murmurs unintelligibly.

Last night something bad happened. At dinner Bermudez paid her much attention. She seemed to react in the usual fashion, interested in him one minute, apparently bored the next. But after dinner, as he showed us around the floodlit gardens of Vargas's decadent palace, it was different. She stayed always close to him, occasionally touching his arm with the back of her hand, and I was jealous. For the first time in my life. The experience was terrifying. My hold on women, and sometimes men, stems partly from my ability to be above jealousy, so it can never be used as a weapon against me. If I am jealous now maybe it means that my affection for Inez has indeed matured into love. The thought is catastrophic.

I begin to wonder, too, about Bermudez. He shows disturbing symptoms. He's already moved into the palace and his uniform is smarter, his speech a little more arrogant. Like many before him he could be falling victim to the narcotic of power.

He is surprisingly unworried by the USA. The *Nimitz* has been pulled back over the horizon. Incursions into San Carlo airspace have decreased. I told him bluntly that those moves were probably designed to lull him into a false sense of security. I told him of the slackening of awareness in the compound. He was calm, merely saying that he would send word to Fombona. He is convinced that the Americans will soon negotiate. Already both the Red Cross and the Swedish ambassador have put out feelers. I remarked that such moves were to be expected. I sensed his irritation at my words, but he was polite. He had to be. He needs us Cubans.

Back at the hotel, after we had made love, Inez lay on her back gazing at the ceiling. Then she said reflectively, "He has the power of death."

"What?"

"Bermudez. They bring him the decisions of the people's courts. He can veto the death penalties or sign them. He has signed more than a hundred. There will be hundreds more; maybe thousands."

She turned to look at me and I could see the awe in her eyes.

Studying her face now, a picture of purity and innocence, I know that she will find that power fascinating. In a disturbed mood I stand up and pack a little cassette recorder into my bag and go out.

Two bodyguards are sitting on stools in the corridor. Both with their heads against the wall. Both asleep. They were assigned to me two days ago. There is much talk in the city of American spies and agents. Should they know of my existence, Bermudez thinks they might try to kill me. Fidel would be angry. These two offer brilliant protection. Not at all gently I kick them both awake and walk on down the corridor.

Outside the truck is waiting. There is another passenger sitting in the back, on sacks of beans; the young Mestizo boy who works in the kitchens. He nods at me nervously. As we pull away I ask, "They let you out of the compound?"

"Yes, sir . . . my mother . . . she is sick."

We bump along the road. He is small and slight. It's hard to judge his age but I think he's less than twenty. He has long, lank, black hair cut jaggedly. He avoids looking at me.

"You don't like working there?"

His eyes flicker towards me and away.

"Why are you going back?"

He moistens his lips. "I fear for my family, sir."

"Ah. So you also are a hostage."

He nods tentatively.

The truck comes to a halt and the doors open.

In the guardhouse I leave my files in the bag but take out the cassette recorder and place it in the centre of the desk. Then I unlock the cell door, and without looking inside go to my chair and sit down.

He appears at the doorway, his beard visibly longer.

"Good morning, Excellency."

He is looking at the recorder. "Calderon, I don't often swear, but if you switch that thing on you'll hear some obscenities."

JASON PEABODY. *San Carlo.*

He waves at the chair. "I don't want to record. I want you to listen to something."

As I walk to the chair he says, "Now Peabody, Ex-President Vargas borrowed a trick from your President Nixon. He had his palace wired up and he taped everything. The revolutionaries found the tape library intact. They're working through it now. Yesterday they gave me this tape. We're going to listen to it and then talk about it."

He leans forward and presses a button. There's a pause and then from the small speaker come the two harsh words, "Sebago shoes."

In an instant I'm taken back sixteen days, to my second day in San Carlo. I had requested a private audience with Vargas, and was shown into a vast room by an aide-de-camp. He indicated a chair in front of an inlaid walnut desk and left. I studied the chair and sat down. Genuine Louis Quatorze, it must have cost enough to feed an entire Mestizo village for five years.

I was kept waiting for five minutes, then Vargas came in through a side door. I stood up and he said triumphantly, "Sebago shoes."

I was momentarily confused, then understood and looked down. "Yes, Mr. President. I always wear them."

He beamed. "So do I. When I'm out of uniform, of course. Best shoes in the world. My embassy in Washington sends me regular shipments. I'll instruct them to include your size."

I started to say something about foreign service regulations but he waved that aside and approached with his hand out. After we shook hands he sat down behind his desk and I resumed my seat.

Vargas had a short body, short neck, short legs. Tight blue and gold bemedalled uniform, the obligatory dark glasses. He lacked only a wide moustache to complete the picture of a banana republic dictator. I recall wondering why most dictators are short.

He said, "I must tell you I am very pleased with your arrival. To be honest your predecessor did not fully understand our special position here and failed to communicate our feelings to your government. I have heard good reports of you, and of course your hatred of communism is well known from your writings."

He stood up and started pacing in front of me. "It is essential that we receive the full military and civil aid package promised by your president. The subversives grow stronger. They terrorize the people; disrupt the economy; spread the cancer of communism."

"Excellency, my government is doing everything possible to get the aid package through. The president himself is spending a lot of time with individual senators. The problem is human rights; the continuous killings and disappearances under your government."

"They're improved," he countered sharply.

"Only marginally. From a hundred and fifty-two last month to a hundred and thirty-one this month, and it's still got four days to run."

Vargas shrugged. "It takes time. There is much passion in the country. My people hate the subversives. It is not always easy to control them."

"But Mr. President, in twelve months there have been more than one thousand five hundred killings and disappearances. Not one person has been convicted or even tried."

He spread his hands. "Courts need proof. It is hard to get."

190

"I'm sure it is. But congress votes in two weeks and I am to prepare a report for them on the progress you are making. And its contents will depend on three conditions."

"Conditions?" Amazement was creeping over his face.

"Yes. For me to send a favourable report, genuine progress will have to be made. First, the killings and abductions must stop. Don't tell me it's impossible. We know they are directed from an office in the north wing of this very building. Second, the university is to reopen, the four detained lecturers to be released, either to resume their duties or be allowed to leave the country. Third, the officers in charge of the massacre of Mestizos in Higo Province last April must be immediately brought to trial."

Vargas stood there like a squat volcano. I wished I could see behind those glasses into his eyes. Abruptly he walked to the high window, turned, and started talking. First the university. It was the womb of revolution, spawning the germs of destruction. He was eloquent in his anger.

My answer was succinct. "You cannot fight communism with ignorance. The university must reopen."

We glared at each other. Then Vargas talked of the death squads. Argentina had stifled communists by using their own methods against them—terror. So had Uruguay and Chile. It worked. The only way to deal with them. They are all vermin.

I answered, "For every death of a genuine communist you kill maybe five innocents. For every death of an innocent you create five communists. It's an equation of disaster."

Vargas gave up on explanations. His anger distilled into cold formality. "Tomorrow my Washington ambassador will convey to the state department our displeasure at your appointment—our inability to work with you. Your career will be finished."

"It's almost over anyway. I retire in a couple of years." I stood up. "Understand me clearly. I represent the country which sustains you. I abhor you and your principles, but I abhor communism more. I will be an instrument in your sustenance, but only under the conditions I outlined."

Now as I look down at the little recorder I hear my parting words, and the click of the door as I went out. The tape curls on until Calderon rouses himself, reaches out and pushes a button.

He slumps back in his seat. Silence. Then he says, "Who would believe those were the words of Jason Peabody, ambassador to San Carlo of the United States of America? A man whose political philosophy is slightly to the right of Ghengis Khan."

"What's so hard to believe?"

He stands up and stretches. "Peabody, you are an enigma. Your country has ambassadors all over the world paying lip service to human rights. You're the least likely candidate to really believe in it, but from the evidence of that tape you do."

"Why should that be difficult to believe?"

He smiles. "Maybe you don't understand yourself. Tell me. If Vargas had not been overthrown, what do you think would have been the result of your little lecture?"

"Not much. He would have toned things down for a while."

"Exactly. After you left, he called his brother in. It's all on tape. He told him to suspend the killings for a couple of weeks, reopen the university but detain the lecturers, and find a couple of junior officers to serve as scapegoats for the Mestizo massacres."

I believe him. It's logical.

Fascinated, he says, "But you genuinely loathed him. Had he done nothing you would still have urged your government to give him aid. Why?"

I point at the recorder. "You heard me. I abhor him. But I abhor communism more."

He sits down again, shaking his head in puzzlement. "Peabody, we are going to talk about this. Now. Maybe for hours. Don't get negative with me. You need to talk. After three days alone you were glad to see me. Don't deny it. I need a name and you are going to give it to me because you will want to."

"Calderon, as usual you delude yourself."

He smiles. "No, Peabody. First understand this. The name you give me will lead me to the others. But don't grieve for them. They will not die: they will be re-educated."

I laugh, genuinely amused. "You're telling me that if I give you a name, which anyway I don't have, then that person will merely be given a strict talking to, and persuaded to give up all his naughty thoughts? Calderon, you insult both my intelligence and your own."

He thinks for a moment and then nods in agreement. "But they won't be maltreated. I'll be doing the interrogation myself. No matter. Now we are going to examine the source of your political beliefs. But first Peabody, why did you keep going to the airport?"

I feel immediate mental discomfort. A child caught in an act of misbehaviour.

Quickly I say, "You'd better change the subject or it's the end of this conversation."

192

DAY EIGHT

COLONEL SLOCUM. *Fort Bragg, USA.*

I'm at work. Sitting in a jeep on the edge of a disused airstrip. Komlosy is next to me. We are both looking up into the clear sky, at the circling ultralights.

"There are more than the twenty men you asked for," Komlosy says.

"Twenty-four, sir. I got four backup men in case of injury during training, or sickness. Watch now, they've cut the engines. They're coming down."

The flock breaks up and rearranges itself into four groups. They separate and begin a spiralling descent. A dozen giant white crosses have been painted about thirty metres apart on the concrete runway. Two men stand to one side talking into handheld radio sets, wearing jeans and windcheaters.

"What are those guys doing?" Komlosy asks. "They're civilians?"

"Uh huh. They're giving me a helping hand, sir. The short one is Larry Newman. The tall one is his partner Bryan Allen. Two of the most adventurous men in aviation. Newman was one of the three guys who flew that balloon over the Atlantic, and Allen won the prize for being the first person to fly across the English Channel using only human power. They're probably the two best ultralight instructors in the world. Some of my squad had flown them before, others hadn't. Believe me they're learning fast. Now watch."

The first two groups are coming in. There's about a ten-knot headwind. They turn gracefully into it. The canard wings lift and they look to be hardly moving as they approach. Silently, one by one, they slide onto the concrete. Most are right on the crosses, some overshoot by a metre or two. One lands a little short. They quickly pull their crafts clear and into line. A minute later the other two groups come in with similar performances.

With satisfaction I say, "Not bad."

The pilots are congregating around Newman and Allen. Komlosy says, "Shall we go over?"

"No, sir. They're being debriefed. Let's wait awhile."

He lights a cigarette. "Colonel, when we're alone you don't have to call me sir. I'm Mike."

"Thanks, Mike. I'm Silas."

We sit in companionable silence for a few minutes, then he says,

193

"They look easy to fly, but I guess it's tricky at night . . . and in combat conditions."

"It's more complicated, sure. You'll see it tonight at the mock-up."

The group of men breaks up. Two of them go back to their machines, start the engines, taxi clear and take off. Allen and Newman stroll across towards us. We get out of the jeep and I make the introductions.

Komlosy says expansively, "I want to thank you guys for what you're doing. It's a great job. Just great."

They mumble a few modest words. Newman grins. "Silas, you picked a bunch of naturals. I sent Brand and Kerr up to do half an hour more. After that I guess everyone should rest up to be ready for tonight."

"OK, we'll see you at dinner. Larry, ask the squad leaders to come over here please."

"Sure."

They walk back to the group. Komlosy and I turn to watch a giant C5 transport lift off a distant runway. As it roars up into the sky I ask, "Mike, can you give me an update on the intelligence situation?"

"Sure. There's quite a bit, but I'd like to do that after I've seen the show tonight. Can tell you one thing though; I pressed your case about the *Nimitz*. It's been pulled back over the horizon, and overflights have been limited to the essential. I guess you made quite an impression on the president. We have a second surveillance satellite in position, so we're pretty well covered."

"Good. Listen, you'll meet all the men tonight, but I want you to meet the squad leaders now."

I take Komlosy's arm and lead him to where four men are lined up at attention five metres away. I sneak a glance at him. He's going to have to take lessons from the president on how to keep a poker face. He looks like he just set eyes on something from outer space.

It's true to say the appearance of these guys would frighten a panzer division. Sacasa is short and slight, looking as though a strong wind might knock him off his feet. But his face would freeze oil. It must have started out bad enough, but after plenty of fist fights plus the close attention of some misdirected napalm he could make a fortune in horror movies. Moncada is also short, but is practically deformed by the shoulders and arms of a professional weightlifter. He has a low forehead and mad, staring eyes. Castenada is tall and slender. He has a thin black moustache and looks as if he is cruelly smiling—but this is a sinister illusion caused by a shrapnel wound.

Gomez has no apparent facial anomalies. In fact he should be handsome, but the mix of features has somehow resulted in a face that approaching strangers cross the street to avoid.

I savour the moment while he recovers, and then I say, "Mr. Komlosy, sir. This is Lieutenant Sacasa; Captain Moncada; Sergeant Castenada; Captain Gomez. Men, you all know who Mr. Komlosy is. Tonight he's going to be watching the exercise. I want a clockwork effort from you and all your men."

Four voices snap out, "Yessir!"

Komlosy confines himself to a lame, "Keep up the great work, men. We're relying on you."

I dismiss them and we climb back into the jeep. As we head for my quarters he mutters, "Silas, where did you find them?"

"They're all long time regular soldiers. Sacasa and Gomez are Chicanos. Moncada and Castenada are of Cuban blood ... they all speak Spanish, they're tough and they know how to lead."

"Is the rest of the squad like them?"

"More or less."

Komlosy shakes his head, speechless.

IT'S JUST AFTER TEN. We're standing on a platform high on a scaffolding tower. Behind us Newman and Allen are discussing the wind conditions. Komlosy is looking down at the mock-up of the San Carlo embassy compound. It's just plywood and canvas but all the measurements and distances are exact.

I point below. "Now, I'll fill you in. Moncada's squad lands there behind the chancery. Castenada's over there by the residence. Sacasa's there behind the apartments. Meanwhile Gomez's squad has approached a thousand feet higher. They circle down slowly. At the first shot they turn on their engines, dive down and circle over the compound dropping grenades on all the rooftops where the guards have emplacements. Their ultras are equipped with small but powerful lights. Once those emplacements are taken out they land and secure a landing zone over there for the choppers."

"How long will the choppers take to arrive?"

"They'll lift off from the *Nimitz* as we make our final approach. We figure four to five minutes. At the same time fixed-wing aircraft and helicopter gunships will be closing out the whole area."

"So how long from landing to evacuation?"

"Eight to ten minutes."

He turns slowly, studying the whole compound. "It's pretty dark out there, Colonel."

"Our boys have light-intensifying glasses, sir. They don't exactly show daylight, but they're damn good and a hell of an advantage."

I glance at my watch and he asks, "They're about due?"

"Yes, sir, any time now. See how far away you can spot them."

He strains his eyes into the darkness, first one direction, then another. Finally he remarks, "I guess they're late."

Very quietly I say, "No, sir. They're here."

I point to a corner of the chancery building. Two black figures glide across the ground towards the entrance. I point again; black figures running towards the residence, others towards the apartments.

"How the hell . . . ?"

His words are cut off as two black shapes glide by, twenty yards in front of our faces. We hear the first shots. Above our heads lights appear, picking out the rooftops. Then sharp explosions and flashes. Komlosy ducks down.

"Just thunder flashes, sir—simulating grenades."

After a few seconds the lights go out. There are explosions and bursts of fire all over the compound. Two minutes later flàres light up in a circle a hundred metres across. There's a clattering over our heads. A single chopper plunges out of the dark sky, slows abruptly and settles to earth. From all points of the compass twenty black-clad figures walk slowly out and form a circle around it. The chopper's rotor slows and stops. There is total silence. Komlosy is gazing down mesmerized.

AN HOUR LATER we are propping up the bar in my quarters. I don't drink a hell of a lot but when I do I like to be on my feet. I built the bar myself out of stripped pine. It's the right height and has a footrest.

We are onto our third Scotch. Komlosy is in a strange mood. At one moment introspective, at another excited and enthusiastic. He's in total awe over what he's just seen. I'm pleased with the exercise, but I don't tell him about what he didn't see: one of Sacasa's squad overshooting and almost hitting the side of the chancery; Moncada's squad arriving more than a minute late; Gomez's men too high when they switched on their lights. I don't tell him this because I want this job so bad it really hurts.

I pour Komlosy another three fingers of Scotch. "So what are the chances we get to go in?"

He swirls the amber liquid in his glass, draws a deep breath and exhales slowly. "If the rescue operation goes ahead, you've got a better than seventy-per-cent chance . . . *if* it goes ahead."

"But why shouldn't it, Mike? It's the obvious option."

196

He sighs. "Silas, you don't know politics. There's a complication—a beauty. Our ambassador in San Carlo, Peabody, is an expert on Cuba, and it so happens that there's a big operation under way against Castro. It involves people high up in the Cuban administration, and Peabody advised on it. He knows their names. And now the Chamarristas have given Castro access to him."

"How do you know?"

"We have a dozen agents in San Carlo including one in the compound who we've finally made contact with. We also had a guy at the airport. He managed to get some photos of disembarking passengers on some of the planes that flew in after the takeover, before we imposed the blockade. One of those photos shows the face of a man called Jorge Calderon...." He bends his head back, stretches his neck, then looks me straight in the eye. "Top interrogator for Cuban intelligence. Apparently very effective."

"And this Calderon is in the compound?"

"He comes and goes every two or three days in the back of a provisions truck."

"Can't our guys knock him off?"

"He's guarded day and night."

"OK, but even he's not going to be torturing an American ambassador ... or is he?"

He shakes his head. "No, he's using psychology, humiliating Peabody, keeping him isolated in the guardhouse. He's almost naked. There's no sanitation and all they feed him is garbage."

"Bastards ... ! But Mike, an ambassador has to be top material. That's not going to make him crack."

He sighs again and lights a cigarette. "A team of psychiatrists have written in-depth profiles on Peabody. Apparently that guy had some kind of tragedy decades ago. It turned him in on himself. He never married ... has no friends ... few acquaintances. He's got a brilliant mind and he buried himself in books and his work. His anti-communism has reached obsessional level ... and in his personal habits he's turned fastidiousness into a fetish. Our experts think that he's prime material for the skills of a man like Calderon. Their report concluded: 'Continued exposure to intense psychological pressure could have a detrimental effect on his mental state.'"

A long silence, then I remark, "The president has quite a choice to make. Does he lose sleep over it?"

He smiles. "I doubt it. He's developed 'switching off' into a fine art. But one thing's for sure, he doesn't want to jeopardize that anti-Castro operation."

"What will he decide, Mike?"

"Nothing. Not for five or six days. During that time the CIA has another operation running in San Carlo. A lovely little operation."

"What are they planning to do?"

"Using the agent in the compound, they're going to try to poison Peabody."

For a moment I don't believe what I've heard. I look at his face; at his eyes and I see that it's true. Komlosy is staring morosely into his glass. He says quietly, "They have to smuggle a special poison down there. One drop and you're dead."

"So when does it happen?"

"They figure five to six days."

"I hope to God they fail!"

"So do I."

DAY NINE

JORGE CALDERON. *San Carlo.*

There's an onshore wind, and from the northwest the big rollers sweep in and crash onto the beach below, sweeping in from Cuba. It's only five hundred miles away, and it tugs at me.

For two days I talked of Cuba. Stayed in the compound for two days and argued, cajoled, threatened. It came to nothing. It was a road I had to go down. After hearing that tape I had to examine the roots of his ideology.

I am standing on the balcony of the hotel room. It is early evening. The light is soft. The sunsets here are like Cuban sunsets: sudden, dramatic, vivid. Then darkness coming down like a warm black sheet. I am experiencing unhappiness. Peabody is the cause of my unhappiness. I cannot break him. He is not my superior but he is my equal.

After hearing the tape we talked for hours. On reflection I talked more than him. That was part of his skill. I talked more than I expected but it was also part of my purpose. An attempt to draw him close to me. So close that he would be vulnerable.

I asked about his parents. He talked of them as though they had been paintings on a wall. There was no feeling to him. No passion. I reminded myself that this was the man who had once loved passionately. Who had recently damned the excesses of Vargas. I played the tape again in front of him. Listened to his words; of how one innocent killed as a communist will create five communists. Then with a chill I realized that the words coming off that tape were equally devoid of emotion. He was simply setting out conditions to force a dictator to be a more acceptable loan recipient.

Now, for a moment I'm close to despair. I have one formidable weapon. But if I misuse it, it's gone for ever. First, I need to draw him close. He must depend on me. There must be a way. I think again about his trips to the airport. Scores of them. There was surely a reason. He spent hours. Last night I pored over an airline schedule trying to find a pattern.

The door slides open behind me and I feel the cool of the air-conditioning on my back. Inez comes up beside me and rests her elbows on the rail. She is another part of my unhappiness, for I think I love her, and I am shamed by the absurdity.

Bermudez has taken to having working dinners. Roberto Bermudez who would be the new Fidel. Last night we were invited—as we are tonight. He enjoys his power and enjoys showing it off. He also competes with me for Inez. He calls her "comrade" with the inflection of a sensualist. She responds with a twitch of her lips and a flick of her eyes in my direction. And I feel pain. Me!

"Don't you think it's exciting Jorge?"

"What?"

"What we are seeing. What we are part of. The transformation of a country. Being at the centre. Knowing history is being made."

Irritably I say, "History is being made in Cuba. You never took much interest there."

"Ah, it's different. This is young. This is now."

"It could also be very short. Bermudez is losing his sense of proportion."

She puts a hand on my arm. "Jorge, you are just irritable because of the American. Because he is not easy for you. You must try harder. Roberto was saying last night how much he hopes you succeed. We must go soon or we'll be late."

I say gently, "Inez, I have to think a little more. Go inside and wait for me. I will come soon."

She squeezes my arm and kisses me on the ear. She never wears perfume but the scent of her skin is in my nostrils.

I wrench my mind away, back to Peabody. I must get it off the witch in the room behind me. I try to concentrate again on his trips to the airport. I try hard to concentrate but the image of her face intrudes. The image of her looking at Bermudez, smiling at him. Ah, the loneliness of jealousy!

The loneliness of jealousy? Suddenly I understand! I am flooded with excitement. I turn to Inez. "I'm going to the compound."

She puts a hand on my arm. "Now? We must be at the palace in half an hour."

"Damn the palace. I'm going to the compound. I must."

Her eyes glitter. "Well, I'm not staying here alone. I'm going to the palace!"

I pick up my bag. "Do what you want."

As I reach the door she says defiantly, "You will be sorry, Jorge Calderon."

She is standing, legs apart, her eyes radiating a single simple message. I am unbelievably sad.

"Yes, Inez. I will."

PEABODY IS SURPRISED to see me, but I think he is not displeased. He comes gingerly out of his cell. His grey beard makes his face appear much thinner.

I have ordered coffee and while we wait I give him the usual assurances that the other hostages are in good health. To his questions about the outside situation I am vague. Of course his government has imposed sanctions and frozen assets. I don't mention the blockade or the sudden diminished activity of the *Nimitz* and its aircraft.

The Mestizo boy brings in the coffee. As Peabody takes his first sip I study him. Am I right? Was my moment of intuition correct? If so, this man in front of me is about to have his brain exposed as in a lobotomy, and I will be able to prepare him for the final phase. If I'm wrong he's going to regard me as a fanciful idiot and my task will be a thousand times harder. It's a risk that's been thrust at me.

While the Mestizo is in the room I keep a deliberate silence, pretending to read something in one of my files. I am tense, vividly aware of the importance of the moment. Then I say, very casually and still looking down at the file, "Peabody, I know why you made all those trips to the airport."

I glance up. There is a startled look in his eyes. Then his eyes drop to the file, and the startled look is gone. He visibly relaxes. He thinks that everything I know is in the file, and he is aware that such knowledge can be in no file. He sips again, puts the mug down and patiently waits for me to make a fool of myself.

I close the file and, in a sombre tone, say, "I would not have believed that a human being, so intelligent, so widely read, so aware of the world, could be . . . so lonely."

He pulls his head back; his whole body shrinks away from me. His eyes narrow as if in pain and I know that I'm right.

"Peabody, you did not go to the airport to meet or watch for any particular person. You went to watch the arrival passengers being welcomed.... Parents greeting children ... and children parents ... grandparents ... wives ... husbands ... and lovers. Peabody, for a brief time each week you were on the fringe of emotion and love. You sat and watched those people embrace, and kiss, and sometimes cry with joy. You never went to the departure hall. You never went to see the tears of sorrow."

He is staring down between his thin knees. No artist or sculptor could create an image of such melancholy.

"Peabody..." He lifts his head. "Peabody. You, who know everything, you who are so strong that you need no one, you had to creep close to the aura of love between strangers; like an animal creeping near to a campfire at night; frightened of the fire but from a distance absorbing a hint of its warmth."

His head sags again. I stand up and slowly walk around the desk. I bend my knees and crouch beside his chair. His hands are resting on his knees. I reach out and cover one of them with mine. I can feel fine bones under dry skin.

Many seconds pass. Then in a choking whisper he asks, "How could you know that?"

I have no simple answer. I came to the knowledge through no logic. I tell him. "I guessed only because I must have the same capacity to isolate my intellect from my emotions. To stoke the fires of one and smother the other. You took that capacity to an extreme. But you are more than twice my age, have travelled a longer road, have smothered until there is barely an ember still alive. And I tell you now, it frightens me. If that can happen to you, so it can happen to me."

I would never have believed I could utter such words, still less that they would be an exact expression of what I feel. I am confused by this. Numb with emotion.

Peabody has moved his other hand and covered mine with it. I look up at his face. He knows what has happened. From the beginning I had set out to do it, to crack through his exterior and expose him to what was inside. I have succeeded. But in cracking him I have cracked myself. Does the influence of Inez have anything to do with this? I must leave here now and think.

I withdraw my hand and straighten up.

"Peabody, I will come to see you in two days. Until then try to think on something. Try to understand that if a man warps his true instincts for years, then the whole philosophy of that man could also be warped. Try to think on that and let us talk about it the next time I see you."

We are looking at each other. He smiles faintly and stands up. At the cell door he turns.

"Calderon, understanding me is one thing. Using that to extract information is another. Goodnight to you."

He goes in and closes the door.

As I cross the compound I try to decide when to use the concluding weapon. It will be devastating. I know that he is close to being ready for it.

Fombona is talking to the guard at the entrance to the residence. I tell him, "I'm leaving in the morning."

He shakes his head. "There are no van deliveries tomorrow. You'll have to go the day after."

"What are you talking about?"

He is grinning. "The deliveries tomorrow have been cancelled. Don't worry, you won't go hungry. We have plenty of food."

I realize Bermudez has sealed me off here. But he is too subtle to move in on Inez tonight. It would be crude, and he knows crudeness will turn her away. He also knows that his isolating me here, his cleverness, will attract her. He understands her character.

Anger threatens to overwhelm me. The ape Fombona must know what's behind this. There's no way I can leave the place except in the back of that van.

As I walk away I tell Fombona, "If Bermudez calls, tell him he's going to regret this."

DAY TEN

JASON PEABODY. *San Carlo*.

I know about the Stockholm Syndrome, about captives being drawn to their captors; sufferers to their tormentors. I think about it for a long time, trying to analyse my feelings. It is different, and sometimes painful, to face weaknesses which I have never admitted. In looking back over four decades I can only see the arid flatness of an emotional desert. Yet since I created it, surely I wanted it? Now I recognize the truth. I never did want it. I built that desert from bitterness and sustained it with false pride.

Finally I decide that what I am going through has nothing to do with the Stockholm Syndrome. Certainly I have drawn close to Calderon but the reality is that right from the beginning he affected me in a remarkable way.

Throughout the early sessions my rage at him was always overlaid by fascination. I count my scratch marks on the wall. It was only ten days ago that he sat in his chair looking at death down the barrel of Fombona's gun as though he was examining a rare and exotic flower. I analyse myself again; try to decide whether it is admiration that has drawn me to him.

It is not. I have admired many men and women for gifts both natural and acquired, but never been emotionally drawn to them. It happened because, like nobody else, he understands me. I suddenly realize with a shock that the emotion I'm feeling is paternal. He understands me the way a son will sometimes understand a father. More mental confusion as I try to work out how this happened. But then I decide not to care. Enough analysis.

It is just after dawn. Natural light is replacing that from the bulb. I wonder again what is happening in the outside world. A rescue plan must be in process. The special forces will be training. Even with satellite surveillance alone they will know the disposition of the hostages and guards. The chances of success must be good.

I hear the sound of the outside door and the clomping of his boots. I get up as the key turns in the lock. He said two days. What is he doing here and why so early? The door is pushed open. I hear him clomping to his chair. There's a little water in the bucket. I splash some on my face and go out.

His face is different. His eyes are not alert as before. It's as though they look in rather than out. He doesn't smile. He is obviously troubled and for a moment I think events are moving. Maybe freedom is on the way.

Then he says, "Peabody, were you ever jealous?"

"Jealous? You mean over a woman?"

"Yes."

"Well, of course." I think about that. It was so long ago.

"Why?"

I can't help but laugh. From anyone else it would be a ridiculous question, but he gives it the weight of earnestness. I answer. "It's human nature to be jealous. With some it's a disease. What's all this about? Are you jealous of someone?"

He ignores the question and asks, "When was the first time you were jealous?"

"Listen Calderon, this is stupid."

He looks up. "Tell me ... please."

He spoke the last word softly, almost painfully. He is surely troubled. I'm shocked again to feel paternal instincts. I delve into my memory.

"I was fifteen. So was she. I dated her a couple of times. We were in high school together. She started dating a football jock who was seventeen, and dropped me."

"You loved her?"

"Hell, no. I thought I did at the time."

"Thought you did!" He is genuinely puzzled. "It makes no sense. Either you did or you didn't."

"Not at all. I thought I was in love three times before it finally happened."

"And that was when you met Amparo?"

"Yes."

He runs his hand through his hair. "I don't understand, Peabody. You were not genuinely in love with that first girl, but you were jealous about her. That's not logical."

I smile. "Logic, love, jealousy. They don't make a good triangle."

"True. What you're saying then, is that it's possible to be genuinely jealous, without being genuinely in love."

I consider that. "Yes, of course. The emotion of jealousy can be falsely stimulated. But you'll only ever know that by hindsight."

He shakes his head. His eyes are focused inward again. He scratches his nose thoughtfully. "How long had you known Amparo before you got this revelation of genuine love?"

Strangely I find I don't mind thinking or talking of her. "After about a month. At first I was attracted by her beauty. Then, after we had been out a few times, I got an idea of her character. Then it just happened."

"Suddenly?"

My mind goes back to the exact date. June 19th, 1958. I describe what happened. "We were sitting in a small bar in a side street off El Prado. A guitarist played softly in a corner, the lighting was subdued. She was wearing a blue and white blouse with a high collar. She turned her head and smiled at me—and in that instant I crashed into love."

As I finish the story he looks morose. "Had you made love to her?"

"No. The first time we made love was an hour later."

He sighs as if this information adds to his problems. My curiosity is acute.

"What's all this about, Calderon? You've been here less than two weeks. Have you already fallen for a local girl?"

"No." He shakes his head sadly. "I brought my problem all the way from Havana."

"You brought a woman with you? Castro allowed that?"

His smile would look well on a death's head. "Fidel warned me about her. He let her come, but he warned me."

I can't help being intrigued. "What has she done?"

He looks at his watch and sighs. "About now, it's just possible that she's climbing out of Bermudez's bed. If not, it's a certainty that by tonight she'll be climbing into it."

"You say it's possible she's with Bermudez. If it's not certain, why don't you go and try to stop her?"

His sad expression instantly changes. "Because that bastard has cancelled the delivery van! I can't get out until tomorrow."

A nice twist. Calderon is breathing more quickly. In this session his poker face is absent.

"This woman is very beautiful?"

"Very. But she's a witch—an animal even."

"So why did you get involved?"

He looks me in the eye. "Peabody, I know you and I guess you know me. You can work it out."

I certainly can. This is the man whose sole reaction to possible death is fascination. He enjoys going to the edge. This woman must be quite something to pull him so close to it. But I'm still puzzled. I ask him, "Have you been in love before?"

"No."

"Been jealous before?"

"No."

"Are you being honest with yourself?"

"Yes, I am." He sighs in disgust. "I'm attractive to women. I've got power over them. I've known many. I've lost count of the number I've slept with. Sometimes . . . occasionally . . . well . . . very occasionally, a woman has left me for another man. I never felt a twinge of jealousy or envy."

I believe him and I'm intrigued. I'm just wondering if he really loves her when he says flatly, "I'm indulging myself. I don't just think I love her. I know it. Peabody, how could I fall in love with an animal?"

"I can't help you there. I'm not an expert. But what are you going to do?"

I watch his face resume the normal Calderon expression. He's probably holding a low pair but it could be four aces. He says, "I'll work it out. Anyway I'm not here to talk about women."

"Calderon, I'll tell you the perfect way you work it out. When you get out of here, take her straight to the airport and fly home with her; meanwhile having given the order for me to be taken from this cesspit and reunited with the other Americans."

"I can't. There are no planes."

Ah! The power of a woman. He's so unsettled he's slipped and shown his low pair. "No planes." So there's a blockade as I suspected. I'll bet he wants to chew his tongue into mincemeat. He tries to recover.

"Peabody, listen to me. I'll do better than reunite you with the others. Give me one name and within half an hour you'll be freshly bathed and shaved; wearing your finest clothes and sitting at your dining-room table eating a sirloin steak from your kitchen. Think about it, man. One name!"

I have to force my senses not to take in the sight and aroma of the dish.

Coldly I tell him, "When I leave this room it will either be to total freedom or to rejoin those Americans who are my responsibility. Do you really believe I would betray my country for a piece of meat?"

DAY FOURTEEN

COLONEL SLOCUM. *Fort Bragg, USA.*

The phone rings. I'm in the bath. It always happens. I heave myself out of the bath, wrap on a towel and drip water through to the study. It's Komlosy.

"You got me out of the bath," I tell him severely.

"Tough luck. Decision's been taken. If the poison operation fails, the rescue goes ahead—soonest. You and your men have been selected."

I feel a surge of relief—and anxiety. "When will we know?"

"In three days from now. You said you needed three weeks, but it's only been twelve days. Will you be ready?"

"Sure, Mike. Since you were here, we've run through the exercise fifteen times. War is like a football game. You train your guys till they're perfect. Then you stop, or they go downhill. My team made the perfect raid three hours ago."

"OK. When we get confirmation, General Simmons will make arrangements to transport you to the *Nimitz*."

Cautiously I ask, "There's no chance this poison thing can be called off?"

His voice sobers. "No. But anyway, get ready to move."

DAY FIFTEEN

JORGE CALDERON. *San Carlo.*

I study the photograph, trying to imagine how it was between them. How she was. It is not difficult. Once again I go over my strategy. It must be exact. He is ready and, in normal circumstances, I would be fully confident of success. But nothing now is normal. It is necessary that I hurt him. Hurt him so deeply that he will reach out to me for comfort. But I have no passion for it. Also in this strategy I have to lie just a little. This should not be a problem, but it is. In past sessions, when I told him the truth, he believed me. Is the opposite true? It is a frightening possibility.

I hear the key in the door and slide the photograph back into the file. Inez comes in with the face of a child leaving a chocolate factory. She leans over and kisses me. The witch has not even bothered to bathe. I smell his cologne.

"You really should have come with us, Jorge. It's a beautiful palace. The furniture is from Spain . . . antique. Even the handles for the doors."

It comes out even before I can think. "And I suppose the bed was a Castilian four poster."

She smiles. Pretty white teeth, perfectly shaped; lips curving into an arc of derision.

"You are so clever, Jorge. Eighteenth century. It is said that Queen Isabella slept in it."

Yet again the jealousy makes me nauseous. I must not show it. When I returned home from the compound yesterday I adopted a nonchalant attitude, saying nothing of my forced containment there. It confused her. She was so sure that I would lose control. I contained my rage with great difficulty. I must continue to do so or I am lost. But now, today, she has again been alone with him.

"Five thousand hectares, Jorge. All coffee. It covers hills and valleys."

Keeping my voice neutral I remark, "And doubtless Bermudez

will now turn it into a commune for the workers who slaved on it for years."

Her black hair swirls as she flounces away to the window. "Doesn't Roberto deserve something? He fought for years. He endured great suffering. You think the people will begrudge him one palace out of thousands? He has given them freedom."

I desperately want her to understand. In the understanding maybe she will turn away from him.

I tell her, "Inez, freedom is equality. There cannot be oppression if there is equality. Ask yourself this. A quarter of a century ago Fidel made his revolution. Does he live in a palace? No. He lives in a small apartment. He owns no great estates . . . no antique furniture. After all these years he works every day; sometimes sixteen hours . . . for the revolution . . . for Cuba. Now, Bermudez is already casting his eye over the country like a vulture. He wants a billion dollars from the Americans. How much will the people see of it?"

She turns, climbs onto the bed and sits cross-legged. "You are jealous of him. You think you are so clever but he is cleverer. You are the same age, but he has already conquered a country; is already the leader of his people. And what have you done? Has your American talked? No! Have you got one name? No! Roberto says that if, after twenty days you have failed, then he will do it. He owes it to Fidel."

"What the hell are you talking about?"

She sees my fury and leans forward, feeding off it. "Roberto thinks you are soft. Why spend twenty days? Fombona will do it in two without leaving marks. Then they will give Peabody an injection, and he will die. They have the drug. It will seem like a heart attack. Even the best doctors cannot tell. Roberto will be very sorry, express much regret and deliver the body with full honours. He knows that Fidel will be grateful."

The scenario rips through my mind. I consider the angles. What *would* Fidel's reaction be? He is truly desperate for that name. The Americans have tried to kill him a dozen times. And the Chamarristas would be doing the deed, not him. For him it would be a windfall. I could persuade him otherwise but I've no means of communication. I believe her. Bermudez would do it. Peabody must talk within four days.

I tell her, "Peabody will not talk under torture."

"Fombona tells him different."

"Fombona is a fool. So is Bermudez."

"He gets what he wants!"

She is wearing a thin cotton blouse. She sees my eyes on it, and

swings her feet to the ground, struts over and stands close to me. "He's a wonderful lover . . . better than you. Jorge Calderon, you are finished . . . a failure. And I like strength. I move from weakness to strength. Something's gone wrong with you, just in a few days. Maybe it's the American. Roberto says the American is stronger than you." She watches me contemptuously as I struggle for control. "Anyway, it's over. I've come to get my clothes. A car is waiting for me. Jorge, you are . . . boring."

She spits in my face.

My control is gone. Some seconds pass. I hardly hear her screams. I don't hear the door opening. I only feel the throat under my thumbs. I don't hear their shouts or feel their hands pulling at me. I only see her eyes blazing triumphant in her reddening face. Then I am stunned with a blow to my head and she pulls away. I am lying on the carpet. She is laughing. My bodyguards help me to my feet. They are mumbling apologies, explaining that they could not let me kill her. I have a terrible pain in my head. I stumble as I walk to the table and pick up my files. An eternity passes while I fumble them into the bag and walk carefully to the door. I don't look at her, but as I leave, her laughter sears my eardrums.

THE MESTIZO IS again in the truck. He looks once at my face and turns away. My hands are still shaking—and my brain. I feel the lead of shame in my belly. Peabody will look at me and guess; will know that I've been beaten by that woman.

By the time we reach the compound I'm more composed. But I have to get my confidence back. The only way is through Peabody. He must give me a name. If I fail and Bermudez succeeds then I am finished in all their eyes—and my own.

Quickly I walk to the guardhouse. I send the sleepy guard away, take out the file and unlock the door to the inner room. I am sitting behind the desk looking at the file when he moves out and stands opposite me. I look up and my resolve is washed away. He is watching me, his head slightly on one side. There is concern in his eyes. Concern for me. I suddenly know what I feel for this man. It goes beyond affection. This man, this capitalist is closer to me than anyone I've ever known.

"What happened to you, Jorge?"

My name "Jorge". It sounds so natural, this first time he uses it. I'm close again to losing control. I have to swallow hard.

"I tried to kill her."

Without taking his eyes off me he carefully sits down.

210

"What did she do?"

"Nothing unexpected. She left me for Bermudez. Her going was in keeping with her character. She was vicious. She enjoyed it."

After a silence he says, "You fell in love . . . so you lost."

In a few words he has painted the exact picture. He makes more brush strokes. "And this loss is your first. You never conceived it possible. You imagined yourself different from other mortals. So it's devastating."

I am pinned and squirming. He has peeled me open.

His voice changes tone. I feel like a boy as he gently says, "Jorge, bless your luck. Had you gone on that way your character would have fossilized . . . like mine. If that witch has taken away your arrogance, or made you aware of it, then she has done you an inestimable service. She may just have turned you into a human being."

It's all going wrong. I know what I have to do and yet I sit and listen. . . . I want to sit and listen and talk for hours; and maybe find the paths I have never seen. With an effort I put coldness into my voice. "Peabody, my situation is immaterial. We both indulge ourselves with emotions. Now circumstances have changed. It is vital, both for me and for you that you give me the name I want."

Very quietly and very firmly he states, "Whatever happens, I will never do that."

I have difficulty looking at him. I centre the file in front of me—position the weapon exactly between us.

"Peabody, you know that name—and the others—because you advised the CIA. You advised them because over decades you have built up a hatred for my country . . . a hatred based on a single tragic incident. That incident never happened."

He is puzzled. "Never happened?"

"No. Amparo Flores did not die in a Cuban prison twenty-five years ago. She died in the finest Cuban hospital two years ago . . . from a cerebral thrombosis."

Tension is immediately in the room. The link between us is broken. I now have to make my little lie. With genuine sorrow I tell him, "A month after she enrolled at Havana University, Amparo Flores became an agent for Fidel Castro. She was a fervent believer in the revolution." I tap the file. "Her first assignment was to seduce a colonel in Batista's national guard and discover troop dispositions for the defence of the city. She carried it out brilliantly. Her second assignment was to seduce a man called Peabody, the political counsellor at the American embassy, and influence him to the cause."

211

He is shaking his head, puzzlement still in his eyes. We are so close now. I force myself on.

"She also carried out that assignment brilliantly." Emphatically I tap the file. "You became almost an advocate for the cause. You fell in love with her." Again I tap the file. "You told her much about American policy—even as you argued against it. To keep you talking she agreed to a bethrothal. And when Havana fell to Castro, *he* persuaded her to continue the assignment. Even urged her to marry you and go on supplying information and influence. She did so for another month. But by then she had met Raul Gomez who had fought with Castro throughout the struggle. They fell in love. You will know his name. He is now assistant minister for agriculture. It was arranged that she should be arrested as a subversive. In due course her death was announced. In reality her name and papers were changed. She married Gomez secretly."

He is a bearded statue, carved into the chair. I pause. It is easier now. I am able to tell him the truth.

"She worked as a teacher. In '63 she had a daughter—Pilar. She also is a teacher ... I know her."

His mouth opens. He is breathing deeply. He shakes his head again. "Jorge, these lies will change nothing. Why try to smear her memory?"

The moment has, at last, arrived. I open the file and slide out the photographs. Eight-by-ten enlargements. I push the first one over. Amparo Flores, aged twenty-seven, sitting in a chair smiling at the camera. She is holding a baby.

I watch as he looks down at it. I wait, judging the moment, then reach out and place the second one on top: Amparo Flores, aged thirty-nine. She is smiling at her tall, teenage daughter who proudly holds a small silver cup won in a school athletics contest.

Peabody is frozen. Very slowly I reach forward and complete the pile with the last photograph: Amparo Flores, aged fifty-two. She is sitting at a restaurant table wearing a white dress, her hair piled high on her head. She is still remarkably beautiful. Her husband, Raul Gomez is on her left. On her right sits Fidel Castro.

Still he doesn't move or utter a sound. This has to be the moment. Irrationally I'm aware that if he actually survives this moment he will be a dead man, murdered by Fombona. To live he has to talk. For this reason, I must nudge him over the top.

"You know these photographs are genuine. No science can fake her face or her expression ... Jason, we did not kill her ... you built a philosophy on a lie...."

212

Still not a flicker from him. His eyes are on the only woman he ever loved, the only person he ever grieved over. On her, on her husband, and on Castro.

The moment is balanced. I dare not say another word. Doubts are building in me when the sound comes: a sob. Then another. His shoulders shake. I watch as he slumps across the desk. I have won. This man hasn't wept for an eternity. I feel no elation. I want to reach out and help, but I cannot. I must continue now. The sobbing has stopped. His cheek is lying on the photographs, his arms around his head. I repeat my words.

"Jason, you built a philosophy on a lie. Your logic was warped by hatred. It's over now. You can be yourself again. You can find the ideals and emotions that you smothered thirty years ago. Jason, give me a name."

He raises his head. "Jorge, whatever I became after that lie; whatever I've done; whatever is done to me, I will never give you the names you want. I know the names; all of them. I will not betray them. I will not betray my country. I know that my country, for all its ills and mistakes is a force for good in this world . . . and I will not betray it."

The quiet conviction of his words finally snaps my control. I scream at his gaunt face, "You are stupid! You are dumb! Just a stupid, dumb American!"

Through the haze of my rage I hear him whisper, "Yes. You know, dumb is defined as mute; silent. When it comes to betraying my country I'm proud to be dumb."

DAY SIXTEEN

JASON PEABODY. *San Carlo.*

I have lost all sense of time. I sit in this chair and look at the wall. I have nothing left now. What a pathetic waste I've been, shuffling around on this earth. Half my life an idealistic fool; the other half a puritanical fop. Because a woman looked at me in a bar one night.

I hear the key turn. He comes in briskly, but his attitude is more resigned than confident. Over the past days I have been sledgehammered into mental change. So has he.

He sits down. "Jason, it is time now to face reality. Your position is not good. I am going to tell you the situation. There is no more time for sparring. Listen, I accept that whatever I do I'm unlikely to get a name from you. What I do now is not a trick. What I do is for you."

"Then why do it?"

He is as numb as I. It shows in his eyes. He says, "I don't want you to die."

"Why?"

He turns his head and looks at the wall. "Bermudez has decided that after twenty days, if I don't have a name, he'll set Fombona on you and extract it—by torture."

His words are incredible. "How can you believe that Bermudez would allow me, an ambassador, to be tortured, knowing the consequences when my government finds out, as they surely must?"

Dismally he completes the picture. "Bermudez is crazy. He'll let Fombona torture you without leaving a mark. Afterwards they inject you with a drug. It will appear that you had a heart attack. Then the militant students will make a regretful announcement and hand over your body to the authorities, who in turn will beat their breasts and give it back to your people."

With a chill I realize he's telling the truth.

He is watching. His eyes see into me. "Jason, this is not a trick. You must believe me. You must give me a name. I cannot protect you if I don't have that name."

I shake my head. "I cannot do it, Jorge." I am surprised by how much conviction I hear in my voice.

Apparently he is not. He nods thoughtfully. There is a long silence while I contemplate my short future and how I will face it.

Then he says firmly, "They will not torture you."

I gaze at him and he gives a wan smile. "They will not torture you because I will leave here in the morning and send to Fidel the names of those two who I suspect the most: Pineda and Samarriba."

His eyes are totally alert as he says the names. While I keep my expression neutral I marvel at his perception. One of them is correct. I shrug negatively.

He continues, "With the names I will send the message: 'Hold until my arrival'. Fidel will do that. He will not let anyone else interrogate them. Of course I may be right in my guesses. Then so much the better. If not, I will drag out the interrogations. When you are free—and I think it will not be too long—then I will be able to tell Fidel the truth and take the consequences."

I am almost paralysed with gratitude. I manage to ask, "What will the consequences be?"

"I don't know, Jason. I cannot imagine what Fidel will do."

I have a feeling of helplessness. He is destroying his own life to save mine. I search around in my mind.

"Jorge, if you are right, and if I get out of here soon, there's a way I can help. The CIA still has a strong presence in Havana. There's a good chance they could get you out. You could have a new life in the States."

He smiles again. "Thanks, but no. My failure here hasn't changed my convictions. I'll go on with my old life ... wherever it leads. You will lead your life—I will lead mine."

JORGE CALDERON. *San Carlo.*

Not for a second did I consider his offer. Whatever has happened, or is to come, I, Jorge Calderon, will not run from it.

There is a tap on the door and I call, "Enter."

I know it is the Mestizo boy and I know what he brings. I ordered it in the residence kitchen half an hour ago.

The boy approaches nervously, puts the tray on the desk between us, then scuttles out. I watch Peabody closely. There is a look of disbelief on his face.

On the tray is a large oval plate, in the centre of which is a juicy sirloin steak flanked by twin hillocks of French fried potatoes. Beside the plate is a wine glass, a bottle of vintage claret and a corkscrew with a silver handle.

He is running his tongue across his lips. He reaches for the bottle of wine and the corkscrew.

I find my own gaze transfixed on the steak. It's a symbol of my failure. I feel a rage building inside me. He is very carefully removing the foil from the bottle. Holding it so as not to disturb the wine. He eases out the cork, unscrews it and raises it to his nose. Satisfied, he places it on the tray, picks up the bottle and half fills the glass. He swirls the wine a little, then lifts it to his nose.

He takes a sip, nods in satisfaction and then says apologetically, "Jorge, I am forgetting myself. Won't you join me? Call for another glass."

My rage explodes. I lunge forward and pull the tray across the desk. Some wine spills from the glass. I can hear my voice, words tumbling out in frustration.

"Damn you. I'm the one who's going to suffer. If I don't get a name, you don't get a steak!"

I grab the knife and fork, cut a piece of meat and raise it to my mouth. It's rare and dripping juice. At the first bite my rage is washed away; also my self-pity. What have I been reduced to? I chew mechanically, swallow and push the tray back.

He is watching me suspiciously. I gesture reassuringly at the plate. He picks up the knife and fork, cuts a slice of meat and puts it in his mouth.

But wait! It is not delicious. I have a bitter aftertaste in my mouth and my gums begin to feel numb. Suddenly I feel the pain—like a white hot knife being plunged into my stomach. I realize in an instant. The Mestizo boy asked me twice in the kitchen: "It's for the ambassador? The American?" The Mestizo boy who's been out of the compound.

Another searing spasm of pain, then I realize that Peabody is chewing. I shout, "No! Wait! You mustn't eat! The meat has been poisoned!"

I hurl myself across the desk, scattering the plate and wine. He goes over backwards with me on top, and lies stunned while I push fingers between his teeth, praying that the meat's still there. It is. I pull it out and throw it across the room. The wine bottle has rolled to the edge of the desk and is spilling its contents. I grab it. His eyes are open now, looking up at me in shock. I push the neck of the bottle against his lips.

"Wash your mouth out. Don't swallow! Wash and spit out."

He sucks the wine in. I roll away from him with spasms of pain spreading out from the centre of my body. My knees come up to my chin. I have never known such pain. I realize with cold clarity that it's the prelude to death.

He is beside me, an arm cradling my head, his voice urgent. "I'll call someone. They'll get you to hospital."

I shake my head. "I'm done, Jason. It was meant for you. Your people tried to kill you."

I can feel death coming. It marches in time to the spasms. I have to tell him. "Jason, I lied ... listen to me. You have to know ... Amparo loved you. It's true she died two years ago ... true she married Gomez ... but she loved you, Jason. She would have married you, wanted to. And Fidel wanted her to ... and keep passing information ... but she couldn't do that to you ... so she chose the other way ... but she loved you ... it's the truth ... please believe me."

Through the agony I feel his other arm come around my shoulders. He holds me tight and says, "I believe you, Jorge."

He does believe me. The pain, like guilt after a confessional, seems to be washed away. I'm aware of my limbs moving but I cannot feel them ... I can only feel his arms holding me....

216

JASON PEABODY. *San Carlo.*

His body convulses. I draw him closer. His face against my chest, my arms holding him. I put my lips to his ear.

"My son ... Jorge ... you are as my son."

His fingers grip me. More convulsions. Then suddenly, abruptly, he is still.

I hold him as time passes. Just twice in over sixty years I have felt bonded to another human being. I run my fingers through his hair. It is damp with my tears.

There is a noise at the door. Fombona crashes in, others crowding behind him. They have to prise Jorge out of my arms.

They take Jorge away. Time passes. I hear a distant, single shot. Then Fombona comes in again. I look up at him standing by the door. His face radiates anticipation.

"You will soon be screaming, pig. Tomorrow I will be bringing some equipment here, and you will scream and scream ... and you will talk."

I resolve at this moment, not to speak another word.

DAY SEVENTEEN

COLONEL SLOCUM. *Fort Bragg, USA.*

I'm waiting beside the cargo plane. My team and all the equipment left three hours ago for the *Nimitz*, just before I got the call to wait so that Komlosy could brief me personally. I'm excited. I've been this way for eight hours, since Komlosy's voice came through telling me that the other operation failed and we're going in.

Now I hear the chopper. It lands about a hundred yards away. Komlosy and General Simmons step down. As the chopper's rotor stops I walk over to meet them. I shake Komlosy's hand and salute Simmons.

Simmons is a tall gangly man approaching sixty, with straw-coloured hair. He addresses me. "Colonel, the commander in chief asked me to convey his entire confidence in you and your men. He is sure that as a result of your forthcoming action our citizens will be safely returned and our country's honour upheld. He is looking forward to welcoming you and your team at the White House."

I've got a lump in my throat and I'm trying to think of a suitable reply when a jeep pulls up. Simmons says, "I'm going to pick up my kit. I'll be back in ten minutes."

He climbs into the jeep and as it pulls away I ask Komlosy, "What happened to the other operation?"

He grins. "Apparently they poisoned the wrong man. Our agents report that the Cuban interrogator was delivered to the morgue."

"And what about our agent in the compound?"

"We have to assume he's dead. He was a young Mestizo who worked in the kitchen."

I'm puzzled. "Why would he take that risk?"

"He was from a very poor family, one of twelve children. We guaranteed his entire family a new life in the States ... so he sacrificed himself."

Komlosy muses for a while, then turns to me.

"Silas, you pull this one off and there's no limit to how far you can go. You know that, don't you?"

I voice a thought that has been in my mind for the past few days. "We'll pull it off, Mike. But after it's over I'm thinking of taking early retirement."

His face shows his surprise. "Why would you do that? Hell, you're only forty-six. Don't you want promotion?"

"No, Mike. I've been in this army since I was eighteen. I don't regret any of it, but I want to do something else."

"What?"

"Don't laugh, but I'm going to be a rancher. Never spent much money—saved most of it. A couple of years back I bought a small spread in Wyoming. Not big, but enough for me. It's tucked in right under the Rockies. It's got a pine-board cabin on it—not much but comfortable. I'll get a couple of dogs and walk behind them of an evening."

He's got a smile on his face.

"What's so funny?"

The smile widens into a grin. "I'm picturing you as a cowboy. Wherever are you going to find a horse big enough to lump you around?"

Thought lines appear across his forehead.

"Silas, you're an enigma. Haven't you got any real close friends?"

"Nope."

"Not one? I would have thought that army life generated a special kind of friendship."

"Mike, army life maybe does just that for most people. I guess I'm a loner."

He looks thoughtfully out across the airfield. With relief I hear the jeep coming. It swings around in front of us and Simmons climbs out. "You ready, Colonel Slocum?"

"Yessir, General."

"I'll see you in the plane then." He turns away and walks to the Trader.

Komlosy holds out his hand. I grip it and say, "Mike, thanks for giving me the chance. I won't let you down."

He smiles. "It's kind of odd being thanked for giving a guy a damned good chance to get killed." His face fades, and he adds quietly, "Good luck, Silas."

I slap him on the back and turn towards the plane. I must be getting soft. I can't say anything because I'm scared my goddam voice will quiver!

THE GENERAL AND I are the only passengers. We sit in companionable silence while the plane climbs to cruising altitude. He's probably thinking about the mission. I'm not. I'm thinking about what I said to Komlosy. About me being a loner. I sure can talk rubbish sometimes. Why do I always have to project the big black tough guy image?

May's words come back through twenty years: "Silas, I don't understand it much either. I know you love me and I sure love you. But Silas, I *need* you, and you don't need me. It's taken me two years to face up to that. And I've got to find a man who needs me . . . just as much as I need him."

I can see her face as she spoke those words. Earnest, sad, intelligent and beautiful. It was five years till I woke up one night and realized that I'd rather have May than a super tough image. Five years! I traced her to a suburb of Fort Lauderdale. She had married an engineer just six months after our divorce came through.

I had to know, so I took some leave, flew over there and hired a car. I located her house and cruised by it a few times. It was a nice home. The husband had to be at work so I parked at the corner and told myself I ought to go over and visit. I sat there for an age telling myself there was nothing wrong with that, but unable to get out of the car. Then she came round the back of the house pushing a baby carriage. She walked down the drive and crossed the street right in front of me. She didn't notice me. She was heart-stoppingly beautiful—and happy.

So I crawled back under my tough image and let all those thoughts wither away. Friendship. What the hell do I know about that?

DAY EIGHTEEN

JASON PEABODY. *San Carlo.*

I try to imagine describing it to someone. How to convey the agony and degradation. Torture stretches our species' depravity beyond any possible comparison. No other animal on earth approaches it. The evil of sadism is confined to mankind and mocks all our pretensions to ascendancy over other creatures.

Torture starts in the mind. As I waited for Fombona, sleep was impossible. I sat with my back to the hard wall and tried to prepare myself. The night passed with dreadful speed.

Shortly after dawn I heard the squeak of the gates and the motor of the truck, Fombona's voice shouting orders. I could feel the coppery taste of fear on my tongue. Then the key turning and Fombona at the door.

With a smile on his face he supervised the installing of his equipment. "Over there," he commanded as two guards struggled to get a heavy canvas-covered object through the door. Grunting with exertion they manoeuvred it over to the far wall.

There followed a high, small-topped table, a canvas bag, and several rolls of thick black cloth. He had the table positioned beside an electric socket and the bag and the cloth were put beside it. The guards were dismissed and the door closed.

Fombona was standing in the centre of the room watching me. "OK, pig. Here's how it is. You give me names or in a few minutes you start to experience pain that you never knew existed."

I took a long, slow swallow and shook my head. Immediately I saw relief in his smile.

"Good!" He chuckled, and turned away rubbing his hands.

"Let us prepare. I will now introduce you to *El Abrazo*—the embracer."

Theatrically he pulled off the canvas cover. It was like a great wooden barrel sliced lengthways and mounted on a stand. Its dark surface was broken by gleaming metal studs spaced about four inches apart. There were leather thongs hanging from the corners.

He fetched the rolls of black cloth and started draping them over the studs. I could feel my limbs going rigid with fear. He walked to the canvas bag and lifted out a black metal box trailing three wires. One ended in a plug. Each of the other two, longer and thicker, was attached to a crocodile clip.

He held the apparatus up for my inspection. With strange clarity I noted the single switch and the dial with its graduated colours: vectors of yellow, blue, green and red.

"Excellency, meet *El Rompecabezas*—the tickler." He nodded with his chin to the barrel. "*El Abrazo* and *El Rompecabezas* are partners. One lovingly embraces ... the other tickles." He put the box carefully onto the table and pointed. "The switch turns on the current. The dial is a rheostat. The yellow sector gives a moderate current. It increases through the blue and green. Red is usually fatal."

He reached down into the bag and took out several rolls of bandages and put them on the table. Then he pulled out a white bundle, unrolled it, and slipped it on—a doctor's coat. He smiled at me and again reached into the bag. This time it was a stethoscope which he hung around his neck.

"Doctor Carlos Fombona at your service, Excellency. I was in fact a medical student for a year. Not a good one but I learned a few things. For a man of sixty-three you are in good health but sometimes *El Rompecabezas* can upset the heart. You will be glad to know that I will keep monitoring yours."

He shouted an order and four guards entered the cell. One of them held a grey blanket loosely over one arm. They were very practised. I was not. One made a feint for my left wrist. I lashed out at him, striking only air and losing my balance. Then darkness as the blanket enveloped my head, and arms clasped me. I kicked out and then hands were gripping my waist and ankles and I was helpless.

I was lifted and laid down on my back, across the studs. The blanket was pulled away and there was Fombona's face leering over me.

"First his ankles. Hold him tight."

I felt something being wrapped around my left ankle.

"Bandages," Fombona remarked. "They will stop the leather from chafing your delicate skin."

They quickly finished the bandaging. I gasped in pain as my arms were forced backwards and down over the slopes of the barrel. With the thongs tied I was stretched as though on a rack, and after only seconds began to feel the aching spread, moving from my arms into my shoulders and across my chest and back. I heard Fombona dismiss the guards; the tramp of feet and the closing of the door. Silence. It was about to happen. Desperately I tried to prepare my mind. Repeated to myself that I would not utter a word, no matter what.

Suddenly my chin was pulled roughly back and fingers were digging in on each side above my jaw, forcing open my mouth. Something hard was pushed in between my teeth and below my tongue. I gagged as I tasted rubber.

"A bone for the dog." His voice was very quiet but very clear. "To stop you biting your tongue . . . and to muffle your screams. Now we make it secure."

I could feel the cloth strips being pulled tight under my ears and fingers fumbling at the nape of my neck as he tied the knots. I closed my eyes, squeezing the lids together, praying for strength. Then I felt his hand on my right foot and the grip of metal on my big toe. I strained against the leather, but I was secured like a pin-stuck butterfly.

He was at my left arm. The clamp of metal on my thumb. I lay still. He was alongside me again, talking in a soft, intimate voice.

"We will begin. Only the yellow sector. In later sessions we will go higher. Remember that. And I want no names now. Don't try to tell me names. This is only to introduce you to *El Abrazo* and *El Rompecabezas*. Don't spoil it by trying to tell me names. . . . Listen for the click."

I drew a breath and held it—and then I heard the click.

The pain was a memory a millisecond after it ended. A memory enclosed in a scream. A searing, cold memory.

In Brazil I once saw gold being smelted. A huge vat of yellow vicious heat. Someone dropped into such a vat would have the same last memory, and be lucky it was the last.

Then he was bending over me, the flat of the stethoscope on my chest. I couldn't see. Sweat stung my eyes. I turned my head and shook it, trying to stop sobbing. He listened for a long time and then straightened. My vision cleared. He was smiling as though at a recovering patient.

"Good. Your Excellency has an excellent heart. That was only two seconds . . . a little introduction. Next time it will be longer. Listen for the click."

For half an hour he tortured and teased. He was beyond evil. He wanted no name. Nothing but the pleasure. When it was over and they had lifted me limp from the barrel, nourishing food was brought. He wanted me healthy. With a sneer he informed me that the next day would be the twentieth day—the Cuban's twentieth day. Where the Cuban failed he would succeed. On that day I would go onto *El Abrazo* and stay there until I talked.

I took the food. A rich vegetable and meat soup. The guards had been ordered not to say a word to me. It was a relief. No words from them. No words from me.

A guard was always in the room sitting on a chair by the door. Eyes always on me; changing every two hours or so. Fombona is taking no chances that I will mark myself.

Now I lie on the palliasse in the centre of the room, the silent guard eight feet away. There is a faint light at the barred window. He will come again soon. I pass through moments of enraged bitterness. What are they doing about me? Those bastards back home? First they try to kill me—then they just leave me here. What the hell are they doing?

The moments of bitterness come and go. So do moments of profound self-pity. Also, at times when I can force away thoughts of the coming torture, I review my life—both with bitterness and self-pity. What a mockery of a life. Almost all of it wasted. I made a smartly pressed suit more important in my life than a caring thought; a perfect cup of coffee superior to a human emotion; a vintage claret preferable to love.

Too late now. The twentieth day has dawned.

DAY TWENTY

COLONEL SLOCUM. *USS* Nimitz.

On boarding the liner *Queen Mary* in New York, Mae West was reported to have asked the captain: "When does this place get to Europe?"

I get the same kind of feeling whenever I'm on one of our big carriers. I'm standing on a city of over six thousand people.

It's a dark night, just after eleven o'clock. There's not a lot of activity up here on the acres of flightdeck. I came to be alone for a while and to try and control my frustration. San Carlo and the compound are just twelve miles away. I'm facing towards them, swaying a little in the gusts of wind caused by a lady called Olga. She's a hurricane which at this time of year has no business lurking around between Venezuela and Haiti. I restrain the urge to go to the met. office again. Those guys are already fed up with my badgering. But being alone is doing nothing for my frustration.

Now the tannoy blares. "Colonel Slocum to report to the admiral's sea cabin."

The message is repeated as I hurry across to the lift. I make my way through the maze of corridors feeling a little apprehensive, and tap on the admiral's door. I hear the barked "enter" and go in.

The admiral's sitting at the head of the table. The *Nimitz*'s captain is on his left, and General Simmons is sitting on his right. They are looking mighty serious. The admiral indicates a chair at the front of the table, and I sit down.

Simmons sighs and says to the admiral, "Allow me to do this, please."

The admiral nods. There is a little pile of papers in front of General Simmons. He shuffles them for a moment, sighs again and says, "Colonel, there's been an ominous development. Reports are flowing into Langley from San Carlo in growing numbers, and our analysts have told us that there's a ninety-per-cent possibility that our ambassador is currently being tortured. In that event it is one-hundred-per-cent certain that the torturer is the leader of the so-called militant students: one Carlos Fombona. He's a known sadist. The national security council is in session and waiting for our recommendations."

For a moment rage threatens to overwhelm me. How can the bastards do that to Peabody? First they abuse and humiliate him. Then our own analysts decide that he's a loser. Then our people try to poison the poor man. And now he's being tortured! He's just a dozen miles away. Frustration wells up in me, and then subsides as I realize what I have to do. The ship's captain is talking.

"I just don't understand why they'd do that. Why take the risk? They must realize the consequences."

Simmons says curtly, "They have compelling reasons, but that's classified information. Our analysts surmise that afterwards they'll fake death by natural causes. It's ..."

I break in flatly, "So we go and get him out now!"

The admiral grimaces. "You seem to forget Hurricane Olga and the weather conditions out there. They exceed the flying parameters of those contraptions of yours."

I retort, "We'll go anyway. Enough of us will get through to do the job."

He shrugs cynically. "You hope."

I lean forward to deliver a few selected words but Simmons cuts them off.

"Colonel! First we'll examine all aspects ... then we'll forward a recommendation to the national security council who'll pass it on to the president for executive decision." He turns to the admiral. "We should get an update from the met. officer."

224

The admiral nods and while the met. officer is sent for I say, "I'd like to have Newman and Allen sit in on this."

"Civilians?" the admiral barks incredulously.

Simmons answers for me. "They're the world's top experts on those contraptions, Admiral. They're on this vessel by executive order."

The admiral stares at him, then shrugs and nods. As the met. officer enters, sits down and pulls out his charts, Simmons picks up the telephone and gives the order.

Newman and Allen arrive in about three minutes, looking scruffy in denims and creased shirts. They sit down with expectant faces, but as I quickly bring them up to date, their expressions turn sombre.

The met. officer takes over with his weather charts. Olga is fat and furious. Although she's lurking some hundred and eighty miles south of us the lines of her outer, circling winds pass over our position. They vary from forty knots to gusts of close on sixty.

He resumes his seat and the admiral asks, "So?"

Newman takes a deep breath and succinctly spells it out.

"Our ultralights would not normally operate in wind speeds of over forty knots—fairly constant knots. My guess is that it could be two, even three days before the wind drops and steadies. There's one factor in our favour. The wind is blowing on shore." He looks at the captain. "I understand you can get this tub up to thirty-six knots?" The captain smiles and nods. Newman smiles back. "OK, so you steam down wind but even picking the right moment it's going to be a very dangerous takeoff." He looks at me. "Those waves out there are going to cause all kinds of low level turbulence. A split second's loss of concentration and you're swimming . . . if you survive the impact." He winces. "And then the landing—enclosed area. You just have to land into the wind. Get a gust at the wrong moment and you get flipped like a tossed coin. You could be losing men from takeoff to landing."

Simmons cuts in. "What losses would you expect? Give me a percentage."

Newman and Allen look at each other. There's a painful silence. Then Newman says, "Between forty and fifty per cent."

Simmons turns to me. "You can expect to lose up to half your men before you hit the compound. That leaves you with ten."

"No, sir. I've got four reserves. If I have twenty-four take off, that's minimum eleven or twelve in the compound. It's enough. We've planned for it. Rehearsed it."

Simmons turns to the admiral. "OK. I'm going to call the White

House and put the situation to the NSC. But there is no way that with those projected losses this can be anything but a volunteer operation." Without looking at me he adds, "I suppose the soldier over there personally volunteers."

"Yessir!"

Was there a hint of a smile on that long face? If so it disappears when he says, "OK. I propose that if we get the go-ahead, and if we get enough volunteers, we proceed as soon as possible this night."

In less than a minute Simmons is in contact with Komlosy at the White House. He is beautifully terse as he maps out the situation. The president's there and he gets a fast decision. He hangs up, looks at me, sighs and says, "Slocum, if enough of your men are suicide-prone you have the president's order to go and get our people out."

Suddenly I panic. I've picked a bunch of wildly diverse individuals. Some for sure will go. But will it be enough? If even half a dozen opt out it'll be a non-starter. I shrug off the thought.

"Most of them are in the hangar, sir. I'll have the others sent there ... let's find out."

AS WE ENTER THE HANGAR my guys are lined up in front of the ultra-lights with the four squad leaders in front. Captain Moncada shouts, "Ten-shun!"

There's a ragged clatter as twenty-four pairs of boots hit the steel deck. I wince. This mob is not exactly a drill instructor's dream.

Simmons says loudly, "At ease!"

Another ragged clatter. He looks along the row of faces. Then in a quiet, clear voice he explains the situation. No calls to patriotism; no stress on national security. Just the torture of our ambassador; their instructors' assessment of up to fifty-per-cent projected losses; a total volunteer operation. No man will ever be looked down upon if he decides not to go. With those projected losses everyone would understand. It's not a suicide mission but comes very close to it.

I think to myself, Hell! He's practically talked them out of it. Some of them are glancing at me. I stare straight ahead.

There is a pause, then Simmons commands sharply, "Ten-shun!"

Yet another ragged clatter. I'm so wound up with the tension that I hardly notice. Simmonds commands, "Volunteers take one pace forward ... hut!"

No drill sergeant working with them ten hours a day for a month could have produced a movement with more precision and unity. Twenty-four left boots come forward. Twenty-four right boots come down beside them in a single reverberating crash. Twenty-four pairs of eyes look straight ahead. The tough old bulls don't show that they're churning up inside with relief, pride and affection.

Even Simmons cannot totally keep the emotion from his voice. "I'm sure your commanding officer is proud of you. So am I . . . and your country will be. Good luck! Go ahead, Colonel."

I look at my watch and step forward.

"OK. There's much to do. The plan will have to be modified." I glance at my watch. "We're losing time. Be at the briefing room in ten minutes."

JASON PEABODY. *San Carlo.*

He no longer bothers to check my heart. All that stopped after he moved the dial up into the blue sector. I have beaten him but will die anyway. I have been slipping in and out of consciousness. They are blessed but frightening moments.

My body rises again as a new shock passes through. My nerves shriek. The scream comes; but my mind defends itself and I pass out.

I come back slowly. Voices murmuring. Fombona talking to the guard in a surly voice. "Go now. Sleep. I am on the edge of the red. I will give him half an hour's rest. At midnight I start again. If he doesn't talk by half past midnight I give him the needle anyway."

A half hour's rest; a half hour's torment; then death. A timetable to peace.

COLONEL SLOCUM. *USS* Nimitz.

The briefing is short. The changes to the plan minimal. We will leave at ten past midnight. I am now going to land behind the west end of the residence. I will take with me our best pilot, a Puerto Rican called Rodriguez, and I will also have Brand and Kerr follow me in. They will then move directly to the front of the chancery while Moncada's squad approach from the back and sides. Rodriguez will follow me to the guardhouse. After I secure the ambassador he will guard him while I join the main assault. Sacasa's squad will assault the apartments where most of the guards should be sleeping. Castenada and his men will cover the residence and act as general troubleshooters.

After my men leave to suit up I spend a few minutes going over timings with the leaders of the back-up groups: the controller of the A6E Intruders and helicopter gunships which will "sanitize" the area around the compound; the pilots of evacuation helicopters; the

228

signals officer; the officer in charge of the rescue of any of my men who are forced down over the sea; and finally Simmons, who is co-ordinating the whole operation. Then the talking is over.

WE'RE GROUPED into attack formation up on the maindeck. The ultralights are in position, held by sailors at each wing tip. Their canvas wings are flapping and shaking in the gusts. They look about as sturdy as butterflies.

I look at my watch. Five past midnight. Everyone's ready. My four squad leaders are in front of me. I remember Wellington's words when he once reviewed some of his troops: "I don't know what they'll do to the enemy, but by God they frighten me."

They're a murderous looking quartet. Webbing festooned with grenades and spare mags. Sawn-off shotguns slung over shoulders. Black faces. Knives in boots. Submachine guns swinging from one hand. Black goggled radio helmets from the other. They're waiting for final orders. There aren't any. I just say, "So let's go do it."

I see flashes of white teeth in the darkness as they turn away. We move out onto the flightdeck and into the wind. The ultras are facing the bow, spread out across the width of the great deck in five flights. Mine is at the front. Newman and Allen are moving between the machines, checking them.

Rodriguez is directly behind me, already seated. On either side of him are Brand and Kerr. Moncada's flight of seven ultralights is behind them. I gave him extra men. With me diverting first to the guardhouse his role is vital in securing the other hostages. Behind him is Sacasa's flight of five, the Castenada five and finally, at the back, Gomez's flight of four.

I have momentary doubts. Should I have given Gomez more? He has to take out the machinegun emplacements on the roofs in the compound. That role is also vital. Damn it; everything is vital! Besides, he and his three men are crack pilots and more than likely to make it.

They're all seated. I raise both my thumbs. The signal to start engines. Apart from the two sailors holding the wing tips there's also a third sailor at the front of each machine, to signal when the engine is running smoothly. There is hardly any noise but one by one their right arms go up. I do a count: twenty-four. All on go. I duck and swing myself into my seat, get as comfortable as my bulk will allow, and switch on. I feel rather than hear the engine kick into life. I ease up the throttle while the sailors take the strain; quickly check the few instruments. Tachometer, wind meter, compass, temperature gauge

229

and glide indicator—A-OK. I glance at my watch. Ten past midnight. Time to go.

Now I concentrate on the wind. A strong gust, then another and then a lull. Another gust, four, five, six seconds, another lull. That's it—let's go!

I pour on the power and the machine surges forward. I'm airborne! In a near panic I struggle with the handlebar controls to stop myself drifting to the left. The bow of the *Nimitz* slides away beneath and I'm looking at a very angry, white-topped sea. The machine bucks upwards and then sinks sickeningly. I feel spray on my hands and I'm looking at the foaming top of a wave right in front of me. I haul back on the bars and climb again. I could be having a bad time in a rodeo. I work the machine a bit higher and it steadies for a while. What's happening to the guys behind? I twist my body and crane my neck around and I'm plunging again sideways. Down on the right handlebar, ease it back. I'm not going to risk another look back. Every goddam gram of concentration is needed to keep this thing and me in the air.

I fight the thing up to five hundred feet. It's no less turbulent but the sudden down drops are now less likely to be fatal. If anyone is still behind me they'll follow me up.

It's getting a bit easier. I'm getting used to it and I'm not snatching at the controls; anticipating instead of just reacting. I check my watch and calculate my surface speed. It's bouncing between seventy and eighty knots. I continue the climb. We'd decided on a ceiling of 3,500 feet. Slowly the altimeter winds up. At a thousand feet conditions are definitely better. The rollercoaster is just a little smoother.

At two thousand feet I can see a darker line on the purple horizon: San Carlo. I'm going to make it. I pray that there are at least nine others behind me. I reach 3,500 feet and ease the throttle. The coast takes shape rapidly. A few lights show up. The outer floodlights on the compound walls? My excitement climbs as they form into a square. I can make out the dark blobs of the individual buildings inside the walls. There it is! The guardhouse. I'm so intent on it I almost forget. I can see the waves pounding on the shoreline below. It's time. I reach up to my helmet and flick on the transmit button. Please God let there be nine behind me!

I call Rodriguez.

"Vampire One to Vampire Two."

Seconds pass. Nothing. I repeat.

"Vampire One to Vampire Two. Come in."

Brand's voice crackles in my ears. "This is Vampire Three. Rodriguez didn't make it. Neither did Kerr."

Nerves racing I call the others. The final count is twelve. Newman and Allen were right. We lost fifty per cent plus one. But we're twelve and we're going in. Simmons on the *Nimitz* will have monitored the radio and by now will be talking to Komlosy in the White House or even the president himself.

As we cross the coast the compound is below me on the left. I reach for the engine cut-off and say, "Vampire One. Engines off."

It takes me a few seconds to get used to the machine in the glide mode, then I'm spiralling sharply down, fighting the handlebars and praying that we all get on the ground in one piece. It comes rushing up at me. I'm lifted by a gust and strain against the handlebars. As I cross the southwest corner of the wall I'm too fast and too low! I ease back the bars, slow, and crab sideways. The building looms in front of me. I correct and I'm down and rolling, pushing out my right leg on the nose wheelbar, turning into the shadow of the wall. A second of relief and self-congratulation, then I'm scrabbling clear, swinging the Ingram submachine gun off my shoulder, cocking it, and straining my ears. Not a sound, not a whisper . . . yes, a whisper. A dark blob glides past me. It's Brand. He's overshot. I draw in my breath as he corrects and the machine bumps onto the ground with a squeal. He comes to a stop six feet from the back wall of the residence. While I listen for any alarm he jumps off and pulls the ultralight close in under the wall.

We creep to the corner of the residence. The guardhouse is about fifty yards away to our right and beyond are the main gates. I can just make out two figures slumped against the wall beside them. Far to our right are the blocks of staff apartments. On top of the nearest one I can make out the hump of a machinegun emplacement, exactly where it should be. I hope that Lewis and Spooner are circling slowly down ready to take it out. Two hundred yards in front of us is the chancery building. As I focus on it, two diamond shapes glide down behind it. OK. Away to our left there's a scuffling sound and a couple of bumps. There's nothing to see. It must be Sacasa's squad going behind the apartments. Time to go. Everything's going to cut loose any second and when it does I want to be at the guardhouse with my man. We set off across the compound at a fast crouch. We reach the back of the guardhouse and creep round the side of the oblong building. I put my head round the corner. Next to the door is a figure sitting slackly in a chair with his chin on his chest. I move back, tap Brand on the shoulder and point with a curving motion round the corner. Then I hold up one finger and parody a sitting man with his chin on his chest. He nods and I see the pale gleam of his Bowie knife. I move clear, he slithers round the corner, and I'm right behind him as he glides up, slips a hand behind the guard's neck, clamps it across his mouth and pulls up and back. There's no sound. He lifts the body clear as it kicks and twists, and lays it quietly on the concrete. I make a sign to him to guard my back and then gingerly turn the door handle. I open it a crack, slide the barrel of the submachine gun in, and nudge it open. The room is lit by a single bulb. It's empty except for a desk and two chairs. On the far side is another door with a key in it. My man is in there.

Suddenly from behind that door I hear a muffled but unearthly sound. A sound out of hell. My skin prickles. I move quickly, my rubber boots making no noise. I put my ear against the door. There's a voice; muffled, but I can make out the words.

"Talk, pig! Talk to me! Give me a name!"

I turn the knob, kick open the door, and raise my gun.

It's a tableau. A thin, naked man strapped over a barrel-shaped thing, face a mask of agony. Standing over him, a big beefy guy wearing a white coat with a stethoscope round his neck. My thumb flicks the submachine gun onto single shot. I hear my voice. "You want a conversation? Talk to me!"

His mouth opens and my bullet cracks right into him, slamming his body back. I'm seeing things through a red haze of anger. I turn and the red haze lifts and urgency washes over me. Peabody's narrowed eyes are watching me, and he seems far away. Gently I remove the crocodile clips attached to his body. I slip out my knife and cut through the leather bindings. He moans terribly as the pressure is eased. Then I bend over him.

"It's over, Mr. Ambassador. I'm taking you out and home. First I've got to see about the other hostages. I'll leave you here, two to three minutes. There'll be a man at the door guarding you. Two to three minutes and I'll be back." His eyes are glazed. "The other hostages, sir. I'd better go."

His eyelids flicker and his head moves slightly. I turn and race through the outer room. Brand is crouched at the door, scanning the compound.

"Anything?"

"There was movement by the apartments. I guess that's Sacasa's squad."

"OK. I'm heading for the chancery. The ambassador's secure but in bad shape. Guard this door and don't move no matter what happens!" I point to the two sleeping figures by the gate. "And keep an eye on those two."

In a crouch I head across the compound. Just then there's a shout from near the chancery; the rapid coughing of an Ingram on automatic; a piercing scream. I flick on my transmission switch.

"Vampire One to Base. Sanitize. Repeat, sanitize. Ambassador secure. Confirm torture. Going into chancery now. Over."

Simmons's voice crackles straight back. "Base to Vampire One. Sanitizing."

It's happening now. There's a splintering of glass. Loud shouting in Spanish. Explosions from the chancery. Lights come on in the sky. Their beams wobble across the compound. On the roof of the chancery I can just see a long barrel rearing upwards. Each light leads to a target. I scream into the mike. "Lewis, Spooner, switch off your lights!" One goes out immediately. The other is slow. The machinegun on the roof clatters and the light twists and then goes out. Three seconds later there's a rending crash behind me. I turn and see the ultralight: a crumpled heap.

I'm twenty yards from the chancery. A series of *crumps* and then a blinding white light from the windows. There's a short flight of steps to the door. I take it in one leap. Inside, I swing right into the reception area and in front of me are about forty people. A kid in jeans is holding a little box frantically twisting a dial. I feel a wave of relief. The explosive jackets really are dummies! Another student guard is groping behind him at his belt. I line up the Ingram and he clutches at his chest as he goes over backwards. His pistol clatters to the floor. Moncada is shouting in Spanish, "Hands on your heads or you die. Hands on your heads!"

My eyes sweep the room. There are only male hostages here. I turn and race back through the door. Two enemy guards on the stairs, both with pistols, both firing. I flick to automatic and squeeze the trigger. They're punched back up the stairs and then roll slackly down.

The door in front of me is open. I run through it discarding the empty mag and clicking in a fresh one. The plan of the building is stamped on my brain. Through another door, down a corridor, and two seconds later I've found the other hostages. The third man of Moncada's squad, Sam Shaw, has his back to me. He's got the situation under control. The seven women are lying on the floor, their hands covering their faces. Two of them are moaning in terror. Another is sobbing. The seven female guards are also on the floor. But they are dead.

Shaw spins round as I come up beside him. With his visor down he looks like something from outer space. I guess I look the same. We both push up our visors. His lean, tanned face is troubled.

"I was alone, sir. I couldn't take any chances. I took 'em all out."

"You did right, Shaw. The original plan called for three men. You did right."

I can hear the clamour of heavy machineguns from above. The rooftop emplacements are still in place. I can also hear the faster staccato rattle of Ingrams, and in the background the deeper sounds of cannon fire and the constant rolling rumble of explosions. The A6Es and helicopter gunships from *Nimitz* are making sure that not even a mosquito gets close to the compound.

I say, "Ladies, you can get up now." Slowly, apprehensively, they start to scramble to their feet. "Ladies, I'm Colonel Slocum, US army. We've come to take you home. Your menfolk are all OK, but it's still very dangerous here. I want you to take off those jackets and follow me. Keep low." They're looking at me with dazed expressions. "Come on, ladies. Move! Quick!"

A little woman with grey hair starts removing the dummy jacket and taking charge. "Come on, everyone, let's go."

I tell Shaw, "Go ahead. Scout to the main entrance and then stay there keeping watch."

He moves off, and I follow a few seconds later with the women crowding behind me. We pass Shaw lying at the door, staring out over his submachine gun into the darkness. When we enter the reception area there's an emotional moment as the women greet their husbands, and then Moncada's shouting at them.

"Get down! Get down all of you. Stay on the floor!"

They sink down clutching each other. There's a babble of voices directed at me. I hold up a hand.

"Listen. Everyone's safe. The choppers will be coming to take you out soon, but there's still fighting. You've got to stay here on the floor till we clean up. Captain Moncada here and his men will look after you and lead you to the choppers. Do exactly what he tells you."

A voice calls, "What about the ambassador?"

"He's sick but safe."

A small cheer goes up. To my left another member of Moncada's team is snapping hand and leg cuffs onto the guards. There's still a hell of a row outside and it's not just coming from the sanitizing. There's at least two heavy machineguns still firing inside the compound. I flick on my transmitter.

"Vampire One to Base. Come in."

"Base to Vampire One. Go ahead."

"Hostages all safe and secure in chancery. Ambassador in poor condition but alive and secure in guardhouse. There are still active enemy machinegun emplacements on rooftops. Over."

Simmons's voice comes back full of excitement and relief. "Well done, Vampire One. You want an airstrike on those rooftops?"

"No way, sir, too risky. We'll do it ourselves. Meanwhile keep the evac. choppers on hold just off the coast."

"OK. Good luck."

I've got to get a situation report.

"Slocum to Lewis. Come in."

"Sir, this is Spooner. Lewis didn't make it."

"OK. Report, Spooner."

"Sir, I got the machineguns on top of the chancery and apartments but then I was hit by fire from the residence and I had to crash land."

"Are you OK?"

"Broke my right leg. But I'm by a corner of the residence. I've got a clear field of fire across the compound to the west of the chancery. Ain't no one gonna cross there."

"Good man. We'll get to you real soon. Castenada, report in."

"Castenada. Apartment building one cleaned out. Fifteen enemy dead, twelve captured. No friendly casualties. Cannot cross to the chancery, we're pinned down by two machineguns on the residence roof."

"OK. Well done. Stay put. Sacasa, report in."

"Sacasa here. Apartment buildings two and three secured. Twenty-two enemy dead. Three captured. Legrand got hit, chest and shoulders, but he's walking. We're also pinned down by those machineguns."

"OK. Stand by."

It's a problem. We must clear the machinegun emplacements from the residence roof. We've got no one inside the building, but Spooner's right on its corner and chancery is only two hundred yards away. I'll do the job myself.

A voice is calling from the floor. "Colonel, Colonel." It's a tough-looking young man with a crew cut. "Gunny Sergeant Cowder, sir. Marine Corps. I have fifteen men here, sir. We'd like to help."

There's not much they can do. We've no weapons to spare but I tell him to collect what he can find from the guards and put himself under the command of Captain Moncada.

Now I've got to get up on that residence roof. I call out. "Where's the embassy admin. officer?"

"Here, Colonel . . . George Walsh."

He's a middle-aged, round-faced guy. I ask, "Is there any way up onto the residence roof apart from the access hatch?"

Walsh shakes his head. Then, suddenly, his face lights up. "Wait. There is. There's a drainage pipe up the back wall to a gutter."

"That's my man." From Moncada I take an extra mag for my Ingram and three more grenades. I switch on the mike and say, "All units, I want blanket fire aimed at the residence rooftop in sixty seconds from now. Keep it up for thirty seconds and then quit." I flick off the switch and tell Moncada, "If I don't make it, you better call in the airstrike."

"Yessir. Good luck."

I move to the door and wait. Abruptly the barrage of covering fire begins. I leap down the steps and start running. Thirty years ago I ran the hundred yards in just under eleven seconds. I reckon I'm doing slightly better now. I strain to move my legs faster and then dive and roll into the cover of the building.

The covering fire eases up and then stops. I move down the building and locate the drainage pipe. Perfect. It's bracketed onto the wall at five foot intervals giving excellent hand and foot holds. The sanitizing aircraft are dropping flares outside the walls. They light the place up too much for my liking. I flick on the transmitter. "Base. Come in."

"Yes, Colonel."

"I'm going up on the roof. There's too much light. Can you ask those guys in the choppers to hold up the flares for a while?"

"Sure thing."

Within seconds it starts to darken. I inch my way up. As I reach the top I get a grip on the gutter and it squeaks but there's still a lot of noise all around the compound. I raise my eyes over the gutter and sweep the rooftop. The two emplacements are at each end, about a hundred feet apart. As I go for one I'll be exposed to the other. Simple: I've got to take them out, one immediately after the other.

I wait for a series of explosions and heave myself up and over the gutter. It squeals. I roll over and scramble to my feet darting a look left and right and reaching for a grenade. As I pull out the pin there's a shout from my left. I lob the grenade, and drop to the ground. The explosion compresses my eardrums. I don't bother to look. I can see the barrel of the other emplacement swing towards me. I lob another grenade at it. Hell! It hits a sandbag on the side and bounces over the roof. I hear the explosion as I scramble to my feet, grabbing for the Ingram. The machinegun barrel is coming into line. I run towards it holding the Ingram high; squeezing the trigger and spraying bullets. There's a scream and then the heavy hammer of the machinegun. He's high, over my head. Still fifteen feet away, he's got time to correct! I'm gonna die! Ten feet. I feel something like a branding iron across my side. Then I'm diving over the sandbags with an empty Ingram. There's two men there. One slumped with blood on his face, the other lunging back from the machinegun and grabbing for a pistol at his belt. My shoulder smacks into him. We sprawl on the concrete. He's getting closer to the pistol. I'm in a rage. I pick him up and throw him off the roof. It's done.

I wait a second while my breathing settles to something approaching normal; then flick the transmission switch. "Vampire One to Base. Compound totally secured. Send in the evac. choppers."

Simmons's exultant voice vibrates in my ears.

"They're on their way, Colonel. Well done. See you soon."

DAY TWENTY-ONE

JASON PEABODY. *San Carlo.*

The black face is above me again. Is it real? I've been slipping in and out of consciousness. It's as though I've been sleeping through a thunderstorm. He's talking.

"Sorry, sir. It took a little longer than I thought. The other hostages are all fine, sir. I'm taking you out of here now."

I hear another voice. "Choppers are down, sir. The women are boarding." Women? Is it really happening?

"Sir. I'm going to carry you. It's going to hurt some. You'll be in the sickbay on the *Nimitz* within minutes."

Ah ... the good ship *Nimitz*. ... I feel his arms working under me. He lifts. Yes, there's pain. But it's sweet pain. I know so much about pain. I'm in his arms. I move my head and rest it against his shoulder. I try to speak.

"What ... what's your ... name?"

"Colonel Silas Slocum, sir. United States army."

"Colonel. ... Don't ... don't leave me, Colonel. Please stay with me. ..."

There's a loud noise. Voices talking. Faces looking at me. I hear his reply, "I won't leave you, sir. I won't leave you."

It's all right. Everything's all right. I let myself slide into the peace of senselessness.

I'M CONSCIOUS AGAIN. I see a white coat, a stethoscope. The scream tears at my throat. A startled face recedes. A furious voice. "You stupid bastard! Get that white coat off!"

Black Slocum again bending over me, holding my hands. "Don't worry, sir. It's not the other one. He's dead, sir. I killed him myself. This is a doctor. He's going to give you an injection. Make you feel better."

He smiles. "We're going to fly you Stateside, sir, to Washington; Walter Reed Army Hospital. You'll be fine. Just fine. But first you've got to have this little injection."

I nod and he moves away slightly; still holding onto my hands. I feel something cool on my arm, then a slight prick. Slocum smiles again.

"It'll make you sleepy. Then we'll load you onto the plane and head for home."

"You're coming too?"

"I sure am. I'll be there all the way."

His face is becoming indistinct. I drift away.

THE ROOM IS LIGHT and airy. Sunlight filters through net curtains. I have woken from a long sleep. I feel like I've slept a lifetime. I am looking at a very white ceiling. I turn my head and now I'm looking at Slocum. I'm not at all surprised to see him. He's sitting in a chair with his head back and mouth open, snoring gently. Softly I call, "Slocum."

He jerks erect. His eyes widen and then his mouth splits in an enormous grin. "I thought you were going to sleep for ever, sir."

"How long has it been?"

"Six days since we left *Nimitz*."

"Could you find some water?"

"Sure, sir. I'll buzz for the head nurse."

He reaches for a bell beside the bed. I say seriously, "You have the right to call me by my first name."

He smiles. "OK, Jason. I'm Silas."

"Silas, if you were me how would you go about thanking a man for what he did?"

He shakes his head. "I wouldn't waste the breath. I'm a soldier. I was doing my job. I'd be real glad if you'd keep that in mind and not embarrass me. I mean it."

I'm trying to think of an answer to that when the door opens and a short, plump, middle-aged woman bustles in.

"Move yourself, Colonel."

He backs away down the bed. She leans over me. "How do you feel?"

"Very well. A little weak I guess. I'd like some water."

Her eyes dart to the bedside table and her mouth tightens in irritation. She picks up the bell and gives it two sharp presses.

"Major Calder will be here in a moment."

"Major Calder?"

"Your doctor."

I'd forgotten I was in a military hospital. She turns to Slocum. "You may leave now, Colonel."

Reluctantly he nods his head. "OK, ma'am. Jason, I'll see you later this evening. Anything you need?"

I shake my head. What the hell can I say to this man? I mutter, "Thanks, Silas ... for everything."

A pretty young nurse opens the door.

"Water," the head nurse says succinctly.

The nurse is back in less than a minute with a flask and a glass. She gets a look from the older woman that says, "I'll be talking to you later." Slocum follows her out and as the head nurse fusses around straightening the bedsheets I ask, "He's been here all the time?"

She sighs. "Yes. Colonel Slocum arrived in the ambulance with you and simply refused to leave. You were in a very bad way, your condition complicated by pneumonia. He even wanted to go into the intensive care unit with you. When you were moved in here two days ago he slept on the couch over there or in the chair."

The door opens and a fair-haired man with a cheerful face comes in. The head nurse says, "This is Major Calder."

He shakes my hand and says heartily, "So the sleeping ambassador has woken. And how do you feel?"

"Really fine. A bit weak but I feel surprisingly well."

He nods. "You surprised all of us. You were four days in intensive care. For the first two you were in an extremely agitated mental state. Your subconscious was in turmoil. Then quite abruptly you passed into a very deep and serene sleep. Then the pneumonia cleared up and all vital signs became normal. You've slept now for four more days. I was getting a little worried."

He's been examining me rapidly but thoroughly while talking. Now he listens to my heart and nods in satisfaction. "You've made a wonderful recovery. Nevertheless such treatment often affects the mind ... sometimes it's a delayed reaction. I'm going to ask our senior psychiatrist to pass by and visit you tomorrow."

I shake my head. "No, thank you, Major. I could have used him a

239

long time ago, but not now. Whatever effect that torture had on my mind, believe me, was beneficial." I smile at him. "Shock treatment is used in mental hospitals to try to bring insane people back to sanity. I guess something like that happened to me."

He's looking very puzzled. He shrugs. "Well, OK, sir. If that's your decision. But if at some future time you experience any difficulties be sure to call us immediately."

"I will, thank you. Can I eat something, doctor?"

"Sure." To the head nurse he says, "That drip can come out. Put him on a light diet and he's to have no visitors until tomorrow afternoon at the earliest."

"Yes, doctor. But Colonel Slocum said he was coming back this evening."

He shrugs resignedly. "Well, you can classify the colonel as a fixture rather than a visitor."

I ask him, "How long will I have to be here, Major?"

He purses his lips. "I want to keep you under observation for at least another week. Besides you need time to build up your strength, and it's better that you do it here where no one will bother you— especially the press. I'll see you this evening."

He leaves and the head nurse says, "I'm going to send you some fresh chicken soup. Is there anything else you'd like?"

My reply is prompted by the major's mention of the press. "Would you have any newspapers? I'd like to catch up on what's been happening."

"Yes. I've kept you the *Washington Post* for the last six days."

I READ THE PAPERS in sequence. The first is full of the rescue; I feel a terrible pang as I learn about the casualties suffered by the rescue team. I also learn that Slocum was wounded. A bullet took a chunk of flesh out of his right side. My condition is reported as being critical. The editorial calls for the immediate invasion of San Carlo.

My condition is still critical on the second day. There's a clamour for Slocum to be interviewed but a bulletin from Walter Reed Army Hospital states that he is still recovering from his wound. Again the editorial calls for the invasion of San Carlo.

The headlines on the third day proclaim the invasion of San Carlo. After a brief battle the capital was taken and the Chamarristas fled to the mountains. An interim government was to be formed and a constitution drawn up, leading to free and fair elections. Slocum's wound was still being treated and in the meantime the president had announced that he was to be awarded the Congressional Medal of

Honor, and all his men were to receive high decorations. Meanwhile the state department had protested to Cuba in the strongest terms about my being abused and interrogated by a member of the Cuban intelligence organization. My condition was now stable and improving. I push aside the later papers. My eyelids are heavy, sleep has become such a warm companion.

I WAKE AT THE SOUND of the door. Slocum is standing there, his arms cradling packages. He manages to raise a finger to his lips, and winks. He deposits the packages on the bed, carefully closes the door and gives me a conspiratorial grin.

"I came in through the service entrance, eluding hospital spies."

From the packages he produces two Big Macs, French fries, packets of cookies, and a bottle of Black Label Scotch. I've never had a Big Mac; always considered fast food plebeian. I chomp into it like a schoolboy. He pours two slugs of whisky and adds some water. It's the first drink I've had for more than three weeks, and it tastes like nectar.

I raise my glass. "Silas, let's drink to your Congressional Medal of Honor . . . richly deserved."

He's sitting on the end of the bed. He sips at his whisky and says, "I got it because I was in command. It's a pity that all my guys couldn't get it."

I'm suddenly conscious of the casualties. I tell him of my guilt and he shakes his head vigorously.

"Jason, considering the conditions we were damned lucky. Only one man was killed in the compound, and those wounded are recovering well with no permanent disability. Two men crashed on takeoff right on the deck of the *Nimitz*: one walked away and the other had a broken ankle. Eleven others went into the sea: eight were saved through brilliant rescue work by the navy, three drowned. In all we had four fatalities—a lot less than we projected."

"Four lives lost. I hate to think about that."

He gives me a very straight look. "I knew those guys well. Let me tell you this. They joined the army to fight. They were all veterans, and they all volunteered for that mission. Right now, wherever they are, they sure as hell don't blame you. They'd rather have died that way than of senility . . . believe me."

I do. He said it simply and sincerely. As he pours more whisky into our glasses, I remark, "Well, Silas, it looks like you're going to end up the most senior black officer in the entire history of the United States armed forces."

He sighs. "I don't know that I want to end up the highest black anything. I'm thinking of retiring."

"Retiring?"

"Sure. I've got a ranch in Wyoming."

"A ranch?"

He grins. "Yeah. And I'm going to be the first cowboy in the West to round up his cattle from an ultralight!"

"Tell me about it."

He tucks the whisky bottle out of sight behind my pillows, sprays the room and dumps the empty paper bags in a trash can. Then he perches on the end of the bed and tells me his plans. His enthusiasm comes through. It's like he's starting a new life, and it reminds me that I'm doing the same. I ask a few questions. They come easily . . . personal questions. An intimacy grows between us as he talks of his life, of his early broken marriage. I marvel that I can feel so close to this man, can see parallels in his life and mine.

Suddenly he leans forward and says earnestly, "Jason, why don't you come down and visit me? Damn it man, you're going to need a good period of recuperation. The air out there is real fresh. . . ." His enthusiasm suddenly fades. "But hell, it's not much of a place I got. I mean just a pine-board cabin . . . with an outhouse an' all that . . . I guess it's not the kind of place you'd . . ."

Quickly, I cut in. "Silas, you invite me and I'll come. You just talked about changing directions in your life. I'm about to do the same. Some things were important to me before; now they're trivial. I don't mind roughing it a bit. I think I might enjoy it."

He grins. My eyes begin to feel drowsy. There's a silence and I doze off.

LATE MORNING. The head nurse comes in and sniffs the air. In seconds she locates the empty paper bags in the waste bin, then she sniffs at the empty whisky glass on the bedside table. Silas, what have you got me into? I feel like a schoolboy caught with his hand in the cookie jar. Mercifully she shifts her attack.

"It's that damned Colonel Slocum! This is the best run hospital in the world and in one week he's turned it into a tavern!"

She stalks around the room, vibrant in her indignation. Then she draws a breath. She gives me a look and I'm absurdly conscious of the bottle of whisky under my pillow.

"He's a lonely man," she says suddenly.

"Colonel Slocum? You think so?"

"Yes."

242

She's bustling again. Pulling and patting the sheets into place. I keep my head firmly on the pillow.

"I've seen others like him in this hospital. Tough as rawhide on the outside and desperately lonely underneath. They pretend to be scared of me because the pretence gives them comfort in their loneliness. Colonel Slocum is like that."

She is standing at the end of the bed, her hands gripping the footrail, her face infinitely sad. Then there's a brief knock on the door and General Simmons comes in.

We exchange pleasantries and he tells me, "I had a call from the White House. The president would like to visit you at seven o'clock this evening."

Immediately I feel nervous. I know the confrontation has to come and I've tried to rehearse it.

I say, "That's OK, General. But no media. I'd like it to be a private visit."

He nods briskly. "So would the president."

I'VE SPENT MUCH OF the afternoon trying to compose my words and clarify thoughts, but when the tap comes on the door my mind is still in turmoil.

The start is melodramatic. General Simmons enters, stands to one side and says portentously, "Mr. Ambassador . . . the president of the United States of America."

That makes me even more nervous but then the president strides in, grins and says, "Hi, Jason. How are you?"

I know what I'm going to say and I'm no longer nervous. I'm propped up against a pile of pillows. I take his outstretched hand and shake it firmly. The general is pushing forward a chair but the president waves it away and perches on the foot of the bed. As the door closes he asks, "They looking after you?"

There's genuine concern in his eyes. I nod. "Very well, Mr. President, thank you."

He's carrying a paper bag. He reaches out and puts it on the bedside table.

"Grapes. I don't know why but hospital visitors always bring grapes. When I was in here I got enough to start a winery!"

We both smile. I cannot sustain the anger that has been smouldering inside me. But still I'm going to get it off my chest. I take a breath but I'm interrupted by a tap on the door. The head nurse bustles in with a tray holding coffee and cups.

She is totally at ease. As she pours the coffee she casts a critical eye over my visitor and says sternly, "You're overdoing it. You look tired. You need at least a week at Camp David."

He smiles affably. "Mary, it won't be for much longer."

She puts two spoonfuls of sugar into his coffee, passes him the cup and goes out. The tension is mounting now. I wonder if he will broach the subject first. He does.

"Jason, you will know that our agent in San Carlo tried to kill you."

"Yes."

He is looking down into his cup as if trying to find an explanation in the black coffee. Harshly he says, "I don't apologize for it. It was an immoral act but sometimes morality has to be tempered to reality. You were in a situation which affected the security of our nation."

He has, with that statement, made my position easier. I was dreading either a denial or an apology. Before this moment I had respected the man. Now I admire him. The anger has left me but quietly I state my belief.

"Mr. President, I don't think that an agency of our government has any business dealing in murder. Reality must never be the master of morality."

I feel disconcerted. The words sounded good in my head, but pompous as I uttered them. He is nodding solemnly.

"Jason, of course you're right. Your case has resulted in a general review of the agency."

He smiles wanly. "Now I didn't come to apologize but to try and make restitution. What can I do?"

"Allow me to take early retirement."

He sighs. He really does look tired. He puts down his cup and stands up, then strides to the door, opens it and sternly calls out, "Tell Colonel Slocum to report here at the double."

He walks to the window and looks out over the city. Without turning he says, "I know of the friendship that's grown between you and Slocum. During the past days you've both had an effect on me and on this country. You may as well hear what I've got to say together. The colonel is waiting to escort me to visit his wounded men. He will be here directly."

A long silence while I wonder what's coming. There's a knock on the door. The president turns and says, "Enter!"

Slocum comes in in full dress uniform and snaps off a salute. The president points to a chair.

"Sit down, Colonel. Last month you paced up and down in my office while I sat and listened to a lecture. Now it's your turn."

Slocum glances at me and then meekly sits down.

The president paces and talks. "Colonel Slocum, I understand you want to take early retirement so you can go ranching in Wyoming. Well, the answer is no. By your lecture and your recent actions you have caused me to institute a major review of our armed forces. You will be involved. These are your orders: You will take one month's leave. On returning to duty you will be promoted to brigadier general and put in command of our rapid deployment force, which you will inculcate by training and example, with your military philosophy and methods. You will do so for four years after which you may retire to your ranch. By that time I too will be retired and will accept an invitation to come to Wyoming and teach you something about cows ... is that understood, Colonel?"

"Yessir!"

The president has stopped pacing. He directs a gaze at Slocum that would penetrate steel plate. The gaze then sweeps round to fix on me.

"Mr. Ambassador, you are a foreign service officer of vast experience. My experts told me that you would crack under torture. You did not. That makes you a very special person. You asked me for early retirement. Now these are your orders: You will take as much leave as you require for rest and recuperation. You will then be appointed ambassador in residence at Georgetown University in recognition of your outstanding ambassadorial service. At the same time you will serve as a special presidential adviser on Latin American affairs until the end of my term of office. At that time you may retire. Those are your orders!"

The words jump out of my throat. "Yes, Mr. President!"

He nods in satisfaction and turns to Slocum. "Right, Colonel. Let's go and see those men of yours."

At the door he turns, grins at me and says, "It seems that the only way to deal with heroes is to give them a good kick in the butt!"

After they've gone, I eat some grapes and decide that I like the prospect. In Georgetown I'll be able to pick my own subject on which to lecture. It will be good surrounded by young people.

And I realize something. We take pieces from all those who affect our lives. I took something from Amparo, from Jorge, and from Slocum. I'm sixty-three years old and at last I feel complete. Through a combination of involvement, humiliation and agony, my life— what's left of it—has been given redemption. I'm not going to waste it now. I'm going to make up for the barren years. I'm going to find out about people—and yes, I like the idea. I drift into a contented sleep.

WHEN I AWAKE LATER that evening shadows slant across the room. The door opens and Slocum comes in like the brother I never had. He puts a thick envelope on the bedside table, sits on the foot of the bed and asks, "So what do you think of your orders?"

"I like them. How about you, General?"

He grins. "Me, too. It's a real chance to do something positive. The cows can wait. But right now I'm off to Wyoming for my month's vacation."

"What's in the envelope?"

He grins. "My address in Wyoming and telephone number, and a United Airline timetable . . . and something I want you to have."

He gets up and holds out his hand and I grip it warmly. I don't know what to say. Here he is giving me presents. I smile. "You'll hear from me, Silas . . . bet on it."

As the door closes behind him I repeat the words in my mind. "Bet on it."

I doze again for a while and then a nurse brings me dinner. She's followed by the head nurse who fusses about straightening the napkins and knives and forks. I remember the envelope and pick it up. It's surprisingly heavy.

I shake its contents onto the bed: a slip of paper, the airline timetable—and a flat velvet box. The head nurse watches curiously and I open it. I catch my breath as I see the blue ribbon and the round gleaming embossed metal.

She murmurs softly, "It's his Congressional Medal of Honor. He gave you that?"

There's a little card with sloping handwriting. It reads, "I've got enough of these things. You deserve it more than I do. Silas."

For a moment I'm speechless. Then I mutter the only words possible. "Of course, I'll have to send it back."

She nods her head slowly. "I guess you will. . . ."

Then I close the box and smile at her. "On second thoughts, I won't send it back."

"No?"

"Definitely not. I'm going to take it back in person . . . just as soon as I'm allowed out of this bed."

A. J. QUINNELL

A. J. Quinnell is the pseudonym of a writer who chooses anonymity for both personal and practical reasons. The plots of his five novels to date, which have been translated into ten languages, move freely over boundaries and cultures. He desires the same freedom for himself. Even his publishers do not know his real identity. We do know that he is British, in his mid-forties, and that he travels widely. We also know that he has an almost obsessive eye for accurate detail.

He says of *Siege of Silence*: "The idea for this novel came several years ago when I read about bank robbers in Stockholm who took several hostages. The siege lasted over a week and finally ended with the robbers' surrender. Astonishingly, during those days, some of the hostages and robbers became mentally (and in one case physically) very close. Psychologists later dubbed this phenomenon 'The Stockholm Syndrome'. This became the major theme of *Siege of Silence*. I simply chose two very disparate characters and put them into a cauldron of confrontation and tension. It's always interesting how a person, very set in his, or her, ways, reacts when routine has been shattered. This is when the real character emerges, whether it be strong or weak. It is also my belief that in any very bitter confrontation, the winner loses something too.

"It was a very difficult book to write because I chose (after several attempts) the format of the first person for all three main characters. This format has its limitations, but I believe it gave the characters a great deal of immediacy. In the early stages, Slocum was to be a minor character, but somehow, as the book got written, he elbowed his way forward.

"Also, I have always been fascinated by hostage rescue attempts, and therefore I put much thought and research into this aspect of the novel. Military experts subsequently studied all phases of the rescue, and I'm pleased to report that they could find no fault with it."

THE SOUND
of
DISTANT CHEERING

A CONDENSATION OF THE BOOK BY

K. M. Peyton

ILLUSTRATED BY PAM MASCO

Everyone in the racing world lives on dreams, and the staff at Brood House stables are no exception. Jeremy Cutbush, the young trainer, struggling to get the business back on its feet, pines nostalgically for the days when he was a successful jockey, and the thunder of hooves and the cheers of the crowd rang in his ears.

Jeremy's faithful stable girl, Rosy Weeks, harbours an impossible dream of owning her very own racehorse, but channels all her energy into looking after her favourite steeplechaser, Roly Fox. For although Roly is past his prime, to Rosy he's the finest, most willing horse that ever lived. And she'd do anything for him.

When Roly is sold to a mean-spirited owner with more concern for his bank balance than the horses who run for him, it's more than Rosy can bear. . . .

1

The sun was low, bright in the sky. The horses were bunched together on the far side of the course, the sun behind them, their shadows long across the cropped grass.

"Midnight King, Greensward and Roly Fox," intoned the commentator. "Roly Fox moving up on the outside, jumped the ditch well and gained two lengths on Greensward, who made a mistake . . ."

The girl, huddled in an ancient ski jacket, squinting into the sun, clutched leading rein and horse blanket with quivering fingers. Roly, my dear Roly, you are going to win this race. I can feel it in my bones.

Sometimes everything comes right, she thought. Once in a while Jeremy will smile; we can dance and shout in the stands, and Roly will stand there, steaming, in the winners' enclosure.

"You think you've got it, and they fall at the last," the man next to her said.

Rosy smiled at him. "He won't fall. Not Roly. He's the winner."

GRACE MADDOX, WATCHING television in the study, saw Jeremy Cutbush's horse win and exclaimed out loud in surprise. Her brother though, who worked for Jeremy, had said the stables were having a poor season. She wondered if anyone in the village had put a fiver on. Roly Fox's price was fourteen to one. How easy to make money, if you chose the right horse!

Grace watched Jeremy, and that odd girl Rosy, looking like a scarecrow, grinning as she led the horse in. If Jeremy looked like that when he won, whatever did he look like when he didn't? Something about Rosy's jacket struck a chord. Grace recognized it as once her own, bought for a skiing holiday in Val d'Isère five years ago. Her mother must have put it in a jumble sale, and now here it was, appearing on television, fallen on hard times. Like the television, which distorted the picture strangely. Unbeautiful as Rosy was, her head was surely not that elongated shape? Rather, it was broad and short from hairline to chin, as Grace remembered it, the nose unimposing, the cheekbones flat and wide apart. Like Nureyev, if one wanted to be generous. She obviously did not realize that she was appearing on television as she flung her arms round the winner's neck and kissed him in a manner more fitting to a Pony Club event than the winners' enclosure at Wincanton. Such lack of sophistication was bad form, by Grace's reckoning. But what could one expect? Rosy was only a village girl. Hugh had said Rosy was basic. She had defended herself with a pitchfork when he had made a pass at her. A pass at *Rosy?* Grace had been surprised. She had been away too long and forgotten how things were.

Not that anything had changed. The study she sat in was still the only warm room in the house. Filled entirely by a rolltop desk with a large sofa pushed hard against it, it served both as living room and dining room in the winter, when the four of them tended to live in it, even eating their dinner watching the box, three on the sofa and one on the floor. It was very embarrassing if anyone called. They were considered quality by the village, Hugh having been to Harrow and herself finished in Switzerland, but they lived like pigs.

MRS. CUTBUSH, DOZING on the sofa before her television set, awoke suddenly and cried out, "The Tetrarch! The Tetrarch wins! Come on, Steve!" She sat bolt upright and stared, looking for the grey horse with white slashes over its flanks that was as clear in her brain's image as if it were present in the room. But nothing . . . only a blurred picture on the screen before her—a horse, true, but not her father's darling. How vividly she remembered the excitement in her father's face as he bent down beside the rails and said close in her ear, "Watch that horse, child. You'll never see anything as fast as that again, ever." And she had lifted her eyes obediently and regarded the wonder horse. The instant, some seventy years ago, passed in total recall through her waking brain, then faded.

She looked at the television screen. Whatever had reminded her of The Tetrarch? she wondered. The fire was nearly out, the racing dull, and she had fallen asleep and forgotten what she was about. Something to do with Rosy, as far as she could remember. Not that it mattered—Rosy would visit soon. Not her grandson, Jeremy, but Rosy, and sometimes Gin, who neither of them had any claim on her at all, but came out of a casual kind of friendship. Not pity—she was sure of that—else she would have shut the door on them, as she had on the vicar and the WI women.

A girl like Rosy seemed to be dancing about on the television screen, holding a horse. But Mrs. Cutbush had forgotten what she had put the television on for. She got up painfully and switched the picture off. Silence had become her friend. Her own company was good enough. And Jasper's.

"Eh, Jasper?" she said out loud.

But the dog had died six months ago.

AFTER THE INITIAL EXCITEMENT, Rosy made a conscious effort to be cool about Roly's winning, slightly ashamed of her elation. But the thrill of it kept making her shiver. She sat crouched up in the cab of the horsebox beside Gin going home, living it over, the vision of her horse coming up the straight with his ears pricked, his stride ever lengthening, going away in the fine, decisive style of a good horse. It had been so long, but she had never lost faith. Roly had been given to her to "do" when she was a new girl at the stable, and the other "lads" had made fun of them both: the dud horse and the art student "lass".

"Time we had a winner," Gin said. "How long is it? Straw Top at Worcester? Nearly two months. It's the law of averages by now."

Rosy stared out at the cold evening, disregarding the law of averages, watching the entirely appropriate magnificence of the evening sky. She always liked going home, even without a winner, the cab growing fuggy and comfortable and the radio blaring. She loved motorways, the endless pattern of lights approaching on the opposite carriageway flashing and sparkling in her vision; she smiled into the evening, and Gin laughed. "You are a nut, Rosy! Kissing old Roly, and on television and all."

"Oh, God, was it?" She laughed too.

"Didn't notice the guv'nor throwing his hat in the air. I think winning hurts him more than losing."

"Of course it hurts. Think, if it had happened to you—"

"I was never in that class. Can't guess—got no imagination."

"You don't need much for that!" Rosy groped for the fruit gums under the dashboard. "Mrs. Palmer should've come. I could have told her he'd win today. It's not right, a horse winning and nobody to cheer."

In the second, third and fourth enclosures owners and friends had swarmed with congratulations, but Roly's owner, Mrs. Palmer, had been in America. As far as Rosy was concerned, *she* was his owner. Nobody knew Roly like she did.

Glancing at her sideways, Gin said, "It's dangerous, you know, how you love Roly."

"But if you're not involved, you don't care, the job's nothing. Just hard labour for life."

"For life? Haven't seen any old 'lasses' of sixty."

"That'll be me one day. Can't see how I'm going to better myself. You need money to be a trainer."

"You'll get married."

"What for? That's just the same thing but for a man. I'd rather do it for a horse."

"There's one man you'd do it for."

"Oh, shut up."

"You scare 'em all off, Rosy, the way you are."

"Good. That suits me."

"Pity the one that gets you."

"There won't be one."

The banter was stock-in-trade. They had known each other since they were born, much too well for marriage to one another. Rosy knew Gin like she knew Roly, even better. Humans were more predictable. Gin—his name was short for Ginger—had met a girl called Beryl in the betting queue at Newbury. He did his courting at occasional race meetings, since he had no car and Beryl lived thirty miles away. It was slow going.

Gin flipped the indicator stalk for leaving the motorway and they heard Roly shift his weight behind them. The journey was easy tonight: no fog, no ice, not even rain. Spring was coming and there would be a couple of months of easier racing before the season ended.

Rosy had adjusted to the tough life, taking it in her stride. It was easier than London, where she had gone after she left school, where everything had been against the grain, the spirit out of its element. She had worked for Jeremy now for three years and was well up in the pecking order, giving way only to Hugh, the assistant trainer, and old Albert, more through respect than anything else. The lads mostly came and went, the best of them aspiring to more successful stables. Rosy aspired too, but could not leave for many reasons, not least because of her horse, Roly.

A car passed them, the driver giving a toot and raising an arm in greeting.

"What kept him?" Rosy asked.

"He was talking to a bloke—they went into the bar."

"Talking? Jeremy?"

"The other bloke was talking."

"A rich Arab?"

"A Yorkshireman."

"More our style." Rosy sighed.

The journey was nearly over. The grind up the last hill was a killer. Jeremy said the place discouraged unwanted visitors. He might have been thinking of owners, but it worked for useful characters like milkmen, newspapermen and charwomen as well. Brood House—it was well named—could no longer call the tune to the village below as it had in earlier times. More sensible people, Jeremy's parents, for example, had abandoned it for purpose-built yards in sunnier climes, but Jeremy, like the place, was washed-up and without a future, and Brood House suited. In the headlights a barn owl lifted off from his perch on one of the stone globes that topped the gateway pillars; the gates had long gone. Gin made the last awkward swing between the pillars, a horse whinnied and Roly, recognizing home, whinnied back from the box.

"Silly old devil!" Rosy climbed in with him, going to his head. "You clever old stupid old horse, you. Come home a winner, have you, and about time too, you gorgeous brute you." She gentled him while Gin opened the doors and let down the ramp. Roly was always keen to get out when the engine died, anxious about where he was. "I love you, Roly, you're wonderful. OK, I'm ready!" She raised her voice for Gin to hear.

The horse thumped down the ramp, whinnying some more. The row he made echoed round the walls, sending roosting pigeons crashing out of the nearest trees. He made for his box, where the straw was deep laid, the haynet full.

Everyone had gone home. There was a light on in the house and Jeremy's car was parked outside, but he did not come out.

"Moody bastard," Gin said to himself, crossing to the feedshed to fetch Roly's supper. Why did he stay to work for a moody bastard like that? He had the experience now to get a decent job, no ties at home, no wife and kids to move. What held him was the place; it was his anchor, his roots—his undoing. He had no adventure in his soul. He was twenty-eight now. Life was passing him by.

"You needn't wait for me," Rosy said when he came back with the feed. "I want to see him settle."

"OK, if you say so."

Stirred up by the excitements of the day, Rosy—unlike Roly Fox—had no inclination to settle down to supper and bed. She leaned over Roly's half-door pretending that his win was the prelude to great improvements in the stable's fortunes. Racing people lived on dreams, from the small breeder to the meanest punter. Every year the dreams came true for somebody, to encourage others to believe that next year it might be their turn. Winning was not the prerogative of the rich; the Queen had not yet bred a Derby winner, yet a Derby winner had been produced by a doctor who kept two mares for a hobby. Hope sprang eternal . . . Rosy saw herself leading Roly in at Cheltenham, making him stand for the photographers. She would receive a couple of thousand from the grateful owners and buy herself a car . . .

Rosy, who never had enough for a new pair of jods, let alone a car, could weave dreams at the drop of a hat. Life was full of opportunities, she was convinced, if the cards were played right. The fact that in twenty-eight years not much had gone right for her was by the way. She was a born optimist.

Optimism kept her longer than was necessary. Was Jeremy waiting till she went, to avoid her? She could see the light in his kitchen from where she stood. She leaned on the stable door, smelling the cold air that came over the top of the downs with its scent of trodden grass and earth and winter dew. Brood House was cold as a tomb. The stables were warmer, with the hot blood of the racehorses in their tattered rugs leavening the draughts, the thick straw snug and the ancient stove in the tackroom ticking over through the night. Rosy did not answer her own question; she did not want to know that Jeremy avoided her when there was no one else around, although the answer was perfectly obvious. Jeremy avoided women full stop. While it was so, Rosy felt no regret, for she knew she was closer to him than any other female, seeing him every day, even on Sundays. One could scarcely ask for more by Rosy's reckoning.

"I can't wait for ever, Roly, can I? He'll come and see you when I've gone and tell you what a grand fellow you are. Quite right too. You are a grand fellow."

She gave him a kiss, a last feel under his rug to make sure he was dry, and went outside. Jeremy's yard, lacking all the paraphernalia of the up-to-date crack yard, looked austerely beautiful in spite of its dilapidation. In the dark the patches of corrugated iron over the roofs were hidden; only the elegant proportions were revealed, the two rows of stables facing each other inside the main gate, overhung by the vast, ancient evergreen oaks that grew in the garden beyond. The garden and the house, reached through an archway with a cracked bell tower threatening life and limb to those who passed below, were generally out of bounds to the stable staff. Jeremy did not encourage communication. Once under the archway, his life was his own.

Rosy looked in on her other horse, a chestnut gelding called Villanelle bought with the Triumph Hurdle in mind but so far having been a great disappointment; he was snatching happily at his hay and turned his head briefly. Rosy only had two to do; the "lads" had three each and any newcomer would come into Rosy's care. But it was over a year now since they had had a new horse.

Rosy fetched her bike, pulled on a battered balaclava and thick gloves. Downhill all the way . . . she knew each pothole intimately and could weave a fast and erratic course without danger. Walking up in the morning gave her time to think. Uphill and downhill—it was racing in a nutshell. Snakes and ladders. She reckoned Brood House was due for a ladder or two.

GRACE SAID, "THAT FATHER of Rosy's—Mr. Weeks—is he all there?"

"Of course he is," Mrs. Maddox said sharply. "Considering he's been a widower for the last ten years, I think he's coped very well."

"Well, I think he's a nutcase," Grace said. "His back garden is full of weeds, all planted out in beds with labels. And his front garden is solid nettles, surrounded by a lavender hedge."

"Wild flowers, not weeds," Mrs. Maddox corrected. "The nettles are for the butterflies."

"We see him on the downs, often, on his hands and knees, gazing at the turf," said Hugh. "Once he put a hurdle across one of the gallops, and told Jeremy not to use it because an orchid was growing there."

"What did Jeremy say?"

"We had to ride round it."

Working at Brood House across the valley, a job he had fallen into by chance after being sent down from his minor university, seemed to content Hugh. At thirty he was already thickening round the waist and thinning on top.

"Do you remember Mrs. Cutbush, Jeremy's grandmother, when she was young?" Grace asked her mother.

"She was about forty when the war ended. I saw her a few times up at Brood House. She was very beautiful and very fierce. There's a painting of her by Munnings hanging in the hall up there, done when she was about twenty, on a horse—fabulous! I wonder if it's still there?"

"Jeremy would have sold it by now, if he's so hard up. It must be worth a bit," said Grace.

"Oh no! Surely not! Sell his grandmother—"

"He would, you know."

"No," said Hugh. "He's a mean bastard but he wouldn't do that. He's got a thing about his roots, the house and that. He'd have gone long ago, if not."

"D'you think? He hasn't got much of a thing about his grandmother. He hardly ever sees her. It's very naughty of him."

"Do you wonder? She's such an old harpy."

"Well, you'd think it would be policy. She must have quite a pile to leave."

"Oh, Grace, how cold-blooded you are!"

"Mother, don't be so old-fashioned! That's probably why Rosy butters her up, and Gin. So she leaves them something."

"That's very unkind."

"Why else then?"

"I think, with Rosy, it's Mrs. Cutbush's old mare, out in the field," Hugh said. "She's frightened the old girl forgets to feed her. What with Jeremy's roots and old Weeks's weeds, Rosy's thing is clapped-out racehorses."

"Whatever do you mean?"

"She gets very neurotic about dud horses being sent to the sales—you know, when their legs have gone or they're just too slow. When they've tried their best, and nobody wants them."

The telephone rang in the hall. Mrs. Maddox went to answer it. "Is Hugh there?"

"It's Jeremy, isn't it? Wait a moment, I'll call him."

She did so. Hugh came, startled. Communication from Jeremy was rare.

"Yes, all right. Who is he, a sheikh? . . . a Yorkshireman? Oh, bad luck. You think she'll sell him if the money's right? Some of these blokes certainly throw it around. Time some came our way . . . OK, best bib and tucker. I'll be up early."

Hugh replaced the receiver.

"What's all that about?" Grace asked.

"Some tycoon chappie saw Roly Fox win today, wants to buy him. He's calling tomorrow. We've all got to pull our fingers out."

WHEN ROSY GOT HOME she realized she had been so wrapped up with Roly's winning that she had forgotten to look in on Mrs. Cutbush's mare.

"Oh, damn!" She hesitated in the kitchen door, in the middle of pulling off her jacket. The kitchen was warm, her dinner was ready, and she was tired, cold and hungry. She looked in the oven. A dish of thick brown rice and wind-inducing white beans steamed gently, not a sight to arouse great enthusiasm. Her father was into vegetarian food and was not an inspired cook, although well-meaning. Rosy always had a good appetite, but was used to a sad sinking of the spirits when sitting down to his cooking. The slightly repellent dish in the oven prompted her to button up her jacket and wind her scarf back on. She put her head round the living-room door. "Hi, I'm back. Just going to feed Silverfish—I forgot. Roly won today. Did you see it?"

"Won, did he? Good for you. I've left your dinner."

"Yes, I saw it. I'll be back in five minutes."

She cycled the hundred yards or so to Mrs. Cutbush's cottage. It had a large garden round it and stood well back from the road. Rosy climbed the gate into the field beyond, trying to skirt the mud. Why on earth did she bother about the old nag? she wondered, at times like this. Interfering it was, Gin said, thinking every horse that wasn't in her care was deprived. To prove him right she found Silverfish happily munching at a large bundle of hay thrown down for her already by her owner. Mrs. Cutbush hadn't forgotten. A thin moon shone into the barn and cast cruel shadows along the mare's rib cage and down her shoulders, delineating the fine bone structure that had contributed to her past glory. She had once stood in winning enclosures at Royal Ascot and Epsom, at York and Goodwood and Newmarket, and had had her photo taken against potted hydrangeas to appear in *Tatler*. Pure white in her old age, she had once been the unusual splashed grey of her great-great-great-grandfather The Tetrarch, which is why Mrs. Cutbush had kept her, past associations meaning more to her as she lost her standing in the racing world after her husband's death. For all her failing memory, Mrs. Cutbush could remember the names and dates and relationships of all the great horses of the past, and Rosy's fascination with horse history had forged the initial link between the two of them. Silverfish had bred six winning foals, but now Mrs. Cutbush could no longer be bothered to send her away to a stallion. "Bring one here, to the door, and we'll breed another," she had said to Rosy.

"They don't do that any more," Rosy told her. "It's the mares that have to travel now."

"Stupid. I can't be bothered."

Silverfish was twenty, but the potential in that gaunt frame never failed to stir Rosy, especially since Mrs. Cutbush had said, once, "You can get her served, if you're so keen." But the stud fees were beyond Rosy's pocket. She had discussed it with Gin, but he had no spare cash either. They had tried a few bets—certain winners—to go towards a stallion fund, but the certain winners had failed to win.

"What would you do with it, anyway? It'd cost you," Gin said.

"We could train it here, give Jeremy a half share."

"You must be joking!"

The practicalities were dismissed. Rosy thought that side of it would solve itself.

Looking at Silverfish in the cold moonlight now, she saw the opportunity within her grasp, yet she could not take advantage of it. She had the will, the knowledge, the devotion . . . but not the money. In a week or two, with the coming of the spring sunshine, the mare would come in season: the moment would be ripe. The opportunity would then pass, and she would be no further forward. She loved the mare for all she represented, laid her arms over the knobby spinal ridge, stroking her muddy coat, and could easily have wept with self-pity.

Silverfish turned her head and butted Rosy affectionately.

"Wasting my time, you idiot mare!" Rosy squelched back down the field, damping her wild aspirations with the thought of the supper that waited in the oven. She got on her bike and free-wheeled back to her house, one of the six council houses that stood in an ugly row beside the road. They were the only modern houses in the village: the rest were old and picturesque and lived in mostly by well-heeled "incomers", only a few by the native elderly, like Mrs. Cutbush.

Mrs. Cutbush was something of a legend, sitting uneasily on the village conscience, for she was downright rude, and ungrateful for any offers of help, yet was over eighty and had, like her horse, a glamorous past much bound up with village history. Her strong personality still made itself felt even now. Her garden flaunted her spirit, sloping conspicuously up from the lane to the cottage, an eye-catching tangle of bright flowers and regimented vegetables amongst which her frail figure could sometimes be seen stooping, grunting and muttering, acknowledging no one. Rosy, interfering when the mare had got too thin for her to bear, had been accepted, bringing down ten bales of Jeremy's good hay which was received with a grace not accorded to the meals on wheels lady.

After the excitements of the day, Rosy was reluctant to finish it, to go in and sit down to her brown rice. She put her bike away and stood in the garden, looking up at the dark ridge of the down that encircled the village and the luminous sky above it. There was a moon somewhere, and the air smelled of spring. Instinctively her eyes went to Brood House, where occasionally a light gleamed from a window, and late in the evening a faint glow from the yard light showed when Jeremy was doing his last stable round, but tonight there was no indication of life.

Once, old people in the village said, the sound of Brood House parties kept them awake at nights; there had been a dance band on the lawn and smart open cars tearing through the lanes full of the Cutbush set. Now there was always silence, except for the screech of the owls that nested in the rotting barns.

There was no wind. Rosy felt she was surrounded by the bright stillness of death. Far away, on the main road, a motorbike engine roared away into the night, receding—someone going somewhere. Fortunate man. Rosy waited until the sound had gone, then put her bike back in the shed and went in for her supper.

2

The following morning a Rolls came up the drive to Brood House and parked outside the front door. Rosy put Villanelle away and got to work on grooming Roly, to show him at his best. He was not, after all, a fantastic-looking beast, but workaday, powerful more than beautiful, and slightly old-fashioned-looking: head large and eyes honest, nose a touch Roman. Yesterday's race seemed to have taken nothing out of him. He looked as well as Rosy had ever seen him.

She was good at grooming, throwing all her weight into each brushstroke to see the gloss on the light bay coat improve. Roly's hard muscle flexed to her vigour, as he stood quietly. His nature was pathetically ingratiating. He had no will of his own, only wanting everyone to be pleased. He hadn't the flame of the great racehorse, but equally he had no guile, no nasty tricks.

"You're a great fellow, Roly," Rosy assured him.

"Action stations," Gin said, looking over the half-door. "Our rich friend in view now, coming your way."

Rosy looked out, pretending she wanted to see the new owner, knowing she wanted to see Jeremy. They were a contrasting pair: Jeremy's slight figure in the battered waxed jacket and well-worn cap dwarfed by the newcomer, a massive man dressed in fine tweeds, with a naturally suspicious expression on his fleshy face. His eyes were very sharp and small, and sparse hair was arranged tactfully over his scalp. He did not smile when he was introduced, nor hold out a hand. A curt nod.

"Rosy, this is John Hawkins. He has come to see Roly Fox. Lead him out, will you?"

Jeremy, Rosy would have said, was on the verge of feeling happy, a rare condition. His pale and interesting—to Rosy, fascinating—face was a shade less drawn than usual, the eyes a hint livelier, with a touch of the old spirit that had once proclaimed him invincible. "Cocksure bastard," Gin had called him in those days, when Rosy had cut out his photo and pasted it on her bedroom mirror . . . "The cocksure bastard'll come a cropper, you wait." So long ago, it seemed, that Rosy could scarcely remember; she had been a child in love. Now, the state was apparently a permanency.

She went in to Roly Fox, untied him and led him out. She chucked him under the chin and got his legs square, and he got the message and held up his head and gazed nobly all round him, selling himself, the silly beast . . . Rosy had a dreadful feeling that he would be much safer with Mrs. Palmer, his present owner, than with Mr. Hawkins.

"He likes the ground soft. We can't run him on hard going," Jeremy was saying. "He's had a spot of leg trouble in the past, but he's fine now, as long as he's treated right."

"It's more often soft than hard in the winter, surely?"

"There are no rules. It's soft now but at this time of year it can dry out very fast. Then we'd run the ones that like it that way, give this one a rest."

"But he's entered for some more races soon?"

"Yes, he is."

A faint sun shone on Roly's bright frame, bringing up the shining muscle that Rosy had nurtured to the detriment of her own femininity: her muscles were as impressive as his, the dust she brushed from his coat furred her own fine skin and eternally gritty hair. She joined the men in regarding her horse as he stood out

obediently, a touch anxious. His big rabbity ears flexed hopefully to catch the admiration in the voices of the spectators.

"He's very much the type I like. Stands over a lot of ground."

Rosy suspected Mr. Hawkins had picked up the phrases without knowing what they meant. Roly made an affectionate lunge towards his outstretched hand and landed some specks of slobber on the Yorkshire tweed. Hawkins withdrew a fraction.

"Walk him out," Jeremy said. "He's a nice mover."

"I'm a nice mover too, Roly," Rosy whispered as they went away down the yard. Had Jeremy noticed? Her quarters were as shapely, her fetlocks as springy.

"Thank you," Jeremy said.

Big deal. At least, unlike some trainers, he was civil to his lads. She led Roly away and saddled him ready to exercise, put his rug on and tied him up. Mr. Hawkins looked at all the other horses and Rosy joined Gin in the tackroom. Hugh Maddox put his head round the door. "The guv'nor's taking that guy up in the Land-Rover. Wants the second string got ready, and Roly Fox is to go too, Rosy, to do a canter. Looks like we've got an interested customer."

There was no time for speculation; they got the horses out and rode straight up onto the downs by the track that led out of the back of the stableyard. Roly was as fresh as if he hadn't raced for weeks. In the sharp canter over the crest of the hill before the watchers in the Land-Rover, Rosy, perched above that smooth machinery with the wind of their passage making her eyes smart, looked to the sky ahead where rooks were tumbling like windblown rags over the horizon and felt her spirits soaring in unison.

"Steady on, old Roly. We're not on a racecourse!"

The long ears switched back in response to her voice, and she laughed out loud. Roly, the way he felt, was laughing too.

STANDING BY THE OPEN car window as Hawkins fastened his seatbelt, Jeremy felt not unhappy.

Then Hawkins said, "You know, of course, that my own jockey rides all my horses? Young Mowbray."

"If you prefer it that way. I have great faith in Dave, though. To my mind, there's none better."

"Well, Mowbray rides all mine."

"Will he ride work for us?"

"Yes, if I tell him."

"Fine."

"Cheers, then."

But it wasn't fine. Jeremy went back under the archway, silent and scowling. He pushed open the front door and stood in the hall beneath the life-size picture of a young woman on a horse. Confidence and spirit radiated from the portrait. The girl was slight, her bearing arrogant, her hands delicate. She had a bundle of untidy golden-red hair pinned up beneath a shapeless twenties sun hat that shaded half her face, darkened the brown, direct eyes. The face was beautiful, the chin pointed, the lips sensuous and curling, mocking. The horse was as arrogant as its rider, and between them they made a dramatic impact upon the unsuspecting visitor coming in through the front door.

"Oh, Gran," Jeremy said out loud.

She was three minutes away by car. On an impulse he drove there, parked outside, and limped up the garden path. She was trying to nail a windblown climbing rose back onto the porch, wielding a huge hammer and a plastic bag of staples. Failing.

"Here, give it to me."

Surprised, she yielded up the hammer.

"Go and make a cup of coffee. I'll do this first."

He did not pretend that he was a devoted grandson. He was a swine to the old girl. She had all the courage that he lacked, facing crippling by age with a resolution he could not find in his own situation. That was why he kept away, he supposed, not wanting to ponder on the comparison. But his mood today was uncertain, excited by the prospects Hawkins had expounded over the smoked-salmon sandwiches, sickened by the thought of having to employ Mowbray to ride. Mowbray the Boy Wonder, who had won the Gold Cup at the age of nineteen.

The rose, an old-fashioned Caroline Testout which Mrs. Cutbush had brought with her from Brood House, was throttled into subjection against the wooden posts of the porch, and Jeremy stepped inside. It was so long since he had called that the dark, low-ceilinged room with its walls solidly packed with racing pictures and mementos came as a shock. There had been no wall big enough for the portrait back at Brood House, but anything she had been able to fit in was there, from the little Stubbs, "Horse and Groom in a Landscape", to all the lesser portraits of horses her husband had trained.

There was a whole wall devoted to photographs of himself, riding winners at Cheltenham, at Newbury and Ascot and, as a boy, at point-to-points from Tweseldown to Cottenham. In all of them he looked fearless and arrogant like the rider in the portrait at home. At eighteen he had grinned at the camera, mud-splashed, victorious, obnoxiously cocky—not unlike Tony Mowbray.

When his gran doddered in with the coffee cups on a tray, he tried hard to see in the stooped figure the girl in his hall, but it was as hard to reconcile the two as it was to recognize the young jockey in the photos as himself. The old claw-like hands, knotted with gardening, rheumatism and general wear, were the same that held the reins in his picture with such silken authority. That dirty bundle of white frizz was the same gleaming gold hair that escaped in artistic tendrils from the sun hat. Oh, Gran! he wanted to cry out— lovely Letitia McAlister on Golden Harvest, where have you gone? And where the cocky rider of Gunshot, winner at Kempton on Boxing Day, triumphant behind a mask of mud?

Letitia McAlister had the excuse of sixty years passing; the rider of Gunshot a shattered pelvis, and disintegration thereafter. Nobody could escape the battering of age, but better people than he had surmounted worse injuries than he had received and lived to be gracious, loved and successful.

"You look peaky, dear," said his grandmother. "Aren't you well?"

"Yes, I'm fine. I've got a new owner, Gran. He's a Yorkshireman and he's bringing me two youngsters off the flat, and he's bought Roly Fox."

"A foreigner?" She pursed her lips. "I don't like foreigners."

He groaned in spirit, having forgotten her eccentricities. "A Yorkshireman is not a foreigner."

Over her mantelpiece was a portrait of her husband, Peter Cutbush, an upstanding, clean-cut Britisher of impeccable antecedents: Winchester, Trinity and, later, the Gloucester Hussars. He had volunteered in 1940 and got killed for his impetuosity, leaving a stableyard at Brood House with a reputation second to none. He had been a golden boy of prewar racing. He and his wife had attracted owners because they themselves were lovely people to know; racing with the Cutbushes was fun and glamorous.

The Cutbush glamour had faded in the next generation. Jeremy thought his own father had perhaps been overshadowed by his parents' powerful personalities. A more stolid and altogether less showy character, he had taken on Brood House after the war at the age of twenty, taking out the licence in the name of the very efficient head lad who nursed him through his first years.

The stable had been moderately successful, but they had turned more and more to the jumping game, because young Cutbush liked to hunt and ride as an amateur himself. He had married an Australian girl, the daughter of an owner, and Jeremy had been their only child. Letitia Cutbush had been a terrible mother-in-law. Still living on the premises, she had tried to run the place as she was used to running it. Jeremy could remember the impressive rows during his boyhood, Letitia's powerful will smashing head-on against the growing doggedness of his father and his wife's loyalty. Between them they all taught him to ride, and fast riding had been his release, his passion. His triumph and his downfall. The photographs round the walls chronicled the life of his grandfather Peter Cutbush, and his own, and completely missed out the intervening generation. Five years ago his parents had emigrated to Australia, but he had refused to go.

"What you need," said his grandmother, between noisy sips of her coffee, "is a wife, to look after you."

"Please, Gran, don't start on that." He remembered now why he never came to see her.

"That gel—Judith Partridge . . . what became of her?"

"She went." Hospital visiting had bored Judith. She liked her men in bed all right, but not hospital beds.

"That was a long time ago," he added.

"Was it?" She looked surprised. She got her sequences of events much muddled these days.

"Seven—eight years ago."

"When was your accident?"

"The same time—eight years ago."

He had been twenty-two, the same age as Tony Mowbray. The thought of employing Mowbray hurt dreadfully. Seeing him ride his horses was going to pull the scabs off the deepest of his wounds because young Mowbray was everything he had once been. The Cutbush glamour had flowered again, briefly, when Jeremy had been riding and winning and everyone had wanted to know him. He had been brave and self-confident. Life had been a party and he had been guest of honour. Until the day he got buried at the last of the railway fences at Sandown Park.

True courage would have seen him through all that, but true courage was not what he possessed. He had not coped. He got up and studied the walls again, taking the coffee cup with him. He found Judith Partridge, gazing up at him as he was led in at Newton Abbot, frankly adoring (or so it seemed), lustrous film-star eyes wide beneath a wild fur hat. She had promised to marry him. So much for promises. Painfully stirred, he moved on, and came to the Stubbs.

"This is worth a fortune, Gran. I hope you lock up well."

"I never go out."

"At night, I mean."

"I've got Jasper."

He didn't argue. "Horse and Groom in a Landscape" was full of serenity, very beautiful. In a park filled with a golden autumn glow, a stallion with eyes as lustrous as Judith Partridge's stood haltered by a boy in livery. The horse was perfectly proportioned, muscled and shining and pictured for posterity in a moment of poise, one foreleg uplifted, mane and tail stirred by an invisible breeze.

"That came from your great-grandfather's place," Mrs. Cutbush said. "That was his grandfather's horse, Lionheart." Casually she added, "I'm going to leave it to Rosy, she loves it so."

Jeremy was deeply shocked. "To *Rosy?*"

"Yes."

"Have you told her?"

"I can't remember. I might have."

Jeremy did not know what to say. He knew Rosy and Gin helped the old girl but had never suspected they were in it for money. Did not suspect it now, in fact. But the Stubbs . . . It was probably worth half a million. Far more than a gift of friendship.

"It's worth an awful lot of money, Gran."

"I'm not short, dear."

"That's not what I meant. Is it insured?"

"The contents of the house are insured."

"Did you tell them you had a Stubbs?"

"I don't remember."

He had a right to the painting. But what had he ever done to deserve it? Far less than Rosy.

"Did you put it in your will, Gran? To leave the picture to Rosy?"

"I think I wrote a note in my desk. I know that you will see to it for me, the few little bequests. It's all quite plain."

He did not know what to say. He did not even know if she had made a will, did not know how much she was worth anyway. He had always assumed that her estate would pass to his father, her only child. He had never thought of her leaving him money, never even thought of the Stubbs until now. Money was a subject that did not interest him much—or so he had always thought. But the idea of the Stubbs going to Rosy was very disturbing. It might be worth mentioning to Rogers, the family solicitor . . . although what sort of a light did that put him in? Damn it, Jeremy thought, what an embarrassing situation!

"Does Rosy come often?"

"Two or three times a week. She does my errands. She stays and talks."

The thought of Rosy doing chores for the old girl, when he scarcely ever looked in, gave him a bad feeling, but he knew he wasn't going to change anything. If she got the Stubbs . . . God dammit, half a million for running a few errands! Don't think about it, he said to himself later, as he ground his way up the drive to Brood House. It was as bad as having to employ Tony Mowbray.

He looked in the tackroom to give a few orders.

"We'll need two boxes got ready for Hawkins's horses. The two end ones, I suppose. They'd better be thoroughly scrubbed out and disinfected. Will you see to it, Gin?"

Gin was a good lad, entirely reliable, which was more than one could say about dreary Hugh, whom Jeremy felt himself lumbered with. Well-meaning and honest—but lazy—Hugh was thick, whereas Gin was sharp as a needle.

"When are they coming, sir?"

"Wednesday, he said."

Without meaning to, Jeremy caught Rosy's eye, as she looked up from her tack-cleaning. She had a way of looking at him which he found slightly disturbing. Now, with the Stubbs in mind, it occurred to him that he ought to rethink Rosy; she was moving into another league. Up to now she had been a hard-working "lass", not one to worry about. He had known her, as he had Gin, ever since he could remember. He could recall her following him about at the local point-to-points, as a girl of fourteen, fifteen; remembered the letter she had sent him when he was in hospital, the regret more fiercely phrased than in most, as if she had some knowledge of how it felt. Her dad, Weeks, a recently retired postman, couldn't be much of a rave to live with. He was to be seen on the downs in his long ex-army shorts, 1940 vintage, muttering to invisible wonders in the earth or, sometimes, meeting other naturalists in unlikely places to look for gromwell and tway-blade. His wife Doreen had died of cancer. She had been taken ill when Rosy was in London at art college and Rosy had come home to help nurse her. People had assumed that Rosy stayed after her mother's death to look after her father, but Jeremy always thought she had stayed because she had decided that country life suited her better than town life.

Rosy was stocky like her mother, with curly brown hair, and a strong face that could have been a boy's. The eyes that regarded Jeremy so steadily were calm and wide, not as striking as Judith Partridge's, but more reassuring. They were blue-grey in colour and hard to read, Rosy being older than she looked and not given to much display of emotion, except where Roly Fox was concerned.

Feeling generous at the thought, he said to her, "Roly ran a blinder yesterday—he seems to have got his confidence at last. All credit to you."

She coloured slightly but said nothing. Last night, when it had mattered, he had gone indoors without a word and waited until she had gone to look at the horse. It was not surprising, he thought, that he had a reputation for being lousy to work for. But it was hard to be gracious when his jealousy burned as deeply as it had yesterday, seeing Dave Perkins bring Roly flying over the last with a jump that could have cleared the Aintree Chair with a foot to spare. Jeremy employed Dave Perkins regularly for the main reason that, although Dave was extremely competent, he seemed to get very little pleasure out of his profession. Jeremy did not want euphoric jockeys. He feared that Tony Mowbray might prove a talkative brat: he was certainly young enough never to have heard of Jeremy Cutbush and his brilliance over fences before being cut off in his prime.

"You'll have to do one of the new horses, Rosy. You can have first choice."

She smiled, looking pleased at the prospect of more work. He made towards the house, but Hugh, coming out of the feedshed, waylaid him. "With the new horses coming—if you're short of anyone to ride, Grace said she'd come up. She's a pretty good rider."

"Grace?"

"My sister. She's at home—at a loose end just now."

"Oh—Grace—yes, sorry. Of course."

That Grace . . . an ill-named female, by Jeremy's reckoning. "Fine. Thanks."

He darted for home, suffering suddenly from a surfeit of human intercourse. Letitia McAlister, back in her prime, watched him cross her track towards the large bleak kitchen and the remains of the smoked salmon sandwiches.

"Did you ask him?"

"Yes," said Hugh.

"What did he say?"

"Oh, nothing much. You know him."

"Not as much as I'd like to," Grace said.

The horsebox from Newmarket made three attempts at clearing the stone pillars into the yard and decided to unload outside.

"Don't know how you do it, mate," the driver said, noticing the resident horsebox safely parked within.

"It's knack," Gin said carelessly, but he was pleased all the same.

Rosy, warm with Jeremy's promise that she had first choice of the newcomers, went out to help unload.

"Which is the best?" she asked the lad who was travelling with them.

"The best is Peppermill, the chestnut. The nicest is the Sagaro colt."

They were a very classy pair, wrapped in dazzling rugs and thick felt bandages that seemed to be part of the deal. Installed in the newly prepared looseboxes, their handsome heads reviewed the new surroundings. They were both superbly bred: Peppermill was by Mill Reef, out of a mare called Peppercorn. They had been stayers on the flat and were now to be schooled over hurdles to see if they could make a new career for themselves.

It wasn't until Rosy was riding out for the first time on Peppermill the next morning that the revelation came to her. Hugh had said take them through the village on the lanes first and do the long hack home over the downs, and Rosy was just beginning to get the feel of the skittery Peppermill—like a pony after Roly—when they came to the gate of Mrs. Cutbush's field. Silverfish was at the top of the field and heard them coming. Rosy saw the mare lift her head and stare and, for a moment, look like her photograph in *Tatler*: the shapely ears pricked up tight, nostrils dilated. Then she gave a plunge and a buck and came down the hill, pulling up at the gate just as Peppermill was passing.

Peppermill let out a deep-throated whinny and swung round, almost catching Rosy unawares. She snatched him up and drove him on with her heels and Gin, laughing, circled his horse and came up on her inside, driving the colt away from the mare. Silverfish let out a piercing whinny behind them.

They trotted to get out of the danger area. "Who said the old girl was past it!" Gin laughed. "Love at first sight—at her age!"

"God, Gin—if only they could! Think of it!"

"No, I won't. And don't you either." He was grinning as he rode beside her. They turned off onto the track up to the downs, and Peppermill started to pull, feeling the grass beneath his feet. On the left they passed the lovely Georgian house belonging to Hugh's family, set in an old-fashioned garden. Grace was going out for the newspapers and watched them closely as they passed.

"She's asked if she can ride out," Gin said to Rosy.

"Whatever for? She's got her dad's hunter if she wants to ride."

"She's after the guv'nor. Like you, Rosy."

"You're joking!"

"Bet I'm not. Why else?"

The news disturbed Rosy, for Grace had a formidable will. Rosy had never thought her attractive, but perhaps her view was not shared. She had sharp features of classic proportions and her colouring was true blonde and rose, with sky-blue eyes.

"She's not what he needs, I'm sure." Sour grapes perhaps. Grace's aggressive drive might be the very thing Jeremy needed.

Rosy put the idea away, unable to contemplate the idea of Jeremy falling for Grace. He'd have more sense . . . but the chemistry of love was a funny business. Silverfish now . . . that was something to think about. If the old mare was in season so strongly, surely she would "take" if she were given a chance? The crazy idea took hold, and would not leave Rosy.

Peppermill was a good sort, a fitting mate for Silverfish. He was not big and rangy like Roly, but built very correctly, neat and powerful in a different sort of way, full of class. He was a very dark chestnut with no white on him save for a small star, a bit fierce in the stable, especially at feeding time, but nothing that Rosy couldn't handle.

"He's to be let down," Hugh announced later as he was measuring the colt's ration. "Get the condition off him, then he can be gelded."

"How long will that take?" Rosy asked.

"About a month, probably."

A month—no time at all!

"JUST WHAT ARE YOU proposing, for goodness sake?" Gin asked, exasperated. "Who is going to agree to it? The colt belongs to Hawkins, I can't see Jeremy asking old Hawkins on your behalf."

"I wasn't thinking of asking anybody."

They were in Gin's kitchen, sitting at the kitchen table over cups of coffee. The room was still full of the lovely lingering aromas of supper: fried bacon and onions and chops and apple pie. Rosy had just come from her father's speciality—curried eggs with bolognese sauce—and was grateful for the coffee to soothe her offended palate.

"There's still such a thing as nature. You've only got to give them a chance when no one's around. Take him down there when she comes in season next time."

"During morning exercise?" Gin's voice was sarcastic.

"There's afternoons when Jeremy and Hugh are away racing— there's no one about at all. No one need ever know."

Gin stared into his coffee. Rosy knew that he was impressed with her thinking.

"Mrs. Cutbush told me I could have the foal—own it—don't you remember? If I got the mare served. Any foal of Silverfish's is worth a lot of money."

"But you couldn't register it—who would give you a covering certificate? You couldn't send it up to Weatherby's, as by Peppermill. What good is it without papers?"

"Oh, there must be a way round that." Her airy dismissal of what Gin saw as an insoluble difficulty annoyed him.

"It's time you grew up! I'm not having a hand in such a crazy idea, and you wouldn't be able to do it by yourself."

"It would be half yours, if you helped."

Rosy was grinning. She did not really believe in the idea herself. "We'd be pretty lucky," she conceded, "to get everything right— Silverfish in season and the chance to get Peppermill to her without anyone seeing. She might not come in season again before Peppermill gets cut."

Gin looked relieved. "You are a nut. Only you would get a notion like that into your head."

"It's not so stupid—not if we could work out how to get the foal registered."

"You'd have to find the right stallion owner and a crook vet— who'd sign the papers for you."

"You know plenty of crooks," Rosy said. "I'd leave that bit to you." She got up and made herself another coffee at the stove. She was in no hurry to go, at home in Gin's house more than in her own. It was a haphazard family—"feckless" her father said. Gin's father was some sort of a dealer in scrap and cars. Sometimes he had a large roll of notes in his pocket; other times they had to buy on credit. There were several brothers and sisters, all married but Gin. They were all on at him to get married, and often told him to marry Rosy, in her presence. Laughs all round. "She's been one of the family for years," they said cheerfully. It was true that, right from being small, she had spent as much time in Gin's house as her own. The confusion, the crowd and the cooking had always attracted her, an only child from a quiet, tidy home.

"How's Beryl?" she asked.

If romance came easily to Rosy, with her patient, useless infatuation for Jeremy Cutbush, it was an altogether different matter for Gin, who was more used to persuading horses than girls. He dreaded both the intimacy and the responsibility of marriage and he liked living at home. Beryl was the only girl who seemed likely to have him, the way he saw it. Whether he wanted her or not he never could decide. At least she knew racing, so she'd know what to expect, but going home to her every night . . . the thought did not uplift him.

He shrugged to Rosy's inquiry, and she laughed.

"You're terribly *slow*. Your ma told me she's going to kick you out of the house if you've not got round to it by next Christmas."

"I'm taking Hallmark to Newbury tomorrow. Beryl will probably be there. I'll try and make a date—borrow Dad's car."

"That's a boy!"

"It's a pity . . ." He hesitated, considered. "You and me, we know each other too well. But if we'd got married when we were kids—twentyish or so, it might have worked."

"I doubt it." Rosy did not encourage the thought. There would be time for regrets when she was fifty, not yet.

When she went home, two houses away, she looked up the hill and saw the light shining through the trees. She glanced at her watch. It was ten, the time Jeremy did his round. Rosy wished she were Roly Fox with that to look forward to every night. She reckoned Jeremy was a good trainer, but he did not attract new owners with his introverted disposition; he did not go looking for them, and they were a rare breed in any case, requiring to be sought out and tempted and offered delectable horses. Hawkins was the first new owner she could remember. It was something of a wonder that Jeremy had taken him on, not sent him away with a flea in his ear. What a waste it all was! Rosy would have despised Jeremy if she did not remember his glorious youth, the fire and courage he had shown before his accident.

The next day Grace came to ride out. Hugh gave her the Sagaro colt, who was quiet and kind and called, perversely, Needles. Grace was madeup as if she were going hunting and wore white breeches and boots and a black velvet riding hat. Gin insisted that she wore a crash helmet, which annoyed her. Rosy watched, interested. There could only be one reason for her wanting to ride work: she was not known to have a passion for horses. When Jeremy came out to see them mounted he merely nodded to her, his usual dour self.

Grace rode well, better than Hugh, who, as usual, was riding the hack, Brown Ale. The two lads, Simon and Trev, were embarrassed by Grace and steered well clear, not knowing whether she was in the same pecking order as themselves or, being Hugh's sister, someone to be kowtowed to. Grace settled in beside Rosy's mount, Villanelle, as they climbed the wide track through the Brood House forest up towards the bare crest of the downs above.

"What does he do?" Grace asked her, nodding at Villanelle. "Not much, by the look of him."

A true estimation, it offended Rosy deeply. "He's a novice hurdler. He's done nothing wrong so far."

Jeremy came up behind them in the Land-Rover and they made room for him to pass.

"Does he never ride now?" Grace asked.

"No. He can't."

"I don't see why not, if there was someone to encourage him—to motivate him—"

Was Grace suggesting he only needed motivating? By the love of a good woman, presumably. Thinking she could see the suggestion of a smile on Grace's face, Rosy fumed, stuck her heels into Villanelle and trotted on, passing the boys. When they got to the top of the slope they trotted to where the Land-Rover was waiting. Jeremy beckoned Rosy over. Grace came with her, but when Jeremy got out he said sharply to Grace, "Ride on," and turned to Rosy.

"Villanelle is not going level."

In her distraction, Rosy had failed to notice. She hated to be found wanting. She stroked the gelding's neck while Jeremy picked up his feet. A stone was wedged against one of his frogs, and Jeremy worked it free with a hoofpick. Rosy looked down on the back of his head and had a great urge to caress the curling dark hair that lay close against his neck. Oh, damn! she thought, damn Grace, for setting off the old weary cycle of frustration. She spent her whole working life damping the ridiculous sparks Jeremy's presence ignited in her system; she had thought the precautions of a lifetime had made her proof. When he straightened up and declared the horse fit, she nodded coldly and looked into his eyes for signs of irresolution, cowardice, meanness and bad temper, but saw only the grey-green independence of his old gran, wanting his own cussed way, not wanting pity, sympathy or even, it seemed, the human face of friendship.

Surprisingly, he smiled, patted Villanelle's neck, and said "OK." Rosy interpreted it—to suit herself—as a conspiracy against Grace, to whom he had not yet extended either smile or word. She returned to the stables in high spirits.

In the tackroom, on the calendar, the week's likely events were pencilled in. She was surprised to see that Hugh was taking Drogo and Straw Top to Worcester the day after tomorrow. Jeremy would go, and she and Gin would have the place to themselves, if they so desired. Silverfish was due to come in season again any minute now. While these conjectures were going through her head, Hugh said, "The vet's coming to cut the two colts on the fourteenth."

Ten days' time. Their only chance was coming up. Rosy stood dumbly before the calendar, in a world of her own. If Silverfish showed tonight, or tomorrow . . . God meant it to happen.

"Are you deaf?"

She blinked.

"I said Mowbray is coming to ride work on Tuesday. Tomorrow."

"Who's Mowbray?"

The boys were laughing. She came to, pulled herself together. "Oh, *him*. The Boy Wonder."

Wednesday was the day that mattered. She wasn't interested in Tuesday.

"To ride your blooming horse. He's its jockey from now on, or is it news to you?"

But Rosy wasn't listening.

"He's not like Perkins. He's whip-happy," Trev said. "I'm glad he's not riding mine."

GRACE, HAVING DELIVERED Needles back to Simon to put away, tossed her crash helmet in at the tackroom door and walked firmly under the clock tower to the door of Brood House. Jeremy's Land-Rover was parked outside. She paused for a moment with her hand on the doorknob, then gave it an experimental twist. The door opened, and she took a step into the hall.

"Coo-ee! Jeremy!"

The portrait that dominated the hall took her by surprise. It was almost as if one were being ridden down, the action of the horse so strong, the figure so vibrant. Grace had never seen a Munnings so impressive. Whatever was it worth? she wondered. Nobody knew whether Jeremy had money or not. By appearances, he had none, save that he owned the decrepit Brood estate and its buildings. Yet Grace knew that his grandparents had made a lot of money and, as far as anyone knew, it was still around. Old Mrs. Cutbush, if appearances were anything to go by, hadn't spent a penny of it. Grace liked money. She was not at all averse to the idea of taking on Brood House and modernizing it, and she thought Jeremy would benefit from the same treatment.

The house had a musty damp smell and was as cheerless as an unused church. Yet it retained, somehow, an innate style. Grace crossed the hall and opened the door into the drawing room. She found herself looking right through the width of the house and out through vast French windows onto neglected lawns. The room was an inspired blend of chic twenties design imposed upon the natural Georgian order. It was strikingly successful. All the same, Grace thought, I would gut it and modernize it; one could not possibly live with so strong a flavour of somebody else. That the somebody else was Letitia Cutbush she had no doubt. The recalcitrant old granny had had rare taste in her youth—or the money to buy it.

She shut the door, and set off in the opposite direction, trying another "Yoo-hoo!"

Jeremy, telephoning a clerk of the course to check on the state of the going, tethered by the telephone cord to the kitchen wall, was outraged by Grace's audacity. She appeared at the kitchen door and stood taking in his sanctuary, apparently unaware that it was out of bounds. Even Hugh had never come further than the hall. He turned his back on her and spun out his conversation. But soon he was forced to replace the receiver and turn round.

"I'm dying for a cup of coffee," Grace said. "Shall I make you one?" Her nerve unnerved him.

"Do what you please."

He meant to be deeply sarcastic but she took the invitation at face value and crossed over to the stove where the percolator was standing. Jeremy pretended to study the racing calendar, but his mind seethed with indignation.

"I like riding out, if I'm of use to you," Grace said, spooning out the coffee as if she had lived at Brood for years. "Hugh said you were shorthanded."

Jeremy grunted, pretending to read attentively.

"It's very cold in here, colder than outside. Haven't you ever thought of putting in central heating?"

She busied herself looking for china in a cupboard that he hadn't opened for years. She set a tray, putting milk in a jug as if she was still passing exams in her expensive finishing school.

"No," he said.

"You're just the same as Dad. He says it's healthy to be cold. It's a very old-fashioned attitude."

If nothing else, Grace was certainly healthy, but her assurance crucified Jeremy.

"Do you take sugar?"

"No."

"No, *thank you*."

"It's my sugar. Why should I thank you?"

"You need sweetening, Jeremy. Why are you so bitter?"

Her eyes glittered with bravado. She wanted him to respond, ready to pounce again.

Like a fool, he responded. "Why did you come in? I didn't ask you. Nobody comes in the house, not even your brother."

"I'm not surprised. It's such a morgue."

"They're not invited."

"But why? You used to have plenty of friends. Why the hermit act? You have made your life very dreary, you have to admit."

She carried the tray to the table, pushing his racing calendar to one side. "I know it's very out of place for me to talk like this, but what a waste, Jeremy!"

"I think you'd better go. I've a lot to do."

"It's a platitude that you only live once. But it's true. You're living just like your old gran. But she's eighty."

She drank her coffee quickly and turned to go.

"I want to help you, Jeremy. Please don't be cross. I'll come again tomorrow and do as I'm told. I won't come in again. Goodbye."

And she turned and pranced out, full of self-assurance, leaving Jeremy livid and ashamed, and deeply disturbed.

3

On her way to work the next day Rosy called in on Silverfish and confirmed that she was in season. Her mind was completely occupied with the God-given opportunity which was presenting itself and she went in to do her horses in a daze.

"You're not serious?" Gin hissed at her when they were fetching their tack.

"Oh, I am! Gin, you must—*must* . . ."

It was not a job one could do single-handed. Gin looked at Rosy and felt himself growing pale.

There was no chance to discuss it then, the others were all agog for the arrival of the Boy Wonder who was to ride Roly Fox on the gallops. At any other time Rosy would have been anticipating this even more than most, but as it was she scarcely noticed when the dark blue MG pulled into the yard and its driver inquired for Mr. Cutbush. Grace, arriving right behind in her battered Mini, got out and, before the approaching Hugh could say anything, said, "Come with me. I'll tell him you're here," and escorted the newcomer away under the archway. She returned almost immediately, leaving Mowbray to enter the hallowed portals alone. Hugh tacked up Needles for her, and Rosy, on Roly Fox, avoided her company as they rode up onto the gallops, not much wanting to talk to anyone. She was so preoccupied with planning how she could get Silverfish in foal that she was not even aware of Roly Fox's new jockey until she was on the gallops and Jeremy was beckoning her over. Mowbray was sitting beside him in the Land-Rover.

"Get down," Jeremy said. "Mowbray is having your horse."

Mowbray was a vision in silver-grey, his anorak fur-lined, blond hair artfully highlighted, a gold chain necklace showing at his throat. Rosy gawped. Ice-blue eyes took in her shabby figure, thawed faintly in acknowledgment.

"Give him a leg-up."

Mowbray settled his helmet and raised an elegantly-booted ankle into her hand. He went into the saddle like thistledown and gathered up the reins. Rosy noticed his whip, a cutting, well-worn affair, and remembered the talk in the tackroom.

"He won't need to use that. He always gives everything. He's absolutely genuine."

"Fine then." Mowbray set off at a trot.

Jockeys came to ride work often, but none of them looked a fraction as beautiful as Tony Mowbray. Rosy looked at Jeremy. "Cor," she said, and grinned.

He actually smiled. "Hop in."

She hopped. They drove up over the crest of the down and sat in silence to watch their new jockey. Rosy felt a deep unease at the thought of her darling now owned by an uncaring businessman and ridden by a whiz kid who had a name to make. Jeremy felt every bit as bad as he had foreseen he would, taking in Mowbray's youth and confidence and natural flair. Under the new arrangement they were likely to win more races, but this fact made neither of them happier. Mowbray did his gallop, took Roly twice over the schooling fences and came back to the Land-Rover looking cocky. He slapped Roly's neck and said, "He's fine. No problems."

If only, Rosy thought.

BY TEATIME GIN HAD accepted the inevitable. The following afternoon the stables would be empty. Even old Albert was going racing: Hugh was taking him because it was his seventieth birthday. Simon and Trev would go home after lunchtime feeding and not be back until four thirty.

"It'll only take half an hour—ten minutes walk down, ten minutes back—we can use the big barn, Silverfish's barn—no one will see. No one will ever kncw," said Rosy.

"What about Mrs. Cutbush?"

"I'll go and talk to her—now. She'll like the idea, I swear she will."

"Gawd! What if—"

"Oh, Gin, shut up! It's such a little risk, compared with what might come out of it. I'm going down to talk to the old girl."

Rosy walked fast down the lane to Mrs. Cutbush's cottage. She banged on the door and went in. The poky little room, crammed with its pictures, always enchanted her with its stamp of past glory. She had minutely studied all the photographs, mostly when Mrs. Cutbush was pottering in the kitchen, and knew where to look for Jeremy on his horses. If—when—their study was too painful she turned always to the eternal golden afternoon of the "Horse and Groom in a Landscape" where everything was as it should be: perfect. Contemplation of the Stubbs never failed to soothe. Even now, one glance gave courage.

Letitia Cutbush was delighted with the idea.

"A Mill Reef colt? Splendid, splendid! Lots and lots of Nasrullah blood—he'll be grandsire on one side and great-grandsire on the other. Nasrullah was third in the Derby the same year my husband was killed. I remember him well. Can you see my glasses anywhere?"

She could remember every date of fifty years back, but lost her glasses all the time, and never knew whether it was Sunday or Thursday. Rosy retrieved the glasses from the top of the china cabinet.

"If I don't like him, mind you, I won't have it. He's not a weed, I hope?"

"No, he's beautifully made, not big, but compact."

"That's what we want. Bring him up in the afternoon. I'll have her ready for you."

Rosy hesitated. "You said—you said—" she was embarrassed. "If I arranged it, the mating—you said the foal—"

"Would be yours," Mrs. Cutbush said. "Yes, that's right. I want you to have it. Like the picture."

Rosy had no idea what she meant by the last sentence but was too relieved to inquire. It was of no importance.

She was half convinced that something would happen to upset the plans the following day, but Jeremy and Hugh departed for Worcester at the appointed hour, taking Albert with them, and at one o'clock Simon and Trev went home on their motorbikes. Rosy sat shaking in the tackroom. The quiet of the stableyard, disturbed only by the steady munching of the horses over their midday feeds, meant that all was in order. Rosy had planned to bridle Peppermill and lead him down but had an attack of the panics, and could not start.

Gin came in. "I'm on my way. By the time you get down there, I'll have her ready and waiting. What's the matter, gel?"

He, the unwilling partner, was now calm and objective, Rosy nervous as a hare.

"Come on, you can't back out now. I'm off."

"OK."

He departed, and Rosy unhooked Peppermill's snaffle. Ears pricked, he looked a handsome devil. Rosy's courage came back, and she slipped the bridle over his ears, talking to him kindly. They walked down the long drive together, the colt curious, Rosy happy now. They came out on the road, but met no one. The village was asleep, the only sign of life Mrs. Cutbush waiting by the gate into Silverfish's field. She wore her ancient jodhpurs, with the old-fashioned winged upper parts, and an even more ancient suede jacket and felt hat.

"If I don't like him—" she said, jutting out the famous chin.

"Look—how can you not?"

Rosy unbuckled his surcingle and pulled back his rug, to show the splendid slope of the shoulder. Mrs. Cutbush groped for her spectacles. Silverfish whinnied from the barn, and Peppermill threw up his head, excited, making the rug fall in a heap under the open gate.

"Oh, very nice!" Mrs. Cutbush leaped into action. "Yes, he'll do splendidly. Come along."

She slammed the gate shut, gathered up the rug and they hurried up the hill towards the barn. Gin came to meet them, grinning.

"Here, wait." He clipped a long rein onto the snaffle rings. "You go and handle the mare—I'll take this end."

Rosy ran. Silverfish was tied up and churning the deep straw. Rosy undid her. "Hold up, old girl! There's no hurry."

Silverfish thought otherwise, and plunged round to face the entrance to the barn. Peppermill came in, amazed, the sweat rising, making deep whickering noises in his throat. As he advanced, Rosy dragged the mare's head round to present her backside, and heard Gin cry out, "Watch yourself!"

Peppermill's front feet missed her by inches. He mounted the mare at a bad angle and fell off sideways, roaring with excitement. Rosy kept the mare in place, rear on, and at the second attempt Peppermill mounted her properly, forelegs on either side. Silverfish stood like a rock, ears flat back, stoic in obedience to nature's pattern.

Rosy had seen it all before but this time the creation was as much hers as the two animals'; she felt as if she was playing God.

"That's it," said Gin. "You won't get another chance, old girl."

Peppermill slithered down, sweating and blowing as if he was standing in the winners' enclosure. Mrs. Cutbush was smiling, having shed about thirty years.

"When will you bring him up again? I'll have her ready."

"We can't. There's no chance of doing it again. We borrowed him—nobody knows about it, only the three of us."

"Jeremy doesn't know?"

"No."

"Oh, that's good! I like that!" Mrs. Cutbush grinned. "Our secret, eh? Well, I like secrets. That's good."

Gin threw Peppermill's rugs on and buckled them up. He and

Rosy felt an urgent need to have the colt back home now the deed was done. Silverfish must take her chance. They turned her loose and watched her walk away towards the best of the spring grass that was coming through down by the stream.

THREE DAYS LATER Rosy went to Newton Abbot with Roly Fox who was running in a handicap chase in his new owner's colours. Tony Mowbray was to ride him and Rosy was worried. Driving down with Gin she remembered someone saying Mowbray was whip-happy.

"Is it true?" she asked Gin.

"Probably. All the young ones are. Anyway, Hawkins—he's in it to win, not like Mrs. Palmer." Gin had Beryl on his mind and wasn't bothered about Rosy's new problem. Beryl had told him the last time he met her that she was fed up and wanted a new job. What if he proposed marriage, just like that? She was a betting lady, and might take a chance. His mother was going to turn him out and he didn't fancy doing his own cooking. There was a cottage on the Brood estate—it had once been the lodge at the bottom of the drive, when the drive had boasted gates at both top and bottom—and Gin reckoned Mr. Cutbush would let him rent it for the time being, until a council house came up. It was a bit ramshackle but nothing he couldn't tart up with a few evenings' work. It would be handy to live on the estate itself. He had visions of nipping down for lunch and coming in at the door to find her waiting in a pretty apron, table laid and covered with the sort of dishes women's magazines taught them to make.

Beryl was betting on a runner in the three o'clock. He couldn't wait to find her. The sun was shining, the air clear and bright, perfect racing weather. The flat boys were taking over and the old steeplechasers were due for their annual holiday, nosing into lush pasture and putting fat over their lean hides. As soon as the weather firmed the ground, Cutbush would shut up shop. May . . . June . . . that was the ideal time to get married, get some fun in before the season started again.

Gin left Rosy to unload Roly Fox and went to look for Beryl. He found her amongst the bookies, a small, skinny figure, too thin, he thought, with smudged shadows under over-large eyes and a rather repulsive ex-punk hairstyle, with blonde dye starting two inches from the roots. He thought he would have to change the hairstyle. That apart, he saw her as attractive, like a little bird, cute and perky.

"Hi, Beryl. Will you marry me?"

She stared at him. "Have you been drinking?"

He was deeply hurt. Having had the idea, he had been thinking about it with such concentration that he had forgotten how very limited their contact had been up to now. The vision of the little lodge house and Beryl in her apron had carried him away.

"Thought you said you wanted to change your job?"

"Why, you going to pay me?"

"Oh, come off it. It's a good offer."

"Bit sudden. Sorry. You gave me a fright. I was just putting a fiver on Gunfleet."

"Our horse'll come good today. Roly Fox. Put it on him."

She studied her card. "He won't beat Gunfleet. He likes it softer."

"Please yourself."

Betting was a mug's game, Gin thought; that was something else he would have to change. "If you've got a spare moment—before they run—we could go down to our horsebox—you know. If your horse isn't in until the last."

"Yes, OK. Just let me put my bets on."

"Come on. You spend too much time in this department."

"The only bit of excitement I get," Beryl giggled.

"I'll give you a bit of excitement."

"All right. I'm coming."

Rosy saw them, knew what they were up to. Sighed angrily. She knew she was not jealous of Beryl, but felt it, in that moment. She bought a cup of coffee, watched the first race, and went back to Roly Fox. He was restless, but in a let's-get-on-with-it mood, not nervous. He liked her to be around, she knew, and stood quietly while she talked to him. She was more nervous than he was, afraid of Tony Mowbray and his winning ways.

The second race was starting and the first runners were back and being washed down. The weather was fine, a warm breeze blowing, and the ground hardening by the minute. The favourite for Roly's race, a grey called Gunfleet, walked by in a navy blue rug trimmed with yellow. Rosy slipped off Roly's mothy day-wear and flung on the Hawkins finery with its woven initials and sharp, bright trim. She was glad her horse looked as smart as he deserved. She led him out and followed Gunfleet down.

Hawkins was in the paddock with a glamorous henna-headed lady by the name of Artemis. Roly Fox, it appeared, was a birthday present for Artemis. Artemis thought he was cute. Tony Mowbray came out and Hawkins said, "You must win for Artemis," and Mowbray said, "Sure, we'll do our best."

Rosy expected Jeremy to give his instructions, but he said nothing, legging the jockey into the saddle in tight-lipped silence. Rosy led Roly Fox away, appalled. Out of earshot she turned and said to Mowbray, "This horse doesn't run any faster if you hit him. He gives everything without that. He's really honest."

"Fine. No problem then."

He gave her a cool smile. Rosy noticed that his face was harder than most, and knew then that his ambition was dangerous. This was a boy on the make, not an old-fashioned horseman in the trade for love of it. There were still plenty of those around, but Roly Fox had struck unlucky.

Rosy unclipped her horse and he bounded out eagerly onto the wide green course. She shook off her pessimism and made for the stands to find Gin and Beryl. She had never formally met Beryl before, but now Gin introduced her and said, "If Roly wins, she's going to marry me."

Rosy thought he was joking.

"The way I see it, getting married carries the same risk as money on a horse. So I've decided your horse shall decide," Beryl giggled happily.

Rosy was appalled at such irresponsibility. When she thought of her rock-fast love for Jeremy Cutbush, Beryl's joke decision made her feel mocked, ridiculous. It was Gin who was going to suffer, she could see. He was crazily in love with the idea of getting married; Beryl happened to be available.

There were ten in the field and five were good horses. Roly had courage on his side, but not the turn of foot that Gunfleet could produce after the last. They went away fast on the firm ground and Mowbray kept Roly well up, placing him to perfection, but on the second circuit, where Rosy judged he should give Roly a bit of a breather before asking for his effort, he gave him a reminder instead and took him to the front. Rosy saw Roly switch his tail, a sign that he was tiring. As they approached the home bend Gunfleet began to make his move, and two of the other horses went after him, all three of them catching up on Roly. The gap between them began to close. Mowbray glanced behind, pulled out his whip and gave Roly a real stinger behind the saddle. Roly lengthened but Gunfleet was travelling very smoothly and catching him fast. As the last jump came up Mowbray gave Roly another belt and booted him into it; he crashed through the top and Gunfleet jumped into contention beside him, so that they picked up together. Both jockeys started to ride for home, whips flailing, and the two tired horses galloped desperately neck and neck up towards the finish, neither being able to pull out any more. Gunfleet's rider dropped his whip, knowing his horse was doing his best, but Tony Mowbray beat Roly all the way to the post, getting there a head in front of his rival. The crowd roared, Gin picked up Beryl and hugged her and said to Rosy, grinning, "Congratulate us, Rosy—we're going to get married!"

Rosy was sick with rage. Winning was one thing—but winning like that . . . She pushed past Gin and Beryl and ran down the steps to meet the returning horses. Gunfleet passed her, head down, heaving. Roly was behind him, so tired that he stumbled. Rosy took the rein. She had never seen Roly so distressed, nostrils distended, flanks working like bellows.

"You didn't have to use the whip like that! You've half killed him!" She could not stop herself flinging the words at Mowbray.

He did not answer, in much the same state as Roly, with no breath for a retort. The crowd liked tight finishes, but Rosy hated them when they came at the end of a long hard race and were ridden without any regard for the horse's future. Many horses never came back after such an experience.

"He didn't need it—you could have won without!"

"Oh, shut up," said Mowbray.

Rosy did so, and made for the winners' enclosure, normally a happy place. Hawkins and Artemis were waiting, all smiles, and Jeremy came forward to greet Mowbray. He did not smile or congratulate him but put a hand on the trembling Roly's neck and let the effusive owner shower her jockey with compliments. Rosy had to position Roly to have his photo taken with Artemis at his head. Her great lipstick smile would appear in gruesome contrast to the horse's exhaustion, which she hadn't the wit to notice. Gin appeared with the rugs and his exuberance at his sudden engagement changed to genuine concern. "Poor old bugger!"

Hawkins pressed a note into Rosy's hand, which was stuffed without a word into her pocket, resisting an instinct to shove it back at him.

"Horses away!"

As she turned Roly for the exit, Jeremy came up and said, "Sorry about that." He put his hand for an instant on her shoulder before turning back to the owners' party, who were inviting him to go and celebrate. Rosy did not know whether to laugh or cry. She and Gin took Roly back to his box and washed him down tenderly. It wasn't until he was dried off and rugged up again that Rosy remembered what the win was responsible for.

"Were you joking—about marrying Beryl if he won?"

"No. She agreed! I said afterwards would she go back on it and she said no. She said she'd marry me whenever I liked."

"You won't have second thoughts?"

"No. I really like her. She doesn't care—worry . . . she likes a bit of fun. Suits me fine."

"I hope so. Congratulations then. I hope it works out."

"Well, why not? It's all a toss-up, however you go about it."

More a toss-up this way than most, Rosy thought, but didn't say. Gin was obviously very pleased with life, and went to kiss Beryl goodbye before they loaded Roly for home. While she was waiting for him, Rosy put her hand in her pocket and discovered the note Hawkins had given her. It was for fifty pounds. She turned it over bitterly, wishing it was the usual fiver, and Roly the jaunty winner as in past, happier days.

JEREMY, AWARE THAT HE had had too much champagne, drove with the extra confidence the condition gave him, too fast and yet with what felt like extraordinary skill and care. Everything was panning out as badly as he had feared. He was unhappy, yet assured of a more optimistic future than he had had for years. Hawkins was thrilled with the afternoon's miserable win and had told him over the champagne that he had bought a chaser called Spinning Wheel, and that Spinning Wheel was destined for Brood House, a classier horse than the old place had boasted since his grandfather's day. This was the sort of break he had once dreamed of.

Flying down the fast lane, he thought of all the conditions he should have made and had failed to do. If Hawkins dictated when and how Spinning Wheel was to run, he had nothing to look forward to at all. It was just his luck to have landed himself an ignorant rich bastard out of the blue, whose wealth was exactly what the stable wanted, but whose attitude was completely unacceptable.

Hawkins had said, "That was a great win! How soon can the horse run again? A week? Ten days?"

"We'll have to see how he comes out of it." But Jeremy already knew, as Rosy had done, that the afternoon's race would knock all the confidence out of Roly, for he was a horse who did best when humoured and encouraged. A nice second, instead of a punishing win, would have been of far more value, more likely to line Hawkins's coffers in the future than what had happened today. Jeremy did not like heavy-betting owners, as it made the game so tense, the horse so vulnerable, yet it was commonplace in racing.

287

Mowbray had beaten Roly home in front because, financially, it mattered a great deal. Jeremy, having expected to greet Mowbray back after the race with the old, consuming jealousy, had felt not jealousy but contempt. The boy rode beautifully, but was greedy for both recognition and money. Jeremy had not ridden for money. To be fair, he had had no need to. He had been brought up in the old school, grounded far back in the way to treat horses. Mowbray's father was a garage mechanic, and Mowbray rode like a motorcyclist.

Having been kept some time talking to his new owners, Jeremy was home no sooner than the horsebox. Gin and Rosy were unloading. Old Albert, out from his cottage at the sound of the engine, was saying, "What's up with him then?"

Roly's uncharacteristic exit down the ramp showed, even in the dusk. He was shivering, nervous, his cockiness knocked out of him.

"That bloody jockey—" Rosy launched into a diatribe that Jeremy felt bound to check, although he agreed with every word.

"Get him comfortable, and I'll come out and have a look at him."

Gin, about to park the horsebox, said, "Sir, can I have a word?"

"Yes?"

"I want to get married, sir. I wondered if there was any chance of renting the lodge house? Until I can get a council house."

"The lodge house? I thought it was derelict."

"I could do it up, sir."

"What girl would want to live in that, for heaven's sake?"

"I could make it OK, sir. She wouldn't mind."

"I didn't know you were courting, Gin?"

"Yes—no, it's a bit quick, like."

Jeremy grinned. "I hope—" But it was no business of his. Gin, young, strong, good-hearted, was the marrying sort. "Yes, I see no reason why not. Not if you think you could make it habitable."

"That's great. Thank you, sir!"

On the way home, Gin stopped his motorbike at the bottom of the drive by the lodge house. In the silence he sat for a moment, his whole being suddenly shaken with a happiness he had never experienced before. It was as if everything had come together; this very place that he had known all his life, was to be his home, with Beryl. A couple of hundred yards away was the yard where he had his job, the job he had enjoyed since he had left school and which was all a part of his small, enclosed, precious existence. Life was exactly how he wanted it to be: secure, full of promise, utterly familiar. It was all meant; God was on his side. He opened up his throttle with a triumphant roar and surged out of the drive.

4

"Do you think she's in foal?"

"Yes, oh yes," said Mrs. Cutbush. "Look at her."

Rosy looked out from the kitchen window, but could not see what Mrs. Cutbush could see. The mare grazed in the soft evening, switching her tail at the midges.

"A filly. She will have a filly."

"How do you know that?"

"She tells me she's due for a filly."

If only, Rosy thought, you could tell what was true and what was not out of Mrs. Cutbush's ramblings. Having delivered what sounded like a judgment based on all the experience of a lifetime, she then turned and called her old dead dog.

"Jasper! Come along! I'll get your supper."

She brought dogfood and put it down on the kitchen floor. Tomorrow she would scoop it up and scrape it into the rubbish bin.

These days she kept talking about Rosy's picture. Every time Rosy looked at the "Horse and Groom in a Landscape" Mrs. Cutbush said, "That's your picture. You like it, don't you?"

"Yes, I love it. It's not mine though. It's yours."

"No. It's yours. I told Jeremy. You're more interested in old times than he is. I told you, that horse was in our family. He belonged to Peregrine Cutbush who asked Stubbs to paint him. My grand-mother told me. That horse, Lionheart—he was by Highflyer. You know who Highflyer was, don't you?"

"He belonged to Mr. Tattersall who founded the Tattersall fortune. He sired three Derby winners."

"There!" said Mrs. Cutbush in admiration. "Jeremy wouldn't have known that. Of course you should have the picture."

Rosy did not see what her general knowledge had to do with it. She had an idea that the picture was worth a lot of money. It belonged by right to Jeremy. The fact that Mrs. Cutbush might be willing it to her disturbed her: she had no ambition to get tangled up in such an embarrassing situation with Jeremy. It would be embarrassing enough if he found out about the foal.

"Well, he will, if it's born," Gin said, when the subject was broached.

"Mrs. Cutbush seems to think the mare is in foal. If she is, I was leaving it to you, remember, to make it legal. To earn your half share. We want a covering certificate from somewhere to register it with. You won't tell anyone about it, will you? Not even Beryl. Don't tell Beryl."

"No." Gin had spent a weekend with Beryl at Bournemouth, and brought her home to meet the family. The wedding date was fixed for May, and Gin was spending all his spare time trying to put the lodge house in order. The thatched roof leaked, the floors had fallen through, the windows were broken. Beryl had found it wanting, apparently, on her visit.

"I've done a lot to it since then. It's better than where she lives now, with her mother in a flat in Newbury. They quarrel all the time. Her mother has boyfriends in and Beryl has to keep out of the way. I met her mother. She's a right slag."

Like mother, like daughter . . . Rosy hoped not, but hadn't Gin's faith. Beryl was a lightweight, too flimsy for foursquare Gin. Rosy, visiting the cottage on her way home, standing in the living room with the smell of fresh wood shavings and paint, recognized its utter tranquillity. It was magical, a perfect love nest, but Beryl would never see it as that. Beryl wasn't in love. Beryl was marrying on a whim. I'm in love, Rosy admitted, I want it; I would die of bliss to live here with my beloved. She rode her bicycle out onto the road in a dream, spinning down the lonely valley where nothing stirred, no action threatened, no clouds loomed . . . *nothing ever happens* . . . Rosy groaned out loud. She would soon be thirty and nothing ever came her way but peace and security, and good nourishing food.

GRACE, IN WHOM SPRING was rousing much the same emotion that was seizing Rosy on her bicycle, suggested to her mother that she might ask Jeremy to dinner.

"Good heavens!" Margaret Maddox, clipping the grass round the dead daffodils, looked up at her daughter in surprise. "Jeremy never comes here."

"You never ask him, so no wonder. I want to marry him."

"Oh, really, Grace. Does he know?"

"Of course not. Have you seen inside Brood House? It's palatial. It could be quite stunning. If you cut all the trees down below the house, you could paint the front a pale colour and it would look out right across the valley. It would be terribly impressive. Jeremy must be worth an awful lot of money. That place, and all the land, the gallops and everything, not to mention the paintings, and Mrs. Cutbush's stuff. She is supposed to have a Stubbs, you know. I want to marry Jeremy, I would be very good for him."

So Grace asked him to dinner. She told him her father might be persuaded into having a chaser for a bit of fun and so, as it was put to him in the nature of a job, he accepted the invitation.

He arrived wearing a dark grey suit and a lemon-yellow shirt with a dark yellow tie, which was very taking indeed. Grace was impressed. Jeremy had instinctive style, which she supposed was inherited from his Cutbush forebears. If she married him, they would make a smart pair. She was now committed to the idea, and intent on carrying through the conquest.

Rather to Grace's relief, he was nicer in the social context than he was at work. Of course, he could not appear as a moody bastard to his owners, as he did to the staff at Brood, so she assumed that he could switch on affability to order, as a requirement of the job.

In fact, having made the initial effort to switch on affability, Jeremy found, as the evening progressed, that he had no difficulty in maintaining it since old Hugh and Margaret were so nice. But Grace had an amazing capacity for picking the subjects of conversation he least wanted to talk about.

"Have you never ridden at all since your accident?" she inquired, as Margaret stacked up plates after the soup.

"No." He had tried it, but wasn't going to tell her anything of his pains, humiliations and lonely tribulation.

"Is there actually any reason why you can't ride now?"

"Probably not." Lack of the necessary grit to accustom his complaining, cockeyed pelvis and rebuilt thighbone to the harsh facts of life aboard a thoroughbred was not an answer he cared to spell out.

"I understand that, actually, if you get over the first agonies it's generally OK. If you persevere. Mary Anstey broke her back in two places and was riding again within six months."

Old Hugh, looking glazed, turned to Jeremy. "Can I top up your glass? Have you had a good season? I suppose it's nearly over now."

"Not very marvellous, no."

"But it'll be better next year," said Grace knowledgeably. "With Mr. Hawkins's horses."

"Perhaps."

"Who is Mr. Hawkins? A new owner?"

"He's a tycoon," said Grace. "He owns Roly Fox and he's just bought Spinning Wheel. We shall have Spinning Wheel at Brood."

Even Colonel Maddox had heard of Spinning Wheel. "That must be good, surely? How has Mr. Hawkins made his money?"

"In fertilizer, I understand."

"Oh, *that* Hawkins? Better not tell Rosy's dad," said old Hugh, amused. "Arch poisoner of the British weed. He makes Killit Plus—it clears whole forests, I understand, let alone a weed."

"Oh dear." Mrs. Maddox had returned with the casserole. "I'm on Mr. Weeks's side in that. But I'm not a vegetarian. If we were all vegetarian, there would be no animals in the fields, which would be very sad. They enjoy themselves before they die. You've only got to look here, in the valley. Sometimes I sit and watch the lambs through the binoculars. They always make me laugh."

"Funny you should say that—I was watching a hunting owl through the binoculars a month or so back and I saw something very strange," Grace said.

"What was that?" Mrs. Maddox asked.

"I saw Rosy leading Peppermill down the road from Brood. Gin met her at the gate of Mrs. Cutbush's field and let her in, and they took him up to the barn. About ten minutes later she led him away again and back home."

There was a long, thoughtful silence.

"When was this?" Jeremy had to know more.

"One afternoon, when you were at the races."

"My grandmother—was she there?"

"Yes."

"This was before—I take it—Peppermill was cut?"

"Mmm, I think so."

"And Silverfish—where was she?"

"In the barn, obviously," said young Hugh. He looked stunned. "What a colossal liberty!"

Jeremy didn't pass comment. He was full of admiration for the ingenuity, the utter simplicity, of the operation—a stroke of genius, to use what was at hand.

"I wonder if it's been successful," Colonel Maddox said. "Odds against, I'd say, the mare that age."

"But how on earth is Mrs. Cutbush going to register it at Weatherby's?" said Hugh.

Margaret laughed. "I can't see a detail like that daunting her. Was it her idea? Or Gin's and Rosy's?"

Jeremy considered. He thought Rosy's, but did not say so.

Grace had rather thought he would be angry but to her disappointment he made no comment at all on the news.

But the evening had been a success in that it hardened her ambition to marry Jeremy: he had fitted very easily into the social background of her own home. Her parents liked him, and Grace had no desire to go away and earn her own living again.

ROLY FOX RAN TWICE in April and won each time. Rosy assumed the third race he ran in Mr. Hawkins's colours would be the last for the season but ten days later he was declared for Worcester.

"There's still heat in his off-fore," she said anxiously to Jeremy. "You've never run him so soon before."

It was the nearest she dared come to telling Jeremy his job.

"He'll be out of novice chases next year. Mr. Hawkins wants to make the most of it."

"He'll break him down."

"I'll be the best judge of that." Jeremy was sharp. Rosy knew he was being overruled by Hawkins.

Roly, hard-raced, had become anxious, and now left a good deal of the feed he had so eagerly scoffed in the past. The silly old devil ran his heart out under Mowbray's urging; large sums of money passed hands and Rosy got a fifty-pound note each time. She accepted it, with murder in her eyes. The "lad" was not in a position to pass comment. Mr. Hawkins did not even know her name.

Tony Mowbray turned up to ride work the day before the race, and as Rosy saddled Roly and led him out, she asked, "Aren't you going up in the Land-Rover?"

"No, I'll ride up with you. It's a nice morning."

Catch him hacking when the rain came in horizontal lines over the top of the hill, Rosy thought . . . all right on a spring morning of soft sunshine, the skylarks whirring, the ramblers with their rucksacks bulging strung like targets on the skyline.

"Cheer up, darling," Mowbray grinned, chewing gum. He rode by instinct and brute strength, but knew little of how horses ticked. Horses did what he asked them to because of the strength of his command over them, but they did not relax with him, or trust him, or seem happy in his hands. Rosy, riding alongside on Villanelle, noticed Roly's anxiety.

"Winning is what counts," said Tony. "These fellows have to earn their keep, you know."

"You can keep a good horse winning for years if he enjoys it. Your way they pack it in after a season."

"There's always youngsters coming on. Trouble with you girls, you get sentimental. Owners want a return—can't pay out these training fees and get no return. It's a business."

"It's a sport. If everyone thought your way—you might as well play a fruit machine, or put it in stocks and shares. The whole attraction of racing is in the nature of the beast. It comes first. If you get that right, the money comes."

"Haven't noticed it in the dump you work for. Not till us businessmen arrived on the scene."

Rosy had difficulty in keeping her temper. Mowbray was grinning and chewing, Roly's long stride beneath him breasting the chalky path that cut in sweeps up the shoulder of the down. With the spring in his coat, the warm breeze lifting his mane, Roly looked, if not beautiful, workmanlike and strong, radiating health and well-being. Surely he was more than a mere business proposition?

"If you're a businessman, don't break Roly down tomorrow. He's not a hundred per cent in his off-fore. It would pay to pull him up if there's any doubt."

"Since when do I take orders from a lad?" The grin vanished. "I take orders from Mr. Hawkins—he pays me, doesn't he?" Mowbray grinned again, scornfully. "You ought to run the Pony Club, not mess around in racing. Racing's for men."

"Excuse me while I'm sick."

"You got a boyfriend?"

"What's that got to do with it?"

"It's what you need—you're too uptight. I'll take you out, if you like. Do you the world of good."

Rosy would have liked to have taken her whip to his insolent face. But she laughed, knowing there was no winning when the argument took this turn, in a man's world. "You're probably right. But no, thank you very much, offer refused."

The following day, Roly was the favourite. Hawkins had made a very large bet. "So has Beryl," Gin told Rosy, looking worried.

"She going to bet when you're married?"

"Not like she does now. We'll have to save our money."

"Hope you've told her."

"Yes, I have."

If Roly had still been owned by Mrs. Palmer, Rosy knew that Jeremy would have withdrawn him, the ground having firmed up too much for him. He looked magnificent in the paddock and the price shortened. Mr. Hawkins stood with Artemis and Jeremy as Rosy led him round. The jockeys came out and Rosy halted Roly to let them through. Tony winked at her.

"Jockeys please mount!"

Rosy turned Roly into the centre, and stood in front of him to keep him still. He was sweating slightly, and too much on his toes for comfort. He swung away from the approaching Mowbray and let out a kick. Jeremy checked the girths, and gave Tony a leg-up.

"Remember what I told you," Hawkins growled at the jockey.

The Sound of Distant Cheering

"You've just got to win, Tony," trilled Artemis. "I'm so excited!
I'm counting on you."

"Yes, ma'am," said Tony, poker-faced.

As Rosy led Roly back onto the paddock path Tony said to her,
"Them as pays the piper calls the tune, darling."

"God, that woman!"

"You look lovely when you're cross."

"Go to hell!"

She let go of Roly too soon, on purpose, and Tony had a tough few
moments controlling him before he got a clear run out onto the
course. Rosy went up into the stand with Gin and Beryl. Beryl was
chewing her fingernails. "If he wins, it'll pay for my wedding dress,
and the bridesmaids'."

"We don't want bridesmaids," Gin said. "A registry office will do,
I've told you."

"Roly'll decide."

"He can't make all your decisions for you, for God's sake. He's
only a horse." Rosy, worried, vented her temper on Beryl.

The ground being hard, the runners went off at a good pace. The
field was not very classy, but there were several horses who were
coming fresh to the spring racing, having rested since November.
Roly was at the end of a fairly hard season. He lay well back for the
first circuit and was left with a good deal to do by halfway. Mowbray
was depending on Roly's superior class and stamina, and when he
went on to chase the leaders the leaders themselves were dropping
back fairly fast. Rosy thought his tactics were going to work, but one
unconsidered horse, a bay called Smokescreen, kept plugging on,
and seemed to have no thought of calling it a day. This was where
Dave Perkins would have opted for second, but Tony Mowbray,
with his large financial interest in winning, started to drive his horse
with all his strength, belting him into the second last with more
ambition than tact. Roly panicked, took off a stride too soon and
went through the top instead of jumping clean. He pecked heavily
on landing, but Mowbray kept his seat and picked him up with great
skill. Smokescreen was at last reaching the end of his tether. Tony
picked up his whip again and slammed Roly down the backside. The
crowd started to roar.

"Oh, God, I hate him!" Rosy was close to tears.

Smokescreen, tiring, battled bravely up to the last, with Roly on
his heels. The bay jumped badly but Roly made a wild, soaring leap
and caught up in midair. They landed side by side and their jockeys
both rode them out to the line without mercy. Roly got his head in

front in the last fifty yards and won for the fourth consecutive time. The crowd adored him, and Beryl was in tears of bliss, her wedding-day glory assured.

With everyone around her singing her dear Roly's praises, Rosy was half proud, half sick, as she ran down the steps to meet him at the gate. He came up to her obviously tender on his off-fore, and exhausted. Everyone crowded round, and she led him into the winners' enclosure to cheers and clapping.

This is what they had always dreamed about, wasn't it? . . . winning and success and interviews on the television. Artemis was in raptures, old Hawkins all smiles, even Jeremy looked pleased. Tony unsaddled and managed to pinch her bottom before he went to weigh in. She led Roly away, and watched how tenderly he walked beside her. Mowbray had broken him down, she was sure.

"Lucky it's the end of the season. He'll have all the summer to get over it," Jeremy said. He came to examine the leg when he got home, running his long, bony fingers down the swelling. "It was that

stumble at the second last, I'm afraid. We'll see what the vet says tomorrow. Keep the hose on it for now and put a compress on it before you go home. I'll look at it again before I go to bed."

He straightened up, and pulled a fifty-pound note out of his pocket. "Hawkins gave me this for you." He smiled. "Does it make it worth it?"

Rosy looked at it stonily. "Not really, no."

"You don't want me to return it?"

"No. I'm not stupid. I just don't like—" She hesitated. She had liked winning, damn it. "*Having* to win, because of the money involved—you know . . ."

"Yes, I know. We'll have to try and educate our Mr. Hawkins. But for now—well, the stable could do with his sort of input. Would you like to do Spinning Wheel, when he comes here?"

"Is he coming?"

"Next season, yes."

"Yes, of course. I'd love to do him."

"You're more conscientious than the boys. These sorts of tips—you deserve them. The boys can do the hurdlers between them."

The win had sweetened Jeremy; it was a long time since he had been so talkative. "Perhaps this is a blessing in disguise for Roly, as he won't be able to race again till next season. He can take a well-deserved rest."

"Yes, perhaps."

As they stood there briefly in the warm loosebox with Roly, the unexpected aura of success was tangible between them, the pride of being responsible for a good horse warming their relationship. Rosy felt it strongly and for a moment a heady vision of the stable's future danced in her mind: cheers all the way and the winners' enclosures at Cheltenham and Ascot and Sandown Park. And she thought suddenly of Silverfish and the foetus that Letitia swore was fastened snugly in her womb and, in the present state of hallucination, saw glory all the way, and a part for herself.

Jeremy patted Roly's neck and departed. Rosy came off her high, and took Roly out into the yard to start hosing his leg. An hour of that, getting cold and bored, brought the long working day to its end, and she cycled home through the dark spring evening with mixed feelings. The fifty-pound note was folded snugly in her pocket, the only sure bonus in a welter of wishful thinking.

ROLY FOX, LET DOWN in condition over a week or two, was eventually turned out to grass with Silverfish for the summer. This was at Rosy's request. His leg recovered. Rosy went to the field in the afternoons and took him down to stand in the stream. She sat on the bank in her shirtsleeves, holding the halter rope and watching the crystal-clear water flowing over his precious ligaments and tendons. She called it work, but knew that it was an excuse for dreaming an hour away. She could feel the sun hot on the back of her neck, and Roly's kind breath on her hand, as she watched the four firmly planted hooves appear to dance in the distortion of the water . . . Did this, then, make up her total happiness, a touch of nature and the love of a good horse? God, where was passion and triumph and the sound of trumpets? In her twenty-eight years she had achieved absolutely nothing, not even a relationship that mattered—save with a horse. Even Gin, up to now her comrade in underachievement, had with his recent marriage become a token success, no longer dissatisfied and self-questioning but confident, a whole man. Was Tony Mowbray's crude diagnosis of what was wrong with her a truth so simple that she could not accept it?

As the sun went down and she walked back up the field, she wondered why she had these ridiculous discontents. She was happy, in truth, liking her job, her lifestyle. The two horses followed her along the narrow track they had made from the stream to the gate, their shadows long over the grass, tails rhythmically switching to the midges: sweet, trusting Roly in his summer gloss-coat and the disdainful, stiff-jointed mare hopefully hiding a secret in her belly.

Rosy went back to her father's fresh nettle soup. She badly missed Gin two doors down and the cheerful interludes in his mother's kitchen. She had visited Gin and Beryl at suppertime one day in their lodge cottage—the "love nest" as it had become known by all—but discovered that, however Beryl had found her way to Gin's heart, it was not via his stomach. Beryl was missing her Newbury supermarkets, and as Gin had not yet managed to find a cheap freezer, he frequently had to borrow his father's car and take her late-night shopping twenty miles away; the village shop was "dirty", according to Beryl.

"She'll get used to it," Gin said to Rosy. "I won't have time to take her shopping when the season starts."

Rosy did not share his confidence. She felt almost motherly towards Beryl, seeing her stranded in the cottage all day, like a kitten up a tree waiting for the fire brigade. But as far as Rosy could see, no fire brigade was to be forthcoming.

"There's no point spending a lot of trouble on this dump, because we're going to get a council house before long," Beryl had told Rosy. She had no nesting instinct, and was content to sit in the bleakly furnished rooms watching the television all afternoon. Racing from Newmarket, from Epsom, from York, from wherever they showed it. Gin never came in to find her cooking or knitting or making cushion covers, only watching the television.

"She'll settle down," he said to Rosy, as he boiled himself a couple of eggs. He was noticeably losing weight. Rosy had more sense than to pass comment, but saw Beryl on two or three occasions in the telephone box at the crossroads, and suspected that she was putting bets on. Gin had said she had given it up.

"It's all right once in a while, if you get the right price, but the way she goes about it—no one can stand that, when you're saving and getting a house together. I've told her, none of that lark, not now it's my money. When she starts work—well, she can risk a bit of her own money now and then."

The idea was that she would work for Jeremy when the season

started again, but by the time the horses began to come in from grass, Beryl was pregnant. Rosy was appalled. Gin admitted that it was a mistake, and Beryl said, "We'll get a council house now." As she had a perfectly adequate house already, Rosy did not think this would follow. She felt sorry for the girl, still too much of a child herself to be bearing another.

Roly Fox came in from grass and Silverfish was almost certainly in foal. Now Rosy realized she might well have a real racehorse on her hands. As she had no money to keep it with, this might prove a difficulty rather than a dream come true, but it was too soon to start worrying on that score. There were other things to worry about—Grace Maddox, for instance.

Grace, according to Gin, was to start work as Jeremy's secretary, with an office in the house.

"She asked him, apparently. He offered her a pittance, thinking she would refuse, but she accepted. So he's lumbered."

Rosy, who had thought she was too old and sensible to feel jealous, now knew differently.

5

Jeremy had been his own secretary for years, carrying everything, computerwise, in his head. He had an ancient typewriter on the end of the kitchen table, and piles of papers on the dresser, kept in place with old kitchen-scale weights. Grace knew he didn't want her. The salary he had offered her was an insult. When she had accepted, she had seen the panic flare in his eyes. The job was difficult, for one coming new to it, but Grace was determined to make no mistakes. She went to stay in Lambourn with friends who ran a racing stable there, and conscientiously learned all she could. She was going to make herself indispensable.

She appropriated a filing cabinet from her father's junk hole and got Hugh to collect it in the stable Land-Rover. She set up office not in the study but in the morning room, because it led out of the kitchen, which was Jeremy's lair. With the door open, she could talk to him from her desk. The room was furnished with a large table and chairs, but very little else. Grace rearranged it with furniture from other rooms, and made what she thought of as a workmanlike den. With her own money she bought a calor-gas heater. She wanted a telephone extension installed, but Jeremy would not agree.

"You can use the one in the kitchen," he said tersely.

Grace did not argue. She was careful to be meek, and as helpful as possible, so that if she went she would be badly missed. She arrived when Jeremy was out with the first string, parked her Mini firmly outside the front door, and went in. By the time Jeremy came back, she had cleaned the kitchen and got the Aga well stoked, the coffee bubbling at the ready, the post and *The Sporting Life* collected from the box down on the road and laid out on the table.

Gradually she started to add the odd round of buttered toast to her offerings, and after a few weeks she was cooking him a full breakfast when he came in, so that he stopped bothering to make something for himself when he got up. From being silent and hostile, he gradually thawed and accepted her as part of the furniture. He came in expecting his breakfast, and knowing that the kitchen would be welcoming and cosy, and the post collected.

When he was out, Grace explored the house. She went up the elegant, curving staircase and visited each bedroom in turn. Jeremy's was a monk-like room that had been his from boyhood, his father's Biggles books stuffed into a bookcase, along with racing year-books and forgotten school textbooks. His own racing silks were still on a hanger behind the door. Yes, thought Grace, the house was ripe for a return to life. Jeremy would never thrive without positive removal from the ghosts of Brood. But how tactfully, how gently, he must be prised away . . . She bristled with mental endeavour, while compelling herself into an unnatural role: quiet, sympathetic, super-efficient. Like a nun. The effort was killing her.

"If you could find time to ride out occasionally," Jeremy said, "it would be a great help."

Grace forced a smile.

The two new geldings, Peppermill and Needles, were ready to start their hurdling careers; Roly was sound and back in work, and Spinning Wheel arrived one afternoon in October. A bright chestnut, all of seventeen and a half hands, he was immediately king of the yard. Rosy could not help but be proud of "doing" such a good horse. He was easy to ride, strong but obedient. It was like sitting on a rock. Tony Mowbray said he was "a lazy old sod", and that he had to work hard with him during a race. "He needs all of three miles—takes two and a half to get into his stride. Not like your Roly Fox."

Tony had discovered what Rosy had told him in the first place, that Roly was all heart and no sense, would die for you before he cracked. It did not mean he was never beaten, for his talent was limited, but he was never beaten for lack of trying. He won his first two races of the season and had added two seconds by Christmas. His leg held up by dint of Rosy's dedicated hosing, and the punters loved him.

"He's my lucky horse," Beryl said, showing Rosy her winnings. The bet was above board, for it had been Gin who put the money on for her.

Beryl liked visitors to relieve her boredom and Rosy called in when she could. Not that the house was very welcoming. With her pregnancy an excuse, Beryl was fast becoming a slut. When Gin told her to get some exercise, for her own good, she said pathetically, "Where to? There's nowhere to go."

Gin thought Beryl would become a new woman when the baby came. Rosy did not argue with him, realizing that he still saw the whining self-centred Beryl through rose-tinted spectacles. It would take more than a baby, Rosy thought, to make Beryl work. Gin had taken over the evening cooking, in self-defence, and Rosy sometimes peeled potatoes for him, for she knew Beryl wouldn't.

"I see Grace is riding out," Beryl remarked one evening when Rosy called in on her way home. "She looks funny on a horse, I reckon. I thought her job was secretary."

"Lots of racing secretaries ride out, don't they?"

"Yeah, well, she's a funny sort. She's after him, don't you think? I reckon she'll get him too, the rate she's going on. Six to four on."

Rosy kept quiet, chilled by the odds Beryl was estimating.

"I asked Gin why he didn't marry you, and he said, no chance, you were in love with Mr. Cutbush. Is that right?"

"Gin and I—it's more like brother and sister, the way we've been. Marriage doesn't come into it. As for Mr. Cutbush—yes, well, I've always admired him, I like working for him, but I suppose I don't actually know him very well."

"You're in love with 'im though?"

"Funny sort of love—"

"Yeah, well, there's all sorts. I mean, I'm not in love, am I, but I'm married—it's a sort of love, you could say. Grace, she's after Mr. Cutbush, she must want him, that's a sort too. But hers isn't like yours, I'd say. So yours is another sort. The proper sort, I suppose, but where does it get you, eh?"

Beryl's candid résumé seemed to Rosy more accurate than she could have attempted on the subject herself. Bleak, realistic—it was hardly cheering. She had never even spoken to Jeremy save in the role of employee; she had never said anything other than yes, sir; no, sir. Even in *Woman's Weekly* they moved faster than that.

JEREMY SENT GRACE out in the second string on a horse called Bellboy, belonging to one of his old ladies, and considered a fairly sensible ride. She came out from the house in her riding gear with a proprietorial air that irked Rosy. It cheered her enormously to realize that Grace did not want to ride out, and was doing it because she had been ordered to.

"Bellboy's easy," she said, fetching Roly out for herself. "And it could be worse—it's not raining."

This was no longer true by the time they emerged from the wooded ride above Brood and took the chalk road up onto the shoulder. The grey winter turf merged into low cloud and driving rain, and it was hard to see for the sharp needles of drizzle. Rosy hunched down into her anorak collar, seeing only Roly's rabbity ears flexing back from the wind, and the solid quarters of Bellboy breasting a steep patch ahead of her. They climbed up over the brow and Gin, leading the ride on Drogo, broke into a trot to hurry on out of the worst of the weather on the summit. Behind him Peppermill gave a couple of bucks and Bellboy for no apparent reason shied violently off the path. Rosy saw him disappear and jerked Roly to a brisk halt. There was a ditch below the road and Bellboy, having lost his footing, was suddenly down in a panic of thrashing hooves. Rosy heard Grace scream.

"Gin! Gin, stop!" Rosy heard her own shriek furled away by the wind as she flung herself off Roly. She threw the reins at Simon. "Get Gin!"

Bellboy was upside down, struggling frantically. All Rosy could see was the mud-splashed belly of the horse and above it a hand flung to the sky, clenched in agony, the only bit of Grace visible.

"God!" Gin loomed above her, straddling the ditch.

"Give me your hands, I'll pull you out," he shouted down to Grace, but she screamed at him, "Don't touch me! Don't touch me!"

"Are you hurt?"

"God, Gin—she wouldn't be making that noise if she wasn't! Can't you get the horse off her?" Rosy sat on Bellboy's head to keep him still, stroking the trembling neck, seeing the terrified white of his eye and his blood-rimmed nostrils.

Gin got into the ditch and disappeared behind Bellboy's up-ended quarters. The horse, apparently trusting Rosy's reassurance, lay still, twitching slightly, his eyes rolling sadly; it occurred to Rosy that he might be more badly injured than Grace. Horses often did not reveal pain . . . Grace screamed like a seagull, beating her hands against the ditch that had trapped her.

Gin surfaced and called Trev to help him, leaving Simon trying to hold four wheeling, frightened horses. They got into the ditch and manhandled Bellboy's backside sufficiently to one side to roll Grace out from beneath.

Whether she was badly hurt or merely frightened Rosy had no way of knowing, for Gin dispatched her to fetch help as quickly as possible. She hastened away on Roly, down the hillside, met Jeremy in the Land-Rover coming out of the wood and told him what had happened. He swore angrily, revealing little sympathy for Grace, and told Rosy to ring for an ambulance.

"Not that they'll get it up there. I'd better go back for a stretcher, in case."

There was one in the tackroom, lodged in the rafters. He put it in the Land-Rover, along with a bundle of horse blankets, and departed at speed, leaving Rosy to do the ringing up. The rain pelted down. Rosy shivered, glad that her job was to wait in the warm for the ambulance to arrive. She stood by the tackroom stove, thinking of Jeremy handling the accident. Trust Grace. Not for Grace the messy ignominy of a broken nose—the only accident that had ever befallen Rosy—even in accidents, Grace opted for the dramatic and impressive. Rosy sighed, and rang up Mrs. Maddox, not wanting to be the one to accompany Grace to hospital in the ambulance. Grace, it turned out, had broken her back.

Rosy heard in the afternoon, from Hugh. Expressing dismay and sympathy, she felt a wicked spasm of delight spark in her dark subconscious. Even for a jockey, that was at least three months out of action, no doubt twice as long for Grace. Bellboy was unharmed.

Two mornings later, when Rosy was putting Spinning Wheel away after exercise, Jeremy came across to the box.

"I'm going to see Grace in hospital tonight, when I get back from Newbury. Would you like to come with me?"

Rosy was stunned. She felt her jaw sag.

Jeremy, looking nervous, said, "I've got to go—I feel bad about it—my fault in a way. But I really dread it. If you come, it'll make it easier. I'm no good at that sort of chat—you know—"

Rosy nodded. "Of course."

"I'll pick you up at your house at about seven. Will that do?"

"Yes."

Rosy tried for the rest of the day to work out why he was asking her. She tried hard not to pretend that he suddenly had become aware of her as somebody other than a conscientious "lad"; she made a point of not putting on anything special, or even as much eyeshadow as she would have worn if Gin had asked her out. It was a job of work, for the stable. By the time he arrived, she had got herself into such a suitable state of nonchalance that she did not hear his knock. Her father went to answer it, and came back with a jocular, knowing look on his face. "Like that, is it?"

"Oh, Dad!" Rosy's venom startled him, startled herself. She fled out of the house and tried unsuccessfully to calm down in the five yards from the door to the gate, where Jeremy waited.

"It's not a nuisance? I'm sorry—"

"No, it's my dad. I'm glad to come. Not your fault—"

In mutual embarrassment they clipped seatbelts and drove towards civilization.

JEREMY HAD ASKED ROSY because Hugh and Margaret Maddox preferred to visit in the afternoon, and he preferred her company to that of tedious young Hugh. One visit to Grace was obligatory, and Rosy's presence would be beneficial, in the same way that it was to nervous horses. For one moment, seeing the expression on Mr. Weeks's face, Jeremy had a panicking suspicion that more was being read into the outing than he intended, but Rosy's demeanour quickly reassured him. She was cool and businesslike, carrying a bag of apples and a small bunch of Christmas roses. They made scarcely any conversation on the drive, save about the day's racing. Jeremy, not used to actually talking to Rosy, felt at a disadvantage; it was strange how little he knew her, although he saw her every day. But his dread of going into the hospital atmosphere occupied his thoughts more than his unease with Rosy, and when they reached the place and parked, he was glad for her to take the initiative, find the ward and the bed, as if she were finding her horse's allocated box at a racecourse stables . . .

The brightness, the sight of suspended femurs and white faces on whiter pillows, revived in him such black memories that he had difficulty in resisting his instinct to turn round and run for his life. God, how he *hated* it!—bringing back the bitterness and the pain of the eternal, centrally heated nights when he had lain and cursed each minute away. Why—oh why—had he never learned to laugh at his misfortune? He was lucky—lucky still to be walking and working, in the only job he knew; he was for ever telling himself so, when the black depression took hold, seeing Mowbray's face as he came to his fences up the home straight, seeing through the binoculars the light in the eye and the smile at the feel of taking off five or six abreast at a dirty black brush fence and the moment's arrest in the glorious thunder of galloping hooves . . . After all the years he still couldn't grow up, and accept.

Rosy was saying all the right things, arranging the flowers, smiling, self-possessed. Grace was looking impressively pale and transparent with suffering, smiling thinly. Yet Jeremy felt no compassion, only irritation. He kept thinking that she intended to marry him, and that she always got her own way; and he could never love her—she was too managing. She brought out the worst in him. With luck the accident would put her off horses and everything to do with them. He felt jumpy and left well before the hour was up, as soon as Rosy ran out of the obvious things to say.

He stood on the hospital steps, taking deep breaths of the outside air. "I should have grown out of it by now."

It was the nearest thing to a personal statement he had ever made, Rosy realized. She had no idea how to answer him.

"Shall we go for a quick drink? There's a nice pub two miles down the road?"

His suggestion, her feelings exactly.

After a whisky, Rosy said, "She wants to marry you, I think."

"You think? I get that impression too, but why? What have I got to offer her, anybody? I like my own company, I'm morose by nature—"

"You weren't before."

"No? Well, perhaps not when you saw me at the races. But I was morose at home, where it was all fighting. My father had a tough time, being the son of very colourful parents, and carrying on in the same profession. Sons should never put themselves in the position of being compared to a successful father. And for my mother, having Letitia as a mother-in-law must have been some cross to bear. From what I've seen of marriage—it holds no appeal for me. Some day, perhaps, when—if—the stable ever gets on its feet and makes some money, but at the moment it's so precarious."

"You're very pessimistic."

"I suppose I am. It would be easier if I knew where I stood."

"How do you mean?"

"In regard to the property. With Letitia. Everything belongs to her."

"Hasn't she made a will?"

"As far as I know, no. Which means it will all go to my father. And at the moment, he seems to need the cash."

Rosy remembered, painfully, the Stubbs. It seemed a good time to mention it. "She keeps saying to me that she wants me to have a picture—the one called 'Horse and Groom in a Landscape'. It worries me. I don't want it, not if it's worth a lot. I only want a memento, if she wants to leave me something. The painting's yours by rights, it belongs to the family."

"The old girl can be very difficult. If she wants to leave you the Stubbs, she will. It's probably worth more than the estate."

"I won't have it. It's ridiculous."

"If she does, I shall have to marry you to get it back."

Afterwards, Rosy wondered if she remembered this conversation correctly. Having to drive, Jeremy did not prolong the call at the pub, and Rosy had just enough alcohol to confuse her, not enough to be bold enough to tell him she would hold him to his suggestion. She supposed Jeremy spoke in jest. He was smiling at the time, not morose at all, but infinitely eligible. She did not reply, the remark leaving her incapable.

When she got home and had escaped to bed, she lay for an hour gazing out at the Brood woods on the hillside, aching for lost opportunities. She cried before she went to sleep, wondering if there was something wrong with her, that she was so inept a hand at making things work out the way she wanted them. Grace's plan had gone awry, but at least she had tried; she had nerve and guts. But she, Rosy, like Jeremy, was one of life's drifters. Tonight they had drifted together but she hadn't even the wit to hold on, throw a line, connect, or whatever. She deserved every bit of the nothing she had achieved in her twenty-nine years.

JEREMY MISSED GRACE badly, especially the breakfasts. To be accurate, he missed the home comforts. Not actually having to confront Grace every morning was a great relief.

He went to see Rogers, the family solicitor, who confirmed that Letitia had not made a will, and that the Stubbs was probably worth about half a million.

"But if she hasn't made a will, the girl won't get it anyway."

"She's written a note, and said she knows I will carry out her few small bequests," Jeremy said.

"That's nothing. The whole lot will go to your father, including the Stubbs."

"Well, so be it. I reckon he'll sell Brood, in that case. He's hard up."

"You ought to make a stand, Jeremy. For Brood, at least, else you'll have no livelihood. I'll go and have a chat with her. There ought to be a will, in any case, whatever she decides."

"She's not going to die tomorrow—probably another ten years to go, by the look of her. It's disgusting to fight over her money. I've never done anything for her. Rosy has more right to the Stubbs than I have if you judge by good works."

"It's not fighting, don't be ridiculous. You're her only grandson. It should be settled, fairly divided. I'll go and see her."

"Good luck. Don't be sordid." Jeremy grinned. He had been at school with Paul Rogers and Paul knew the score.

LETITIA THOUGHT PAUL ROGERS wanted to read the electricity meter and got him a stool to stand on, and a torch.

"No, Mrs. Cutbush, I'm Paul Rogers, your solicitor. I was passing so I thought I'd drop in, as I know you can't get about like you used to. I'm an old friend of Jeremy's."

"Did he send you?"

"No. Heavens, no!" He gave his professional laugh.

"There's nothing wrong?" she asked.

"Not at all."

"I'll make a cup of tea then."

He might have known . . . he was here for the afternoon and might as well make the best of it. While she was in the kitchen he studied the pictures on the walls and decided that the Stubbs, although smaller than most, was a very decent painting, in perfect condition. It would surely make a bomb at Sotheby's . . . he winced at its vulnerability here in the dilapidated cottage.

"Do you lock up?" he asked her when she eventually arrived with a silver teapot on a tray.

"Jeremy asked me that, when he was here. There's a key under the flowerpot on the doorstep that Gin and Rosy use when they come. Nobody else comes as a rule. I'm not very popular, you know."

She smiled maliciously. She was unkempt in a rather dashing style, in clothes that had once been so expensive they had lasted a lifetime, rubbed and faded but indubitably classy. She still had beautiful legs and ankles, clad in dark woollen stockings and pointed leather brogues.

On her thin hands, knotted with alarming blue veins, she wore a second fortune in rings, loose now but stopped from falling off by painfully swollen knuckles. For a granny she was far from cosy and homespun, a different kettle of fish from the blue-rinse ladies in apricot courtelle and woolly slippers for whom he was in the habit of making out wills.

308

"I am glad you have come, because I want to make a will," she said.

Paul Rogers could not believe his luck.

"My mare is in foal, and I want it legal—that the foal belongs to Rosy Weeks. Also that picture, when I die." She indicated the Stubbs.

Paul waited hopefully. "And the estate?"

"That doesn't matter. I don't care about that. Only the foal and the picture."

"The picture is probably worth as much as the estate."

"It doesn't matter. Money doesn't matter at all to me, Mr. Rogers." Her dark eyes, far from faded, widened with contempt and majesty in such a way that Paul's professional patter died in his throat.

"The animals—and the picture. We can do the rest another time. I am not intending to die for some time, you know. You can come to tea more often, Mr. Rogers, and we can discuss it."

He was pretty sure she knew that he did not care for this idea at all. He tried every argument in the book to prevent her willing the Stubbs to Rosy, but to no avail. The deed was done. The visit a disaster. He reported to Jeremy. Jeremy laughed.

"You'll have to marry her," Paul said. "What's she like?"

"She'd make a good trainer's wife. I might have come round to thinking about it, but it's impossible now. It would be highly embarrassing. It's not as if I've ever spoken to her, save to give her orders."

"Good grounding for marriage. You must go and talk to your granny, Jeremy—she's a nutter. I talked till I was blue in the face, telling her it would all go to the Inland Revenue anyway unless she wrapped it up properly now, but she's got a mind above the Inland Revenue apparently. It's up to you, lad. I can come round and change the will any time, just give me a ring and I'll be on my way."

"Serves me right for meddling."

The news did nothing to cheer Jeremy. Better to have drifted, as before, not really expecting much, but with a faint hope. Hope was now extinguished. He had no will to fight Letitia over her money, for God's sake. All now depended on making good with the stable. Good for him, really. High time he came out of mourning for his pelvis and learned ambition. But Rosy, in spite of his instinctive protest, took on a new significance in his life and he could no longer think of her as one of the lads. How exactly he could think of her, he had no idea.

6

"Look." Mrs. Cutbush pointed to Silverfish's belly as the mare drank ice-cold water out of the field trough, and Rosy saw the indignant thump of the foal moving inside her. She laughed. "It's an active little beggar."

"Sharp. Strong. She's never had a sickly foal." Mrs. Cutbush had fed the mare and looked after her with renewed interest. With the fresh life growing in Silverfish, the old woman seemed to have taken a new lease of life herself.

Rosy was divided between being excited and deeply worried about the responsibilities of rearing and making this possibly valuable animal legal. But no doubt between Gin, Mrs. Cutbush and herself some plan might take shape.

While the foal inexorably grew to term in the old mare's worn body, Gin worried about the similar growth taking place in Beryl's inadequate frame, and when Rosy tried to pin him down about finding a way of faking the foal's papers he said, "Oh, for God's sake, Rosy, haven't I got enough troubles at the moment?"

Rosy hesitated. She no longer talked to him as she had once done; with marriage he had aged five years and his once-open, cheerful face was now habitually drawn.

"What troubles? Is it Beryl?"

They were alone in the tackroom, just before departing for lunch. The boys had gone and Rosy had come to fetch her jacket.

"I suppose I can tell you. Yes. It's not all roses being married to Beryl, you know."

"Oh, yes, Gin, I do know. I've got eyes in my head."

"I don't seem to have made her happy. When I get home she'll be in bed, as like as not, to keep warm, no dinner made, no work done, nothing. She's made me put down for a council house in town, ten miles away—what'll I do then, if we get it? I haven't even got a car yet. She's betting with the housekeeping—says it's only a quid or two and she's won more than she's lost, but I know that's not true. When I tell her she mustn't, she sets up this terrible argument—what else is there to do in this godforsaken hole, with no one to talk to, nowhere to go . . . it's getting me down, I can tell you. My family don't take to her, say she's lazy."

"They might feel differently when a grandchild is born.—"

"There's ten already. What's another? It'll be all comparisons. She won't do anything right. This baby's a disaster, I can tell you, Rosy."

Rosy wanted to put her arms round him and give him a kiss, but thought they would probably both weep. There was nothing to say. She could think of no comfort for Gin. For once her own life seemed promising. The difficulty of making the foal a legal member of the British Stud Book seemed, as he indicated, a very small matter beside his domestic problems.

The stable had a winner at Cheltenham in March, to make a season's score of seventeen, the best ever. Roly Fox covered himself in glory and Artemis gave Rosy a gold brooch in the shape of a little Pegasus. Rosy was still torn by Roly's foolish courage in racing. He was rarely clever enough to win except by herculean effort, and was far more game than the dour Hawkins deserved. Even with winning the man did not become more lovable, always preoccupied by how much return he was getting from the bookmakers.

"If that's what success does, perhaps we don't want it," Jeremy remarked, as near a joke as he had been known to utter.

But Jeremy smiled more often, and when Rosy heard that the convalescent Grace was being regularly visited by one of her ex-ski-instructors, her optimism increased. The threat of Grace taking up her duties again next autumn was the one dark cloud in the sky.

Rosy called one afternoon to visit the recumbent Grace and clashed with the ski instructor by chance. He was blond, bronzed and muscled, a New Zealander introduced as Ed, and Rosy got the strong impression that Grace now saw her future in a flat in Earl's Court rather than at Brood.

She lay gracefully on a sofa in the window overlooking the valley, basking in Ed's obvious admiration, and Rosy had to admit that Ed was an impressive catch, far more showy than Jeremy, although possibly he might prove a short-distance performer. He reminded Rosy of Mowbray, who still offered her his sexual services whenever he had the chance, cornering her in Roly's loosebox with roving hands which Rosy deftly fielded. He took no offence. "Who're you saving yourself for then? Who'd you go to bed with?" he asked.

"No one."

"You're joking? You have—you're not telling me you never—?"

"No, I'm not telling you that, you cheeky so-and-so."

She was past the speedy thrash in the hayloft that his young blood desired. She had gone through that period during her London student days and did not consider herself by any means inexperienced, only inexperienced in her true commitment. An affair with Tony Mowbray did not promise to alter that.

311

SILVERFISH'S LOVE LIFE came splendidly to fruition one freezing early morning, when the mare's strained breath hung in white clouds and tiny hooves protruded hesitantly into the cold world, so that Rosy pleaded and wept, and Mrs. Cutbush, having waited in the straw for so long that spiders' trails spun from her damp hair, moved at last to declare she would go and make some bacon sandwiches.

"What, *now?*" Rosy wailed.

"She's always slow. By the time I come back, she'll be born."

Rosy, unfamiliar with the habits of birth, sat in the straw with her arms huddled round her legs, shivering with cold and anxiety. Silverfish, who knew far more about it than she did, looked bored rather than distressed, in fact thoroughly sour, her frosty eyelashes veiling her gaze, nostrils dilated with irritation. At intervals she heaved enormous sighs. Rosy felt much in sympathy, and somewhat remorseful to have interrupted the noble old girl's well-deserved retirement to put her through this wretched business again. But practice told: after a deeper sigh than usual, some angry groans and tetchy kicking into the straw, the forelegs of the foal started to slither forward, and Rosy could see a neat little muzzle resting exactly in the right place over the knees. She watched, fascinated, putting her hand on the mare's quivering tail and encouraging her, half sick with excitement. "Come on, come on, you old beauty."

And Silverfish crossly made her final effort, and the foal was delivered in a wet heap, both hideous and magnificent, to Rosy's incredulous relief and overwhelming joy. She watched the strange bedraggled creature stretch itself free, legs at all angles like a grasshopper's. Silverfish lifted herself up in the straw and looked dispassionately at what she had produced, gave it a careless push in the hindquarters with her nose, and lay back again with another of her world-weary sighs.

Rosy supposed her reaction was a trifle hysterical, and was glad there was no witness to it. When Mrs. Cutbush arrived with the bacon sandwiches, she had recovered herself and was cool and collected. Both animals were on their feet in the thin, pearly light that was struggling into the barn.

"It's a filly," Rosy said. "Like you said."

"Tiny. She's tiny." Mrs. Cutbush shook her head, but could not help smiling. She gave one of the bacon sandwiches to Silverfish.

The foal was dark in colour, with a tiny white star between her nostrils: she might turn out to be a grey, or she might be dark chestnut like Peppermill. She was, indubitably, very small. Like Hyperion, Rosy reminded herself . . . size was no criterion. She had the blood of classic winners in her veins. Perhaps it was the bacon sandwiches, but Rosy felt a glow creeping into her bloodstream as she stood in the doorway of the big barn watching the old mare and her equally ancient owner. Mrs. Cutbush, who had actually seen The Tetrarch race, could see his descendant now taking her first milk. She looked to Rosy suddenly very frail after the long vigil, blue veins showing in her temples, eye sockets hollow with weariness, like Silverfish's own. A less militant lady Rosy would have instinctively kissed; as it was, she took her arm and said softly, "You must be tired? I am. She'll be all right if we leave her now. She can go out when she's ready."

The barn was open to the field. Silverfish dictated her own coming and going and had chosen herself to foal indoors rather than out. They had been up most of the night. Rosy, who wanted to run with joy, tempered her triumph to the old girl's shaky progress back to the house.

"I'll just have forty winks, till breakfast time. In the chair."

Rosy made up the fire and brewed tea which they drank together. The room smelled of old leather and old books and old age.

When it was time for work, Rosy left Mrs. Cutbush dozing in her chair. Silverfish was outside already, walking slowly down to the river, her shadow long over the soaking grass. The mist was dispersing before the fine April sunrise, as sweet a picture of promise as nature could contrive, laced with larks' song and the crunch of frosty grass underfoot. The new filly pressed close to her dam, her eyes wide to the world's perfection, unaware of what she was born for, the merciless effort that would be asked of her, the hopes that were pinned on her delicate, uncertain frame.

TO ROSY THE BIRTH of a son to Beryl was an anticlimax after seeing her filly born, but she made the approved expressions of congratulation and admiration. This was not difficult, for the child was a splendid creature, in no way the mewling scrap that Rosy had somehow expected. He thrived on Beryl's offerings of tinned milk, tinned soup, chips and Jaffa biscuits, and laughed as soon as was humanly possible at the enchanting world he inhabited. Rosy, who had never liked babies until now, was bowled over by Kes, as Beryl called him. ("After a film," she said. "Kes was a bird," Rosy said. "Oh, no. Kes was the boy.")

She volunteered to babysit so that Gin could take Beryl out sometimes, or wheeled Kes down during the summer afternoons to visit Silverfish and her filly, and the fat, lazy Roly Fox who had been turned out in the mare's field again. Sometimes Beryl went out in the afternoon and would not be back when Rosy returned with the baby, so Rosy fed Kes on the unsuitable concoctions she found in Beryl's refrigerator. Beryl said she went for walks on the downs— "It's so marvellous to feel free again," she exclaimed, and indeed she seemed to have flowered: once more birdlike and spry, with freckles across her nose, back into her jeans and T-shirts. She even made a dab at a bit of housekeeping, made ham salad for Gin, and kept the baby clean. Rosy was relieved, and presumed her former sullen laziness had been caused by pregnancy and winter combined. And yet . . . there was something other, something breathless and secretive about Beryl's transformation.

Gin bought a car, and said to Rosy, "Beryl put a bet on. She put the whole bloody maternity allowance on. If I'd known I'd have killed her, but it came up. I can't get over it! For God's sake don't spread it around. My ma would kill her. I've told 'em I got a bonus at work. Don't know whether to laugh or cry."

Cry, Rosy reckoned, if the girl couldn't kick the habit. She guessed that after her bonanza, Beryl was losing the housekeeping money fast. For someone who bet as Beryl did the wins were invariably overtaken by the losses.

JOHN WEEKS LAY on the edge of a small declivity on the downs, hidden in a tangle of thorns and brambles that made a good hide for watching birds. Weeks liked this isolated spot, and settled there quite often when the weather was right.

On this particular August morning the air was heat-hazy and still. John, in his voluminous shorts, long socks turned down over the tops of his boots to reveal his stringy brown legs, was never bored communing with nature. He loved the uncultivated forest of Brood, the undisturbed nature of the valley, and examined it inch by inch through his binoculars.

The only people he saw on the downs were exercisers of racehorses, and an occasional walker, and he knew that few of them saw him, for he prided himself on melting into his surroundings, seeing things that nobody else saw.

Today he was held captive in his shrubbery of gorse by the unexpected arrival of a young man and a young woman who came up through the trees. Walkers always kept to the ridge above Brood, and he thought these were walkers who had missed the way and would pass by him and keep going until their route converged with the route proper. But they stopped in the depression below him and threw off their clothes and made love with passionate abandon. They were only thirty feet away and John Weeks, who had watched every sort of copulation through his binoculars, from fox and vixen to dragonfly, from grass snake to magpie, with fascinated, biological interest, was horrified by the human spectacle. He shut his eyes in disgust and lay helplessly in his hide until, in the aftermath, he recognized the girl, and guessed who the man was.

THE FILLY FOAL was Rosy's pride and joy. She was sharp as a needle, pushy and nosy and bold, and her galloping over the uneven pastures of her home was both impressive and nerve-racking. Rosy was used to chasers and the little filly's fine legs looked to Rosy much too delicate for the wild action they were put to. But she thrived, a splendid "doer", although she remained small. By autumn when she got her second coat it was apparent that she would be a grey like her dam. Rosy called her Secret, but the shy connotation was not very suitable. She decided to register her as Dark Secret—should she ever overcome her difficulties in that direction.

"Look, I'd see to it if I knew someone, but at the moment I just don't want any more trouble on my plate." Gin was uncooperative. "There's no hurry. It's not as if we're going to sell her, is it? We'll sort it out next year."

He had scarcely been to see the filly, too preoccupied to take an interest. When racing started again he was glad to get away in the horsebox, growing more cheerful as the miles clocked up away from home. He and Rosy enjoyed the old relationship during the long, fuggy hours in the cab, talking about the horses and racing, but not about love and life, nor betting. During the hours away, with Spinning Wheel or Peppermill or Roly Fox dozing to the engine roar that engulfed them, Rosy producing fruit gums, and coffee from a thermos to perch on the dashboard, Gin would mellow. The nearest he ever came to comment on his situation was, "Life is what you make it, I suppose." Accompanied by a deep sigh.

GRACE DID NOT APPEAR again at Brood House all winter. As soon as she was fit she departed with Ed to the snow slopes of France, to housekeep, presumably, for a more appreciative male. Rosy was deeply satisfied by this turn of events.

Jeremy, working under more pressure for the formidable Mr. Hawkins, seemed suddenly more cheerful. To keep Hawkins's horses racing so hard was a challenge to his skill as a trainer, and when they started to get winners at Newbury and Sandown Park and Cheltenham as well as at the more modest courses, his temperament improved along with their results. The work load was heavy in the yard but everyone seemed to thrive on the pressure.

"Except the horses," as Gin remarked gloomily in the tackroom. "We might get a rest when he's broken them all down. He thinks they are bloody motorbikes."

After three runs in six weeks on ground harder than was good for him, Roly's leg was giving trouble. Rosy spent hours hosing it in the yard, to keep at bay the dreaded heat. Quite often she rode him down to Silverfish's field and stood him in the river. This was in her own time, during the afternoons, and she did not think of it as extra work. But one day Jeremy saw her as he was driving past, and he stopped and came across the field to speak to her. Seeing him

316

coming, followed by Silverfish and the filly, Rosy recognized an element of fantasy in the encounter—all her prize loves congregating on the riverbank in one magic moment. Pure pantomime: a dark, rain-heavy afternoon, the earthy smell of the river, swollen and fast-running, the grass churned and trodden where the mare had come to drink. Jeremy approached with his uneasy gait, not quite a limp, his old cap pulled close, frowning.

"You charge overtime for this?" He half smiled, as human as Rosy had ever known him.

"No. Pure love."

"It's the best thing going."

He stood companionably, pulling Silverfish's ear as she pushed at his pockets. He gave her a Polo mint and the filly pushed in, nipping. He gave her one, cuffed her on the muzzle. Seeing Rosy sitting there on Roly Fox, he saw them as "Horse and Groom in a Landscape", entirely appropriate. She deserved the picture; she would get it, for all he intended to do about it, but the business had singled her out, made her no longer one of the lads. It had made a barrier. He was more aware of her now.

He was about to thank Rosy for the extra trouble she was taking and depart, when he remembered the extraordinary disclosure Grace had made over the dinner table, and felt the moment was too opportune to resist.

"Who does she take after? Not Silverfish, for sure. Who did Letitia get the mare served by?"

Rosy did not reply. In the dusk Jeremy sensed her embarrassment. "It wasn't Peppermill, was it?"

She still said nothing.

"Better not let Hawkins know, else he'll want five thousand in stud fees."

"He doesn't know!"

"No. News to me if he does. It's true though?"

"Yes. I—I—it seemed too good to miss—"

"Stroke of genius. What are you going to do about her papers?"

"Gin was going to find some crook vet but now he's not so keen. I don't know really. It's a bit of a problem."

"I might find you somebody . . . some obscure stallion. Nobody with a good one would take the risk. It won't enhance her value, I'm afraid. Are you going to sell her?"

"I don't know."

Rosy could see Jeremy was amused. It was an enormous relief, suddenly, that he knew. "How did you find out?"

"Someone told me, who saw you. Pure chance. Don't worry about it." He stood assessing the filly as she cantered sharply away up the field. He laughed as she put in a couple of bucks. Silverfish wheeled away and trotted after her. "You can sell me a share. We'll run her on the flat."

Did he mean it? Rosy felt the blood rushing to her head, the dizzy vision of sharing the owners' stand with Jeremy almost too much for her. But he was laughing, joking.

"I'll do what I can about a stallion. Have to be very careful, but I'm sure I can find someone."

He departed, and Rosy followed him to the gate. He opened it and fended off the mare and foal while she went through. It was nearly dark. She trotted Roly along the grass verge and turned into the Brood drive. She was excited, warmed by her encounter. She hugged Roly when she untacked him. He looked magnificent in the electric light, hard and fit and shining like a billiard ball. She felt, for once, incredibly lucky at the way things were going.

It was the nature of racing that this state of mind was short-lived. Roly went to Sandown and won, battling his heart out as usual, and came home distressed. The next day there was heat in his foreleg, he left his feed, and Rosy took him out in the afternoon to graze on Jeremy's lawn. She bitterly resented that such a man as Hawkins should own a horse like Roly. Most horses—the ones with any sense—packed it in when they were treated as he had been treated.

"You're so bloody stupid, Roly, killing yourself for that oaf. He'll sell you for dogfood when you've crocked yourself up."

The horse stopped grazing and gave her an affectionate rub with his thick head, nearly pushing her over. She laughed, and scratched his nose.

Roly was entered at Lingfield in a fortnight's time, and Cheltenham three weeks after that. Jeremy wanted to take him out of Lingfield to give him a chance for Cheltenham, but Hawkins would not hear of it. He had invited some business friends to Lingfield, and Roly was a part of the entertainment. "No point, if I haven't a horse running, for God's sake."

So Rosy put heavy bandages on Roly's forelegs. She watched him go down to the start with lump in her throat, knowing that the fatal weakness on her part of actually loving her horse was about to have its inevitable repercussion. She stood with Gin as usual, close to tears. With luck the leg would hold out, or perhaps he would go tender early on and be pulled up without much damage. But Roly did it the hard way, as he inevitably did, jumping like a stag until

318

the second last, when he stood off too far, fiddled a stride, jumped awkwardly and landed very steeply, off-fore leading. Even before he had recovered and run on, Rosy knew the damage was done. Mowbray pulled him up at once—which showed how bad it was, for Roly had been in front and looked like being in the frame. The crowd roared with dismay and Tony dismounted. Rosy ran.

"Don't blame me. I couldn't have pulled up any quicker!" Mowbray gave her a defensive, almost sympathetic smile.

Roly, all steamed up, danced round them on three legs, not able to stand still, not understanding the pain. Tony took his saddle off and put the sweat rug on; buckling it in front.

"Sorry, Rosy, honest," he said, before departing.

Did she look so bad? Rosy had never felt bleaker in her life, but sentiment had no place in public. Jeremy was hurrying through the fringes of the crowd towards her, Gin with him. They were still well down the course, away from the public, a forlorn group watched perhaps by a few interested parties through binoculars. A horse written off, shoulders shrugged. Memories were only a week or two long in racing . . . on with the next. As Tony had said at the start, there were plenty of youngsters coming along.

Jeremy came up without a word, felt the leg, watched as Rosy tried to lead Roly out. The horse could put no weight on it at all. It hung, almost as if broken. Roly tried, stumbled, and fell to grazing as if he had not eaten for a week.

"Go and fetch the box," Jeremy said to Gin. "And get the vet down here on your way. With luck he's already coming."

Mr. Hawkins did not even come to see. He rang up three days later, and forgot to send the fifty-pound note.

Roly was injected with painkillers, and bandaged, He could not leave his box, fretted, would not eat, grew thin and miserable. Spinning Wheel went to Cheltenham and won a good race. Mr. Hawkins came down to see him, actually patted his sleek neck, and patted Rosy on the back. She nearly bit his hand. He glanced over Roly's door and shook his head. "He might as well go to the sales. Ascot in July—he'll be walking sound by then, don't you think?"

"He'll run again, given time. We could turn him out here for eighteen months," Jeremy said.

"What, and charge me keep all that time? I'm not a mug, Cutbush."

"It wouldn't cost you much. He's done you well. He deserves a chance."

"I can't wait that long. Get him back by next season, perhaps—"

319

"Unlikely, I'm afraid. It'll take at least a year."

"And then it's likely to go again. No. It doesn't interest me. Get him sound and send him to the sales. Someone else can take a chance with him, and I'll get another youngster."

Jeremy avoided Rosy's eyes.

Two days later, as if to placate her, he told her he had acquired her filly a respectable document. "She's by Understanding. Look, all down in writing."

"Who's Understanding?"

"Best I could do. He died of a twisted gut three months ago, the owner doesn't care and the vet who signed the certificate is retiring any day now and did it for a bottle of whisky. The stallion has the same bloodline as Peppermill—goes back to Nasrullah, Nearco, so if anyone ever breeds from your filly they won't go too far wrong. If you sell her, the fact that she's by Understanding won't make you a big price, but beggars can't be choosers. The fact that she's out of Silverfish might make up for it."

Rosy was relieved. The filly was becoming a worry to her, for she was now a yearling, and if she was going to race she would have to go into training at the end of the year. She was tough and hard and fast and everything a budding owner might desire. But Rosy doubted more and more if the budding owner was going to be herself.

"I could do with the money if we sell her," Gin said.

"What, for Beryl's betting?" Rosy could not help the sharp retort, for Gin reminded her at frequent intervals that he had a half share in the filly.

"It's not that," said Gin. "We owe money on everything. It's not for betting, just to clear up some of the debts."

"You know it won't. It'll go the same way."

"What can I do?"

There was no answer to that. Not with Kes as part of the set-up. Gin doted on Kes, and Beryl, for all her faults, was not a bad mother. She was good with Kes and he thrived on his strange diet and his outings up on the downs. On mild mornings Beryl pushed his pram up the rutted track through the Brood woodlands, and the wide-eyed baby, parked in the bushes, laughed at the antics she got up to with the man who was waiting for her. Tony was always in a hurry, glancing at his watch.

"I'm riding in the first race at Wincanton, Beryl. Let go of me!" He ran back down one of the old gamekeeper's tracks to where he left his car in a clearing nicely hidden from the main road. The affair was good for a laugh and kept him fit.

ROLY WAS DULY ENTERED for the Ascot July sales and Rosy tried not to think about his departure. She kept telling herself he could have broken his neck and departed this life some four or five months ago instead of merely doing in a tendon, but the argument was no comfort. She always thought horses killed racing at least died at full stretch, enjoying themselves, better than the ones like Roly who, clapped-out, turned to less heady careers in hacking stables or the yards of middle-aged ladies who went in for dressage. If he went to a good home she might bear it quite well, or so she convinced herself. But as the day came nearer she grew more and more depressed, and spent long hours with him in the stream so that his leg would show up as sound as possible. Not that he could be sold with a warranty, but she would do her best by him.

Another summer on, and what had seemed so sweet the summer before was now all doubt and disillusion. Word went round that Grace had left Ed and was coming home again. "That's all I need!" Rosy raged, and the chill river seemed to infect her spirits with a dread of the future, revealing the simple allegiances round which her life revolved as pathetic and insubstantial: her horses, her dreams of Jeremy, even her timeworn friendship with Gin who was growing daily more hard-pressed, bitter and shifty, caught in the oldest trap of all. What narrow horizons, what lack of ambition, what a sad waste of the passions and achievements of which she was sure she was capable . . . If Grace came back, she would have to get another job, and meet another set of people, and forget Jeremy.

It was almost with a sense of relief that the date for Roly's disposal arrived. She dreaded the day, but was glad it had come at last. She had brought Roly in from the field for the last few days, to get his coat clean and a stable sheen on it. He looked rested and well and trusting. When they loaded him, he thought he was going to the races. He did not know he was never coming back.

Once in the horsebox and on their way, Rosy broke down and wept. Gin was not sympathetic. "He's only got half my troubles, for God's sake."

Rosy did not like Gin any more, she decided. She felt much better after a good cry, and knew she was safe for the rest of the day. Jeremy was driving over, and before Jeremy she would keep cool and proud.

Poor Ascot horses, she thought, many going for a few hundred in spite of their decent records and honest eyes. There were just too many horses . . . the sight depressed her. Why did people breed so many? Was the thrill of racing, at bottom, sheer greed? She never could make up her mind, seeing the way Hawkins's mind worked, and yet knowing that there were considerations and glories way above mere money. Granted, she was sentimental, but other people revealed mushy hearts—she was not the only person obsessed by the likes of Roly Fox. She could not bring herself to lead him round and left the job to Gin. But she stayed with him in the stable until his number was near.

"Cheer up," said Jeremy, gently. "The worst hasn't happened yet. There are some decent people interested in him."

He had driven over to see how it went; he looked nervous, probably worried she was going to make a fool of them both by crying, but she no longer felt like it, merely cold and sick. They went into the sale ring and sat and watched two eleven-year-olds go for a few hundred each. They both had decent records, and terrible legs, and their racing days were over.

Rosy could see Roly walking round outside in the sunshine. It was a lovely day and he was on his toes, thinking it must be racing, yet he was rounded with summer grass. He looked magnificent. Her heart started to pump as Gin brought him in and the auctioneer began to read from the catalogue. "This is a good horse! The owner making way for young stock, but there's a lot of races in this one yet."

Roly stared about him as he walked round, surprised, interested, full of goodwill towards the human race. The bidding started at one thousand, and went on steadily. Rosy tried to see who was bidding. A lot of men stood in the entrance to the ring, and the auctioneer was looking there, and up into the stand behind her. She turned round, craning.

"Who are they?" she asked Jeremy.

"One of them is—" He mentioned a very decent trainer. Rosy's optimism lurched.

"Two thousand nine hundred, two thousand nine hundred, any advance on two thousand nine hundred?"

The invisible man behind made it three thousand, and the price went up again, but more slowly.

Someone behind Rosy said, audibly, "That's the horse that broke down at Lingfield, isn't it?"

"Is it? Probably. You wouldn't sell a horse like that if it were still any good. I wouldn't anyway."

The decent trainer dropped out. It was left to the invisible man behind.

"Three thousand two hundred. Are we all finished at three thousand two hundred?"

He waited, for what seemed to Rosy an age.

The hammer fell. "Sold to the gentleman—" The auctioneer peered upwards. "Smith," he muttered to his clerk. Rosy turned round.

"Who is it?" she asked Jeremy. "Who's Smith?"

Jeremy was frowning. They got up and pushed their way outside. Another horse was already in the ring and nobody was interested in Roly any more. Roly was wondering when the race was going to start. He danced around and Rosy took his rein.

"Who is Smith?"

Gin, glowering, said, "He's a bloody—"

"Cutbush?" Smith was a burly, rough-spoken man in a crumpled waxed jacket and a tweed hat. He said to Rosy, "My lad will take him." He drew aside with Jeremy, and Rosy heard him say, "This leg now . . ." She was left with the lad, a similarly hulkish, unsmiling boy of about eighteen who produced his own headcollar and changed it quickly. His handling was rough and sharp.

"He's very kind," Rosy said, belligerently.

The boy grunted, chucked her the removed headcollar and led Roly away without a word. Rosy stood watching. The horsebox that received Roly was a clapped-out wreck. Though she had vowed not to cry again, Rosy felt as if she had turned to stone.

"That's a betting stable," Gin said dourly. "Load of crooks. Smith ...
you know him. Had that good mare, Blue Eucalyptus."

"She got killed?"

"Yeah. There was some funny business, but nobody proved
anything."

"What do you mean? How can—"

"Come on, I'll buy you a lunch." Jeremy was back, speaking
tenderly.

"Is he as awful as he looks, that Smith?"

"He's not what you might call one of the country's top ten
trainers, no. I'm sorry. I thought Nichols was going to get him."

Rosy followed the two men blindly into the canteen. All around
them sat nice, fresh-faced, middle-aged people who had come to
pick up hunters, or keen young ladies who wanted a nice hack.
Suddenly the place seemed to be teeming with prospective homes,
kind and true. There was nobody else like Smith in sight. Why did
he have to pick Roly? Blind misery overcame her. She pecked at her
steak pie, and Jeremy did not offer to drive her home. He let her go
back in the horsebox with Gin.

JEREMY FELT TOO BAD to drive her home. Roly had stood a good
chance of getting a fairish home, handsome and kind as he was, duff
leg or not. But it was just in the nature of things that, when it
mattered so desperately to Rosy, a profiteer like Smith had picked
on him for his nefarious plans. Hawkins was of the same ilk. Jeremy
felt uncomfortable about Hawkins, not wanting an owner like him,
but needing his financial support. Oh, God, who would be in the
racing game! It was so magnificent at its best, seedy—to put it
kindly—at bottom. Human greed ruined it; the exploitation of one
of the kindest, gamest animals on earth for money. Yet without the
money motive, racing would not exist.

As he drove now, remembering Rosy's bleak face, old agonies of
his own flooded back, of a much-loved pony he had outgrown at
sixteen which, sold on to slapdash owners, had died neglected in a
field, of tetanus. Even at that age he had wept every night in bed for
a week when he found out, and the memory still brought back a
dreadful ache. It was no good thinking that the animal brain worked
in the same fashion as the human brain, for that was patently
rubbish. But he had failed that pony, by any standards, just as now
he was thinking he had failed Roly.

The day was not one to remember with pride and joy.

Smith had a small stable of about twelve horses on the outskirts of

Wolverhampton, and ran most of his horses in sellers and ill-paid handicaps. Asking around, Rosy built up a picture of a meanly run establishment from which horses ran with great variations of form, ridden mostly by a weasel-faced jockey called Parkins who was known to be suspect and got few rides otherwise. Why she troubled to find out these details which caused her only distress Rosy had no idea, save through a sort of perversity.

To distract herself she spent a lot of time with the filly, now registered with Weatherby's as Dark Secret. She was very forward, and Rosy wanted to get ahead with handling her so that she would be easy to break in when the time came. She weaned her from old Silverfish and kept her up at Brood in Roly's old box, leading her out every day and getting her to accept a bit, and saddle and girths. Jeremy would not accept any money for her keep, but made no further offer to take a share in her, or train her. Gin wanted to sell.

"Neither of us can afford to put her into training."

"We might if Jeremy were to take a third share."

"The guv'nor? He won't. Have you asked him?"

"No."

Rosy knew she must ask him. Jeremy had friends who trained on the flat . . . he could fix it . . . perhaps.

"Sir, can I have a word?"

She was grooming Peppermill at the time. Her voice shook. Jeremy was on his way back to the house, the moment opportune.

He said, "Come to the house with me. I'm expecting a telephone call."

She dropped her tools in the manger and darted after him. She had never set foot in the house before and was stunned by the portrait of Letitia, struck by the spark of the old Jeremy that she saw in the portrait's expression.

"She's like you!"

Jeremy was amused. "God forbid! I don't seem to hit it off with the old lady these days. Not like you."

Rosy was embarrassed, thinking of the Stubbs, thinking he thought she was after the old girl's money. She followed him into the kitchen, trying not to stare. It was harrowing to be on his home ground, painful beyond expectation. She had forgotten what she had come for, seeing all the homely things: his battered typewriter, socks hanging to dry on the rail of the Aga, some Alpen shaken into a bowl and a bottle of milk on the table.

"Excuse the mess. Do you want coffee? I'm going to make one."

"Yes. Thank you."

"What's the matter?"

Everything, she thought desperately. "It's the Silverfish filly. I don't know what to do about her."

"How can I help?"

"I don't know if you can. It's worth asking—I just thought—I mean, it's worth a try, whether you could—you want—to have a—a share in her, to race her? I can't afford to put her into training. I thought you might—" It sounded quite dreadful. She pulled herself resolutely together. "I think I've got to sell her, but I thought I'd ask if you can think of any way I could afford to race her myself?"

There. In a nutshell. Train her for me free. For love. Help me. I love you. Love me, love my horse.

"Have a seat," Jeremy said.

Did she look as if she was about to fall over? Her knees were trembling. Jeremy was fiddling with the coffee percolator.

"You mean—if I train her? You'd like me to train her?"

"I just wondered if it was possible—if I did all the work? Would I have enough money? I know it costs a fortune ordinarily."

"Well, I've got a licence. Why not?" He wasn't shocked, offended, embarrassed. Not even put out. "Why not?" he said. "Do you take sugar?"

"One please."

"We could try it, couldn't we? See if she's any good. That's where the money is, after all, if the legs run fast enough. Old Letitia would love it, eh?"

Rosy could not believe it. Jeremy put the coffee down on the table and came and sat opposite her.

"She's very well bred." He smiled.

Rosy could think of nothing to say. All these weeks of worrying and now Jeremy taking up the cause for a lark.

"One thing about you, Rosy, you go for what you want. I had been thinking for the last couple of years that Silverfish was being wasted, and didn't lift a finger to do anything about it."

Is that how he saw her? She who irresolutely through life achieved nothing . . . She drank some coffee, wished it was brandy. Now was the moment to propose, obviously. Grace would have.

Jeremy moved the milk bottle away from her elbow. "Sorry this place is so scruffy. All will be changed when Grace gets back." He spoke with irony, but Rosy heard no more than the actual words.

"Grace is coming back?"

"So she has announced. Give her a week and we'll be all shipshape and shining. She is very efficient is Grace."

So. The euphoria was short-lived. Grace would get him this time. Rosy sat back, trying to hurry with her coffee, not wanting Jeremy to divine her thoughts. He was being uncommonly nice this morning—was it the prospect of having Grace back? Perhaps not. He had been thawing gradually over the last couple of years, whether because of Hawkins and the success the stable had achieved, or because he was mellowing anyway she did not know.

"Talk of the devil," Jeremy murmured.

Outside on the gravel Grace's Mini was parking in its assured place hard outside the front door.

"Yoo-hoo! Jeremy!"

It was worth it, Rosy supposed, to see the expression on Grace's face when she came in and saw the two of them drinking coffee together. Shock, fury and blatant cover-up—brittle smile and fluttering eyelashes.

"Jeremy! Why, Rosy! How lovely to see you again!" Insincerity shone from her gorgeous blue eyes. "Can I help myself to coffee? Just like old times."

"I'm just going," Rosy said, swallowing fast.

"Oh, no. Have another."

Rosy suspected Jeremy was enjoying himself at her expense. Grace took a mug and filled it for herself, very obviously not refilling Rosy's. She turned the full glare of her beauty on Jeremy and gave him a smile that cut Rosy right out of the kitchen.

Jeremy said, "Rosy's got new status, Grace. She's an owner. We're going to train her filly for the flat."

"You mean Silverfish's filly, by—"

"Understanding. That's right."

In that moment Rosy realized who had told Jeremy about Peppermill's visit to Letitia's.

"How exciting!"

Grace was having a hard time. Her eyes raked over Rosy, seeing her afresh, her status enhanced. One could see the challenge accepted; Grace loved a challenge. Did Jeremy read it too? He very deliberately refilled Rosy's coffee cup. Grace noticed. She passed the sugar nobly. "Hugh tells me you've lost your Roly Fox. To a not very nice stable, he said."

Sweet smile. Her dart nicely on target. Rosy, her mind now tuned to Dark Secret, felt the wound opened, remorse sprung. There was no glib answer. Jeremy said nothing and there was a long silence.

Rosy made her exit as soon as possible, her mind hammering to new possibilities. The season was just getting under way, the horses all back in work and fit to race. Come the cold weather Dark Secret would have to be brought in and started in work. The prospect was glorious. Working with Jeremy, her place with the owners and trainers, not out in the back, taking a tip, touching the forelock. *My* filly, *my* colours . . . the mind soared. She called in on her little racehorse on the way down for lunch. The filly was all sweetness for a handful of oats, fickle, still tiny, but all quality. Her winter coat was steel dark, but with splotches of rusty chestnut over her quarters, a hark-back to The Tetrarch, or to Peppermill.

"The guv'nor said he'll train her!" Rosy told Gin, when they came back for evening stables.

"You're joking?"

"No. 'Why not', he said."

"It'll cost us a bomb."

"No. He didn't say so. We can do the work—I can, anyway."

Rosy wished Gin wasn't involved. She knew he wanted to send the filly to the December sales, and make a few quick thousands. But without him she would never have gone through with the mating; no good regretting his involvement now. She only wanted his enthusiasm, nothing else. It was plain who was going to put the hours in.

Grace took up where she had left off. She too put in the hours: to catch Jeremy, to get Jeremy organized, make herself indispensable. She got him two new owners, and set to work charming Mr. Hawkins. "You *need* Hawkins," Grace told Jeremy crisply.

Hawkins took to calling, taking a drink with Grace and Jeremy in the newly primped kitchen, now sparkling clean and boasting magazine touches of colour and character: a string of onions and a bowl of lemons. Artemis, apparently, had got the push, like Roly Fox. Hawkins inspected Spinning Wheel, Peppermill and Needles, and Rosy got a twenty-pound note for pointing out which was which.

Jeremy knew he was being manipulated, knew that if he married Grace he would go from strength to strength. Largely Grace's strength. She was ruthless and highly efficient. It was very difficult to resist what was happening. In her role as secretary she was, in effect, only running on one cylinder—the thought of her being given carte blanche to run the place, and himself, entirely, through marriage, was awe-inspiring. Jeremy knew he was mellowing with time and success, his hankering to be back in the saddle dissolving with age—for he was now at the age when most jump jockeys retired—but whether he would ever mellow enough to take Grace as a wife he doubted. He was content to let things run. For now he kept her firmly in her secretary/housekeeper role, and talked to her like an employer.

Strangely, to Rosy he now talked less like an employer, more as an accomplice.

Grace noticed this and throttled back. She grew quieter and less obvious, and wore skirts instead of trousers. Jeremy noticed the improvement but was too guileless to guess the reason why.

ON RACING DAYS Rosy looked out for Mr. Smith of Wolverhampton, and was not cheered by what she saw. His horses were undernourished and scurfy and ran mainly in sellers, losing when they were expected to win and winning when they were expected to lose. He always had a plausible excuse for the stewards, and if he was a crook, he was too petty to cause a lot of trouble. Of Roly Fox there was no sign.

Usually Smith's horses were attended by the surly youth who had taken Roly from Rosy at Ascot. Once she asked the youth if Roly Fox was all right and he said, "Yeah, he's OK," and walked away scowling. But one dark December day at Towcester a horse running in Smith's name was attended by a girl, a depressed-looking blonde in tight jeans called Tracy, and when she brought her runner back to the stables, Rosy accosted her. She was washing her horse down in a very inefficient fashion, the horse restive and exhausted. Rosy tactfully offered to hold him for her.

"Thanks awfully." She looked as exhausted as the horse.

"You got a horse in your yard called Roly Fox?"

"Yeah, I think so."

"How is he? I used to do him."

"Oh. He's got a bad leg."

"He's not in training then? Is he turned out?"

"No. He's in training."

"How can he be?"

"Mr. Smith swims him."

"Oh." Rosy knew this was an accepted system of training these days, but did not suspect Mr. Smith had a stable swimming pool, a very expensive piece of equipment. "Where does he take him?"

"He swims him in the river."

"In the river! This time of year?"

"Yeah. He tows him from a dinghy."

"Does he like it?"

"Not much, I shouldn't think." The girl giggled. "I wouldn't, would you?"

"What about the cold?"

"He dries him off in the pig barn. It's heated, for the piglets. He ties him up there when he gets him home. S'warm as toast."

Rosy considered this amazing information. If Roly was standing up to the unorthodox treatment, it should be doing his leg a lot of good. "When's he going to run then? This season?"

"Oh, I think so."

"Will you let me know when, in advance? So's I can make sure I see him."

"Yeah, if you like."

"I'll give you my phone number. Here." Rosy scrabbled in her pocket and wrote her telephone number on her racecard. She had a fiver in her purse. She tucked it in the card and gave it to Tracy. "Put it in your pocket. Don't forget. I really mean it."

"Looks like it. Thanks."

Rosy was torn by Tracy's information. She could not stop thinking of old Roly being towed along behind a dinghy, in an ice-cold river. She reported to Jeremy, who was intrigued. "Well, he's a tough old bugger. It might work a treat. I wonder what Smith's planning for him?"

"When he does run, can I have the day off to go and see him?"

"Of course."

By Christmas the Brood horses had won ten races. Hawkins gave Rosy a hundred pounds, which she put to her Dark Secret fund.

Grace invited Jeremy for Christmas. Rosy invited Letitia. Neither invitation was accepted. Christmas was no holiday at the stables, with three runners on Boxing Day, but Rosy cooked a turkey herself and asked Gin and Beryl round, and took a plateful down to Letitia. It was not a success, her father not approving of the turkey, nor of Beryl. Gin was in an equally sour mood. Beryl did not help matters by studying form for the Boxing Day racing—she was going to have a bet because it was Christmas. The atmosphere was deadly, overlaid by loud television bonhomie. Rosy, aware that it was through her invitation that this gruesome afternoon was taking place, went out with Kes in the buggy, ostensibly to give his mother a break, in reality to give herself one.

It was a raw, cloudy day and the village was deserted. Rosy wheeled Kes down to Letitia's cottage, and opened the door with the key under the flowerpot. The house was in darkness, but the room warm, the fire glowing.

"Mrs. Cutbush?"

The old lady was in the chair by the fire. Rosy could see her by the light from the small flame, her eyes glittering. Tears ran down her cheeks.

Rosy knelt down in front of her. "Are you all right?"

"Yes, dear."

"Why are you crying?"

"It's time I was dead."

"No. Oh, no!" Rosy had never seen Mrs. Cutbush without her fight. It frightened her.

"I want Peter."

"Look. Don't cry." Rosy scrambled up. She put on a small wall light, went back to the front door and pulled the buggy inside. She lifted Kes out and took him over to the old lady.

"I've brought you a visitor."

She sat on the floor and held Kes up so that he stood by Letitia's knee. With impeccable manners he held his arms up to her, not minding her fierce face and her whiskers and her old-ladies' smell. He was undoubtedly an enchanting baby, in spite of being by Gin out of Beryl.

"It's not yours, is it?"

"No. It's Gin's. You know Gin."

"Yes, I know Gin. Well. Fancy."

Letitia considered Kes and the baby stared back, unblinking, entirely well-disposed.

"That's a nice child."

"Yes. Here." Rosy knelt up and lifted Kes onto Letitia's lap. Kes reached for one of Letitia's rings, pulling the finger up to his mouth. Letitia smiled.

Rosy felt bad, that she had left her all alone after delivering the dinner, but at the same time impatient. Letitia was Jeremy's pigeon, for heaven's sake—certainly on Christmas Day.

As if the message had exploded in some way in the ether, Jeremy appeared, like the good fairy in a pantomime—a tentative knock at the door and an uncertain hail, "Gran?"

He came in. Rosy felt herself go scarlet in the gloom. She scrambled up from the floor, seeing Jeremy equally startled and embarrassed. Her emotions stretched already by this curious afternoon, Rosy felt a surge of pure, stinging, sexual love overtake her, an agony of wanting—of having wanted for so long. Her heart raced, robbing her of both speech and sense. She had to turn away and stoke the fire.

"Fancy," said Letitia. "All these visitors."

"I've come to drink your health, Gran. Apologize for my neglect and all that."

Jeremy suddenly noticed Letitia's tears, felt furious to be found wanting on Christmas Day, and as if by instinct his eyes turned to the Stubbs painting, seeking reasurrance in the eternal peace that abounded in the landscape of his ancestors. Rosy saw the direction of his glance and her acute embarrassment over her sexual feelings was immediately replaced by an equal embarrassment at being caught in the act of courting the old woman for her possessions—or so it could be construed. Jeremy noticed her reaction and knew what she was thinking. His happy visit was disastrous, even before a conversation was started.

The bottle of Cointreau he had brought was a life-saver. Rosy fetched the glasses from the cabinet and set them on the old brass trivet in the hearth. Her ferocious assault on Letitia's stove had resulted in a cheerful burst of flame. Jeremy poured the drinks generously and they sat on the hearthrug in the firelight reviving the festive atmosphere. It worked. Gazing into flames had a distinctly soothing effect—indeed, glowing, after the Cointreau.

"Marvellous stuff," said Jeremy.

"Reminds me of hunting. I always put this in my flask," said Letitia, and Rosy saw her again as the Munnings girl, fearless across country. Fearless too in old age, except on Christmas Day. Rosy took Kes off her, and he lay quietly in her arms watching the fire. Any likely conversation being spiked with danger, nothing was said. And just as Rosy saw Letitia's eyes close and the empty glass fall sideways in her lap, she felt Kes grow heavy with sleep in her arms. She was effectively alone with Jeremy. Momentary panic slithered into amusement and pleasure and the ominous—a touch inebriated—shiver of desire. The ill-tempered day had flowered . . . how unpredictable it all was. She could not move, because of Kes, and sat cradling him, smiling into the flames.

From where he sat Jeremy saw Rosy crouching on the hearth with the Stubbs picture on the wall behind her. He too was aware that they were virtually alone in a distinctly inviting situation, but it was as if old Stubbs was on guard.

Strangely, Rosy now seemed quite different from the reliable girl in the stable he had taken for granted for the last few years. Taken out of context, he saw her suddenly as someone entirely congenial and attractive. She was strong, trustworthy, loyal and unstrident. All the virtues. With brandy coursing through his bloodstream he felt an ardour unknown since the days of Judith Partridge overtake him. Yet such was his perpetual condition of self-doubt and self-denial that he could not overcome habitual caution. In fact he felt that his uncommon stirrings were perhaps a sentimental weakness due to the combination of its being Christmas Day and of having had too much to drink before lunch.

"I haven't fed Jasper," Letitia said suddenly, and sat up, the Cointreau glass falling into the hearth. It smashed on the flags. Kes woke and started to cry.

"I must go back. Beryl will wonder what I'm doing," Rosy said.

Jeremy swept up the glass. He thought of asking Letitia to go back home with him, but abandoned the idea immediately. Brood House did not appeal, with or without Letitia. He had been out all day and lunched in a hotel with racing friends, and when Rosy departed with Kes, he felt bereft and abandoned. He knew the godly thing to have done would have been to stay and get Letitia's tea and watch television with her, but even while the thought was going through his head he was putting on his coat and departing.

Out in the garden he tried to sort out his feelings through an alcoholic haze. Rosy Weeks! He wanted babies and a warm home, and someone in bed to talk to. What was he doing with his life?

He had to go back and feed the horses because everyone had the evening off, and when he had done that he drove to the Maddoxes very fast, and introduced himself into their postprandial torpor.

Margaret Maddox greeted him warmly at the front door, while Grace reached wildly for her high heels, and raced upstairs to do her face before Jeremy saw her. Margaret was genuinely pleased to see Jeremy, because he was so nice. She couldn't help giving him a hug and a kiss, and he looked a little surprised. "Let me get you a drink. What will you have?"

Jeremy's yearning for family comforts was suddenly granted: this gracious house, full of Margaret's comfortable touches, warmth and affection . . . he felt pleased to belong. When Grace came down she stood in the doorway showing herself off, simulating surprise, and then offering a welcome both effusive and sexual, pressing her lips softly against his own, so that he realized that all he wanted was perfectly attainable. If he were to ask Grace to marry him, tonight, she would accept. The trouble was, he preferred her mother.

Friends arrived and Margaret and old Hugh took more drink to sustain them. They ate mince pies, young Hugh put on some music and old Hugh went out for more logs. Jeremy went to help him, but Grace was in the kitchen, starting to make coffee, and she called out to him as he crossed the hall, so loudly that he could not possibly pretend not to hear. Reluctantly he went in. Grace wore a frilly apron and was flushed and looked rather magnificent. The bright blonde hair tumbled. When she came up to him he caught her in his arms just as she was obviously hoping he would. Her kiss was far more passionate than his own, so that he had to adjust, allow his natural impulses to take over and stop thinking about the consequences. He kissed her neck, and started to work his way down, but the coffee boiled over and Hugh could be heard thumping the log basket down in the hall so he had to come up for air. He was surprised, and rather pleased with himself.

"Oh, Jeremy!" Grace was ecstatic as she dived for the coffee.

Whatever had he been wasting time for? he wondered. He had not been entirely celibate since Judith Partridge, but had certainly forgotten the taste of passion and excitement.

They made the coffee together, and carried it in to the music and chatter. Christmas certainly had something to answer for, he thought as he had another Cointreau.

7

Jeremy felt bad about Rosy. The two or three minutes sitting on the hearth with her in his grandmother's house had made an impression, fleeting, elusive, but remembered quite clearly. Whether Rosy had been aware of anything he had no idea. He had avoided speaking to her since, because he did not know how to treat her. He felt bad about Roly Fox too, and not too good about the Silverfish filly which Gin desperately wanted to sell, being so deep in debt— not a sound start for a partnership. Jeremy knew of no way to help Gin, and reflected sadly on the perils of marriage. Which brought him back to Grace.

Grace wanted to marry him.

"Why?" Jeremy asked her, lifting his head from between her rather flat breasts on one of the evenings he had taken her upstairs to occupy Letitia's marriage bed ("Staying late to do the entries"). "What difference would it make?"

"It would regularize the situation."

"I am a very indecisive person. I like it as it is now."

"Oh, Jeremy, that's the trouble with you. You would get on so much better if you—" she hesitated, remembering that people did not like to be told what was wrong with them.

"Married you?"

"Went for what you really wanted. I could help you in so many ways."

This was true. The house was actually habitable now Grace had possession. There was hot water in the tap, bread in the breadbin, a new ribbon for the typewriter. The well-ordered household undermined his resistance. Marrying Grace would be simple and undemanding. The Maddox family would embrace him. Grace would enchant owners and cook them delicious lunches, look good in the paddock, and keep immaculate books. The marriage was obviously meant.

He turned away from Grace and lay with his hands behind his head. He played with the words on his tongue: "All right. Let's get married." But said nothing.

Grace waited, frowning. She found Jeremy infuriatingly elusive. Sometimes she wanted to shake him. But she took long calming breaths, and turned to him, pressing herself against his slender body and smiling tightly. "I do love you, Jeremy."

He did not think she knew the meaning of the word love. Remembering Judith Partridge, he knew only too well that the essential ingredient was lacking between them. He did not say anything.

Her eyes glittered. "Have you always been so undemonstrative?"

He smiled at her and stroked her hair gently, knowing he must get up in a minute and do his round of the horses. This nightly ten o'clock habit was apt to annoy Grace. Cautiously he slid away from her, with a casual, "Must go and do the rounds."

Grace gritted her teeth and buried her face in the pillow.

Going out into the night, Jeremy felt the spring-touched breeze off the downs fresh in his face, and his whole being gave an impulsive shiver of delight. What it meant he had no idea, but he whistled as he made his way to the first loosebox.

PUSHING HER WAY through the paddock crowds at Towcester, Rosy cursed her compulsive determination to see Roly Fox run again, knowing how it would distress her. He was entered for a three-mile handicap but in recent months had become so ill-considered that the bookies were offering him at twenty to one. Even Beryl was not betting on him this time. Brood House had no runners, but Rosy had asked for the afternoon off and begged a lift from a friend of her father's who was going to Northampton on business. How she was going to get home she had no idea.

I'm round the bend, she thought. In love with a bloody horse. She had tried not to think about him, but his stupid, honest face haunted her. She had tried earnestly to shift her allegiance to Dark Secret, but the filly wanted no friends. She was as haughty as her dam, and no one would ever do her down. She had no will to please, to do her best, like Roly; she was all hot blood and give-me-my-way.

Why do I do this? Seeking out Roly in the paddock was no joy; seeing his sad eyes as he went past was misery indeed. All his zest and bounce were now extinguished; he walked lethargically, hardly bothering to remove his gaze from the buttocks of the horse in front. She tried to convince herself that it was all in the mind . . . she tried every argument in the book, and remained unconvinced. Roly was unhappy and so was she.

Smith, she thought, looked dead worried. The field was not a classy one; in his prime Roly could have beaten them with ease, but Roly was now a has-been. Before the jockeys mounted Smith had a long, animated discussion with his jockey, Parkins, and then Roly was led through and cantered down to the start. Rosy, on an impulse, followed Smith and stood by him in the stand, waiting for the off.

The ground was soft, which suited Roly. On the first circuit he was running well enough, pushed by Parkins, and by the time they came round the bottom on the last circuit and hit the hill again he was in the lead. But the testing course was cruel to horses not in the top of condition and rivals Roly could once have shaken off with ease lobbed after him only a couple of lengths adrift. Rosy could see that it was going to be a hard race, and a glimpse of Smith convinced her that Roly was intended to win—Smith was tight-lipped and tense and muttering oaths.

Parkins started to ride like a demon, legs and arms flailing. Roly came to the last and jumped bravely, but was virtually on three legs as he made his way to the post. Two other horses hung to his girth and the crowd roared; Parkins's whip whistled into the dull hide, and Rosy wept.

"You bastard!" But Smith did not hear her, white from the tension. At twenty to one he had made his pile. Roly, like the good servant he was, had played his part, and could now go on the scrap heap which was all he was good for. Rosy pushed her way through to the winners' enclosure and saw Roly limp home, bewildered by pain. Smith made a show of concern over the leg, while his lad held Roly's head, and Roly stood heaving. Rosy went to him and, even in his state of distress, the old horse lifted his head and shoved his muzzle into her outstretched hand. But the lad pulled him roughly away and said, "You've no right here."

He swore at her. Rosy opened her mouth to reply in what would have been an unwise fashion, but a hand descended on her shoulder and a voice said tersely, "Shut up."

It was Jeremy.

"Come away or you'll get yourself into trouble." He put his arm round her and steered her firmly out of the enclosure and away from the crowd. Rosy, all screwed up, was ungrateful and said angrily, "Did you see what happened?"

"Yes, I did. That's the way of the world, Rosy. Come and have a drink."

"Don't you care?"

"I'm sorry about Roly, that such a decent animal should be used in that way, yes, but now he's played his part I daresay he'll be turned out and have a rest. He certainly won't be able to race again for a while."

Rosy tried to pull herself together, much surprised by the arrival of Jeremy out of the blue.

She followed him to the bar. "I know you think I'm a fool, but that horse—he's special."

"Think straight, and you'll see that nothing's as bad as it seems. He's worth pretty well nothing at all at the moment. Perhaps you could scrape up enough cash to make an offer, if it means that much to you."

He left her and went to buy the drinks, and Rosy stood staring out of the window towards the paddock, where the horses were already circling for the next race. Could it be as simple as that? With Hawkins's tips she had saved up a thousand or so, which was meant to be going towards running the filly. She was not a complete pauper.

When Jeremy came back she said, "Can we go and talk to Smith, before he goes?"

"No. Give him a day or two. You have to sleep on these things. Cool it, Rosy, or he'll take you for a ride."

He took her to a table and sat her down, and Rosy wanted to ask what he was doing at Towcester, but did not like to. Perhaps Grace was lurking somewhere. He smiled. "You should have had your money on."

Rosy had a mental vision of Beryl reading of Roly's win at twenty to one when for the first time she hadn't bet on him, and nearly choked on her whisky.

"Poor Beryl! I persuaded her he wasn't worth a bet!"

Jeremy laughed. "Do her good! Do you want a lift home, or are you with anyone?"

"No, I'm not. Thank you."

Sitting beside him in the fuggy interior of his Audi, Rosy was aware that the events of the day were rather special, but the mixture was wearying, and she could not remember, when she got home, whether anything significant had taken place. Jeremy was a changed character these days, considerate and positively outgoing, and Rosy put it down to the relationship with Grace. He was as good as married, it seemed, and it was only a matter of time before the union actually took place. He never said how he had come to be at Towcester.

When she got home she felt very depressed and restless. She ate and washed up and it was still too early to go to bed. She went out into the garden and stared up at Brood House on the hillside. But all was in darkness, and Jeremy—no doubt—out gallivanting with Grace, his beloved.

While she was undressing to get into bed, Rosy heard the telephone ring downstairs. No one rang so late. She went down to answer it with slight apprehension. She lifted the receiver, and heard the sound of money going into a callbox.

"It's me, Trace. You gave me a fiver once, to tell you about Roly Fox."

"Oh, yes, thanks. I went to Towcester today. I saw him."

"Yeah, well. I thought you might like to know, he's going to the knacker's in the morning. Lorry's coming at nine." The telephone went dead.

Rosy stood with it in her hand, frozen. What had Jeremy said? Sleep on it, cool it. But the likes of Smith, having got what they wanted, did not hang around. Roly was only fit for the knacker's after that race, and every oat spent on him now was money down the drain. Rosy rang Jeremy's number at Brood House. The ring went on and on. He was in bed with Grace, Rosy guessed, and let it ring. On and on.

At last, an irritable voice, "Yes? Cutbush speaking."

Rosy, shivering, said, "Roly Fox is going to be put down in the morning."

"What? Is that Rosy?"

"Yes. At nine o'clock."

"Oh, God. The swine. What do you want then? To go up there?"

"Yes. Yes, please, I do." There was a long silence.

"OK. Suppose I pick you up at—say—seven thirty. That should do. I'll ring Hugh and he can see to things. We could be back soon after ten. Suit you?"

"Yes. Oh, yes."

"I'll call for you. That'd be best."

"All right."

She would be ready. She was ready now. She did not even want to undress. Suppose Jeremy got a puncture, or overslept. Suppose the knacker came early and they missed him? Rosy went back to bed and lay awake, shivering under the blankets. Either it was very cold or she had something wrong with her. She had Roly wrong with her. Roly on the brain, Roly in the heart; she was demented, Roly was only a horse. Yet Jeremy had not scoffed, nor even debated coming. That thought helped. She thought she would never go to sleep, but in fact slept heavily when dawn came, and awoke to the alarm feeling drugged and heavy. She dragged herself out of bed and went to the window. Mist lay thickly over the valley, the downs above shouldering out into the sky like icebergs over an ocean. She could hear the stream that ran through the village—where she had stood Roly all through the summer—and she could smell the damp, strong promise of spring. Life was full of promise, but Roly was for the knacker's today.

Rosy pulled on her working clothes and went downstairs quietly, not waking her father. She made herself some coffee but could not eat anything. She felt sick, like when she was at school, before exams. The worse she felt, the more she despised herself. All for a bloody horse!

Jeremy arrived on the dot. He was bright-eyed and freshly shaved, business-like and unsentimental. Rosy got into the car and fastened her seatbelt.

"What are we going for?" Jeremy asked. "We must know what we intend to do. Do you want to make an offer for Roly, to buy him?"

"Yes. I've got more than carcass money, which is all Smith is going to get."

"That's right. He won't get the insurance to pay if he has him put down—although I doubt if he insures his horses. What if he asks a big price?"

"Why ever should he?"

"Oh, Rosy, don't be so innocent! You want him badly. It shows, you know, arriving before nine o'clock with a chequebook in your hand. You're dealing with a shark."

"I've got a thousand pounds. And Dark Secret. That's all."

"That's more than he'll get from the knacker. We'll just have to keep our fingers crossed. Play it by ear. Perhaps I'm doing the man an injustice."

Jeremy drove fast, hurtling through the spring morning, past fields of lambs and dripping woods and brimming watermeadows all smelling of new life and rebirth and an optimistic future. Rosy sat in silence, in a turmoil of doubt and despair.

Smith's yard was as she had envisaged it, a muddle of do-it-yourself buildings round a muddy yard, a shaggy manure heap prominent, a squat bungalow by the gate, guarded by a mangy, barking dog chained to a kennel. Half a dozen horses were about to go out on exercise, and Smith was emerging from the bungalow as Jeremy pulled up.

"Shall I do the talking?" Jeremy offered. "I think it would be best."

"Yes."

"Stay here then."

Jeremy got out and went to greet Smith. Rosy sat shrinking in her seat, shivering. She saw the two men talking for a minute or two, then Smith gestured to one of the lads to lead out on exercise without him, and he went back into the house with Jeremy. When they had gone, the dog stopped barking and went back into its kennel. For a few minutes the yard was empty and silent. Then a lorry came up the road and turned into the drive. The name on the front was the name of the slaughterer. The driver got out and went to the bungalow, and the dog started barking again. Smith came to the door and said something to the driver who went back to the lorry, got in the cab and pulled out a packet of cigarettes. The dog went on barking. Rosy watched all this as if she were watching a play on television.

When the lorry driver was about halfway through his cigarette Jeremy came out of the house alone and came back to Rosy. He got into the driving seat.

"I told you," he said.

"What is it?"

"He wants the price he paid for him, three thousand two hundred. I've knocked him down to three thousand. It's up to you, Rosy. I can help you out for the time being, but in the long run, I can't afford to pay two thousand out for a dud horse. I wish I could."

"I would have to sell the filly."

"We could stall. Let him load Roly and go to the knacker's. At the last moment, he might change his mind. But then if we were to follow, he'd know how badly we want the horse. I'm afraid it's a bit of an impasse."

"Three thousand? The filly would fetch enough, wouldn't she? I know Gin wants to sell her."

"Oh, yes, I reckon she'd fetch that."

Jeremy did not press her. He did not tell her how stupid she was, what a waste of money it was, that Roly was worth nothing.

There was a stubborn bit of her that—seeing what a fool she was quite clearly—could not give in. "Yes, tell him he can have the money. If you can loan me the two thousand until we sell—"

"That's no problem."

Jeremy went back into the bungalow. He was away for about ten minutes. Then he came out with Smith, who went to the lorry driver and said something to him. The driver put out his cigarette, started up his engine and departed. Jeremy came back to the car. "That's it then. Three thousand pounds, and he'll deliver him tonight, after racing."

Rosy smiled.

She felt wonderful. Having thrown away her hard-earned tips, all her hopes of the filly, she felt marvellous.

"I'm sorry I'm such a fool," she said. But she couldn't stop grinning.

Jeremy glanced at her and smiled too. "Money isn't everything."

ROLY'S LEG WAS AS BAD as Rosy had seen in her lifetime, and for a couple of weeks the tacit opinion in the yard was that it would have been kinder to have let Smith have his way. Only Gin was delighted at the way things had turned out, with the decision to sell Dark Secret. The filly was entered for Tattersalls' next sale at Newmarket, early in May. Rosy hardened her heart against what might have been, only grateful that she had the means to pay Jeremy back. Or assumed she had the means . . . it was hard to foresee what sort of price the filly would fetch.

"I think you're crazy, honestly," Grace announced, pausing to regard Rosy in her eternal chore, playing the cold water hose over Roly's swollen leg. "Throwing away all that money, and the filly too. Still, I suppose you'll never be short, not with the Stubbs Letitia is leaving you. It must be worth a bomb."

"Who said she's leaving it to me?"

"She's made her will, saying so. Hasn't she told you?"

"Not that she's made a will. I don't want it—it's always belonged to the family."

Grace laughed. "Oh, Rosy! You must be joking! You don't want it? You don't expect me to believe that?"

"I don't mind a memento or a hundred quid or something. But not the picture. It's too valuable, it's a family thing. How do you know about the will? Nobody's told me."

"Jeremy told me."

Grace was feeling at her most bitchy, Jeremy having taken to treating her more like a secretary than a lover lately. She was making no progress with him at all and was trying to screw herself up to give him an ultimatum.

"You don't believe everyone thinks that you do all that for Letitia out of neighbourliness? Even Jeremy can't stand the sight of her. She's such a bad-tempered old bag. But she needs someone to help her, and I suppose if you're prepared to put the time in, you deserve what she—"

Without thinking twice, Rosy switched the hose and turned it on Grace. The jet hit her full in the mouth and turned her further conversation into a choking howl of anger. Rosy stood staring, astonished at her own impulse. She took her finger off the jet and the water fell away, soaking Grace's tweeds and filling her shoes and gurgling down the drain.

For a moment Rosy thought Grace was going to hit her. Seeing her rage, stunned by her malice, Rosy felt a heartening swoop of pure joy, suddenly aware that someone as sound as Jeremy would never marry a bitch like Grace. It just wasn't possible.

"I'm sorry, but you asked for that."

She went back to Roly's leg again, turning her back. Grace flounced away, and found herself in the path of Mr. Hawkins's Rolls, just scraping through the gateway. The window purred down and Hawkins said, "Grace, my dear! How are you?"

Glancing up, Rosy saw Grace make a great effort to look as if being soaked by a cold-water hose was part of everyday occurrences at Brood.

"Just a slight accident with the hose—I must go in and change."

Even in such an extremity it came naturally to Grace to toss her wet hair back and smile brightly, because Hawkins was a male.

"Thought I'd just look in on Spinning Wheel—passing near, you know." He smiled at Rosy as she untied Roly to lead him back to his box. "This isn't one of mine, it it?"

If he was to produce his fifty-pound note, Rosy thought she would throw it back in his face. Hawkins did not even recognize Roly Fox, the gamest horse he was ever likely to lay eyes on, who had won him a small fortune in bets. She turned her back on the man and led Roly back into his box. She crouched in the straw, her fingers working neatly and tenderly as she rebandaged the damaged leg, trying not to think of Grace discussing her with Jeremy, finding out about the picture. Surely Jeremy did not think she had helped Letitia with an eye to getting a reward? Grace might, but surely not Jeremy.

She finished the bandage off, much disturbed, and laid her cheek briefly on Roly's neck, sniffing his hide gratefully. He was poor and skinny and dead lame, but the misery had gone from his eyes and his rabbity ears were interested in life once more. He butted her with his bonehead, and Rosy gave him a last caress before hurrying on to attend to the horses she was paid to look after.

SITTING ON A STRAW BALE outside Dark Secret's box at Park Paddocks, Newmarket, waiting for customers, Rosy had to admit that a spring day in the heartland of racing England had much to recommend it. The silken grass lawns rolled gently between yards of beautifully appointed looseboxes. This was the smart end of racing, where horses raced on summer turf and racegoers strolled in summer dresses and shirtsleeves and sat out on flower-bedecked terraces clinking the ice in their drinks. Rosy had had visions that she too might grace a paddock as an owner with Jeremy this summer, but her visions were now away in the clouds: her assets were for sale.

"Tell me why, with a mare like Silverfish, Mrs. Cutbush put her to a no-hoper like Understanding?"

An elegant woman studying the catalogue was talking to her companion, an expensively suited, dark-skinned man. Rosy had overheard this remark several times.

The man said, "I'm not interested in an Understanding."

"Pity," said the woman, looking at Dark Secret over the door. "She's very nice."

They strolled away, leaving Rosy depressed. Dark Secret was well grown and very good-looking, and Rosy could only hope that it was on these qualities she would raise the bids, along with her illustrious dam. The less said about the bogus sire the better.

"Funny time of year to sell a two-year-old." An incredibly handsome, blond youth with a gnarled, broken-nosed older man paused by the box.

"That can mean anything. She looks fit, doesn't she? Sharp."

"The dam's got a lot of form. Grand-dam won the Thousand

344

Guineas and the St. Leger. Perhaps the genes are ready to spring again, Dad. That's how it works sometimes."

"Or the line dies out, more often. We'll have a look at her, if you like."

Rosy sprang up and led Dark Secret out into the yard. She stood to be examined, lipping at Rosy's hand. Nobody could fault her looks and condition, thanks to Rosy's hard work. Her spring coat had settled on grey, a dark steel grey still mottled over her quarters with faint splashes of light and dark. Some viewers had not liked this oddity, but the more discerning were impressed by the apparent throwback to The Tetrarch through six generations. Rosy walked and trotted her, and she went obediently, all spring and contained fire, action long and smooth. How could they not admire?

They did. "Very nice. Very nice." Pencillings in the catalogue.

Rosy put her away, encouraged. The boy looking after the mare in the next-door box came back from lunch and said he would show Dark Secret for her to any interested parties if she wanted to go and get a cup of tea, so Rosy wandered off and looked at some of the competition. Gin had disappeared, in spite of promises to relieve. Jeremy had said he would come.

Rosy leaned on the paddock rail where the animals soon to go into the ring were paraded before entering. She thought how smooth and well-mannered it all was, compared to the world of steeplechasing. Perhaps, when Jeremy married Grace and she herself left Brood, she would turn to flat racing.

The loudspeaker intoned the bids from inside the ring: the voice of inexorable selling, the smooth professional patter that hid all the human folly, ambition, chance and glory that underlaid the thoroughbred breeding industry.

"Had many customers looking?"

Expecting Gin, Rosy found Jeremy.

"Yes. Quite a few."

"That's a good sign. She shows herself so well."

Rosy no longer called Jeremy "sir". She was not sure why this was. Over the past year something had altered in their relationship. The business with Roly, and now with Dark Secret, seemed to have led them into a special kind of friendship. She did not suppose in her wildest dreams that Jeremy thought there was anything significant in it. But he no longer treated her as just a lad, more of a head lad, if it had to be declared in racing parlance. They got on well, in the same way as she had once got on well with Gin. At thirty, she thought, she was beginning to grow up.

"You never know your luck," he said. "She's ready to run, after all. She looks good. You might be able to retire after this."

"Do you think?"

"Well, perhaps it's best not to be too hopeful. Have you had anything to eat?"

"I think I'll just get a snack and go back. I don't want to miss any buyers."

Jeremy escorted her to the bar and bought her sausage rolls and coffee, and then said he had people to see and would come back when the filly was due in the ring. Rosy supposed Grace was around, but when it was time to take Dark Secret out to the parade ring Jeremy came back with Gin. It was evening, fine and warm, and the crowds were back from the races and filling the sales building. Rosy was nervous.

"Shall we go and find a seat?" Jeremy suggested.

Gin had charge of the filly. They left him, climbed up the staircase into the sales ring and took a seat opposite the entrance. There were four lots to go before Dark Secret, and Rosy sat in mounting apprehension while Jeremy scanned the buyers for any likely faces.

When Dark Secret came in she hesitated at the strangeness of her surroundings, but Gin soothed her and she walked on boldly, showing off her swinging walk. Looking down on her, Rosy reckoned she had done a good job, engineering such a filly. The auctioneer read out her description and dwelt on the erstwhile fame of the dam as instructed, listing Silverfish's other winning progeny, ignoring the sire, and then vigorously pointing out the good action, conformation and condition. Rosy's pulse was starting to thump uncomfortably.

"A two-year-old, in training and ready to run straightaway for her new owner. This is a great opportunity . . ."

He tried to start her at five thousand, dropped to four, to three, and got his first bid, by which time Rosy was in a sweat of agony. From the three the bids climbed steadily to six, to seven, where one bidder dropped out. There was a long holdup, the auctioneer very patient, pleading and cajoling, then someone else came in at eight and the bidding climbed steadily to twelve thousand. By this time Rosy was feeling quite sick with excitement.

Jeremy glanced at her and grinned. "I reckon you'll be retiring after this."

"I can't believe it!"

She had been so terrified the filly would not make her even the two thousand she owed Jeremy. Now, splitting with Gin, she was four thousand to the good.

"Twelve thousand five hundred? Thank you, sir. The bid is on my right . . ."

Dark Secret had her admirers. The price danced up to fifteen thousand, and hovered there. Rosy had her eyes on the tickertape figures spluttering on the indicator board, hardly daring to breathe. Gin was looking poker-faced as he hurried round to the filly's long, powerful stride.

"Sixteen thousand? Thank you. I am bid sixteen thousand."

Rosy thought, Six thousand guineas. I have six thousand guineas for myself. It was a fortune.

The bidding went to another five hundred. And another.

At seventeen thousand five hundred it stopped. The auctioneer brought his hammer down.

Rosy looked at Jeremy, jubilant, and he put his arm round her and gave her a hug. "Well done! I'm really pleased for you."

Rosy found it hard to believe. She went down the stairs behind Jeremy, walking very carefully, trying to stop the idiotic grin bursting over her face. Outside the exit doors Gin was waiting with Dark Secret. Grace and Mr. Hawkins were standing with him.

"What a splendid price!" Grace called out, all smiles. "Wasn't it much better than you expected?"

"Yes. A lot."

"Well done, Gin. Congratulations," Jeremy said. Gin looked happier than he had done since he was married. Perhaps the thought struck Jeremy, for he added, "Don't let that wife of yours spend it all now."

"I will not, sir. It's great news. Eh, Rosy?"

"Oh, Gin!" Rosy gave him a hug. "Isn't it lovely?"

"Yeah—until she wins the Oaks!"

Laughs all round. An elderly groom came up to take Dark Secret. "For Mr. Pemberton's stable. We'll be taking her home right away. Two miles up the road—she's not got a long journey."

He was kindly, gentle, a real groom. Mr. Pemberton, apparently, was the man with the broken nose and the blond son.

Grace, with two men in attendance, drinks and dinner in the offing, was in her element. Rosy, watching her, knew perfectly well that she was toying with the idea of telling Hawkins how Dark Secret had been bred. If Hawkins had been able to tell one horse from another, it should have struck him how like Peppermill the filly was; he would not have needed Grace's advice. But Jeremy, sensing the same mischief, took Grace firmly by the arm and said to Rosy, "You'll go back in the box with Gin?"

"Yes."

"A good day's work. Well done."

With which he departed with Grace and Mr. Hawkins, and Rosy was back to her station again. She took her leave of her lovely filly, thinking of the money and not of the cold morning Silverfish first took the little thing out into the frosty air . . . *my* filly, she thought stubbornly, whatever happens afterwards. And she made for home with Gin, perched in the familiar lorry, trying to realize that things weren't quite the same any more.

8

"Will you come to Ascot with us, if we take you in the car? To see Dark Secret run?"

"Eh?" Letitia was at the field gate when Rosy came in the evening to check on Roly Fox.

"We've just been talking about it. It was Gin's idea. We're going in the car and he said ask you. Like old times. It's Royal Ascot week—Dark Secret is entered for the Queen Mary Stakes. Can you believe it?"

Excited herself, Rosy knew the old girl could not make head nor tail of what she was talking about. Leaning beside her on the gate, she spelt it all out slowly, looking down the field towards the river where Silverfish and Roly Fox grazed side by side, tails switching rhythmically to the evening midges.

"We'd look after you, so you won't get too tired. We'll get seats in the grandstand, do it properly. What do you think? When did you last go to Ascot? Silverfish won at Ascot, didn't she?"

"Hmm." The old girl frowned into the evening. "Peter won't be there."

"No." Peter had been dead for forty years.

"Someone will have to feed Jasper."

"We can leave his food down. He'll be all right."

"I'll think about it."

"You must! You'll love it, to see it all again. The Queen and everything."

"The King. He spoke to us, you know. He shook hands with us."

Was it cruel, starting old memories? How could you tell, trying to figure how the tiring brain worked, what was good for it, what bad?

"Fancy, our filly being entered for the Queen Mary! They must think highly of her."

Dark Secret had run once, at Newmarket, and been fourth in a large field. Jeremy had been very impressed. Rosy kept thinking about it, warmly. If they had kept Dark Secret, would she still have come fourth at Newmarket and be entered for the Queen Mary? Who could tell?

"I'll sleep on it," Mrs. Cutbush said.

"You do that. And say yes in the morning."

Rosy walked down to the river and Roly came towards her, friendly and accommodating. His leg was improving very slowly, he had put on weight and the old sheen was back on his hide. He was now as happy as a horse could be, back with his old companion, Silverfish. Rosy still found that walking through this field in the evening or early morning, to see the horses, gave her pleasure out of all proportion. If she went to work elsewhere, there would be a great loss. She felt she belonged here, on this ground, where Dark Secret had first seen the light of day, and the old horses found solace. It was a part of her. How stupid, mocked her common sense. She kept meaning to look for a new job. But never did.

When she called on Mrs. Cutbush the next day she was astonished to find her wearing a short-sleeved, full-skirted dress in white cotton with a pattern of red tulips splashed gaily over it. On her head was a red straw hat with a wide brim, a bunch of cherries with dark green leaves decorating one side, the grey hair escaping in loops beneath. Her sticklike arms, which Rosy had never seen uncovered, protruded from the caped shoulderline to reveal the pathetic frailty of the ancient frame; equally spindly legs in shiny stockings supported the strange edifice, shod in dirty white satin shoes of ancient design.

"The shoes don't fit any more. They pinch me," she said. "I wore this rig-out the last time I went to Ascot."

"It's fantastic!" Rosy was touched. It was funny, but not to be laughed at. "You look marvellous!"

Letitia allowed her to take the dress home to wash and iron, and Rosy tactfully shortened it a little at the same time. To her great relief, Letitia agreed to wear one of her classy but ancient long cardigans over the dress—"You aren't used to having your arms bare. You don't want to get a chill." It was a deep plum colour, and calmed the initial impact of the bright tulips considerably. A pair of leather sandals found in the back of the wardrobe completed the picture, still eye-catching but—Rosy hoped—no longer grotesque.

Bizarre. It was OK to be bizarre, after all, especially when, in the past, you had led your own horses into the winners' enclosure.

At the last moment Rosy panicked about the outing and mentioned it to Jeremy. "I should have told you. You don't think it'll be too much for her? We just thought it would be such a splendid day out."

"God, Rosy, it's a fantastic idea! I'm ashamed the thought never crossed my own mind. You're a saint. Actually, I had thought of going with Grace. Shall we arrange to meet? You bring Gran out to the paddock to see the filly, and I'll try and find you. Get a place in plenty of time and you can sit her down."

"I'll try. Yes. I'll look out for you."

On the Wednesday morning of Royal Ascot week the motley racegoers from Brood packed into Gin's ancient Cortina. Mrs. Cutbush sat in the front, holding her hat, while Gin in his wedding suit and a rather dubious blue tie, fastened her seatbelt solicitously. Beryl read *The Sporting Life* in the back, noting that Dark Secret was offered at ten to one. Kes had been left with Gin's mother.

It was a perfect day, clear and cloudless, a slight breeze keeping the temperature at a comfortable level. Rosy blessed it, having been afraid that Letitia might be tempted to shed her cardigan. When they arrived Gin set his passengers down at the members' entrance and arranged to meet them when he had parked the car. Rosy and Beryl took Letitia to the nearest bar and Gin joined them as planned, ready for his first pint.

"There's no point the four of us being tied to the old girl," Rosy whispered to Gin. "Leave her to me. You and Beryl go and do your own thing and I'll meet you here after the last."

Rosy took Letitia up into the grandstand to watch the royal party arrive in their horse-drawn carriages. She gave her her own binoculars, and Letitia peered diligently in all directions, muttering and exclaiming. Her eyes glittered like a child's. Rosy sat back, thinking that in Letitia's day it had been no different: the throng of racing's richest participators, a galaxy of obvious wealth and privilege from the rows of Rollers in the car parks to the champagne corks popping in the bars: the sport at its most picturesque. Yet behind the glitter, in the stables, on the gallops, the whole business worked in exactly the same way as they worked at Brood. The top dressing was incidental . . . a charade that—to a real racegoer—cluttered one of the year's very best meetings.

Getting Letitia to the paddock to meet Jeremy was a major operation in the crush. Holding her firmly by her skinny arm, Rosy took her down the stairs and out across the crowded lawns. She got to the all-important oval of tree-shaded turf before the preceding race finished, and seated her on one of the toadstool-like seats in front of the rails. Already three fillies were being led round. One of them was Dark Secret.

"Look, that's her! Silverfish's filly!"

Behind them the crowd roared its winner home, and Dark Secret paused in her step, her ears pricking up to the noise. She was as beautiful a thoroughbred as Rosy had ever set eyes on. The groom who had taken her from Newmarket was leading her, smiling, gentling her with words.

"Hi, Gran, you made it! How does it feel to be back here again?" As good as his word, Jeremy joined them before the crush started, with Grace at his side. He was wearing formal dress, and Grace was bedecked in canary frills, showing a lot of flat brown chest. Rosy saw her eyes rake Letitia's splendid show of tulips and the resplendent hat, saw the mirth bursting, suppressed, felt the malice. Seeing Rosy's face, Grace froze over.

"Your grandfather won the Queen Mary before the war," Letitia said to Jeremy. "With a filly by Mr. Jinks. His grandsire was The Tetrarch, you know. He did like that strain."

The other fillies came in, nervous, flirting with their bits, eyes staring at the bright crowd. The paddock filled with owners and trainers. Rosy glimpsed the blond young man in grey tails, and his broken-nosed father. Their trainer was one of the top five, and their jockey was a household name. Bright as a parakeet, he flipped up into the saddle and rode down past Letitia on the rails.

"Good luck, young man!" she called out boldly, and the crowd around them stared and tittered. The jockey touched his cap, to Rosy's amazement. They were not normally given to hearing remarks from the crowd.

"You'll never get her back into the grandstand in time," Jeremy said as the fillies left the paddock and the huge crowd surged back to their vantagepoints. "Shall we go and stand by the rails? We'll see the finish, at least. It's only five furlongs, after all. Hardly worth going into the grandstand for a minute's worth of racing. We'll hear the commentary."

They guided Letitia across the grass to the railside, where indeed they would see nothing until the finish itself.

Rosy listened to her heart pounding. She had never been so nervous about a horse racing, not even dear Roly. She'll end down the field, she told herself—a high-class race like this, don't hope for anything. It's impossible. The prize money was nearly thirty thousand pounds. We're in the big league. She'll win because we sold her . . .

"They're under starter's orders!" Oh, God!

"They're off!"

Rosy felt the blood thundering in her ears like the thunder of hooves on the hard turf. For the whole minute before they came into view she stood hardly breathing, screwed up with praying, eyes shut tight. The name Dark Secret was somewhere in the jumbled commentary, but the voice was all at sea, as she was herself. She felt fingers digging into her arm, Jeremy's voice bawling. "Come on, my girl! Dark Secret!"

Rosy heard screaming, and realized that it was herself.

The familiar, heart-wrenching crescendo of flying hooves overlaid the great crowd's roar as the field exploded into view, a tangle of colour and action. One filly came clear. She shot from the pack like a bullet fifty yards from the post and went on flying when the others had spent their strength, hurtling away down the wide green course as if she had another circuit to run.

"Dark Secret wins by three—four lengths! White Hyacinth second, Amritzar, Pagan Princess . . ."

"She's won!" Rosy flung herself into Jeremy's arms. He hugged her, kissed her, danced a wild circle, picked his grandmother up and kissed her.

"Your Silverfish has done it again, Gran! What a mare! What a filly! What a breeder! Congratulations, Rosy!"

Rosy found she was crying—tears of joy, half hysterics. The brilliance of the turf, the jockeys' silks and the Ascot dresses, whirled inside her head, and she was reaching for the fragile Letitia, thinking giddily, The excitement will kill her! "Are you all right, Mrs. Cutbush?"

"I'm very well, thank you."

"Shall we go and see her in the winners' enclosure? Oh, please!"

The crowd was thronging back. Rosy took the old lady's arm on one side and Jeremy took the other, and they hurried, half lifting the old lady over the grass. An officious gateman put a rope across their way to stop the crowd pressing up from the grandstand and they were caught on the wrong side. Jeremy went on shoving.

"This is Mrs. Cutbush, the breeder of the winner. Please let her through."

The gateman raised his bowler. "Mrs. Cutbush, congratulations, madam."

He lifted the rope back to let them through, and put it back just before Grace could make it.

"There, Gran, you're back in the winners' enclosure where you belong."

Jeremy introduced her to the excited, handsome boy, and his equally excited father, and the famous trainer, all waiting for their winner. Jeremy introduced Rosy too. "She broke in the filly. She handled her from a foal." They were enchanted with the amazing figure of their filly's breeder, her eyes sparkling, the red straw hat tipping rakishly over one eye with the cherries failing to counter-balance on the other side. Watching her, Rosy ached suddenly for these smart people to see her as Munnings had seen her in her youth, with her beautiful, imperious gaze, her lovely, sensitive hands and radiant red hair. But the newsmen were enchanted and camera bulbs were popping all over the place.

They drew back when Dark Secret was led in, to keep out of the picture, slipping away to a decent distance to admire their famous filly as she danced and cavorted in Ascot's place of honour.

"If I don't go to the lavatory soon, dear," Letitia said suddenly to Rosy, "I'll wet my drawers."

"I'll take you. We'll go now." She explained the situation to Jeremy.

"I'd better go and find Grace. I'll look for you in the grandstand for the next race then. Which end will you be?"

They made the best rendezvous they could, and Rosy set off with Letitia. The queue was enormous. "You can go through, I'll take you," Rosy said. "I'll ask the attendant."

Letitia battled her way through and a kindly attendant held the next door open for her, ahead of the crowd. Rosy slumped against a washbasin, still wrapped in the dream of winning. She still felt faint at this magic stroke of success, though she knew that when the gloss of the amazing day had worn off, she was going to be left with something close to heartbreak. If a filly like Dark Secret carried through with the promise she had just shown, she was likely to make half a million racing and command three times that to go to stud when she was finished. She, Rosy Weeks, had thrown away the chance of becoming a millionaire.

"Your gran's a long time in there, dear," said the attendant. "Do you think she's all right? Do you want to give her a call?"

Rosy looked up anxiously, unaware of how long she had stood gazing into space. She tried the door but it was locked.

"Mrs. Cutbush? Are you all right?"

No answer. Rosy knocked heavily, and shouted.

"Perhaps she's fainted. It's so hot," said the attendant. "I'll fetch a chair and we can look over the door."

Everyone was agog, staring. Rosy was deeply afraid. "I'll climb up. Give it to me." She shoved the chair against the door and lifted herself high to see over. Below her, huddled against the door, lay a heap of white and scarlet. The crazy hat covered her face, the bright cherries flung forward on the tiles.

"I'll ring through to first aid," the attendant said.

"Please, if you give me a leg-up, I can climb over."

A large horsy lady in grey silk pushed forward and gave Rosy a professional leg-up, so she got a knee over the top of the door. She lowered herself with infinite care, one leg reaching for the lavatory seat. Balanced, holding the partition, she could reach forward and unlatch the door. But Letitia lay against it, and it could not be opened.

"You shouldn't move her, dear! Wait for the first aid men. They know what to do."

They hustled in, practised, important, the crush giving way. They looked over, appraising the situation, while Rosy stood on the lavatory seat. They took the door off its hinges and lifted it gently away. Letitia rolled forward and the hat slithered sideways showing a paper-white face, blue lips. They knelt over her, feeling for her pulse amongst the bright tulips.

"She's alive? She's not—"

"Yes, she's breathing, dear. Not too good though. Let's have some room, please. Can we clear a space?" Between them they secured Letitia onto the stretcher and lifted it. Rosy kept close, following them out. An ambulance with its blue light flashing was waiting, curious crowds staring.

"Where are you taking her?"

"We'll just run her into the hospital, to be on the safe side. Looks like more than a fainting fit, the pulse isn't good."

"Shall I come?"

"You're welcome, dear. We'll want her particulars."

"But I must tell her grandson—he's here, I must find him. We were meeting him in a minute—"

Rosy's panic would not go away. She needed Jeremy, not only for Letitia, but for herself.

"You come along when you've found him, love. We'll take her on in, I think that's best."

For all their calm voices, they were not wasting any time, the stretcher in place, doors closed, engine running. The ambulance departed, and Rosy was left distraught, blindly making for the grandstand and up to the place she had arranged with Jeremy. To her infinite relief, she saw him standing just below, with Grace, talking to some people. She ran down again.

"Whatever's the matter?"

"Mrs. Cutbush—your gran—she's been taken ill. They've taken her to hospital—"

"Oh, no!" Jeremy's face contorted with anguish.

"There," said Grace, "I said it was stupid."

"I shall have to go. Excuse me, Grace. You can get a lift home with someone, I'm sure."

"I arranged to meet Gin in the bar after the last," Rosy said. "He'll take you back."

Jeremy was already hurrying down the steps. She ran after him. "I'm coming too. I can't stay."

They pushed their way out, Jeremy taking Rosy's arm to guide her. She was in tears. "It was all my fault! I thought—she's so strong—"

"Don't blame yourself, Rosy! Didn't you see her face? She was loving it. The day of her life! Whatever happens, don't regret anything." He paused in his hurry, turned to her and gave her a little shake. "It was lovely of you to arrange it. She'll never forget. Whatever happens, it wasn't a mistake, Rosy."

When they got to the hospital, they were told she was still unconscious. A doctor spoke to them briefly. "It doesn't look too good. A slight heart attack . . . she's been taken up to intensive care."

A nurse asked them for her particulars, which Jeremy gave, then they sat waiting in an office, and were offered cups of tea. Eventually the doctor came back and said, "There's nothing you can do for the time being. Perhaps you could come back later, say, at six o'clock, and then we might be able to tell you what the situation is. If she's stable by then, you could go home."

"Very well."

They went back to the car.

"Grace was right, I suppose," Rosy said.

"Grace is always right," Jeremy said, without joy. "I don't fancy going back, do you? We'll go somewhere quiet."

The roads in and out of Ascot all seemed to lead through woodland and heath. They found a convenient lay-by and parked the car, and walked along a path through bracken and trees. The late afternoon was now very hot and still, but the woods were mercifully cool. They came to an opening where the turf was fine and dry, and a large oak had fallen. Jeremy dropped down and settled himself with his back to the trunk, pulling off his tie.

"Poor old Letitia. Shame I never could get on with her. My loss, not hers."

"Oh, God, I hope she's all right!"

"Don't worry, Rosy. Everything's for the best, whatever."

Rosy dropped down onto the turf. Her brain was in turmoil; the peace of the woodland was blessed, after the shocks and confusion of the day. She lay curled on the turf, smelling the scent of the hot grass and the crushed bracken, the crumbly peaty soil. From the distance came the faint voice of the commentator from the races and, presently, the sound of distant cheering. Rosy saw Dark Secret again, and shivered.

As if he knew, Jeremy said, "We should have kept that filly."

"Yes. But it's what you just said. Everything's for the best. Roly was going to the knacker's."

"Money's not everything. We said so before."

The last race was over. On the still air now there was only the humming of a bee, the whine of a mosquito.

"If Letitia dies, I shall lose Brood. I shall lose everything. I've never done anything about it, all my fault. Whatever will Grace say?"

"Doesn't she know?"

"She thinks it's all mine."

Rosy smiled into the turf. If Letitia died, she would inherit the Stubbs which was worth half a million. Suddenly, the afternoon was unreal. She did not want Letitia to die.

"I shall have to find another place. Or give up," Jeremy said.

Rosy concentrated on taking long, steady breaths, to make her pulse stop thudding. Her mind could not absorb everything calmly, not least that she was alone with Jeremy in a peaceful, isolated place, and he was confiding to her whole regions of his private life, of which Grace knew nothing. He was looking away and she could not see his eyes, but in her mind she could see the pale grey-green irises, the dark eyelashes and well-defined eyelids. He had a hard-used look, youthful and yet with the beginnings of wisdom, a touch wary, a thread or two of grey. She knew she loved him as much as she had ever loved him; nothing in her was cured or discouraged after all this time. Perhaps now, this half hour or so—was the most she would ever have, and it was taken up with preoccupations of life

357

and death, and larger things than mere infatuation. She would love him if he had nothing, if she had nothing too, if everything was bleak and hopeless in front of them, if they had to live without a roof to their name. She thought she had a touch of the sun. She shut her eyes and said nothing.

From the road, the hum of traffic leaving the races now interrupted the silence. The day was over, fortunes lost, fortunes made, trainers triumphant, trainers in despair.

"Please don't let Letitia die!" Rosy prayed as she lay with her face turned into the turf. "Please don't let Letitia die!"

GRACE SAT PEEVISHLY in the back of Gin's Cortina in the crawling queue making for the M4 and listened irritably to Gin's boring agitation over the state of Letitia Cutbush.

"God, if she dies! And we thought it was such a great idea! Rosy'll be in a terrible stew. She'll think it's all her fault."

"It will be, as I see it," Grace said. "It was her idea."

"Yeah, but Letitia saw Dark Secret win, didn't she? It must have been fantastic for her."

"You'll be wishing you hadn't sold that filly, I imagine?"

"Yeah—well—"

Beryl had already had her say on that count, and Gin did not want to dwell on it. Beryl had a good return on her hefty bet but every time she thought of the prize money the filly had won, and her enhanced value, tears came into her eyes.

As he sat staring at the backside of the car in front, drumming his fingers on the wheel, Gin's mind turned to other permutations of the day's happenings.

"If the old girl dies, we might be out of a job, Beryl. Did you think of that?"

"Good riddance to that place, I'd say."

"Why d'you say that?" Grace inquired.

"She owns the place, doesn't she? And she always told us she hadn't made a will, she wasn't going to die, there was plenty of time. So I suppose it will all go to Mr. Cutbush senior, in Australia," said Gin.

"Are you sure?" Grace's voice was sharp.

"Only going by what she said. You can never tell—she used to ramble quite a lot. Say one thing one day and another the next. You know what they're like, when they're old."

Grace did not speak again. She felt that if she said anything, she would spit gobbets of fire.

ROSY AND JEREMY went back to the hospital at six and sat with Letitia until she died, at ten o'clock. She did not recover consciousness, but lay quite still, smiling faintly. For some reason, the red hat with the cherries was perched on the radio over the top of the bed.

It was a happy death, if such a thing could be. She only stirred once in the four hours they watched her, and said, "Feed Jasper." Just before she died she said something else. Rosy thought it was "Peter," and hoped Letitia was going to meet her beloved husband, for ever fixed in her mind at the age of forty-five. If it had not been for Jeremy, Rosy would have been devastated.

"Nobody could go better than that, Rosy," he said gently. "Think of it—how she might have become. She would have hated to be dependent, you must see that, and in a year or two . . ."

Rosy took the red hat, and they went back to the car. The air was cool and still and it was the twilight dark of midsummer. They drove back past the silent grandstands and the empty course, with the windows open, the night air blowing in, and Rosy felt the tears trickling down her cheeks. The smell of the woods in the half dark, Jeremy sitting beside her, the memory of Dark Secret flying past the winning post, Letitia's face in the winners' enclosure . . . it was all a tangle of triumph and disaster, joy and grief, which overwhelmed her as the car sped on out towards the motorway. Jeremy glanced at her, wound up the windows, and drove in silence, fast along the empty roads.

9

The following morning Rosy woke with a blinding headache and did not want to think about what had happened. Jeremy had said not to come in, but there were several jobs that needed doing. She remembered Jasper's dogfood in Letitia's kitchen: it must be cleared away before it stank the place out. She cycled down there on her bike, and walked up to Letitia's front door. The rose over the porch was in magnificent bloom, its drooping pink heads too heavy to hold up, scattering petals. The garden looked splendid—poor Letitia!

"Oh, damn!" Rosy swore, feeling the wretched grief flattening the beauty of the morning. She groped for the key under the flowerpot, let herself into the house and went through into the kitchen. She cleared the dogfood, and put it in the dustbin. Poor old Jasper, he would now be forgotten for ever. She tidied up, threw out a few bits of food that might go bad, and went back towards the front door. Halfway through the living room, she realized that where the Stubbs picture had hung on the wall, there was now an empty patch where the wall had faded to the exact size of the picture.

She stopped. Had Jeremy taken it for safety? He always said it was foolish to leave such a valuable object so poorly guarded. A burglar? Rosy felt her panic rising

She locked the house behind her and cycled up to Brood. Gin was in the yard, clearing out the haybarn ready for a new delivery. Rosy had rung him when she got home and told him about Letitia.

"Have you been into Mrs. Cutbush's? The picture's gone, the Stubbs."

"No. Of course not. Bloody hell, the valuable one?"

"I must tell Jeremy."

There was no sign of Grace, nor her car. Jeremy was in the kitchen, making his own breakfast.

"Hi. I thought you were Grace. She doesn't seem to be coming today."

"The picture's gone. The Stubbs."

"What's up? What do you mean?"

"Someone's taken it. Did you take it, for safety?"

"No. Why ever should I? Never crossed my mind." Jeremy pulled out a chair for her. "Sit down, take it easy. It's gone missing—your picture? Your fortune, Rosy?"

"It's not that. I never did want it. But I didn't want it stolen either."

"And now it's gone? Does Gin know anything about it? He knows about the key."

"He said he didn't."

"I'll call him, see if he's any ideas."

Jeremy went out and Rosy leaned her elbows on the table, feeling as bad as she had the evening before. Sunlight filled the kitchen, polishing the new pine surfaces, glowing on a jugful of roses. There had been no roses before Grace. Jeremy came back with Gin.

"Have you seen Grace? Did you bring her home last night?" Jeremy asked him.

"Yes. I brought her here, to collect her Mini. Then she drove home."

"I rang her this morning, but no one answered." Jeremy sighed. "I wonder where she is. Oh, hell, I suppose I'll have to ring the police. They'll take hours asking questions. I can't believe anyone nicked it though. Is Hugh in today?"

"He was going up to Newmarket with Hawkins."

"Oh, that's right. OK, Gin, carry on. I'll ring the police."

Gin hesitated. "Perhaps you should wait until Grace comes. She might know something."

"All right. That's a point. I'll try phoning her again."

Gin went out and Jeremy rang the Maddox number. It was answered. "Hello. Margaret? Is Grace around this morning? I thought she was coming in?"

Long pause.

"Yes. It was all a bit of a disaster. She told you? Yes, she died in the evening. I got back too late to ring . . . yes, yes . . . thank you. . . . Grace left an hour ago? Oh, no, I expect she's called in somewhere. Thank you. Yes, thank you. I'll call later and talk about it." He put the telephone down.

"Bloody Grace. Just when I really need her. What shall we do, Rosy? Your picture. Letitia left it to you, you know. She made a will to say that, but not about anything else. She said she'd do all that later."

"Are you really going to lose Brood?"

"I think so. My father never cared twopence for the place, and is frightfully short of money. It'll be on the market as soon as he hears." He sat on the edge of the table, looked at Rosy thoughtfully, for a long time. A lot of flippant remarks went through his head, about marrying her for her Stubbs, but now she hadn't got it they none of them seemed very tasteful. She was the least material-minded person he had ever met. She had not touched the money she had received for the filly, nor even yet voiced any regrets about selling Dark Secret. It was the first thing that had occurred to Grace, when he had rejoined her after the race: she had kept saying over and over how dreadful to have sold the filly—how absolutely ghastly to have passed up all that money. She really wanted to get her hands on Brood. Rosy was not like that at all. Even now he guessed that if she was given the choice again between Dark Secret, knowing how valuable she was, and saving old Roly Fox from the knacker's, she would opt for Roly.

"What are you thinking about?" he asked her.

"It's awful you losing Brood. It—it belongs to you."

"What about you losing the Stubbs?"

She shrugged.

Jeremy could not help laughing. "Look, let's go down to the cottage again, and have a look round. I can't believe just any old burglar walked in and took that picture."

Rosy got up. The panic had subsided, now that matters were in Jeremy's hands. They drove down the steep hairpin turns through the tunnel of trees. Outside Gin's cottage, Kes sat in the middle of the drive. Jeremy pulled up.

"I'll take him in." Rosy scrambled out and picked him up, hugging him. "Where's your mum? What's she up to?"

Beryl came to the door, surprised. "Where you going to, with the guv'nor?"

"We're going to the cottage. Someone's been in and pinched the picture, the Stubbs."

Beryl swung Kes into her arms, and laughed. In a mock whisper, she said, "I reckon his ladylove took it! She wasn't half narked when Gin said the guv'nor would lose Brood if the old girl died. She thought it was his! I could tell—she didn't speak all the way home, but her face! That was a picture an' all—I don't know about Stubbs though! I won a monkey on our filly—wasn't that great?"

Rosy got back into the car. She was shocked by what Beryl had said, but could hardly repeat it to Jeremy. She was silent on the short drive, preoccupied with disturbing thoughts, and followed Jeremy reluctantly up the long path to the front door. Once inside, Jeremy studied the blank space on the wall.

"Well, Rosy, you weren't dreaming." He looked serious. "It's probably worth more than Brood."

"We're equal then," Rosy said, and grinned.

"Damn it, I don't know why you're laughing!"

"It's better than crying."

If he went on standing there, looking at her like that, Rosy thought she would pass out. Every time they met in this cottage she found his presence overpowering. She had to retreat, the closeness of the small room and all its memories pressing in on her unbearably. She went out of the door and round the side of the house to the gate into the field. She leaned on it, looking down her beloved field to the two horses grazing, the ridiculous axis of her life. Jeremy came after her.

"What's wrong?" he asked.

"I love you."

"What?"

"I just love you. I can't bear it. It's awful."

He leaned on the gate beside her, looking down the field. She supposed he was thinking about Grace. She, Rosy, had done a Grace, staking a claim, proclaiming her need. But she could not regret it. The relief was balm.

Jeremy put his arm round her and gave a little squeeze as he had done on several occasions. But the arm did not relinquish her this time. The fingers caressed the nape of her neck, her hair, an earlobe, very gentle, tentative. Rosy felt hormones taking charge, her control faltering, the sun burning, the field shaking.

"Rosy?"

She turned to him and he put both arms round her very quickly, no longer gentle, but as quaking as she, experiencing everything that was absent from his coupling with Grace, the illusion of the sky coming down, the sun burning, the field shaking. Not the illusion but the conviction that this was how love ought to be, flowering out of want, money no object.

They neither of them said a word, but kissed passionately in the morning sunshine, until the two horses came up and nudged them over the gate, and they remembered they were on the way to the police station.

LETITIA'S FUNERAL WAS the biggest social occasion in the village since the Maddox wedding in 1950. Not only did the whole village attend, but also many elderly racing people from her past; most of Jeremy's owners, including Mr. Hawkins; the new owners of Dark Secret and, last but not least, the suntanned Peter Cutbush junior from Australia, her son and heir. Margaret and Hugh had offered their home for a reception afterwards, and Margaret made a buffet lunch; it was more suitable than Brood, and within walking distance of the church. Grace had helped her, and now sat in the church between her parents and Mr. Hawkins. Rosy sat at the back with her father, refusing Jeremy's invitation to sit with him and his father. She did not want to give the village anything else to gossip about: they had enough with Letitia's dramatic departure and the theft of her Stubbs.

It was not an unhappy occasion—how could it be? What a way to go, they all said, the perfect end of a racing lady. A pity it was in the lavatory, but that was beside the point, it was only the initial collapse. She had died with dignity, as she had lived. The vicar stood up and said all these things, and the congregation sat eyeing each other, looking forward to the chat and food and drink to come, enjoying the spectacle of the ancient church with the sun streaming in through the stained glass, and the impeccable organ-playing of the young man who was imported for important occasions.

Rosy sat in a state of trance, the service drifting over her head. Since his father had arrived, Jeremy had confirmed that Brood was

363

to be sold. Peter Cutbush was claiming all that Letitia had left, except the old cottage which he said Jeremy was welcome to— "Don't let it be said I didn't leave you a roof over your head!" He was a hard but quite jovial man. There had been no falling out. He told Jeremy he would try to leave him a reasonable pile when he went, but for now, he could use the money. Jeremy was philosophical. No, he did not want to go to Australia. He would get by. His father was relieved to see that he was a lot happier than he remembered him in the past.

The Pembertons, owners of Dark Secret, eating vol-au-vents on Margaret's immaculate lawn in the crush afterwards, said to Rosy, "What a character! We shall never forget her, standing there at Ascot in those amazing tulips—the expression on her face! She was like a queen. If I was eighty-something, you know, I wouldn't mind going out like that. The only pity is, she won't be there to see the filly run again."

"At Epsom next year," said the blond son, grinning. "She'll be an Oaks contender, we hope. We're going to nurse her for the big one. A pity the old lady won't see that."

"Her dam is in a field down the road, if you'd like to see her." Rosy said. "I could take you down, before you leave."

"Great! We'd love that. We'd really love that."

The sire was also at grass in a field further down the valley, did they but know it, but Rosy was not saying anything on that score. If Dark Secret was destined for fame, how fortunate that Jeremy had declared her sire to be of the same bloodline as was actually the case, for it would matter when she became a brood mare.

"I understand Mr. Cutbush will have to give up Brood House with the old lady dying. We have a couple of chasers, to keep us amused in the winter—we wouldn't mind sending them to Mr. Cutbush next season, if he gets another yard."

The magic words all small trainers wanted to hear . . .

Rosy took the Pembertons down to see Silverfish, and when they had departed she sat on by the riverbank in the late-afternoon sunshine. She felt very tired. She had scarcely seen Jeremy, his father having arrived only hours after he had got the news of Letitia, but she nursed the memory of his embracing her at the field gate.

She lay on her back on the grass, having removed her tights and shoes, shut her eyes and listened to the soft tumble of the river below her, and the steady cropping of the two horses close by, thinking how inconsequential life appeared to be, nobody much in charge of what happened to them, but making the best of circumstances as they arose. After all his years of hard work, Jeremy's business was down the drain, they had all lost their jobs, their futures, their ridiculous fortunes. Yet she was not unhappy. She was in a state of suspension, not able to think clearly about anything any longer. Her brain needed a rest. I will clear it, she thought, lie here and think of absolutely nothing at all.

"Rosy."

Her concentration on absolutely nothing was so determined that she did not hear the voice until it repeated her name. She opened her eyes. Jeremy stood there, against the sun, looking down on her.

"I thought you'd be here."

She did not say anything. He sat down beside her. He was in white shirtsleeves, the funeral tie discarded. Roly Fox came up and stood nudging his shoulders, then wandered on to take a drink from the river. Rosy sat up and kept her eyes carefully on the drinking horse, his black tail switching from side to side.

"The Pembertons say they'll send you a couple of chasers this season, if you've got a yard."

"Really?"

"I brought them to meet Silverfish. They've just gone."

Jeremy picked a piece of grass, and chewed it thoughtfully.

"But I haven't got a yard." He searched for some edible clover, picked another stalk. "I thought, while I'm being divested of everything, I might as well divest myself of Hawkins as well. He offered to buy Brood, keep me on there. Can you imagine? I couldn't sink lower than that. I told him to try Hugh."

"You're better off without a man like that."

"My feelings exactly. He is my living though." He looked at Rosy and smiled. "I know what you're going to say: money isn't everything."

Rosy smiled too, shrugged. "No."

She said, "You've got this. You could build a few boxes at the top of the field. There's room. Say yes to Mr. Pemberton."

Jeremy turned and surveyed the rolling six acres or so of Letitia's field. He rolled over and lay on his stomach, looking up at the level patch at the top, and the decrepit barn where Silverfish had borne her foal. The scent of Letitia's straggling lavender bushes came faintly on the air. He lay still, considering, for what seemed to Rosy a very long time. Roly came out of the stream and walked slowly past, making for the barn where Silverfish had already gone to find shade. They were great mates these days.

"I'd need a head lad," he said at last. "Would you take the job?"

"Yes, I would."

"Living in?"

"Yes," she said.

"Whoever took the Stubbs," Jeremy said, "did us a good turn. I could never have asked you . . . I've got nothing."

"Nor me."

He smiled at her, and his expression gradually changed, the smile broadening. He seemed to shed his years and to Rosy he was the boy in the curling photos, riding in his winner, passionate and triumphant.

"I'll make you out a contract, straightaway."

"Yes, sir," she said.

The "Horse and Groom in a Landscape" lay, as they spoke, where it was to lie for ten years before being discovered: in the loft of Letitia's cottage. Grace, who had hidden it there in a splendid fit of spite after returning from Ascot, was already in Brood House, mentally measuring up for carpets and curtains while Hawkins (she must learn to call him John) clasped her to his paunch.

A crack of sunlight filtered beneath one of the cottage tiles and played on the face of the groom and his timeless gaze, fixed now upon a cistern lagged in old horse blankets. No surprise, naturally, was registered. He in his day had been, no doubt, party to vicissitudes of human nature stranger than those that had brought about his incarceration in this dusty setting.

And his horse cavorted for eternity, the bold eyes for ever alight, waiting patiently for daylight and his just due, once more, of admiration and love.

K. M. PEYTON

Small of stature, but bubbling with enormous enthusiasm and a lively sense of humour, Kathleen Peyton is a delightful person to meet. Laughter punctuates the conversation as she talks about her lifelong passion for horses and racing. Then, for a moment, an uncharacteristic frown crosses her brow as she tries to analyse her fondness for these animals. "It's an obsession, I suppose. I can't explain it. It must be in my blood. Even if I didn't ride or go racing, I'd just want to look at horses, talk to them, have something to do with them."

It was a love that began in her childhood, but for years it had to remain just a dream. "When I was a child growing up in Surbiton, my parents couldn't afford to pay for riding lessons. I used to save up all my pocket money for one ride on Wimbledon Common during each school holiday." She also occupied her spare time writing stories about horses and illustrating them with her own drawings. A collection of well-worn exercise books filled with her neat, youthful handwriting has survived to this day. She laughed as she showed me her first attempt at a novel: a few folded sheets of paper portentously titled, "Greystar. The Life Story of a Racehorse. With illustrations by the auther" (sic). She was seven when she wrote it. At the age of seventeen she had her first book published, and she has been writing ever since.

Kathleen Peyton (right) introduces me to Essie and Pip

After leaving school she went to art school in Manchester, where she met her future husband Michael, who today is a cartoonist and keen sailor. Together they travelled widely before settling in Essex to bring up their two daughters.

Until very recently Kathleen Peyton wrote exclusively for children, and is probably best known for her prize-winning *Flambards* trilogy which was made into a television serial. Success in her writing has brought about the fulfilment of her childhood dreams, and from her desk she can see her very own horses grazing: two grey mares, Essie and Pip, which she rides regularly, and a twenty-four-year-old chestnut, fondly referred to as "the lodger", who, like Roly Fox in *The Sound of Distant Cheering*, was rescued and given a good home at the end of his working career.. "I think it's dreadful," she says vehemently, "that horses who have served people well for years should be thrown on the scrapheap."

When I visited her on a chilly day in February, she was anxiously waiting for the weather forecast, hoping that the postponement of the season's steeplechasing due to frozen ground would soon end. She owns a share in a racehorse called Wise Words, and such is her fondness for him that it is an unbearable deprivation not to see him run. He's come second on five occasions. To see him win and to hear the sound of cheering ringing in her ears, is one more dream that Kathleen Peyton hopes just might come true any day now.

Sue Yde-Poulsen

NIGHT
of
ERROR

A CONDENSATION OF THE BOOK BY
DESMOND BAGLEY

ILLUSTRATED BY GERRY HAYLOCK

Mike Trevelyan and his brother Mark
have never seen eye to eye. Even a shared
fascination for the sea which has lead them
both into careers as oceanographers has
failed to bridge the rivalry dividing them
since childhood. It nevertheless comes as
a shock to Mike to learn of Mark's death
on an unnamed atoll in the Pacific.
And when witnesses begin to
come up with conflicting stories, his
suspicions are aroused. Was Mark murdered?
What had he discovered that was so
important to a band of South Americans
that they are willing to kill to
get their hands on it?
Setting out on a sea voyage to the Pacific
islands where his brother disappeared,
Mike finds himself caught up in a situation
of increasing menace as he draws closer
and closer to the truth—and a
remarkable oceanographical discovery.

CHAPTER ONE

I heard of the way my brother died on a wet and gloomy afternoon in 1962. The sky was overcast and it had become dark much earlier than usual.

I was standing at my office window watching the mist-shrouded Thames, wishing I could get out of London and its greyness and back to sea under tropical skies, when the telephone rang.

Helen, my brother's widow, was on the line, and she sounded hysterical. "Mike, there's a man here—a Mr. Kane—who was with Mark when he died. I think you'd better see him." Her voice broke.

"All right, Helen; shoot him over. I'll be here until six—can he make it before then?"

There was an indistinct murmur, then Helen said, "Yes, he'll be at the institute before then. Thanks, Mike. Oh, and there's an advisory note from British Airways—something has come from Tahiti. I think it must be Mark's things. I posted the slip to you this morning—will you look after it for me? I don't think I could bear to."

"I'll look after everything," I said.

She rang off and I put down the receiver slowly, then leaned back in my chair. Helen seemed distraught about Mark and I wondered what this man Kane had told her. All I knew was that Mark had died somewhere in French Oceania, on a remote island near Tahiti; the British consul there had wrapped it all up and the Foreign Office had got in touch with Helen as next of kin. She had fallen apart at the news, even though her marriage had caused her nothing but misery.

Judging by the way she was behaving, she must have loved Mark despite everything; but then, he had a way with women.

One thing was certain—his death wouldn't make me distraught. I had long ago steered clear of him and all his devious plans which had only one end in view—the glorification of Mark Trevelyan.

I put him out of my mind, and got down to my figures. People think of scientists—especially oceanographers—as being constantly in the field making esoteric discoveries. They never think of the office work entailed—and if I didn't get clear of this routine work I'd never get back to sea.

At a quarter to six there was a knock on the door. I opened it and a man said, "Mr. Trevelyan?"

Kane was tall and haggard, about forty, and dressed in rough seaman's clothing. As we shook hands I could feel calluses and thought that perhaps he was a sailing man—steam seamen don't have much occasion to do rough work. I said, "I'm sorry to have dragged you across London on a day like this, Mr. Kane."

"That's all right," he said in a raw Australian accent. "I was coming up this way."

I sized him up. "I was just going out. What about a drink?"

He smiled. "That 'ud be fine. I like your English beer."

We went to a nearby pub and ordered a couple of beers. He sank half a pint and gasped luxuriously.

"Would I be correct if I said you'd done your time in sail?" I asked.

He laughed. "Too right you would. How do you know?"

"I've sailed myself; I suppose it shows somehow."

"Then I won't have to explain too much detail when I tell you about your brother. I didn't tell Mrs. Trevelyan all of it—some of it's pretty grim. But I suppose you want to know the whole story?"

"I'd better know everything."

Kane finished his beer and cocked an eye at me. "Another?"

"Not for me just yet. You go ahead."

He ordered another beer and said, "Well, we've got a schooner, my partner and me, and we do a bit of trading. We were in the Tuamotus—they're east of Tahiti."

"Yes. I know where they are," I said.

"OK. Well, we thought there was a chance of picking up a few pearls so we were cruising round the inhabited islands. Most of 'em don't have names—not names that we can pronounce. Anyway we were passing one when a boy in a canoe hailed us—a Polynesian, you know—and Jim talked to him. Jim Hadley's my partner. He speaks the lingo—I don't savvy it too good myself. What the boy said was that there was a white man on the island who was very sick, and so we went ashore to have a look at him."

"That was my brother?"

"Too right."

"What was wrong with him?"

Kane shrugged. "We didn't know at first, but it turned out to be appendicitis, after we got a doctor to him. If you could call the man a doctor. He was a drunken old no-hoper who'd been living in the islands for years. He wasn't on that island though; Jim had to go fifty miles to get him while I stayed with your brother."

Kane took a long pull at his beer. "Your brother said he was some sort of scientist—something to do with the sea."

"Yes, an oceanographer, like me."

"Too right. Anyway, he told me that he was alone on the island. He said he'd been dropped there to do some research and he was due to be picked up any time."

"Why didn't you take him to the doctor instead of bringing the doctor to him?" I asked.

"We didn't think he'd make it," answered Kane simply. "A little ship like ours bounces about a lot, and he was pretty sick."

"I see," I said.

"There wasn't much I could do for him, beyond cleaning him up. We talked a lot—that was when he asked me to tell his wife."

"Surely he didn't expect you to make a special trip to England?"

"Oh no," said Kane. "I was coming to England anyway. I'd won a bit of money at cards, and I always wanted to see the old country. Jim dropped me at Panama and I bummed a job on a ship that was coming to England."

He smiled ruefully. "I won't be staying here as long as I thought—I dropped a packet in a poker game coming across. I'll stay until my cash runs out and then I'll go back to Jim and the schooner."

I said, "What happened when the doctor came?"

"Oh, sure. I got off track. Well, Jim brought this old no-good back and he operated. Pretty rough it was too; the doc's instruments weren't any too good."

The thought of some drunken doctor cutting Mark open with blunt knives wasn't a pretty one. "So my brother died," I said.

"Not right away. He seemed OK after the operation, then he got worse. The doc said it was peri . . . peri . . ."

"Peritonitis?"

"That's it. He went delirious and died two days later."

Kane looked into his glass. "We buried him at sea. It was stinking hot and we couldn't carry the body anywhere—we hadn't any ice. The doctor said he'd see to all the details. I mean, it wasn't any use for Jim and me to go all the way to Papeete—that's the main town on Tahiti. The doc knew all we knew."

"You told the doctor about Mark's wife—her address and so on?"

Kane nodded. "But when I spoke to her today she said she'd only just heard—that's the islands' postal service for you. You know, Mr. Trevelyan never gave us nothing for her, no personal stuff, I mean. We wondered about that. But she said some gear of his is on the way—that right?"

"It might be," I said. "There's something at Heathrow. I'll probably pick it up tomorrow. When did Mark die, by the way?"

Kane reflected. "Must have been about four months ago. I reckon it was the beginning of May."

"Do you remember the doctor's name? Or where he came from?"

Kane frowned. "He was a Dutchman; runs a hospital on one of the islands—my word, I can't remember the name of that either."

"It's of no consequence. I can get it from the death certificate." I finished my beer. "The last I heard of Mark he was working with a Swede called Norgaard. You didn't come across him?"

Kane shook his head. "Only your brother. You think this Norgaard was supposed to pick him up when he'd finished his job?"

"Probably," I said. "It's been very good of you to take the trouble to tell us about Mark's death, and thanks for looking after him. I wouldn't like to think he died alone."

"Aw, look," said Kane, embarrassed, "we couldn't do anything else now, could we?"

I gave him my card. "I'd like you to keep in touch," I said. "Perhaps when you're ready to go back I can help you with your passage. I have plenty of contacts with the shipping people."

I said goodbye and ducked into the lounge bar in the same pub. I wanted a few quiet thoughts over another drink.

I thought of Mark dying a rather gruesome death on that lonely Pacific atoll. God knows that Mark and I didn't see eye to eye but I wouldn't have wished that fate on my worst enemy. And yet there was something odd about the whole story, a sour note. For instance, what had happened to Norgaard? It wasn't standard procedure for a man to be left entirely alone on a job. I wondered what Mark and Norgaard had been doing in the Tuamotus. They had published no papers, so perhaps their investigation hadn't been completed. I made a mental note to ask old Jarvis, my boss, about it. He knew everything that went on in the profession.

But something else was niggling at the back of my mind that I couldn't resolve. I chased it around for a bit but nothing happened, so I finished my drink and went home.

THE NEXT DAY I arrived at the office bright and early. I was opening the post when one of the girls brought in a welcome visitor. Geordie Wilkins had been my father's sergeant in the commandos during the war, and after my father was killed he had taken an interest in my brother and me. Mark, typically, had been contemptuous of Geordie, but I liked him and we got on well together.

He had retired after the war, and had bought a 200-ton brigantine which he chartered, to rich Americans mostly, at an exorbitant price. It had been a while since I'd last seen him.

"Where have you sprung from this time, Geordie?" I asked after we had exchanged greetings.

"The Caribbean," he said. "I've brought *Esmerelda* over for a refit. I'm in between charters, thank goodness."

"Where are you staying?"

"With you—if you'll have me."

"Don't be an idiot," I said. "You know you're welcome. We seem to have struck lucky this time—I have to do a bit of writing which will take a week, and then I've got three weeks' leave."

He rubbed his chin. "Why don't we push off somewhere?"

"That's a great idea," I said. "I've been dying to get away. Wait while I read this letter, would you?"

The letter I had just opened was from Helen, and it contained the advisory note from British Airways. There was something to be collected from Heathrow which had to clear customs. I looked up at Geordie.

"Did you know that Mark is dead?"

He looked startled. "Dead! When did that happen?"

I told him all about it and he said, "A sticky end—even for Mark." He immediately apologized. "Sorry—I shouldn't have said that."

"Quit it, Geordie," I said irritably. "You know how I felt about Mark; there's no need to be mealy-mouthed with me."

"Aye. He was a bastard, wasn't he? How's his wife taking it?"

"She's pretty broken up."

"It beats me what women saw in him," said Geordie bluntly. "He treated 'em like dirt and they begged for more."

"Some people have it, some don't," I said.

He took the paper out of my hand. "Got a car I can use? I'll get my gear from *Esmerelda* and then pick this stuff up for you."

I tossed him my car keys. "Thanks. It's the same old wreck—you'll find it in the car park."

When he had gone I went up to see Jarvis. He was cordial. "You've done a good job, Mike. I've looked at your stuff and if your correlations are correct I think we're on to something."

"Thank you."

He leaned back in his chair and started to fill his pipe. "You'll be writing a paper, of course?"

"I'll do that while I'm on leave," I said, and then changed tack. "Can you tell me anything about a fellow called Norgaard? I think he's a Swede working on ocean currents."

"Wasn't he the chap working with your brother when he died?"

"That's the man."

Jarvis pondered, then shook his head. "I haven't heard anything of him lately; he certainly hasn't published. I'll make a few inquiries and let you know what I find out."

And that was that. I didn't know why I had taken the trouble to ask Jarvis about Norgaard unless it was still that uneasy feeling that something was wrong. It probably didn't mean anything anyway, and I put it out of my mind as I walked back to my office.

It was getting late and I was about ready to leave when Geordie returned. "Here it is," he said, and heaved an ancient suitcase onto my desk.

I looked at the case warily. "What's inside?"

"Not much. Some clothes, a few books and a lot of pebbles. And there's a letter addressed to Mark's wife." He opened the case, handed the letter to me, and started to haul out the contents—a couple of tropical suits, several shirts, three textbooks on oceanography and a couple of notebooks in Mark's handwriting.

I looked at the letter. "I'd better open this," I said. "We don't know what's in it and I don't want Helen to get any more shocks."

Geordie nodded and I slit the envelope. I read the letter aloud. It was short and rather abrupt:

Dear Mrs. Trevelyan,

I am sorry to tell you that your husband, Mark, is dead, although you may know already by the time you get this. Mark was a good friend to me and left some of his things in my care. I am sending them all to you.

Sincerely,
P. Nelson

"Do you know this chap, Nelson?" Geordie asked.

"Never heard of him."

Geordie reached into the suitcase. "Then there are these." He dropped a dozen or so potato-like objects onto the desk, some of which rolled off onto the carpet. "You'll probably make more sense of these than I can," he said as he stooped to pick them up.

"Manganese nodules," I said. "Very common in the Pacific."

"Are they valuable?"

I laughed. "If you could get at them easily they might be—but you can't, so they aren't. They lie on the seabed at an average depth of about fourteen thousand feet."

He looked closely at one of the nodules. "I wonder where Mark got these, then? That's a bit deep for skin-diving."

"They're probably souvenirs of the IGY—the International Geophysical Year. Mark was a physical chemist on one of the IGY ships in the Pacific." I took one of the notebooks and flipped through it. Most of the pages seemed to be covered with mathematical equations.

I tossed it back into the open suitcase. "Let's get this stuff packed away, then we'll go home."

We put everything back and carted the case down to my car. On the way home Geordie said, "What about a show tonight?"

"If you can get tickets," I said. "I don't feel like queueing."

"I'll get them," he said confidently. "Look, drop me right here and I'll see you at the flat in half an hour or so."

I dropped him off and when I got home I took Mark's suitcase and Geordie's gear up to the flat. For some time I pottered about, estimating what I'd need for a trip away. Then, after a while, I found myself looking at the suitcase. I picked it up, put it on the bed, opened it and considered the few remnants of Mark's life. As I lifted up a jacket, a small leather-bound notebook fell out of the breast pocket.

I picked it up and examined it carefully. It had obviously been used as a diary but most of the entries were in shorthand—Pitman's, but adapted in an idiosyncratic way, probably so that it would be incomprehensible to anyone but Mark.

Occasionally there were chemical and mathematical notations, and every now and then there was a mysterious drawing. I couldn't make much sense out of any of it.

I put the diary on my chest of drawers and turned to the larger notebooks. They were much more interesting. Apparently, Mark was working on a theory of nodule formation that, to say the least, was harebrained—certainly from the point of view of orthodox physical chemistry.

Presently I heard Geordie come in. He popped his head into the bedroom and said triumphantly, "I've got the tickets. Let's have a slap-up dinner first and then go to the theatre."

"Good idea," I said, and threw the notebooks and the clothing back into the suitcase.

Geordie nodded at it. "Find anything interesting?"

I shoved the case under the bed. "Nothing, except that Mark was going round the bend. He'd got hold of some idea about nodules and was going overboard about it."

IT WAS A GOOD DINNER and a better show, and we drove home in high spirits.

I parked the car outside the flats and got out. There was a thin drizzle of rain. As I looked up at the sky, I stiffened. "Geordie, there's someone in my flat."

He looked up at the third floor and saw what I had seen—a light moving at one of the windows.

"Come on," I said, and ran up into the foyer.

Geordie caught my arm as I pressed for the lift. "Let's do this properly. You wait one minute and then go up in the lift. I'll take the stairs—we should arrive on your floor at the same time. Covers both exits."

I grinned and saluted. "Yes, sergeant."

I went up in the lift and stepped out into the lighted corridor. Geordie had made good time up the stairs. He motioned me to keep the lift door open and reached inside to press the button for the top floor. The lift went up. He grinned. "Anyone leaving in a hurry must use the stairs now. Got your key?"

I passed it to him and we walked to the door of my flat, treading softly. Geordie cautiously inserted the key into the lock, gave it a twist, threw open the door and plunged inside.

As I followed I heard a shout—"*Ojo!*"—and the next thing I knew, there was a blinding flash in my eyes and I was grappling with someone at the kitchen door. Whoever it was hit me on the side of the head. I felt dizzy for a moment but held on, thrusting forward and bringing my knee up sharply.

I heard a gasp of pain and above it the roar of Geordie's voice from further into the flat—possibly the bedroom.

I let go my grip, struck out with my fist, and yelled in pain as my knuckles hit the kitchen door. My opponent squirmed out from where I had him pinned and disappeared through the front door.

Things were happening too fast. I could hear Geordie swearing at the top of his voice and the crash of furniture. A light tenor voice

378

called, *"Huid! Huid! No disparéis! Emplead cuchillos!"* Then someone banged into me in the darkness, and I struck out again.

I knew now that this assailant would certainly have a knife and possibly a gun, and I went berserk—it's wonderful what the adrenal glands will do in an emergency. In the light from the corridor I glimpsed an upraised knife and chopped viciously at the wrist. There was a howl of pain and the knife clattered to the floor.

Something was swung at the side of my head again and I went down as a black figure jumped over me. If he hadn't stopped to kick at my head he would have got clean away, but I moved to avoid his boot and caught his leg, and he went sprawling into the corridor.

I dived after him and got between him and the stairs. He stood in a crouch looking at me, his eyes darting about, searching for escape. Then I saw what he must have swung at my head—it was Mark's suitcase.

Suddenly he turned and ran, towards the blank end of the corridor. I've got him now, I thought exultantly, and went after him at a dead run. But I had forgotten the fire escape.

I tackled him rugby-fashion so that I floored him just short of it. The fall knocked the breath out of me, and as I was shaking my head in dizziness, he tossed Mark's case into the darkness.

By the time I regained my feet I was between him and the metal staircase and he was facing me. His right hand darted to his pocket and I saw the gun as he drew it. I jumped for him and he sidestepped, frantically trying to clear the gun from his pocket—but the foresight must have caught on the lining.

Then I hit him hard on the jaw and he teetered on the top step of the fire escape. I hit him again and, to my horror, he jack-knifed over the railing. It seemed a long time before I heard the dull thump as he hit the ground.

There was a scurry of footsteps and I turned to see Geordie darting down the stairs. "Leave them," I shouted. "They're armed!"

But he didn't stop and all I heard was the thud of his feet as he raced down the staircase.

Suddenly a gunshot echoed up the stairwell. I started down the stairs at top speed, and found Geordie in the foyer. He was sitting on the floor staring at his hand. Blood was spurting from the end of his little finger.

"The bastard shot me!" he said incredulously.

"Are you all right?" I asked.

He was wrapping his finger in a handkerchief which was turning red. "I'm OK," he said. "You can't call this a mortal wound."

"I think I killed one of them," I said emptily. "I knocked him off the fire escape. He fell from the third floor."

Geordie looked at me closely. "We'd better go and have a look."

We went out into the street and walked quickly round to the alley into which the fire escape led. As we turned the corner there was a sudden glare of light and the roar of an engine.

"Look out!" yelled Geordie, and he flung himself sideways.

I saw two great headlamps rushing at me from the darkness of the alley and I frantically flattened myself against the wall. The car roared past, turned the corner and was gone.

I eased myself from the wall, taking a deep shaky breath. In the light of the street lamp I saw Geordie pick himself up.

"This lot aren't ordinary burglars," he said, brushing himself down. "They're too persistent. Where's this fire escape?"

We walked slowly up the alley and found the man I had knocked over the edge. His head was twisted at an impossible angle and there was a deep bloody depression in the skull.

"No need to look any further," Geordie said. "He's dead."

"AND YOU SAY THEY were speaking Spanish?" said the inspector.

I nodded wearily. "As soon as we entered the flat someone shouted, 'Look out!' and then I was in the middle of a fight. A bit later another man shouted, 'Get out of here, don't shoot—use your knives.' I think it was the man I knocked off the fire escape."

The inspector looked at me thoughtfully. "How good is your Spanish, Mr. Trevelyan?"

"Pretty good," I said. "I was based in Spain about four years ago and I took the trouble to learn the language."

I looked about the flat—it was a wreck. What hadn't been broken by the burglars had been smashed during the fight. A chair with no legs lay against one wall and broken glass littered the carpet. Geordie, who sported a natty bandage on his little finger, sat in an armchair. A couple of uniformed constables stood stolidly in the corners and a plain-clothes man was blowing powder about the place with an insufflator.

"How many of them were there?" the inspector asked.

"I had a go at two," I said. "But I think that one of them had a bash at Geordie first. It's difficult to say—it happened so fast."

Geordie said unexpectedly, "There were four of them."

The inspector looked at him with raised eyebrows.

"I saw three men in the car. One driving and two getting in in a hurry. With one dead in the alley—that makes four."

"Ah yes," said the inspector, whose watchful grey eyes suddenly turned on me like gimlets. "You say the dead man threw a suitcase into the alley?"

"That's right."

"We haven't found it, Mr. Trevelyan."

"The others must have picked it up. That's when they nearly ran us down."

He nodded. "What was in the suitcase—do you know?"

"Some stuff belonging to my brother. Clothing, books—geological samples."

The inspector sighed. "Anything important or valuable?"

I shook my head. "I doubt it."

"What about the samples?"

"They appeared to be manganese nodules of a type often to be found on the ocean bed. They're very common."

"And valuable?" he persisted.

"I don't think that anyone with knowledge of them would regard them as valuable," I said. "I suppose they might be if they were generally accessible, but it's too hard to get at them through two or three miles of water."

The inspector seemed at a loss. "How do you think your brother will regard the loss of those specimens, and his other things?"

"He's dead," I said.

The inspector sharpened his attention. "Oh? When did he die?"

"About four months ago—in the Pacific. Mark was an ocean-ographer like myself."

"Um," said the inspector. "Is there anything else missing?"

"Not that I know of."

Geordie spoke up. "I think we were too quick for them. So one of them grabbed the first thing he saw and tried to make a getaway."

I was careful not to mention that the suitcase had been hidden under my bed.

It was not until 3:00 am that we got rid of the police. The inspector wasn't satisfied but neither he nor any of his colleagues could pin down what was wrong. Come to that—neither could I! His last word to me as he left the flat was, "There's been a fatality here, Mr. Trevelyan. I shall expect both you and Mr. Wilkins to hold yourselves in readiness for the inquest. You are not under arrest," he added in such a way as to make me feel that I was.

When we were alone Geordie said, "He'll be looking for an expert on manganese nodules. He thinks there's something fishy there. Tell me, these nodules—are they really valueless?"

381

"I told him the truth," I said. "But Mark seemed to have some curious ideas about nodule formation . . . Still, the notebooks are gone and I can't study his theories without them."

Then suddenly I remembered something. "Wait a minute," I said and went into the bedroom. Sure enough, there it was—the little leather-bound diary, still lying on my chest of drawers. The police had probably thought it was mine, and hadn't touched it.

I took it in to Geordie. "They didn't get this. I found it in one of Mark's suit pockets. What do you make of it?"

He opened the book with interest but his enthusiasm died as he scanned the pages.

"That's Mark's Pitman variation," I explained. "I doubt if old Isaac himself could make anything of it."

"What are all the drawings?"

"Mark was an inveterate doodler," I said, then lapsed into silence as I mulled over the events of the previous day, trying to piece them together.

"Geordie, think about this," I said at last. "Mark dies, and Norgaard, his colleague, disappears. Jarvis knows all the gossip of the profession, and if he says he hasn't heard anything of Norgaard then it's unlikely that anyone else has either."

"Do you know anything about Norgaard?" asked Geordie.

"Only that he's an oceanographer. He's a Swede, but he was on an American ship during the IGY survey."

"What's his speciality?"

"Ocean currents. He can dredge up a bit of water and tell you which way it was flowing a million years ago last Wednesday."

"And Mark was like yourself—an analytical chemist. Why would he team up with Norgaard?"

"I don't really know," I said slowly, thinking of the unlikely theory indicated in Mark's missing notebooks.

"All right," Geordie said. "Norgaard's disappeared—you think. What else have you got?"

"The next thing is Kane. Kane turns up and we have a burglary. He knew Mark's stuff was coming—I told him."

Geordie chuckled. "And how do you tie in the four Spanish burglars with Kane?"

"I'm damned if I know." There was another silence while I marshalled my thoughts. "I wish I could get hold of Kane. I think there's something odd about him. But I don't know what it is."

"Mike, I think your imagination is working overtime," Geordie said decisively. "I don't believe Norgaard has mysteriously disappeared—I think he's somewhere writing a thesis on prehistoric water. As for Kane, you've got nothing but a blind hunch. But I'll tell you what I'll do. If Kane is a seaman he's probably somewhere in dockland. I'll ask my crew to nose around a bit."

"Thanks, Geordie," I said. "I'll have to ring Helen tomorrow. She's not going to like hearing that Mark's stuff has been stolen, so I'll play it down—tell her it was all worthless anyway."

"Are you going to pass the notebook on to her?"

I shook my head thoughtfully. "What notebook? As far as she's concerned, it was all stolen. She could never make anything of Mark's scribblings—but maybe I can."

I HAD NIGHTMARES that night.

I dreamed of a lovely Pacific island and a Dutch doctor who was chasing me, brandishing a rusty kitchen knife.

I woke with a yell. I was breathing deeply, taking in great gulps of air, and I could feel a slick film of sweat all over my body. But I knew at last what was wrong with Kane's story.

The bedroom door opened and Geordie said, "What's going on?"

I switched on the bedside light and said, "Come in, Geordie. I'm all right—just a nightmare. But I remembered something."

"What?"

I lit a cigarette. "Mark had his appendix out years ago."

Geordie looked startled. "But the death certificate..."

"I don't know anything about the death certificate. I haven't seen it yet, so I don't know if it's a fake. But I know that Mr. Kane is a fake."

"Are you sure?"

"I still know the doctor who operated on Mark. I'll give him a ring and check on it—but I'm sure."

"Perhaps this Dutch doctor made a mistake," offered Geordie.

"You can't take out an appendix that isn't there," I said acidly. "Anyway, he'd have seen the scar the moment he made his examination, and he'd know the appendix had already been removed. No doctor would sign a certificate that could be so easily disproved—no one is as incompetent as that."

"Aye. If he'd wanted to cover up something, he'd have put down the cause of death as fever or something you couldn't prove. But we don't know what he put on the death certificate."

"We'll soon find out. They sent it to Helen. And now I want to find Kane more than ever."

"I'll do my best," said Geordie. He didn't sound too hopeful.

CHAPTER TWO

First thing next morning I received a telephone call from the institute. It was a fellow named Simms. "Dr. Trevelyan, I've taken over your office while you're away and you've left something behind. I don't know if you want it . . ."

"What is it?" I asked.

"A manganese nodule. One of the cleaners found it under your desk and gave it to me. What should I do with it?"

"Stick tight to it," I said. "I'll pick it up. It's got some relation to work I'm engaged on. Thanks for calling."

I turned to Geordie. "All is not lost," I said. "We've got a nodule. When you dropped some in my office, you left one under the desk."

"I don't see what all the fuss is about. All along you've been insisting that they're worthless."

"There are too many mysteries connected with this lot to suit me. I'm going to take a closer look."

As I breakfasted I rang Helen and asked her to read out Mark's death certificate. It was in French, of course, and she had some difficulties over the handwritten parts, but we got it sorted out.

"What was the cause of death?" Geordie asked.

"Peritonitis following an appendectomy. And that's impossible. The doctor's name is Hans Schouten. The certificate was signed in Tanakabu, in the Tuamotus."

"That's a long way from here."

"But Kane isn't. Do your best to find him, Geordie."

I dressed and drove down to the institute, retrieved the nodule from Simms and then went down to the laboratories. I was going to analyse this lump of rock down to the last trace elements. First I photographed it in colour from several angles and took a casting of it in latex—that took care of the external record. Then I cut it in half with a diamond saw. Not entirely unexpectedly, in the centre was a shark's tooth, neatly cut in two. One of the pieces I put in the rock mill, and while it was being ground to the consistency of fine flour, I polished and etched the flat surface of the other piece. Then I went to take photomicrographs of the etched surface.

I was busy for another couple of hours, but by early afternoon everything was well under way. Luckily I had had the place to myself the whole time. Normally I would have used the services of a laboratory technician, but this was one job I wanted to do myself. And it was fortunate that I had taken that precaution because what I finally found astounded me. I looked incredulously at the table of figures that was emerging.

I meticulously cleaned and put away every piece of equipment I had used. I did not want to leave any evidence of what I'd been up to. That done, I phoned the flat.

Geordie answered. "Where the devil have you been?" he demanded. "We've had cops, press, insurance people—the lot."

"Have they gone now?"

"Aye."

"Good. I don't suppose you found Kane?"

"You suppose rightly. But if you're so suspicious of him why don't you go to the police?"

"I don't want to do that right now. I'm coming home, Geordie. I've got something to tell you."

"Have you eaten, boy?"

I suddenly realized that I hadn't eaten a mouthful all day. I felt very hungry. "I've been too busy," I said.

"I thought so. I'll tell you what: I'll cook up something in this kitchen of yours—one of my slumgullions."

"Thanks. That'll be fine."

When I entered the flat later that evening I was greeted by a mouth-watering aroma. "It'll be ready in about an hour," Geordie called out from the kitchen, "so you can tell me your news before we eat. I'll be out in two ticks."

I went to the cabinet for the whisky bottle and two glasses, then took my old school atlas from the bookshelf. Ink-blotted and politically out-of-date as it was, it would still suit my purpose. I put it on the table and turned to the pages which showed the Pacific.

Geordie came out of the kitchen and I beckoned to him. "Sit here. I want to tell you something important."

He sat down obediently. I poured two whiskies and said, "I'm going to give you a little lecture on basic oceanography. At the bottom of the oceans—particularly the Pacific—there exists a fortune in metallic ores in the form of small lumps lying on the seabed." I took the half-nodule from my pocket and put it on the table. "Like this lump here. Every oceanographer knows about them. They were discovered as far back as 1870."

Geordie picked up the nodule and examined it. "What's this white bit in the middle?"

"A shark's tooth."

"How the hell did it get in the middle of a piece of rock?"

"That comes later," I said impatiently, "in the second lesson. Now

these lumps are composed mainly of manganese dioxide, iron oxide and traces of nickel, cobalt and copper, but to save time they're usually referred to as manganese nodules. The sheer quantity of them on the seabed is incredible."

I turned to the atlas and moved my forefinger along the shoreline of the Americas, starting at Chile and moving north towards Alaska. "Proved deposits here, at an average of one pound a square foot, cover an area of two million square miles and involve twenty-six *billion* tons of nodules."

I swept my finger out to Hawaii. "This is the mid-Pacific Rise. Four million square miles—fifty-seven *billion* tons of nodules."

"Hell's teeth," said Geordie. "Those figures are incredible."

I moved my finger south again, to Tahiti. "Fourteen million square miles in the central and southeastern Pacific. Two hundred *billion* tons of nodules. Like grains of dust in the desert."

"There must be a snag. Otherwise somebody would have scooped up the nodules for their content."

I smiled. "Oh yes, there are snags. The average depth at which these things lie is over fourteen thousand feet. That's a good deal of water to go through, and the pressure on the bottom is terrific. But it could be done. An American engineer proposed dropping a thing like a giant vacuum cleaner and sucking the nodules to the surface. The capitalization on a scheme like that would run into millions and the profit would be marginal at one pound of nodules per square foot of ocean bed."

Geordie said, "But you have a card up your sleeve."

"Let me say this. The information I've given you is based on IGY surveys, and the one pound per square foot is an approximation."

I stabbed my finger at the eastern Pacific. "The Soviet Institute of Oceanology found three point seven pounds of nodules per square foot right there. You see, the stuff lies in varying concentrations. Here they found five pounds per square foot, here they found eight."

Geordie had been listening with keen interest. "That sounds as though it brings it back in line as an economic proposition."

I shook my head. "No, it doesn't. Manganese isn't in short supply, and neither is iron. If you started picking up large quantities of nodules, you'd saturate the market, the price would slip accordingly, and you'd be back where you started—with a marginal profit. The big metals firms and mining houses—the only people with enough capital to do anything about it—aren't interested. They already run manganese mines on land, and if they started anything like this they'd wreck their own land-based investments."

"Where is all this getting us?" asked Geordie.

"Have patience. Now, I said there are traces of other metals in these nodules—copper, nickel and cobalt. You can forget the copper. But here, in the southeast Pacific, the nodules run to about one point six per cent nickel and about point three per cent cobalt. The mid-Pacific Rise gives as much as two per cent cobalt. Keep that in mind because I'm going to switch to something else."

"For heaven's sake, Mike, don't spin it out too long."

"I'm coming to it," I said. "All the figures I've given you are based on the IGY surveys. Guess how many sites they surveyed."

"I couldn't begin to make a guess," said Geordie.

I took a sip of whisky. "A lousy sixty sites in sixty-four million square miles of the Pacific!"

Geordie stared at me in disbelief. "Is that all?"

"That's all. The orthodox oceanographer says that the ocean bed doesn't vary greatly from place to place—what you find at site X, you're pretty certain to find at site Y."

I tapped the atlas. "I've always been suspicious of that kind of reasoning. Admittedly, the ocean bed is pretty much of a piece, but I don't think we should rely on that, sight unseen. I'm banking on there being places where nodules lie fifty pounds to the square foot—and Mark knew of such places, if I interpreted his notes correctly."

"I think you had a point to make about cobalt, Mike. What is it?"

I let my excitement show. "This is the clincher. The highest assay for cobalt in any nodule has been just over two per cent." I touched the half-nodule on the table with my finger. "I assayed this one today. It checked out at *ten* per cent cobalt. Cobalt, Geordie, is worth more than all the other metals put together—and the rocket metallurgists can't get enough of it!"

WE ATE GEORDIE'S STEW and very good it was, and by midnight we had just about talked the subject to death.

At one stage I returned to a sore point. "I wish Mark's notebooks hadn't been pinched."

Geordie sucked on his pipe. "I could do with knowing why they were pinched—and who pinched them."

"Then you agree that it has something to do with Mark's death?"

"It must, boy. Your brother got hold of something valuable..."

"...and was murdered for it," I finished. "But who killed him? Kane? That's unlikely—it's an odd murderer who travels half-way round the world to inform the family. If only we could get hold of that doctor."

"He's on the other side of the world."

I said softly, "I think Mark came across a hell of a big deposit of high-cobalt nodules. His theories were a bit startling, but they intrigue me. I'd like to organize an expedition. A find like this would hit oceanography like evolution hit biology. Also, there could be billions to be made out of it."

Geordie wasn't ready to be enthusiastic. "So you think it's as good as that?"

"As good as that," I said firmly. "There's enough at stake for quite a few murders."

"How much would such an expedition cost?"

"Let's see. A ship—plus about fifty thousand for special equipment—plus stores and running expenses."

"Running expenses for how long?"

I smiled wryly. "Who knows in a thing like this? Of course, I wouldn't be going entirely blindfold. I know a lot of places where there aren't any high-cobalt nodules. And there's also what I can recall of Mark's theories—perhaps they're not so fantastic after all. Plus there's this." I held up Mark's little diary, which I was keeping on my person.

Geordie slapped his hands together suddenly. "All right, boy. If you can find the capital—and who knows where you'll find money like that—I can provide the ship. Would *Esmerelda* do?"

"Do! Why, she'd be perfect." I tried not to show my excitement too much. "But why should you come into this? It's a chancy business, you know."

He laughed. "You did mention a few billions. And tourist charters aren't much fun after a bit. I suppose you have some ideas about finance? Without a tame banker it's a non-starter."

"As a matter of fact, I do. I saw Clare Campbell the other day— she's in town with her father, attending a conference. He's my goal."

"Who is he?"

"Jonathan Campbell. A Scottish-Canadian mining man. Mark worked for him for a while after the IGY—something to do with a mining venture in South America."

Geordie cocked his head inquiringly. "So he's got money?"

"He's loaded. He lost a packet in the South American business— something to do with mines being nationalized—but I think he's got enough left to take a gamble on something new."

"How well do you know this fellow Campbell, Mike?"

I shook my head. "I never actually met *him*, but I met his daughter once. Mark had her in tow. They seemed to be pretty close."

"I see. And how long did Mark work for Campbell?"

"About a year and a half. Then he pushed off into the South Pacific and teamed up with Norgaard."

"But if Campbell's a mining man, what makes you think he'll finance a deep-sea adventure?"

"Metals are his business," I said. "He's dabbled in tin and copper and had a go at platinum. At the moment he's concentrating on alloy metals—titanium, cobalt, vanadium and stuff like that. Now that rocketry is big business there's a boom in these metals. He's a canny Scot, all right. He organizes field expeditions into remote places, spots a body of ore, puts a million or so into proving and development, then pulls out and sells to the real big boys at a profit."

Geordie rubbed his chin meditatively. "You know, if we do go on this caper, I'd like to include a couple of blokes I know from the old days in my crew. Ian Lewis perhaps."

I remembered a tall, gangling Scotsman. "What's he doing now?"

"Oh, he had a place in the Scottish wilderness that he said he'd be glad to leave. You know, I reckon I could get half a dozen of your dad's old mob, all trained fighters and some of them seamen. They may be getting older, but they're not that old and they're all ex-commandos."

"What do you think you're doing—setting up a private army?"

"Might not be a bad idea," he said. "If last night is a sample of what to expect, we might need an army!"

I sighed. "All right, Sergeant Wilkins. But hold your hand until we get Campbell tied up. We can't do anything without money."

"Ah yes, the money," said Geordie, and looked very sad.

THE FOLLOWING MORNING I had a visit from the inspector. He was cagey and suspicious, but very casual. I think his trouble was that he didn't really know what to be suspicious of.

"Know anyone in South America?" he asked.

"Not offhand," I said.

"Um. The man you killed may have been a South American not a Spaniard. His clothes were labelled from Lima, Rio and Montevideo."

"Who was he?"

The inspector shook his head. "That we don't know, Mr. Trevelyan. Or anything else about him, yet." He changed tack. "I've found out everything there is to know about manganese nodules."

"Then you know more than I do," I said dryly. "They're not really my line. Did you find it interesting?"

He smiled sourly. "Not very—they're about as valuable as road gravel. Are you sure there wasn't anything else in that suitcase that might have been of value?"

"It was just junk, Inspector."

"Looks as though Mr. Wilkins might have been right, then. You surprised the burglars before they could pinch anything else."

I said noncommittally, "I think you're right."

"The inquest will be next Wednesday," he went on. "You'll get an official notification, both you and Mr. Wilkins."

"We'll be there."

Then he left and I thought about South America. That was nearer the Pacific than Spain, but it made no particular sense to me. And then I thought of Mark's connection with Jonathan Campbell, and Campbell's connection with some South American mining venture. But it still made no sense and for the time being I gave up.

Finding a rich Canadian in London was easier than finding a poor Australian. The institute gave me the telephone number of the conference centre where Campbell was supposed to be, and they in turn gave me the name of his hotel. I had him at the third phone call. He was blunt and curt. Yes, he could give me half an hour at eleven that morning. His tone indicated that if I was wasting his time I'd be kicked out in the first two minutes.

At eleven I was shown up to Campbell's suite at the Dorchester. He opened the door himself. "Come in, Trevelyan."

He led the way into a room fitted out as a temporary office, and seated himself behind the desk, gesturing me to sit opposite. He was a stocky man of about sixty with a lined, tanned face, frosty blue eyes and iron-grey hair. Only the slightest accent indicated his transatlantic origin.

I decided that directness was the best policy. I produced the half-nodule and put it on his blotting pad, saying, "This assays at ten per cent cobalt."

He picked it up and looked at it carefully, then asked, "Are you any relation of the Mark Trevelyan who worked for me a while back?"

"He was my brother."

"Was?"

"He's dead. He died about four months ago—in the Pacific."

Campbell frowned. "Sorry to hear that. He was a good scientist."

I detected a reserve in his voice, and thought that here was someone else who had seen through my brother.

He carried on looking at me rather than at the specimen. "Trevelyan—I've heard the name more recently. Oh yes!" He

391

turned and produced a tabloid newspaper from a shelf. "Are you the Trevelyan mentioned here?"

I saw the headline, SCIENTIST KILLS BURGLAR, and nodded.

He put aside the paper and then came back to business. "This is a manganese nodule. There are billions of them lying at the bottom of the Pacific. There are quite a few in the Atlantic, too."

"Not many there," I said. "And the quality's poor. Too much sedimentation."

"True." He tossed the stone and caught it. "The highest cobalt assay to date is a fraction over two per cent. That was found in nodules from the central Pacific. Where did this one come from?"

I wasn't going to provide him with *that* information quite so easily, so I just looked at him blankly and shook my head. He suddenly gave a very charming smile which transformed his face. "All right, I tried," he said. "You'd be surprised how often the direct approach works. Do you know why I'm able to reel off facts about manganese nodules?"

"I was wondering."

"Your brother told me about them," he said. "He wanted me to finance an expedition a couple of years back. I must say I was tempted."

"Why didn't you?"

He hesitated, then said, "I had just lost a packet in South America. It caught me off balance, and until I reorganized I didn't have any liquid capital. About that time your brother left my company, and when I *did* have the cash to fund the expedition, I found he hadn't given me enough information to go on by myself."

"I hope you're better placed now," I said, "because that's why I've come to you—to ask you to fund an expedition."

He touched the nodule. "I must say you've brought more than your brother did. He talked a good story but he never showed any concrete evidence. You say this assayed at ten per cent cobalt?"

"I assayed it myself yesterday—the other half, that is."

"Mind if I have this assayed independently?"

"Not at all," I said equably.

He laughed. "All right, Trevelyan, I won't need to. I believe what you say."

"I must tell you though, Mr. Campbell, that what you've got in your hand is *all* the evidence I have to show."

His hand clenched around the nodule. "Now you begin to interest me. Why don't you tell me your story?"

I told him everything, holding nothing back. He listened in

absolute silence until I had finished, and then said, "Now let's see if I've got all this straight. One, your brother died out in the Pacific; two, a man called Nelson whom you have never heard of sent you a case which contained notebooks and nodule samples; three, Kane shows up and pitches what is clearly a cock-and-bull yarn because your brother had already had his appendix removed; four, the suitcase is stolen by presumed South Americans with additional violence including one killing; five, you retain *one* nodule, analyse it and find a fantastic percentage of cobalt; and six, you also retain a diary of your brother's which you can't even read."

He looked at me for a long time and then said gently, "And on the basis of this you want me to invest maybe a million dollars."

I nodded.

"Have you got that diary here?"

I took it from my breast pocket and handed it to him. He flicked through it. "Who taught your brother to write shorthand?" he asked disgustedly. "St. Vitus?"

"Basically it's Pitman's," I said. "But Mark adapted it."

Campbell tossed the diary onto his desk. "Maybe a cipher expert can sort it out. Let me hang on to it for a while." He turned in his swivel chair and looked out of the window towards Hyde Park. There was a long silence until he spoke again.

"You know, what really interests me in this improbable story of yours is those South Americans," he said unexpectedly. "South America has been unlucky for me. I lost nearly ten million there. That's when Mark's expedition went down the drain. And now Mark has come back—in a sense—and more South Americans are involved. I don't believe in coincidence." He paused, continuing to stare reflectively out over the park, then he swung back to his desk and pointed to the nodule. "What's the iron-oxide content of this?"

"Thirty-two per cent by weight."

"That does it. The cobalt will make the venture economically feasible, but we'll also get a cheap high-grade iron ore, a heck of a lot of manganese, plus some copper, vanadium and anything else we can pick up. Cheap metals, billions of dollars' worth and cheaper than anyone else can produce. It can be tied into one neat, strong package—but it needs careful handling and secrecy. I shall have to consider the complications of international law regarding offshore mining. Financing. Distribution. Markets."

"Then you're willing to finance an expedition?" I asked. It was almost too easy, I thought, and I was right.

"I don't know yet. I want to make some investigations of my own.

393

Maybe I can find Kane for you. Besides, you killed a man, remember." His smile this time was more grim than charming. "Let's wait for the inquest before deciding anything."

IT WAS SIX DAYS to the inquest. To fill in the time I got down to writing the paper that I was supposed to turn out.

Geordie wasn't having any luck tracing Kane. "It's hopeless," he said to me. "A needle in a haystack would be easier to find."

But on the morning of the inquest Kane was found—or rather, he found me.

He called at the flat just as I was leaving for the court—Geordie had already left and was to meet me there. Kane was looking a little the worse for wear, with bloodshot eyes and stubble on his cheeks. He coughed raspingly and said, "Sorry to trouble you, Mr. Trevelyan, but you did say I was to keep in touch."

I looked at him in astonishment and choked back the questions that were on the tip of my tongue. As I invited him inside, I did a bit of fast thinking. Geordie and Campbell had as much at stake in this as I had, and besides I wanted witnesses when I questioned Kane. I decided to play it softly.

I made myself smile pleasantly. "Had enough of England, Mr. Kane?" I asked.

"I've had a bonzer time," he said. "But my stay's over, Mr. Trevelyan. I got to gambling again. I'll never learn. You said you might be able to arrange a passage for me. I wondered . . ."

"Do you have to get back to the Pacific immediately?"

For some reason that didn't please him. "Not specially, no."

"I have a friend who has a yacht he's fitting out. He and I hope to get in some sailing together, and I think he needs crew. How would that suit you?"

He took the bait eagerly. "That'ud be just fine, Mr. Trevelyan!"

I put a writing pad in front of him. "Write down your address so that I can get the skipper to contact you. He'll want to interview you but I'll put in a good word. How's that?"

He scribbled something on the pad. "Thanks a lot, Mr. Trevelyan."

"That's all right," I said generously. "You've earned it."

I showed him out, and then left for the court hearing.

The inquest was straightforward. A doctor gave evidence of death, then I went on the stand, followed by Geordie. We both stuck to the facts and didn't elaborate, then the police had their turn.

I glanced round the courtroom and saw Campbell sitting at the back. He nodded to me, then turned his attention back to the proceedings.

The inspector made an appearance and confirmed that he had found a gun in the right-hand coat pocket of the deceased. Then the lack of identity of the dead man was briefly discussed.

There was a surprise witness, at least to me—Jarvis, my boss, appeared to give expert testimony. He told the coroner what manganese nodules were, explained that they had little value, and even produced one to show what the things looked like.

At the end of the hearing, the coroner took little time to decide that death was due to justifiable manslaughter. He wound everything up with a speech to the effect that no man has the right to take the law into his own hands, and that if a little more care had been taken a death could have been averted. However, what was done was done. I was free to leave the court without a stain on my character.

We all stood when he swept out and there was a general drift towards the doors. An official elbowed his way up to me and gave me a note. It was very brief. *"See you at the Dorchester. Campbell."*

I passed the note to Geordie. "I hope this means what I think it means," I said. "I've got a lot to tell you."

We left the court building and, once outside, I saw Professor Jarvis. I ran to catch up with him, Geordie behind me.

Jarvis saw me coming and waited for me to join him.

"Well, that went off all right, my boy," he said.

"You did your bit—thank you."

"Silly fools," he grumbled. *"Everyone* knows that those nodules are basically worthless—not an economic proposition at all. By the way, I made a few inquiries about that chap, Norgaard. But he seems to have disappeared off the face of the earth."

"When was the last you heard of him?"

"About six, seven months ago—when he was with your brother in the islands round Tahiti."

"When did Norgaard start working with Mark?" I asked.

"Now let me see. It must have been nearly two years ago. Yes, that was it—after Mark had to leave the IGY project he went to Canada to work for Jonathan Campbell for two years, then he left to join up with Norgaard. What they were doing I don't know—they didn't publish anything."

I seized on something he had said. "What do you mean—*had* to leave the IGY?"

Jarvis looked embarrassed. "Oh, I shouldn't have said that."

"I'd like to know. It can't hurt Mark now."

Jarvis regarded the tips of his highly polished shoes. "Well, I never did get to the bottom of it—it was hushed up, you know—but apparently Mark fudged some of his results."

"Faked his figures?"

"That's right. It was found by sheer chance. Of course he had to leave. But we . . . the IGY agreed not to make any more of the matter, so he was able to get the job in Canada after he resigned."

"So that's why he left the IGY before the survey was over. I wondered about that. What was he working on at the time?"

Jarvis shrugged. "I don't recall, but it certainly had to do with the underwater surveys. Manganese nodules, perhaps? You know, I never did trust your brother, and the fact that he cooked his books didn't surprise me a bit."

"That's all right—lots of people didn't like Mark," I said. "I wasn't too keen on him myself."

Jarvis nodded. "Still, my boy, I don't mistrust the whole Trevelyan family. You're worth ten of your brother. Now, forget all this and enjoy your leave."

"Thanks, Prof," I said warmly.

We shook hands and he strode off down the street.

I turned to Geordie. "What do you make of that?"

"Norgaard vanished just about the same time that Mark kicked the bucket. I wonder if . . ."

"I know what you're thinking, Geordie. Is Norgaard dead too? I do hope Campbell has good news for us—I want to do some fieldwork in the islands. Come on, come with me to see him."

CAMPBELL WAS LESS CRUSTY than at our first meeting. "Well," he said, as we entered his suite, "I see you're not exactly a hardened criminal, Trevelyan."

"Not a stain on my character." I introduced Geordie, and the two men sized one another up with interest. "Mr. Wilkins is willing to contribute a ship—and skipper her, too," I said.

"I'm glad someone has faith in your crazy story."

"What about you?" I asked.

He ignored that, and got down to business.

"I knew I could trust my hunch about your South Americans," he began. "I've got a pretty good intelligence network, and I've discovered that Suarez-Navarro, a South American mining house, are fitting out a research ship in Darwin at this very moment. I've tangled with them before—they're a crowd of unscrupulous thugs. Why would they be fitting out an oceanographical research ship?"

"Nodules," said Geordie succinctly.

"How unscrupulous?" I asked. "Would they stoop to burglary?"

Campbell folded his hands together. "I'll tell you the story and let you judge for yourselves. Once I had a pretty good set-up in South America, never mind just where. The mines were producing well, and I ploughed a lot of money into the area in the interests of good labour relations. I built a couple of schools, a hospital and all the civilized trimmings. Those Indian miners had never had it so good, and they responded well.

"Suarez-Navarro cast an eye on the operation and liked the look of it. They went about things in their own smelly way, though. They had a troubleshooter, a guy called Ernesto Ramirez. He greased a few palms, supported the army, and suddenly there was a new government—which promptly expropriated the mines in the interests of the national economy—or that's what they said. Anyway, I never got a cent out of it. They just took the lot and Ramirez vanished.

"Then the government wanted somebody to run the mines, so Suarez-Navarro offered to take on the job out of the kindness of their hearts. For a hefty percentage of the profits.

"They closed the schools and the hospital—those things aren't profitable, you see—and pretty soon they had a strike on their hands. That brought Ramirez back fast. He called in the army, there was quite a bit of shooting, and then there was suddenly no strike—just fifty dead Indians and their widows."

Campbell smiled grimly. "Does that answer your question about the scruples of Suarez-Navarro?"

I nodded.

Suddenly Campbell seemed to go off at a tangent. "I'm attending a conference here in London, on mineral resources. It's a Commonwealth deal but other interested parties have been invited to send observers. Suarez-Navarro have sent two, and another one arrived last week. His name is Ernesto Ramirez." Campbell's voice was hard. "Ramirez isn't a conference man, he's Suarez-Navarro's muscleman. Do I make my point?"

Geordie and I both nodded intently.

"Well, just to make sure I'm going to hammer it home. I put someone on to watch Ramirez and was told that the fellow called Kane you told me about had a two-hour talk with Ramirez yesterday. So it seems they're in league. We had Kane followed to his digs and I have the address."

I reeled it off.

397

My tactic was effective. Campbell said, "What?" disbelievingly, and Geordie gaped at me. I enjoyed my moment.

"Kane came to visit me this morning," I explained, then told them both what had happened. I turned to Geordie. "I suggest you get him down to the docks and have a serious talk with him."

Campbell frowned. "No, you don't," he said. "Don't ask him anything. Don't you see what's happening?"

Geordie and I shrugged.

"Ever heard of industrial espionage? Of course you have. Every big outfit runs a spy system. I do it myself—don't much like it, but I've got to keep up with the hard-nosed bastards in the business. Now let's reconstruct what's been happening. You got hold of something you shouldn't have—from the point of view of Suarez-Navarro. Ramirez hotfoots it to England—he arrived the day before Kane came to see you, so it's quite probable they came together. Kane comes to you to find out if Mark's stuff has arrived yet, and you tell him it has. He spins you a yarn as cover—it doesn't really matter what it is—and reports back to Ramirez. Then Ramirez tells his boys to snatch the stuff but you surprise them in the middle." Campbell lifted his eyebrows. "Does that make sense so far?"

Geordie said, "It makes sense to me."

I said nothing. I was a little more doubtful.

Campbell continued, "But something goes wrong—they leave the diary and one nodule. Ramirez doesn't know this, but he does know you've contacted me and that all sorts of inquiries have started—including questions in court about nodules. Oh yes, I bet he was there—or one of his spies. You see, he'd keep a tail on you just to see if you did anything out of the ordinary—and you did. So what does Ramirez do now?"

"I'll buy it," I said. "What does he do?"

"He lays Kane alongside you again," explained Campbell. "You gave him the perfect opportunity—you invited Kane to join your crew. But what Ramirez doesn't know is that you were suspicious of Kane right from the start, and this gives *us* a perfect opportunity. We employ Kane, feed him information. We also keep him underfoot and don't lose him again. That's why you mustn't ask him any awkward questions—not right now, anyway."

I thought about this for a long time. "Does this mean you're financing us?"

"You're darn right it does," snapped Campbell. "And I'm coming along for the ride. If Suarez-Navarro are going to all this trouble they must be on to something big. I'll put up half a million dollars—or whatever it takes—and I ask only one thing. That we get there, and do it, before they can."

He turned to Geordie. "Now, tell me about your ship, Captain."

"It's a brigantine," said Geordie. "About two hundred tons."

Campbell's jaw dropped. "But that's a little sailing ship!"

"Take it easy," I said. "A lot of research vessels are sailing ships. There happens to be a sound economic reason."

"All right. Let's hear it," said Campbell.

"A research ship never knows exactly where it's going," I began. "We might find ourselves dredging a thousand miles away from the nearest land. Station-keeping and dredging take power and fuel. You *could* use an engine-powered ship to do the job but it would cost you—oh, a million pounds plus. Geordie's boat will be fine."

"That makes sense, Trevelyan," Campbell said. "What will you need in the way of equipment?"

So we got down to it. The biggest item was the winch, which was to be installed amidships, and storage space for 30,000 feet of cable below it. There was also to be a laboratory for on-the-spot analysis of the nodules we dredged up.

Very little was said concerning the location of the strange treasure we were after, and I knew that I alone could come up with anything of use there. I had some heavy studying ahead of me.

"I've been thinking about Kane," I said presently. "Your review of the situation was wrong on one point."

"What's that?" said Campbell.

"You said that Kane spun me a yarn as cover, and that it didn't matter what it was. That's not entirely so. Mark's death certificate states the cause of death as appendicitis which, as I explained to you, is impossible. Kane and Schouten both told the same lie. I'd like to know just how Mark really did die."

"By God, you're right," said Campbell. "We'll get it out of Kane as soon as he's served his purpose."

Geordie grunted. "We're going into the Pacific," he said. "Maybe we'll get it out of Schouten."

CHAPTER THREE

It was nearly three months before we were ready to get away. When I handed in my resignation, old Jarvis didn't take it too well, but he accepted the situation with reluctance. I wished I could have told him what I was doing, but that was impossible.

Geordie recruited his crew. He had kept on four of his own lads and had of course taken on Kane. Of the other six that he added, all were ex-commandos from my dad's wartime gang.

Ian Lewis detached himself from his croft with alacrity and Geordie made him first mate; he'd had years of experience under sail. Ex-corporal Taffy Morgan came along; one night during the war he had killed six Germans with a commando knife, earning himself the MM. Danny Williams had also won the MM, although I never found out what for. Then there was the burly bulk of Nick Dugan, an Irishman. Bill Hunter also turned up—he had made a name for himself as an underwater demolitions expert and was the only other regular sailing man in the team. And there was Jim Taylor, another explosives wizard.

They were all into their forties, like Geordie, but seemed as tough and fit as ever. I was confident that if we ran into trouble we could handle it.

Geordie was confident too of welding them into a good sailing crew. What any of them lacked in knowledge they'd soon pick up. The enthusiasm was certainly there—although for the time being they knew nothing of the complications in which we were entangled. It was a straight research and survey trip to them all, including Kane, and any hints Geordie may have given his special team they kept strictly to themselves. As Campbell had predicted, Kane was sticking as close to us as a leech; Geordie had simply told him that there was a berth for him if he cared to cross the Atlantic with us, and he had jumped at the opportunity.

Campbell went back to Canada as soon as the mineral conference ended, and was planning to meet us in Panama. Before he left England he had a talk with me. "Suarez-Navarro have a good intelligence service," he said. "You'll be watched and they'll know everything you do as soon as you do it. It can't be helped. It's a case of we know that they know that we know, and so on."

"Talking of what we know," I said, "have you made any progress with Mark's diary?"

Campbell snorted. "I gave it to a cipher expert and he's having his troubles with Mark's peculiar shorthand. But he says he can crack it, given time. What I wish I knew was how Suarez-Navarro got on to this whole thing in the first place."

My own thoughts were that Mark, cheated out of Campbell's backing—for he would have seen Campbell's loss only in terms of his own disappointment—had approached Suarez-Navarro himself. But I wasn't sure and decided to keep my thoughts to myself.

So Campbell went off to Canada to attend to his business affairs, and we speeded up ours as much as possible. It was with great relief that I heard Geordie announce one day that we were at last ready for sea. All he needed to know was where to head for.

I said, "Do you know the Blake Plateau?"

"Never heard of it."

"It's off the coast of the southeastern United States. There are nodules there, although they're poor quality, not like the ones in the Pacific. We'll test our gear there, and if there's anything wrong we can get it fixed in Panama."

"Right, boy. Let's go and scoop up some poor-quality wealth from the bottom of the sea."

"I can't wait," I said.

WE MADE A FAIR and untroubled crossing of the Atlantic. The crew's spirits ran high, and Kane fitted in well and seemed as willing as the others. Knowing that they were all curious as to our purpose I gave occasional deliberately boring lectures on oceanography, touching on a number of research subjects, so that the matter of manganese nodules was obscured. Only two people showed an interest in what I had to say, and to them I spoke in private about our quarry. One was Geordie, of course, and the other, to my satisfaction, was Bill Hunter, our diving expert. I knew that his interest and involvement might well be crucial.

One afternoon they both joined me in the laboratory, at my request, to learn a little more about manganese nodules.

Geordie picked up the one which I'd cut in half—I had brought a few on board to help my explanation along—and pointed to the white central core.

"I suppose you'll tell me again that it's a shark's tooth in the middle of this rock. You never did get around to explaining how it got there, did you?"

I smiled. "It happens often. A shark dies and its body drifts down; the flesh rots or is eaten, the bones dissolve—what bones a shark has, it's cartilage really—and by the time anything reaches the very bottom there's nothing left but teeth. They are made of sodium triphosphate and are insoluble in water. There are millions of them on any ocean bed." I opened a box. "Look here," I said and gave Geordie a larger white bone. It was as big as the palm of his hand and curiously convoluted.

"What's this?" he asked.

Bill answered. "It's whale's earbone. I've seen 'em before."

"Right, Bill. Also made of sodium triphosphate. We sometimes find them at the core of larger nodules—but more often it's a shark's tooth and most frequently a bit of clay."

"So the manganese sticks to the tooth," said Geordie. "How long does it take to make a nodule?"

"Estimates vary from one millimetre every thousand years to one millimetre every million years—which makes it one of the slowest chemical reactions known."

"Do you mean that if you find a nodule with a half-diameter of ten millimetres formed round a tooth, the shark lived ten million years ago? Were there sharks then?" Geordie asked in fascination.

"Oh yes, the shark is one of earth's oldest inhabitants."

We talked a little more about nodules and then I dropped the subject. They had a lot to learn and it would be easier for them if it came in small doses.

We did our testing on the Blake Plateau. There were only minor problems, and generally I was happy with the way things were going. I got some nodules up, which were the usual low-quality stuff that's always pulled out of the Atlantic, and among the debris of ooze, red clay and deposits we found enough sharks' teeth and whales' earbones to give everyone on board a handful of souvenirs.

Both Geordie and Bill Hunter were becoming more and more interested in the nodules, so I soon arranged for another session with them.

"Why does manganese lump together?" Geordie asked.

I laughed. "It's complicated; I'll try to explain it as simply as I can. Do you know what a colloid is?"

Two headshakes.

"Look. If you put a teaspoon of sugar into water, you get a sugar solution—that is, the sugar breaks down to the molecular level and mixes intimately with the water. In other words, it dissolves. Right?"

"Right."

"Now, if you have a substance that won't dissolve in water but is divided into very fine particles, much smaller than can be seen in a microscope, that's a colloid."

"I see the difference," Geordie said.

"All right. Now, all colloidal particles carry an electric charge. These charges make the colloidal particles of manganese dioxide clump together in larger and larger units. They also tend to be attracted to any electrically conductive surfaces such as a shark's tooth or a bit of clay. Hence the nodules."

"Where does the manganese come from?" asked Bill.

"From rivers, from underground volcanic fissures, from rocks on the seabed. The sea is a big chemical broth. In certain localized conditions the sea becomes alkaline and the manganese in the rocks leaches out and dissolves in the water..."

"You said it doesn't dissolve."

"Pure metallic manganese *will* dissolve as long as the conditions are right—in what chemists call a 'reducing atmosphere'. Just believe me, Geordie. But when currents carry the dissolved manganese into 'oxidizing atmospheres' where the water is more acid, the manganese combines with oxygen to form manganese dioxide which *is* insoluble and so a colloid is formed. And then the process goes on as I've described."

He thought about that. "What about the copper and nickel and cobalt and other stuff that's in the nodules?"

"Well," I said, "all these metals have certain affinities for each other. What happens is that as the colloidal particles grow bigger they scavenge the other metals—entrap them. Of course, this is happening over a pretty long period of time."

"Say a hundred million years or so," said Geordie ironically.

"Well, that's the orthodox view. But I think it could happen faster than that," I said slowly. "Given the right conditions, though just what these conditions would be I'm not sure. I have seen peculiarities that indicate rapid growth. Anyway that's one of the objects of this trip—to find out."

What I didn't say in Bill's hearing was that the peculiarities I had seen were contained in Mark's prize nodule. I was beginning to grope towards a theory of nodule formation which, though still vague, was tremendously exciting. I was anxious to know how Campbell's cipher expert had made out in translating Mark's diary.

TEN DAYS AFTER LEAVING the Blake Plateau we docked at Panama, where Campbell was waiting for us as planned.

"I've booked you into my hotel for a night or so," he told me. "There's no reason why you shouldn't have a last taste of luxury before the big job. Geordie too, if he wants it. I'll expect you both to dinner—you can't miss the hotel, it's the Colombo, right on the main street."

He steered me into a waterfront bar, and soon I was sitting thankfully in front of a large glass of cold beer.

Campbell wasted no time. He produced a biggish envelope from his jacket. "I had photostats made of the diary pages," he said. "The original's in a bank vault in Montreal."

403

He emptied the envelope. "I got the translation done. My cipher expert hopes he's got the scientific bits right."

"We'll soon find out." I was stiff with eagerness.

Campbell handed me a neatly bound booklet. "It looks screwy to me. It had better make sense to you or this whole expedition is a bust already."

I glanced through the booklet. "This is going to be a long job," I said. "I'm not going to be able to make any snap judgments here and now; I'll study it this afternoon. Right now I want to go back to *Esmerelda*, pack my gear and go and take a shower."

If he was disappointed he didn't show it—clearly what I said made sense. And so it was not until I was lying on the bed in my blessedly cool hotel room a couple of hours later that I finally opened the envelope.

The translation was complete except for a few gaps here and there, but it didn't improve matters as much as I'd hoped. The thing was written in a kind of telegraphese which didn't make for easy reading. It was, on the whole, an ordinary diary covering the last few months of Mark's life. There were references to shore leave, films seen, all in brusque lack of detail, the people mentioned by initials only. It was fairly uninteresting on the surface.

Then there were entries made at sea. Here the diary turned professional, with roughly scribbled equations and analyses of seabed material, mostly sea ooze. I waded on feeling that I might be wasting my time until, towards the end, I found myself looking at something remarkable. It was an analysis of a nodule, and the figures were startling. They read: "*Manganese—28%; iron—32%; cobalt—8%; copper—4%; nickel—6%; other—22%. Wow!*"

"Wow!" indeed.

There followed analyses of four more nodules, all equally rich. I did some calculating and found the average cobalt in the five nodules to be a fraction under nine per cent. The copper and nickel weren't to be laughed at either. I didn't yet know much about the economics of recovery but it was evident that this might be a paying proposition even with relatively primitive methods of dredging, depending on the depth of water. With sophisticated equipment it would be better than owning a goldmine. But there was one snag—nowhere did Mark say where these riches were located.

Scattered through the typewritten pages was the phrase, "*Picture Here*", and a number, and at the end there were reproductions of rather strange drawings—more doodles than drawings—as well as a statement by the cipher expert about them:

404

It is probable that these drawings are pictograms or rebuses which indicate place names. Of the 32 drawings, I believe I have successfully identified 24.

To illustrate: the rough sketch of the gas mantle with word GRATIS beneath may well refer to the Australian town of Fremantle; the bearded man with the sword and the baby is probably Solomon, referring to the biblical story, and may indicate the Solomon Islands; the bearded man looking at a monkey may be a reference to Darwin, Australia.

The fact that all these names occur in the same quarter of the globe is a further indication that one may be on the right track in such surmising. Other names tentatively identified are also to be found in the same area.

Tracings of the drawings, together with possible identifications are attached. To solve the eight unidentified drawings one would need a more precise knowledge of the Pacific.

I looked up Mark's analyses of two of the non-standard nodules again. Coming immediately after them were the numbers 28 and 29. I turned to the relevant drawings. One was of a voluptuous wench wearing a Phrygian cap with underneath it the words, *"The Fair Goddess"*. The other was a rather bedraggled-looking American eagle with the inscription, *"The Disappearing Trick"*. Neither was identified.

I knew that Mark's ship had been based in Australia during the IGY survey—hence, possibly, the Australian references. He'd probably been in the Solomons. Did he go as far as Easter Island? I checked the drawings and found a rabbit trying to hatch an egg, a traditional symbol of Easter. That was one the expert had spotted too.

It was a big area in which to find *The Fair Goddess* or *The Disappearing Trick*.

I thought about Mark and his brilliant but strangely twisted mind which delighted in complexity and deception. He had certainly been up to something fishy—no high-cobalt results had come out of the IGY investigations, and yet he had such results.

My thoughts were interrupted by Geordie banging at the door. "Aren't you ready yet?" he demanded as he entered the room. "We've got a dinner date with Campbell."

"Goodness, the time's slipped away."

"Found anything?"

I looked up. "Yes, I've found something, but it looks as though we still have to play guessing games. I'll tell you about it when we're all together. Give me ten minutes to get dressed."

"Come to the lounge. Campbell wants to meet us there."

THE HOTEL LOUNGE was discreetly lit and in one corner a trio was playing soft music. Over drinks I brought Campbell and Geordie up to date concerning our manganese nodule. "I've come to the conclusion that our nodule isn't very old," I said.

"How old?" Campbell demanded.

"He always talks in millions," said Geordie.

"Not more than fifty thousand years," I said flatly. "I'll stake my reputation on it. Somewhere in the Pacific these things are growing at an explosive rate."

"Explosive," said Geordie incredulously. "Do you call fifty thousand years explosive?"

"From a geological standpoint it's very fast. It's highly unusual, though, and very important."

"Why so?" Campbell asked.

"Look, the whole Pacific is covered with these nodules which have been growing slowly over millions of years. Now we have one which has grown in a fraction of that time. There must be a specific reason for it. My guess is that it's the result of purely local conditions, and that these nodules are growing at the same rate there even now."

"I can't see that that helps us much."

"It helps us this much. It means we can cut out vast areas— millions of square miles—where I *know* that no peculiar conditions exist in the sea. I'll go along with orthodox oceanography on that one; the seabed is pretty regular. What we've got to watch for is the oddity."

"Got any idea what kind of oddity?"

I nodded. "I have vague ideas that I'm not prepared to put into words just yet," I said. "Maybe I'll get something from the diary translation. It may only need one word to make the whole picture clear—like the last piece in a jigsaw puzzle."

"We'll come back to that later," Campbell said. "Meanwhile, I've been keeping tabs on Suarez-Navarro. Ramirez left London and joined their ship."

"Where are they now?" Geordie asked.

"Still in Darwin—doing nothing. I don't get it." He glanced up as he spoke. Approaching our table was a young woman whom I recognized as his daughter. Campbell introduced us. "Clare, this is Michael Trevelyan, and our captain, Geordie Wilkins."

Geordie shook hands gravely. As I took her hand she looked at me carefully but did not react to my name at all. I was about to remind her that I had met her once before in Vancouver, with Mark, but took my cue from her and made my greeting noncommittal.

While drinks were being ordered, I assessed her. She was really beautiful—tall, with black hair and straight brows over grey eyes. Her mouth was generous with mobile corners, a mouth made for laughter, and she dressed with that deceptive simplicity which means money.

We all chatted for a short time, and I saw that there was something wary and watchful about her. I felt that it concerned me.

Presently Campbell said, "Gentlemen, you had better know that I've told the whole story to Clare. She's my right hand. What's more, when I join ship she's coming along as well." Geordie looked dismayed and glanced at me.

"Why not?" I said evenly. "We could do with an extra hand in the lab, Miss Campbell . . ."

"Clare, please. Are you Michael or Mike?"

"Mike, always."

Geordie finally had his say. "Have you been to sea before, Miss— er, Clare?" he asked sternly. Clare bore it equably.

"Yes, I have—for long trips, too. I've got all my own gear and you'll believe me when you see how worn-out it all is."

Geordie was routed.

Campbell broke in impatiently at this point. "What about the diary, Mike? You've read through it, I suppose."

"There are interesting possibilities opening up."

"Such as?"

"The diary was written partly while Mark was with the IGY survey. I believe he got hold of those high-cobalt nodules at that time, found out their value, and decided to keep the knowledge to himself. He suppressed the evidence."

Campbell seemed perturbed. "Do you really think your brother would do a thing like that?" he said stiffly. "He struck me as a very fine scientist."

"Mark was never too scrupulous," I said. "He had a mind that made a corkscrew look like a straight edge. He wanted something from you and he was showing his cleanest face."

"Well, you knew him best," said Campbell.

Clare's face was calm, showing only a polite interest, but her tense jawline caught my notice.

I said, "Well, whatever you thought of Mark, we're faced with a

407

problem put to us by him, and we can only solve it by understanding the way his mind worked." I had them all riveted now. "Let me tell you something that I'll bet you don't know—Mark was kicked out of the IGY for falsifying figures."

"I didn't know that," exclaimed Campbell.

"It's true," I said. "Professor Jarvis, my boss at the institute, told me about it. After leaving the IGY, Mark went to work for you—he was using you. He hoped you'd put up the money for an expedition. But he couldn't show you the nodules because you'd want to know how he had obtained them. And that was by stealing them from the people who paid his salary."

Campbell began to look baffled. "He never showed me anything. He talked a good story though."

"That's right. And you nearly fell for it. But you couldn't finance his expedition, and so he left you."

There was silence while Campbell digested what I had said.

"I think Mark tried the same ploy on Suarez-Navarro. In fact I think he and Norgaard were sailing round the islands near Tahiti, waiting for the Suarez-Navarro ship that's in Darwin right now."

"All right, you've made your point. What next?" Campbell asked.

"Well, we could find out where Mark's IGY ship dredged, and drop our dredge in the same places. But I don't think it will be any of the sites they actually surveyed or word of the nodules would have come out already. No, I think it was a trial site, one they weren't serious about, and probably didn't even make a record of."

We all sat in gloom for a while. The faint drift of music changed tempo and a woman began to sing with the trio. Her voice was nice and I turned to watch her.

"It seems we're back where we started—all we have to go on is the diary," said Clare suddenly.

"We'll discuss it over dinner," Campbell decided, to my relief.

THE MEAL WAS DIGESTIBLE which was more than any of us could say for the diary. Clare asked if she could have it for bedside reading. "I like that sort of thing," she said. "Puzzles, jigsaws."

"You're welcome," I told her, thinking that her knowledge of Mark might be useful. "I want a break from it."

I was pleased that as the evening wore on she seemed to lose some of her reserve. We were at the coffee stage when a waiter came up to the table. "Is one of you gentlemen Mr. Trevelyan?"

"I am."

"There's a young lady in the foyer asking to see you."

I got up, "I don't know anyone in Panama. It's probably a mistake," I said. "Excuse me."

There were several people in the foyer including more than one young lady, but no one approached me. I crossed to the desk and said, "My name's Trevelyan. I understand someone wants me."

The clerk pointed with his pen, indicating that I should come into the office behind the desk. The young lady waiting there was the singer who had been entertaining us in the lounge.

"I am Mike Trevelyan. You wanted to speak to me?"

I could see she was nervous. She was rather slight, with hollows under her dark eyes. But there was an appealing quality about her—I think the best word would be winsome.

"I'm sorry to trouble you—I saw your name in the register—I wondered if you were any relation of Mark Trevelyan? From Tahiti?"

"I'm his brother," I said. "Obviously you—know Mark?" I didn't know if she knew of his death and I felt it would be unkind to throw it at her without warning.

She nodded, gripping her hands together. "Yes, I knew him very well. Have you just come from England?"

"Yes."

"Do you know if his wife got the suitcase I sent?"

I stared at her in amazement. "I thought you were a man! So you are P. Nelson! You already know about Mark's death, then," I added gently.

She nodded, and for a moment we were silent, then she smiled and some of the tension left her face.

"So the case did arrive all right?"

"It arrived, thank you," I said. I didn't say that it had been stolen immediately afterwards because I didn't know just where she might stand in the complexity of Mark's affairs.

"Miss Nelson, what about having a drink with me? I'd like to know more about Mark and what he was doing out in Tahiti."

She looked at her watch. "I could spare half an hour. Then I've got another stint in the lounge."

I sent a waiter back to Campbell and the others with a message, then we went to a small bar a little way down the street. I ordered drinks and we settled down in an alcove. "You're an American, aren't you?" I said.

"Yes. And you're from—Cornwall. You talk the same way Mark did. I used to tease him about that sometimes."

"Where did you meet him?"

"In Tahiti. I was working a little joint in Papeete. Mark used to come in with his sidekick, and we got pretty—friendly."

"Who was his sidekick?"

"A Swedish guy, Sven Norgaard. But this was, oh, maybe two years ago, when we first met."

About the time he left Campbell, I calculated. I said, "I'm interested in how Mark died. Can you tell me anything about it—if it doesn't distress you too much?"

"Oh, that's all right," she said in a tremulous voice. "He died of appendicitis out in the Tuamotus—didn't you know that?"

"Yes—but how did you know?"

"I didn't believe it at first, but they let me see the death certificate."

"Who are 'they'? Who told you in the first place?"

"A schooner came in with the news. And I went down to the government bureau to see the proof. You see, I thought he might have just gone away."

"Did the doctor who operated on Mark come to Papeete himself?"

She shook her head. "Not much point, was there? I mean, it's over two hundred miles and he's the only doctor out there. He wouldn't make that journey just to bring the news back."

This clashed with Kane's story: according to him the doctor had dealt with the certificate and the authorities. Or had he? I thought back to what Kane had said—that he and his partner, Hadley, had left it all to the doctor. Perhaps it only meant sending the papers back on the next convenient transport.

I said, "Did you know the men on the schooner?"

She was silent for a bit and then said, "Why are you asking me all these questions, Mr. Trevelyan?"

"I think there's something very odd about the whole affair."

"You think he was murdered, don't you?" she asked flatly.

I decided that I might as well be honest. I nodded. "You think so too, Miss Nelson?"

There was a long pause. "Yes," she whispered, and started to cry. I took her hand in mine.

"I was living with Mark," she explained. "Oh God, I *loved* him."

"Were you happy with him, Miss Nelson?" I asked.

Amazingly, a smile appeared. "Oh, I was. Please—call me Paula."

"And I'm Mike."

We were silent for a few moments, then she said, "I suppose it all started when Sven was killed—"

"Norgaard? Killed!"

"Yes. He was found out on the reef, outside Papeete, with his head bashed in. At first everyone thought it was the sea—they thought he'd been washed off his feet and had his head smashed on the rocks. Then they decided he might have been murdered. The police began asking questions and they came to Mark. He said he knew nothing about it. It didn't seem to worry him."

I took a deep breath. "Paula, do you think that Mark killed Sven?"

She hesitated, then shook her head. "No, it *couldn't* have been Mark. I know he could get very angry—even violent—but he couldn't have killed Sven. They were partners. But that night Mark disappeared from Tahiti. And then we heard that he was dead. I've already told you how that was."

"Who brought you the news of Mark's death—in that schooner?"

"A man called Hadley. He said that he and his partner had found Mark dying out in the islands."

This was the break—the evidence that showed Kane to be a liar. There could have been an honest mistake about the death certificate, but not about this. Kane had told me that he and Hadley had left things to the doctor.

I said, "Hadley's partner—was he called Kane?"

"I don't know, I never met him. I knew Hadley, though. He came to visit Mark often."

"He did!" I ejaculated. This was a new development.

"Oh sure. Mark and Sven used to hire Hadley's boat and go off for weeks at a time with him."

"You've no idea where they went, I suppose?"

"Mark never talked to me about what he did," she said.

"One more thing. What led you to think Mark had been murdered?"

"It was Hadley," she said. "He came to my place and said he wanted Mark's things. I didn't see any reason why he should have Mark's stuff so I gave him the air. He was mad but he couldn't do anything because I had friends with me. But he scared me. So I sent Mark's suitcase home to his wife." There was pain in her voice. "Hadley came back and beat the daylights out of me—he was a real bastard. He searched my place but of course there wasn't anything there."

"You mean—he actually beat you up?"

"Yes." She shuddered at the memory. "Well, then I got real scared because I'd said too much. I said I had proof that he was lying—that Mark hadn't died the way he said. Hadley looked at me in a real funny way and said he'd be back—with friends. So I packed a few things and got out. Next morning there was a trading schooner leaving for Panama at five o'clock and I was aboard by four."

"What was that proof you had, Paula?"

She said what I guessed she was going to say. "Mark had had his appendix out. I saw the scar. He couldn't have died that way."

"I knew about that, too. Mark had his appendix out years ago."

Paula glanced at her watch. "I have to get back."

"Thanks, Paula. You've helped me a lot. Do you think that Hadley killed Mark and Sven Norgaard?"

"I do," she said intensely.

"Have you any idea why?"

She shrugged. "No idea—but I'm sure he did it."

We returned to the hotel lounge. Paula rejoined the trio, and I sat down with Geordie and Clare. "Pop's gone to bed," Clare explained. "It's late and he gets tired."

Paula began to sing in her pleasant, husky voice.

"Nice voice she's got," said Clare, smiling mischievously. "We noticed you escorting her out of the foyer."

"Her name is P. Nelson," I said. Geordie choked over his coffee.

I put Clare in the picture regarding the name, then said, "She thinks Mark was murdered, and his partner Norgaard too. And she thinks they were both killed by Hadley, this partner of Kane's. But the official police view in Tahiti seems to be that Mark might have killed Norgaard—and that Mark died by accident while on the run. It's a mess."

"Good heavens," said Geordie. "What's the girl doing here?"

"Ran away from Hadley."

Clare looked over towards Paula, who was still singing.

"How well did she know Mark?"

"Pretty well. She was another of his girlfriends," I said unthinkingly. I could have bitten my tongue out the moment I spoke.

NEXT MORNING AT BREAKFAST Campbell came down with a cable in his hand. "Suarez-Navarro have started to move," he said. "Their ship has left Darwin, bound for New Guinea. Would your nodule deposit be anywhere near there?"

"Possibly," I said. "From what I could gather from the notebooks Mark was linking nodule formation with vulcanism, and there's a hell of a lot of volcanos in that part of the world."

"Do you think Mark was right in that theory?" asked Campbell.

"I don't know," I admitted. "It's all very theoretical. There's nothing against it in principle."

412

Campbell muttered, "When I get an unqualified answer from a scientist I suppose the world will be coming to an end. Now, what's all this about the girl last night? Clare's told me a little."

So I filled them in and we sat back, disturbed by the story. We were running into something which was getting steadily nastier.

Clare said, changing the subject, "Mike, I've been giving the diary some thought and I think I've come up with something." She laid out the diary and drawings in front of us. "I've been working backwards, from where we know Mark was, to see if we can identify any more of the drawings. The very last one looks like a monocle, and I think it means Tahiti."

"Why would it mean Tahiti?" asked Campbell.

"Tahiti is one of the Society Islands. And a monocle is the epitome of the upper-crust, 'society' bloke."

I laughed. "Crude but effective. Go on."

"Numbers 31 and 30 I can't work out at all. One's a cow and one's a—well, it's this." She pointed to an object like an irregular, flattened semicircle standing on a flat base. It was connected to the cow with the word "OR", and made no sense at all.

"Then we come to these. *The Fair Goddess* and *The Disappearing Trick*, a woman and an eagle."

I interrupted her. "They are the two that come immediately before Mark's high-cobalt assay figures. I think they may be crucial."

"Good," she said briskly. "I've been thinking about the woman. I think she could be La France—you know, Uncle Sam for America, John Bull for Britain and this female—Marianne—for France. You see her in newspaper cartoons."

Campbell looked at the drawing intently. "You may have something there. What's the extent of French territory in the Pacific?"

"French Oceania," I said. "About a million square miles of it, including Tahiti, Bora-Bora, the Tuamotus, the Marquesas. You'd have to get it down much closer than that."

"The Marianas Islands," said Geordie glumly.

Clare looked thrilled. "Where are they?"

"A long way off. Almost alongside the Philippines," I said. "The place we're looking for can't be there, or why was Mark so far away from it? We want something down this way."

"What's this about a goddess? Marianne isn't one."

"Let's go through a list of goddesses," I suggested. "There's Venus for a start. Is there a Venus Island?"

Geordie grinned. "I've heard of the Good Ship Venus, but never of an island."

"What about Aphrodite?" asked Clare.

We all thought about that. "Nothing doing," said Geordie finally.

"It could be a French name," said Campbell.

"Or a Polynesian name. Or a Polynesian goddess," I added.

We tried, but we couldn't even make a start on the Polynesian deities, not having a single degree in anthropology between us.

Clare gazed fiercely at the drawing. "All right, one last try. Let's go through it once more."

We all groaned.

"Demeter," muttered Campbell, whose attention was waning.

Still nothing doing.

Clare gave a shout of laughter. "I've got it—she's not La France at all, she's Athena, the Roman goddess of justice. Mark used 'fair' in the sense of 'fair play'."

"But Athena wasn't Roman," objected Campbell. "She was Greek."

"The Roman equivalent was Minerva—what about that?" I said quickly.

Geordie thumped the table and burst out laughing. "My God! I should have seen it before. *Récife de Minerve*, of course!"

Campbell said, "You mean there is such a place?" He rubbed his hands, his interest rekindled. "Now we're getting somewhere—where is it? Down this way?"

"Down south of the Tuamotus," said Geordie.

"Is it worth a trip?" Campbell asked me. "You're the expert."

I thought that it was only a remote possibility that we'd hit on the right spot on our very first guess, but we had to start somewhere. "It could have possibilities," I said. "It partly depends on where it is, which is what Geordie's going to tell us."

"Are you kidding?" said Geordie. "*Récife de Minerve*, or Minerva Reef, is a hidden shoal. Nobody knows where it is. There's an account of it in the Pacific Islands *Pilot*. I've got a copy on board. I'll go and get it."

While Geordie fetched the book, I decided to have another word with Paula, who had left a note for me containing her phone number. I used the phone in the hotel foyer. "Paula, it's Mike. I'd like to talk to you again. Now, if I can."

"Sure," she said. "I'll see you in that little bar up the street."

She was waiting for me, sitting at the same table. "Hi," she said. "What's on your mind?"

I ordered coffee for both of us. She looked decidedly less tense this morning, and had obviously made up her mind that I was an ally.

414

"We're leaving tomorrow, most likely to sail to Tahiti," I began. "And Hadley is on my mind. I could pass him on the street without recognizing him. What I need is a pair of eyes."

She said in a small voice, "You want me to go back to Tahiti?"

I nodded. "But not without an escort. I'm here on a small ship crewed by the toughest mob outside the Mafia—most of them are ex-commandos. If you come with us I'll assign two of them as your permanent bodyguards when we get there. If Hadley tries anything he'll learn something he never knew about fighting."

I thought that having Paula on board would be tricky with Kane around, but she said they had never met and it was worth the risk.

"You'll have female company, by the way. The girl we were with last night—she's coming too."

Paula bit her lip. "Oh Mike, I'd be scared. Besides, I'm on contract here, though it's up in a few weeks. I don't want to run out on a contract."

I said, "If it's the money you're worried about, we'll pay all your expenses. If you want, we can even buy out your contract."

"I'm not thinking of money." She thought for a moment, then sat back and looked determined. "Mark was the only man I've ever loved—and I think he loved me. I'd certainly like to see his killer caught."

"Good girl! Look, why not come over when your contract is up in a few weeks' time? Do cruise ships go from here to Tahiti?"

"Wait a minute—I'll see if I can find out."

She left the bar, and was back in five minutes.

"There's a smallish cruise ship, the *Eastern Sun*, coming through here in a few weeks. It'll stop at Papeete."

That suited me. It would be a few days before we left Panama, and then we might be dredging for several weeks around Minerva Reef. I got the date of the *Eastern Sun*'s arrival in Tahiti and promised Paula that we would be there before her.

"I'm glad to have you on our team, Paula," I said.

"There's more to this than just Mark's death, isn't there?" she said shrewdly.

"A lot more. I'll tell you about it in Tahiti."

We said goodbye and I walked slowly back to the hotel, enjoying the exotic scenes around me. I lunched alone in the dining room, but presently Clare and her father came in. Soon we were joined by Geordie carrying a copy of Bill Robinson's *To the Great Southern Sea*.

"Here's the bit," he said. "I've looked up Minerva Reef in the *Pilot* too, but I left that on board for later. Here is what Robinson has to say about Minerva. This was published in 1957, by the way."

He passed the book to Clare, indicating a paragraph. She read it aloud to us:

"Minerva is one of those shoals of doubtful position and uncertain existence known as 'vigias'. Vigias are the bane of navigators, for one is never sure where they are, or if they are there at all. A ship named the *Sir George Grey* was assumed lost there in 1865, although the British navy failed to locate a reef there a few years later. In 1890 the German bark *Erato* saw the shoal. It was again seen breaking heavily in 1920 ten miles from the position reported by *Erato*."

Clare stopped reading and Campbell said, "Do you mean to tell me that while we're on the verge of going to other planets there's a shoal like this that hasn't been located?"

"That's right," said Geordie. "There are lots of them."

"It's amazing," said Campbell. "But if Mark found it, so can we."

"*If* he did," I said. "You see, if an IGY survey ship had found Minerva I'm sure they'd have reported it, and they didn't. But it doesn't mean they didn't dredge around there," I added hastily to three disappointed faces. "You'd probably only be able to see it in a flat calm, with the tides right. Still, we have to make a start somewhere, and it would be fun to find Minerva."

KANE CAME TO SEE ME before we left Panama.

I had kept clear of him on the voyage from England, finding it intolerably creepy to have the possible murderer of Mark underfoot, but this was one contact I had been hoping for. Geordie had only agreed to take Kane as far as Panama and now we were waiting to see what his next move would be. He appeared at my cabin one morning and said, "Mr. Trevelyan, could I have a word?"

"What is it?"

"There was a message waiting for me here in Panama from my partner, Jim Hadley. Jim's down in New Guinea and he says he can't come up this way for a while, so I wondered if I could stick with you a bit longer. Maybe you'll be putting in some place that's nearer for Jim—Tahiti, maybe? That 'ud suit us both."

"I don't see a problem. You're welcome to stay on."

"Gee, thanks, Mr. Trevelyan."

I told Campbell and Geordie that Kane would be staying on. "Right, we'll keep him under our thumb," said Campbell. "Not much chance of him knowing where we're going if *we* don't know, and he can't pass the word on from out there."

The next day we set sail on a voyage of uncertain duration to an unknown destination which might, or might not, exist.

CHAPTER FOUR

We left Panama under sail and made good time at first, but after a day or so we found ourselves becalmed in a sea of glass. We stuck it for twenty-four hours and then went ahead under power. Using the engines was a pity, because it would leave so much less fuel for station-keeping and dredging, but in Campbell's view time was as precious as fuel, and I couldn't disagree with him. I had Paula to think of.

Campbell had sent a spate of cables from Panama to his agents, asking them to keep their eyes on the movements of Suarez-Navarro's ship, and once we were at sea he became nervous. He was unused to being cut off from the telephone. We had a powerful radio telephone, but he didn't want us to use it for fear Suarez-Navarro would monitor the broadcasts. News did finally come that they had dropped anchor in Port Moresby, Papua, and were sitting tight. Campbell was as worried by their inactivity as he would have been if they had been constantly on the move.

Esmerelda forged on through the placid seas at a steady nine knots, and it wasn't long before we picked up a southerly trade wind and headed southwest under sail.

As the days went by the wind shifted easterly until we knew we were in the true trade winds. We hoisted the big square sails on the foremast and *Esmerelda* picked up her heels.

These were Kane's home waters and he was free with his advice on weather conditions. "A bit further on we'll get revolving storms," he said. "They're not very big—but my word they're fast. You've got to keep your eyes peeled."

Campbell turned out to be a poor sailor and spent a great deal of time on his bunk regretting that ships had ever been invented. Clare, on the other hand, was a good sailor. She worked hard on deck and was greatly appreciated by all the crew. She helped cook and kept watch like the rest of us, but she also studied the books in *Esmerelda*'s small library.

One evening she and I talked together and I got another look at my brother, through her eyes.

It was one of those incredible nights you find in the tropics. There was a waning moon and the stars sparkled like a handful of diamonds cast across the sky. The wind sang in the rigging, the water talked and chuckled to *Esmerelda*, and a white-foamed wake with patches of phosphorescence stretched astern.

I was standing in the bows when Clare joined me. She looked across the sea path of the moon and said, "I wish this voyage would go on for ever."

"It won't. There's a limit even to the size of the Pacific."

"When will we get to Minerva?"

"We'll be in the vicinity in a week if the weather keeps up."

"What if we're wrong about that drawing?"

"We'll just have to think of something else. Figuring out Mark's mental processes was never an easy job at the best of times."

She smiled. "I know."

"How well did you know Mark?"

"Pretty well," she said. "In the end I decided he was a thorough-going bastard."

I was startled and at the same time surprised. "What happened?"

She said reflectively, "It was the usual thing. It must happen a thousand times a day somewhere in the world, but when it happens to you it hurts. I went overboard for Mark—he was so very attractive. I was all wrapped up in rosy dreams, hearing the distant chime of wedding bells, when I discovered he was already married—maybe not happily—but married."

I said softly, "He was using you, to get at your father. It's not surprising behaviour from Mark."

"I know that now. I wish I'd known it then. Mark and I had a lot of fun, and I thought it was going to go on for ever," she said bitterly.

"And then Mark vanished."

"That's right. I never saw him again. And now he's dead—his body lies somewhere out there . . . ."

"Take it easy," I said. It was time to change the subject. I used the standard approach. "Tell me about yourself, Clare. When did your mother die?"

"When I was six."

"Who brought you up? Your father was away a lot, wasn't he?"

"Oh, I've been everywhere with Pop. He brought me up."

"That must have been some experience."

"It was fun. I had to spend a lot of time in boarding schools, but I always went to Pop during the vacations. Sometimes we went on a skiing holiday, sometimes to Europe, Australia or South America. It was tricky at times. Pop has had his ups and downs—he hasn't always been rich. Only last year I found out that once, when he was on a crest, he put aside a fund for me. Even when he was busted he never touched it, no matter how much he needed money."

"He sounds a fine man."

"I love him," she said simply. "When the Suarez-Navarro mob put the knife into him it was the first time I was old enough to understand defeat."

"He seems to have survived."

"He's tough," she said proudly. "You can't keep Pop down, and you can bet that in the end Suarez-Navarro will be sorry they ever heard of him. Pop always bounces back. But enough about the Campbells. What about the Trevelyans—about you?"

"What about me? I'm just a plodding scientist."

We both laughed.

"Why did you become an oceanographer?"

"I suppose I've always been in love with the sea."

"And Mark? What made him one? I don't think I've ever known two brothers that were more different."

I said, "Mark was eaten up with ambition. Some of it was jealousy of me, though Heaven knows what he had to be jealous about. I was two years older, and when we were children he nearly beat himself to death trying to keep up, physically and mentally—the psychology boys would term it 'sibling rivalry'. With Mark it took an unhealthy turn. He seemed to see his whole life in terms of competition with me. It hasn't always been easy having a brother like Mark. People sometimes confuse us—to my detriment."

"And his advantage."

"Why, thank you, lady," I said, and bowed. Our relationship suddenly took a step forward.

We continued to chat, in a relaxed, easy fashion, and by the time Clare went below to her cabin I had a better understanding of both her and her father. Campbell was a difficult man to assess, but I felt more than ever that he was a man to be trusted.

And then there was Clare herself. I wondered if she could bring herself to trust another Trevelyan.

AS KANE HAD PREDICTED, we entered a region of small revolving storms. They ranged from mere waterspouts, ten yards across, to monsters fifty feet in diameter. *Esmerelda* would be foaming along beneath a brilliant blue sky when the horizon would darken and within minutes the water would be dark and wind-lashed. When the

420

storm had gone there would be rainbows plunging into the sea and the faithful trade wind would pick up again, driving us deeper into the heart of the Pacific towards the southeast corner of French Oceania.

Sixteen days after leaving Panama, Geordie announced, "We're nearly there. We'll enter the search area this afternoon."

We had decided not to tell the crew too much, so Geordie gathered them together and said merely that I wanted to look for a particular water condition, but that everyone was to be on the watch for shoals. His request may have sounded strange, but willingly they organized for extra eyes on each watch.

I was in the chartroom early the next morning with Campbell and Geordie, studying the chart and the Pacific Islands *Pilot*.

"The *Erato* spotted Minerva here—that was in 1890," said Geordie. "But in 1920 another ship placed Minerva here. There's a difference of ten miles. Now, let's put both of these sightings into the middle of a rectangle, ten miles by twenty. That'll give us two hundred square miles to search. We'll start on the outside and work our way in."

Campbell said, "Let's get to the heart of the matter. Let's go right to each of these positions and see what's there."

But Geordie decided against that. "I'm not going anywhere near those two positions unless the sea is calm. We might find Minerva too quickly and rip the bottom out of *Esmerelda*."

"We've got the echo sounder," I said. "That should tell us where the water's shoaling."

"Come on, you're the oceanographer," said Geordie. "You should know that these shoals are the tops of undersea mountains. There'll probably be deep water within a quarter of a mile of Minerva. We could be sailing in twenty fathoms and a spire of coral could rip our guts out."

"You're right," I said. "Minerva's probably a budding atoll. Give her another million years and she'll be a proper island."

"We can't wait a million years," said Campbell acidly. "All right, you're the skipper, Geordie. We'll do as you suggest."

THAT EVENING, AS WE ATE our dinner on deck, I was bombarded with questions from the crew. They were all curious and I thought they'd be more enthusiastic if they were in the know—of one piece of the story at least. I was also curious as to what Kane's reaction would be.

"All right, chaps," I told them. "We're looking for something a bit offbeat."

They were intent.

"Ever heard of Minerva?" I asked.

Kane raised his head sharply. *"Récife de Minerve!"* he said in a barbarous French accent. "Are you looking for that? I wish us all luck then." He chuckled, enjoying his moment of superiority.

I told them briefly about Minerva's tantalizing history.

"What's the idea, anyhow?" Danny Williams wanted to know.

I said, "Well, oceanographers like me are always interested in mysteries—that's how we make our living. The waters round a newly forming island are fascinating, you know."

They accepted this, and presently everyone fell silent. After a time Kane came over to join me, dropping his voice to address me alone. "Er—this got anything to do with your brother, Mr. Trevelyan?" he asked, as though idly.

I was wary. "Why do you ask?"

"Well, he died not very far from here. Wasn't he looking for something with another bloke?"

I looked into the darkness towards the northeast where the Tuamotus lay. "Yes, he died near here, but I don't think that he had anything to do with Minerva."

Kane chuckled derisively. "Looking for Minerva! That's like looking for a needle in a haystack." Getting nothing more from me, he moved away.

We started on the search early the next morning. Geordie had the man up the foremast relieved every hour because the glare from the sea could cause eyestrain. He stationed another man in the bows with strict instructions to keep a watch dead ahead—he didn't want Minerva to find us. That might be catastrophic.

The day was a dead loss. Minerva was sighted only to turn out to be dolphins playing in the waves. Otherwise there was nothing.

The next day was the same. The last leg of the search took us directly over both reported positions, and we were anxious because the wind had veered northerly and the waves were confused, showing whitecaps. In the evening we held a conference in the chartroom.

"What do you think?" asked Campbell. He was brusque and edgy.

Geordie looked at me. "We're probably within five miles of Minerva right now. You said that the conditions that created our prize nodules were local. So let's drop the dredge around here and see what we can find. We could be right on top of your 'locality'."

"You're right, Geordie. Of course we can dredge and keep a look-out for Minerva at the same time."

Next morning I got the winch ready for operations. We dredged two sites that day and five the next. On two occasions work was interrupted when something was sighted that looked like a coral reef, but in both cases this turned out to be masses of a greenish algae floating on the surface.

I was kept very busy in the lab analysing the stuff we were bringing up, which often included volcanic particles amongst the other material—this pleased me as it bore out some of the theories I was turning over in my mind. We recovered many nodules but test results were poor—high manganese, low cobalt.

At breakfast on the third day of dredging, Geordie said, "We've only been dredging west of where we think Minerva is—how about a stab at the eastern side?"

I agreed and we motored across the few miles. The sea was calm, which would make the search easier. I had a spell at the wheel—I wasn't much of a practical seaman and I wanted to learn while I could—and Clare was sitting talking to me. "Isn't this the life," she said. "I had flying fish for breakfast this morning."

"Your dad isn't enjoying the trip," I observed.

"Poor Pop, he's so disappointed. He's—"

"Go left! Go left! Go to port!"

Danny Williams's excited voice soared up from the bows.

I spun the wheel desperately and *Esmerelda* heeled violently as she came round. To my relief Ian, who was next to me, took over at the wheel. Shouts and the thud of bare feet told me that the whole crew was tumbling up onto deck to see what was happening. I noticed the echo sounder and saw the indicator light spin round the dial. It looked as though the bottom was coming up to hit us.

Ian let *Esmerelda* continue to go about until the foaming area in the sea was well behind us, and the indicator light of the echo sounder spun the other way. He throttled the engine down and I took a deep steadying breath. Geordie and Campbell came running along the deck.

"What the dickens was that?" Geordie shouted.

"I think we've found her," I gasped. "Unless it's more fish—"

Ian said, "No, it was a reef—about a foot sticking out."

Campbell looked aft and saw what we were all trying to get a better glimpse of. "Is *that* Minerva?" he asked incredulously.

Some of the crew looked equally baffled.

"What did you all expect—the Statue of Liberty?" I asked.

"Wherever it is we're there!" Geordie was exultant. He said to Ian, "I want you to keep *Esmerelda* just where she is. If we lay off a couple of miles we'll never find Minerva again. It's lucky it's almost low water, otherwise the reef wouldn't show at all."

"There'll be coral clusters all round," I said. "And deep water between them and the actual reef. There'll be a lagoon beyond that. An atoll is forming." I saw that they were all taking an interest, so I expanded. "The rock spear that was underneath us can't have been there very long, or it would have been higher—you'd have an island here. This coral has only just started to form."

Geordie said suspiciously, "What do you mean by 'only just'?"

"Within the last five or ten thousand years—I'll know better when I can take a closer look at it."

Campbell gestured to me that he wanted a private word, so I extricated myself from the excited crew and followed him below.

"How does this tie in with the nodules?" he asked. "Do you think we're going to be luckier now?"

I said soberly, "That's just the trouble. I don't see how we can be. Most nodules are very old, but Mark's was comparatively young. He had a theory which I'm beginning to grasp, to do with them forming very fast as a result of volcanic action. Now there's been volcanic action here all right, but much too long ago for my taste. There's been time for a long slow coral growth."

"So this is a false alarm," said Campbell gloomily.

"Maybe not. I could be wrong. We can only find out by dredging."

SO WE DREDGED—all round Minerva. But the operation was negative; there were no nodules at all.

I was unperturbed. I thought that there probably had been nodules in the area, but the upthrust of our friendly reef had queered the pitch. I decided to try further out, away from the disturbance.

This time we began to find nodules, but I quickly became depressed. "This is standard stuff," I told Campbell. "High manganese—low cobalt. But we'll do it thoroughly." So day after day the dredging went on, with the results of my assays continuing to be unfruitful.

Then one evening Geordie and I consulted with one another. We had been out from Panama for over three weeks, and I was anxious to get to Tahiti before Paula arrived. So we decided to call a halt to the dredging and to turn towards Tahiti the next morning.

"What shall we do then—after Papeete?" asked Geordie.

"I've been thinking a lot about that," I said. "If it hadn't been for that diary, Minerva Reef would be the last place I'd look for high-cobalt nodules, but Mark's scribbling has hypnotized us."

424

"Do you think he was on the wrong track?"

"I don't know what track he was on—that's the devil of it. I only leafed through those notebooks of his before they were stolen, and I couldn't absorb much in that time. But one thing did keep cropping up, and that was the question of vulcanism."

"You mentioned that before," said Geordie. "Are you going to put me in the picture?"

"I think another little lecture is in order—I'll deliver it to Campbell and Clare as well. The three of you come in here after dinner, Geordie, and put a lad on watch, to keep Kane away."

And so later that same evening I faced my small class, with a map of the world's seabeds unrolled on the chart table.

"The Pacific is full of nodules, while the Atlantic hasn't many," I began. "Orthodox thinking puts this down to sedimentation, and that's not entirely wrong, because if the sedimentation rate is high then the nodules stop growing—they get covered up and lose contact with the seawater—the colloidal medium. The sedimentation rate in the Atlantic is pretty high. But I don't think that's the entire explanation of the lack of nodules there. I want to show you something."

We all bent over the map.

"One fact about the Pacific stands out a mile; it's ringed with fire." My pencil traced a line, beginning in South America and moving north. "The Andes are volcanic, and so are the Rockies." My pencil hovered over the North American Pacific coast. "Here's the San Andreas Fault, the cause of the San Francisco earthquake of 1906." My hand moved in a great arc across the North Pacific. "Active volcanos are here, in the Aleutians and all over Japan. New Guinea is very volcanic and so are all the islands about there." I swept my hand further south. "New Zealand—volcanos, geysers, hot springs. Go south again to the Antarctic and you have Mount Erebus and Mount Terror, two big volcanos."

I turned my attention eastward. "The Atlantic is pretty quiescent, volcanically speaking, except for the Icelandic area. There was the enormous Mount Pelée eruption down here in the Caribbean but that's only just off the Pacific ring. The only place you find nodules in any quantity is on the Blake Plateau—and the interesting thing is that the plateau is exactly where the current runs into the Atlantic from the Caribbean, which I've already mentioned as being volcanic. I know that a high-cobalt area exists and I'll stake my reputation that we find it in a volcanic area."

Campbell said, "As I understand you, the nodules in the Pacific have been growing over millions of years as a result of long-ago volcanic activity. But you think there are places where nodules might grow faster due to recent volcanic activity?"

"That's right—and they'll be high-cobalt, high-nickel and so on because of the fast growth. The metals are entrapped before they have a chance to be dispersed into the waters of the Pacific."

"Um. That still doesn't tell us where to look."

"I want to stick around the western Pacific," I said intensely. "There are plenty of known undersea vents here." I had another reason to remain, of course—I wanted to begin my investigation into my brother's death.

Presently Geordie spoke up. "All right, let's get on to Tahiti and decide what to do when we get there," he said with finality.

WE FIRST HEADED SOUTH to skirt the Tuamotus. Geordie didn't want to sail through the islands unless he had to; the name, he told us, meant "The Dangerous Isles", and they were every bit as dangerous as the name implies, a vast area of coral atolls and sharp-toothed reefs, not all of them charted.

I judged we should arrive in Papeete, which is the capital of French Oceania, just about the same time as the *Eastern Sun*. We had all been at sea a long time and felt the urge to tread firm ground again. So it was with relief that everyone heard Geordie's announcement that Tahiti would be sighted at any time. We were having lunch on deck. Clare sat a little way from the rest of us, studying Mark's drawings. She had copied the photostatted drawings into her own notebook.

"Land—dead ahead!" Taffy Morgan hailed, and we all scrambled to our feet to get our first sight of Tahiti. We stood lounging at the rails when Kane came over to Clare.

"You left this on the table, Miss Campbell. It could blow over the side."

He held out her open notebook, with many of Mark's drawings in full view. We were all very still, looking at it.

Clare said coolly, "Thank you, Mr. Kane."

"I didn't know you could draw, miss."

"I can't, not very well."

Kane grinned and flicked at the open pages. "Doesn't look like it," he agreed. "That's a pretty cow, mind you, but it's a pretty scraggy-looking falcon."

Clare managed a smile as she took the book from him. "I'll never be an artist," she said.

Kane walked away and I let my breath out slowly. Clare said in a soft voice, "I am sorry."

"Clare, of all the silly things to do," Campbell muttered.

"I don't think it matters," I said calmly. "It's not the actual diary—none of Mark's handwriting shows. And for all we know Kane isn't aware that the diary ever existed. If he's a low man on the totem pole he wouldn't know everything."

Clare looked at the drawing again, and suddenly a smile displaced her look of tension. "Now that he's mentioned the cow, I think I may have one of Mark's awful puns figured out."

She pointed to the cow and its companion, the squashed semi-circle. "I read somewhere that another name for the Tuamotus is the Low Islands. That's what this flattish object is, a low island. Then he's put OR—and drawn the cow. It's two drawings for the same place—the Tuamotus."

"I don't understand. What are you saying?" Campbell demanded.

"Cows moo—they low." And she burst out laughing. I had to join her, and even her father started to smile as he saw the joke. We put the incident with Kane out of our minds and turned our thoughts to cold beer ashore.

Papeete, the Pearl of the Pacific, is a pleasant town, and its setting is magnificent. Arriving there we tied up almost in the main street and there are not many ports where you can do that. Looking over the harbour you can see the island of Moorea nine miles away, a volcano which exploded in the past leaving a jumble of spires and peaks leaning at impossible angles—one of the most splendid sights in the world.

As we waited for customs clearance, Campbell was fretful, anxious to go ashore and see if there was anything for him at the post office, especially word of the Suarez-Navarro expedition. I wasn't too patient myself. I had questions to ask the authorities.

At last a customs officer arrived, gave us a leisurely scrutiny and departed, leaving us free to go ashore. I asked him when the *Eastern Sun* was due, and he said, "The cruise boat, m'sieur? I 'ave 'eard on ze radio. She is due tomorrow."

I spoke to Geordie before everyone vanished. "Who are the two toughest chaps you have?"

"Ian Lewis and Jim Taylor," he said promptly.

"Paula Nelson will be arriving tomorrow. I want you to go and meet her. Take Ian and Jim, and bring her back here—unhurt."

He nodded. I knew Paula would be in good hands.

"We don't know how long we'll be staying here," I added, "so warn the crew not to stray. Now I'm going ashore to try for an interview with the governor."

I collected a file from my cabin and set out for Government House, which I discovered to be a rambling edifice set in a large garden.

As I expected, I had a tussle with batteries of underlings and secretaries, but I was at long last summoned to a meeting with the governor of French Oceania. He was a cadaverous Frenchman with a thin hairline moustache, sitting behind an imposing desk cluttered with papers. He stretched his hand out to me.

"Please sit down, Monsieur Trevelyan."

"Thank you for seeing me, Monsieur—er—"

"Moreau. Now, how can I help you, Monsieur Trevelyan?" His English was fluent, with hardly a trace of a French accent.

"About ten months ago my brother died in the Tuamotus. There appears to be some mystery about his death."

Moreau raised his eyebrows. "Mystery, Monsieur Trevelyan? I am afraid I have no knowledge of the death of your brother. For one thing I am merely acting governor. The governor of French Oceania is away on leave. Also one would not recall the details of every death in so large a jurisprudence as this one."

I managed to express my disappointment without actually dismissing myself from his office, which had clearly been his wish, and he settled back to hear me out.

"We will have something in our files," he said when I had finished, and picked up a telephone. While he was speaking I opened my own file and sorted out documents.

He replaced the receiver. "You spoke of a mystery, Monsieur Trevelyan."

"My brother died on an unnamed atoll. He was treated by a Dr. Schouten who lives on an island called Tanakabu. Here is a copy of the death certificate." I passed a photostat across the desk.

He studied it. "This seems to be quite in order."

"Yes, it's a well-filled-in form," I said sardonically. "It states that my brother died of peritonitis following an operation to remove a burst appendix."

I was interrupted by the appearance of a clerk who put a file on Moreau's desk. He opened it and scanned the contents. "I see the British Foreign Office asked for details. Here is the letter and my superior's reply. All seems in order, Monsieur Trevelyan."

I pushed another photostat across the desk. "This is an attested copy of a statement made by an English doctor to the effect that he removed my brother's appendix several years ago."

Suddenly it sank in. Moreau picked up the photostat. He read it several times and then put it down. "It looks as though Dr. Schouten made a mistake," he said slowly. He spread his hands. "I've never met him—he never comes to Tahiti. He is a Dutchman who has lived in the islands for about twenty years, ministering to the people of the Tuamotus group."

I sensed that he knew more. "He has a problem, hasn't he? Is he an alcoholic?"

"He drinks, yes—but everyone does. I drink myself," said Moreau, in mild rebuke. He was not going to commit himself.

"Did he come to Papeete to report my brother's death?"

Moreau consulted his file. "No, he didn't. He sent a letter together with the death certificate."

"So no one saw my brother except Dr. Schouten, and Kane and Hadley, the men who found him. And no one has questioned them?"

Moreau leaned forward and asked coldly, "Are you aware, Monsieur Trevelyan, that at the time of your brother's death he was suspected of murder and was a fugitive from the police?"

"I did hear that. It must have been convenient for your police department to have such a tidy closing of the case. But you will admit that there is something wrong with the death certificate."

Moreau picked up the doctor's statement. "True, a man cannot have his appendix removed twice. I will appoint an officer to interview the doctor." He made a note on his pad. "It will be done as soon as he next goes out to the Tuamotus."

"When will that be?" I asked.

"In about three months' time."

"Three months!"

"We are busy men, Monsieur Trevelyan. I administer an area of over a million square miles and—"

"All I'm asking is that you investigate my brother's death!"

"It will be done," he said levelly. "And we will find that the doctor has made an honest mistake. Perhaps he confused two patients on the same day. It would be a pity to ruin him for one mistake. We need doctors in the islands, Monsieur Trevelyan."

I realized I was up against a stone wall. The whole affair would be hushed up, covered in a web of red tape.

I wrote my lawyer's address on a piece of paper. "I would be obliged if you would let me know the results of your investigation. You can write to that address."

"I will let you know, Monsieur Trevelyan." He stood up, clearly dismissing me.

I went immediately to the British consul, but got no joy from him. He was urbane and civil, pointing out that everything Moreau had said was true and that the only thing to do was to wait. "I'll have to speak bluntly, Mr. Trevelyan," he said. "Your brother was on the run from the police. When he died, complete with death certificate signed by a qualified medical man, the police called off the hunt, quite naturally so in my opinion. The administration has a lot on its plate, but they'll get around to investigating the new evidence you've brought them sooner or later."

"When the trail is totally cold."

"I do see your point," he said. "I don't think I can do anything about it. But I'll try."

And with that I had to be content.

WHEN I REBOARDED *Esmerelda*, Clare was on deck and she said sunnily, "Isn't this a beautiful place?"

"It stinks," I said sourly. "It's these colonial French. Justice—but at a snail's pace. The British aren't much better."

"No dice with the governor?"

"Oh, they'll make an investigation in three months—or three years. He's worried that if he looks too closely he might have to arrest the doctor for unprofessional conduct and he doesn't want to do that, so he's sweeping the whole thing under the carpet in the hope that it'll be forgotten."

She was sympathetic and after a while I felt cheerful enough to ask her to dine with me. To my delight she agreed. I excused myself and went in search of Geordie, whom I found tinkering with the engine. I told him what had happened.

He wiped the oil from his hands and said, "Then it looks as though you're stymied."

"Looks like it, as far as authoritative aid goes."

"Now's the time to put some pressure on Campbell. You won't get anywhere without him if you want to see Schouten. It's a pity you can't scare up some good scientific reasons for going to Tanakabu."

"I'll work on it," I said morosely.

That evening Clare and I took ourselves off for an enjoyable dinner during which we both avoided any mention of the voyage, and got to know each other better.

Campbell had booked himself and Clare into a hotel for the time we were to stay in Papeete, so at the end of the evening I escorted Clare to her new temporary home and came back to the ship feeling weary but reasonably happy.

EARLY THE NEXT MORNING I saw the *Eastern Sun* enter harbour. Geordie disappeared with Ian and Jim to meet Paula, and I wandered on deck to find Danny Williams just reboarding.

"Morning, Mike," he said. "Just back from my detective stint."

"What do you mean?"

"The skipper arranged for some of us lads to keep an eye on Kane. Yesterday he was at the post office, and then he holed up in a spot called Quin's Bar. I've sent Bill down to hang around Quin's again— we think it's his meeting place. Yesterday he was asking for someone there."

I nodded in satisfaction.

After a while Campbell came on deck with Clare, and I decided that this was as good a time as any to work on him. But he anticipated me. "Clare tells me you want to go and see Schouten."

I nodded at Clare. I hadn't told her, but she must have been reading my mind. I was grateful. "Under the circumstances, it might be a good idea," I said.

Campbell frowned. "I don't know about that." He produced a letter. "Suarez-Navarro are on the move again—heading towards Rabaul in New Britain. They should be there by now."

"Do you know if they're doing any dredging?"

He shook his head. "My man doesn't say."

"Do you want to follow them?"

"You don't seem to know where to go next, and apparently Ramirez does. Maybe we should follow him," said Campbell.

I looked up and saw a party coming on board, Paula diminutive between Ian and Jim, Geordie carrying her suitcase. "Paula Nelson's here," I said. "Let's see where this leads us. If she can identify Hadley for me, we may not have to go and see Schouten."

I introduced Paula to Campbell and Clare.

"We're glad to see you, Miss Nelson," Campbell said. "Did you have a good trip?"

"It was wonderful! I've never been on a cruise ship before."

Before she had a chance to say anything more I saw Nick Dugan come up and speak urgently to Geordie, who then levelled a pair of binoculars at the harbour mouth. I left Paula with the Campbells and joined Geordie at the rails.

Nick said, "There's the man who was talking to Kane in Quin's Bar." He pointed. "He's just gone on board a schooner—and they're getting under way."

I took the glasses and focused them on the schooner. A big bull of a man was standing at the wheel, apparently bellowing orders to his crew. I had a sudden intuition and called Paula over, thrusting the binoculars into her hands.

"Look at that ship and tell me if you can identify anyone."

She gave a shuddering gasp. "It's Jim Hadley," she said. "And that's his schooner, the *Pearl*."

Campbell snatched the glasses and had a look himself.

"Where's Kane?" I asked urgently.

"Still at Quin's Bar, last time I saw him," Nick said.

Ian Lewis had joined us and seemed eager to go on an immediate chase. "How soon can we get under way, skipper?" he asked.

"There's no need to go chasing after him," said Geordie. "I saw that schooner in Panama. He's following us, damn him."

Ian looked at Geordie. "Skipper, I think it's time we all knew what is going on," he said gently.

Geordie and I exchanged glances. It was indeed high time.

He said, "Ian, gather the lads together and we'll put you in the picture. I'll be happier with you lot in the know."

"Why don't you all come to my hotel this afternoon," said Campbell, taking over as he liked to do. "We'll pool information. You too, Miss Nelson. And, Mike, I want a word with you now."

He led me aside and said, "I feel as though we're losing out on this thing. I thought we could use Kane to feed Ramirez phoney information, but it's not working out that way. Kane is reporting our every movement, and we're learning nothing."

I laughed. "I bet his report puzzles Ramirez. He'd have a hell of a job trying to find the last place we dredged."

"But what's Ramirez *doing* in Rabaul?"

"Waiting to follow us, is my guess—when he thinks we've hit pay dirt. I'm sure Suarez-Navarro don't know any more than we do, or they'd be there, dredging. But this all started with Mark's death and Schouten was present. I think we should talk to him, if only to clear up some unanswered questions."

Campbell nodded. "All right, it's worth the risk. We'll go."

I was delighted with Campbell's decision. We went over to rejoin the two girls, who had been chatting together with Geordie.

"We're going to Tanakabu," I told them. Geordie and Clare looked pleased. Paula, of course, only looked puzzled.

I had an idea. "Paula, you're going to join in the briefing this afternoon. After all, you have a lot to contribute. But we may be going off soon after that, and as I've brought you here I can't just leave you. Would you like to come to Tanakabu with us?"

Paula looked uncertain.

"Think about it," I said encouragingly. "We eat well and you won't have to sleep in a hammock."

She agreed to come with us. I was pleased, and I also felt that she was probably the only one of us who had faith in Mark. It would be good to have someone along who was on his side.

"What do we do about Kane?" Geordie asked.

"We take him with us, if he asks to go. Which he will. After I've talked to Schouten we ask Kane some pointed questions. Until then you just watch him, Geordie."

CHAPTER FIVE

We sailed the next day for the Tuamotus, after announcing that we were heading for Indonesia in slow stages. This piece of disinformation was for the benefit of Kane, who had reacted as predicted by asking to come along on our next leg.

We sailed through the pass in the reef and out into the open sea, continuing west until we were out of sight of land. Then Geordie gave the order to change course northwards towards Tanakabu.

Clare liked the Tuamotus. "It's just like a movie," she said happily as she viewed an atoll on the horizon. "Couldn't we go in closer, and have a look?"

I took her elbow. "Come here. I'd like to show you something." In the chartroom I pointed out our position. "Here's that atoll you saw on the horizon. You see the marks here, extending out about three miles from it. Do you know what they are?"

"Yes, of course. Coral reefs," she said.

"Exactly," I agreed. "Nasty and sharp. I'm as near to that atoll now as I'd like to be. We only touch on the ones with mapped entrances, otherwise you need local knowledge." Suddenly I thought of Hadley. Was he following us?

"I hope we're not making a mistake by heading for Tanakabu," Clare said soberly.

"We may not find out anything concerning manganese nodules, but I hope we'll find out something about Mark. And one thing may lead to another." I changed the subject. "How are you getting on with Paula?"

Clare was silent for a moment, then said, "I thought I wouldn't like her—you know, two of Mark's girlfriends should be wanting to scratch each other's eyes out. I find I do like her, though. Anyway, I was never in love with Mark, it was an infatuation. When I found out what a lousy creep he could be my feelings for him died. That isn't love. Paula knew what he was and loved him in spite of it. That takes real love—I never had it. We're not rivals any more."

As for Paula, she was relaxed and enjoying herself on board. Occasionally she sang for us in the evenings and took pleasure in her small touch of limelight.

When we left the main clutter of islands, Geordie was able to set a course for Tanakabu without worrying overmuch about grounding. Kane was aware of this manoeuvre and spoke to me about it. "Where are we heading for, more research grounds?"

"The boss wants to have a look at Tanakabu," I said. It was dangerous but Kane would find out soon enough.

His eyes shifted. "Has this anything to do with your brother?"

I raised my eyebrows. "Why should it?"

"Well, old Schouten lives on Tanakabu."

"Does he?"

"Yeah, but I suppose the old bloke's dead by now. He was hitting the bottle pretty hard when I saw him."

"He's still alive, as far as I know," I said. I was tempted to play him further but fought the instinct.

Kane withdrew thoughtfully, and a few minutes later I saw him heading below, apparently for some private cogitation in his cabin.

On the evening of the third day we were close to Tanakabu. The sun was dipping into the sea as Geordie scanned the reef with binoculars. "We'll go in under power. The pass is a bit too narrow for comfort under sail. Stand by to hand the sails in, Ian."

Geordie was still looking hard at the sea-pounded reef when Shorty Powell, our radio man, came up. "I picked up a funny transmission, skipper," he said. "It mentioned us."

Geordie swung round. "What did it say?"

Shorty grimaced. "That's it, I don't know. I just caught a few words—'... on board *Esmerelda*. She's...' I tell you one thing, though. I'd lay ten to one it was an Australian talking."

"I think we'd better get Mr. Campbell in on this," said Geordie.

So we called him up and poor Shorty got the grilling of his life. "Well, how far away do you think it was?" Campbell insisted.

Shorty shrugged. "You can't tell that, not unless you've got two directional fixes on the station. But when you spend half your life listening out you get a kind of instinct. I'd say it was from a low-powered station close by."

"All right, thanks, Shorty. Stay around that frequency. Maybe you can pick up something else," said Geordie.

As Shorty left and Geordie turned back to his navigation Campbell spoke to me. "It must have been Hadley on the radio," he said. "I'd give my back teeth to know who he was talking to—someone on land there, I suppose."

We abandoned speculation as by then we were going in through the pass. It was getting dark and Geordie was on edge. The darkness coupled with the four-knot current made the passage very tricky, but we got through into the lagoon and dropped anchor opposite the lights of a village. A small fleet of canoes came out to meet us and soon a number of Polynesians were climbing on deck.

I had decided not to wait until morning, but to act right away. It was evening, perhaps the best time to see a busy doctor, and there was the fear of Hadley catching up with us to spur me to action. I raised my voice. "Where can I find Dr. Schouten?" I asked.

There was an increased babble and a stocky man with a wide grin pushed his way to the front. "These boys don' spik English," he said. "They spik Française. I spik English. I bin to Hawaii."

I said, "My name is Mike—what's yours?"

"I are Piro."

"All right, Piro. Where do I find Dr. Schouten?"

"The doctor?" Piro waved his hand. "He round the other side water. He in—*hôpital*."

"How can I get there?"

"You come wit' me—I take you in jeep."

I looked into the darkness. "How far is it?"

Piro shrugged. "Not far. Twenny minute maybe." He was suddenly cautious. "You pay me?"

"Yes, I'll pay you." I turned to Campbell and said, "I may as well see Schouten tonight. Tell Geordie to keep a close eye on Kane— don't let him get away. I'll take an escort—Jim Taylor, I think." I said this because he was the handiest, and grabbing him by the arm I told him about our errand.

Campbell looked closely at me, then gripped my shoulder. "Be careful, Mike. Don't take any chances."

"I won't," I promised.

We dropped over the side into Piro's canoe, a leaky and unstable craft. Once ashore, Piro introduced us to his proudest possession— his jeep. We climbed in and he started the engine which banged and spluttered. He threw in the gears with a jerk and we were off, bouncing along the beach.

After a while we turned inland and though I lost sight of the sea I could still hear the roar of the surf, in between the car noises. After a few minutes we came back onto a beach and Piro pointed ahead. "There is *hôpital*."

In the distance was a large cluster of lights. I said, "That's a big hospital for a small island, Piro."

"Ho, plenny boys come from other islands—ver' sick. Many lepers there, an' boys wit' swells."

A leper colony! I shivered. I knew that leprosy isn't particularly infectious, but I didn't feel like driving into a colony.

Piro wasn't worried though, and drove blithely into the hospital grounds, pulling up in front of a long low-roofed shack. "Schouten is there," he said. "You wan' I wait?"

"Yes," I answered. "I won't be long. Jim, don't come with me—but be ready if I call you."

"Sure thing, Mike." Jim leaned back and offered Piro a cigarette.

I walked up two steps onto a long veranda and knocked on the door. A voice said, "*Ici! Ici!*" and I walked along the veranda to where I thought the sound had come from. At the far end, a door was open. I walked in and found a big man seated at a desk, writing by the light of a Coleman lamp. His face was scarred and lined and he had two deep clefts from his nose to the corners of his mouth. There was a half-empty brandy bottle and a full glass at his elbow.

"Dr. Schouten?" I said.

He looked up. "*Oui?*"

"I'm sorry. I have very little French. Do you speak English?"

He smiled and it transformed his ravaged face. "*Ja*, I speak English." He stood up and offered me his hand. "It's not often we get strangers on Tanakabu." His accent was Dutch but his English was fluent.

"We just came in," I said.

"I know. I saw the lights of your ship as you came through the pass, and then I heard Piro's jeep coming." He turned and opened a cupboard. "Will you have a drink?"

I said, "My name is Trevelyan."

Schouten dropped the glass he had taken from the cupboard and it smashed on the floor. He swung round sharply and I saw that his eyes were furtive and haunted.

"Praise be to God," he mumbled. "I thought you were dead."

I looked at him in surprise. "Dead! Why should I be dead?"

He sat at the desk, his hands clutching the edge. "They said you were dead," he said softly. "I wrote out the death certificate—here at this desk. Mark Trevelyan was the name. You died of peritonitis." He looked up at me and there was fear in his eyes.

Then I caught on—he thought I was Mark! I said gently, "I'm Michael Trevelyan—Mark was my brother."

He gave a long shuddering sigh, then his gaze dropped to the glass on his desk and he picked it up and drained it in one.

I said, "Perhaps you'd better tell me about it." He gave no answer, merely hunching his shoulders and avoiding my eyes. "You must tell me what happened," I pursued. "My brother didn't have appendicitis. But you forged a death certificate. Why?"

He hunched over the desk and remained silent.

"My God, what kind of a doctor are you?"

He shook his head slowly, then closed his eyes as if in pain.

"What happened to Mark?"

He opened his eyes and looked at me bleakly. "I can't tell you."

"All right," I said. "You're coming with us—we're going back to Papeete and you'll tell your story to the governor. I'm putting you under civilian arrest."

Schouten pushed back his chair abruptly and stood up. "You don't understand. I *can't* leave the hospital and the people here—some of them would die. I'm the only doctor here."

I looked at him without pity. "You should have thought of that before you killed my brother."

His mouth twitched. "I'm a peaceful man, Mr. Trevelyan. I didn't kill your brother."

"Then for Heaven's sake, what's the matter with you? Why won't you tell me what happened?"

He sat back down and buried his face in his hands. When he raised his head I saw that his cheeks were streaked with tears. He said with difficulty, "I cannot leave the hospital, Mr. Trevelyan. You see, they said they'd burn it."

"Burn the hospital! Who said that?"

"What could I do? I couldn't let them burn it, could I?" What I saw in his eyes made me begin to pity him.

"I couldn't help it," he went on. "They made me do it—I had no choice. It was covering up a crime or losing the hospital." He threw his arms out. "I thought my patients were more important than bringing a murderer to justice. Was I right?"

"What happened to my brother?" I said in an even voice.

"You must promise protection for the hospital," he insisted.

"Nothing will happen to the hospital. What happened to Mark?"

"He was murdered. On a schooner out in the lagoon."

I let out my breath in a long sigh. Now it was in the open. I said slowly, "Tell me what happened."

So Schouten told me. It was a sad and cruel story.

"The schooner came through the pass early last year. She entered the lagoon and dropped anchor just opposite the hospital—out there." He nodded towards the sea.

"Two men came ashore. One was about your size, the other was a big man. They said there had been an accident and a man was dead. They wanted a death certificate. I said I'd come aboard, but the big man said no, it wasn't necessary, the man was already dead, and all they wanted was a bit of paper to say so."

Schouten smiled slightly. "I laughed and said what they wanted was impossible—the body must be seen by a doctor. Then the big man hit me. I couldn't do anything—I'm not young any more."

"I understand," I said. "Tell me, were their names mentioned?"

"The big man was called Jim, the other man called him that. And another name was mentioned, but I forget."

"All right. What happened then?"

"I got up and he hit me again, knocking me to the floor, sat me in this chair and told me to write a death certificate."

My lips tightened. I was certain that the big man was Hadley and the other was Kane.

"I asked why I couldn't see the body and the other man laughed and said it was a mess and would turn the stomach even of a doctor. Then I knew there was something very bad going on. I guessed they had killed someone and wanted a death certificate."

I nodded. "What happened then?"

"The big man kept on hitting me until the other made him stop. He said that was not the way to do it. He wiped the blood from my face, and while the big man sat drinking he talked to me about the hospital. He said it was a good hospital and that it was doing good work in the islands. Then he asked what would happen if there was no hospital on Tanakabu, and I said it would be a very bad thing—many people would die."

Schouten caught my hand and said appealingly, "I told him freely. I didn't know what he wanted."

"Go on," I said tightly.

"The big man started to laugh and then he said, 'You sign that certificate or we'll burn the whole bloody hospital.' "

Schouten dropped his head into his hands. "What could I do? The big man kept lighting matches as he talked to me."

I was angry, more angry than I'd ever been in my life before. If Kane and Hadley had been in that room then I'd have killed them both without mercy.

"So you signed the death certificate?"

"*Ja.* I made it out as they wanted. The big man hit me again and the other man said, 'If you breathe a word about this we'll come back, and you know what will happen to this collection of grass shacks you call a hospital.' Then the big man set fire to the thatch over there and while I tried to beat it out they left."

"Did you see them again?"

Schouten nodded sombrely. "The big man—yes. He has been back—three times. He says he is keeping an eye on me. He comes and drinks my brandy and lights matches. I didn't dare tell the police. I was frightened for the hospital."

I ran over his terrible story in my mind. "You don't remember the other name you heard?"

He shook his head. "No, but I think it was the third man on the boat. He didn't come ashore but I saw him on the deck of the schooner—a very tall, thin man with a hooked nose, very dark. I saw him only once, when the boat was coming in."

I thought about that, but it didn't ring any bells. I said, "I'm sorry about what happened, Dr. Schouten. But you realize you will have to tell the authorities?"

He nodded heavily. "I realize it now. But I was so afraid for my patients. I am still afraid." He looked me in the eye. "What is to prevent these men from coming back?"

"I know who they are," I said. "They won't trouble you again."

He hesitated and then said, "I will write a letter which you can take to Papeete. You understand, I cannot leave the hospital."

"I understand." This would make Moreau sit up and take notice. I would be very pleased to deliver Schouten's letter in person. "I must go back to my ship now. I'll come back for the letter in the morning."

Schouten inclined his head. "As you wish."

I got up to go, and then just as I got to the door, he said, "One moment, Mr. Trevelyan. Something has just come back to me."

He rose from his desk. "You were asking about the other name— the one they mentioned. The big man spoke it."

"What was it?"

"It was a strange name—it sounded Spanish. It was Ramirez."

WHEN JIM TAYLOR AND I got back to *Esmerelda* some of the canoes were still alongside and there was an air of festivity on deck, with crew and locals apparently sharing their evening meal. Campbell, Clare and Paula were waiting at the rail as I climbed on board, and they saw at once that I was not in a happy mood.

"Where's Kane?" I asked Campbell in a low voice.

"Geordie's given him a job below. What happened?"

I said, "That bastard—and Hadley—killed Mark."

Paula drew in her breath, and Campbell said, "Are you sure?"

I remembered the tears on Schouten's cheeks. "I'm sure. It's a filthy story. Ramirez was involved too."

Campbell started. "How do you reckon that?"

"Can you describe him?"

"Sure. He's tall and thin with a beak like an eagle. He's got a deep scar on the left side of his face."

"That does it. He was there when Mark was killed. Schouten saw him and described him, all but the scar, and Hadley mentioned his name. Ramirez is tied up in all this. But first I want Kane."

I went down into the forecastle but Kane wasn't there. The crew searched the ship, but there was no sign of him.

"He's skipped," said Ian.

"Geordie—where's Geordie?" I asked.

But Geordie had vanished too.

I ran up on deck to find that several of the locals were still hanging around. I shouted for Piro and he emerged from the pack.

"Can you help us find two men on the island?" I asked.

Piro shrugged. "You pay—we find."

With that he dropped into his canoe with two or three of our men. Ian, meanwhile, was directing several of the crew as they lowered our inboard launch over the side.

"Come here," Campbell said and took me under a light. He opened his hand and I saw a round of ammunition in his palm. "I found this on the floor by Kane's bunk. He must have dropped it in his hurry. That means he's armed."

"Then we must stop these natives making a search," I said. "We don't want any deaths." I turned to race along the deck but he held my arm, pushing something heavy into my hand.

"Here's a gun," he said. "Can you shoot?"

I stuffed it into the pocket of the anorak I was wearing. "I'll soon find out, won't I? You'd better stay here."

"Son," said Campbell. "I'm not as old as that—not yet."

We dropped into the launch and looked ashore. Little spots of light were moving in the darkness. "Damn, they've started to search," I said to Ian. "And Kane's armed."

"Let's go then." The engine started and we sped shorewards.

When the boat grounded on the beach, Piro was waiting, his face alive with excitement, "Found 'im," he said.

"Which one?" I asked quickly.

He gestured. "The big one—up in hut now."

I sighed with some thankfulness. That would be Geordie. "Piro, can you call your men off—stop them? They must not find the other man. He has a gun." Piro made a quick sign to one of his friends, who lifted a large conch shell to his lips. A mournful sound boomed out, and I saw the spots of light begin to drift back to the village.

We found Geordie in one of the huts. His face was a dreadful mess, with deep cuts across his forehead and cheeks. I think he had concussion because he rambled as he spoke. He had seen Kane slipping ashore in one of the canoes and had followed in another. He hadn't had time to call anyone because he was afraid of losing him. He had followed as Kane skirted the village and entered the trees, and then he had been ambushed.

"Who ambushed you?" I asked.

"It—must have been Hadley. A man as big as an elephant," said Geordie painfully. "He stepped from behind a tree and took me by surprise. Then he—spun me round to face him and started to hit me." Geordie was trailing off, but he recovered. "With the gun. A revolver. He hit me a couple of times on the head and I—passed out."

I stood up. "I think we'd better get you back to the ship."

Two of our crew moved in, gently lifted him and set off for the launch. The others began to gather in the hut. I spoke urgently to Piro. "Is there another boat here—the *Pearl*?" I asked. If Hadley had returned several times Piro was sure to know his boat. Piro's answer shocked us all.

"Yes, it came 'ere. It gone by *hôpital*—one, two hour."

"Well I'm damned," exclaimed Campbell. "Hadley must have come through the pass behind us—in the dark and without lights. He's a good seaman."

A man ran into the hut and spoke to Piro rapidly in his own language. Piro looked upset and gestured to me to come outside, where he pointed into the darkness. There was a redness in the sky on the horizon. "*Hôpital*, he burn," he said.

"Hadley's set fire to the hospital!" I shouted.

The others crowded out to exclaim at the sight.

"How can we get there—fast—all of us?"

"Big canoe," said Piro. "Go fast." He ran off.

Campbell looked at the red glow in the sky. "Is Hadley crazy—why did he do that?" he demanded.

"He threatened to do it. No time to tell you now. We're going in canoes. Piro's gone to organize it. Where's Ian?"

441

His soft Highland voice sounded at my shoulder. "I'm here."

"Take one canoe and go back to *Esmerelda*. I want her down at the hospital as fast as you can make it."

He ran off. Piro touched me on the arm. "Come to canoes."

Most of us could crowd into the launch, and the big canoe took the rest as well as a lot of Piro's men—it held twenty of us. The rowers put their backs into it and it skimmed across the water at a great speed, easily keeping up with the launch.

The three miles or so to the hospital took only twenty minutes, but by that time the whole place was on fire. We could see people running about, outlined against the flames, and I wondered how many survivors there were. I was so intent on the scene that I didn't see the ship. Campbell shook me by the shoulder and pointed.

A schooner was anchored in the lagoon just near the hospital. We wouldn't have seen her in the darkness but for the raging fire which gleamed redly on her white hull. I shouted to Campbell, "What should we do—go to the schooner or the hospital?"

"The hospital—we must save the patients."

The canoe slid onto the beach and we all splashed ashore. I saw that Campbell had produced an automatic pistol. I took out the revolver he had given me and pounded towards the fire, barely able to keep up with the racing commandos.

I ran for the open space between two burning huts and came in sight of the hospital's own landing place. A boat was just moving out and I heard the revving of an outboard motor.

"They're getting away," I yelled. Campbell squatted in a half-crouch and took aim at them with his pistol, then straightened up and shook his head. "Too far. I wish I had a rifle."

"But we can't let them get away," I raged.

Campbell grabbed me roughly by the arm. "Come on!"

I took one last look at the boat disappearing in the direction of *Pearl* and then raced up the beach after the others. I heard someone shouting. "You can't put those fires out—save the people!" and I ran across to Schouten's house.

It was no use. The place was enveloped in fire, a roaring mass of flames shooting up into the night sky. I ran round the house to see what it was like at the back, and stumbled across a woman who was sitting in the path cradling Schouten's head in her lap. Her dress was scorched and torn and her wails rose above the crackle of the flames. *"Aaaah, le pauvre docteur, le pauvre docteur!"* When she saw me she gave a cry, scrambled to her feet and ran away screaming into the darkness beyond the hospital.

442

I dropped to one knee beside Schouten. He had been shot through the head, and his jaw was torn away.

I rose and stumbled off, weak and trembling. Nick Dugan rushed up, his face blackened with smoke. "You all right?"

"I'll—do."

"Look, Mike—there's *Esmerelda.*"

I looked across the water and saw her coming up fast, under power. *Pearl* was still moving slowly out to sea and I could see from the changing angle of *Esmerelda's* bow that Ian meant to try to stop her by coming hard alongside or even ramming her.

But the schooner was picking up speed, and just before the moment of impact *Pearl* seemed to spin smartly sideways and *Esmerelda's* bowsprit only grazed her side. As the two ships passed one another there was a fusillade of shots from *Pearl* and an answering staccato rattle from our ship. I wondered who had guns.

Then *Pearl* was safely out of reach, heading across the lagoon for the pass in the reef. *Esmerelda* gave up the chase and turned towards the shore: it was too dangerous to follow the schooner in the dark.

DAWN REVEALED CHAOS. Smoke still spiralled skywards from the gutted buildings and the survivors huddled together on the beach. Piro had done a count, and the death roll numbered fifteen.

We were all weary, scorched and depressed as we sat drinking hot coffee, brought ashore from *Esmerelda*. We had worked through the night to save as many of Schouten's patients as we could, but it still seemed as if our efforts were inadequate. We didn't have enough food on board to provide for everyone but we had distributed what we could, and the villagers had brought provisions of their own for the shocked survivors. The few men whom Schouten had trained were performing heroic feats of first aid but much more was needed. And we had received a bad shock of our own—the morning light revealed that our ship's radio had been smashed, presumably by Kane before he jumped ship. There was no way to send for help, save by going in person.

"This wouldn't have happened if we hadn't come here," Campbell said slowly.

At that moment, Clare came towards us, carrying a first-aid kit. She looked drawn and pensive. "Mike, your hands are burned raw," she said. "I'll bandage them."

I looked at my hands. I hadn't noticed before, but now they were starting to hurt. She began to dress my hands and spoke with her head down as she worked.

443

"Pop, I guess this is where you get busy with your chequebook."

I said harshly, "A chequebook isn't going to bring fifteen people back to life."

"You men are fools," she said angrily as she smeared a cool emulsion on my hands. "What's done is done, and *you* didn't do it. But the hospital is gone, and what's going to happen to the people here? Somebody has to do something for them."

"I'm sorry, Clare," I said. "But what can we do?"

Campbell dug his hands into his pockets. "There'll be another hospital—a good one. And doctors, and good equipment. I'll endow the whole thing." He got up and walked away down the beach.

"Tell me what happened on board," I said to Clare when we were alone. "I didn't know we had guns."

"Several of the men have them, besides Pop's little armoury."

"Who was doing the shooting from *Esmerelda*?"

"A couple of the crew—and me," she said shortly.

I raised my eyebrows. "You?"

"I'm a good shot. Pop taught me." She began to bandage my hands. "I think I shot someone—I think it was Kane." Suddenly her voice broke. "Oh, Mike, it was awful. I've never shot at a man, only at targets. It was..."

I was entangled in bandages but I somehow managed to get an arm round her and she buried her head on my shoulder. "He deserved what was coming to him, Clare. Did you kill him?"

She raised her head and her face was white and tear-streaked. "I don't think so—the light was bad and everything happened so fast. I think I may have hit him in the shoulder. But—I was *trying* to kill him, Mike."

"It's all right, Clare," I said. "Just remember killing doesn't come easy to people like us. We're not mad dogs like Kane or Hadley, but when we do come up against mad dogs I think it's our duty to try and stop them in any way we can—even if the only way is by killing them."

She pulled herself together. "You're right, Mike. Thanks."

Suddenly I wished that the whole business was over. How Mark came to die, where his stupid treasure of cobalt lay, none of it mattered. I wanted to be done with the whole affair—bar Clare. But a burned-out hospital littered with corpses wasn't the best place to tell a girl that you were falling in love with her. I would have to wait for a calm sea and romantic moonlight.

She saw the expression in my eyes and looked away quickly, but I think she could read it all there. She said, "We've got to go through

444

with this now, Mike. We can't let Suarez-Navarro get away with what they've done."

"I know, but I'm glad it won't last for ever, Clare. There'll be better days coming. Were any of our chaps hurt besides me?"

"A few scrapes. None worse than you," she told me.

"Good. We must set off for Papeete, then. The local people will have to carry on as best they can until we can get help sent from Tahiti." I left her and went to where Piro was standing.

"What will you do now?" I asked him.

"We build again—many huts. But no doctor . . ."

I said, "Piro, Mr. Campbell is going to send doctors. You will get a proper hospital. But first we must go back to Papeete and tell the police what happened here."

We buried the dead in the hospital cemetery and Schouten was given a grave in a special place apart from the others. It was clear that the islanders mourned him deeply. By the time we left that afternoon most of the patients had vanished into other homes.

As Ian conned *Esmerelda* out through the pass of Tanakabu, Shorty Powell came on deck, white-faced. "I've got something to show you," he told me, and took me down to Kane's cabin. On the bunk lay a brown-painted gadget.

"It's a walkie-talkie, surplus American stock, selling for about fifteen dollars. The range on land is about five miles but on water you can keep contact for up to ten miles," Shorty explained.

"So that's how Hadley's schooner turned up so opportunely! And that's what that transmission was that you picked up."

I was examining the radio when Paula came looking for me. "Geordie's asking for you," she said. She looked tired, having spent all morning helping Clare on that dreadful beach.

I found Geordie sitting up in his bunk, his eyes peering brightly at me through a mass of bandages. He'd been told about the fire and the smashed radio, but was avid for more information.

"How are you feeling?" I asked him.

"Not so bad, considering. But I haven't heard the whole story yet. What happened last night between you and the doctor?" he demanded. I realized with a start that I hadn't had time to pass on Schouten's terrible story to anybody, so I summoned Paula, Clare and Campbell to the cabin. They heard me out in stunned silence.

"They must be off their heads," said Geordie at the end.

"It's Hadley who's the lunatic," I said. "Kane's cleverer than we thought him to be." I told Geordie about the walkie-talkie.

Campbell said, "We've been played for suckers and I don't like

445

that one little bit. But I think they've outreached themselves in setting fire to the hospital. I have a feeling that Hadley ran amok, and Ramirez isn't going to like it when he finds out."

"I've been thinking," said Geordie. "According to Schouten, Kane and Hadley murdered Mark and Ramirez was in on it. Why do you think they killed Mark?"

I said, "I've been thinking about that too. Poor Schouten said that when he asked to see the body Hadley laughed and said it would turn the stomach even of a doctor. What would that mean to you?"

"Knowing what we do of Hadley—torture."

"And why should they torture Mark? I think they wanted to know where the high-cobalt nodules were to be found."

"Would Mark tell them?" Campbell asked.

"I don't know. He'd look after his own skin, but he was capable of being very scornful of people like them—he may not have realized that they really meant business until it was too late."

"You mean you think that Hadley went too far—and Mark died before he could talk?" asked Geordie.

"I think so. They clearly don't know the location of the nodules or they wouldn't be tailing us. So they buried their mistake, terrorized Schouten to keep him quiet, and sent Hadley to get Mark's stuff, hoping for leads there. Hadley bungled it and let the gear slip out of his fingers—thanks to you, Paula—and so Ramirez went to England to get it back, using Kane as contact man."

"It all seems to fit," Geordie said. He lay back on his bunk looking suddenly exhausted, so we left him.

WE MADE A QUICK PASSAGE and all went well until we were within about two hours of Papeete. I was in my cabin when word came down for me to get on deck fast. Ian, who was acting skipper, pointed to a boat that was cruising around us in a circle. "It's up to something, Mike," he said to me. "It looks official."

He handed me binoculars and I saw that it was a naval patrol boat, with a four-pounder quick-firer mounted on the foredeck. As I looked, it turned to approach us directly. When it was about fifty yards away, an officer by the wheelhouse raised a loudhailer and a spate of French crossed the water. I raised my arms to indicate that I didn't understand. Another man took the loudhailer and shouted in English, "Heave to, *Esmerelda*, or we will fire."

"What the devil!" I exploded. But one couldn't argue with a four-pounder. Ian gave orders and sails came tumbling down everywhere as crewmen rushed up on deck, Campbell among them.

"What's going on?" he asked loudly.

"We're being boarded by the French navy," I said. "If we don't stop they'll open fire—the man said so."

The patrol boat came alongside, lines went across, and an officer jumped on board followed by three sailors with submachine guns.

"Monsieur Trevelyan?" the officer barked.

I stepped forward. "I'm Michael Trevelyan."

"You are under arrest."

I looked at him dumbfoundedly. "What for?"

Campbell stepped forward aggressively. "Now look here—" he began. The officer gestured and the sailors lifted their weapons. There were ominous snicks as the safety catches were released. Ian caught Campbell's shoulder and he was silenced.

The officer said to me, "You will learn about it in Papeete. You will please come aboard my boat." He turned to Ian. "You will accompany us in under power. These men will stay on board with you. You will attempt nothing foolish, please."

I looked into the man's cold grey eyes and realized that he wasn't kidding, so I swung myself over the side and into the launch. I was searched, then led to a cabin. Once inside I heard the door being locked.

There were no portholes in my cabin and I couldn't hear much either, but our arrival at the jetty was unmistakable, and I braced myself for whatever was coming. Within a few minutes I was brought up into the sunshine of Papeete. *Esmerelda* was tied up alongside us, and a police car was waiting for me.

I was taken immediately and without any formalities into a cell at the police station and left there. A couple of hours passed and then two policemen escorted me to a large office, to confront an angry-looking man behind a desk. The nameplate on this desk told me that he was Jacques Chamant, Chief of Police.

"Sit down," he ordered.

"I want to see the British consul!" I said. "I answer no questions without his presence."

"I stand on no ceremony with you, Trevelyan. There has been a massacre at Tanakabu, which you started."

I stared at him, outraged. "Are you crazy?"

He leaned his elbows on the desk. "I have a dossier here on you. You came to Papeete last week and made some very serious accusations against Dr. Schouten. You were told that someone would take steps to verify your vilifications, but that was not good enough for you. You cleared Papeete with the stated intention of sailing westward, but instead you went to Tanakabu, had a quarrel with Schouten—and murdered him. To cover your tracks you set fire to his house, and the entire hospital caught fire resulting in many deaths. Your crew is implicated in this as well. You are all guilty men."

I blinked, stunned by his accusations. We had made a very fast return trip to Papeete and as far as I knew there were no radio telephones on Tanakabu, so there was only one way the police could know what had happened there. I seized on a couple of things Chamant had said and made the best use of them that I could.

"Do you know exactly how many were killed? Have you had any direct contact with the island?" I asked rapidly.

He hesitated and I knew I was on the right track.

"How did you learn about the massacre? Was it from a man called Hadley—off a ship called the *Pearl*?"

That went straight to the mark. Chamant said, "I do not see that it makes any difference, but you are correct. Mr. Hadley described the terror on Tanakabu. He stated that he barely escaped with his own life and that you attempted to run his ship down."

I sensed a faint thread of doubt in his voice and pressed on. "You say I quarrelled with Dr. Schouten. What evidence is there? I left him after a long talk; he was alive and well. There was a witness to that, an islander called Piro, who will also verify that we came back to save the hospital when it was burning. You have no right to arrest me. Or any of us!" He was listening intently and did not interrupt me. "Why don't you study that file, Monsieur Chamant? Hadley was the man who is supposed to have found my brother, but *I* say he was his murderer—Schouten told me so. I can't prove that now, but I can prove everything else."

"We have already sent a police patrol boat to Tanakabu. But you still have a great deal to explain, Monsieur Trevelyan."

I said, "I've got plenty to tell you! Hadley and his mate Kane— they're the ones you want. They murdered Sven Norgaard, they murdered my brother, they murdered Schouten and they killed fourteen patients in his hospital—burned them alive!"

I slumped back, shaking and fighting for self-control. There was silence for a moment.

"Where is Hadley now?" I asked, trying to stay on the offensive.

Chamant regarded me closely, then gave instructions to one of my police escorts in rapid French. The officer left the room smartly. Chamant looked at me. "I am not yet ready to believe you. But we will speak again with Monsieur Hadley, I assure you. Meantime, I ask you to explain this, if you can."

The remaining policeman brought a small box to the desk. When it was opened, it revealed four guns and several boxes of ammunition.

"We found them on *Esmerelda*. Not a cargo for a scientific expedition, Monsieur Trevelyan."

I made a weak gesture. There didn't seem to be much to say.

"You had better tell me the story."

So I did, leaving out all reference to our search for manganese nodules, and to Ramirez and Suarez-Navarro. I thought that made it all far too complicated. I said only that Hadley, who had chartered a boat to my brother and Norgaard, had quarrelled with them for reasons unknown, murdered both of them and implicated the Dutch doctor in his crime. I had come to seek the truth and had run into a hornet's nest. Chamant made some notes but said little.

When I finished he said, "You will write all this down and sign it, please. I am going to allow you to return to your ship, but you and all your crew are confined to quarters on board."

He was interrupted by the return of the officer he had sent out, who came and whispered agitatedly to him. They both got up to look out of the window and went on speaking in urgent undertones, in French. Somehow I guessed what they were talking about.

"You've let Hadley get away, haven't you?" I asked.

Chamant turned to face me. "He has apparently left. You must understand that there was no reason to hold him, after he gave us the information."

Something told me that Monsieur Chamant was deeply troubled. He had blotted his own copybook rather badly. I was furious and exultant at the same time.

He gave instructions for me to be taken back to *Esmerelda*, and I was only too happy to go. I went on board to find armed police dotted about, a couple on deck and more on the quayside.

I went straight to the saloon and over breakfast I told the crew what had happened. My news cheered everyone up amazingly, for although we were all technically still under arrest, it was clear that we weren't in any real trouble, thanks to the evidence I had given the police chief.

Later that afternoon the guards began to let us out on deck for exercise. Things were looking up, and we all turned in that night a great deal happier than we'd been at the start of the day.

A SENIOR POLICE OFFICIAL came on board the next morning and took formal statements from everyone. A short while later a doctor came to see Geordie. Campbell cornered him and asked innumerable questions about the hospital on Tanakabu, and about the possibility of getting another doctor to go out there soon.

At some time in the afternoon Geordie sent word that he'd like to see me and so I went to his cabin. He was propped up in his bunk surrounded by nautical books. His face was still heavily bandaged but he was obviously much stronger.

"Sit down, boy," he said. "I think I've found something."

He handed me volume two of the Pacific Ocean *Pilot* opened at a particular page, and I began to read where he pointed. Before I had got to the bottom of the page my eyebrows had lifted in surprise. "Very interesting, Geordie—but why?"

He said carefully, "I think that's the explanation of the other drawing in the diary. If it seems to fit in with your professional requirements, that is."

It did.

"Let's get the boss in on this," I said.

I got up, went to round up Campbell and Clare and brought them back to the cabin. "OK, Geordie. Begin at the beginning."

"I was thinking about Kane," Geordie said. "I remembered that when he saw Clare's drawings he'd called one of them a 'scraggy falcon'. We all saw it as an eagle, didn't we? So I checked on falcons in the *Pilot* and found there is a Falcon Island, so called because it was discovered by HMS *Falcon* in 1865."

Clare said, "But where's the 'disappearing trick'?"

"That's the joke," I said. "Falcon Island disappears."

"Now wait a minute," said Campbell, a little alarmed. "We've had enough of this nonsense with Minerva."

"It's not quite the same thing," said Geordie. "*Récife de Minerve* is a shoal—exact position unknown. Falcon Island has had its position measured to a hair—but it isn't always there."

"What the devil do you mean by that?" Campbell exploded.

Geordie grinned at me. "You tell them—you're the expert."

"Falcon Island is the top of a submarine volcano of the cinder type," I said soberly. "Every so often it erupts and pumps out a few billion tons of ash and cinders, enough to form a sizable island." I referred to the *Pilot*. "In 1889 it was over a mile square and about a hundred and fifty feet high; in April 1894 there wasn't anything except a shoal, but by December of the same year it was three miles long, one and a half miles wide, and fifty feet high."

I pointed to the pages. "There's a long record of its comings and goings. In 1949 for instance it had vanished and there were nine fathoms of water in the same position."

I passed the book to Campbell. "What seems to happen is that the island gets washed away. The material that comes out of the volcano is pretty friable and a lot of it is soluble in water."

He said, "Does this tie in with your theory about the nodule formation?"

"It ties in perfectly. If these eruptions have been happening once every, say, twenty years, for the last hundred thousand years, that's an enormous amount of material being pumped into the sea. What metals there are would be scavenged and concentrated in the process of nodule formation."

Campbell looked baffled. "First you come up with a reef that might or might not be there, and now a disappearing island! What's the present state of this freak?"

I looked at Geordie.

"I don't know," he said. "I'll check the *Pilot* supplements—but they're often printed behind the times. The locals may know."

"Where is Falcon—when it is available?"

"In the Friendly Islands," I said, "which are also known as the Tonga Islands. Falcon's about forty miles north of Tongatapu, the main island of the group."

Campbell frowned. "That's a long way from Rabaul, where the Suarez-Navarro crowd is. And it's a long way from here, where Mark was."

I said mildly, "It's halfway between."

Just then a vagrant breeze from the open porthole flipped back a page or so of the *Pilot* and I happened to glance down. I looked at the page incredulously and began to laugh.

"For goodness sake, what's so funny?" asked Campbell.

I dumped the book into Geordie's hands and he too began laughing. I said, "Look—Minerva Reefs, two hundred and sixty miles south-west of Tongatapu—that puts them only about three hundred miles from Falcon Island."

"You mean there's *another* Minerva?"

"That's exactly what I mean."

Geordie gave the book to Campbell, "They're fully mapped. They're on a plateau twenty-eight miles long. It's hard ground—shell, coral and volcanic cinders."

"Just like Falcon Island," I put in. "But much, much older and well established."

"There's no mention of nodules," Campbell said.

"These are naval records and the navy wouldn't dredge for them."

There was a rising air of jubilation in the small cabin.

"Well, that does it," said Campbell. "When we can get out of here, we head for the Friendly Islands." He looked at us all fiercely. "But this time there'd better be no mistakes."

FOUR DAYS LATER Campbell and I were taken ashore and driven to the police station where Monsieur Chamant was awaiting us.

He was quite pleasant. "We have sent a patrol boat to Tanakabu," he began. "Our findings there are consistent with your statements. I note that Monsieur Trevelyan called off the search as soon as he found that Kane was armed, which is a point in your favour. I also found that you saved many lives at the hospital, and that you were all aboard your ship when the doctor was shot and the fires started."

It was good news, and as near to an apology as we'd ever get.

"When can we leave?" asked Campbell.

Chamant shrugged. "You can go whenever you want. If we had Kane and Hadley here you would be expected to stay and give evidence at their hearing, but..."

"But you haven't found them," I said bitterly.

"If they are in French Oceania we will find them. But the Pacific is large."

"We're heading west towards the Friendly Islands," Campbell told him. "If we see them we'll let the authorities know."

We returned to *Esmerelda* with the welcome news of our release. The radio had been repaired and we had a lot of planning to do before we could set sail for the Friendly Islands, one of which might, or might not, be there.

CHAPTER SIX

It was good to be at sea again, pounding along under the unfailing impulse of the trade wind. We had decided to head first for Tongatapu, the main island in the group. It was a passage of about six days, and we soon settled into shipboard routine.

Geordie was up and about. Although his face looked like the map of a battlefield he was fit enough otherwise, and took over the command from Ian, who had gloried in his brief spell as skipper. Kane's disappearance had lifted the last reserve of secretiveness, and everyone was now in the know, including Geordie's original crewmen, as we felt that it was only fair to warn them of possible danger ahead.

We raised the island of Tongatapu on the morning of the sixth day out of Papeete. Nuku'alofa, the capital and southern port of entry of the Friendly Islands, is on the north side of Tongatapu, so Geordie changed the heading of *Esmerelda*.

He said to me, "There's a paragraph in the *Pilot* that says you have to keep a sharp lookout for undersea volcanic activity and new shoals in these waters."

I smiled. "Sounds good from my point of view."

"Not so good from mine. I have to skipper this ship."

But we entered the anchorage without sighting anything unusual, tied up and waited for the port officials. Nuku'alofa was a typical Pacific island town, its wooden houses with their galvanized iron roofs for ever frozen in a late-Victorian matrix. At one time it had looked as though Nuku'alofa was going to be the chief trading port of the western Pacific; but Suva, in the Fiji Islands, eventually came out on top, possibly for no more profound reason than that it was an easier name to pronounce. At any rate, Nuku'alofa lost its chance and lapsed into a timeless trance.

Once free to go ashore, Campbell headed for the post office as usual. I went off with the two girls who were going to book in at an hotel.

I said, "We may be based on Nuku'alofa for some time. Maybe I'd better get a room and see if Geordie wants one, too."

The hotel was pleasantly cool with big electric fans lazily circulating the air. At the reception desk we ran into trouble when we asked for five rooms. There had been an unprecedented rush on accommodation just recently and they had only three rooms, one single and two doubles. I said to Clare, "That's all right, if you don't mind doubling up with Paula again. Geordie and I will share and your father can have the single."

The girls agreed, and I arranged to meet them in an hour or so. In the meantime I went upstairs to soak in a hot bath. When I came downstairs I found them in the lounge with Campbell, who had a sheaf of correspondence in his hand and a worried look on his face.

"I think we've come to the wrong place," he said abruptly, as I joined them and sat down.

I signalled to a waiter for beer. "What's the trouble?"

He unfolded a cable. "The Suarez-Navarro crowd have moved to Nouméa in New Caledonia."

I raised my eyebrows. "I wonder what they're doing there?"

"I don't know. According to what we've figured they don't know where the stuff is either, so why on earth are they drifting round the Pacific?"

"It looks as though they're as lost as we are."

I glanced through the door of the lounge and saw the receptionist working on his accounts. I said, "Excuse me for a minute," and went into the foyer where I had an interesting little chat with him, which included the passing of a discreet backhander across the counter. I returned to the lounge, sat down and took a long draught of cold beer. Then I said, "We're in the right place."

They all stared at me. "How do you know?"

I said, "One Ernesto Ramirez has booked half a dozen rooms in this hotel. I thought it a bit odd that the hotel should be so full right now, so I checked up on it. Ramirez booked the rooms and paid handsomely for them in advance; he wrote that he didn't know exactly when he was coming, but that the rooms must be kept free."

"I don't understand," said Campbell. "If he's got rooms here, what's he doing in Nouméa?"

"I think he's been stooging around in this area all the time, waiting to see where we'd go without being too close to us."

"But we've not been here a day," said Clare. "How could he know we were in? And why come so close now?"

"We saw several ships as we came across, and we made no secret of our destination. My guess is that he's been fed the information somehow. As to why he's closing with us, that I can't guess. But what he doesn't know is that *we* know he's coming."

Campbell put down his empty glass with a click. "He must know we've arrived. We've got to get going as soon as we can."

I saw Geordie enter the foyer and waved him over to us. He put a little glass jar on the table with a hand stained black with grease, and said, "We've got trouble."

"Sit down and have a beer," I said.

Geordie sat down. "I *would* like one," he admitted as he unscrewed the top of the jar and pushed it over to me. "Rub some of that grease between your fingers and tell me what it feels like."

I scooped up a little on my forefinger and rubbed it with my thumb. It seemed gritty.

"Where did you get this?" I asked.

"It came from the main bearings of the winch motor," said Geordie. "The grease in the bearing of the winch drum is the same—doctored with carborundum."

"If we'd used the winch the whole thing would have seized up. What put you onto it?" I asked.

"Partly routine maintenance. But I also thought about what I'd do if I were Kane and wanted to put a stop to Mr. Campbell's project. I decided I'd have a look at the winch. I never thought I'd find grinding powder mixed with the bearing grease."

"How long will it take to fix?"

"A week," said Geordie. "We'll have to strip the winch right down, and that's a big job. But that's not what worries me. I wonder what else Kane might have done that we haven't found yet?"

"Geordie's right," said Campbell. "We can't take anything on trust. The whole ship must be checked out."

I drained my glass. "Let's get to it."

We went back to *Esmerelda*, rounding up crewmen along the way, and I immediately went below to the laboratory. I gave it a thorough going over, but all my equipment was in order.

Ian came down with fuel-oil samples from the main tanks. "Skipper wants these tested," he said.

"Tested for what?"

He grinned. "Anything that shouldn't be in fuel oil."

I poured the samples into Petri dishes and burned them. The sample from the port tank left a gummy mess at the bottom.

I went on deck to see Geordie. "The port fuel tank's been got at," I told him. "I think it's been doctored with sugar."

Geordie swore. "I thought we were using an awful lot of sugar. So that's where it went. How's the starboard tank?"

"It seems all right."

"We might have found out sooner—the hard way," said Geordie. "But all the fuel we've used has come from the tank in the engine room, and we just kept topping that up when we were in port."

Campbell came up. "What are the long faces for?"

I told him and he cursed violently.

"We dump it," I said. "We can't dump it in harbour—so we go to sea and dump it. Then we'll have to wash out the tank because there's probably a lot of undissolved sugar lying at the bottom of it."

"Do that," said Campbell. "How long do you think it'll take us to get ready for sea again?"

We did some figuring and and the answer was a little more than a week. Campbell shrugged. "That's it then. But we've lost our lead. We'll be lucky to get out of here before Ramirez turns up."

"He may wait until we go," I said.

But guessing was futile, and we left it at that.

NEXT DAY WE WENT TO SEA and pumped out both main tanks and refilled them with water from the freshwater tanks. I checked for sugar and found an appreciable quantity in the water of the port tank, so we pumped out again and went back to Nuku'alofa. We filled up with fresh water once more, and put back out to sea.

I still found a little undissolved sugar in the tank, so we did it all again. By this time I reckoned we were clean so we put back to port, where we filled up with new fuel oil.

While Geordie and one team were checking the winch and its auxiliary equipment, Ian set another group to stripping *Esmerelda* and inspecting all the rigging. They found nothing wrong.

Seven days after we had discovered Kane's sabotage, Geordie said, "That does it. We're ready for sea."

When we assembled in the hotel lounge that evening Campbell asked me about the next move. "How do we go about it?"

"I'm working on the assumption that there may be something between Falcon Island and Minerva," I said. "That's a distance of three hundred miles. I suggest we go to Falcon and take a bottom sample every ten miles on a direct course to Minerva."

"So our first step is to find Falcon Island."

I became thoughtful, shook my head and presently said, "No, I've changed my mind. I think we'll start at Minerva Reefs—do it the other way round."

"Why would you do that? Why should it matter?" Campbell asked.

"Well, if the high-cobalt nodules are anywhere near Falcon, why did Mark mention Minerva at all? I think the nodules are quite a distance from Falcon, close to Minerva perhaps. And when Mark indicated them in his diary he thought of the source first—which is Falcon—and then the vicinity, Minerva."

"But it's also possible that the nodules aren't situated on a direct course between Falcon and Minerva," said Campbell.

"OK," I said, "this is what we do. We leave here and sail due west until we hit the track between Falcon and Minerva. We turn towards Minerva and take samples every ten miles. If we don't find anything then, we go round Falcon and come back on a parallel course, sampling all the way. How's that?"

We agreed that that's what we would do, and then went in for dinner. Towards the end of the meal Clare nudged me and murmured, "Look over there. The waiters have just put two tables together. There are places for eight."

"Ramirez!" I exclaimed.

She nodded. "Could well be. Don't tell Pop. I want us to get him away quietly. He'll get mad if he sees Ramirez."

"You'd better get him up to bed then—if you can. Geordie and I will check out now and go back to *Esmerelda* to push things on—

we'll try and leave early tomorrow morning. You must be there."

Ramirez and his group didn't come into the dining room while we were there, and Clare and Paula got Campbell upstairs without his being aware that he was being moved like a chess piece. As soon as they'd gone I said to Geordie, "Clare's been Sherlocking, and we think Ramirez has arrived." I indicated the waiting table.

We settled up at the desk and then went to our room to pack. I took one of two .38 revolvers which Campbell had entrusted to me and tossed it to Geordie. "This is for you."

Halfway down the winding stairs I halted and put out my hand to stop Geordie. The foyer was full of people and I heard a drift of conversation. It was in Spanish. We waited until the crowd had moved into the dining room, led by a tall, thin, hawklike man who must have been Ramirez. I felt a wave of anger at the sight of him.

We found Ian on the deck of *Esmerelda*. Geordie asked him, "Any new ships come in during the last hour or so?"

"Aye," said Ian. "That one." He pointed across the water and I saw the dark silhouette of a boat, about the same size as *Esmerelda*, anchored a little way out.

"That is Suarez-Navarro's," said Geordie, and Ian stared at him aghast. "I want a watch—two men on each side and a lookout up the foremast. And I don't want any extra lights—I don't want to show that anything out of the ordinary is happening. I want us ready to move at a moment's notice. How many of the crew are on board?"

"Most of the lads, and I can round up the others easily enough."

"Do that, right away."

"Aye aye, sir," said Ian smartly, and went below.

Geordie looked across at the other boat. "I wonder if Hadley's over there—or Kane?" he said softly.

"They weren't in Ramirez's party in the hotel. Perhaps they're too scared to come ashore—there must be warrants out for them in every port in the Pacific by now. On the other hand, there's no reason for them to be on board that boat at all. Hadley's still got the *Pearl*, remember, and we have no proof that they joined up with Ramirez after leaving Papeete."

"True," said Geordie glumly.

"I've got things to do in the lab," I said. "I'll see you later."

I HAD BEEN WORKING for an hour when Geordie and Ian came in to see me. "We've got an idea," Geordie said. "The boys think that Kane and Hadley may be across there, on Ramirez's ship. They want to go and get them."

"They can't do that! Anyway, they're probably not there."

"But suppose they are? It would solve a lot of problems. We hand Kane and Hadley over to the police and that scuppers Ramirez. He'll be too busy explaining why he's harbouring a couple of wanted murderers to be able to follow us."

I thought about it and shook my head. "No, it's too risky, too close to piracy. Campbell wouldn't like it at all."

"Look," said Geordie, "the boys are all steamed up. They didn't like what those two did on Tanakabu, and they didn't like the week's work they've had to put in here because of Kane. I don't know if I can stop them."

"Suppose Kane and Hadley aren't on that ship after all?"

"We'll be bound to learn something to our advantage." I noticed Geordie was now including himself in the venture.

Ian said, "Ach, Mike, it's all laid on. It'll be easy."

"Oh, it's all laid on, is it? Would you mind telling me what the pair of you have been up to?"

Ian looked at Geordie, who said, "Well, it's like this, Mike. I sent a couple of boys ashore to scout around, and they found a lot of the Suarez-Navarro crew in a pub, drinking themselves silly."

"No Kane or Hadley?"

"No one spotted them. Anyway with the lot that's at the hotel, I knew there were precious few bodies left on Ramirez's ship. So I sent Taffy and Bill Hunter out in a boat to have a look. Bill's the best swimmer we've got." He chuckled suddenly. "Do you know what he did? He hauled himself aboard, had a good look round the deck, then let himself into the water and came back to report. That's the sort of watch they're keeping over there."

"It would have to be done very quietly," I mused.

"Ach, that's no trouble," said Ian. "We're a quiet lot."

"Well, what about it?" said Geordie imploringly.

"It's a darn silly idea, but I'll agree to it—on two conditions. One— no killing. If you find Kane or Hadley we hand them over to the police alive. Two—if we don't find them you get back here fast. We'll have to get the hell out of Nuku'alofa anyway—Ramirez will be looking for us. That means, three—that Campbell and the girls will have to be got aboard."

Geordie's face fell. "That means the whole thing's off. He'll never stand for it, not with the girls along."

"He doesn't have to know about it—if we get him on board at just the right time."

"The right time being when it's too late to stop us," said Geordie.

"Mike, laddie, you're going to have a devil of a time explaining to the old man what we're doing."

"I'll leave the explanations until afterwards," I said. "I've got another condition, number four—I'm coming with you. I've got scores to settle myself."

THE TIMING WAS TRICKY. We didn't know how long Ramirez and company were going to stay in the hotel, nor even if they intended returning to their ship that night. And Campbell and the girls had to be got out of the hotel under the nose of Ramirez—another tricky bit. So we made a plan.

I had a word with Nick Dugan, whom Geordie had picked to bring Campbell from the hotel. "Keep an eye on Ramirez," I told him. "If any of them make a move to go back to their ship, you nip down to the waterfront and flash a signal to us. We'll be starting off at eleven thirty. At exactly that time you get into Mr. Campbell's room and give him a note which I'll write. I settled all our bills, so he and the girls needn't stop at the desk. Get them back here as fast as you can—and don't let Ramirez or any of his crowd see you."

"I understand," said Nick.

We were ready in good time. Six of us were going—Geordie, Ian, Taffy, Jim, Bill Hunter and myself. Danny Williams would be left in command of *Esmerelda* and the rest of Geordie's non-commando crew.

I said to him, "Danny, if anything goes wrong, get out of here as fast as you can, once Mr. Campbell and the girls and Nick are back on board, even if it means leaving us behind. Mr. Campbell mustn't be involved in this, you understand?"

"I gotcha," he said. "But you'll be all right."

Geordie was getting anxious. "What time is it?" he asked.

I looked at the luminous hands of my watch. "Eleven twenty-eight."

"Let's go," he said. "It'll be a doddle."

We dropped into the larger of our two dinghies. Ian and Taffy took the oars and we headed quietly across the harbour. Soon the dinghy glided to a stop. Bill Hunter was dressed in dark clothing and all I saw of him was the flash of his teeth in the moonlight as he slipped over the side into the water.

"Are you sure this torch is waterproof?" Geordie murmured.

"It's OK," Bill replied. "I'll give you a flash as soon as I'm aboard."

He moved away without a single splash and we sat quietly waiting for his signal. It seemed a long time coming and as I sat there, I began to wonder what I was doing in this Pacific harbour, contemplating an act of piracy.

I tried to relax, never taking my eyes off Ramirez's ship. Suddenly there was a faint flicker of light.

"That's it, " said Geordie softly. "Pull together. Gently now."

We moved in under the measured strokes of the oars until the side of the ship loomed above us. Something hit my face and I started violently. Geordie said in my ear, "Be still."

I felt him moving about and he said in a low murmur that was much more effective than a whisper, "Bill's dropped us a line. Make fast there."

Jim, in the bows, made fast and Geordie said, "I'll go first." He disappeared into the blackness above us. Ian followed and then it was my turn. I found that they were using a rope ladder that hung just above our dinghy. I had got used to the darkness and with the dim glow of the riding lights I could see fairly well. I reached the top of the ladder. There was no one on deck, but a murmur of voices came from aft.

Someone moved to join us and Bill's voice, soft and unexpectedly close, said, "I've copped one. He won't wake up for a long time."

The other three had arrived on deck and Geordie said, "Split into pairs—I'll take Mike. We'll do the old backward-forward trick."

"What's that?" I asked, pitching my voice as low as he had done.

"Quiet! Someone's coming. Jim and Taffy—you take him."

I watched the two figures snake across the deck and vanish into the shadows. Then I heard what Geordie's quicker ear had caught much earlier—footsteps coming along the deck from aft. The man came in sight round the corner of the deckhouse; he was carrying a mug in his hand, being careful not to spill its contents.

Suddenly a black shape rose up in front of him and Taffy said gently, "Well now, that's a nice thought—bringing me coffee."

The man backed up in amazement. He was about to speak when something flickered at the side of his head and he raised his hands to claw at his neck. Taffy expertly caught the falling mug.

The man staggered two paces along the deck and collapsed. Jim and Taffy dragged him over to us.

"That's two—how many more do you reckon, Bill?" Geordie asked.

"There were five on deck when I was here before. But I don't know about below."

Jim and Taffy were gagging and trussing their victim. Geordie said, "We'll finish that. You go aft and clear the deck."

They drifted away and I helped Geordie finish the job. The man was unconscious and I whispered, "What did Jim do to him?"

"Stunned him, using a silk cloth with a weight in one corner. We learned that trick from an Indian instructor. He'll recover OK."

There was a muffled thump from aft and Geordie clicked his tongue. "Someone's being a bit too noisy. Come on, I want to see if Jim and Taffy have done their job properly."

We walked aft as though the ship belonged to us. Geordie said softly, "Never dodge about when there's no need. Nothing looks more suspicious." He slowed as he came to the deckhouse where a stream of light splashed on the deck from the door. He peered cautiously round the edge of the door, then snorted. "I might have known," he said resignedly. "What do you think you're doing, Taff?"

Geordie stepped into the deckhouse and I followed to find that it led straight to the galley. Taffy was sawing at a loaf of bread. "Making myself a sandwich, skipper," he said.

"You cormorant. How many did you get?"

"Two."

"Kane? Hadley?"

"Not a sign. If they're aboard, they're below."

"Well, let's clean up down there," said Geordie. "It only needs one of 'em to decide he'd like a nice breath of sea air and come up on deck. When you've finished your supper, Mr. Morgan, we'd all be grateful if you got back on the job."

"Yes, sergeant," said Taffy.

Geordie and I went to the wheelhouse and found the others. Ian was unscrewing the central holding bolt of the wheel-bearing with an adjustable spanner. He looked up and said, "Might as well cause a bit of inconvenience while we're here." He withdrew the bolt and casually tossed it overboard, then spun the wheel. "They'll have a wee bit of trouble in their steering, I'm thinking."

"Very nice," said Geordie. "But let's get the job finished first. Mike and I will take the forehatch and clean out the fo'c'sle. Ian and Bill, take this hatch here. Jim, you'll find Taffy in the galley—you take midships. We'll all go below simultaneously, I'll give the signal. Come on, Mike."

When we got to the forehatch Geordie paused. "We'll give the others a minute to get ready."

I looked aft along the deck. It was very quiet. I thought how easy it had been—so far.

"Come on," Geordie said softly, "follow me."

He lifted up the hatch gently and went down the companionway.

The forecastle was dimly lit by a single lamp and appeared full of shadowy shapes. When I got to the bottom of the steps I found Geordie fastening the door which led to the midships accommodation by means of a small wooden wedge which he took from his pocket. The door fastened, he glanced round the forecastle. Tiers of bunks, three high, lined the triangular space formed by the bows of the ship. There was a snoring noise and Geordie turned quickly, then crept forward. He was looking at a middle berth upon which a villainously unshaven seaman was sleeping. He put his lips close to my ear and said, "Check the other bunks."

I tiptoed round the forecastle, looking into every bunk, but found no one else. I got back to Geordie and shook my head.

He said loudly, "All right, let's wake up the sleeping beauty." He shook the man by the shoulder. "Come on, chum. Prepare to meet thy doom." As the man opened his eyes, Geordie hit him on the chin with a fist like a hammer.

He rubbed his knuckles and said, "I never like to hit a sleeping man. It seems a bit unfair." The seaman was out cold.

"Right, let's see what there is midships." Geordie took the wedge out of the door and opened it. We checked all the compartments we came across, but found nothing. We carried on until suddenly there was a shadow at the end of the passage and Taffy came into sight. "What did you get?" demanded Geordie.

Taffy was eating an apple. He said, "Ian put one laddie to sleep—he wasn't Kane and not big enough to be Hadley."

"Damn! The bastards aren't here, then," snapped Geordie. "By the way, where's Jim?"

"In the engine room," said Taffy.

"Good. You go up on deck and keep watch. The crew will probably be coming back soon and Ramirez might nip back to check up."

We went aft and found Ian going through a desk in one of the bigger cabins. "Ramirez lives here," he told us.

The desk gave us nothing of interest so we glanced through his clothing quickly. It was rather too elegant and extensive a wardrobe for shipboard life. "Have you found our birds?" asked Ian as we worked.

"Neither of them," I said. "Campbell is going to be mad."

Ian was disconsolate. "My mannie wasn't Hadley. He had a black beard."

I was looking down and saw Geordie pulling back the carpet, revealing a recessed ring bolt. "What's down there?" I asked.

"Let's find out." Geordie grasped the ring bolt and pulled, opening a trapdoor. He took a torch from his pocket and flashed it down the hole. We looked in silence, and then Geordie pulled out a sub-machine gun. "Good heavens! This is a battleship!"

Five minutes later we were surrounded by enough weapons to start a small war. There were four submachine guns, fifteen rifles, half a dozen pistols and a dozen hand grenades.

Geordie said thoughtfully, "You were a pretty good armourer in your time, Ian. How would you put this lot out of action?"

"With the bolt-action rifles you just throw the bolts away. With the others we smash the firing pins."

"Why not throw the lot overboard?" I asked.

Geordie cocked his head at me. "We'll do that too, but this mob will then do some skin-diving and I want it to be a wasted effort. Get cracking, Ian. We've spent enough time here."

We were ready to leave fifteen minutes later after quietly dropping the useless guns over the side. Ian was rolling the last of the bolts he'd taken from the rifles into torn strips of cloth and stuffing them into his pockets when Taffy suddenly held up a hand. "Quiet," he said softly. "There's a boat coming."

Then I heard the faint creak of rowlocks and the splash of oars. I looked anxiously towards Geordie.

"We take them," he announced. "We can't have the game given away too soon." He issued instructions and we retreated into the deck shadows. There was a soft bump as the boat reached the boarding ladder, and a few moments later I saw the outline of a man against the night sky. I drew in my breath. It was Kane.

"He's mine," I murmured to Geordie, who nodded. I moved forward in a crouch. Kane walked forward along the deck and just as he passed me I straightened up and gave him a tap on the shoulder. He turned and I let him have it on the jaw. Ian tapped him on the head with something as he started to collapse and all in one movement, as it seemed, rolled him into a piece of canvas.

Geordie looked over the railings and saw that Kane had been alone in the dinghy. "We must get out of here fast. If the police find out what we've done, we're for it. We'll take Mr. Kane with us."

We piled into our boat and as we passed under the stern of Ramirez's ship I looked up and saw her name painted there—*Sirena*. Halfway across the harbour I had a sudden thought. "Geordie, what was Jim doing in the engine room?"

"Nothing much," he said. Jim grinned in the half-light and I was about to say something when Geordie interrupted. "Heave—we haven't much time." He seemed in a devil of a hurry.

AS WE CLIMBED the bulwarks of *Esmerelda* Geordie was already giving orders. "Get the engine started. Slip all lines bar the bowline. Get that dinghy up smartly now."

Campbell was on to me in a rage. "What the dickens is going on?"

"Some direct action," I said coolly.

"You idiotic fools! You'll get us all jailed."

"Better jailed than dead," I said. "You don't know what we found on that ship." I heard a throb as Geordie started the engines.

"I don't care what you found," fumed Campbell. "Do you realize you've committed an act of piracy?"

In the same moment Ian came running along the deck. "Mr. Campbell, sir. Yon man on the jetty—he wants a wee crack wi' you."

We both looked ashore in alarm and saw a solitary figure standing just where our gangplank lay. It was Ernesto Ramirez.

Campbell recognized him at once, and took my arm. "Mike, tell Geordie to stop the engines, will you?" He seemed in complete control of himself as he walked towards the gangplank and I shouted, "Hold it, Geordie! The boss has a visitor." I followed Campbell.

Ramirez was alone, leaning on a bollard. Obviously he hadn't yet been on *Sirena*—there hadn't been time for that, and he was too composed. "Well?" asked Campbell coldly.

Ramirez smiled up at him. "I just came to wish you farewell. I thought you would be leaving about now."

He walked up the gangplank and stepped onto the deck, elegant in a white tropical suit. "I thought I should warn you," he said. "I have plans and I do not wish you to interfere with them. Why don't you give up and go away?"

Campbell's voice was icy. "I'm not concerned with your plans."

"You know what I mean, Mr. Campbell. We met in battle before and you came off worst. You will again unless you get out of my way."

My mouth was dry. I said, "Ramirez, you're a murderer and I'm going to see you pay for it."

He raised his eyebrows. "Murder?" he queried mockingly. "That is libel, Mr. Trevelyan. Whom am I supposed to have murdered?"

"My brother, for one," I said hotly.

Ramirez threw back his head and laughed. "My dear sir, I'm willing to go into any court in the world on a charge like that." He laughed again. "You have no proof—no proof at all."

That was only too true. The only man who had met Ramirez on Tanakabu was Dr. Schouten—and he was dead.

Geordie tugged at my sleeve agitatedly. "We've got to get away—now. Before that thing goes bang."

"What thing, for goodness sake?"

He drew me aside and said, "Jim had a small charge of plastic explosive—he slapped it against the crankcase of their engine."

"It'll rouse the whole harbour!"

"But we'll have gone—nothing to do with us." There was urgency in his voice.

I looked across at Ramirez and said to Geordie, "I think you ought to have the privilege of cleaning your own deck."

Geordie caught on immediately and went to the gangplank where Campbell and Ramirez were locked in a furious argument. I noticed Geordie dab his hand on the winch drum and then signal surreptitiously to Ian and Taffy. He placed himself in front of Ramirez. "I'm the master of this ship—and I'm particular about filth on my decks. I'd be pleased if you'd leave." He put out his hand and smeared it down the front of Ramirez's white jacket, leaving a trail of black oil. "You're dirty, Mr. Ramirez."

Ramirez was so shocked that he just stood there.

Geordie said, "I think Mr. Ramirez needs a wash—don't you, lads?" They got the idea fast. Four of them were on to him. I saw Ramirez's hand go to his pocket as quick as lightning, but Danny was faster and his hand came down in a mighty chop. A pistol clattered onto the deck. Then Ramirez was lifted off his feet and carried to the side. They swung him twice and over he went, with a great splash.

Geordie wasted no time. He turned, picked up Ramirez's pistol and began chopping out orders again. "Gangplank in. Ian, get the wheel. Cast off forrard. Engine slow ahead."

Esmerelda got under way even while Campbell was still staring over the side. "Well, I'm damned," he said, staring at Geordie.

As we drew level with *Sirena*, anchored in the harbour, there was a dull *thump*, which carried over the water. At the same time there was a flicker of lights from a dinghy arriving alongside. The crew returning, no doubt, to find a shambles.

Silence held us until we were well past all shipping and then a babble of noise went up as everyone's tongue was loosened. The excitement on board was electric.

CHAPTER SEVEN

"You pack of fools," said Campbell. "Whatever possessed you to do a crazy thing like that?"

Ian shuffled his feet, Geordie was clearly unrepentant and I

467

suspected we were in for a tongue-lashing, and didn't relish the thought. The lights of Nuku'alofa were falling astern as *Esmerelda* ran at full speed. Danny Williams was at the wheel while Campbell gathered the three of us together to take us to task.

"Well," Geordie began, "we thought it would be a good idea to go and get hold of either Kane or Hadley and—"

"Kane! Hadley! You won't find them with Ramirez. He won't chance being linked with those two, not now he won't."

I grinned at Geordie. "Where did you put Kane, by the way?" I asked casually.

"We're making a brig. For now he's under guard in my cabin."

Campbell's jaw dropped. "You mean you've *got* Kane?"

"Of course," I said. "We thought we'd hand him over to the Tongan police but circumstances—ah—precluded that."

"What circumstances?"

"Ramirez's ship got a bit bent," I said. "One of us had an accident with some explosive."

"That thump we heard? As we left harbour? You blew up his ship?"

"Oh no, nothing like that," said Geordie placatingly. "There's a bit of a hole in their engine crankcase, that's all. They won't be following us in a hurry."

"They won't have to," said Campbell. "Ramirez must be seething mad, thanks to you fools. By now he'll be presenting himself at the nearest police station, still in his wet clothes, claiming assault and piracy. I should say that within the hour there'll be a fast patrol boat coming right after us. And we won't get out of it as we did in Tahiti—this time we *are* in the wrong."

We looked at each other in silence.

"Or maybe he won't," said Campbell slowly. "Not after what I told him back there." He jerked his head astern. "I said the Tahitian police knew about Hadley and Kane and that they had witnesses who'd seen Ramirez with them at Tanakabu, the first time they went there." He grinned at us. "It hit home."

"I don't know anything about any witnesses," I said.

"There were no witnesses. But I told Ramirez that the police had already linked him with the events on Tanakabu, and that if he went to the cops in Tonga with any kind of story about us pirating his ship, and if we were picked up, then we'd get the Tahitian police down here fast."

"We know he was at Tanakabu," Georgie agreed. "We know Schouten saw him."

468

"Exactly," said Campbell. "And how does he know that someone else didn't see him? He can't take the chance—he'll lie low."

I said, "He won't go to the police while we have Kane. He wouldn't dare let Kane get into the hands of the police. And something else. Maybe the raid wasn't as stupid as you think." I gestured to Ian. "Trot out your collection of ironmongery."

Ian delved into various pockets and brought out the bolts he had taken from the rifles. Campbell's eyes widened as he saw the mounting pile they were making on the deck.

"He had *ten* rifles?"

"Fifteen," I corrected. "The others were automatic action. We smashed them and dropped them over the side. Plus four sub-machine guns and a lot of pistols."

Geordie dug into his pocket and produced a hand grenade. "There were a few of these too. I hung onto a couple."

Campbell's eyes flashed as he stared at the grenade in Geordie's hand. "Be careful with that, or you'll blow us all up. Let's go down to the saloon and have a drink—it's pretty late."

"No," I said. "I want to talk to Kane—now. And I want to be sober when I do it."

Campbell, Geordie and I went down to the cabin, to find Jim and Nick Dugan on guard. Kane was terrified. He was huddled at the end of Geordie's bunk as though by making himself smaller he wouldn't be noticed. He looked haggard, unshaven and ill, and carried his right arm awkwardly—I remembered that Clare had shot him. His eyes slid away when I looked at him.

"Listen to me, Kane," I said. "You're going to tell us the truth. We'll work on you until you do. Have I made myself clear?"

He licked his lips and croaked incoherently.

"Give him a whisky, Geordie," I said. He drank some of it and sat up straighter, but with no less fear in his face.

"I'll talk," he whispered at last.

"All right," I said deliberately. "We'll start at the beginning. You went to London to find Helen Trevelyan and then me. Why?"

"Jim boobed," he said. "He let that suitcase get away. There were the books and the stones in it. We had to get them back."

"You and Ramirez and some of his cutthroats, right?"

"Yeah, that's right."

"But you didn't get them all, did you? Did Ramirez know that?"

"He said—you must have something else. Didn't know what."

"So he laid you alongside me to try and find out what I had?"

"Yeah. And to pass word where you went, any time I could."

Now Kane was volunteering information, and it was getting easier.

"You smashed our radio, didn't you?" I asked.

"Yeah, I was told to."

"And brought Hadley in the *Pearl* onto our track?" We already knew this but I let him confirm it.

"Why did you tell the Papeete police that we'd burned the hospital?" I continued. "Surely you knew that we'd disprove that."

He looked exasperated. "That was Jim. I told him it wouldn't wash. You can't tell him anything."

I veered off on another track. "That time you saw Miss Campbell's drawings on deck, you identified one as a 'scraggy falcon'. Why did you say that?"

He was taken aback. "I dunno—did it have something to do with Falcon Island, maybe?"

"Go on. Why should it have?"

"I—it was on my mind, see. Ramirez said once that Falcon Island was where we would be going after we'd got rid of you lot."

"'Got rid of'? How was he going to do that? And why?"

"I dunno. Something about those stones you've been pulling out of the sea—those nodules. He had to ditch you before he could go to Falcon Island, cos that's where they were. My word, Mr. Trevelyan, I don't know what it's all about!"

Behind me I heard Campbell let out his breath. "Do you know exactly where the nodules are?" I asked.

"No, the top brass would never let me in on that."

I could believe that. Kane was much too far down the line to have access to such information. I changed my tack again and suddenly shot the question, "Who killed my brother?"

Kane's mouth twitched. "It was Jim—and Ramirez. They killed him." He looked mortally sick.

"And you helped them."

He shook his head violently. "I had nothing to do with it!"

"Look, Kane, stop lying to us. You were with Hadley when he went to Schouten to get the death certificate, weren't you?"

He nodded unwillingly.

"Then you were in on Mark's death, damn you!"

"I didn't kill him. It was Jim—Ramirez fixed it all up."

"Who killed Schouten?"

The answer came promptly. "It was Jim—Jim Hadley."

"And of course you didn't set fire to the hospital and burn fourteen people to death?"

470

"I didn't," said Kane, "It was Jim—he's a devil. He's crazy."

"But you were there."

Kane was sweating and his whole face quivered. "I told you I was."

"And you'll be sentenced as an accessory. Now, who killed Sven Norgaard?"

Kane didn't answer for a moment. Then he said, "I dunno for sure—I wasn't there. It was Jim or—or your brother."

"*My brother?*"

"The cops were looking for him, weren't they?" cried Kane defensively. "He might have done it for all I know."

"Tell me more about my brother. Why was he killed?"

"Ramirez didn't—didn't tell me. But I think he was holding out on something Ramirez wanted. I think it had something to do with those stones. I never—never killed him or nobody!"

"Well," I said wearily, "so you didn't kill anyone and you're as pure as driven snow. I think you're a liar, and I warned you what would happen if you lied. Think about that."

Kane flinched and I said, "Anyone got any more questions?"

Campbell said harshly, "I can't think of anything right now. Later, maybe."

"Geordie?" He shook his head.

Campbell said harshly, "I wouldn't make any attempt to break out, Kane. The crew here don't like you and they may shoot to kill if they see you, so stay put."

We left the cabin. Once outside we looked at one another bleakly. "I could do with that drink now," I said heavily.

We sat in the saloon for a while, letting tiredness wash over us. Then Geordie had Kane removed to a small cabin which had been stripped of everything bar a bunk, and which had a padlock on the door, so that we were free to turn in to our own bunks. It was already dawn.

THE NEXT DAY, over a late breakfast, I spoke to Clare and Paula about the events of the previous night. "You got back to the ship smartly," I said. "Well done."

"Nick was great. But maybe not so well done—Ramirez must have seen us leaving the hotel," said Clare.

"Not necessarily. He must have spotted *Esmerelda* right away. He knew we were here. I'm still not sure why he finally joined us. He surely didn't think we'd give up and go away, or hand over our knowledge, simply for the asking," I mused.

Clare said, "From what I know about him, he probably decided to bring things to a confrontation, just to see how we might react to his baiting."

"Where were you during the big excitement?"

"Pop was mad as a bull when we came on board and he found out what was going on. He was sure it would end up in trouble, so he made us both go down below and promise to stay there." She giggled. "We saw Ramirez go overboard though—it was fantastic."

Clare caught my hand across the table, and I wanted desperately to be alone with her. At that moment, as if by prearrangement, Campbell appeared and our hands slid apart.

We were soon joined by Geordie, and together he and I filled Campbell in on the details of our raid on *Sirena*. When we'd finished, Campbell actually chuckled. "My God, I wish I'd been there." He turned to Geordie. "How long do you give Ramirez to repair the damage?"

"A very long time if he has to depend on facilities in Nuku'alofa. That engine will never run again, if Jim placed his charge correctly."

"He'll have a new engine flown in with a crew to install it," predicted Campbell. "I give him three weeks—four at the most—to be at sea again, and on our tail."

"The sea is big. He may never find us," I said.

"He knows something about Falcon Island, and he will guess that we do too. But let's hope you're right," said Campbell. "And let's also hope that Ramirez didn't run to the cops."

Geordie said, "It looks as though he kept mum. A patrol boat would have caught up with us by now."

Campbell folded his hands on the table. "Now let's talk about Kane. I don't think he knows anything much—and he's a danger to us all every moment he's on board. I want to get him to write a statement. And then I want to put him off somewhere."

Geordie said, "I agree with you, Mr. Campbell. Let's have a look at the charts—see where we can drop him off."

Geordie found what he was after almost immediately. Among the northern islands of the Tongan group lay the small islet of Mo'unga'one. It had, according to the *Pilot*, one village and a beach where landing in good weather was possible. We could find nothing wrong with the idea, and so Geordie set about changing our course slightly while Campbell went down to talk to Kane. I didn't want to face him again that morning.

Campbell came back presently and sat down.

"It's fixed," he said. "He'll write anything we want, he says, but

I've told him to stick to the facts as he knows them. He doesn't in the least mind incriminating his great friend Jim Hadley. He's got a touch of fever from that bullet wound, but nothing a few days' rest cure on a tropical island won't fix. The local people will look after him for a backhander of some kind, till we can pick him up or send the cops for him."

We lay off Mo'unga'one for a morning while Geordie and three of the crew took Kane ashore. He didn't seem at all concerned as to how long he'd have to stay there.

We got under way again and soon Geordie said, "We're almost on the track between Falcon Island and Minerva now. All being well, we should be able to start dredging tomorrow—if you want to."

"We might as well start," said Campbell. "That's what we're here for. Come and have some coffee in the saloon, Mike. I want to talk to you."

As I poured the coffee he said, "We should be all right as long as we stay out at sea. It's when we put into any port Ramirez will discover us again. Of course, he might get lucky and find us out here—and that's what I want to talk to you about."

I lifted my eyebrows. He continued. "Our crew's a tough mob, and I know they can fight if they have to—but will they stand a chance?"

"It depends on the kind of fighting," I said. "We might have cleaned Ramirez out of weapons, and we might not. If he comes up against us with any kind of armament we've probably had our chips. If it's a matter of hand-to-hand fighting, we've got a good chance, even though he has a crew of fifteen. Our lot are trained fighting men, most of them. Ramirez has waterfront scum."

"I hope you're right. But I'd like to have a talk to our crew. A man should know what he's fighting for."

"They know what they're fighting for," I said softly. "They saw the hospital at Tanakabu."

"True. But they don't know the extent of what we're searching for. And there's no harm in mentioning a fat bonus at the end of all this—whether we dredge lucky or not."

I said, "They'll all be about when we put the dredge over the side. You could talk to them then."

We had the winch made ready for dredging early the next day, and at ten o'clock Campbell had the whole crew gathered before him on deck. He stepped up onto the winch and sat on the control seat, looking down on the men.

"You all know a little about what we're looking for on this expedition," he said. "But not everything." He held up a nodule.

"This is a manganese nodule and the seabed is covered with them. This particular nodule is worthless, but the ones we're looking for are worth a hell of a lot of money.

"Now, I want you to get this straight. Ramirez is going after these nodules for the money—and so am I, make no mistake about that. The difference is that I think there's enough for all and I'm not greedy. I won't bother Ramirez if he won't bother me, but he seems to be spoiling for a fight."

I had my own ideas about that statement. I was quite certain that Campbell didn't want Suarez-Navarro to have any part of the find, but perhaps on moral rather than on economic grounds.

"Now, I want you boys to know that whether we strike lucky or not, there's going to be a sizable bonus at the end of this trip—you can call it danger money. If we do strike rich, I'll be forming a corporation to exploit the find, and I'll put five per cent of the stock aside to be divided among this crew. That may not seem much, but let me tell you it won't be peanuts. You may all end up millionaires."

There was a babble of talk and a spate of handclapping. Geordie said, "I think I can speak for all of us, Mr. Campbell: that's a very generous gesture. We're with you all the way."

A chorus of approval swept the deck. Campbell held up his hand for silence. "That's settled then. If any of you want to know more about these nodules you'd better ask Mike. And now I think we'd better get on with the job before *Sirena* shows up."

On the first drop the dredge touched bottom at 13,000 feet and when we hauled it up there were plenty of nodules in it.

I took the first few samples down to the lab, while the crew secured the dredge and *Esmerelda* got under way again. I hadn't been working long when Paula and Clare came in.

"We came to see if we could help," said Clare.

I rubbed my chin. Neither would be able to use the spectroscope without training, but they could help with other tasks. "I hope you're good dishwashers," I said, and waved at the glassware. "This lot needs taking down and cleaning after every run."

"I'll do that," said Paula.

I turned to Clare and said, "There's an awful lot of record-keeping to be done. Could you cope?"

"Sure. No problem."

I was pleased. This would help speed up the work considerably, and there was a long grind ahead. The result of the first dredge was about average, just what an oceanographer would expect to find in a normal Pacific nodule.

474

Clare and I went on deck to get a breath of fresh air and were just in time to see the dredge go over the side for a second time that morning. We sat down on the foredeck and she said, "Pop told me what you asked Kane. Do you think he was telling the truth?"

"Not a chance. He was lying through his teeth."

She said, "You didn't expect him to admit to killing anyone, did you? Of course he would lie."

"That isn't what I meant, Clare. I don't think he did kill anyone— not directly. I don't think Kane has enough guts."

"Then you think he was lying about something else."

"That's right—but I'm damned if I know what it is. It was just something about his manner when I questioned him about Mark. There was a look of fear in his eyes."

Clare shivered, and I reached for her hand. There was no romantic moon shining across the water as I would have liked; instead we were in the hard white glare of the tropical sun. There was no love song echoing from the saloon, just the rhythmic clanking of the winch and the throb of a diesel. Nevertheless I said, "Clare, if we come out of this successfully I'd like to get to know you better—much better."

She slanted her eyes at me. "And if we don't come through successfully—will you never want to see me again?"

"That's not a nice way to put it."

"That's the way I have to put it."

I said nothing, fumbling for the right words.

"This is rather a new experience for me," said Clare with a warmth of humour in her voice. "I've never had to work at it myself. Most times I've had to fend off the advances—"

"I'm not making . . ." I was about to reply angrily until I suddenly realized that she was teasing me. Her eyes were alight with mischief—and, I thought in astonishment, with fondness. I said lamely, "Clare, there are all sorts of . . ."

She waited but I was still fumbling.

"Complications? But we could weather them all. Oh Mike, you're an awful fool—but I love you all the more for it."

I said after a pause, "Damn it, Clare, it isn't the way I intended this."

"Why don't you just say what's on your mind, Mike?"

So I did. "Will you marry me, Clare?"

She hung her head for a moment and then looked at me. "Of course I will," she said. "I thought you'd *never* get to the point. Girls are only supposed to propose in leap year, but I nearly had to break that rule."

I felt exhilarated and weak simultaneously. "Well, I'll be damned," I said, and we both burst out laughing. I wanted to do the obvious thing and take her in my arms, but there was little privacy, so we simply clutched each other's hands.

Clare said, "Mike, let's not tell anyone just yet. Pop has enough on his mind right now. I think he'll be fine about it but I want to be sure when we tell him, and nobody else should know first."

I agreed with her. I can't remember us walking back down to the laboratory—I think we floated.

WE STOPPED AND DREDGED every ten miles on the way to Minerva Reefs. I worked a sixteen-hour day, taking my meals in the laboratory.

We dredged—and dredged—and dredged. Then we hit shoal ground at nearly 4,000 feet. Geordie said laconically, "Minerva Bank."

"Nice navigating," I said. "Now we dredge all round it."

We retraced our track to the edge of Minerva Bank and started to circle it at a distance of about ten miles, dredging in deep water. Geordie worked it out on the chart. "That's about sixteen times we drop—say four days."

Five days later we had made the full circle and still hadn't found anything. Campbell was getting nervous again. "Are you *sure* we're in the right place?" he asked me, not for the first time.

"No, I'm not sure," I said sharply. I was on edge too. "I'm not sure of anything. I've got theories, but no certainties."

"What do we do next, then?" he persisted.

"We go back towards Falcon on a parallel track."

"Why don't we zigzag back using the course we came on as a centre line? First sample one side, then the other," Geordie suggested.

"That's a reasonable idea," I said. "Let's do that."

So we went back to the same boring routine. The winch motor whined, the bucket went over the side and a couple of hours later came up with its load which I then proceeded to prove worthless. There were plenty of nodules, but not the gold-plated ones.

Geordie was worrying about the winch gear. "We're overworking it," he told Campbell and me. "I'm scared the cable will break soon if we don't give it a thorough cleaning and oiling."

Campbell heard him out, and said, "No. We must carry on as long as we have the headway. You'll have to do your best, Geordie."

I knew what was on his mind. We had been at sea now for over two weeks and Ramirez would soon be ready to sail. So we carried on, zigzagging back towards Falcon, dredging the seemingly profitless Pacific.

And then we hit it!

My voice shook as I called the vital figures out to Clare. "Cobalt—4.32 per cent."

She looked up, startled. "Did I hear correctly, Mike?"

I said shakily, "This is it—4.32 per cent cobalt!"

We looked at each other wordlessly. At last I said, "We'll assay again from that last load. More than once. Paula! I want everything washed down again." And the three of us threw ourselves into a routine that was suddenly anything but boring.

The results were dotted around my first one: 4.38—4.29—four times I tested, and every test checked out.

"I must tell Geordie," I said. "He's got to change course."

I dashed up on deck. Ian was at the wheel. "Whoa up!" I shouted. "We're going back to the last site."

His eyes widened. "You've found something?"

"That I have! Where's Geordie?"

"He's off watch—in his cabin."

I left Ian to supervise the change of direction and pounded below. But Geordie wasn't impressed. "Four per cent is a long way from ten," he said.

"It's twice the percentage that's been found in any nodule before, Geordie, apart from the one we had in London. We must have struck the edge of the concentration."

"Well—what now?"

"We go back and cruise that area, keeping an eye on the echo sounder. That'll probably tell us something."

Geordie swung out of his bunk. "Come on, let's tell the boss."

Campbell had already been told. We found him in the lab with the girls, looking at the figures. He turned as we came in, his eyes bright with expectation. "Have we really found it, Mike?"

I said carefully, "We've found something. Whether it's what we're looking for is another thing." I pulled out the chart I had been making from the echometer. "There's a ridge running along here, roughly north-south," I said. "The top is within nine thousand feet of the surface. We picked up our prize nodule here, on the east side of the ridge at eleven thousand feet. I'd like to sail at right angles to the ridge, striking east. I'd like to see how the depth of water goes."

"You think the depth might have something to do with this?"

"It might. The deepest place would be the natural accumulation area for the greatest volume of nodules hereabouts, rather than the

477

shallowest areas—even though there's never more than one layer of thickness of nodules anywhere."

"I thought they'd be lying in great piles."

"Sorry, no," I said. "That's never been found. The best evidence from deep-sea photographs is that there are parts of the seabed which are lumpy underneath the sediment layer, indicating that many more nodules might be buried there, but in that case they'd have stopped growing anyway, being cut off from their lifeline—the seawater itself. But don't worry, the billions of tons I promised you will be there, even if they do lie only one layer thick. There are lots of things we have to find out first, though."

We arrived in the vicinity of the last site with members of the crew, rather ludicrously, peering at the ocean as if it could tell them something.

Geordie said, "Right—now which way?"

I drew a pencil line on his chart. "Follow that course, please."

As we sailed I watched the trace of the echometer with intense concentration. The line showed a gradual deepening of water. After we had gone about ten miles the bottom began to come up again from 13,000 feet. I made sure it wasn't just a local condition and then said, "I want to go back two miles."

"OK," Geordie said, and gave brisk orders. We were doing most of this work under engine, as it was tricky for sail.

Campbell looked at my tracing. "What do you think?"

"There's some sort of valley down there," I said. "We've come from a ridge, crossed the valley and begun to climb up towards the opposite ridge. I want to go back and dredge where it's deepest—it's about 13,000 feet there."

By now everyone knew what was in the wind and there was a lot of tension as the dredge went down. Ian was at the winch and Geordie himself at the wheel, keeping *Esmerelda* on station. It seemed a particularly long time before Ian, watching the cable tension meter, slipped the winch out of gear and said, "She's bottomed."

I could visualize the dredge at the bottom of the abyss, scraping forward in utter darkness, gathering the nodules and debris into its maw like a vast-jawed prehistoric creature.

Then the job was done and Ian had the winch in gear again. The drum started to turn. It seemed to take ages, and the tension increased until our nerves fairly twanged. Thirteen thousand feet is nearly two and a half miles. It takes a long time to haul a full dredge up from that depth. Normally nobody took any notice until the bucket came inboard, but this time everyone's attention was riveted, and when at last the dredge broke surface there were many willing hands to bring the haul in.

Geordie handed over the wheel to Danny and ran forward to help release the load. A cascade of nodules swept onto the deck, together with a lot of slimy mud.

"How long, Mike?" asked Campbell.

"The usual three hours. I can't do it any faster."

In fact it took longer. The lab wasn't very big and we had enough trouble with the three of us working there. Campbell insisted on coming in and watching, and wherever he stood or sat he was in the way. In the end I bundled him out, despite his protests, but I could hear him pacing up and down in the passageway.

At the end of three and three quarter hours I opened the door and said, "Congratulations, Mr. Campbell. You've just become the father of a 9.7 per cent cobalt nodule."

His eyes lit up. "We've hit it! By God, we've hit it!"

"Bang on the nose," I agreed happily.

He leaned against the bulkhead and sighed deeply. "I never thought we'd make it." After a few moments his brain started to function again and he said, "What's the density?"

"Ten pounds to the square foot. That'll keep you busy for the next few years."

His smile grew jubilant. "Come up to the saloon, the three of you. Let's have a drink on it. And get Geordie down here, too."

Paula followed Campbell out of the lab, but Clare and I managed to linger in the passage long enough for a quick hug and kiss before joining them. Geordie arrived a moment later, beaming.

Campbell opened the drinks cabinet, and set about filling glasses with great energy. "To you, Mike. You've done a great job," he said expansively.

"It isn't finished yet," I warned. "We've got to find the extent of the deposit."

Geordie cocked his head at me. "Where do we go from here?"

I said, "Ninety degrees from your last course—to the south. We came from a ridge and dredged in the deepest part of a valley. Now I want to run along the valley to see how far it stretches each way. We'll dredge at intervals along the course. Tell the watch to keep an eye on the echometer and to keep to the deepest water they can. We'll go for about twenty-five miles."

Geordie went up on deck to pass on the instructions—and the news of the nodules.

When he came back into the saloon, Campbell pointed to the

cabinet. "Pour your own," he said. Geordie grinned and picked up a bottle.

I rolled a nodule onto the table. "Geordie's a bit doubtful as to the value of this. I promised I'd get you to talk figures."

Campbell jabbed at the nodule with one finger. "It doesn't look like much. But it contains nearly ten per cent cobalt. We don't know much about anything else that's in it because Mike's only checked for cobalt, but as far as we know there should be a fair amount of copper and vanadium and a lot of iron—and manganese too, of course. The gross recoverable value will run to about four hundred dollars a ton."

Geordie was still not convinced. "That doesn't seem too valuable to me. I thought it was really valuable—like gold or platinum."

Campbell grinned delightedly and took a little slide rule from his pocket. "You'd say the density would be pretty consistent over a wide area, wouldn't you, Mike?"

"Oh yes. You can fairly well rely on that."

"And what would you call a wide area?"

I shrugged. "Oh, several square miles."

Campbell looked at Geordie under his brows, then bent over the slide rule. "Now, let's see. At ten pounds a square foot— that makes it—say, fifty-six million dollars a square mile."

Geordie, who was in the act of swallowing a sip of whisky, suddenly coughed and spluttered.

At last he recovered his breath. "Man, that's money!"

I saw the two girls looking at Campbell with astonishment, and something occurred to me. I said to Paula, "You're in on this too, you know."

She gaped at me. "But I've—I'm not—"

Campbell said, "Why, yes, Paula. You're one of the crew. Everybody on this ship gets in on the deal."

Her astonishment must have been too great for her to contain, for she burst suddenly into tears and ran blindly from the saloon. Clare cast us a happy smile and went after her.

I could see that Geordie was trying to work out the fifteenth part of five per cent of fifty-six million dollars—and failing in the attempt. I said, "That four hundred dollars a ton is a gross value. We have to deduct the cost of dredging and processing, distribution and all sorts of extras. Got any ideas on that?"

"I have," Campbell said. "The main problem is the dredging—a drag line dredge like the one we're using, but bigger, isn't much use at this depth. You waste too much time pulling it up. It would be best to use a hydraulic dredge. My boys did a preliminary study and

480

reckoned they could suck nodules to the surface from 14,000 feet for ten dollars a ton or less. Then you have to add all sorts of other costs, such as processing, marketing, transport. We'd want to develop and build our own dredges, we'd need survey ships, and we'd have to build a processing plant. I would have to float a company capable of digging into its pocket to the tune of some forty million dollars."

Geordie and I gaped at him. "Good heavens! Can you lay your hands on that much?" I asked.

"I can with what we have to show here. There will be a lot of guys on Wall Street eager to jump into a thing like this."

He got up and went to a porthole to look out over the sea. "Tonga's back there. They'll benefit by being the ones most likely to get the processing plant built in their territory. It'll mean a huge income in many ways, once it's built, so I should think they will be happy to cooperate.

"There's another thing—nodules are still forming out there, and they'll go on doing so. Maybe for once we'll be able to run a mining operation without raping the planet." He came back to the table and picked up his glass. "And that's an achievement to be proud of. Let's drink to it."

WE STAYED IN THE AREA for another week, dredging the submarine valley at selected spots. A much more detailed survey would be done later—all I was aiming at was to put limits on the area and to find out roughly how rich and how consistent it was.

Once, when I was having a breather on deck, Paula joined me.

"I don't know what came over me the other day, Mike—you know, when Mr. Campbell said I had a share in everything. I never thought of being rich," she said. "I never had the time, I guess. I've always been on the move—the States, Australia, Tahiti."

"Well, Paula," I said warmly, "what will you do with your new-gotten wealth?"

She was silent for a while and then said, "I think I'll go home."

"Where's home?"

"In Oregon. Just a small town called Medford. I haven't been there for years—and I should never have left it."

"Why did you leave, Paula?"

She laughed. "Oh, it's a real cliché. When I was sixteen I won a local beauty competition. That gave me a swelled head and a big mouth—you should have heard me talk about how I was going to knock 'em cold in Hollywood. But I went to Hollywood and it knocked *me* cold! There are too many girls like me there."

481

"What happened after Hollywood?"

"I drifted around singing in night spots." I was saddened by the bitter resignation in her voice. "That place where you found me in Panama—that was the best-paid job I ever had."

"And you left it—just because I asked you to?"

"Why not? It was Mark, you see. Oh, I know he was a no-good. But—I loved him. I wanted to do whatever I could for him."

I remained quiet. There was nothing I could say to that.

"Yes," she went on. "I think I'll go home. I always boasted I wouldn't go back until I was a success. I guess they'd call me a success now, Mike?" There were tears in her eyes.

"You've always been a success," I said gently.

She sniffed a bit and then shook her head briskly. "I'd better go back to work. But thanks."

I watched her walk along the deck. At a touch on my elbow I turned to find Geordie.

"What's on your mind, Geordie?"

"I want to talk to you about our next move," he said. "We can't stay out here much longer, Mike. The winch desperately needs attention, and we're low on water and fuel. We'll have to put into port somewhere pretty soon."

"Yes, my lab stocks are running low too. Let's put it to the boss."

Campbell said, "That's it then. But we don't go back to Nuku'alofa, in case Ramirez is still there, or hunting for us in that area. We'll go to Fiji—to Suva."

I hesitated. "Fine, but I'd like to have a look at Falcon."

"What for?"

"Well, it's responsible for all this, and it could well give us a lead to other high-cobalt areas hereabouts once we find out something about the mechanisms of this thing."

He laughed. "OK, Mike, I guess you've earned it. If Geordie gives you the go-ahead we'll go to Suva by way of Falcon."

Geordie wasn't too certain. He pulled out his charts, measured distances, and grumbled, "How long do you want to stay there?"

"Let's see—there'll be no need to dredge. It's very shallow over the site. A good swimmer like Bill Hunter could go down and collect the samples I want by hand—it won't be more than a few fathoms. We could be away again in just a few hours."

So Geordie set a course northwards for Falcon Island.

That evening in the saloon I said, "I'd like to summarize what I've found. Can you stand another short lecture?"

My seminar settled down to hear me out in a state of contentment, and I produced my charts and notebook. "The high-cobalt nodules seem to be concentrated in a valley twenty miles wide and a hundred miles long."

Clare, whom I had discovered to be a quick natural mathematician, said in astonishment, "That's two thousand square miles."

"Quite an area," I agreed. "The richness of the nodules varies roughly with the depth of the water, from about two per cent at the top of the ridges to a peak of about ten per cent in the valley bottom. The density varies in a different way. At the extreme north of the valley the density is only half a pound per square foot. At the other end it peaks out at fifty pounds per square foot."

Campbell said, "Still at ten per cent cobalt?"

"On the valley bottom, yes."

"Hot diggety!" he exclaimed. "A quarter of a billion bucks a square mile!"

He and Clare were smiling in delight, Geordie and Paula looked dazed—the figures were so fantastic.

Campbell shook his head in wonder. "This is fantastic. We'll need a detailed survey, though—with you to head it up."

"I'd be proud to," I said. I thought of the advanced equipment and systems I could use and inwardly rejoiced.

Campbell said, "I've been thinking this thing out. For centuries people like me have been taking metals out of the earth and putting nothing back. We've been greedy—the whole of mankind has been greedy. Now we've got hold of something different and we mustn't spoil it. Ten per cent of our profits will go to an independent, non-profit-making organization which will push my ideas further. We have to find a way to take that stuff out of the sea without disturbing the environment more than we can help, and a way to put something back—by way of recompense."

"There's one thing I can think of immediately," I said. "There are phosphorite nodules as well. You can make good fertilizer out of them, but so far no one has thought of a way of dredging them commercially. We could get them up with the rest, and you could be doing agriculture a bit of good."

"That's exactly the type of thing I mean," Campbell exclaimed. "You've gone to the heart of it—research is what's needed." His eyes crinkled. "How would you like to head up a new foundation?"

"Good grief! I'm a field man, not an administrator."

"You wouldn't be an administrator. I wouldn't waste your time on that. I can hire managers, but you'd be in charge of research."

"Then nothing would stop me taking it on," I said, dazzled.

"That's my boy." He lifted the bottle and inspected it critically. "Nearly the last of the Scotch. Never mind, I expect we can get some more in Suva."

I WAS BELOW WHEN I heard the engine start, so I strolled on deck to find Geordie at the wheel. It was a calm evening, without a breath of wind. "It's lucky you kept some fuel back," I commented, looking at a steadying sail hanging limply.

"Got a few gallons up my sleeve—I always save a little. Mike, what's the depth of water at Falcon?"

"I don't know, Geordie. It varies from year to year. The *Pilot* gives the depth in 1949 as about fifty-four feet, with no sign of the island at all, but it was there in 1941."

He wasn't happy with this. "We'll have to go very canny then."

"We've been around shoals before, Geordie. And we know exactly where this one ought to be—so what's the problem?"

"I don't like this weather."

I looked across at the setting sun, and then to the east. The sky was cloudless and everything was peaceful. "What's wrong?"

"I dunno," he said. "I've just got a feeling. I don't like that yellow tinge on the horizon. Maybe there's a storm coming up."

He called to Taffy and handed the wheel over to him. "Keep a close watch on that echo sounder, Taff," he said. "We should be nearly there. Ian, set a watch out. If there's nothing before dark, we'll circle back and come up again in the morning."

The morning brought more of the same weather—or lack of it. It was calm, quiet and peaceful as we gathered on deck to watch for any telltale breakers while Geordie motored slowly ahead. Presently he throttled the engine back to less than three knots. The echo sounder showed a hundred fathoms.

He said quietly, "The bottom's coming up. Only fifty fathoms." He throttled back the engine still further.

Clare asked, "Is this Falcon Island?"

"Dead ahead," I told her. "But you won't see anything—just another bit of sea."

"Twenty fathoms," called Jim at the echo sounder.

Geordie had taken the wheel and he cursed suddenly. "What the hell's going on?"

"What's the matter?" I asked.

"I can't keep the old girl on course."

I looked across the sea path to the rising sun. The sea had a black, oily look and seemed as calm as ever, but then I noticed small eddies and ripples here and there—it was a strange and disturbing sight. I felt *Esmerelda* moving under me, and she seemed to be travelling sideways instead of forwards.

As Jim called out, "Ten fathoms," Geordie put the engine out of gear and we glided to a halt. Jim was calling steadily, "Nine fathoms ... eight ... seven ..." At six and a half Geordie touched the engine into reverse and the sounder came back up to hover at seven fathoms. "This is it," he said. "As far as I'll go." He sounded bothered. "Is Bill ready?"

Diving in six fathoms—thirty-six feet—was going to be no problem to Bill, who was already kitted up in a wet suit and aqualung. He had orders to take down a couple of sample bags and bring me back a little of anything he could see—I didn't expect nodules, but the cinder- and shell-laden bottom material would be fascinating. I had expected him to take someone else down with him but he preferred to dive alone.

"Where you want a buddy most is on the surface," he had told me, overturning most of my accepted beliefs at a stroke. "You get disorientated pretty fast down there, even in clear water like this, and half the time you're not in sight of one another."

So we'd put the smaller dinghy into the water and it was from there that Bill would launch himself into the sea. Now, as he prepared to climb into the dinghy, he paused, sniffing the air, and commented, "Someone hasn't washed their socks lately."

There was a heavy, sulphurous smell in the atmosphere. Geordie and I looked at each other and he said, "Sulphur, Mike?"

"Well, this is a known volcanic region," I said. "I suppose it's always a bit niffy."

Ian spoke, pointing out to the horizon. "You can almost see it in the air, skipper." The sky low down was brightening into the dawn but there was a strange yellow tinge to it.

Jim and Rex Larkin rowed the dinghy a few yards off from *Esmerelda*. Bill sat on the thwart, gave the traditional thumbs-up sign, and toppled backwards into the sea. For a few moments we could see his body sinking. He had just disappeared when Geordie said hoarsely, "Stop him! Don't let him dive!"

It was too late. Several heads turned to stare at Geordie, who had suddenly gone ashen and was wrestling with the wheel.

"We're spinning!" Geordie said, and I saw then what he meant.

Esmerelda was sweeping round in a complete circle, not very fast, but in the grip of a colossal eddy. And at the same time I saw a column of mist, darkening even as it rose, that appeared as if by magic out of the sea half a mile or so away from us. There were shouts of alarm, and I clung to a stanchion to steady myself as we spun about.

Almost as soon as it happened it ceased, and *Esmerelda* was rocking tipsily, but steadying up again. I saw other little eddies appear and vanish on the sea's disturbed surface, and the smell of sulphur was suddenly pungent. I heard Geordie shouting, "Ian! We've got to get an anchor down! We'll lose the dinghy and Bill if we start drifting."

I heard the anchor cable rattle out of the hawser pipe almost as he spoke, tethering *Esmerelda* to the shallow bottom. The dinghy rocked heavily and I saw a line being thrown to keep her in contact with us.

Geordie called, "We'll have to get Bill up fast!" But he had gone down without a line, and there didn't seem to be any way to do so. Some of the crew were swinging out the motor launch, and I guessed that Geordie would use this more seaworthy craft to take up the dinghy crew, leaving the smaller boat in tow.

"How long will he stay down?" I asked, staring over the side. The whole surface of the water was rippling and beginning to chop.

"Not long," Geordie said, tensely. "The moment he breaks surface we'll have him out. With any luck there'll be enough disturbance down below to encourage him to come up quickly. Thank God it's shallow—at least he won't have a decompression problem."

Campbell appeared and demanded, "What's happening?"

"Wait a moment—I'll explain later." I was mesmerized by the column rising from the sea, which blackened steadily, like the smoke of an oily fire. I knew without a doubt that if there was no underwater disturbance to bring Bill to the surface, there was another phenomenon that would work as well—the sea would be rising in temperature to several degrees above its normal state. I knew that I was looking at the beginning of an underwater volcanic eruption.

Geordie guessed it too, and a ripple of awareness ran through the crew, who were scanning the water near us, looking anxiously for Bill's reappearance.

"There he is!" called Danny, pointing.

We watched as Rex and Jim, who were still in the dinghy, pulled Bill in. Nick Dugan, in the motor launch, waited to tow them back to the ship. Suddenly there was a totally unexpected interruption as Taffy Morgan shouted, "Ship on the starboard beam!"

I spun round incredulously and pounded across the deck. Out of the smoke and steam that drifted across the sea, shielding her until the last moment, the bulk of *Sirena* came bearing down on us.

"Damn it! We're trussed up here for the slaughter," Campbell said in disbelief.

Geordie ran up the deck. "Slip that cable!" he bawled.

But there wasn't enough time. *Sirena* was slewing round to lay alongside us. She didn't quite make the turn and her bowsprit stabbed at us viciously. There was an almighty crash and *Esmerelda* shuddered violently as she lurched sideways in the water.

I was thrown against Geordie and we both went down in a tangle of arms and legs. I scrambled to my feet, the breath knocked out of me, and saw that our yardarm was locked in *Sirena*'s shrouds.

There was a roar of angry voices and a flood of men poured across the deck from *Sirena*. I saw the flash of knives in the enveloping glow of a fantastic yellow light.

CHAPTER EIGHT

It was a short fight and a bitter one.

In the fraction of a second before they were on to us Geordie roared, "Stand together, lads!" Moments later, I was grappling with a hefty brute who wielded a gleaming knife.

If he had come at me from underneath I might have been disembowelled, but he used the unsound overarm stab. I saw the knife coming down, grasped his wrist and pulled, sending him off balance. I did a neat sidestep, and he reeled into the scuppers, his knife clattering onto the deck.

I looked around. In the chaos, which was indescribable, I saw Campbell go down under a vicious blow from a belaying pin . . . and then I saw the unmistakable bulk of Jim Hadley.

He had got hold of Clare and was twisting her arm behind her back. She was screaming with pain, and there was a glaze of terror in her eyes.

I was about to plunge across the deck when there was a staccato rattle of shots and everything seemed to pause momentarily. I took the opportunity to yell, "Stop fighting, lads. They have Clare."

The tumult began again, only to be halted by another fusillade of shots. A voice called, "Very wise, Mr. Trevelyan." Then came a rapid spate of Spanish, which I was too dazed to follow.

I looked hastily around. *Sirena*'s men seemed to be everywhere, far more of them than of us. Three of our men lay on the deck without moving. We had been defeated in less than three minutes.

Ramirez moved across towards me with two armed men at his

back. "We meet under different circumstances, Mr. Trevelyan," he observed with a mocking smile.

I ignored him. "Everyone all right, lads?"

There was a low murmur. Then Taffy, who was crouched beside one of the prone figures, looked up, white-faced. "They've killed Danny," he said.

Ramirez stood in front of me, nodding appreciatively. "You have sense, Mr. Trevelyan. You've lost and you know it."

Campbell moaned and tried unsuccessfully to lift himself up. Ramirez strolled over to look down at his old adversary, then pointed to Taffy, still crouched over Danny's body. "You—carry the old man into the saloon," he said brusquely.

Taffy and Ian between them got Campbell up. There seemed to be something wrong with his leg. As he lifted his head I saw an ugly blotch of blood on his left temple, and rage rose in my throat.

Ramirez gestured to Geordie with his pistol. "You too—into the saloon. And Mr. Trevelyan, too. We mustn't forget you."

A rifle muzzle poked me in the back and I walked helplessly towards the companionway. I turned my head and saw Hadley pushing Clare forward. He had a heavy pistol trained on her neck. I wondered where Paula was.

In the saloon I helped Taffy and Ian to lay Campbell on the settee. His eyes were open but unfocused. I said, forcing my voice to a normal conversational pitch, "The old boy's had a nasty knock. You'll find some water in the drinks cabinet, Ian."

I looked around for Clare and found her coming to my side. Hadley had let her go and she was very pale but composed. Our hands found each other's for an instant. Then she went to her father, and began to sponge his head with a cloth which she dipped at intervals into the jug of water Ian was holding for her.

Paula was thrust into the saloon. She stumbled and nearly fell as her guard gave her a brutal shove. Then he took up a position near the door, his rifle pointing at us. I took her arm to steady her. "Paula—are you all right?"

"I guess so," she said in a low voice. "I saw them putting four of our crew in the cable hold—and they've hauled in the motor launch, so they've got Nick Dugan."

It wasn't surprising that Ramirez had spotted Nick in the launch and fetched him back. But there were still Jim and Rex in the dinghy, and Bill Hunter. I had a faint surge of hope—had Ramirez missed them? And if so, could they stay hidden in that misty, turbulent sea?

I crossed over to Taffy, who was helping Clare, and made to assist him. "Looks as though this is an officers' party, Taffy. You and Ian had better stay pretty quiet unless you want to join the rest of the boys—they're in the cable hold."

He nodded. "We'll be all right."

Suddenly there was a lot of movement and shouting on deck. Ian looked up speculatively. "I'm thinking they're having trouble, skipper. There's one hell of a tangle at the masthead."

That was all to the good. The longer they took to separate the two ships, the more time we would have to think of a way out of this situation. There were two armed guards in the room with us, both of whom looked as though they'd murder their grandmothers for two pesetas. I knew they'd have no qualms about shooting us if we tried to escape.

Presently, there was a rattle at the door and one of the guards opened it. Ramirez came in. "I trust you are comfortable," he said solicitously.

"Let's not have any blarney," I said bluntly. "What's the next move, Ramirez?"

He smiled, and seemed to be enjoying a huge joke. "Why, I have to introduce you to someone."

He leaned out of the door and beckoned to someone in the passage. He turned back to me and said, "I told you once that you shouldn't make libellous statements that you couldn't substantiate." The man who came into the room was about my size, dark and heavily bearded. He carried my laboratory notebook in one hand.

"I think you all know Mr. Mark Trevelyan," said Ramirez.

As I looked into my brother's eyes my heart seemed to miss three full beats, and then I felt the hairs bristle on the nape of my neck.

The silence in the saloon was total. Ian was the first to stir. "That's the mannie I found ..."

His voice trailed off as Mark switched his eyes to him. "Ah, Ian Lewis. So it was you who clobbered me, was it?"

The whole pattern of events of the last few months had suddenly been shuffled like the pieces of a kaleidoscope, to present an entirely new picture.

I glanced round at the others. Clare gave Mark one long measured look, then made a small contemptuous sound and turned back to her father. Campbell took her by the wrist protectively, never taking his eyes off Mark. He said nothing.

Ian glowered at Mark with black anger in his eyes, while Geordie merely stared speculatively at him. Paula made a move as if to go to him, but shrank back and hid in the shadows at Geordie's back.

Mark was watching me. "Hello, Mike," he said soberly.

I said, "Mark, for God's sake. I—"

He was urbane where I was dumbfounded. He lifted the notebook and some papers in his hand. "I've been rooting about in your laboratory. So kind of you to have done the preliminary survey for me. I couldn't have done it better myself. We seem to have struck it rich, Mike. There may be billions in all this, don't you agree?"

I spoke through a dry throat. "You're a bastard, Mark."

He looked around. "And who else have we? Ah, my dear old boss, Mr. Campbell—and Clare. I'm sorry you had to be here, Clare."

She refused to look at him and said nothing. That irked Mark and he shrugged petulantly, turned away and peered behind Geordie. "And who's the young lady sitting in the shadow?" he asked.

He moved round the table and stopped suddenly. His face went pale. "Paula!" he whispered. He turned his head quickly to Ramirez. "You didn't tell me she was aboard."

"Just another woman," Ramirez said casually. They glared at one another and I had an insight into their relationship.

Paula stood up. "Mark! I thought you were dead. Why didn't you come to me, Mark? Why didn't you trust me?"

Ramirez laughed softly.

Mark looked troubled. "I'm truly sorry," he said. "Sorry you had to be on this ship."

Paula took a step forward. "But Mark, I . . ."

Ramirez snapped out a curt phrase in Spanish and one of the guards lifted his rifle. The meaning was unmistakable.

Paula stopped dead. Mark looked away from her and she slowly fell back into a chair and buried her face in her hands. I heard the racking sobs that shook her, and saw Clare move to put her arm around her shoulders.

"We all thought you were dead, Mark," I said. "Why did you do it?"

"I had to die," he said. "The police were after me and getting a little too close, so I conveniently killed myself."

"You did kill Sven Norgaard, then?"

"The fool wanted to *publish*. Him and his scientific integrity—he wanted to give it all away, billions of dollars that belonged to me—to *me*. I made the discovery, didn't I?" His voice tailed off, and then he added softly, "We had an argument—at first in words, and then it came to blows. The next thing I knew was that he'd cracked his head open on the coral. I didn't mean to kill him. All I ever wanted to do was to shut him up."

490

We all stared at the egomaniacal horror that was my brother. "And then I killed myself," he went on. "The police would never look for a dead murderer. Wasn't that clever of me, Mike?"

"It was stupid," I said. "But then you always were stupid."

His hand crashed on the table and we all jerked at the sudden violence. Only Ramirez watched him unmoved and dispassionate. "It wasn't stupid!" he yelled. "It was a damn good idea! But I'm surrounded by bungling idiots."

"Like Kane and Hadley," I said.

"That's right, them," he agreed, suddenly calm again. "Those stupid fools gave me appendicitis, of all things."

"But it was you who bungled it," I said. "You should have told them precisely what to say."

Mark betrayed for the first time his lack of authority. "It had nothing to do with me," he said sullenly. "Ernesto fixed it." He laughed. "But you all thought I was dead, anyway. And poor old Ernesto here was being blamed for my murder."

Ramirez straightened, his face cold. "This is a pointless conversation," he muttered.

Mark said, "Let me have my fun, old boy. It isn't often a corpse can hold an inquest on himself. I'm getting a kick out of it."

I rubbed my ear—there seemed to be something getting in the way of my hearing. Mark's voice seemed to vibrate in a curious way as he went on, "My inquest. Let's develop this interesting theme."

"Yes, let's do that," said Campbell suddenly.

I turned to find him sitting up on the settee. "Let's consider the burning of the hospital and the murder of a doctor and his patients."

Mark flinched. "I didn't do that. I didn't even know about it until afterwards. It was Hadley again."

"Hadley again," I said caustically. "You sound as pure as Kane."

Ramirez picked up my reference to Kane and was looking at me inquiringly. "You have spoken to Kane again, Mr. Trevelyan? He was supposed to come to me in Nuku'alofa, but I didn't see him there."

"Yes, we've seen him," I said. "He's told us a great deal—enough to condemn the lot of you, so think carefully about how you're planning to deal with us, Ramirez."

"Might one ask where he is?"

"Where you won't find him, and all ready to sing like a bird."

He looked thoughtful and did not speak for a moment.

Campbell said, "You've decided that you can't leave us alive, haven't you? You've already killed several people—another dozen or

491

so won't make any difference. But you won't get away with it. We've covered our tracks. My agents have sealed letters which will be handed to the police if I don't turn up soon. There's going to be a thorough investigation if I go missing."

Ramirez threw back his head and laughed. "You're an old fool, Campbell," he said brutally. "The barometer has dropped three points in the last hour. There's a storm coming up. You're going to be lost at sea—the lot of you. We will not be anywhere near here. There will be no proof—no proof of anything."

Campbell shuddered and Clare pulled a little closer to him. Watching Ramirez, I was fascinated by a movement outside the porthole behind his head. Nobody else seemed to see it. There was a face out there. An eye winked. Bill Hunter was back on board.

He was a hidden ace and I didn't want Ramirez to become aware of him. I cautiously lifted my hand to my mouth, coughed, and then made a slow downward movement, being careful not to jerk. The eye winked again and the face disappeared.

Again there was that vibration in my ears, as though there were some sort of aural interference, and not far away there was a sound as though an engine were letting off steam. *Esmerelda* shuddered and the noises on deck increased suddenly.

To my horror Ramirez strode over to look out of a porthole. I tensed, but then he turned back and started to speak, and I realized he'd not seen anything untoward.

"As soon as these idiots of mine have parted the two ships, we go our separate ways," he said coolly. "We will point your nose into that storm out there." He turned on Geordie. "We have borrowed an idea from you, Captain. We will set the explosive charge against your hull, and the storm will do the rest."

Geordie said nothing.

There was a clatter of heavy boots on the companionway followed by a thump on the door. At a gesture from Ramirez one of the guards opened it and Hadley came in. He bent to whisper something to Ramirez, who immediately turned to look out of the porthole again. I thanked God that Bill had kept out of sight.

Ramirez turned back. "The storm seems to be getting worse." He smiled and said to Mark, "This is lucky, you know. How else should a survey ship be wrecked but in investigating Falcon Island a little too closely at the wrong time?"

He turned on his heel and left the saloon, followed by Hadley.

Geordie watched them go and transferred his attention to Mark. "What makes you think I'm going to sit back and let you wreck my ship and murder my crew? If I'm going to be killed I might as well take you with me." He began to rise from his chair. With Ramirez's departure a curious change had come into the atmosphere. It was as if we could all recognize that where Ramirez had real authority, Mark had only a veneer of toughness over an insecure personality.

As Geordie started to rise Mark snapped out a command in Spanish and the guards' rifles lifted to the ready.

Geordie continued to rise and Ian started to get up as well.

Mark spoke again in Spanish and one of the guards fired his rifle, apparently without aim. The noise was appalling and we flinched back as the bullet struck the cabin floor by Geordie's foot. I spoke sharply. "Cut it out, Geordie—you haven't a chance. You can't move faster than a bullet."

Geordie glared at me but I made a quick slashing gesture with my hand and, taking a chance, winked at him. He sat down again, as did Ian. I knew that I had succeeded in alerting them.

"Mind if I smoke?" I asked. I put my hand into my pocket and stopped as a rifle barrel was pointed unwaveringly at me. "For God's sake, Mark, can't I even have a cigarette?"

He looked amused. "Smoking's bad for you, Mike. Go ahead—but you'd better have nothing but cigarettes in your hand when you pull it out."

Slowly I withdrew my hand as he spoke to the guards again. The rifle barrel dropped a little and I opened the packet and put a cigarette in my mouth. At that moment I saw Bill's face at the porthole again. The rifle shot must have brought him back.

I put my hand to my pocket again and said to the man with the rifle, "*Fosforos.*" He made no objection and I managed to get the matches out without being threatened.

I lit the cigarette and said, "Look, Mark. You know everybody cooped up in this saloon. Some have been your friends—others have been more than friends. What kind of a man are you?"

"What can I do?" he asked. "Do you think I want to see you all killed? It's out of my hands—Ramirez is in control."

Campbell's voice was cutting. "He washes his hands—the new Pontius Pilate."

This was my chance. To speak to Campbell I had to half turn away from Mark and the guards in a natural fashion. "Mark will join us anyway," I said. "Ramirez doesn't need him any more—he only needs my notes—and I'm quite sure he'll want to rub out *any* witness to all this, including Mark."

I was printing on the back of the cigarette packet, with the stub of a pencil I had taken from my pocket with the matches, the words "CABLE HOLD". Campbell caught on fast. He shook his fist at Mark to divert attention. "You bastard!" he shouted.

"Shut up," said Mark venomously.

I held up the cigarette packet towards Campbell and said, "Take it easy. Have one?"

"No, no," he brushed my offer aside, but the job was done. Bill had had a clear vision of my message over Campbell's shoulder. I prayed that he had good eyesight. Clare saw the message, too, and bent her head towards Paula. I saw her whisper in the other girl's ear, apparently soothing her.

I risked another glance at the porthole, and saw that the face had gone, to be replaced by a hand. The middle finger and thumb were joined in a circle. Bill had got my message. He now knew that the others were in the cable hold and hopefully he might be able to free them. It was a slim chance but it was all we had. I had to give him time to act, and I reckoned that the only thing we could do was to get Mark talking again.

I said, "You always knew where that high-cobalt nodule formation was, didn't you?"

"I only knew approximately. I wasn't the only one doing assays on that IGY ship, and I couldn't get all the information I wanted."

"Who had the bright idea to look for us here? We could have been anywhere. You couldn't know where we were."

He laughed. "Couldn't I? I know you like a book, Mike. I knew that you'd find the deposit given time to survey properly—so I gave you that time. We've been here for nearly two weeks waiting for you to turn up."

"How did you get entangled with Ramirez?" We already knew the answer but it kept him talking.

"Campbell couldn't finance me, and Suarez-Navarro could. It was as simple as that. Suarez-Navarro were going to provide Sven and me with a proper survey ship." He thumped the papers and notebook. "Meantime that fool decided that he wanted to publish. You see, he didn't know much about Suarez-Navarro, and that's the way I wanted it. We got into an argument and you know the rest."

As Mark spoke something else was penetrating my consciousness. There was a whistling sound in the distance—high-pressure steam was escaping somewhere. Mark must have heard it too because he turned to look out of the porthole. What he saw over the water made him acutely unhappy. "Damn them," he muttered. "What are they doing on deck? This is no time to be hanging around here."

494

His nervousness increased and he conferred with one of the guards in a low voice. The guard opened the saloon door and went out.

There was a light reflected on Mark's face as he looked out of the porthole again.

I said, "What's going on out there, Mark?"

His voice was strained. "It looks as though Falcon is going to bust loose."

I suddenly felt cold. Mark and I were probably the only two people on either ship who had any understanding of what that might mean. "How close are we?" I asked.

"Maybe a quarter of a mile. It's happened a couple of times this week already. But it's never amounted to much."

We were much too close to Falcon. To Ramirez and Hadley it might seem a safe distance, but Mark and I knew what volcanic eruptions could do. No wonder Mark was scared. So was I.

The whistling and belching suddenly increased and *Esmerelda* lurched, her joints squealing a protest. She swung round, still locked with *Sirena*. There was a sudden blast of an acrid sulphurous smell in the air, then *Esmerelda* gave another great lurch and went over almost on her beam ends. I slithered helplessly towards the side of the saloon. There were sounds of bedlam above decks.

Esmerelda righted herself and we fell back in a jumble of bodies. I heard Campbell groan. It must have been terrible for him in his condition. Geordie was up first. He grasped an ashtray, hurled it at the guard, and then leaped the length of the saloon. The guard's rifle had fallen onto the deck and he tried frantically to retrieve it. He had his fingers on the butt when Geordie kicked him on the jaw.

With the guard temporarily out of action, Geordie snatched up the rifle and turned it on Mark who backed sullenly into a corner of the saloon. He knew he was defeated, and sat down on the floor without a word. Paula moved over to speak to him.

I turned and stared anxiously out to sea. There was a haze of steam in the near-distance and sullen black clouds beyond. The sea was choppy, and around the steam there was a white roil of froth. The smell was terrible.

I looked back into the room. Ian and Clare were helping Campbell back onto the settee. Paula was talking to Mark and Geordie was searching the guard. Taffy was missing.

"Geordie, where's Taffy?"

"He slipped out a moment ago. I think he's gone to help Bill."

"What we need now," I said, "is a plan of action. Bill should be at the cable hold by now, and with luck Rex, Jim and Taffy are with him.

Maybe they've been able to do something. And there's us—three men and a rifle."

"Four men," snapped Campbell, getting to his feet. "And if they haven't searched our cabins there'll be guns in them."

He was right. Clare looked from her father to me. "I'm coming with you," she said.

"Clare, you can't . . ."

She cut in decisively. "I'm a pretty good shot too, remember? You're going to need all the help you can get." She was determined to stay close to me and her father, and I couldn't argue with her. If it came to the worst, for her and for the rest of us, death by a bullet was preferable to drowning in a scuttled ship.

Paula was still talking to Mark. "Paula," I told her, "you stay here with him."

"Come on," Geordie said. "We haven't much time. Me first, then Ian and Mr. Campbell. Mike, you bring up the rear."

Geordie opened the door and we followed him cautiously into the passageway. He hadn't gone more than a few feet when he stopped, stepped over something and then moved on. It was the body of the guard who had left the saloon. He must have met up with Taffy.

Campbell's cabin hadn't been searched. There were three guns, his own and Clare's, and the one Geordie had taken from Ramirez back in Nuku'alofa. Father and daughter loaded their weapons.

In our cabin Geordie and I found our two pistols untouched. "Now we've a fighting chance," said Campbell.

We crept out into the passageway and Geordie turned on me and said, "Mike, I want us to take a look at Falcon. Ian, cover our rear. Mr. Campbell, you and Clare keep watch down here. Shoot anybody who tries to come down that passageway."

We slipped quietly on deck and I got my first full look at Falcon. The yellow glow was diminishing, but there was a lot more steam, and sheets of a rain-like substance were falling. In the middle of it all dense black smoke billowed upwards with streaks of red intermingled with it. The whistle of high-pressure steam was deafening, the smell gut-wrenching. I stared in utter fascination.

Geordie, more concerned with his ship than with Falcon, was looking at the foremast. "What a mess!" he exclaimed.

The two masts were almost separated and seemed to be locked only somewhere high up. *Sirena* leaned over *Esmerelda* at an angle, and there was a hellish tangle of line, broken spars and general debris scattered everywhere. The motor launch still hung astern but there was no sign of our dinghy.

There was nobody at the wheel but I could see Ramirez's men at the foot of each mast. Some were up the masts working to free the wreckage. I hoped they were too occupied to look down and spot us.

"They're still busy," I murmured. "Let's make for the winch. We can hide there while we try to open the cable hold."

"We'll have to chance it," said Geordie and gestured to Ian to follow us. We ran forward in a crouch, keeping to the shadow of the deckhouse. Geordie paused, caught my arm and pointed. There was a slight movement in the shadow of the winch drum.

"Bill—or Taffy," he murmured.

A hand came out into the light and fumbled with the fastenings of the hatch cover.

"I'm going to the other side," I said to Geordie. "Cover me."

Suddenly a rumble came across the water from Falcon and the red flashes of light in the black cloud flared higher. Voices were raised in alarm and there was a stampede of running footsteps. The diversion was perfectly timed. I crept along the deck and flattened myself close to the hatch. Groping for the catches, I saw that my companion was Bill Hunter. Taffy was crouching nearby in the shadows. I had released one catch and was attacking the other when there was a sharp crack of gunfire and a thunder of feet. Ian and Geordie were on their knees, firing at *Sirena*'s men who had caught sight of us and who were pounding aft in our direction.

A contorted face loomed over me, the butt of a rifle poised near my head. I jerked to one side. Then I heard the distinctive "spaat" of Campbell's target pistol and my assailant crashed on top of me.

I shoved his body aside and grabbed for the hatch. The second catch came free and Bill and I flung the cover open. Four men came tumbling out of it.

Geordie shouted, "Aft! Get aft!"

We all tumbled down behind the deckhouse. More shots rang out. The rest of *Sirena*'s crew retreated back to the mast as covering fire came from on board their ship. Geordie looked us over, counting heads, and to my intense pleasure the face of Jim Taylor was amongst them. One of the dinghy crew was safe, at least.

Sporadic fire came from *Sirena*. Geordie ducked as a bullet sent splinters flying just above his head.

"This is no good," he said. "We don't have enough cover, and we're running out of ammo."

Then came three methodically spaced shots from Campbell's pistol. There was a scream from *Sirena*'s yardarm and a figure hurtled to the deck.

497

Geordie got us moving aft, leaving Nick and Ian to cover our retreat. In the companionway Campbell was reloading his pistol as we swarmed below. He motioned us aside and aimed at the yardarm again, crouching to steady himself. Another body plummeted down, this time into the sea.

"That's the lot," he said. He looked drawn and near the end of his endurance. Clare was standing by him with her pistol in her hand. The alarm in her face subsided when she saw us. I caught her and held her briefly.

A short time later Nick and Taffy reported that *Esmerelda* was clear of enemies, below decks at least. With the exception of my brother, who was still in the saloon with Paula.

Geordie went to reconnoitre the forward companionway and was soon back with a report. "They've retreated—they're all aboard *Sirena*. I didn't see any sign of Ramirez, but Hadley's all over the place, bellowing orders. We're going to have to get clear of *Sirena* and away as soon as we can." He swung round to Bill. "How did you get back on board? And where's Rex? Is he OK?"

It took him a moment to reply. "I'm sorry, skipper—we lost him," he said grimly. "We saw some of *Sirena*'s lot take over the launch. They held guns on Nick Dugan, threw him a line and hauled him in. They hadn't seen us, so I got Rex and Jim to slip over the dinghy side and we swamped her. Jim and I got back on board OK, up our ladder, but when *Esmerelda* lurched over, Rex let go. Geordie, I—"

499

"You did your best," said Geordie curtly. Feeling sick and depressed I left them and went up to take another look at Falcon.

The distance to the belching gout of smoke seemed less. Either we were dragging our anchor, which was very likely with the extra weight of Sirena alongside, or the area of eruption was enlarging— an even more alarming prospect.

I went back down to Geordie. "We've got to get out of here before Falcon really starts acting up."

He looked out across the sea. "It's weird, I'll grant you, but is it that serious? Lots of observers have seen eruptions at sea before now. And Mark said it's been going on for days already."

"This is just an overture," I said. "There's no time now for a lecture on undersea vulcanology. But I don't think we should be around when the finale's being played."

"Well, whoever's in command over there—Ramirez or Hadley— will want to get free as much as we do. They're in danger too. And I don't think they'll find it easy to retake us now, or blow us up as they threatened. Ramirez may just cut his losses."

Geordie was right, and I waited in silence, aware that a plan was forming in his mind. At last he said, "I reckon we should call a truce. If we send a man up on the mast they won't fire at him if they know why he's going up there."

"What's the good of sending one man up? They've had a dozen men up there for an age and they haven't achieved much."

"I've got an idea," Geordie said, looking at Jim who had just joined us. He pointed to the masts. "See that yardarm, Jim, where it's tangled with the rigging? Could you blow it off if you fastened a hand grenade on each side of the spar?"

Jim peered at the spars doubtfully. "It would be a bit tricky, skipper. Grenades aren't meant for that sort of thing. The spars are steel tubing."

"It would weaken the spar though, wouldn't it?" Geordie persisted.

"It wouldn't do it any good, if that's what you want."

"Suppose I have the engine going and put a strain on the yardarm after the grenades are blown, do you think that would do the trick?"

"I reckon it might," said Jim. "If the grenades were placed right."

"You'll have a go then? You're our expert."

"I'll give it a bash—if they don't shoot me."

"Good," said Geordie. "We'll take care of that. You gather together what you need and I'll get those grenades. Mike, you'll be the best man to negotiate. Try to settle an armistice."

500

I wondered if Ramirez would realize that if he let us go he might never catch up with us again. We would forever be a threat to his freedom. He might never agree to such terms. And we were very vulnerable—underarmed, undermanned, and in no position to dictate terms. Then I thought of Clare, and how precious she had become to me. Whatever else, I was determined that she should survive.

I crawled into the wheelhouse, keeping below window level, and raised the loudhailer. "Ahoy, *Sirena*!" I shouted. "Can you hear me?"

A shot was fired at the wheelhouse. I heard the smash of broken glass and a small shower of it fell near me. There was shouting and then silence. The only sound came from the ships as they creaked and groaned together, and from the hissing of the volcano.

"Ramirez! I want to talk to you."

"Yes," said a harsh voice. "What do you want?"

"That volcano—it's going to erupt at any moment."

"I know." He sounded frustrated and I almost smiled with relief. He'd cooperate.

"We have an idea. We want to send a man up the foremast. We can clear that rigging."

His voice was full of suspicion. "How can you do that?"

I did not intend to tell him our plan. I called, "We have an expert here. We want you to guarantee that he won't be shot at."

There was a long silence. Someone tapped me on my shoulder and pushed a note into my hands. It was from Geordie and read, "Got to slip the anchor. Quiet as possible. Good luck."

The silence was broken by Ramirez. "All right, we don't shoot."

I called, "Ramirez, if our man is shot at, you'll be dead within the hour. Every man here will make you his personal target."

"You terrify me." Was he laughing? "You can send your man up the mast in five minutes. I will arrange things at this end."

I crawled out of the wheelhouse and joined Geordie, who had Campbell beside him. "What do you think?" asked Geordie.

"I think he'll hold off," I said. "He's in as big a jam as we are and he knows it."

Jim joined us and we waited, huddled at the corner of the wheelhouse. The minutes ticked by as we listened to the ominous rumblings and hissing from the sea. I turned to Geordie. "We're only forty-odd miles from Nuku'alofa—a fast boat could reach us in a couple of hours. What's the chance of sending a radio message?"

Geordie's voice was bitter. "The radio was the first thing they smashed. Shorty's trying to whip up a spark transmitter out of the wreckage, but it'll take time."

When we had one more minute left, I crawled back into the wheelhouse and took up the loudhailer again. "Ramirez! Our man's going forward now. No shooting."

"No shooting," he agreed. "I have told my men."

I watched through the window as Jim walked to the foremast, a satchel slung over his shoulder. He climbed the mast steadily. Almost all our crew were watching from various hidden vantagepoints, several with rifles or pistols handy. Jim reached the yardarm, paused, then swung the satchel in front of him and put his hand inside. He'd have to clip his way through some of the tangle first.

On board *Sirena* there was no one in sight; like us, they must have been staying under cover.

There was a sudden lurch of the two ships as an eddy caught us. I hoped Jim had a firm handhold. At the same time there was a babble of voices from *Sirena's* wheelhouse, and Hadley came running on deck carrying a submachine gun. Swiftly he raised it and fired a burst at our foremast.

Jim toppled from the yardarm, falling with limbs awry to slam across the starboard bulkhead.

There was an angry roar from *Esmerelda* and guns began firing.

Hadley stepped back into the shadow, and sprayed the rest of the magazine across our decks, then he vanished into cover.

I catapulted myself out of the wheelhouse towards Geordie and Campbell. Geordie was speechless and full of grief. Campbell was snarling, "The bastard, he's a maniac!"

"I'll have his guts," Geordie said stiffly.

The firing from our crew died away and I saw faces staring, stunned by the horror of what they'd seen. Two men broke cover to go and collect Jim's body. No one shot at them. Slowly I followed the others below for a council, and found Clare waiting for us in the passageway. She came and clung to me and I held her tightly.

"Dear God, Mike—Pop—what happened up there?"

"Jim's been killed," Campbell said shortly. "Hadley's lost all control. There's no knowing what he'll do next. But I'll bet those men over there are even more scared of him than we are. I think Ramirez will have him dealt with, for their own safety."

Geordie was keeping silent. He was still obviously shocked and angry over Jim's death. Then Campbell suddenly said to him, "Don't forget we're drifting now. You've slipped the anchor," and that brought him to his senses. An expression of worry replaced his glare of bitter hatred. "My God, we could drift right into that storm! We've got to get the foremast out of its housing, clear the shrouds, the lot. Dump it all overboard. It'll hamper *Sirena* if she tries to give chase. Taffy! Nick!" His voice rose in command. The men gathered round, and he began to give orders for freeing *Esmerelda*.

I turned to Clare. "What about Paula and Mark?" I asked quietly. "Where are they?"

Clare nodded towards the saloon. "They're still in there. Mark won't give us any trouble. I've never seen him so subdued. I guess he wants to keep out of Ramirez's way for now."

"There are all the signs that Falcon will get rougher soon. I want you to get both of them up on deck—it'll be safer than staying below. And stay with your father, Clare. Keep them all together." I kissed her and she headed into the saloon without a word.

Geordie and the men went to see what they could do about freeing *Esmerelda* up on deck, and I followed. On board *Sirena* there was frantic activity as men struggled with equipment at the base of the foremast. A similar scene was being enacted on our ship. I started to go forward and make myself useful.

And then Falcon blew.

There was a mighty roar as thousands of tons of water exploded into superheated steam. A bright flickering glare shone on us and a pillar of steam ascended into the sky.

The first wave reached us in less than fifteen seconds. As I staggered, grabbing for support, I saw it racing down towards *Esmerelda*. It was monstrous, rearing mast-high, and approaching with the speed of an express train.

I flattened myself on the open deck as the wave broke against *Esmerelda*. She heaved convulsively and ground against *Sirena*. There was a rending crash. A flood of scalding water washed over the deck, and I writhed in pain.

Then the wave passed us and the ships dipped in the afterwash, creaking and groaning. There were four more huge waves, but none as high as the first. I staggered to my feet.

The waves had done what we had failed to do. *Sirena* was bobbing in the water about fifty yards away from us. *Esmerelda* was free. She had no foremast; it had been plucked out by the roots.

But every time *Sirena* rolled there was a crash that sent a shudder through her. Our foremast was hanging there, still tethered to her mast by a cat's cradle of lines and spars. As I watched, a surge of water sent it slamming against her hull like a battering ram. She wouldn't survive much more of that treatment.

I moved away from the rail, and stumbled over a body lying in the scuppers. Nick lay there with blood oozing from a wound on his forehead. As I turned him over he groaned and opened his eyes. He must have had a constitution like an ox because, in spite of the contusion, he began to struggle to his feet at once.

I urged him on. "Let's look for the others!" and he nodded. We turned and then stood frozen in amazement as we caught a glimpse of Falcon. There was *land* back there. Land that glowed a dull red shot with fiery streaks and that surrounded the pit of Hell itself—a vast crater which spewed forth red-hot cinders and streams of lava. Falcon was building an island once more.

Nothing could stop the outpouring of that huge gaping red mouth, but the sea did its best, pitting water against fire, and the result was an inferno of noise. There was a great ear-splitting hiss accompanied by a rumbling bass from the depths of the chasm.

Great gouts of fire leapt up from the crater, half hidden behind the red mist, and the water boiled as it encountered the blazing heat. Mighty columns of tephra, all the pent-up material that Falcon could fling into the air, erupted in spasms, hurling ash, magma and boulders high into the sky. A hazy brown cloud of fragmentary pumice hung over all, obscuring the sun.

Esmerelda was pitching as helplessly as *Sirena*. Black figures moved on both decks, outlined against the red glow of Falcon, and I felt a great leap of relief. For a moment it had seemed that Nick and I were the only two people alive.

As we made our way forward, featherlike flakes drifted from the sky, as if, incongruously, it had begun to snow. I brushed one from my shoulder; it was a flake of ash. The air was becoming poisonous with fumes, the stink of sulphur and the worse stench of sulphuretted hydrogen. Great bubbles were rising from the seabed and breaking on the surface, adding a dangerous smoke to the haze of steam. I realized with horror that we were not drifting closer to the source of the eruption—it was expanding under the sea, coming to meet us.

There was a shattering roar from Falcon as a second vent opened, only a few hundred yards away from the two ships. Nick and I clung to handholds during the first swamping wave of hot steamy water and then emerged gasping into the fetid air. He was nursing one arm and my rib cage was alive with pain, but we'd survived. Figures struggled to their feet on our foredeck, and I recognized Ian and Geordie among them.

A plume of water suddenly shot up from the sea not ten feet to starboard and drops of warm gritty water fell on me. Another waterspout shot up a little further out, and then another. It was as if we were under shellfire. The whole angry sea was pockmarked as though by a mighty rain, as rocks hurled high in the air from Falcon's second vent fell on the two ships. Smoke wreathed about us and steam coiled everywhere.

Nick and I managed to join the others. Of cuts and bruises there were plenty, but everyone was on his feet again. Except Geordie, who'd vanished. I caught someone's arm.

"Geordie—what's happened to him?"

"Gone to try and start the engine," Taffy bellowed in my ear. A moment later there was a steady rhythmic throb underfoot as our engine started. The sound gave me a wild surge of hope.

A fresh rain of tephra assailed us. Three or four larger flaming rocks crashed down on *Sirena*'s deck. She was almost level with us and her rails were lined with men. Several of them jumped into the sea itself, some trying to reach our decks.

"Bring lines!" Ian yelled, and I pounded after him to the ship's side as he and Nick began throwing lines over the rails. One man battling in the water seized a trailing end and Ian and Shorty dragged him on board. Nick threw another line out. *Esmerelda* was buffeted by a sudden wave and his feet slid across the deck. He cannoned into me and we both crashed down against the railing.

Then another wave poured across us, tipping *Esmerelda* the other way. Nick and I slid away from the railings together, half submerged in the gritty water that was cascading over the deck.

Hands helped me to stand up, and one of them was Clare's. "Mike—are you all right?"

"I'm OK." I was panting and spluttering. But I was comfortably aware that our engine was still running, and that Geordie was backing us steadily away from *Sirena*.

Clare gave me a fierce hug and I winced.

"Mike—you're hurt?"

"Don't worry, it's nothing. But go carefully with those hugs."

Campbell limped up to us, his face blackened with smoke, his clothes scorched and sodden. He and I exchanged a look over Clare's head and he smiled. "How's Paula?" I asked him. "And Mark?"

"Both all right. No more casualties," he said grimly. "The boys pulled two of *Sirena*'s men aboard and two others jumped across."

Taffy was helping Nick to his feet. Apart from his arm which was obviously crippled, and the abrasion on his face, there seemed to be little wrong with him. Taffy said, "We've sent all the enemy below and Ian's got 'em locked in our homemade brig."

I said, "Surely they aren't any danger to us now?"

"Well, there could be trouble," said Taffy. "We've got—"

A stunning crash interrupted him. A fresh pillar of smoke and steam boiled skywards from almost dead ahead of us. Our ship rocked wildly as another barrage of waves hit the decks. *Sirena* reemerged from this last assault on fire in several places.

I'll lay odds that Geordie Wilkins must be the best seaman ever to put his hands on a wheel. With consummate skill and an astonishing use of gear and throttle, he edged *Esmerelda* nearer and nearer to the doomed *Sirena*. As we closed in we saw that one of Falcon's barrages must have sheared right through the rigging and brought down the main gaff. Struggling men lay pinned to the deck. Others were frantically trying to release them, but the fires were closing in, eating their way along the deck timbers.

Clare screamed, "Look—Ramirez!"

A man was staggering across *Sirena*'s deck. Oblivious to the cries and struggles of his crew he never took his eyes from *Esmerelda*. Through the smoke I saw that he was carrying a rifle. His torn clothing was scorched and bloodstained, and his face was a mask of fury. He aimed the rifle across the water.

I flung myself down, shielding Clare, and I heard the gunfire, sharp and crisp. It was followed by a terrible grinding roar, louder than anything we had heard before. We staggered to our feet in time to see Falcon play its most horrible trick.

It was Geordie, intent on his delicate steering, who first saw the danger. *Esmerelda* sheered off violently as he spun the wheel away from the swirling eddy that was threatening to engulf us. Then he pushed the throttle in until the engine was pounding at maximum speed, to carry us away from the current.

Behind us I saw *Sirena* jar to a sudden halt, and Ramirez was flung across the deck. The ship rose grotesquely in the air and tipped over on her side, looking like a small sailing boat stranded by the tide. But this was no sandbank. It was a bed of writhing red-hot lava.

Ramirez was flung overboard into the raging lava and vanished instantly. *Sirena* went up like a funeral pyre, as banks of smoke and steam rolled across to blot her out of sight.

IT WAS THREE HOURS before we were well clear of Falcon. In that time we extinguished the fires, hurled the worst of the debris overboard, and brought some faint semblance of order to the ship.

Now there were a couple of matters that could not, for all my wishing, be put off much longer. Mark had to be dealt with. And

Hadley. Taffy had informed me that he was one of the men who had leaped to our deck, and he was being held in the brig with the others from *Sirena*.

Mark and Paula had stayed in the saloon during the whole of the encounter with Falcon. I pulled myself to my feet and went below. Paula looked up as I entered. Her face was drawn and shadowed.

"Are we safe yet, Mike?" she asked.

"Pretty well. You should both come up on deck and get some air. It's remarkably peaceful up there now."

She and Mark got up together. He was very pale under his heavy beard, and said nothing. I led the way on deck and they followed. We stopped outside the shattered deckhouse and stood together looking astern at the distant cloud of smoke.

"I wish I'd seen it from up here," Mark said. He sounded wistful.

"It was fantastic, but too close for comfort," I said. "I'm going to tape my observations as soon as I can. Do you know what happened to *Sirena*?"

"Clare told us," Paula said, and shuddered. Mark seemed unmoved.

"Mark," I said abruptly. "I have to talk to you."

"I'll go," Paula offered.

Mark took her arm and held it. "Stay with me," he said. She was the only one he could be sure was on his side, and he needed a friend. He turned to me and a hint of the old arrogance was back in his voice. "What's it going to be? A lecture on decency?"

I felt grim and tired. "Ease off, Mark. I'm not going to lecture you. But we have to work some things out before we land."

I wanted above all to lie down, to sleep for a week. I was physically exhausted, but the onus of Mark was an even heavier burden. We stared at one another in stalemate.

My jumbled thoughts were interrupted by a scream from below. Taffy and a couple of others came past us at a run and dived down the companionway.

Suddenly there was a crash from below, and Hadley burst through the burned-out galley and onto the deck. He had a kitchen knife in his hand. I backed away as he came at me.

I booted him on the shin but it was like trying to stop a truck. He leaped at me, his knife hovering near my throat. I clawed at his face desperately. Suddenly he lost his balance and we both crashed to the deck. Nick had seized Hadley's ankle from behind and yanked his foot out from under him. I rolled free and Hadley got the full force of a bullet from Ian's gun in his belly.

Astonishingly, he regained his feet and swooped for the knife which lay on the deck. For a near-fatal instant we were all paralysed. Then with an unearthly scream of rage and agony he plunged towards Mark, his knife flashing viciously in the sunlight.

Mark flung Paula aside and met the attack full on. The knife sank into his side and he collapsed without a sound. The weapon fell to the deck. Hadley took two paces backwards, clutching his stomach, and then in a full back arch he went over the railings into the sea.

I stood shakily, my breath coming in short painful gasps. Clare and Bill Hunter were first at my side. Paula ran to Mark, who was conscious and trying to sit up.

Geordie arrived at a run and Taffy told him what had happened. "My fault, skipper. I let Hadley out. We heard a man screaming in the brig and I thought someone was hurt. I went in with Bill but Hadley escaped—there was no restraining him."

Bill said, "No wonder that poor devil was screaming. Hadley had near taken his arm out of its socket—to get us to open up."

"Well," Geordie said briskly, "that's the last of them. The others won't make any trouble. Now, lads, back to work."

They dispersed slowly. Geordie turned to me and said softly, "The last of them—bar Mark. What are you going to do about your brother, Mike?"

I looked at him bleakly. "I don't know. First I must see how badly he's hurt. But I can't just hand him over to the police."

"I don't think you've any choice, laddie."

"I guess not. But it's a hell of a thing to have to do."

Clare, her arm comfortingly firm around my rib cage, waited in silence for me to come to a decision. I said, "I'll have to talk to him alone. Take Paula with you, Clare. Look after her. And keep everyone away from us for a while, would you, Geordie?"

Mark was sitting propped up against the railing with Paula by his side. I waited until the two girls had gone below to join Campbell. Then I squatted beside him. "How is it?" I asked.

"Not good," he said breathlessly. He was sheet-white.

"Mark, thank you for saving Paula."

"Don't thank me. That was my business." He did not want to hear praise from me. "I told you Hadley was off his rocker."

"Well, he's out of it now. Ramirez, too. Which leaves only you, Mark. And it puts me in a devil of a fix."

I expected his usual sneering retort, but he surprised me by saying, "I know that, Mike. I've caused you a lot of grief, and I'm sorry. I'm likely to cause you a lot more as long as I live."

508

"No, I—"

"Which won't be long. I'm no doctor, but I know that much."

"Mark, we'll be back in port soon and you'll be in medical hands." He was less arrogant than I had ever known him, and I was dismayed.

"Don't be a fool, Mike," he said. "It's not going to make things easier for you if you suddenly turn up with your long-lost, murdered brother, is it?"

I knew he was right. I shrank from the thought of turning him over to the police, but I could see nothing else to do.

"Mike, I have one chance, just one, to make things easy for you. I've never done anything for you before. You have to give me this one chance." He swayed a little. "Mike, I'm going to die."

"Mark, you don't know—"

"Hear me out." His voice shook. "Remember, I'm already a dead man. Without me you have every chance of coming clean out of all this. There will be nobody to contradict your story. You were sailing to meet up with Ramirez on a survey expedition, and got caught up in the shambles of Falcon. By now the world will know it's blown. There'll be ships coming to look, the lot. You can wipe out all traces of a gunfight. And you can persuade those prisoners you've got on board to shut up." He drew in a harsh breath. "Do I have to spell it out for you? I can do one thing for you, if you'll help me now."

"Help you to do what?"

"Help me to die."

I had known. "Mark, I can't kill you."

"You won't need to."

Something glittered in front of my eyes. It was the kitchen knife Hadley had used on Mark, bloody at the tip but winking in the sunlight. I swallowed, a hard lump in my throat.

"What—do you want me to do?"

"Get me over the side, into the sea. It'll be as quick for me as it was for Hadley."

Silently I got up and began to pace the deck. He watched me carefully, saying nothing, giving me time. This was the only completely unselfish thing he would ever have done in his life. But it gave me a dreadful choice.

At last I came back to him.

"All right, Mark. God forgive me, I'll help you."

"Good." He became brisk. "Don't let anyone see us. The story will be that I climbed over on my own, after you'd gone."

I could find nothing to say. Mark gave a short, hard cough, his head drooped, and for an instant I thought he had already died. And then he raised his head and looked me in the eye. For the only time in my adult life our gazes locked without antagonism.

It only took a couple of moments. There was nobody in sight. I got him over to the railing and we both looked down into the sea. I remember thinking how quiet it was.

He hooked one leg over the rail, and I helped steady him as he lifted the other across. For an instant I held him.

"Goodbye, Mike," he said clearly.

I let go. He fell backwards and disappeared into the spray. I turned blindly away and with my head in my hands huddled down by the side of the deckhouse.

After a while I stood up shakily. It was done. I turned to leave.

The knife had disappeared.

I stood for a moment riveted, then swung round to look at the deck where Mark had been lying. There was, when I came to think of it, very little blood.

In two strides I was at the rail, looking aft. The motor launch which had been running in tow was gone, and the painter dangled loosely over the stern. Across the water I thought I could see a tiny dancing speck, but I couldn't be sure.

Slowly I walked aft and hauled in the painter. The end of it was newly severed and just beginning to fray.

There was fuel in the launch, and rations, for it had always had the function of a lifeboat. There were fishing lines, blankets, flares, a first-aid kit. There was everything needed for survival.

I stood at the railing and bid my brother a final, ironic farewell. And yes, I wished him luck.

DESMOND BAGLEY

Desmond Bagley first wrote *Night of Error* in 1962, but withheld it from publication because he wanted to make revisions. Ideas for other novels distracted him and the revision was still unfinished when he died in 1983. Thanks to his wife the long-shelved manuscript, with his notes incorporated, has now been published posthumously, to the delight of his fans.

A friend of Bagley's once said that his books read like fictionalized versions of the National Geographic Magazine, because they were so full of detailed research into technical subjects. Bagley's reply was: "I am an entertainer, not a pedagogue. I don't know if my readers are instructed while reading my books—that is not my aim. I do know that while doing research in odd corners of the world, I am giving myself a liberal education."

And educate himself he did. From humble beginnings as a miner's son in Kendal, where he was born in 1923, Bagley went on to leave school at fourteen. He was apprenticed as a printer's devil, and then spent the war years making parts in a Spitfire factory. Determined to broaden his horizons, he departed at the end of the war for South Africa, where he did a variety of jobs including coal and asbestos mining, before entering journalism by writing a series of talks on scientific subjects for Durban's radio station. From Durban he moved to Johannesburg where he became a freelance reporter, and met his future wife, Joan.

It was in 1963, when Bagley was forty, that he first found success as a novelist with the publication of *The Golden Keel*. Like his subsequent novels, it bore the Bagley hallmarks of being strong on action, skilfully crafted and painstakingly researched, and it set him on the first stage of a writing career that was to place him among the highest-paid writers of fiction in the world.

Throughout his life he travelled widely, learning as much as he could about subjects as varied as genetic engineering, computer science and, for *Night of Error*, oceanography. In 1965 he returned with his wife to Britain, settling first in Devon, where he produced a string of best-sellers, and then in Guernsey where he lived until his death. As an author who has succeeded in both entertaining *and* informing a wide audience, he will be much missed.